D0045694

More Praise for Nationwide Bestsellers by MICHAEL CRICHTON

THE ANDROMEDA STRAIN

"Science fiction, which once frightened because it seemed so far-out, now frightens because it seems so near. *The Andromeda Strain* is as matter-of-fact as the skull-and-crossbones instructions on a bottle of poison—and just as chillingly effective."
—*Life*

"Hideously plausible suspense . . . [that] will glue you to your chair."
—*Detroit Free Press*

"Relentlessly suspenseful. . . . A hair-raising experience."
—*Pittsburgh Press*

THE TERMINAL MAN

"A fascinating, splendidly documented thriller." —*The New Yorker*

"A brilliantly achieved and all-too-believable modern *Frankenstein.*"
—*Book-of-the-Month Club*

"A superb thriller. . . . It will make you think—and shudder."
—*John Barkham Reviews*

THE GREAT TRAIN ROBBERY

"So compelling . . . I found myself not only captivated but charmed."
—*The New York Times*

"It is marvelous fun! It is written with grace and wit . . . style and subtlety. . . . A work of intelligence and craftsmanship."
—*Los Angeles Times*

"A sure-fire gripper!" —*Wall Street Journal*

THREE COMPLETE NOVELS

MICHAEL CRICHTON

THREE COMPLETE NOVELS

MICHAEL CRICHTON

THE ANDROMEDA STRAIN
THE TERMINAL MAN
THE GREAT TRAIN ROBBERY

WINGS BOOKS
NEW YORK • AVENEL, NEW JERSEY

This edition contains the complete and unabridged texts of the original editions.
They have been completely reset for this volume.

This omnibus was originally published in separate volumes under the titles:

This 1993 edition is published by Wings Books,
distributed by Outlet Book Company, Inc., a Random House Company,
40 Engelhard Avenue, Avenel, New Jersey 07001,
by arrangement with Alfred A. Knopf, Inc.

Random House
New York · Toronto · London · Sydney · Auckland

Printed and bound in the United States of America

Library of Congress Cataloging-in-Publication Data

Crichton, Michael, 1942–
[Novels. Selections]
Three complete novels / Michael Crichton.
p. cm.
Contents: The Andromeda strain—Terminal man—The great train robbery.
ISBN 0-517-08479-1
I. Title.
PS3553.R48A6 1993
813′.54—dc20 92-38676
CIP

8 7 6 5 4 3 2 1

CONTENTS

THE ANDROMEDA STRAIN
1

THE TERMINAL MAN
233

THE GREAT TRAIN ROBBERY
435

THE ANDROMEDA STRAIN

for

A.C.D., M.D.,

who first proposed

the problem

The survival value of human intelligence has never been satisfactorily demonstrated.

—JEREMY STONE

Increasing vision is increasingly expensive.

—R. A. JANEK

ANDROMEDA STRAIN

ANDROMEDA STRAIN

THIS FILE IS CLASSIFIED TOP SECRET

Examination by unauthorized persons
is a criminal offense punishable
by fines and imprisonment up to
20 years and $20,000.

DO NOT ACCEPT FROM COURIER
IF SEAL IS BROKEN

The courier is required by law
to demand your card 7592. He
is not permitted to relinquish
this file without such proof of
identity.

MACHINE SCORE REVIEW BELOW

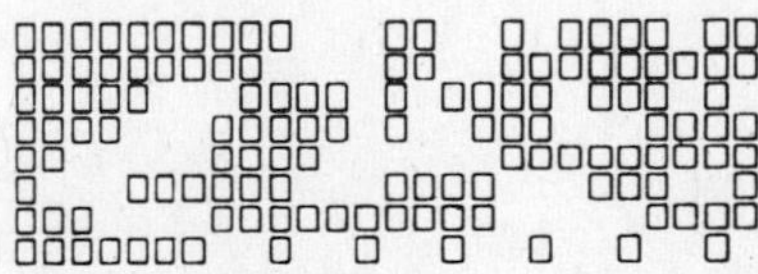

ACKNOWLEDGMENTS

This book recounts the five-day history of a major American scientific crisis.

As in most crises, the events surrounding the Andromeda Strain were a compound of foresight and foolishness, innocence and ignorance. Nearly everyone involved had moments of great brilliance, and moments of unaccountable stupidity. It is therefore impossible to write about the events without offending some of the participants.

However, I think it is important that the story be told. This country supports the largest scientific establishment in the history of mankind. New discoveries are constantly being made, and many of these discoveries have important political or social overtones. In the near future, we can expect more crises on the pattern of Andromeda. Thus I believe it is useful for the public to be made aware of the way in which scientific crises arise, and are dealt with.

In researching and recounting the history of the Andromeda Strain, I received the generous help of many people who felt as I did, and who encouraged me to tell the story accurately and in detail.

My particular thanks must go to Major General Willis A. Haverford, United States Army; Lieutenant Everett J. Sloane, United States Navy (Ret.); Captain L. S. Waterhouse, United States Air Force (Vandenberg Special Projects Division); Colonel Henley Jackson and Colonel Stanley Friedrich, both of Wright Patterson; and Murray Charles of the Pentagon Press Division.

For their help in elucidating the background of the Wildfire Project, I must thank Roger White, National Aeronautics and Space Administration (Houston MSC); John Roble, NASA Kennedy Complex 13; Peter J. Mason, NASA Intelligence (Arlington Hall); Dr. Francis Martin, University of California (Berkeley) and the President's Science Advisory Council; Dr. Max Byrd, USIA; Kenneth Vorhees, White House Press Corps; and Professor Jonathan Percy of the University of Chicago (Genetics Department).

For their review of relevant chapters of the manuscript, and for their technical corrections and suggestions, I wish to thank Christian P. Lewis,

Goddard Space Flight Center; Herbert Stanch, Avco, Inc.; James P. Baker, Jet Propulsion Laboratory; Carlos N. Sandos, California Institute of Technology; Dr. Brian Stack, University of Michigan; Edgar Blalock, Hudson Institute; Professor Linus Kjelling, the RAND Corporation; Dr. Eldredge Benson, National Institutes of Health.

Lastly, I wish to thank the participants in the Wildfire Project and the investigation of the so-called Andromeda Strain. All agreed to see me and, with many, my interviews lasted over a period of days. Furthermore, I was able to draw upon the transcripts of their debriefing, which are stored in Arlington Hall (Substation Seven) and which amounted to more than fifteen thousand pages of typewritten manuscript. This material, stored in twenty volumes, represents the full story of the events at Flatrock, Nevada, as told by each of the participants, and I was thus able to utilize their separate viewpoints in preparing a composite account.

This is a rather technical narrative, centering on complex issues of science. Wherever possible, I have explained the scientific questions, problems, and techniques. I have avoided the temptation to simplify both the issues and the answers, and if the reader must occasionally struggle through an arid passage of technical detail, I apologize.

I have also tried to retain the tension and excitement of events in these five days, for there is an inherent drama in the story of Andromeda, and if it is a chronicle of stupid, deadly blunders, it is also a chronicle of heroism and intelligence.

M.C.
Cambridge, Massachusetts
January 1969

DAY 1

CONTACT

Chapter 1

The Country of Lost Borders

A man with binoculars. That is how it began: with a man standing by the side of the road, on a crest overlooking a small Arizona town, on a winter night.

Lieutenant Roger Shawn must have found the binoculars difficult. The metal would be cold, and he would be clumsy in his fur parka and heavy gloves. His breath, hissing out into the moonlit air, would have fogged the lenses. He would be forced to pause to wipe them frequently, using a stubby gloved finger.

He could not have known the futility of this action. Binoculars were worthless to see into that town and uncover its secrets. He would have been astonished to learn that the men who finally succeeded used instruments a million times more powerful than binoculars.

There is something sad, foolish, and human in the image of Shawn leaning against a boulder, propping his arms on it, and holding the binoculars to his eyes. Though cumbersome, the binoculars would at least feel comfortable and familiar in his hands. It would be one of the last familiar sensations before his death.

We can imagine, and try to reconstruct, what happened from that point on.

Lieutenant Shawn swept over the town slowly and methodically. He could see it was not large, just a half-dozen wooden buildings, set out along a single main street. It was very quiet: no lights, no activity, no sound carried by the gentle wind.

He shifted his attention from the town to the surrounding hills. They were low, dusty, and blunted, with scrubby vegetation and an occasional withered yucca tree crusted in snow. Beyond the hills were more hills, and then the flat expanse of the Mojave Desert, trackless and vast. The Indians called it the Country of Lost Borders.

Lieutenant Shawn found himself shivering in the wind. It was February, the coldest month, and it was after ten. He walked back up the road toward the Ford Econovan, with the large rotating antenna on top. The motor was idling softly; it was the only sound he could hear. He opened the rear doors and climbed into the back, shutting the doors behind him.

He was enveloped in deep-red light: a night light, so that he would not be blinded when he stepped outside. In the red light the banks of instruments and electronic equipment glowed greenly.

Private Lewis Crane, the electronics technician, was there, also wearing a parka. He was hunched over a map, making calculations with occasional reference to the instruments before him.

Shawn asked Crane if he were certain they had arrived at the place, and Crane confirmed that they had. Both men were tired: they had driven all day from Vandenberg in search of the latest Scoop satellite. Neither knew much about the Scoops, except that they were a series of secret capsules intended to analyze the upper atmosphere and then return. Shawn and Crane had the job of finding the capsules once they had landed.

In order to facilitate recovery, the satellites were fitted with electronic beepers that began to transmit signals when they came down to an altitude of five miles.

That was why the van had so much radio-directional equipment. In essence, it was performing its own triangulation. In Army parlance it was known as single-unit triangulation, and it was highly effective, though slow. The procedure was simple enough: the van stopped and fixed its position, recording the strength and direction of the radio beam from the satellite. Once this was done, it would be driven in the most likely direction of the satellite for a distance of twenty miles. Then it would stop and take new coordinates. In this way, a series of triangulation points could be mapped, and the van could proceed to the satellite by a zigzag path, stopping every twenty miles to correct any error. The method was slower than using two vans, but it was safer—the Army felt that two vans in an area might arouse suspicion.

For six hours, the van had been closing on the Scoop satellite. Now they were almost there.

Crane tapped the map with a pencil in a nervous way and announced the name of the town at the foot of the hill: Piedmont, Arizona. Population forty-eight; both men laughed over that, though they were both inwardly concerned. The Vandenberg ESA, or Estimated Site of Arrival, had been twelve miles north of Piedmont. Vandenberg computed this site on the basis of radar observations and 1410 computer trajectory projections. The estimates were not usually wrong by more than a few hundred yards.

Yet there was no denying the radio-directional equipment, which located the satellite beeper directly in the center of town. Shawn suggested that someone from the town might have seen it coming down—it would be glowing with the heat—and might have retrieved it, bringing it into Piedmont.

This was reasonable, except that a native of Piedmont who happened upon an American satellite fresh from space would have told someone—reporters, police, NASA, the Army, *someone*.

But they had heard nothing.

Shawn climbed back down from the van, with Crane scrambling after him, shivering as the cold air struck him. Together, the two men looked out over the town.

It was peaceful, but completely dark. Shawn noticed that the gas station and the motel both had their lights doused. Yet they represented the only gas station and motel for miles.

And then Shawn noticed the birds.

In the light of the full moon he could see them, big birds, gliding in slow circles over the buildings, passing like black shadows across the face of the moon. He wondered why he hadn't noticed them before, and asked Crane what he made of them.

Crane said he didn't make anything of them. As a joke, he added, "Maybe they're buzzards."

"That's what they look like, all right," Shawn said.

Crane laughed nervously, his breath hissing out into the night. "But why should there be buzzards here? They only come when something is dead."

Shawn lit a cigarette, cupping his hands around the lighter, protecting the flame from the wind. He said nothing, but looked down at the buildings, the outline of the little town. Then he scanned the town once more with binoculars, but saw no signs of life or movement.

At length, he lowered the binoculars and dropped his cigarette onto the crisp snow, where it sputtered and died.

He turned to Crane and said, "We'd better go down and have a look."

Chapter 2

Vandenberg

Three hundred miles away, in the large, square, windowless room that served as Mission Control for Project Scoop, Lieutenant Edgar Comroe sat with his feet on his desk and a stack of scientific-journal articles before him. Comroe was serving as control officer for the night; it was a duty he filled once a month, directing the evening operations of the skeleton crew of twelve. Tonight, the crew was monitoring the progress and reports of the van coded Caper One, now making its way across the Arizona desert.

Comroe disliked this job. The room was gray and lighted with fluorescent lights; the tone was sparsely utilitarian and Comroe found it unpleasant. He never came to Mission Control except during a launch, when the atmosphere was different. Then the room was filled with busy technicians, each at work on a single complex task, each tense with the peculiar cold anticipation that precedes any spacecraft launch.

But nights were dull. Nothing ever happened at night. Comroe took advantage of the time and used it to catch up on reading. By profession he was a cardiovascular physiologist, with special interest in stresses induced at high-G accelerations.

Tonight, Comroe was reviewing a journal article titled "Stoichiometrics of Oxygen-Carrying Capacity and Diffusion Gradients with Increased

Arterial Gas Tensions." He found it slow reading, and only moderately interesting. Thus he was willing to be interrupted when the overhead loudspeaker, which carried the voice transmission from the van of Shawn and Crane, clicked on.

Shawn said, "This is Caper One to Vandal Deca. Caper One to Vandal Deca. Are you reading. Over."

Comroe, feeling amused, replied that he was indeed reading.

"We are about to enter the town of Piedmont and recover the satellite."

"Very good, Caper One. Leave your radio open."

"Roger."

This was a regulation of the recovery technique, as outlined in the Systems Rules Manual of Project Scoop. The SRM was a thick gray paperback that sat at one corner of Comroe's desk, where he could refer to it easily. Comroe knew that conversation between van and base was taped, and later became part of the permanent project file, but he had never understood any good reason for this. In fact, it had always seemed to him a straightforward proposition: the van went out, got the capsule, and came back.

He shrugged and returned to his paper on gas tensions, only half listening to Shawn's voice as it said, "We are now inside the town. We have just passed a gas station and a motel. All quiet here. There is no sign of life. The signals from the satellite are stronger. There is a church half a block ahead. There are no lights or activity of any kind."

Comroe put his journal down. The strained quality of Shawn's voice was unmistakable. Normally Comroe would have been amused at the thought of two grown men made jittery by entering a small, sleepy desert town. But he knew Shawn personally, and he knew that Shawn, whatever other virtues he might have, utterly lacked an imagination. Shawn could fall asleep in a horror movie. He was that kind of man.

Comroe began to listen.

Over the crackling static, he heard the rumbling of the van engine. And he heard the two men in the van talking quietly.

Shawn: "Pretty quiet around here."
Crane: "Yes sir."
There was a pause.
Crane: "Sir?"
Shawn: "Yes?"
Crane: "Did you see that?"
Shawn: "See what?"
Crane: "Back there, on the sidewalk. It looked like a body."
Shawn: "You're imagining things."

Another pause, and then Comroe heard the van come to a halt, brakes squealing.

Shawn: "Jesus."
Crane: "It's another one, sir."
Shawn: "Looks dead."
Crane: "Shall I—"
Shawn: "No. Stay in the van."

His voice became louder, more formal, as he ran through the call. "This is Caper One to Vandal Deca. Over."

Comroe picked up the microphone. "Reading you. What's happened?"

Shawn, his voice tight, said, "Sir, we see bodies. Lots of them. They appear to be dead."

"Are you certain, Caper One?"

"For Christ's sake," Shawn said. "Of course we're certain."

Comroe said mildly, "Proceed to the capsule, Caper One."

As he did so, he looked around the room. The twelve other men in the skeleton crew were staring at him, their eyes blank, unseeing. They were listening to the transmission.

The van rumbled to life again.

Comroe swung his feet off the desk and punched the red "Security" button on his console. That button automatically isolated the Mission Control room. No one would be allowed in or out without Comroe's permission.

Then he picked up the telephone and said, "Get me Major Manchek. M-A-N-C-H-E-K. This is a stat call. I'll hold."

Manchek was the chief duty officer for the month, the man directly responsible for all Scoop activities during February.

While he waited, he cradled the phone in his shoulder and lit a cigarette. Over the loudspeaker, Shawn could be heard to say, "Do they look dead to you, Crane?"

Crane: "Yes sir. Kind of peaceful, but dead."
Shawn: "Somehow they don't really look dead. There's something missing. Something funny . . . But they're all over. Must be dozens of them."
Crane: "Like they dropped in their tracks. Stumbled and fallen down dead."
Shawn: "All over the streets, on the sidewalks . . ."
Another silence, then Crane: "Sir!"
Shawn: "Jesus."
Crane: "You see him? The man in the white robe, walking across the street—"
Shawn: "I see him."
Crane: "He's just stepping over them like—"
Shawn: "He's coming toward us."
Crane: "Sir, look, I think we should get out of here, if you don't mind my—"

The next sound was a high-pitched scream, and a crunching noise. Transmission ended at this point, and Vandenberg Scoop Mission Control was not able to raise the two men again.

Chapter 3

Crisis

Gladstone, upon hearing of the death of "Chinese" Gordon in Egypt, was reported to have muttered irritably that his general might have chosen a more propitious time to die: Gordon's death threw the Gladstone government into turmoil and crisis. An aide suggested that the circumstances were unique and unpredictable, to which Gladstone crossly answered: "All crises are the same."

He meant political crises, of course. There were no scientific crises in 1885, and indeed none for nearly forty years afterward. Since then there have been eight of major importance; two have received wide publicity. It is interesting that both the publicized crises—atomic energy and space capability—have concerned chemistry and physics, not biology.

This is to be expected. Physics was the first of the natural sciences to become fully modern and highly mathematical. Chemistry followed in the wake of physics, but biology, the retarded child, lagged far behind. Even in the time of Newton and Galileo, men knew more about the moon and other heavenly bodies than they did about their own.

It was not until the late 1940's that this situation changed. The postwar period ushered in a new era of biologic research, spurred by the discovery of antibiotics. Suddenly there was both enthusiasm and money for biology, and a torrent of discoveries poured forth: tranquilizers, steroid hormones, immunochemistry, the genetic code. By 1953 the first kidney was transplanted and by 1958 the first birth control pills were tested. It was not long before biology was the fastest-growing field in all science; it was doubling its knowledge every ten years. Farsighted researchers talked seriously of changing genes, controlling evolution, regulating the mind—ideas that had been wild speculation ten years before.

And yet there had never been a biologic crisis. The Andromeda Strain provided the first.

According to Lewis Bornheim, a crisis is a situation in which a previously tolerable set of circumstances is suddenly, by the addition of another factor, rendered wholly intolerable. Whether the additional factor is political, economic, or scientific hardly matters: the death of a national hero, the instability of prices, or a technological discovery can all set events in motion. In this sense, Gladstone was right: all crises are the same.

The noted scholar Alfred Pockran, in his study of crises *(Culture, Crisis and Change)*, has made several interesting points. First, he observes that every crisis has its beginnings long before the actual onset. Thus Einstein published his theories of relativity in 1905–15, forty years before his work culminated in the end of a war, the start of an age, and the beginnings of a crisis.

Similarly, in the early twentieth century, American, German, and Russian scientists were all interested in space travel, but only the Germans recognized the military potential of rockets. And after the war, when the German rocket installation at Peenemünde was cannibalized by the Soviets and Americans, it was only the Russians who made immediate, vigorous moves toward developing space capabilities. The Americans were content to tinker playfully with rockets—and ten years later, this resulted in an American scientific crisis involving Sputnik, American education, the ICBM, and the missile gap.

Pockran also observes that a crisis is compounded of individuals and personalities, which are unique:

> It is as difficult to imagine Alexander at the Rubicon, and Eisenhower at Waterloo, as it is difficult to imagine Darwin writing to Roosevelt about the potential for an atomic bomb. A crisis is made by men, who enter into the crisis with their own prejudices, propensities, and predispositions. A crisis is the sum of intuition and blind spots, a blend of facts noted and facts ignored.
>
> Yet underlying the uniqueness of each crisis is a disturbing sameness. A characteristic of all crises is their predictability, in retrospect. They seem to have a certain inevitability, they seem predestined. This is not true of all crises, but it is true of sufficiently many to make the most hardened historian cynical and misanthropic.

In the light of Pockran's arguments, it is interesting to consider the background and personalities involved in the Andromeda Strain. At the time of Andromeda, there had never been a crisis of biological science, and the first Americans faced with the facts were not disposed to think in terms of one. Shawn and Crane were capable but not thoughtful men, and Edgar Comroe, the night officer at Vandenberg, though a scientist, was not prepared to consider anything beyond the immediate irritation of a quiet evening ruined by an inexplicable problem.

According to protocol, Comroe called his superior officer, Major Arthur Manchek, and here the story takes a different turn. For Manchek was both prepared and disposed to consider a crisis of the most major proportions.

But he was not prepared to acknowledge it.

Major Manchek, his face still creased with sleep, sat on the edge of Comroe's desk and listened to the replay of the tape from the van.

When it was finished, he said, "Strangest damned thing I ever heard," and played it over again. While he did so, he carefully filled his pipe with tobacco, lit it, and tamped it down.

Arthur Manchek was an engineer, a quiet heavyset man plagued by labile hypertension, which threatened to end further promotions as an Army officer. He had been advised on many occasions to lose weight, but had been unable to do so. He was therefore considering abandoning the Army for a career as a scientist in private industry, where people did not care what your weight or blood pressure was.

Manchek had come to Vandenberg from Wright Patterson in Ohio, where he had been in charge of experiments in spacecraft landing methods. His job had been to develop a capsule shape that could touch down with equal safety on either land or sea. Manchek had succeeded in developing three new shapes that were promising; his success led to a promotion and transfer to Vandenberg.

Here he did administrative work, and hated it. People bored Manchek; the mechanics of manipulation and the vagaries of subordinate personality held no fascination for him. He often wished he were back at the wind tunnels of Wright Patterson.

Particularly on nights when he was called out of bed by some damnfool problem.

Tonight he felt irritable, and under stress. His reaction to this was characteristic: he became slow. He moved slowly, he thought slowly, he proceeded with a dull and plodding deliberation. It was the secret of his success. Whenever people around him became excited, Manchek seemed to grow more disinterested, until he appeared about to fall asleep. It was a trick he had for remaining totally objective and clearheaded.

Now he sighed and puffed on his pipe as the tape spun out for the second time.

"No communications breakdown, I take it?"

Comroe shook his head. "We checked all systems at this end. We are still monitoring the frequency." He turned on the radio, and hissing static filled the room. "You know about the audio screen?"

"Vaguely," Manchek said, suppressing a yawn. In fact, the audio screen was a system he had developed three years before. In simplest terms, it was a computerized way to find a needle in a haystack—a machine program that listened to apparently garbled, random sound and picked out certain irregularities. For example, the hubbub of conversation at an embassy cocktail party could be recorded and fed through the computer, which would pick out a single voice and separate it from the rest.

It had several intelligence applications.

"Well," Comroe said, "after the transmission ended, we got nothing but the static you hear now. We put it through the audio screen, to see if the computer could pick up a pattern. And we ran it through the oscilloscope in the corner."

Across the room, the green face of the scope displayed a jagged dancing white line—the summated sound of static.

"Then," Comroe said, "we cut in the computer. Like so."

He punched a button on his desk console. The oscilloscope line changed character abruptly. It suddenly became quieter, more regular, with a pattern of beating, thumping impulses.

"I see," Manchek said. He had, in fact, already identified the pattern and assessed its meaning. His mind was drifting elsewhere, considering other possibilities, wider ramifications.

"Here's the audio," Comroe said. He pressed another button and the audio version of the signal filled the room. It was a steady mechanical grinding with a repetitive metallic click.

Manchek nodded. "An engine. With a knock."

"Yes sir. We believe the van radio is still broadcasting, and that the engine is still running. That's what we're hearing now, with the static screened away."

"All right," Manchek said.

His pipe went out. He sucked on it for a moment, then lit it again, removed it from his mouth, and plucked a bit of tobacco from his tongue.

"We need evidence," he said, almost to himself. He was considering categories of evidence, and possible findings, contingencies . . .

"Evidence of what?" Comroe said.

Manchek ignored the question. "Have we got a Scavenger on the base?"

"I'm not sure, sir. If we don't, we can get one from Edwards."

"Then do it." Manchek stood up. He had made his decision, and now he felt tired again. An evening of telephone calls faced him, an evening of irritable operators and bad connections and puzzled voices at the other end.

"We'll want a flyby over that town," he said. "And a complete scan. All canisters to come directly. Alert the labs."

He also ordered Comroe to bring in the technicians, especially Jaggers. Manchek disliked Jaggers, who was effete and precious. But Manchek also knew that Jaggers was good, and tonight he needed a good man.

At 11:07 P.M., Samuel "Gunner" Wilson was moving at 645 miles per hour over the Mojave Desert. Up ahead in the moonlight, he saw the twin lead jets, their afterburners glowing angrily in the night sky. The planes had a heavy, pregnant look: phosphorus bombs were slung beneath the wings and belly.

Wilson's plane was different, sleek and long and black. It was a Scavenger, one of seven in the world.

The Scavenger was the operational version of the X-18. It was an intermediate-range reconnaissance jet aircraft fully equipped for day or night intelligence flights. It was fitted with two side-slung 16mm cameras, one for the visible spectrum, and one for low-frequency radiation. In addition it had a center-mount Homans infrared multispex camera as well as the usual electronic and radio-detection gear. All films and plates were, of course, processed automatically in the air, and were ready for viewing as soon as the aircraft returned to base.

All this technology made the Scavenger almost impossibly sensitive. It could map the outlines of a city in blackout, and could follow the movements of individual trucks and cars at eight thousand feet. It could detect a submarine to a depth of two hundred feet. It could locate harbor mines by wave-motion deformities and it could obtain a precise photograph of a factory from the residual heat of the building four hours after it had shut down.

So the Scavenger was the ideal instrument to fly over Piedmont, Arizona, in the dead of night.

Wilson carefully checked his equipment, his hands fluttering over the controls, touching each button and lever, watching the blinking green lights that indicated that all systems were in order.

His earphones crackled. The lead plane said lazily, "Coming up on the town, Gunner. You see it?"

He leaned forward in the cramped cockpit. He was low, only five hundred feet above the ground, and for a moment he could see nothing but a blur of sand, snow, and yucca trees. Then, up ahead, buildings in the moonlight.

"Roger. I see it."

"Okay, Gunner. Give us room."

He dropped back, putting half a mile between himself and the other two planes. They were going into the P-square formation, for direct visualization of target by phosphorus flare. Direct visualization was not really necessary; Scavenger could function without it. But Vandenberg seemed insistent that they gather all possible information about the town.

The lead planes spread, moving wide until they were parallel to the main street of the town.

"Gunner? Ready to roll?"

Wilson placed his fingers delicately over the camera buttons. Four fingers: as if playing the piano.

"Ready."

"We're going in now."

The two planes swooped low, dipping gracefully toward the town. They were now very wide and seemingly inches above the ground as they began to release the bombs. As each struck the ground, a blazing white-hot sphere went up, bathing the town in an unearthly, glaring light and reflecting off the metal underbellies of the planes.

The jets climbed, their run finished, but Gunner did not see them. His entire attention, his mind and his body, was focused on the town.

"All yours, Gunner."

Wilson did not answer. He dropped his nose, cracked down his flaps, and felt a shudder as the plane sank sickeningly, like a stone, toward the ground. Below him, the area around the town was lighted for hundreds of yards in every direction. He pressed the camera buttons and felt, rather than heard, the vibrating whir of the cameras.

For a long moment he continued to fall, and then he shoved the stick forward, and the plane seemed to catch in the air, to grab, and lift and climb. He had a fleeting glimpse of the main street. He saw bodies, bodies everywhere, spreadeagled, lying in the streets, across cars . . .

"Jesus," he said.

And then he was up, still climbing, bringing the plane around in a slow arc, preparing for the descent into his second run and trying not to think of what he had seen. One of the first rules of air reconnaissance was "Ignore the scenery"; analysis and evaluation were not the job of the pilot. That was left to the experts, and pilots who forgot this, who became too interested in what they were photographing, got into trouble. Usually they crashed.

As the plane came down into a flat second run, he tried not to look at the ground. But he did, and again saw the bodies. The phosphorus flares were burning low, the lighting was darker, more sinister and subdued. But the bodies were still there: he had not been imagining it.

"Jesus," he said again. "Sweet Jesus."

The sign on the door said DATA PROSSEX EPSILON, and underneath, in red lettering, ADMISSION BY CLEARANCE CARD ONLY. Inside was a comfortable sort of briefing room: screen on one wall, a dozen steel-tubing and leather chairs facing it, and a projector in the back.

When Manchek and Comroe entered the room, Jaggers was already waiting for them, standing at the front of the room by the screen. Jaggers was a short man with a springy step and an eager, rather hopeful face. Though not well liked on the base, he was nonetheless the acknowledged master of reconnaissance interpretation. He had the sort of mind that delighted in small and puzzling details, and was well suited to his job.

Jaggers rubbed his hands as Manchek and Comroe sat down. "Well then," he said. "Might as well get right to it. I think we have something to interest you tonight." He nodded to the projectionist in the back. "First picture."

The room lights darkened. There was a mechanical click, and the screen lighted to show an aerial view of a small desert town.

"This is an unusual shot," Jaggers said. "From our files. Taken two months ago from Janos 12, our recon satellite. Orbiting at an altitude of one hundred and eighty-seven miles, as you know. The technical quality here is quite good. Can't read the license plates on the cars yet, but we're working on it. Perhaps by next year."

Manchek shifted in his chair, but said nothing.

"You can see the town here," Jaggers said. "Piedmont, Arizona. Population forty-eight, and not much to look at, even from one hundred and eighty-seven miles. Here's the general store; the gas station—notice how clearly you can read GULF—and the post office; the motel. Everything else you see is private residences. Church over here. Well: next picture."

Another click. This was dark, with a reddish tint, and was clearly an overview of the town in white and dark red. The outlines of the buildings were very dark.

"We begin here with the Scavenger IR plates. These are infrared films, as you know, which produce a picture on the basis of heat instead of light. Anything warm appears white on the picture; anything cold is black. Now then. You can see here that the buildings are dark—they are colder than the ground. As night comes on, the buildings give up their heat more rapidly."

"What are those white spots?" Comroe said. There were forty or fifty white areas on the film.

"Those," Jaggers said, "are bodies. Some inside houses, some in the street. By count, they number fifty. In the case of some of them, such as this one here, you can make out the four limbs and head clearly. This body is lying flat. In the street."

He lit a cigarette and pointed to a white rectangle. "As nearly as we can tell, this is an automobile. Notice it's got a bright white spot at one end. This means the motor is still running, still generating heat."

"The van," Comroe said. Manchek nodded.

"The question now arises," Jaggers said, "are all these people dead? We cannot be certain about that. The bodies appear to be of different temperatures. Forty-seven are rather cold, indicating death some time ago. Three are warmer. Two of those are in this car, here."

"Our men," Comroe said. "And the third?"

"The third is rather puzzling. You see him here, apparently standing or lying curled in the street. Observe that he is quite white, and therefore quite warm. Our temperature scans indicate that he is about ninety-five degrees, which is a little on the cool side, but probably attributable to peripheral vasoconstriction in the night desert air. Drops his skin temperature. Next slide."

The third film flicked onto the screen.

Manchek frowned at the spot. "It's moved."

"Exactly. This film was made on the second passage. The spot has moved approximately twenty yards. Next picture."

A third film.

"Moved again!"

"Yes. An additional five or ten yards."

"So one person down there is alive?"

"That," Jaggers said, "is the presumptive conclusion."

Manchek cleared his throat. "Does that mean it's what you think?"

"Yes sir. It is what we think."

"There's a man down there, walking among the corpses?"

Jaggers shrugged and tapped the screen. "It is difficult to account for the data in any other manner, and—"

At that moment, a private entered the room with three circular metal canisters under his arm.

"Sir, we have films of the direct visualization by P-square."

"Run them," Manchek said.

The film was threaded into a projector. A moment later, Lieutenant Wilson was ushered into the room. Jaggers said, "I haven't reviewed these films yet. Perhaps the pilot should narrate."

Manchek nodded and looked at Wilson, who got up and walked to the front of the room, wiping his hands nervously on his pants. He stood alongside the screen and faced his audience, beginning in a flat monotone: "Sir, my flybys were made between 11:08 and 11:13 P.M. this evening. There were two, a start from the east and a return from the west, done at an average speed of two hundred and fourteen miles per hour, at a median altitude by corrected altimeter of eight hundred feet and an—"

"Just a minute, son," Manchek said, raising his hand. "This isn't a grilling. Just tell it naturally."

Wilson nodded and swallowed. The room lights went down and the projector whirred to life. The screen showed the town bathed in glaring white light as the plane came down over it.

"This is my first pass," Wilson said. "East to west, at 11:08. We're looking from the left-wing camera which is running at ninety-six frames per second. As you can see, my altitude is falling rapidly. Straight ahead is the main street of the target . . ."

He stopped. The bodies were clearly visible. And the van, stopped in the street, its rooftop antenna still turning slow revolutions. As the plane continued its run, approaching the van, they could see the driver collapsed over the steering wheel.

"Excellent definition," Jaggers said. "That fine-grain film really gives resolution when you need—"

"Wilson," Manchek said, "was telling us about his run."

"Yes sir," Wilson said, clearing his throat. He stared at the screen. "At this time I am right over target, where I observed the casualties you see here. My estimate at that time was seventy-five, sir."

His voice was quiet and tense. There was a break in the film, some numbers, and the image came on again.

"Now I am coming back for my second run," Wilson said. "The flares are already burning low but you can see—"

"Stop the film," Manchek said.

The projectionist froze the film at a single frame. It showed the long, straight main street of the town, and the bodies.

"Go back."

The film was run backward, the jet seeming to pull away from the street.

"There! Stop it now."

The frame was frozen. Manchek got up and walked close to the screen, peering off to one side.

"Look at this," he said, pointing to a figure. It was a man in knee-length white robes, standing and looking up at the plane. He was an old man, with a withered face. His eyes were wide.

"What do you make of this?" Manchek said to Jaggers.

Jaggers moved close. He frowned. "Run it forward a bit."

The film advanced. They could clearly see the man turn his head, roll his eyes, following the plane as it passed over him.

"Now backward," Jaggers said.

The film was run back. Jaggers smiled bleakly. "The man looks alive to me, sir."

"Yes," Manchek said crisply. "He certainly does."

And with that, he walked out of the room. As he left, he paused and announced that he was declaring a state of emergency; that everyone on the base was confined to quarters until further notice; that there would be no outside calls or communication; and that what they had seen in this room was confidential.

Outside in the hallway, he headed for Mission Control. Comroe followed him.

"I want you to call General Wheeler," Manchek said. "Tell him I have declared an SOE without proper authorization, and ask him to come down immediately." Technically no one but the commander had the right to declare a state of emergency.

Comroe said, "Wouldn't you rather tell him yourself?"

"I've got other things to do," Manchek said.

Chapter 4

Alert

When Arthur Manchek stepped into the small soundproofed booth and sat down before the telephone, he knew exactly what he was going to do—but he was not very sure why he was doing it.

As one of the senior Scoop officers, he had received a briefing nearly a year before on Project Wildfire. It had been given, Manchek remembered, by a short little man with a dry, precise way of speaking. He was a university professor and he had outlined the project. Manchek had forgotten the details, except that there was a laboratory somewhere, and a team of five scientists who could be alerted to man the laboratory. The function of the team was investigation of possible extraterrestrial life forms introduced on American spacecraft returning to earth.

Manchek had not been told who the five men were; he knew only that a special Defense Department trunk line existed for calling them out. In order to hook into the line, one had only to dial the binary of some number. He reached into his pocket and withdrew his wallet, then fumbled for a moment until he found the card he had been given by the professor:

IN CASE OF FIRE
Notify Division 87
Emergencies Only

He stared at the card and wondered what exactly would happen if he dialed the binary of 87. He tried to imagine the sequence of events: Who would he talk to? Would someone call him back? Would there be an inquiry, a referral to higher authority?

He rubbed his eyes and stared at the card, and finally he shrugged. One way or the other, he would find out.

He tore a sheet of paper from the pad in front of him, next to the telephone, and wrote:

$$2^0 \quad 2^1 \quad 2^2 \quad 2^3 \quad 2^4 \quad 2^5 \quad 2^6 \quad 2^7$$

This was the basis of the binary system: base two raised to some power. Two to the zero power was one; two to the first was two, two squared was four; and so on. Manchek quickly wrote another line beneath:

2^0	2^1	2^2	2^3	2^4	2^5	2^6	2^7
1	2	4	8	16	32	64	128

Then he began to add up the numbers to get a total of 87. He circled these numbers:

2^0	2^1	2^2	2^3	2^4	2^5	2^6	2^7
1	2	4	8	16	32	64	128 = 87

And then he drew in the binary code. Binary numbers were designed for computers which utilize an on-off, yes-no kind of language. A mathematician once joked that binary numbers were the way people who have only two fingers count. In essence, binary numbers translated normal numbers —which require ten digits, and decimal places—to a system that depended on only two digits, one and zero.

2^0	2^1	2^2	2^3	2^4	2^5	2^6	2^7
1	2	4	8	16	32	64	128
1	1	1	0	1	0	1	0

Manchek looked at the number he had just written, and inserted the dashes: 1-110-1010. A perfectly reasonable telephone number.

Manchek picked up the telephone and dialed.

The time was exactly twelve midnight.

DAY 2

PIEDMONT

Chapter 5

The Early Hours

The machinery was there. The cables, the codes, the teleprinters had all been waiting dormant for two years. It only required Manchek's call to set the machinery in motion.

When he finished dialing, he heard a series of mechanical clicks, and then a low hum, which meant, he knew, that the call was being fed into one of the scrambled trunk lines. After a moment, the humming stopped and a voice said, "This is a recording. State your name and your message and hang up."

"Major Arthur Manchek, Vandenberg Air Force Base, Scoop Mission Control. I believe it is necessary to call up a Wildfire Alert. I have confirmatory visual data at this post, which has just been closed for security reasons."

As he spoke it occurred to him that it was all rather improbable. Even the tape recorder would disbelieve him. He continued to hold the telephone in his hand, somehow expecting an answer.

But there was none, only a click as the connection was automatically broken. The line was dead; he hung up and sighed. It was all very unsatisfying.

Manchek expected to be called back within a few minutes by Washington; he expected to receive many calls in the next few hours, and so remained at the phone. Yet he received no calls, for he did not know that the process he had initiated was automatic. Once mobilized, the Wildfire Alert would proceed ahead, and not be recalled for at least twelve hours.

Within ten minutes of Manchek's call, the following message clattered across the scrambled maximum-security cabler units of the nation:

■■■■■■■U N i T■■■■■■■■

TOP SECRET

CODE FOLLOWS
AS
CBW 9/9/234/435/6778/90
PULG COORDINATES DELTA 8997

MESSAGE FOLLOWS
AS
WILDFIRE ALERT HAS BEEN CALLED.
REPEAT WILDFIRE ALERT HAS BEEN
CALLED. COORDINATES TO READ
NASA/AMC/NSC COMB DEC.
TIME OF COMMAND TO READ
LL-59-07 ON DATE.

FURTHER NOTATIONS
AS
PRESS BLACKFACE
POTENTIAL DIRECTIVE 7-L2
ALERT STATUS UNTIL FURTHER NOTICE

END MESSAGE

■■■■■■■■■■■

DISENGAGE

This was an automatic cable. Everything about it, including the announcement of a press blackout and a possible directive 7–12, was automatic, and followed from Manchek's call.

Five minutes later, there was a second cable which named the men on the Wildfire team:

■■■■■■■U N I T■■■■■■■■

TOP SECRET

CODE FOLLOWS
AS
CBW 9/9/234/435/6778/900

MESSAGE FOLLOWS
AS
THE FOLLOWING MALE AMERICAN
CITIZENS ARE BEING PLACED
ON ZED KAPPA STATUS. PREVIOUS
TOP SECRET CLEARANCE HAS BEEN
CONFIRMED. THE NAMES ARE +

STONE, JEREMY ■■81
LEAVITT, PETER ■■04
BURTON, CHARLES ■L51
CHRISTIANSENKRIKECANCEL THIS LINE CANCEL
TO READ AS
KIRKE, CHRISTIAN ■142
HALL, MARK ■L77

ACCORD THESE MEN ZED KAPPA
STATUS UNTIL FURTHER NOTICE

END MESSAGE END MESSAGE

In theory, this cable was also quite routine; its purpose was to name the five members who were being given Zed Kappa status, the code for "OK" status. Unfortunately, however, the machine misprinted one of the names, and failed to reread the entire message. (Normally, when one of the printout units of a secret trunk line miswrote part of a message, the entire message was rewritten, or else it was reread by the computer to certify its corrected form.)

The message was thus open to doubt. In Washington and elsewhere, a computer expert was called in to confirm the accuracy of the message, by what is called "reverse tracing." The Washington expert expressed grave concern about the validity of the message since the machine was printing out other minor mistakes, such as "L" when it meant "I."

The upshot of all this was that the first two names on the list were accorded status, while the rest were not, pending confirmation.

Allison Stone was tired. At her home in the hills overlooking the Stanford campus, she and her husband, the chairman of the Stanford bacteriology department, had held a party for fifteen couples, and everyone had stayed late. Mrs. Stone was annoyed: she had been raised in official Washington, where one's second cup of coffee, offered pointedly without cognac, was accepted as a signal to go home. Unfortunately, she thought, academics did not follow the rules. She had served the second cup of coffee hours ago, and everybody was still there.

Shortly before one A.M., the doorbell rang. Answering it, she was surprised to see two military men standing side by side in the night. They seemed awkward and nervous to her, and she assumed they were lost; people often got lost driving through these residential areas at night.

"May I help you?"

"I'm sorry to disturb you, ma'am," one said politely. "But is this the residence of Dr. Jeremy Stone?"

"Yes," she said, frowning slightly. "It is."

She looked beyond the two men, to the driveway. A blue military sedan was parked there. Another man was standing by the car; he seemed to be holding something in his hand.

"Does that man have a gun?" she said.

"Ma'am," the man said, "we must see Dr. Stone at once, please."

It all seemed strange to her, and she found herself frightened. She looked across the lawn and saw a fourth man, moving up to the house and looking into the window. In the pale light streaming out onto the lawn, she could distinctly see the rifle in his hands.

"What's going on?"

"Ma'am, we don't want to disturb your party. Please call Dr. Stone to the door."

"I don't know if—"

"Otherwise, we will have to go get him," the man said.

She hesitated a moment, then said, "Wait here."

She stepped back and started to close the door, but one man had already slipped into the hall. He stood near the door, erect and very polite, with his hat in his hand. "I'll just wait here, ma'am," he said, and smiled at her.

She walked back to the party, trying to show nothing to the guests. Everyone was still talking and laughing; the room was noisy and dense with smoke. She found Jeremy in a corner, in the midst of some argument about riots. She touched his shoulder, and he disengaged himself from the group.

"I know this sounds funny," she said, "but there is some kind of Army man in the hall, and another outside, and two others with guns out on the lawn. They say they want to see you."

For a moment, Stone looked surprised, and then he nodded. "I'll take care of it," he said. His attitude annoyed her; he seemed almost to be expecting it.

"Well, if you knew about this, you might have told—"

"I didn't," he said. "I'll explain later."

He walked out to the hallway, where the officer was still waiting. She followed her husband.

Stone said, "I am Dr. Stone."

"Captain Morton," the man said. He did not offer to shake hands. "There's a fire, sir."

"All right," Stone said. He looked down at his dinner jacket. "Do I have time to change?"

"I'm afraid not, sir."

To her astonishment, Allison saw her husband nod quietly. "All right."

He turned to her and said, "I've got to leave." His face was blank and expressionless, and it seemed to her like a nightmare, his face like that, while he spoke. She was confused, and afraid.

"When will you be back?"

"I'm not sure. A week or two. Maybe longer."

She tried to keep her voice low, but she couldn't help it, she was upset. "What is it?" she said. "Are you under arrest?"

"No," he said, with a slight smile. "It's nothing like that. Make my apologies to everyone, will you?"

"But the guns—"

"Mrs. Stone," the military man said, "it's our job to protect your husband. From now on, nothing must be allowed to happen to him."

"That's right," Stone said. "You see, I'm suddenly an important person." He smiled again, an odd, crooked smile, and gave her a kiss.

And then, almost before she knew what was happening, he was walking out the door, with Captain Morton on one side of him and the other man on the other. The man with the rifle wordlessly fell into place behind them; the man by the car saluted and opened the door.

Then the car lights came on, and the doors slammed shut, and the car backed down the drive and drove off into the night. She was still standing by the door when one of her guests came up behind her and said, "Allison, are you all right?"

And she turned, and found she was able to smile and say, "Yes, it's nothing. Jeremy had to leave. The lab called him: another one of his late-night experiments going wrong."

The guest nodded and said, "Shame. It's a delightful party."

In the car, Stone sat back and stared at the men. He recalled that their faces were blank and expressionless. He said, "What have you got for me?"

"Got, sir?"

"Yes, dammit. What did they give you for me? They must have given you something."

"Oh. Yes sir."

He was handed a slim file. Stenciled on the brown cardboard cover was PROJECT SUMMARY: SCOOP.

"Nothing else?" Stone said.

"No sir."

Stone sighed. He had never heard of Project Scoop before; the file would have to be read carefully. But it was too dark in the car to read; there would be time for that later, on the airplane. He found himself thinking back over the last five years, back to the rather odd symposium on Long

Island, and the rather odd little speaker from England who had, in his own way, begun it all.

In the summer of 1962, J. J. Merrick, the English biophysicist, presented a paper to the Tenth Biological Symposium at Cold Spring Harbor, Long Island. The paper was entitled "Frequencies of Biologic Contact According to Speciation Probabilities." Merrick was a rebellious, unorthodox scientist whose reputation for clear thinking was not enhanced by his recent divorce or the presence of the handsome blond secretary he had brought with him to the symposium. Following the presentation of his paper, there was little serious discussion of Merrick's ideas, which were summarized at the end of the paper.

> I must conclude that the first contact with extraterrestrial life will be determined by the known probabilities of speciation. It is an undeniable fact that complex organisms are rare on earth, while simple organisms flourish in abundance. There are millions of species of bacteria, and thousands of species of insects. There are only a few species of primates, and only four of great apes. There is but one species of man.
>
> With this frequency of speciation goes a corresponding frequency in numbers. Simple creatures are much more common than complex organisms. There are three billion men on the earth, and that seems a great many until we consider that ten or even one hundred times that number of bacteria can be contained within a large flask.
>
> All available evidence on the origin of life points to an evolutionary progression from simple to complex life forms. This is true on earth. It is probably true throughout the universe. Shapley, Merrow, and others have calculated the number of viable planetary systems in the near universe. My own calculations, indicated earlier in the paper, consider the relative abundance of different organisms throughout the universe.
>
> My aim has been to determine the probability of contact between man and another life form. That probability is as follows:

FORM	PROBABILITY
Unicellular organisms or less (naked genetic information)	.7840
Multicellular organisms, simple	.1940
Multicellular organisms, complex but lacking coordinated central nervous system	.0140
Multicellular organisms with integrated organ systems including nervous system	.0078
Multicellular organisms with complex nervous system capable of handling 7 + data (human capability)	.0002
	1.0000

> These considerations lead me to believe that the first human interaction with extraterrestrial life will consist of contact with organisms similar to, if not identical to, earth bacteria or viruses. The consequences of such contact are disturbing when one recalls that 3 per cent of all earth bacteria are capable of exerting some deleterious effect upon man.

Later, Merrick himself considered the possibility that the first contact would consist of a plague brought back from the moon by the first men to go there. This idea was received with amusement by the assembled scientists.

One of the few who took it seriously was Jeremy Stone. At the age of thirty-six, Stone was perhaps the most famous person attending the symposium that year. He was professor of bacteriology at Berkeley, a post he had held since he was thirty, and he had just won the Nobel Prize.

The list of Stone's achievements—disregarding the particular series of experiments that led to the Nobel Prize—is astonishing. In 1955, he was the first to use the technique of multiplicative counts for bacterial colonies. In 1957, he developed a method for liquid-pure suspension. In 1960, Stone presented a radical new theory of operon activity in *E. coli* and *S. tabuli*, and developed evidence for the physical nature of the inducer and repressor substances. His 1958 paper on linear viral transformations opened broad new lines of scientific inquiry, particularly among the Pasteur Institute group in Paris, which subsequently won the Nobel Prize in 1966.

In 1961, Stone himself won the Nobel Prize. The award was given for work on bacterial mutant reversion that he had done in his spare time as a law student at Michigan, when he was twenty-six.

Perhaps the most significant thing about Stone was that he had done Nobel-caliber work as a law student, for it demonstrated the depth and range of his interests. A friend once said of him: "Jeremy knows everything, and is fascinated by the rest." Already he was being compared to Einstein and to Bohr as a scientist with a conscience, an overview, an appreciation of the significance of events.

Physically, Stone was a thin, balding man with a prodigious memory that catalogued scientific facts and blue jokes with equal facility. But his most outstanding characteristic was a sense of impatience, the feeling he conveyed to everyone around him that they were wasting his time. He had a bad habit of interrupting speakers and finishing conversations, a habit he tried to control with only limited success. His imperious manner, when added to the fact that he had won the Nobel Prize at an early age, as well as the scandals of his private life—he was four times married, twice to the wives of colleagues—did nothing to increase his popularity.

Yet it was Stone who, in the early 1960's, moved forward in government circles as one of the spokesmen for the new scientific establishment. He himself regarded this role with tolerant amusement—"a vacuum eager to be filled with hot gas," he once said—but in fact his influence was considerable.

By the early 1960's America had reluctantly come to realize that it possessed, as a nation, the most potent scientific complex in the history of the world. Eighty per cent of all scientific discoveries in the preceding three decades had been made by Americans. The United States had 75 per cent of the world's computers, and 90 per cent of the world's lasers. The United States had three and a half times as many scientists as the Soviet Union and spent three and a half times as much money on research; the U.S. had four times as many scientists as the European Economic Community and spent seven times as much on research. Most of this money came, directly or indirectly, from Congress, and Congress felt a great need for men to advise them on how to spend it.

During the 1950's, all the great advisers had been physicists: Teller and Oppenheimer and Bruckman and Weidner. But ten years later, with more money for biology and more concern for it, a new group emerged, led by DeBakey in Houston, Farmer in Boston, Heggerman in New York, and Stone in California.

Stone's prominence was attributable to many factors: the prestige of the Nobel Prize; his political contacts; his most recent wife, the daughter of Senator Thomas Wayne of Indiana; his legal training. All this combined to assure Stone's repeated appearance before confused Senate subcommittees—and gave him the power of any trusted adviser.

It was this same power that he used so successfully to implement the research and construction leading to Wildfire.

Stone was intrigued by Merrick's ideas, which paralleled certain concepts of his own. He explained these in a short paper entitled "Sterilization of Spacecraft," printed in *Science* and later reprinted in the British journal *Nature*. The argument stated that bacterial contamination was a two-edged sword, and that man must protect against both edges.

Previous to Stone's paper, most discussion of contamination dealt with the hazards to other planets of satellites and probes inadvertently carrying earth organisms. This problem was considered early in the American space effort; by 1959, NASA had set strict regulations for sterilization of earth-origin probes.

The object of these regulations was to prevent contamination of other worlds. Clearly, if a probe were being sent to Mars or Venus to search for new life forms, it would defeat the purpose of the experiment for the probe to carry earth bacteria with it.

Stone considered the reverse situation. He stated that it was equally possible for extraterrestrial organisms to contaminate the earth via space probes. He noted that spacecraft that burned up in reentry presented no problem, but "live" returns—manned flights, and probes such as the Scoop satellites—were another matter entirely. Here, he said, the question of contamination was very great.

His paper created a brief flurry of interest but, as he later said, "nothing very spectacular." Therefore, in 1963 he began an informal seminar group that met twice monthly in Room 410, on the top floor of the University of California Medical School biochemistry wing, for lunch and discussion of the contamination problem. It was this group of five men—Stone and John Black of Berkeley, Samuel Holden and Terence Lisset of Stanford Med, and Andrew Weiss of Stanford biophysics—that eventually formed the early nucleus of the Wildfire Project. They presented a petition to the President in 1964, in a letter consciously patterned after the Einstein letter to Roosevelt, in 1940, concerning the atomic bomb.

University of California
Berkeley, Calif.
June 10, 1964

The President of the United States
The White House
1600 Pennsylvania Avenue
Washington, D.C.

Dear Mr. President:

Recent theoretical considerations suggest that sterilization procedures of returning space probes may be inadequate to guarantee sterile reentry to this planet's atmosphere. The consequence of this is the potential introduction of virulent organisms into the present terrestrial ecologic framework.

It is our belief that sterilization for reentry probes and manned capsules can never be wholly satisfactory. Our calculations suggest that even if capsules received sterilizing procedures in space, the probability of contamination would still remain one in ten thousand, and perhaps much more. These estimates are based upon organized life as we know it; other forms of life may be entirely resistant to our sterilizing methods.

We therefore urge the establishment of a facility designed to deal with an extraterrestrial life form, should one inadvertently be introduced to the earth. The purpose of this facility would be twofold: to limit dissemination of the life form, and to provide laboratories for its investigation and analysis, with a view to protecting earth life forms from its influence.

We recommend that such a facility be located in an uninhabited region of the United States; that it be constructed underground; that it incorporate all known isolation techniques; and that it be equipped with a nuclear device for self-destruction in the eventuality of an emergency. So far as we know, no form of life can survive the two million degrees of heat which accompany an atomic nuclear detonation.

Yours very truly,

Jeremy Stone
John Black
Samuel Holden
Terence Lisset
Andrew Weiss

Response to the letter was gratifyingly prompt. Twenty-four hours later, Stone received a call from one of the President's advisers, and the following day he flew to Washington to confer with the President and members of the National Security Council. Two weeks after that, he flew to Houston to discuss further plans with NASA officials.

Although Stone recalls one or two cracks about "the goddamn penitentiary for bugs," most scientists he talked with regarded the project favorably. Within a month, Stone's informal team was hardened into an official committee to study problems of contamination and draw up recommendations.

This committee was put on the Defense Department's Advance Research Projects List and funded through the Defense Department. At that time, the ARPL was heavily invested in chemistry and physics—ion sprays, reversal duplication, pi-meson substrates—but there was growing interest in biologic problems. Thus one ARPL group was concerned with electronic pacing of brain function (a euphemism for mind control); a second had prepared a study of biosynergics, the future possible combinations of man and machines implanted inside the body; still another was evaluating Project Ozma; the search for extraterrestrial life conducted in 1961–4. A fourth group was engaged inpreliminary design of a machine that would carry out all human functions and would be self-duplicating.

All these projects were highly theoretical, and all were staffed by prestigious scientists. Admission to the ARPL was a mark of considerable status, and it ensured future funds for implementation and development.

Therefore, when Stone's committee submitted an early draft of the Life Analysis Protocol, which detailed the way any living thing could be studied, the Defense Department responded with an outright appropriation of $22,000,000 for the construction of a special isolated laboratory. (This rather large sum was felt to be justified since the project had application to other studies already under way. In 1965, the whole field of sterility and contamination was one of major importance. For example, NASA was building a Lunar Receiving Laboratory, a high-security facility for Apollo astronauts returning from the moon and possibly carrying bacteria or viruses harmful to man. Every astronaut returning from the moon would be quarantined in the LRL for three weeks, until decontamination was complete. Further, the problems of "clean rooms" of industry, where dust and bacteria were kept at a minimum, and the "sterile chambers" under study at Bethesda, were also major. Aseptic environments, "life islands," and sterile support systems seemed to have great future significance, and Stone's appropriation was considered a good investment in all these fields.)

Once money was funded, construction proceeded rapidly. The eventual result, the Wildfire Laboratory, was built in 1966 in Flatrock, Nevada. Design was awarded to the naval architects of the Electric Boat Division of General Dynamics, since GD had considerable experience designing living quarters on atomic submarines, where men had to live and work for prolonged periods.

The plan consisted of a conical underground structure with five floors. Each floor was circular, with a central service core of wiring, plumbing, and elevators. Each floor was more sterile than the one above; the first floor was nonsterile, the second moderately sterile, the third stringently sterile, and so on. Passage from one floor to another was not free; personnel had to undergo decontamination and quarantine procedures in passing either up or down.

Once the laboratory was finished, it only remained to select the Wildfire Alert team, the group of scientists who would study any new organism. After a number of studies of team composition, five men were selected, including Jeremy Stone himself. These five were prepared to mobilize immediately in the event of a biologic emergency.

Barely two years after his letter to the President, Stone was satisfied that "this country has the capability to deal with an unknown biologic agent." He professed himself pleased with the response of Washington and the speed with which his ideas had been implemented. But privately, he admitted to friends that it had been almost too easy, that Washington had agreed to his plans almost too readily.

Stone could not have known the reasons behind Washington's eagerness, or the very real concern many government officials had for the problem. For Stone knew nothing, until the night he left the party and drove off in the blue military sedan, of Project Scoop.

"It was the fastest thing we could arrange, sir," the Army man said.

Stone stepped onto the airplane with a sense of absurdity. It was a Boeing 727, completely empty, the seats stretching back in long unbroken rows.

"Sit first class, if you like," the Army man said, with a slight smile. "It doesn't matter." A moment later he was gone. He was not replaced by a stewardess but by a stern MP with a pistol on his hip who stood by the door as the engines started, whining softly in the night.

Stone sat back with the Scoop file in front of him and began to read. It made fascinating reading; he went through it quickly, so quickly that the MP thought his passenger must be merely glancing at the file. But Stone was reading every word.

Scoop was the brainchild of Major General Thomas Sparks, head of the Army Medical Corps, Chemical and Biological Warfare Division. Sparks was responsible for the research of the CBW installations at Fort Detrick, Maryland, Harley, Indiana, and Dugway, Utah. Stone had met him once or twice, and remembered him as being mild-mannered and bespectacled. Not the sort of man to be expected in the job he held.

Reading on, Stone learned that Project Scoop was contracted to the Jet Propulsion Laboratory of the California Institute of Technology in Pasadena in 1963. Its avowed aim was the collection of any organisms that might exist in "near space," the upper atmosphere of the earth. Technically speaking, it was an Army project, but it was funded through the National Aeronautics and Space Administration, a supposedly civilian organization. In fact, NASA was a government agency with a heavy military commitment; 43 per cent of its contractual work was classified in 1963.

In theory, JPL was designing a satellite to enter the fringes of space and collect organisms and dust for study. This was considered a project of pure science—almost curiosity—and was thus accepted by all the scientists working on the study.

In fact, the true aims were quite different.

The true aims of Scoop were to find new life forms that might benefit the Fort Detrick program. In essence, it was a study to discover new biological weapons of war.

Detrick was a rambling structure in Maryland dedicated to the discovery of chemical-and-biological-warfare weapons. Covering 1,300 acres, with a physical plant valued at $100,000,000, it ranked as one of the largest research facilities of any kind in the United States. Only 15 per cent of its findings were published in open scientific journals; the rest were classified, as were the reports from Harley and Dugway. Harley was a maximum-security installation that dealt largely with viruses. In the previous ten years, a number of new viruses had been developed there, ranging from the variety coded Carrie Nation (which produces diarrhea) to the variety coded Arnold (which causes clonic seizures and death). The Dugway Proving Ground in Utah was larger than the state of Rhode Island and was used principally to test poison gases such as Tabun, Sklar, and Kuff-11.

Few Americans, Stone knew, were aware of the magnitude of U.S. research into chemical and biological warfare. The total government expenditure in CBW exceeded half a billion dollars a year. Much of this was distributed to academic centers such as Johns Hopkins, Pennsylvania, and the University of Chicago, where studies of weapons systems were contracted under vague terms. Sometimes, of course, the terms were not so vague. The Johns Hopkins program was devised to evaluate "studies of actual or potential injuries and illnesses, studies on diseases of potential biological-warfare significance, and evaluation of certain chemical and immunological responses to certain toxoids and vaccines."

In the past eight years, none of the results from Johns Hopkins had been published openly. Those from other universities, such as Chicago and UCLA, had occasionally been published, but these were considered within the military establishment to be "trial balloons"—examples of ongoing research intended to intimidate foreign observers. A classic was the paper by Tendon and five others entitled "Researches into a Toxin Which Rapidly Uncouples Oxidative Phosphorylation Through Cutaneous Absorption."

The paper described, but did not identify, a poison that would kill a person in less than a minute and was absorbed through the skin. It was recognized that this was a relatively minor achievement compared to other toxins that had been devised in recent years.

With so much money and effort going into CBW, one might think that new and more virulent weapons would be continuously perfected. However, this was not the case from 1961 to 1965; the conclusion of the Senate Preparedness Subcommittee in 1961 was that "conventional research has been less than satisfactory" and that "new avenues and approaches of inquiry" should be opened within the field.

That was precisely what Major General Thomas Sparks intended to do, with Project Scoop.

In final form, Scoop was a program to orbit seventeen satellites around the earth, collecting organisms and bringing them back to the surface. Stone read the summaries of each previous flight.

Scoop I was a gold-plated satellite, cone-shaped, weighing thirty-seven pounds fully equipped. It was launched from Vandenberg Air Force Base in Purisima, California, on March 12, 1966. Vandenberg is used for polar (north to south) orbits, as opposed to Cape Kennedy, which launches west to east; Vandenberg had the additional advantage of maintaining better secrecy than Kennedy.

Scoop I orbited for six days before being brought down. It landed successfully in a swamp near Athens, Georgia. Unfortunately, it was found to contain only standard earth organisms.

Scoop II burned up in reentry, as a result of instrumentation failure. Scoop III also burned up, though it had a new type of plastic-and-tungsten-laminate heat shield.

Scoops IV and V were recovered intact from the Indian Ocean and the Appalachian foothills, but neither contained radically new organisms; those collected were harmless variants of S. *albus*, a common contaminant of normal human skin. These failures led to a further increase in sterilization procedures prior to launch.

Scoop VI was launched on New Year's Day, 1967. It incorporated all the latest refinements from earlier attempts. High hopes rode with the revised satellite, which returned eleven days later, landing near Bombay, India. Unknown to anyone, the 34th Airborne, then stationed in Evreux, France, just outside Paris, was dispatched to recover the capsule. The 34th was on alert whenever a spaceflight went up, according to the procedures of Operation Scrub, a plan first devised to protect Mercury and Gemini capsules should one be forced to land in Soviet Russia or Eastern Bloc countries. Scrub was the primary reason for keeping a single paratroop division in Western Europe in the first half of the 1960's.

Scoop VI was recovered uneventfully. It was found to contain a previously unknown form of unicellular organism, coccobacillary in shape, gram-negative, coagulase, and triokinase-positive. However, it proved generally benevolent to all living things with the exception of domestic female chickens, which it made moderately ill for a four-day period.

Among the Detrick staff, hope dimmed for the successful recovery of a pathogen from the Scoop program. Nonetheless, Scoop VII was launched soon after Scoop VI. The exact date is classified but it is believed to be February 5, 1967. Scoop VII immediately went into stable orbit with an apogee of 317 miles and a perigee of 224 miles. It remained in orbit for two and a half days. At that time, the satellite abruptly left stable orbit for unknown reasons, and it was decided to bring it down by radio command.

The anticipated landing site was a desolate area in northeastern Arizona.

Midway through the flight, his reading was interrupted by an officer who brought him a telephone and then stepped a respectful distance away while Stone talked.

"Yes?" Stone said, feeling odd. He was not accustomed to talking on the telephone in the middle of an airplane trip.

"General Marcus here," a tired voice said. Stone did not know General Marcus. "I just wanted to inform you that all members of the team have been called in, with the exception of Professor Kirke."

"What happened?"

"Professor Kirke is in the hospital," General Marcus said. "You'll get further details when you touch down."

The conversation ended; Stone gave the telephone back to the officer. He thought for a minute about the other men on the team, and wondered at their reactions as they were called out of bed.

There was Leavitt, of course. He would respond quickly. Leavitt was a clinical microbiologist, a man experienced in the treatment of infectious disease. Leavitt had seen enough plagues and epidemics in his day to know the importance of quick action. Besides, there was his ingrained pessimism, which never deserted him. (Leavitt had once said, "At my wedding, all I could think of was how much alimony she'd cost me.") He was an irritable, grumbling, heavyset man with a morose face and sad eyes, which seemed to peer ahead into a bleak and miserable future; but he was also thoughtful, imaginative, and not afraid to think daringly.

Then there was the pathologist, Burton, in Houston. Stone had never liked Burton very well, though he acknowledged his scientific talent. Burton and Stone were different: where Stone was organized, Burton was sloppy; where Stone was controlled, Burton was impulsive; where Stone was confident, Burton was nervous, jumpy, petulant. Colleagues referred to Burton as "the Stumbler," partly because of his tendency to trip over his untied shoelaces and baggy trouser cuffs and partly because of his talent for tumbling by error into one important discovery after another.

And then Kirke, the anthropologist from Yale, who apparently was not going to be able to come. If the report was true, Stone knew he was going to miss him. Kirke was an ill-informed and rather foppish man who possessed, as if by accident, a superbly logical brain. He was capable of grasping the essentials of a problem and manipulating them to get the necessary result; though he could not balance his own checkbook, mathematicians often came to him for help in resolving highly abstract problems.

Stone was going to miss that kind of brain. Certainly the fifth man would be no help. Stone frowned as he thought about Mark Hall. Hall had been a compromise candidate for the team; Stone would have preferred a physician with experience in metabolic disease, and the choice of a surgeon instead had been made with the greatest reluctance. There had been great pressure from Defense and the AEC to accept Hall, since those groups believed in the Odd Man Hypothesis; in the end, Stone and the others had given in.

Stone did not know Hall well; he wondered what he would say when he was informed of the alert. Stone could not have known of the great delay in notifying members of the team. He did not know, for instance, that Burton, the pathologist, was not called until five A.M., or that Peter Leavitt, the microbiologist, was not called until six thirty, the time he arrived at the hospital.

And Hall was not called until five minutes past seven.

It was, Mark Hall said later, "a horrifying experience. In an instant, I was taken from the most familiar of worlds and plunged into the most unfamiliar." At six forty-five, Hall was in the washroom adjacent to OR 7, scrubbing for his first case of the day. He was in the midst of a routine he had carried out daily for several years; he was relaxed and joking with the resident, scrubbing with him.

When he finished, he went into the operating room, holding his arms before him, and the instrument nurse handed him a towel, to wipe his hands dry. Also in the room was another resident, who was prepping the body for surgery—applying iodine and alcohol solutions—and a circulating nurse. They all exchanged greetings.

At the hospital, Hall was known as a swift, quick-tempered, and unpredictable surgeon. He operated with speed, working nearly twice as fast as other surgeons. When things went smoothly, he laughed and joked as he worked, kidding his assistants, the nurses, the anesthetist. But if things did not go well, if they became slow and difficult, Hall could turn blackly irritable.

Like most surgeons, he was insistent upon routine. Everything had to be done in a certain order, in a certain way. If not, he became upset.

Because the others in the operating room knew this, they looked up toward the overhead viewing gallery with apprehension when Leavitt appeared. Leavitt clicked on the intercom that connected the upstairs room to the operating room below and said, "Hello, Mark."

Hall had been draping the patient, placing green sterile cloths over every part of the body except for the abdomen. He looked up with surprise. "Hello, Peter," he said.

"Sorry to disturb you," Leavitt said. "But this is an emergency."

"Have to wait," Hall said. "I'm starting a procedure."

He finished draping and called for the skin knife. He palpated the abdomen, feeling for the landmarks to begin his incision.

"It can't wait," Leavitt said.

Hall paused. He set down the scalpel and looked up. There was a long silence.

"What the hell do you mean, it can't wait?"

Leavitt remained calm. "You'll have to break scrub. This is an emergency."

"Look, Peter, I've got a patient here. Anesthetized. Ready to go. I can't just walk—"

"Kelly will take over for you."

Kelly was one of the staff surgeons.

"Kelly?"

"He's scrubbing now," Leavitt said. "It's all arranged. I'll expect to meet you in the surgeon's change room. In about thirty seconds."

And then he was gone.

Hall glared at everyone in the room. No one moved, or spoke. After a moment, he stripped off his gloves and stomped out of the room, swearing once, very loudly.

Hall viewed his own association with Wildfire as tenuous at best. In 1966 he had been approached by Leavitt, the chief of bacteriology of the hospital, who had explained in a sketchy way the purpose of the project. Hall found it all rather amusing and had agreed to join the team, if his services ever became necessary; privately, he was confident that nothing would ever come of Wildfire.

Leavitt had offered to give Hall the files on Wildfire and to keep him up to date on the project. At first, Hall politely took the files, but it soon became clear that he was not bothering to read them, and so Leavitt stopped giving them to him. If anything, this pleased Hall, who preferred not to have his desk cluttered.

A year before, Leavitt had asked him whether he wasn't curious about something that he had agreed to join and that might at some future time prove dangerous.

Hall had said, "No."

Now, in the doctors' room, Hall regretted those words. The doctors' room was a small place, lined on all four walls with lockers; there were no windows. A large coffeemaker sat in the center of the room, with a stack of paper cups alongside. Leavitt was pouring himself a cup, his solemn, basset-hound face looking mournful.

"This is going to be awful coffee," he said. "You can't get a decent cup anywhere in a hospital. Hurry and change."

Hall said, "Do you mind telling me first why—"

"I mind, I mind," Leavitt said. "Change: there's a car waiting outside and we're already late. Perhaps too late."

He had a gruffly melodramatic way of speaking that had always annoyed Hall.

There was a loud slurp as Leavitt sipped the coffee. "Just as I suspected," he said. "How can you tolerate it? Hurry, please."

Hall unlocked his locker and kicked it open. He leaned against the door and stripped away the black plastic shoe covers that were worn in the operating room to prevent buildup of static charges. "Next, I suppose you're going to tell me this has to do with that damned project."

"Exactly," Leavitt said. "Now try to hurry. The car is waiting to take us to the airport, and the morning traffic is bad."

Hall changed quickly, not thinking, his mind momentarily stunned. Somehow he had never thought it possible. He dressed and walked out with Leavitt toward the hospital entrance. Outside, in the sunshine, he could see the olive U.S. Army sedan pulled up to the curb, its light flashing. And he had a sudden, horrible realization that Leavitt was not kidding, that nobody was kidding, and that some kind of awful nightmare was coming true.

For his own part, Peter Leavitt was irritated with Hall. In general, Leavitt had little patience with practicing physicians. Though he had an M.D. degree, Leavitt had never practiced, preferring to devote his time to research. His field was clinical microbiology and epidemiology, and his specialty was parasitology. He had done parasitic research all over the world; his work had led to the discovery of the Brazilian tapeworm, *Taenia renzi*, which he had characterized in a paper in 1953.

As he grew older, however, Leavitt had stopped traveling. Public health, he was fond of saying, was a young man's game; when you got your fifth case of intestinal amebiasis, it was time to quit. Leavitt got his fifth case in Rhodesia in 1955. He was dreadfully sick for three months and lost forty pounds. Afterward, he resigned his job in the public health service. He was offered the post of chief of microbiology at the hospital, and he had taken it, with the understanding that he would be able to devote a good portion of his time to research.

Within the hospital he was known as a superb clinical bacteriologist, but his real interest remained parasites. In the period from 1955 to 1964 he published a series of elegant metabolic studies on *Ascaris* and *Necator* that were highly regarded by other workers in the field.

Leavitt's reputation had made him a natural choice for Wildfire, and it was through Leavitt that Hall had been asked to join. Leavitt knew the reasons behind Hall's selection, though Hall did not.

When Leavitt had asked him to join, Hall had demanded to know why. "I'm just a surgeon," he had said.

"Yes," Leavitt said. "But you know electrolytes."

"So?"

"That may be important. Blood chemistries, pH, acidity and alkalinity, the whole thing. That may be vital, when the time comes."

"But there are a lot of electrolyte people," Hall had pointed out. "Many of them better than me."

"Yes," Leavitt had said. "But they're all married."

"So what?"

"We need a single man."

"Why?"

"It's necessary that one member of the team be unmarried."

"That's crazy," Hall had said.

"Maybe," Leavitt had said. "Maybe not."

They left the hospital and walked up to the Army sedan. A young officer was waiting stiffly, and saluted as they came up.

"Dr. Hall?"

"Yes."

"May I see your card, please?"

Hall gave him the little plastic card with his picture on it. He had been carrying the card in his wallet for more than a year; it was a rather strange card—with just a name, a picture, and a thumbprint, nothing more. Nothing to indicate that it was an official card.

The officer glanced at it, then at Hall, and back to the card. He handed it back.

"Very good, sir."

He opened the rear door of the sedan. Hall got in and Leavitt followed, shielding his eyes from the flashing red light on the car top. Hall noticed it.

"Something wrong?"

"No. Just never liked flashing lights. Reminds me of my days as an ambulance driver, during the war." Leavitt settled back and the car started off. "Now then," he said. "When we reach the airfield, you will be given a file to read during the trip."

"What trip?"

"You'll be taking an F-104," Leavitt said.

"Where?"

"Nevada. Try to read the file on the way. Once we arrive, things will be very busy."

"And the others in the team?"

Leavitt glanced at his watch. "Kirke has appendicitis and is in the hospital. The others have already begun work. Right now, they are in a helicopter, over Piedmont, Arizona."

"Never heard of it," Hall said.

"Nobody has," Leavitt said, "until now."

Chapter 6

Piedmont

At 9:59 A.M. on the same morning, a K-4 jet helicopter lifted off the concrete of Vandenberg's maximum-security hangar MSH-9 and headed east, toward Arizona.

The decision to lift off from an MSH was made by Major Manchek, who was concerned about the attention the suits might draw. Because inside the helicopter were three men, a pilot and two scientists, and all three wore clear plastic inflatable suits, making them look like obese men from Mars, or, as one of the hangar maintenance men put it, "like balloons from the Macy's parade."

As the helicopter climbed into the clear morning sky, the two passengers in the belly looked at each other. One was Jeremy Stone, the other Charles Burton. Both men had arrived at Vandenberg just a few hours before—Stone from Stanford and Burton from Baylor University in Houston.

Burton was fifty-four, a pathologist. He held a professorship at Baylor Medical School and served as a consultant to the NASA Manned Spaceflight Center in Houston. Earlier he had done research at the National Institutes in Bethesda. His field had been the effects of bacteria on human tissues.

It is one of the peculiarities of scientific development that such a vital field was virtually untouched when Burton came to it. Though men had known germs caused disease since Henle's hypothesis of 1840, by the middle of the twentieth century there was still nothing known about why or how bacteria did their damage. The specific mechanisms were unknown.

Burton began, like so many others in his day, with *Diplococcus pneumoniae*, the agent causing pneumonia. There was great interest in pneumococcus before the advent of penicillin in the forties; after that, both interest and research money evaporated. Burton shifted to *Staphylococcus aureus*, a common skin pathogen responsible for "pimples" and "boils." At the time he began his work, his fellow researchers laughed at him; staphylococcus, like pneumococcus, was highly sensitive to penicillin. They doubted Burton would ever get enough money to carry on his work.

For five years, they were right. The money was scarce, and Burton often had to go begging to foundations and philanthropists. Yet he persisted, patiently elucidating the coats of the cell wall that caused a reaction in host tissue and helping to discover the half-dozen toxins secreted by the bacteria to break down tissue, spread infection, and destroy red cells.

Suddenly, in the 1950's, the first penicillin-resistant strains of staph appeared. The new strains were virulent, and produced bizarre deaths, often by brain abscess. Almost overnight Burton found his work had assumed major importance; dozens of labs around the country were changing over to study staph; it was a "hot field." In a single year, Burton watched his grant appropriations jump from $6,000 a year to $300,000. Soon afterward, he was made a professor of pathology.

Looking back, Burton felt no great pride in his accomplishment; it was, he knew, a matter of luck, of being in the right place and doing the right work when the time came.

He wondered what would come of being here, in this helicopter, now.

Sitting across from him, Jeremy Stone tried to conceal his distaste for Burton's appearance. Beneath the plastic suit Burton wore a dirty plaid sport shirt with a stain on the left breast pocket; his trousers were creased and frayed and even his hair, Stone felt, was unruly and untidy.

He stared out the window, forcing himself to think of other matters. "Fifty people," he said, shaking his head. "Dead within eight hours of the landing of Scoop VII. The question is one of spread."

"Presumably airborne," Burton said.

"Yes. Presumably."

"Everyone seems to have died in the immediate vicinity of the town," Burton said. "Are there reports of deaths farther out?"

Stone shook his head. "I'm having the Army people look into it. They're working with the highway patrol. So far, no deaths have turned up outside."

"Wind?"

"A stroke of luck," Stone said. "Last night the wind was fairly brisk, nine miles an hour to the south and steady. But around midnight, it died. Pretty unusual for this time of year, they tell me."

"But fortunate for us."

"Yes." Stone nodded. "We're fortunate in another way as well. There is no important area of habitation for a radius of nearly one hundred and twelve miles. Outside that, of course, there is Las Vegas to the north, San Bernardino to the west, and Phoenix to the east. Not nice, if the bug gets to any of them."

"But as long as the wind stays down, we have time."

"Presumably," Stone said.

For the next half hour, the two men discussed the vector problem with frequent reference to a sheaf of output maps drawn up during the night by Vandenberg's computer division. The output maps were highly complex analyses of geographic problems; in this case, the maps were visualizations of the southwestern United States, weighted for wind direction and population.

Discussion then turned to the time course of death. Both men had heard the tape from the van; they agreed that everyone at Piedmont seemed to have died quite suddenly.

"Even if you slit a man's throat with a razor," Burton said, "you won't get death that rapidly. Cutting both carotids and jugulars still allows ten to forty seconds before unconsciousness, and nearly a minute before death."

"At Piedmont, it seems to have occurred in a second or two."

Burton shrugged. "Trauma," he suggested. "A blow to the head."

"Yes. Or a nerve gas."

"Certainly possible."

"It's that, or something very much like it," Stone said. "If it was an enzymatic block of some kind—like arsenic or strychnine—we'd expect fifteen or thirty seconds, perhaps longer. But a block of nervous transmission, or a block of the neuromuscular junction, or cortical poisoning—that could be very swift. It could be instantaneous."

"If it is a fast-acting gas," Burton said, "it must have high diffusibility across the lungs—"

"Or the skin," Stone said. "Mucous membranes, anything. Any porous surface."

Burton touched the plastic of his suit. "If this gas is so highly diffusible . . ."

Stone gave a slight smile. "We'll find out, soon enough."

Over the intercom, the helicopter pilot said, "Piedmont approaching, gentlemen. Please advise."

Stone said, "Circle once and give us a look at it."

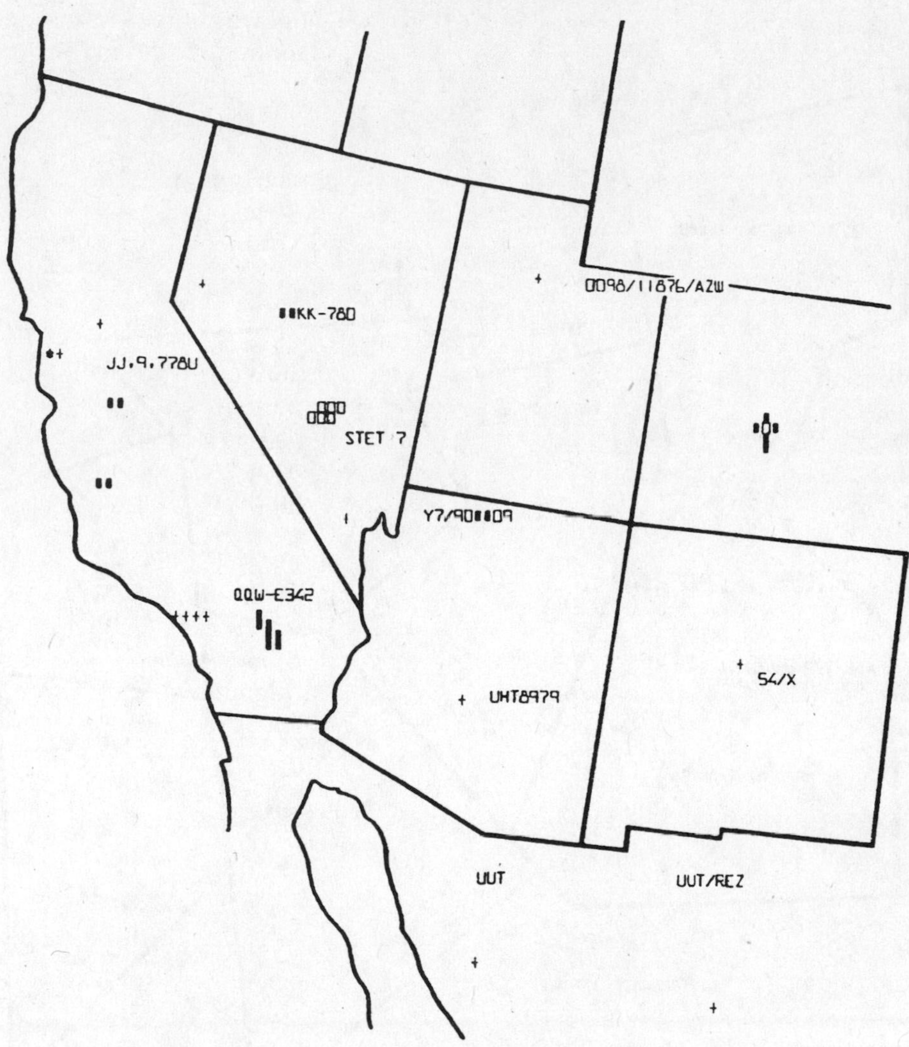

A NOTE ON THE OUTPUT MAPS: these three maps are intended as examples of the staging of computer-base output mapping. The first map is relatively standard, with the addition of computer coordinates around population centers and other important areas.

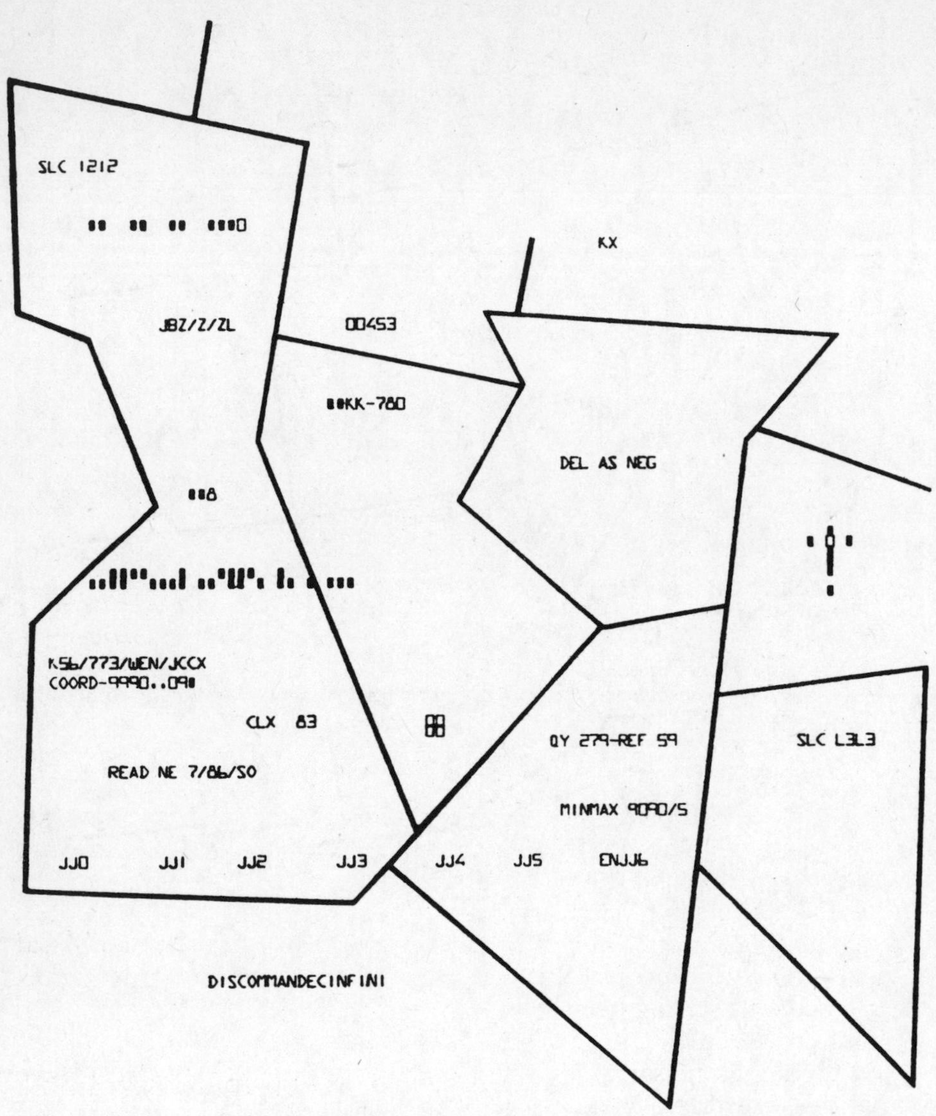

The second map has been weighted to account for wind and population factors, and is consequently distorted.

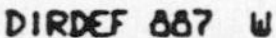

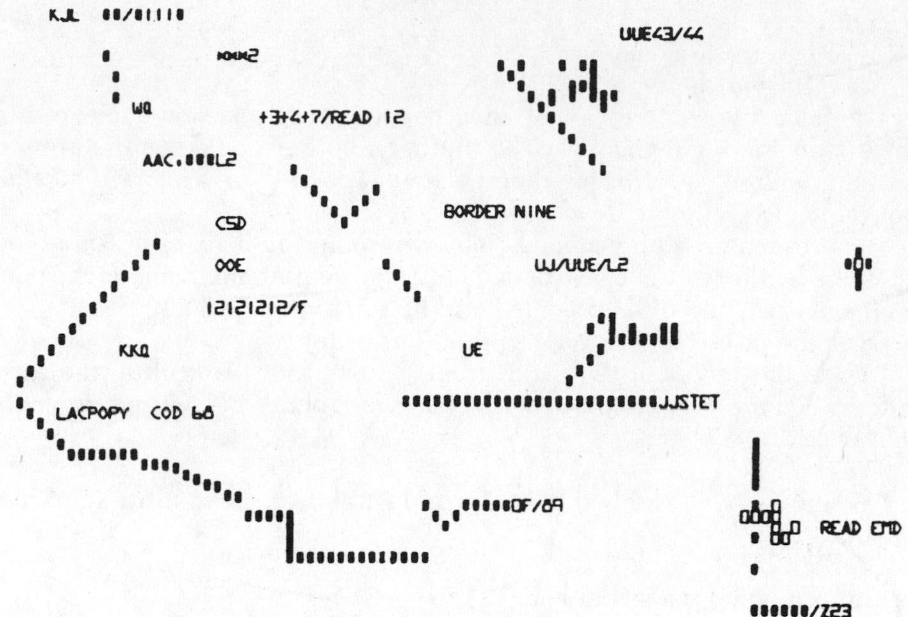

The third map is a computer projection of the effects of wind and population in a specific "scenario." None of these output maps is from the Wildfire Project. They are similar, but they represent output from a CBW scenario, not the actual Wildfire work.

(courtesy General Autonomics Corporation)

The helicopter banked steeply. The two men looked out and saw the town below them. The buzzards had landed during the night, and were thickly clustered around the bodies.

"I was afraid of that," Stone said.

"They may represent a vector for infectious spread," Burton said. "Eat the meat of infected people, and carry the organisms away with them."

Stone nodded, staring out the window.

"What do we do?"

"Gas them," Stone said. He flicked on the intercom to the pilot. "Have you got the canisters?"

"Yes sir."

"Circle again; and blanket the town."

"Yes sir."

The helicopter tilted, and swung back. Soon the two men could not see the ground for the clouds of pale-blue gas.

"What is it?"

"Chlorazine," Stone said. "Highly effective, in low concentrations, on aviary metabolism. Birds have a high metabolic rate. They are creatures that consist of little more than feathers and muscle; their heartbeats are usually about one-twenty, and many species eat more than their own weight every day."

"The gas is an uncoupler?"

"Yes. It'll hit them hard."

The helicopter banked away, then hovered. The gas slowly cleared in the gentle wind, moving off to the south. Soon they could see the ground again. Hundreds of birds lay there; a few flapped their wings spastically, but most were already dead.

Stone frowned as he watched. Somewhere, in the back of his mind, he knew he had forgotten something, or ignored something. Some fact, some vital clue, that the birds provided and he must not overlook.

Over the intercom, the pilot said, "Your orders, sir?"

"Go to the center of the main street," Stone said, "and drop the rope ladder. You are to remain twenty feet above ground. Do not put down. Is that clear?"

"Yes sir."

"When we have climbed down, you are to lift off to an altitude of five hundred feet."

"Yes sir."

"Return when we signal you."

"Yes sir."

"And should anything happen to us—"

"I proceed directly to Wildfire," the pilot said, his voice dry.

"Correct."

The pilot knew what that meant. He was being paid according to the highest Air Force pay scales: he was drawing regular pay plus hazardous-duty pay, plus non-wartime special-services pay, plus mission-over-hostile-territory pay, plus bonus air-time pay. He would receive more than a thousand dollars for this day's work, and his family would receive an additional ten thousand dollars from the short-term life insurance should he not return.

There was a reason for the money: if anything happened to Burton and Stone on the ground, the pilot was ordered to fly directly to the Wildfire installation and hover thirty feet above ground until such time as the Wildfire group had determined the correct way to incinerate him, and his airplane, in midair.

He was being paid to take a risk. He had volunteered for the job. And he knew that high above, circling at twenty thousand feet, was an Air Force jet with air-to-air missiles. It was the job of the jet to shoot down the helicopter should the pilot suffer a last-minute loss of nerve and fail to go directly to Wildfire.

"Don't slip up," the pilot said. "Sir."

The helicopter maneuvered over the main street of the town and hung in midair. There was a rattling sound: the rope ladder being released.

Stone stood and pulled on his helmet. He snapped shut the sealer and inflated his clear suit, puffing it up around him. A small bottle of oxygen on his back would provide enough air for two hours of exploration.

He waited until Burton had sealed his suit, and then Stone opened the hatch and stared down at the ground. The helicopter was raising a heavy cloud of dust.

Stone clicked on his radio. "All set?"

"All set."

Stone began to climb down the ladder. Burton waited a moment, then followed. He could see nothing in the swirling dust, but finally felt his shoes touch the ground. He released the ladder and looked over. He could barely make out Stone's suit, a dim outline in a gloomy, dusky world.

The ladder pulled away as the helicopter lifted into the sky. The dust cleared. They could see.

"Let's go," Stone said.

Moving clumsily in their suits, they walked down the main street of Piedmont.

Chapter 7

"An Unusual Process"

Scarcely twelve hours after the first known human contact with the Andromeda Strain was made at Piedmont, Burton and Stone arrived in the town. Weeks later, in their debriefing sessions, both men recalled the scene vividly, and described it in detail.

The morning sun was still low in the sky; it was cold and cheerless, casting long shadows over the thinly snow-crusted ground. From where they stood, they could look up and down the street at the gray, weathered wooden buildings; but what they noticed first was the silence. Except for a gentle wind that whined softly through the empty houses, it was deathly silent. Bodies lay everywhere, heaped and flung across the ground in attitudes of frozen surprise.

But there was no sound—no reassuring rumble of an automobile engine, no barking dog, no shouting children.

Silence.

The two men looked at each other. They were painfully aware of how much there was to learn, to do. Some catastrophe had struck this town, and they must discover all they could about it. But they had practically no clues, no points of departure.

They knew, in fact, only two things. First, that the trouble apparently began with the landing of Scoop VII. And second, that death had overtaken the people of the town with astonishing rapidity. If it was a disease from the satellite, then it was like no other in the history of medicine.

For a long time the men said nothing, but stood in the street, looking about them, feeling the wind tug at their oversized suits. Finally, Stone said, "Why are they all outside, in the street? If this was a disease that arrived at night, most of the people would be indoors."

"Not only that," Burton said, "they're mostly wearing pajamas. It was a cold night last night. You'd think they would have stopped to put on a jacket, or a raincoat. Something to keep warm."

"Maybe they were in a hurry."

"To do what?" Burton said.

"To see something," Stone said, with a helpless shrug.

Burton bent over the first body they came to. "Odd," he said. "Look at the way this fellow is clutching his chest. Quite a few of them are doing that."

Looking at the bodies, Stone saw that the hands of many were pressed to their chests, some flat, some clawing.

"They didn't seem to be in pain," Stone said. "Their faces are quite peaceful."

"Almost astonished, in fact," Burton nodded. "These people look cut down, caught in midstride. But clutching their chests."

"Coronary?" Stone said.

"Doubt it. They should grimace—it's painful. The same with a pulmonary embolus."

"If it was fast enough, they wouldn't have time."

"Perhaps. But somehow I think these people died a painless death. Which means they are clutching their chests because—"

"They couldn't breathe," Stone said.

Burton nodded. "It's possible we're seeing asphyxiation. Rapid, painless, almost instantaneous asphyxiation. But I doubt it. If a person can't breathe, the first thing he does is loosen his clothing, particularly around the neck and chest. Look at that man there—he's wearing a tie, and he hasn't touched it. And that woman with the tightly buttoned collar."

Burton was beginning to regain his composure now, after the initial shock of the town. He was beginning to think clearly. They walked up to the van, standing in the middle of the street, its lights still shining weakly. Stone reached in to turn off the lights. He pushed the stiff body of the driver back from the wheel and read the name on the breast pocket of the parka.

"Shawn."

The man sitting rigidly in the back of the van was a private named Crane. Both men were locked in rigor mortis. Stone nodded to the equipment in the back.

"Will that still work?"

"I think so," Burton said.

"Then let's find the satellite. That's our first job. We can worry later about—"

He stopped. He was looking at the face of Shawn, who had obviously pitched forward hard onto the steering wheel at the moment of death. There was a large, arc-shaped cut across his face, shattering the bridge of his nose and tearing the skin.

"I don't get it," Stone said.

"Get what?" Burton said.

"This injury. Look at it."

"Very clean," Burton said. "Remarkably clean, in fact. Practically no bleeding . . ."

Then Burton realized. He started to scratch his head in astonishment, but his hand was stopped by the plastic helmet.

"A cut like that," he said, "on the face. Broken capillaries, shattered bone, torn scalp veins—it should bleed like hell."

"Yes," Stone said. "It should. And look at the other bodies. Even where the vultures have chewed at the flesh: no bleeding."

Burton stared with increasing astonishment. None of the bodies had lost even a drop of blood. He wondered why they had not noticed it before.

"Maybe the mechanism of action of this disease—"

"Yes," Stone said. "I think you may be right." He grunted and dragged Shawn out of the van, working to pull the stiff body from behind the wheel. "Let's get that damned satellite," he said. "This is really beginning to worry me."

Burton went to the back and pulled Crane out through the rear doors, then climbed in as Stone turned the ignition. The starter turned over sluggishly, and the engine did not catch.

Stone tried to start the van for several seconds, then said, "I don't understand. The battery is low, but it should still be enough—"

"How's your gas?" Burton said.

There was a pause, and Stone swore loudly. Burton smiled, and crawled out of the back. Together they walked up the street to the gas station, found a bucket, and filled it with gas from the pump after spending several moments trying to decide how it worked. When they had the gas, they returned to the van, filled the tank, and Stone tried again.

The engine caught and held. Stone grinned. "Let's go."

Burton scrambled into the back, turned on the electronic equipment, and started the antenna rotating. He heard the faint beeping of the satellite.

"The signal's weak, but still there. Sounds over to the left somewhere."

Stone put the van in gear. They rumbled off, swerving around the bodies in the street. The beeping grew louder. They continued down the main street, past the gas station and the general store. The beeping suddenly grew faint.

"We've gone too far. Turn around."

It took a while for Stone to find reverse on the gearshift, and then they doubled back, tracing the intensity of the sound. It was another fifteen minutes before they were able to locate the origin of the beeps to the north, on the outskirts of the town.

Finally, they pulled up before a plain single-story wood-frame house. A sign creaked in the wind: Dr. Alan Benedict.

"Might have known," Stone said. "They'd take it to the doctor."

The two men climbed out of the van and went up to the house. The front door was open, banging in the breeze. They entered the living room and found it empty. Turning right, they came to the doctor's office.

Benedict was there, a pudgy, white-haired man. He was seated before his desk, with several textbooks laid open. Along one wall were bottles, syringes, pictures of his family and several others showing men in combat uniforms. One showed a group of grinning soldiers; the scrawled words: "For Benny, from the boys of 87, Anzio."

Benedict himself was staring blankly toward a corner of the room, his eyes wide, his face peaceful.

"Well," Burton said, "Benedict certainly didn't make it outside—"

And then they saw the satellite.

It was upright, a sleek polished cone three feet high, and its edges had been cracked and seared from the heat of reentry. It had been opened crudely, apparently with the help of a pair of pliers and chisel that lay on the floor next to the capsule.

"The bastard opened it," Stone said. "Stupid son of a bitch."

"How was he to know?"

"He might have asked somebody," Stone said. He sighed. "Anyway, he knows now. And so do forty-nine other people." He bent over the satellite and closed the gaping, triangular hatch. "You have the container?"

Burton produced the folded plastic bag and opened it out. Together they slipped it over the satellite, then sealed it shut.

"I hope to hell there's something left," Burton said.

"In a way," Stone said softly, "I hope there isn't."

They turned their attention to Benedict. Stone went over to him and shook him. The man fell rigidly from his chair onto the floor.

Burton noticed the elbows, and suddenly became excited. He leaned over the body. "Come on," he said to Stone. "Help me."

"Do what?"

"Strip him down."

"Why?"

"I want to check the lividity."

"But why?"

"Just wait," Burton said. He began unbuttoning Benedict's shirt and loosening his trousers. The two men worked silently for some moments, until the doctor's body was naked on the floor.

"There," Burton said, standing back.

"I'll be damned," Stone said.

There was no dependent lividity. Normally, after a person died, blood seeped to the lowest points, drawn down by gravity. A person who died in bed had a purple back from accumulated blood. But Benedict, who had died sitting up, had no blood in the tissue of his buttocks or thighs.

Or in his elbows, which had rested on the arms of the chair.

"Quite a peculiar finding," Burton said. He glanced around the room and found a small autoclave for sterilizing instruments. Opening it, he removed a scalpel. He fitted it with a blade—carefully, so as not to puncture his airtight suit—and then turned back to the body.

"We'll take the most superficial major artery and vein," he said.

"Which is?"

"The radial. At the wrist."

Holding the scalpel carefully, Burton drew the blade along the skin of the inner wrist, just behind the thumb. The skin pulled back from the wound, which was completely bloodless. He exposed fat and subcutaneous tissue. There was no bleeding.

"Amazing."

He cut deeper. There was still no bleeding from the incision. Suddenly, abruptly, he struck a vessel. Crumbling red-black material fell out onto the floor.

"I'll be damned," Stone said again.

"Clotted solid," Burton said.

"No wonder the people didn't bleed."

Burton said, "Help me turn him over." Together, they got the corpse onto its back, and Burton made a deep incision into the medial thigh, cutting down to the femoral artery and vein. Again there was no bleeding, and when they reached the artery, as thick as a man's finger, it was clotted into a firm, reddish mass.

"Incredible."

He began another incision, this time into the chest. He exposed the ribs, then searched Dr. Benedict's office for a very sharp knife. He wanted an osteotome, but could find none. He settled for the chisel that had been used to open the capsule. Using this he broke away several ribs to expose the lungs and the heart. Again there was no bleeding.

Burton took a deep breath, then cut open the heart, slicing into the left ventricle.

The interior was filled with red, spongy material. There was no liquid blood at all.

"Clotted solid," he said. "No question."

"Any idea what can clot people this way?"

"The whole vascular system? Five quarts of blood? No." Burton sat heavily in the doctor's chair and stared at the body he had just cut open. "I've never heard of anything like it. There's a thing called disseminated intravascular coagulation, but it's rare and requires all sorts of special circumstances to initiate it."

"Could a single toxin initiate it?"

"In theory, I suppose. But in fact, there isn't a toxin in the world—"

He stopped.

"Yes," Stone said. "I suppose that's right."

He picked up the satellite designated Scoop VII and carried it outside to the van. When he came back, he said, "We'd better search the houses."

"Beginning here?"

"Might as well," Stone said.

It was Burton who found Mrs. Benedict. She was a pleasant-looking middle-aged lady sitting in a chair with a book on her lap; she seemed about to turn the page. Burton examined her briefly, then heard Stone call to him.

He walked to the other end of the house. Stone was in a small bedroom, bent over the body of a young teen-age boy on the bed. It was obviously his room: psychedelic posters on the walls, model airplanes on a shelf to one side.

The boy lay on his back in bed, eyes open, staring at the ceiling. His mouth was open. In one hand, an empty tube of model-airplane cement was tightly clenched; all over the bed were empty bottles of airplane dope, paint thinner, turps.

Stone stepped back. "Have a look."

Burton looked in the mouth, reached a finger in, touched the now-hardened mass. "Good God," he said.

Stone was frowning. "This took time," he said. "Regardless of what made him do it, it took time. We've obviously been oversimplifying events here. Everyone did not die instantaneously. Some people died in their homes; some got out into the street. And this kid here . . ."

He shook his head. "Let's check the other houses."

On the way out, Burton returned to the doctor's office, stepping around the body of the physician. It gave him a strange feeling to see the wrist and leg sliced open, the chest exposed—but no bleeding. There was something wild and inhuman about that. As if bleeding were a sign of humanity. Well, he thought, perhaps it is. Perhaps the fact that we bleed to death makes us human.

For Stone, Piedmont was a puzzle challenging him to crack its secret. He was convinced that the town could tell him everything about the nature of the disease, its course and effects. It was only a matter of putting together the data in the proper way.

But he had to admit, as they continued their search, that the data were confusing:

A house that contained a man, his wife, and their young daughter, all sitting around the dinner table. They had apparently been relaxed and happy, and none of them had had time to push back their chairs from the table. They remained frozen in attitudes of congeniality, smiling at each other across the plates of now-rotting food, and flies. Stone noticed the flies, which buzzed softly in the room. He would, he thought, have to remember the flies.

An old woman, her hair white, her face creased. She was smiling gently as she swung from a noose tied to a ceiling rafter. The rope creaked as it rubbed against the wood of the rafter.

At her feet was an envelope. In a careful, neat, unhurried hand: "To whom it may concern."

Stone opened the letter and read it. "The day of judgment is at hand. The earth and the waters shall open up and mankind shall be consumed. May God have mercy on my soul and upon those who have shown mercy to me. To hell with the others. Amen."

Burton listened as the letter was read. "Crazy old lady," he said. "Senile dementia. She saw everyone around her dying, and she went nuts."

"And killed herself?"

"Yes, I think so."

"Pretty bizarre way to kill herself, don't you think?"

"That kid also chose a bizarre way," Burton said.

Stone nodded.

Roy O. Thompson, who lived alone. From his greasy coveralls they assumed he ran the town gas station. Roy had apparently filled his bathtub with water, then knelt down, stuck his head in, and held it there until he died. When they found him his body was rigid, holding himself under the surface of the water; there was no one else around, and no sign of struggle.

"Impossible," Stone said. "No one can commit suicide that way."

Lydia Everett, a seamstress in the town, who had quietly gone out to the back yard, sat in a chair, poured gasoline over herself, and struck a match. Next to the remains of her body they found the scorched gasoline can.

* * *

William Arnold, a man of sixty sitting stiffly in a chair in the living room, wearing his World War I uniform. He had been a captain in that war, and he had become a captain again, briefly, before he shot himself through the right temple with a Colt .45. There was no blood in the room when they found him; he appeared almost ludicrous, sitting there with a clean, dry hole in his head.

A tape recorder stood alongside him, his left hand resting on the case. Burton looked at Stone questioningly, then turned it on.

A quavering, irritable voice spoke to them.

"You took your sweet time coming, didn't you? Still I am glad you have arrived at last. We are in need of reinforcements. I tell you, it's been one hell of a battle against the Hun. Lost 40 per cent last night, going over the top, and two of our officers are out with the rot. Not going well, not at all. If only Gary Cooper was here. We need men like that, the men who made America strong. I can't tell you how much it means to me, with those giants out there in the flying saucers. Now they're burning us down, and the gas is coming. You can see them die and we don't have gas masks. None at all. But I won't wait for it. I am going to do the proper thing now. I regret that I have but one life to kill for my country."

The tape ran on, but it was silent.

Burton turned it off. "Crazy," he said. "Stark raving mad."

Stone nodded.

"Some of them died instantly, and the others . . . went quietly nuts."

"But we seem to come back to the same basic question. Why? What was the difference?"

"Perhaps there's a graded immunity to this bug," Burton said. "Some people are more susceptible than others. Some people are protected, at least for a time."

"You know," Stone said, "there was that report from the flybys, and those films of a man alive down here. One man in white robes."

"You think he's still alive?"

"Well, I wonder," Stone said. "Because if some people survived longer than others—long enough to dictate a taped speech, or to arrange a hanging—then you have to ask yourself if someone maybe didn't survive for a very long time. You have to ask yourself if there isn't someone in this town who is *still* alive."

It was then that they heard the sound of crying.

At first it seemed like the sound of the wind, it was so high and thin and reedy, but they listened, feeling puzzled at first, and then astonished. The crying persisted, interrupted by little hacking coughs.

They ran outside.

It was faint, and difficult to localize. They ran up the street, and it seemed to grow louder; this spurred them on.

And then, abruptly, the sound stopped.

The two men came to a halt, gasping for breath, chests heaving. They stood in the middle of the hot, deserted street and looked at each other.

"Have we lost our minds?" Burton said.

"No," Stone said. "We heard it, all right."

They waited. It was absolutely quiet for several minutes. Burton looked down the street, at the houses, and the jeep van parked at the other end, in front of Dr. Benedict's house.

The crying began again, very loud now, a frustrated howl.

The two men ran.

It was not far, two houses up on the right side. A man and a woman lay outside, on the sidewalk, fallen and clutching their chests. They ran past them and into the house. The crying was still louder; it filled the empty rooms.

They hurried upstairs, clambering up, and came to the bedroom. A large double bed, unmade. A dresser, a mirror, a closet.

And a small crib.

They leaned over, pulling back the blankets from a small, very red-faced, very unhappy infant. The baby immediately stopped crying long enough to survey their faces, enclosed in the plastic suits.

Then it began to howl again.

"Scared hell out of it," Burton said. "Poor thing."

He picked it up gingerly and rocked it. The baby continued to scream. Its toothless mouth was wide open, its cheeks purple, and the veins stood out on its forehead.

"Probably hungry," Burton said.

Stone was frowning. "It's not very old. Can't be more than a couple of months. Is it a he or a she?"

Burton unwrapped the blankets and checked the diapers. "He. And he needs to be changed. And fed." He looked around the room. "There's probably a formula in the kitchen . . ."

"No," Stone said. "We don't feed it."

"Why not?"

"We don't do anything to that child until we get it out of this town. Maybe feeding is part of the disease process; maybe the people who weren't hit so hard or so fast were the ones who hadn't eaten recently. Maybe there's something protective about this baby's diet. Maybe . . ." He stopped. "But whatever it is, we can't take a chance. We've got to wait and get him into a controlled situation."

Burton sighed. He knew that Stone was right, but he also knew that the baby hadn't been fed for at least twelve hours. No wonder the kid was crying.

Stone said, "This is a very important development. It's a major break for us, and we've got to protect it. I think we should go back immediately."

"We haven't finished our head count."

Stone shook his head. "Doesn't matter. We have something much more valuable than anything we could hope to find. We have a survivor."

The baby stopped crying for a moment, stuck its finger in its mouth, and looked questioningly up at Burton. Then, when he was certain no food was forthcoming, he began to howl again.

"Too bad," Burton said, "he can't tell us what happened."

"I'm hoping he can," Stone said.

They parked the van in the center of the main street, beneath the hovering helicopter, and signaled for it to descend with the ladder. Burton held the infant, and Stone held the Scoop satellite—strange trophies, Stone thought, from a very strange town. The baby was quiet now; he had finally tired of crying and was sleeping fitfully, awakening at intervals to whimper, then sleep again.

The helicopter descended, spinning up swirls of dust. Burton wrapped the blankets about the baby's face to protect him. The ladder came down and he climbed up, with difficulty.

Stone waited on the ground, standing with the capsule in the wind and dust and thumpy noise from the helicopter.

And, suddenly, he realized that he was not alone on the street. He turned, and saw a man behind him.

He was an old man, with thin gray hair and a wrinkled, worn face. He wore a long nightgown that was smudged with dirt and yellowed with dust, and his feet were bare. He stumbled and tottered toward Stone. His chest was heaving with exertion beneath the nightgown.

"Who are you?" Stone said. But he knew: the man in the pictures. The one who had been photographed by the airplane.

"You . . ." the man said.

"Who are you?"

"You . . . did it . . ."

"What is your name?"

"Don't hurt me . . . I'm not like the others . . ."

He was shaking with fear as he stared at Stone in his plastic suit. Stone thought, We must look strange to him. Like men from Mars, men from another world.

"Don't hurt me . . ."

"We won't hurt you," Stone said. "What is your name?"

"Jackson. Peter Jackson. Sir. Please don't hurt me." He waved to the bodies in the street. "I'm not like the others . . ."

"We won't hurt you," Stone said again.

"You hurt the others . . ."

"No. We didn't."

"They're dead."

"We had nothing—"

"You're lying," he shouted, his eyes wide. "You're lying to me. You're not human. You're only pretending. You know I'm a sick man. You know you can pretend with me. I'm a sick man. I'm bleeding, I know. I've had this . . . this . . . this . . ."

He faltered, and then doubled over, clutching his stomach and wincing in pain.

"Are you all right?"

The man fell to the ground. He was breathing heavily, his skin pale. There was sweat on his face.

"My stomach," he gasped. "It's my stomach."

And then he vomited. It came up heavy, deep-red, rich with blood.

"Mr. Jackson—"

But the man was not awake. His eyes were closed and he was lying on his back. For a moment, Stone thought he was dead, but then he saw the chest moving, slowly, very slowly, but moving.

Burton came back down.

"Who is he?"

"Our wandering man. Help me get him up."

"Is he alive?"

"So far."

"I'll be damned," Burton said.

They used the power winch to hoist up the unconscious body of Peter Jackson, and then lowered it again to raise the capsule. Then, slowly, Burton and Stone climbed the ladder into the belly of the helicopter.

They did not remove their suits, but instead clipped on a second bottle of oxygen to give them another two hours of breathing time. That would be sufficient to carry them to the Wildfire installation.

The pilot established a radio connection to Vandenberg so that Stone could talk with Major Manchek.

"What have you found?" Manchek said.

"The town is dead. We have good evidence for an unusual process at work."

"Be careful," Manchek said. "This is an open circuit."

"I am aware of that. Will you order up a 7-12?"

"I'll try. You want it now?"

"Yes, now."

"Piedmont?"

"Yes."

"You have the satellite?"

"Yes, we have it."

"All right," Manchek said. "I'll put through the order."

Chapter 8

Directive 7-12

Directive 7-12 was a part of the final Wildfire Protocol for action in the event of a biologic emergency. It called for the placement of a limited thermonuclear weapon at the site of exposure of terrestrial life to exogenous organisms. The code for the directive was Cautery, since the function of the bomb was to cauterize the infection—to burn it out, and thus prevent its spread.

As a single step in the Wildfire Protocol, Cautery had been agreed upon by the authorities involved—Executive, State, Defense, and AEC—after much debate. The AEC, already unhappy about the assignment of a nuclear device to the Wildfire laboratory, did not wish Cautery to be accepted as a program; State and Defense argued that any aboveground thermonuclear detonation, for whatever purpose, would have serious repercussions internationally.

The President finally agreed to Directive 7-12, but insisted that he retain control over the decision to use a bomb for Cautery. Stone was displeased with this arrangement, but he was forced to accept it; the President had been under considerable pressure to reject the whole idea and had compromised only after much argument. Then, too, there was the Hudson Institute study.

The Hudson Institute had been contracted to study possible consequences of Cautery. Their report indicated that the President would face four circumstances (scenarios) in which he might have to issue the Cautery order. According to degree of seriousness, the scenarios were:

1. *A satellite or manned capsule lands in an unpopulated area of the United States.* The President may cauterize the area with little domestic uproar and small loss of life. The Russians may be privately informed of the reasons for breaking the Moscow Treaty of 1963 forbidding aboveground nuclear testing.

2. *A satellite or manned capsule lands in a major American city.* (The example was Chicago.) The Cautery will require destruction of a large land area and a large population, with great domestic consequences and secondary international consequences.

3. *A satellite or manned capsule lands in a major neutralist urban center.* (New Delhi was the example.) The Cautery will entail American intervention with nuclear weapons to prevent further spread of disease. According to the scenarios, there were seventeen possible consequences of American-Soviet interaction following the destruction of New Delhi. Twelve led directly to thermonuclear war.

4. *A satellite or manned capsule lands in a major Soviet urban center.* (The example was Stalingrad.) Cautery will require the United States to inform the Soviet Union of what has happened and to advise that the Russians themselves destroy the city. According to the Hudson Institute scenario, there were six possible consequences of American-Russian interaction following this event, and all six led directly to war. It was therefore advised that if a satellite fell within Soviet or Eastern Bloc territory the United States not inform the Russians of what had happened. The basis of this decision was the prediction that a Russian plague would kill between two and five million people, while combined Soviet-American losses from a thermonuclear exchange involving both first- and second-strike capabilities would come to more than two hundred and fifty million persons.

As a result of the Hudson Institute report, the President and his advisers felt that control of Cautery, and responsibility for it, should remain within political, not scientific, hands. The ultimate consequences of the President's decision could not, of course, have been predicted at the time it was made.

Washington came to a decision within an hour of Manchek's report. The reasoning behind the President's decision has never been clear, but the final result was plain enough:

The President elected to postpone calling Directive 7-12 for twenty-four to forty-eight hours. Instead, he called out the National Guard and cordoned off the area around Piedmont for a radius of one hundred miles. And he waited.

Chapter 9

Flatrock

Mark William Hall, M.D., sat in the tight rear seat of the F-104 fighter and stared over the top of the rubber oxygen mask at the file on his knees. Leavitt had given it to him just before takeoff—a heavy, thick wad of paper bound in gray cardboard. Hall was supposed to read it during the flight, but the F-104 was not made for reading; there was barely enough room in front of him to hold his hands clenched together, let alone open a file and read.

Yet Hall was reading it.

On the cover of the file was stenciled WILDFIRE, and underneath, an ominous note:

THIS FILE IS CLASSIFIED TOP SECRET.
Examination by unauthorized persons
is a criminal offense punishable
by fines and imprisonment up to
20 years and $20,000.

When Leavitt gave him the file, Hall had read the note and whistled.
"Don't you believe it," Leavitt said.

"Just a scare?"

"Scare, hell," Leavitt said. "If the wrong man reads this file, he just disappears."

"Nice."

"Read it," Leavitt said, "and you'll see why."

The plane flight had taken an hour and forty minutes, cruising in eerie, perfect silence at 1.8 times the speed of sound. Hall had skimmed through most of the file; reading it, he had found, was impossible. Much of its bulk of 274 pages consisted of cross-references and interservice notations, none of which he could understand. The first page was as bad as any of them:

THIS IS PAGE 1 OF 274 PAGES

PROJECT: WILDFIRE
AUTHORITY: NASA/AMC
CLASSIFICATION: TOP SECRET (NTK BASIS)
PRIORITY: NATIONAL (DX)
SUBJECT: Initiation of high-security facility to prevent dispersion of toxic extraterrestrial agents.
CROSSFILE: Project CLEAN, Project ZERO CONTAMINANTS, Project CAUTERY

SUMMARY OF FILE CONTENTS:

By executive order, construction of a facility initiated January 1965. Planning stage March 1965. Consultants Fort Detrick and General Dynamics (EBD) July 1965. Recommendation for multistory facility in isolated location for investigation of possible or probable contaminatory agents. Specifications reviewed August 1965. Approval with revision same date. Final drafts drawn and filed AMC under WILDFIRE (copies Detrick, Hawkins). Choice of site northeast Montana, reviewed August 1965. Choice of site southwest Arizona, reviewed August 1965. Choice of site northwest Nevada, reviewed September 1965. Nevada site approved October 1965.

Construction completed July 1966. Funding NASA, AMC, DEFENSE (unaccountable reserves). Congressional appropriation for maintenance and personnel under same.

Major alterations: Millipore filters, see page 74. Self-destruct capacity (nuclear), page 88. Ultraviolet irradiators removed, see page 81. Single Man Hypothesis (Odd Man Hypothesis), page 255.

PERSONNEL SUMMARIES HAVE BEEN ELIMINATED FROM THIS FILE. PERSONNEL MAY BE FOUND IN AMC (WILDFIRE) FILES ONLY.

The second page listed the basic parameters of the system, as laid down by the original Wildfire planning group. This specified the most important concept of the installation, namely that it would consist of roughly similar, descending levels, all underground. Each would be more sterile than the one above.

THIS IS PAGE 2 OF 274 PAGES

PROJECT: WILDFIRE

PRIMARY PARAMETERS

1. THERE ARE TO BE FIVE STAGES:

Stage I: Non-decontaminated, but clean. Approximates sterility of hospital operating room or NASA clean room. No time delay of entrance.

Stage II: Minimal sterilization procedures: hexachlorophene and methitol bath, not requiring total immersion. One-hour delay with clothing change.

Stage III: Moderate sterilization procedures: totalimmersion bath, UV irradiation, followed by two-hour delay for preliminary testing. Afebrile infections of UR and GU tracts permitted to pass. Viral symptomatology permitted to pass.

Stage IV: Maximal sterilization procedures: total immersion in four baths of biocaine, monochlorophin, xantholysin, and prophyne with intermediate thirty-minute UV and IR irradiation. All infection halted at this stage on basis of symptomatology or clinical signs. Routine screening of all personnel. Six-hour delay.

Stage V: Redundant sterilization procedures: no further immersions or testing, but destruct clothing $\times 2$ per day. Prophylactic antibiotics for forty-eight hours. Daily screen for superinfection, first eight days.

2. EACH STAGE INCLUDES:

1. Resting quarters, individual
2. Recreation quarters, including movie and game room
3. Cafeteria, automatic
4. Library, with main journals transmitted by Xerox or TV from main library Level I.
5. Shelter, a high-security antimicrobial complex with safety in event of level contamination.
6. Laboratories:

a) biochemistry, with all necessary equipment for automatic amino-acid analysis, sequence determination, O/R potentials, lipid and carbohydrate determinations on human, animal, other subjects.

b) pathology, with EM, phase and LM, microtomes and curing rooms. Five full-time technicians each level. One autopsy room. One room for experimental animals.

c) microbiology, with all facilities for growth, nutrient, analytic, immunologic studies. Subsections bacterial, viral, parasitic, other.

d) pharmacology, with material for dose-relation and receptor site specificity studies of known compounds. Pharmacy to include drugs as noted in appendix.

e) main room, experimental animals. 75 genetically pure strains of mice; 27 of rat; 17 of cat; 12 of dog; 8 of primate.

f) nonspecific room for previously unplanned experiments.

7. Surgery: for care and treatment of staff, including operating-room facilities for acute emergencies.
8. Communications: for contact with other levels by audiovisual and other means.

COUNT YOUR PAGES
REPORT ANY MISSING
PAGES AT ONCE
COUNT YOUR PAGES

As Hall continued to read, he found that only on Level I, the topmost floor, would there be a large computer complex for data analysis, but that this computer would serve all other levels on a time-sharing basis. This was considered feasible since, for biologic problems, real time was unimportant in relation to computer time, and multiple problems could be fed and handled at once.

He was leafing through the rest of the file, looking for the part that interested him—the Odd Man Hypothesis—when he came upon a page that was rather unusual.

THIS IS PAGE 255 OF 274 PAGES

BY THE AUTHORITY OF THE DEPARTMENT OF DEFENSE THIS PAGE FROM A HIGH-SECURITY FILE HAS BEEN DELETED

THE PAGE IS NUMBER: two hundred fifty-five/255

THE FILE IS CODED: Wildfire

THE SUBJECT MATTER
DELETED IS: Odd Man Hypothesis

PLEASE NOTE THAT THIS CONSTITUTES A LEGAL DELETION FROM THE FILE WHICH NEED NOT BE REPORTED BY THE READER.

MACHINE SCORE REVIEW BELOW

Hall was frowning at the page, wondering what it meant, when the pilot said, "Dr. Hall?"

"Yes."

"We have just passed the last checkpoint, sir. We will touch down in four minutes."

"All right." Hall paused. "Do you know where, exactly, we are landing?"

"I believe," said the pilot, "that it is Flatrock, Nevada."

"I see," Hall said.

A few minutes later, the flaps went down, and he heard a whine as the airplane slowed.

Nevada was the ideal site for Wildfire. The Silver State ranks seventh in size, but forty-ninth in population; it is the least-dense state in the Union after Alaska. Particularly when one considers that 85 per cent of the state's 440,000 people live in Las Vegas, Reno, or Carson City, the population density of 1.2 persons per square mile seems well suited for projects such as Wildfire, and indeed many have been located there.

Along with the famous atomic site at Vinton Flats, there is the Ultra-Energy Test Station at Martindale, and the Air Force Medivator Unit near Los Gados. Most of these facilities are in the southern triangle of the state, having been located there in the days before Las Vegas swelled to receive twenty million visitors a year. More recently, government test stations have been located in the northwest corner of Nevada, which is still relatively isolated. Pentagon classified lists include five new installations in that area; the nature of each is unknown.

Chapter 10

Stage 1

Hall landed shortly after noon, the hottest part of the day. The sun beat down from a pale, cloudless sky and the airfield asphalt was soft under his feet as he walked from the airplane to the small quonset hut at the edge of the runway. Feeling his feet sink into the surface, Hall thought that the airfield must have been designed primarily for night use; at night it would be cold, the asphalt solid.

The quonset hut was cooled by two massive, grumbling air conditioners. It was furnished sparsely: a card table in one corner, at which two pilots sat, playing poker and drinking coffee. A guard in the corner was making a telephone call; he had a machine gun slung over his shoulder. He did not look up as Hall entered.

There was a coffee machine near the telephone. Hall went over with his pilot and they each poured a cup. Hall took a sip and said, "Where's the town, anyway? I didn't see it as we were coming in."

"Don't know, sir."

"Have you been here before?"

"No sir. It's not on the standard runs."

"Well, what exactly does this airfield serve?"

At that moment, Leavitt strode in and beckoned to Hall. The bacteriologist led him through the back of the quonset and then out into the heat again, to a light-blue Falcon sedan parked in the rear. There were no identifying marks of any kind on the car; there was no driver. Leavitt slipped behind the wheel and motioned for Hall to get in.

As Leavitt put the car in gear, Hall said, "I guess we don't rate any more."

"Oh yes. We rate. But drivers aren't used out here. In fact, we don't use any more personnel than we have to. The number of wagging tongues is kept to a minimum."

They set off across desolate, hilly countryside. In the distance were blue mountains, shimmering in the liquid heat of the desert. The road was pock-marked and dusty; it looked as if it hadn't been used for years.

Hall mentioned this.

"Deceptive," Leavitt said. "We took great pains about it. We spent nearly five thousand dollars on this road."

"Why?"

Leavitt shrugged. "Had to get rid of the tractor treadmarks. A hell of a lot of heavy equipment has moved over these roads, at one time or another. Wouldn't want anyone to wonder why."

"Speaking of caution," Hall said after a pause, "I was reading in the file. Something about an atomic self-destruct device—"

"What about it?"

"It exists?"

"It exists."

Installation of the device had been a major stumbling block in the early plans for Wildfire. Stone and the others had insisted that they retain control over the detonate/no detonate decision; the AEC and the Executive branch had been reluctant. No atomic device had been put in private hands before. Stone argued that in the event of a leak in the Wildfire lab, there might not be time to consult with Washington and get a Presidential detonate order. It was a long time before the President agreed that this might be true.

"I was reading," Hall said, "that this device is somehow connected with the Odd Man Hypothesis."

"It is."

"How? The page on Odd Man was taken from my file."

"I know," Leavitt said. "We'll talk about it later."

The Falcon turned off the potted road onto a dirt track. The sedan raised a heavy cloud of dust, and despite the heat, they were forced to roll up the windows. Hall lit a cigarette.

"That'll be your last," Leavitt said.

"I know. Let me enjoy it."

On their right, they passed a sign that said GOVERNMENT PROPERTY KEEP OFF, but there was no fence, no guard, no dogs—just a battered, weather-beaten sign.

"Great security measures," Hall said.

"We try not to arouse suspicion. The security is better than it looks."

They proceeded another mile, bouncing along the dirt rut, and then came over a hill. Suddenly Hall saw a large, fenced circle perhaps a hundred yards in diameter. The fence, he noticed, was ten feet high and sturdy; at intervals it was laced with barbed wire. Inside was a utilitarian wooden building, and a field of corn.

"Corn?" Hall said.

"Rather clever, I think."

They came to the entrance gate. A man in dungarees and a T-shirt came out and opened it for them; he held a sandwich in one hand and was chewing vigorously as he unlocked the gate. He winked and smiled and waved them through, still chewing. The sign by the gate said:

GOVERNMENT PROPERTY
U.S. DEPARTMENT OF AGRICULTURE
DESERT RECLAMATION TEST STATION

Leavitt drove through the gates and parked by the wooden building. He left the keys on the dashboard and got out. Hall followed him.

"Now what?"

"Inside," Leavitt said. They entered the building, coming directly into a small room. A man in a Stetson hat, checked sport shirt, and string tie sat at a rickety desk. He was reading a newspaper and, like the man at the gate, eating his lunch. He looked up and smiled pleasantly.

"Howdy," he said.

"Hello," Leavitt said.

"Help you folks?"

"Just passing through," Leavitt said. "On the way to Rome."

The man nodded. "Have you got the time?"

"My watch stopped yesterday," Leavitt said.

"Durn shame," the man said.

"It's because of the heat."

The ritual completed, the man nodded again. And they walked past him, out of the anteroom and down a corridor. The doors had hand-printed labels: "Seedling Incubation"; "Moisture Control"; "Soil Analysis." A half-dozen people were at work in the building, all of them dressed casually, but all of them apparently busy.

"This is a real agricultural station," Leavitt said. "If necessary, that man at the desk could give you a guided tour, explaining the purpose of the station and the experiments that are going on. Mostly they are attempting to develop a strain of corn that can grow in low-moisture, high-alkalinity soil."

"And the Wildfire installation?"

"Here," Leavitt said. He opened a door marked "Storage" and they found themselves staring at a narrow cubicle lined with rakes and hoes and watering hoses.

"Step in," Leavitt said.

Hall did. Leavitt followed and closed the door behind him. Hall felt the floor sink and they began to descend, rakes and hoses and all.

In a moment, he found himself in a modern, bare room, lighted by banks of cold overhead fluorescent lights. The walls were painted red. The only object in the room was a rectangular, waist-high box that reminded Hall of a podium. It had a glowing green glass top.

"Step up to the analyzer," Leavitt said. "Place your hands flat on the glass, palms down."

Hall did. He felt a faint tingling in his fingers, and then the machine gave a buzz.

"All right. Step back." Leavitt placed his hands on the box, waited for the buzz, and then said, "Now we go over here. You mentioned the security arrangements; I'll show them to you before we enter Wildfire."

He nodded to a door across the room.

"What was that thing?"

"Finger- and palm-print analyzer," Leavitt said. "It is fully automatic. Reads a composite of ten thousand dermatographic lines so it can't make a mistake; in its storage banks it has a record of the prints of everyone cleared to enter Wildfire."

Leavitt pushed through the door.

They were faced with another door, marked SECURITY, which slid back noiselessly. They entered a darkened room in which a single man sat before banks of green dials.

"Hello, John," Leavitt said to the man. "How are you?"

"Good, Dr. Leavitt. Saw you come in."

Leavitt introduced Hall to the security man, who then demonstrated the equipment to Hall. There were, the man explained, two radar scanners located in the hills overlooking the installation; they were well concealed but quite effective. Then closer in, impedence sensors were buried in the ground; they signaled the approach of any animal life weighing more than one hundred pounds. The sensors ringed the base.

"We've never missed anything yet," the man said. "And if we do . . ." He shrugged. To Leavitt: "Going to show him the dogs?"

"Yes," Leavitt said.

They walked through into an adjoining room. There were nine large cages there, and the room smelled strongly of animals. Hall found himself looking at nine of the largest German shepherds he had ever seen.

They barked at him as he entered, but there was no sound in the room. He watched in astonishment as they opened their mouths and threw their heads forward in a barking motion.

No sound.

"These are Army-trained sentry dogs," the security man said. "Bred for viciousness. You wear leather clothes and heavy gloves when you walk them. They've undergone laryngectomies, which is why you can't hear them. Silent and vicious."

Hall said, "Have you ever, uh, used them?"

"No," the security man said. "Fortunately not."

They were in a small room with lockers. Hall found one with his name on it.

"We change in here," Leavitt said. He nodded to a stack of pink uniforms in one corner. "Put those on, after you have removed everything you are wearing."

Hall changed quickly. The uniforms were loose-fitting one-piece suits that zipped up the side. When they had changed they proceeded down a passageway.

Suddenly an alarm sounded and a gate in front of them slid closed abruptly. Overhead, a white light began to flash. Hall was confused, and it was only much later that he remembered Leavitt looked away from the flashing light.

"Something's wrong," Leavitt said. "Did you remove everything?"

"Yes," Hall said.

"Rings, watch, everything?"

Hall looked at his hands. He still had his watch on.

"Go back," Leavitt said. "Put it in your locker."

Hall did. When he came back, they started down the corridor a second time. The gate remained open, and there was no alarm.

"Automatic as well?" Hall said.

"Yes," Leavitt said. "It picks up any foreign object. When we installed it, we were worried because we knew it would pick up glass eyes, cardiac pacemakers, false teeth—anything at all. But fortunately nobody on the project has these things."

"Fillings?"

"It is programmed to ignore fillings."

"How does it work?"

"Some kind of capacitance phenomenon. I don't really understand it," Leavitt said.

They passed a sign that said:

YOU ARE NOW ENTERING LEVEL I
PROCEED DIRECTLY TO IMMUNIZATION CONTROL

Hall noticed that all the walls were red. He mentioned this to Leavitt.

"Yes," Leavitt said. "All levels are painted a different color. Level I is red; II, yellow; III, white; IV, green; and V, blue."

"Any particular reason for the choice?"

"It seems," Leavitt said, "that the Navy sponsored some studies a few years back on the psychological effects of colored environments. Those studies have been applied here."

They came to Immunization. A door slid back revealing three glass booths. Leavitt said, "Just sit down in one of them."

"I suppose this is automatic, too?"

"Of course."

Hall entered a booth and closed the door behind him. There was a couch, and a mass of complex equipment. In front of the couch was a television screen, which showed several lighted points.

"Sit down," said a flat mechanical voice. "Sit down. Sit down."

He sat on the couch.

"Observe the screen before you. Place your body on the couch so that all points are obliterated."

He looked at the screen. He now saw that the points were arranged in the shape of a man:

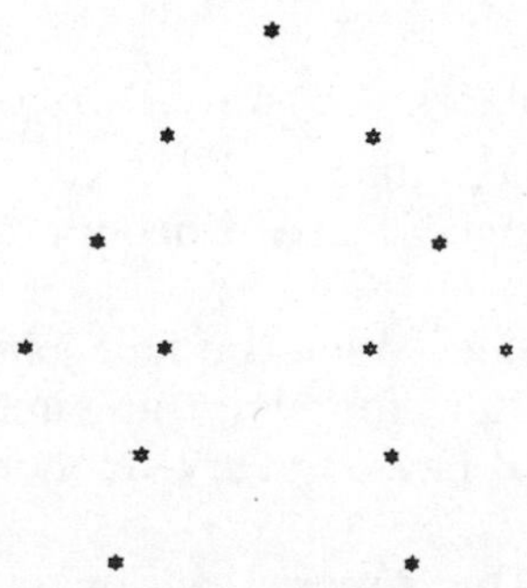

*

*   *

*   *

*   *   *   *

*   *

*   *

He shifted his body, and one by one the spots disappeared.

"Very good," said the voice. "We may now proceed. State your name for the record. Last name first, first name last."

"Mark Hall," he said.

"State your name for the record. Last name first, first name last."

Simultaneously, on the screen appeared the words:

SUBJECT HAS GIVEN UNCODABLE RESPONSE

"Hall, Mark."

"Thank you for your cooperation," said the voice. "Please recite, 'Mary had a little lamb.' "

"You're kidding," Hall said.

There was a pause, and the faint sound of relays and circuits clicking. The screen again showed:

SUBJECT HAS GIVEN UNCODABLE RESPONSE

"Please recite."

Feeling rather foolish, Hall said, "Mary had a little lamb, her fleece was white as snow, and everywhere that Mary went, the lamb was sure to go."

Another pause. Then the voice: "Thank you for your cooperation." And the screen said:

ANALYZER CONFIRMS IDENTITY
HALL, MARK

"Please listen closely," said the mechanical voice. "You will answer the following questions with a yes or no reply. Make no other response. Have you received a smallpox vaccination within the last twelve months?"

"Yes."

"Diphtheria?"

"Yes."

"Typhoid and paratyphoid A and B?"

"Yes."

"Tetanus toxoid?"

"Yes."

"Yellow fever?"

"Yes, yes, yes. I had them all."

"Just answer the question please. Uncooperative subjects waste valuable computer time."

"Yes," Hall said, subdued. When he had joined the Wildfire team, he had undergone immunizations for everything imaginable, even plague and cholera, which had to be renewed every six months, and gamma-globulin shots for viral infection.

"Have you ever contracted tuberculosis or other mycobacterial disease, or had a positive skin test for tuberculosis?"

"No."

"Have you ever contracted syphilis or other spirochetal disease, or had a positive serological test for syphilis?"

"No."

"Have you contracted within the past year any gram-positive bacterial infection, such as streptococcus, staphylococcus, or pneumococcus?"

"No."

"Any gram-negative infection, such as gonococcus, meningeococcus, proteus, pseudomonas, salmonella, or shigella?"

"No."

"Have you contracted any recent or past fungal infection, including blastomycosis, histoplasmosis, or coccidiomycosis, or had a positive skin test for any fungal disease?"

"No."

"Have you had any recent viral infection, including poliomyelitis, hepatitis, mononucleosis, mumps, measles, varicella, or herpes?"

"No."

"Any warts?"

"No."

"Have you any known allergies?"

"Yes, to ragweed pollen."

On the screen appeared the words:

ROGEEN PALEN

And then after a moment:

UNCODABLE RESPONSE

"Please repeat your response slowly for our memory cells."

Very distinctly, he said, "Ragweed pollen."

On the screen:

RAGWEED POLLEN   CODED

"Are you allergic to albumen?" continued the voice.

"No."

"This ends the formal questions. Please undress and return to the couch, obliterating the points as before."

He did so. A moment later, an ultraviolet lamp swung out on a long arm and moved close to his body. Next to the lamp was some kind of scanning eye. Watching the screen he could see the computer print of the scan, beginning with his feet.

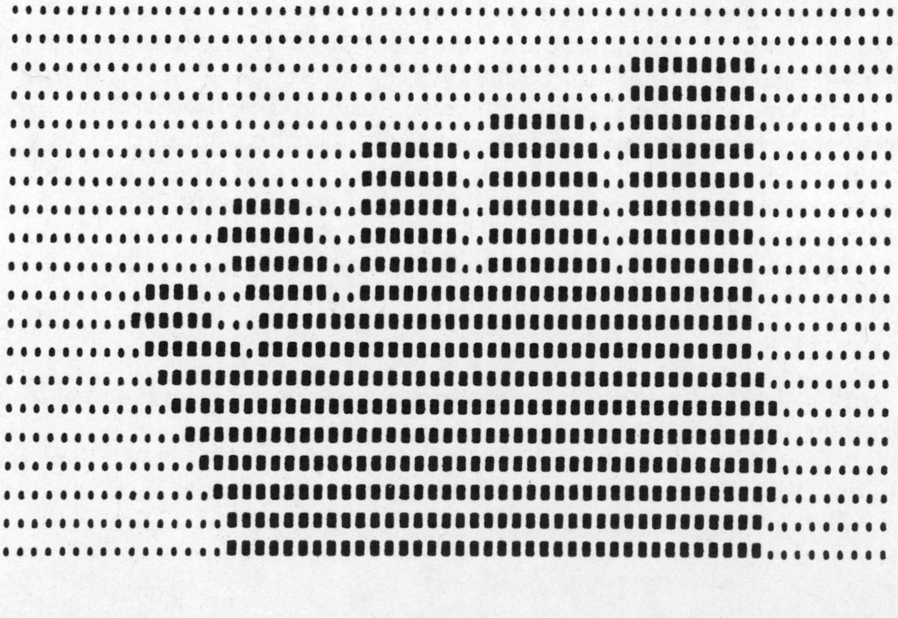

"This is a scan for fungus," the voice announced. After several minutes, Hall was ordered to lie on his stomach, and the process was repeated. He was then told to lie on his back once more and align himself with the dots.

"Physical parameters will now be measured," the voice said. "You are requested to lie quietly while the examination is conducted."

A variety of leads snaked out at him and were attached by mechanical hands to his body. Some he could understand—the half-dozen leads over his chest for an electrocardiogram, and twenty-one on his head for an electroencephalogram. But others were fixed on his stomach, his arms, and his legs.

"Please raise your left hand," said the voice.

Hall did. From above, a mechanical hand came down, with an electric eye fixed on either side of it. The mechanical hand examined Hall's.

"Place your hand on the board to the left. Do not move. You will feel a slight prick as the intravenous needle is inserted."

Hall looked over at the screen. It flashed a color image of his hand, with the veins showing in a pattern of green against a blue background. Obviously the machine worked by sensing heat. He was about to protest when he felt a brief sting.

He looked back. The needle was in.

"Now then, just lie quietly. Relax."

For fifteen seconds, the machinery whirred and clattered. Then the leads were withdrawn. The mechanical hands placed a neat Band-Aid over the intravenous puncture.

"This completes your physical parameters," the voice said.

"Can I get dressed now?"

"Please sit up with your right shoulder facing the television screen. You will receive pneumatic injections."

A gun with a thick cable came out of one wall, pressed up against the skin of his shoulder, and fired. There was a hissing sound and a brief pain.

"Now you may dress," said the voice. "Be advised that you may feel dizzy for a few hours. You have received booster immunizations and gamma G. If you feel dizzy, sit down. If you suffer systemic effects such as nausea, vomiting, or fever, report at once to Level Control. Is that clear?"

"Yes."

"The exit is to your right. Thank you for your cooperation. This recording is now ended."

Hall walked with Leavitt down a long red corridor. His arm ached from the injection.

"That machine," Hall said. "You'd better not let the AMA find out about it."

"We haven't," Leavitt said.

In fact, the electronic body analyzer had been developed by Sandeman Industries in 1965, under a general government contract to produce body monitors for astronauts in space. It was understood by the government at that time that such a device, though expensive at a cost of $87,000 each, would eventually replace the human physician as a diagnostic instrument. The difficulties, for both doctor and patient, of adjusting to this new machine were recognized by everyone. The government did not plan to release the EBA until 1971, and then only to certain large hospital facilities.

Walking along the corridor, Hall noticed that the walls were slightly curved.

"Where exactly are we?"

"On the perimeter of Level I. To our left are all the laboratories. To the right is nothing but solid rock."

Several people were walking in the corridor. Everyone wore pink jumpsuits. They all seemed serious and busy.

"Where are the others on the team?" Hall said.

"Right here," Leavitt said. He opened a door marked CONFERENCE 7, and they entered a room with a large hardwood table. Stone was there, standing stiffly erect and alert, as if he had just taken a cold shower. Alongside him, Burton, the pathologist, somehow appeared sloppy and confused, and there was a kind of tired fright in his eyes.

They all exchanged greetings and sat down. Stone reached into his pocket and removed two keys. One was silver, the other red. The red one had a chain attached to it. He gave it to Hall.

"Put it around your neck," he said.

Hall looked at it. "What's this?"

Leavitt said, "I'm afraid Mark is still unclear about the Odd Man."

"I thought that he would read it on the plane—"

"His file was edited."

"I see." Stone turned to Hall. "You know nothing about the Odd Man?"

"Nothing," Hall said, frowning at the key.

"Nobody told you that a major factor in your selection to the team was your single status?"

"What does that have to do—"

"The fact of the matter is," Stone said, "that you are the Odd Man. You are the key to all this. Quite literally."

He took his own key and walked to a corner of the room. He pushed a hidden button and the wood paneling slid away to reveal a burnished metal console. He inserted his key into a lock and twisted it. A green light on the console flashed on; he stepped back. The paneling slid into place.

"At the lowest level of this laboratory is an automatic atomic self-destruct device," Stone said. "It is controlled from within the laboratory. I have just inserted my key and armed the mechanism. The device is ready for detonation. The key on this level cannot be removed; it is now locked in place. Your key, on the other hand, can be inserted and removed again. There is a three-minute delay between the time detonation locks in and the time the bomb goes off. That period is to provide you time to think, and perhaps call it all off."

Hall was still frowning. "But why me?"

"Because you are single. We have to have one unmarried man."

Stone opened a briefcase and withdrew a file. He gave it to Hall. "Read that."

It was a Wildfire file.

"Page 255," Stone said.

Hall turned to it.

Project: Wildfire

ALTERATIONS

1. Millipore Filters, insertion into ventilatory system. Initial spec filters unilayer styrilene, with maximal efficiency of 97.4% trapping. Replaced in 1966 when Upjohn developed filters capable of trapping organisms of size up to one micron. Trapping at 90% efficiency per leaf, causing triple-layered membrance to give results of 99.9%. Infective ratio of .1% remainder too low to be harmful. Cost factor of four- or five-layered membrance removing all but .001% considered prohibitive for added gain. Tolerance parameter of 1/1,000 considered sufficient. Installation completed 8/12/66.

2. Atomic Self-Destruct Device, change in detonator close-gap timers. See AEC/Def file 77-12-0918.

3. Atomic Self-Destruct Device, revision of core maintenance schedules for K technicians, see AEC/Warburg file 77-14-0004.

4. Atomic Self-Destruct Device, final command decision change. See AEC/Def file 77-14-0023. SUMMARY APPENDED.

SUMMARY OF ODD MAN HYPOTHESIS: First tested as null hypothesis by Wildfire advisory committee. Grew out of tests conducted by USAF (NORAD) to determine reliability of commanders in making life/death decisions. Tests involved decisions in ten scenario contexts, with prestructured alternatives drawn up by Walter Reed Psychiatric Division, after n-order test analysis by biostatistics unit, NIH, Bethesda.

Test given to SAC pilots and groundcrews, NORAD workers, and others involved in decision-making or positiveaction capacity. Ten scenarios drawn up by Hudson Institute; subjects required to make YES/NO decision in each case. Decisions always involved thermonuclear or chem-biol destruction of enemy targets.

Data on 7420 subjects tested by H_1H_2 program for multifactorial analysis of variance; later test by ANOVAR program; final discrimination by CLASSIF program. NIH biostat summarizes this program as follows:

It is the object of this program to determine the effectiveness of assigning individuals to distinct groups on the basis of scores which can be quantified. The program produces group contours and probability of classification for individuals as a control of data.
Program prints: mean scores for groups, contour confidence limits, and scores of individual test subjects.

K G Borgrand

K.G. Borgrand, Ph.D. NIH

RESULTS OF ODD MAN STUDY: The study concluded that married individuals performed differently from single individuals on several parameters of the test. Hudson Institute provided mean answers, i.e. theoretical "right" decisions, made by computer on basis of data given in scenario. Conformance of study groups to these right answers produced an index of effectiveness, a measure of the extent to which correct decisions were made.

Group	Index of Effectiveness
Married males	.343
Married females	.399
Single females	.402
Single males	.824

The data indicate that married men choose the correct decision only once in three times, while single men choose correctly four out of five times. The group of single males was then broken down further, in search of highly accurate subgroups within that classification.

Group	Index of Effectiveness
Single males, total	.824
Military:	
commissioned officer	.655
noncommissioned officer	.624
Technical:	
engineers	.877
ground crews	.901
Service:	
maintenance and utility	.758
Professional:	
scientists	.946

These results concerning the relative skill of decision-making individuals should not be interpreted hastily. Although it would appear that janitors are better decision-makers than generals, the situation is in reality more complex. PRINTED SCORES ARE SUMMATIONS OF TEST AND INDIVIDUAL VARIATIONS. DATA MUST BE INTERPRETED WITH THIS IN MIND. Failure to do so may lead to totally erroneous and dangerous assumptions.

Application of study to Wildfire command personnel conducted at request of AEC at time of implantation of self-destruct nuclear capacity. Test given to all Wildfire personnel; results filed under CLASSIF WILDFIRE: GENERAL PERSONNEL (see ref. 77-14-0023). Special testing for command group.

Name	Index of Effectiveness
Burton	.543
Leavitt	.601
Kirke	.614
Stone	.687
Hall	.899

Results of special testing confirm the Odd Man Hypothesis, that an unmarried male should carry out command decisions involving thermonuclear or chem-biol destruct contexts.

When Hall had finished reading, he said, "It's crazy."

"Nonetheless," Stone said, "it was the only way we could get the government to put control of the weapon in our hands."

"You really expect me to put in my key, and fire that thing?"

"I'm afraid you don't understand," Stone said. "The detonation mechanism is automatic. Should breakthrough of the organism occur, with contamination of all Level V, detonation will take place within three minutes *unless* you lock in your key, and call it off."

"Oh," Hall said, in a quiet voice.

Chapter 11

Decontamination

A bell rang somewhere on the level; Stone glanced up at the wall clock. It was late. He began the formal briefing, talking rapidly, pacing up and down the room, hands moving constantly.

"As you know," he said, "we are on the top level of a five-story underground structure. According to protocol it will take us nearly twenty-four hours to descend through the sterilization and decontamination procedures to the lowest level. Therefore we must begin immediately. The capsule is already on its way."

He pressed a button on a console at the head of the table, and a television screen glowed to life, showing the cone-shaped satellite in a plastic bag, making its descent. It was being cradled by mechanical hands.

"The central core of this circular building," Stone said, "contains elevators and service units—plumbing, wiring, that sort of thing. That is where you see the capsule now. It will be deposited shortly in a maximum-sterilization assembly on the lowest level."

He went on to explain that he had brought back two other surprises from Piedmont. The screen shifted to show Peter Jackson, lying on a litter, with intravenous lines running into both arms.

"This man apparently survived the night. He was the one walking around when the planes flew over, and he was still alive this morning."

"What's his status now?"

"Uncertain," Stone said. "He is unconscious, and he was vomiting blood earlier today. We've started intravenous dextrose to keep him fed and hydrated until we can get down to the bottom."

Stone flicked a button and the screen showed the baby. It was howling, strapped down to a tiny bed. An intravenous bottle was running into a vein in the scalp.

"This little fellow also survived last night," Stone said. "So we brought him along. We couldn't really leave him, since a Directive 7-12 was being called. The town is now destroyed by a nuclear blast. Besides, he and Jackson are living clues which may help us unravel this mess."

Then, for the benefit of Hall and Leavitt, the two men disclosed what they had seen and learned at Piedmont. They reviewed the findings of rapid death, the bizarre suicides, the clotted arteries and the lack of bleeding.

Hall listened in astonishment. Leavitt sat shaking his head.

When they were through, Stone said, "Questions?"

"None that won't keep," Leavitt said.

"Then let's get started," Stone said.

They began at a door, which said in plain white letters: TO LEVEL II. It was an innocuous, straightforward, almost mundane sign. Hall had expected something more—perhaps a stern guard with a machine gun, or a sentry to check passes. But there was nothing, and he noticed that no one had badges, or clearance cards of any kind.

He mentioned this to Stone. "Yes," Stone said. "We decided against badges early on. They are easily contaminated and difficult to sterilize; usually they are plastic and high-heat sterilization melts them."

The four men passed through the door, which clanged shut heavily and sealed with a hissing sound. It was airtight. Hall faced a tiled room, empty except for a hamper marked "clothing." He unzipped his jumpsuit and dropped it into the hamper; there was a brief flash of light as it was incinerated.

Then, looking back, he saw that on the door through which he had come was a sign: "Return to Level I is NOT Possible Through this Access."

He shrugged. The other men were already moving through the second door, marked simply EXIT. He followed them and stepped into clouds of steam. The odor was peculiar, a faint woodsy smell that he guessed was scented disinfectant. He sat down on a bench and relaxed, allowing the steam to envelop him. It was easy enough to understand the purpose of the steam room: the heat opened the pores, and the steam would be inhaled into the lungs.

The four men waited, saying little, until their bodies were coated with a sheen of moisture, and then walked into the next room.

Leavitt said to Hall, "What do you think of this?"

"It's like a goddam Roman bath," Hall said.

The next room contained a shallow tub ("Immerse Feet ONLY") and a shower. ("Do not swallow shower solution. Avoid undue exposure to eyes and mucous membranes.") It was all very intimidating. He tried to guess what the solutions were by smell, but failed; the shower was slippery, though, which meant it was alkaline. He asked Leavitt about this, and Leavitt said the solution was alpha chlorophin at pH 7.7. Leavitt said that whenever possible, acidic and alkaline solutions were alternated.

"When you think about it," Leavitt said, "we've faced up to quite a planning problem here. How to disinfect the human body—one of the dirtiest things in the known universe—without killing the person at the same time. Interesting."

He wandered off. Dripping wet from the shower, Hall looked around for a towel but found none. He entered the next room and blowers turned on from the ceiling in a rush of hot air. From the sides of the room, UV lights clicked on, bathing the room in an intense purple light. He stood there until a buzzer sounded, and the dryers turned off. His skin tingled slightly as he entered the last room, which contained clothing. They were not jumpsuits, but rather like surgical uniforms—light-yellow, a loose-fitting top with a V-neck and short sleeves; elastic banded pants; low rubber-soled shoes, quite comfortable, like ballet slippers.

The cloth was soft, some kind of synthetic. He dressed and stepped with the others through a door marked EXIT TO LEVEL II. He entered the elevator and waited as it descended.

Hall emerged to find himself in a corridor. The walls here were painted yellow, not red as they had been on Level I. The people wore yellow uniforms. A nurse by the elevator said, "The time is 2:47 P.M., gentlemen. You may continue your descent in one hour."

They went to a small room marked INTERIM CONFINEMENT. It contained a half-dozen couches with plastic disposable covers over them.

Stone said, "Better relax. Sleep if you can. We'll need all the rest we can get before Level V." He walked over to Hall. "How did you find the decontamination procedure?"

"Interesting," Hall said. "You could sell it to the Swedes and make a fortune. But somehow I expected something more rigorous."

"Just wait," Stone said. "It gets tougher as you go. Physicals on Levels III and IV. Afterward there will be a brief conference."

Then Stone lay down on one of the couches and fell instantly asleep. It was a trick he had learned years before, when he had been conducting experiments around the clock. He learned to squeeze in an hour here, two hours there. He found it useful.

* * *

The second decontamination procedure was similar to the first. Hall's yellow clothing, though he had worn it just an hour, was incinerated.

"Isn't that rather wasteful?" he asked Burton.

Burton shrugged. "It's paper."

"Paper? That cloth?"

Burton shook his head. "Not cloth. Paper. New process."

They stepped into the first total-immersion pool. Instructions on the wall told Hall to keep his eyes open under water. Total immersion, he soon discovered, was guaranteed by the simple device of making the connection between the first room and the second an underwater passage. Swimming through, he felt a slight burning of his eyes, but nothing bad.

The second room contained a row of six boxes, glass-walled, looking rather like telephone booths. Hall approached one and saw a sign that said, "Enter and close both eyes. Hold arms slightly away from body and stand with feet one foot apart. Do not open eyes until buzzer sounds. BLINDNESS MAY RESULT FROM EXPOSURE TO LONG-WAVE RADIATION."

He followed the directions and felt a kind of cold heat on his body. It lasted perhaps five minutes, and then he heard the buzzer and opened his eyes. His body was dry. He followed the others to a corridor, consisting of four showers. Walking down the corridor, he passed beneath each shower in turn. At the end, he found blowers, which dried him, and then clothing. This time the clothing was white.

They dressed, and took the elevator down to Level III.

There were four nurses waiting for them; one took Hall to an examining room. It turned out to be a two-hour physical examination, given not by a machine but by a blank-faced, thorough young man. Hall was annoyed, and thought to himself that he preferred the machine.

The doctor did everything, including a complete history: birth, education, travel, family history, past hospitalizations and illnesses. And an equally complete physical. Hall became angry; it was all so damned unnecessary. But the doctor shrugged and kept saying, "It's routine."

After two hours, he rejoined the others, and proceeded to Level IV.

Four total-immersion baths, three sequences of ultraviolet and infrared light, two of ultrasonic vibrations, and then something quite astonishing at the end. A steel-walled cubicle, with a helmet on a peg. The sign said, "This is an ultraflash apparatus. To protect head and facial hair, place metal helmet securely on head, then press button below."

Hall had never heard of ultraflash, and he followed directions, not knowing what to expect. He placed the helmet over his head, then pressed the button.

There was a single, brief, dazzling burst of white light, followed by a wave of heat that filled the cubicle. He felt a moment of pain, so swift he hardly recognized it until it was over. Cautiously, he removed the helmet and looked at his body. His skin was covered with a fine, white ash—and then he realized that the ash was his skin, or had been: the machine had burned away the outer epithelial layers. He proceeded to a shower and washed the ash off. When he finally reached the dressing room, he found green uniforms.

Another physical. This time they wanted samples of everything: sputum, oral epithelium, blood, urine, stool. He submitted passively to the tests, examinations, questions. He was tired, and was beginning to feel disoriented. The repetitions, the new experiences, the colors on the walls, the same bland artificial light . . .

Finally, he was brought back to Stone and the others. Stone said, "We have six hours on this level—that's protocol, waiting while they do the lab tests on us—so we might as well sleep. Down the corridor are rooms, marked with your names. Further down is the cafeteria. We'll meet there in five hours for a conference. Right?"

Hall found his room, marked with a plastic door tag. He entered, surprised to find it quite large. He had been expecting something the size of a Pullman cubicle, but this was bigger and better-furnished. There was a bed, a chair, a small desk, and a computer console with built-in TV set. He was curious about the computer, but also very tired. He lay down on the bed and fell asleep quickly.

Burton could not sleep. He lay in his bed on Level IV and stared at the ceiling, thinking. He could not get the image of that town out of his mind, or those bodies, lying in the street without bleeding . . .

Burton was not a hematologist, but his work had involved some blood studies. He knew that a variety of bacteria had effects on blood. His own research with staphylococcus, for example, had shown that this organism produced two enzymes that altered blood.

One was the so-called exotoxin, which destroyed skin and dissolved red cells. Another was a coagulase, which coated the bacteria with protein to inhibit destruction by white cells.

So it was possible that bacteria could alter blood. And it could do it many different ways: strep produced an enzyme, streptokinase, that dissolved coagulated plasma. Clostridia and pneumococci produced a variety of hemolysins that destroyed red cells. Malaria and amebae also destroyed red cells, by digesting them as food. Other parasites did the same thing.

So it was possible.

But it didn't help them in finding out how the Scoop organism worked.

Burton tried to recall the sequence for blood clotting. He remembered that it operated like a kind of waterfall: one enzyme was set off, and activated, which acted on a second enzyme, which acted on a third; the third on a fourth; and so on, down through twelve or thirteen steps, until finally blood clotted.

And vaguely he remembered the rest, the details: all the intermediate steps, the necessary enzymes, the metals, ions, local factors. It was horribly complex.

He shook his head and tried to sleep.

Leavitt, the clinical microbiologist, was thinking through the steps in isolation and identification of the causative organism. He had been over it before; he was one of the original founders of the group, one of the men who developed the Life Analysis Protocol. But now, on the verge of putting that plan into effect, he had doubts.

Two years before, sitting around after lunch, talking speculatively, it had all seemed wonderful. It had been an amusing intellectual game then, a kind of abstract test of wits. But now, faced with a real agent that caused real and bizarre death, he wondered whether all their plans would prove to be so effective and so complete as they once thought.

The first steps were simple enough. They would examine the capsule minutely and culture everything onto growth media. They would be hoping like hell to come up with an organism that they could work with, experiment on, and identify.

And after that, attempt to find out how it attacked. There was already the suggestion that it killed by clotting the blood; if that turned out to be the case, they had a good start, but if not, they might waste valuable time following it up.

The example of cholera came to mind. For centuries, men had known that cholera was a fatal disease, and that it caused severe diarrhea, sometimes producing as much as thirty quarts of fluid a day. Men knew this, but they somehow assumed that the lethal effects of the disease were unrelated to the diarrhea; they searched for something else: an antidote, a drug, a way to kill the organism. It was not until modern times that cholera was recognized as a disease that killed through dehydration primarily; if you could replace a victim's water losses rapidly, he would survive the infection without other drugs or treatment.

Cure the symptoms, cure the disease.

But Leavitt wondered about the Scoop organism. Could they cure the disease by treating the blood clotting? Or was the clotting secondary to some more serious disorder?

There was also another concern, a nagging fear that had bothered him since the earliest planning stages of Wildfire. In those early meetings, Leavitt had argued that the Wildfire team might be committing extraterrestrial murder.

Leavitt had pointed out that all men, no matter how scientifically objective, had several built-in biases when discussing life. One was the assumption that complex life was larger than simple life. It was certainly true on the earth. As organisms became more intelligent, they grew larger, passing from the single-celled stage to multicellular creatures, and then to larger animals with differentiated cells working in groups called organs. On earth, the trend had been toward larger and more complex animals.

But this might not be true elsewhere in the universe. In other places, life might progress in the opposite direction—toward smaller and smaller forms. Just as modern human technology had learned to make things smaller, perhaps highly advanced evolutionary pressures led to smaller life forms. There were distinct advantages to smaller forms: less consumption of raw materials, cheaper spaceflight, fewer feeding problems . . .

Perhaps the most intelligent life form on a distant planet was no larger than a flea. Perhaps no larger than a bacterium. In that case, the Wildfire Project might be committed to destroying a highly developed life form, without ever realizing what it was doing.

This concept was not unique to Leavitt. It had been proposed by Merton at Harvard, and by Chalmers at Oxford. Chalmers, a man with a keen sense of humor, had used the example of a man looking down on a microscope slide and seeing the bacteria formed into the words "Take us to your leader." Everyone thought Chalmers's idea highly amusing.

Yet Leavitt could not get it out of his mind. Because it just might turn out to be true.

Before he fell asleep, Stone thought about the conference coming up. And the business of the meteorite. He wondered what Nagy would say, or Karp, if they knew about the meteorite.

Probably, he thought, it would drive them insane. Probably it will drive us all insane.

And then he slept.

Delta sector was the designation of three rooms on Level I that contained all communications facilities for the Wildfire installation. All intercom and visual circuits between levels were routed through there, as were cables for telephone and teletype from the outside. The trunk lines to the library and the central storage unit were also regulated by delta sector.

In essence it functioned as a giant switchboard, fully computerized. The three rooms of delta sector were quiet; all that could be heard was the soft hum of spinning tape drums and the muted clicking of relays. Only one person worked here, a single man sitting at a console, surrounded by the blinking lights of the computer.

There was no real reason for the man to be there; he performed no necessary function. The computers were self-regulating, constructed to run check patterns through their circuits every twelve minutes; the computers shut down automatically if there was an abnormal reading.

According to protocol, the man was required to monitor MCN communications, which were signaled by the ringing of a bell on the teleprinter. When the bell rang, he notified the five level command centers that the transmission was received. He was also required to report any computer dysfunction to Level I command, should that unlikely event occur.

DAY 3

WILDFIRE

Chapter 12

The Conference

"Time to wake up, sir."

Mark Hall opened his eyes. The room was lit with a steady, pale fluorescent light. He blinked and rolled over on his stomach.

"Time to wake up, sir."

It was a beautiful female voice, soft and seductive. He sat up in bed and looked around the room: he was alone.

"Hello?"

"Time to wake up, sir."

"Who are you?"

"Time to wake up, sir."

He reached over and pushed a button on the nightstand by his bed. A light went off. He waited for the voice again, but it did not speak.

It was, he thought, a hell of an effective way to wake a man up. As he slipped into his clothes, he wondered how it worked. It was not a simple tape, because it worked as a response of some sort. The message was repeated only when Hall spoke.

To test his theory, he pushed the nightstand button again. The voice said softly, "Do you wish something, sir?"

"I'd like to know your name, please."

"Will that be all, sir?"

"Yes, I believe so."

"Will that be all, sir?"

He waited. The light clicked off. He slipped into his shoes and was about to leave when a male voice said, "This is the answering-service supervisor, Dr. Hall. I wish you would treat the project more seriously."

Hall laughed. So the voice responded to comments, and taped his replies. It was a clever system.

"Sorry," he said, "I wasn't sure how the thing worked. The voice is quite luscious."

"The voice," said the supervisor heavily, "belongs to Miss Gladys Stevens, who is sixty-three years old. She lives in Omaha and makes her living taping messages for SAC crews and other voice-reminder systems."

"Oh," Hall said.

He left the room and walked down the corridor to the cafeteria. As he walked, he began to understand why submarine designers had been called in to plan Wildfire. Without his wristwatch, he had no idea of the time, or even whether it was night or day. He found himself wondering whether the cafeteria would be crowded, wondering whether it was dinner time or breakfast time.

As it turned out, the cafeteria was almost deserted. Leavitt was there; he said the others were in the conference room. He pushed a glass of dark-brown liquid over to Hall and suggested he have breakfast.

"What's this?" Hall said.

"Forty-two-five nutrient. It has everything needed to sustain the average seventy-kilogram man for eighteen hours."

Hall drank the liquid, which was syrupy and artificially flavored to taste like orange juice. It was a strange sensation, drinking brown orange juice, but not bad after the initial shock. Leavitt explained that it had been developed for the astronauts, and that it contained everything except air-soluble vitamins.

"For that, you need this pill," he said.

Hall swallowed the pill, then got himself a cup of coffee from a dispenser in the corner. "Any sugar?"

Leavitt shook his head. "No sugar anywhere here. Nothing that might provide a bacterial growth medium. From now on, we're all on high-protein diets. We'll make all the sugar we need from the protein breakdown. But we won't be getting any sugar into the gut. Quite the opposite."

He reached into his pocket.

"Oh, no."

"Yes," Leavitt said. He gave him a small capsule, sealed in aluminum foil.

"No," Hall said.

"Everyone else has them. Broad-spectrum. Stop by your room and insert it before you go into the final decontamination procedures."

"I don't mind dunking myself in all those foul baths," Hall said. "I don't mind being irradiated. But I'll be goddammed—"

"The idea," Leavitt said, "is that you be as nearly sterile as possible on Level V. We have sterilized your skin and mucous membranes of the respiratory tract as best we can. But we haven't done a thing about the GI tract yet."

"Yes," Hall said, "but suppositories?"

"You'll get used to it. We're all taking them for the first four days. Not, of course, that they'll do any good," he said, with the familiar wry, pessimistic look on his face. He stood. "Let's go to the conference room. Stone wants to talk about Karp."

"Who?"

"Rudolph Karp."

Rudolph Karp was a Hungarian-born biochemist who came to the United States from England in 1951. He obtained a position at the University of Michigan and worked steadily and quietly for five years. Then, at the suggestion of colleagues at the Ann Arbor observatory, Karp began to investigate meteorites with the intent of determining whether they harbored life, or showed evidence of having done so in the past. He took the proposal quite seriously and worked with diligence, writing no papers on the subject until the early 1960's, when Calvin and Vaughn and Nagy and others were writing explosive papers on similar subjects.

The arguments and counter-arguments were complex, but boiled down to a simple substrate: whenever a worker would announce that he had found a fossil, or a proteinaceous hydrocarbon, or other indication of life within a meteorite, the critics would claim sloppy lab technique and contamination with earth-origin matter and organisms.

Karp, with his careful, slow techniques, was determined to end the arguments once and for all. He announced that he had taken great pains to avoid contamination: each meteorite he examined had been washed in twelve solutions, including peroxide, iodine, hypertonic saline and dilute acids. It was then exposed to intense ultraviolet light for a period of two days. Finally, it was submerged in a germicidal solution and placed in a germ-free, sterile isolation chamber; further work was done within the chamber.

Karp, upon breaking open his meteorites, was able to isolate bacteria. He found that they were ring-shaped organisms, rather like a tiny undulating inner tube, and he found they could grow and multiply. He claimed that, while they were essentially similar to earthly bacteria in structure, being based upon proteins, carbohydrates, and lipids, they had no cell nucleus and therefore their manner of propagation was a mystery.

Karp presented his information in his usual quiet, unsensational manner, and hoped for a good reception. He did not receive one; instead, he was laughed down by the Seventh Conference of Astrophysics and Geophysics, meeting in London in 1961. He became discouraged and set his work with meteorites aside; the organisms were later destroyed in an accidental laboratory explosion on the night of June 27, 1963.

Karp's experience was almost identical to that of Nagy and the others. Scientists in the 1960's were not willing to entertain notions of life existing in meteorites; all evidence presented was discounted, dismissed, and ignored.

A handful of people in a dozen countries remained intrigued, however. One of them was Jeremy Stone; another was Peter Leavitt. It was Leavitt who, some years before, had formulated the Rule of 48. The Rule of 48 was intended as a humorous reminder to scientists, and referred to the massive literature collected in the late 1940's and the 1950's concerning the human chromosome number.

For years it was stated that men had forty-eight chromosomes in their cells; there were pictures to prove it, and any number of careful studies. In 1953, a group of American researchers announced to the world that the human chromosome number was forty-six. Once more, there were pictures to prove it, and studies to confirm it. But these researchers also went back to reexamine the old pictures, and the old studies—and found only forty-six chromosomes, not forty-eight.

Leavitt's Rule of 48 said simply, "All Scientists Are Blind." And Leavitt had invoked his rule when he saw the reception Karp and others received. Leavitt went over the reports and the papers and found no reason to reject the meteorite studies out of hand; many of the experiments were careful, well-reasoned, and compelling.

He remembered this when he and the other Wildfire planners drew up the study known as the Vector Three. Along with the Toxic Five, it formed one of the firm theoretical bases for Wildfire.

The Vector Three was a report that considered a crucial question: If a bacterium invaded the earth, causing a new disease, where would that bacterium come from?

After consultation with astronomers and evolutionary theories, the Wildfire group concluded that bacteria could come from three sources.

The first was the most obvious—an organism, from another planet or galaxy, which had the protection to survive the extremes of temperature and vacuum that existed in space. There was no doubt that organisms could survive—there was, for instance, a class of bacteria known as thermophilic that thrived on extreme heat, multiplying enthusiastically in temperatures as high as 70° C. Further, it was known that bacteria had been recovered from Egyptian tombs, where they had been sealed for thousands of years. These bacteria were still viable.

The secret lay in the bacteria's ability to form spores, molding a hard calcific shell around themselves. This shell enabled the organism to survive freezing or boiling, and, if necessary, thousands of years without food. It combined all the advantages of a space suit with those of suspended animation.

There was no doubt that a spore could travel through space. But was another planet or galaxy the most *likely* source of contamination for the earth?

Here, the answer was no. The most likely source was the closest source—the earth itself.

The report suggested that bacteria could have left the surface of the earth eons ago, when life was just beginning to emerge from the oceans and the hot, baked continents. Such bacteria would depart before the fishes, before the primitive mammals, long before the first ape-man. The bacteria would head up into the air, and slowly ascend until they were literally in space. Once there, they might evolve into unusual forms, perhaps even learning to derive energy for life directly from the sun, instead of requiring food as an energy source. These organisms might also be capable of direct conversion of energy to matter.

Leavitt himself suggested the analogy of the upper atmosphere and the depths of the sea as equally inhospitable environments, but equally viable. In the deepest, blackest regions of the oceans, where oxygenation was poor, and where light never reached, life forms were known to exist in abundance. Why not also in the far reaches of the atmosphere? True, oxygen was scarce. True, food hardly existed. But if creatures could live miles beneath the surface, why could they not also live five miles above it?

And if there were organisms out there, and if they had departed from the baking crust of the earth long before the first men appeared, then they would be foreign to man. No immunity, no adaptation, no antibodies would have been developed. They would be primitive aliens to modern man, in the same way that the shark, a primitive fish unchanged for a hundred million years, was alien and dangerous to modern man, invading the oceans for the first time.

The third source of contamination, the third of the vectors, was at the same time the most likely and the most troublesome. This was contemporary earth organisms, taken into space by inadequately sterilized spacecraft. Once in space, the organisms would be exposed to harsh radiation, weightlessness, and other environmental forces that might exert a mutagenic effect, altering the organisms.

So that when they came down, they would be different.

Take up a harmless bacteria—such as the organism that causes pimples, or sore throats—and bring it back in a new form, virulent and unexpected. It might do anything. It might show a preference for the aqueous humor of the inner eye, and invade the eyeball. It might thrive on the acid secretions of the stomach. It might multiply on the small currents of electricity afforded by the human brain itself, drive men mad.

This whole idea of mutated bacteria seemed farfetched and unlikely to the Wildfire people. It is ironic that this should be the case, particularly in view of what happened to the Andromeda Strain. But the Wildfire team staunchly ignored both the evidence of their own experience—that bacteria mutate rapidly and radically—and the evidence of the Biosatellite tests, in which a series of earth forms were sent into space and later recovered.

Biosatellite II contained, among other things, several species of bacteria. It was later reported that the bacteria had reproduced at a rate twenty to thirty times normal. The reasons were still unclear, but the results unequivocal: space could affect reproduction and growth.

And yet no one in Wildfire paid attention to this fact, until it was too late.

Stone reviewed the information quickly, then handed each of them a cardboard file. "These files," he said, "contain a transcript of autoclock records of the entire flight of Scoop VII. Our purpose in reviewing the transcript is to determine, if possible, what happened to the satellite while it was in orbit."

Hall said, "Something happened to it?"

Leavitt explained. "The satellite was scheduled for a six-day orbit, since the probability of collecting organisms is proportional to time in orbit. After launch, it was in stable orbit. Then, on the second day, it went out of orbit."

Hall nodded.

"Start," Stone said, "with the first page."

Hall opened his file.

AUTOCLOCK TRANSCRIPT
PROJECT: SCOOP VII
LAUNCHDATE:
ABRIDGED VERSION. FULL TRANSCRIPT
STORED VAULTS 179-99, VDBG COMPLEX
EPSILON.

HOURS MIN SEC PROCEDURE

T MINUS TIME

0002 01 05 Vandenberg Launchpad Block 9, Scoop Mission Control, reports systems check on schedule.

0001 39 52 Scoop MC holds for fuel check reported from Ground Control.

STOP CLOCK STOP CLOCK. REAL TIME LOSS 12 MINUTES.

0001	39	52	Count resumed. Clock corrected.
0000	41	12	Scoop MC holds 20 seconds for Launchpad Block 9 check. Clock not stopped for built-in hold.
0000	30	00	Gantry removed.
0000	24	00	Final craft systems check.
0000	19	00	Final capsule systems check.
0000	13	00	Final systems checks read as negative.
0000	07	12	Cable decoupling.
0000	01	07	Stat-link decoupling.
0000	00	05	Ignition.
0000	00	04	Launchpad Block 9 clears all systems.
0000	00	00	Core clamps released. Launch.

T PLUS TIME

0000	00	06	Stable. Speed 6 fps. Smooth EV approach.
0000	00	09	Tracking reported.
0000	00	11	Tracking confirmed.
0000	00	27	Capsule monitors at g 1.9. Equipment check clear.
0000	01	00	Launchpad Block 9 clears rocket and capsule systems for orbit.

"No point in dwelling on this," Stone said. "It is the record of a perfect launch. There is nothing here, in fact, nothing for the next ninety-six hours of flight, to indicate any difficulty on board the spacecraft. Now turn to page 10."

They all turned.

TRACK TRANSCRIPT CONT'D
SCOOP VII
LAUNCHDATE:—
ABRIDGED VERSION

HOURS	MIN	SEC	PROCEDURE
0096	10	12	Orbital check stable as reported by Grand Bahama Station.
0096	34	19	Orbital check stable as reported by Sydney.
0096	47	34	Orbital check stable as reported by Vdbg.
0097	04	12	Orbital check stable but system malfunction reported by Kennedy Station.
0097	05	18	Malfunction confirmed.
0097	07	22	Malfunction confirmed by Grand Bahama. Computer reports orbital instability.
0097	34	54	Sydney reports orbital instability.
0097	39	02	Vandenberg computations indicate orbital decay.
0098	27	14	Vandenberg Scoop Mission Control orders radio reentry.
0099	12	56	Reentry code transmitted.
0099	13	13	Houston reports initiation of reentry. Stabilized flightpath.

"What about voice communication during the critical period?"

"There were linkups between Sydney, Kennedy, and Grand Bahama, all routed through Houston. Houston had the big computer as well. But in this instance, Houston was just helping out; all decisions came from Scoop Mission Control in Vandenberg. We have the voice communication at the back of the file. It's quite revealing."

TRANSCRIPT OF VOICE COMMUNICATIONS
SCOOP MISSION CONTROL
VANDENBERG AFB
HOURS 0096:59 TO 0097:39
THIS IS A CLASSIFIED TRANSCRIPT.
IT HAS NOT BEEN ABRIDGED OR EDITED.

HOURS	MIN	SEC	COMMUNICATION
0096	59	00	HELLO KENNEDY THIS IS SCOOP MISSION CONTROL. AT THE END OF 96 HOURS OF FLIGHT TIME WE HAVE STABLE ORBITS FROM ALL STATIONS. DO YOU CONFIRM.

HOURS	MIN	SEC	COMMUNICATION
0097	00	00	I think we do, Scoop. Our check is going through now. Hold this line open for a few minutes, fellows.
0097	03	31	Hello, Scoop MC. This is Kennedy. We have a stable orbit confirmation for you on the last passby. Sorry about the delay but there is an instrument snag somewhere here.
0097	03	34	KENNEDY PLEASE CLARIFY. IS YOUR SNAG ON THE GROUND OR ALOFT.
0097	03	39	I am sorry we have no tracer yet. We think it is on the ground.
0097	04	12	Hello, Scoop MC. This is Kennedy. We have a preliminary report of system malfunction aboard your spacecraft. Repeat we have a preliminary report of malfunction in the air. Awaiting confirmation.
0097	04	15	KENNEDY PLEASE CLARIFY SYSTEM INVOLVED.
0097	04	18	I'm sorry they haven't given me that. I assume they are waiting for final confirmation of the malfunction.
0097	04	21	DOES YOUR ORBITAL CHECK AS STABLE STILL HOLD.
0097	04	22	Vandenberg, we have confirmed your orbital check as stable. Repeat the orbit is stable.
0097	05	18	Ah, Vandenberg, I am afraid we also confirm readings consistent with system malfunction on board your spacecraft. These include the stationary rotor elements and spanner units going to mark twelve. I repeat mark twelve.
0097	05	30	HAVE YOU RUN CONSISTENCY CHECK ON YOUR COMPUTERS.
0097	05	35	Sorry fellows but our computers check out. We read it as a real malfunction.
0097	05	45	HELLO, HOUSTON. OPEN THE LINE TO SYDNEY, WILL YOU. WE WANT CONFIRMATION OF DATA.

HOURS	MIN	SEC	COMMUNICATION
0097	05	51	Scoop Mission Control, This is Sydney Station. We confirm our last reading. There was nothing wrong with the spacecraft on its last passby here.
0097	06	12	OUR COMPUTER CHECK INDICATES NO SYSTEMS MALFUNCTION AND GOOD ORBITAL STABILITY ON SUMMATED DATA. WE QUESTION KENNEDY GROUND INSTRUMENT FAILURE.
0097	06	18	This is Kennedy, Scoop MC. We have run repeat checkouts at this end. Our reading of system malfunction remains. Have you got something from Bahama.
0097	06	23	NEGATIVE, KENNEDY. STANDING BY.
0097	06	36	HOUSTON, THIS IS SCOOP MC. CAN YOUR PROJECTION GROUP GIVE US ANYTHING.
0097	06	46	Scoop, at this time we cannot. Our computers have insufficient data. They still read stable orbit with all systems going.
0097	07	22	Scoop MC, this is Grand Bahama Station. We report passby of your craft Scoop Seven according to schedule. Preliminary radar fixes were normal with question of increased transit times. Please hold for systems telemetry.
0097	07	25	HOLDING, GRAND BAHAMA.
0097	07	29	Scoop MC, we are sorry to say we confirm Kennedy observations. Repeat, we confirm Kennedy observations of systems malfunction. Our data are on the trunk to Houston. Can they be routed to you as well.
0097	07	34	NO, WE WILL WAIT FOR HOUSTON'S PRINTOUT. THEY HAVE LARGER PREDICTIVE BANKING UNITS.
0097	07	36	Scoop MC, Houston has the Bahama Data. It is going through the Dispar Program. Give us ten seconds.
0097	07	47	Scoop MC, this is Houston. The Dispar Program confirms systems malfunction. Your vehicle is now in unstable orbit with increased transit time of zero point three seconds per unit of arc. We are analyzing orbital parameters at this time. Is there anything further you wish as interpreted data.

HOURS	MIN	SEC	COMMUNICATION
0097	07	59	NO, HOUSTON. SOUNDS LIKE YOU'RE DOING BEAUTIFULLY.
0097	08	10	Sorry, Scoop. Bad break.
0097	08	18	GET US THE DECAY RATIOS AS SOON AS POSSIBLE. COMMAND WISHES TO MAKE A DECISION ON INSTRUMENTATION TAKEDOWN WITHIN THE NEXT TWO ORBITS.
0097	08	32	Understand, Scoop. Our condolences here.
0097	11	35	Scoop, Houston Projection Group has confirmed orbital instability and decay ratios are now being passed by the data trunk to your station.
0097	11	44	HOW DO THEY LOOK, HOUSTON.
0097	11	51	Bad.
0097	11	59	NOT UNDERSTOOD. PLEASE REPEAT.
0097	12	07	Bad: B as in broken, A as in awful, D as in dropping.
0097	12	15	HOUSTON, DO YOU HAVE A CAUSATION. THAT SATELLITE HAS BEEN IN EXCELLENT ORBIT FOR NEARLY ONE HUNDRED HOURS. WHAT HAPPENED TO IT.
0097	12	29	Beats us. We wonder about collision. There is a good wobble component to the new orbit.
0097	12	44	HOUSTON, OUR COMPUTERS ARE WORKING THROUGH THE TRANSMITTED DATA. WE AGREE A COLLISION. HAVE YOU GUYS GOT SOMETHING IN THE NEIGHBORHOOD.
0097	13	01	Air Force Skywatch confirms our report that we have nothing around your baby, Scoop.
0097	13	50	HOUSTON, OUR COMPUTERS ARE READING THIS AS A RANDOM EVENT. PROBABILITIES GREATER THAN ZERO POINT SEVEN NINE.
0097	15	00	We can add nothing. Looks reasonable. Are you going to bring it down.

HOURS	MIN	SEC	COMMUNICATION
0097	15	15	WE ARE HOLDING ON THAT DECISION, HOUSTON. WE WILL NOTIFY AS SOON AS IT IS MADE.
0097	17	54	HOUSTON, OUR COMMAND GROUP HAS RAISED THE QUESTION OF WHETHER ******************************
0097	17	59	[reply from Houston deleted]
0097	18	43	[Scoop query to Houston deleted]
0097	19	03	[reply from Houston deleted]
0097	19	11	AGREE, HOUSTON. WE WILL MAKE OUR DECISION AS SOON AS WE HAVE FINAL CONFIRMATION OF ORBITAL SHUTDOWN FROM SYDNEY. IS THIS ACCEPTABLE.
0097	19	50	Perfectly, Scoop. We are standing by.
0097	24	32	HOUSTON, WE ARE REWORKING OUR DATA AND NO LONGER CONSIDER THAT**********IS LIKELY.
0097	24	39	Roger, Scoop.
0097	29	13	HOUSTON, WE ARE STANDING BY FOR SYDNEY.
0097	34	54	Scoop Mission Control, this is Sydney Station. We have just followed the passby of your vehicle. Our initial readings confirm a prolonged transit time. It is quite striking at this time.
0097	35	12	THANK YOU, SYDNEY.
0097	35	22	Bit of nasty luck, Scoop. Sorry.
0097	39	02	THIS IS SCOOP MISSION CONTROL TO ALL STATIONS. OUR COMPUTERS HAVE JUST CALCULATED THE ORBITAL DECAY FOR THE VEHICLE AND WE FIND IT TO BE COMING DOWN AS A PLUS FOUR. STANDBY FOR THE FINAL DECISION AS TO WHEN WE WILL BRING IT DOWN.

Hall said, "What about the deleted passages?"

"Major Manchek at Vandenberg told me," Stone said, "that they had to do with the Russian craft in the area. The two stations eventually concluded that the Russians had not, either accidentally or purposely, brought down the Scoop satellite. No one has since suggested differently."

They nodded.

"It's tempting," Stone said. "The Air Force maintains a watchdog facility in Kentucky that tracks all satellites in earth orbit. It has a dual function, both to follow old satellites known to be in orbit and to track new ones. There are twelve satellites in orbit at this time that cannot be accounted for; in other words, they are not ours, and are not the result of announced Soviet launches. It is thought that some of these represent navigation satellites for Soviet submarines. Others are presumed to be spy satellites. But the important thing is that Russian or not, there are a hell of a lot of satellites up there. As of last Friday, the Air Force reported five hundred and eighty-seven orbiting bodies around the earth. This includes some old, nonfunctioning satellites from the American Explorer series and the Russian Sputnik series. It also includes boosters and final stages—anything in stable orbit large enough to reflect back a radar beam."

"That's a lot of satellites."

"Yes, and there are probably many more. The Air Force thinks there is a lot of junk out there—nuts, bolts, scraps of metal—all in more or less stable orbit. No orbit, as you know, is completely stable. Without frequent corrections, any satellite will eventually decay out and spiral down to earth, burning up in the atmosphere. But that may be years, even decades, after the launch. In any event, the Air Force estimates that the total number of individual orbiting objects could be anything up to seventy-five thousand."

"So a collision with a piece of junk is possible."

"Yes. Possible."

"How about a meteor?"

"That is the other possibility, and the one Vandenberg favors. A random event, most likely a meteor."

"Any showers these days?"

"None, apparently. But that does not rule out a meteor collision."

Leavitt cleared his throat. "There is still another possibility."

Stone frowned. He knew that Leavitt was imaginative, and that this trait was both a strength and a defect. At times, Leavitt could be startling and exciting; at others, merely irritating. "It's rather farfetched," Stone said, "to postulate debris from some extragalactic source other than—"

"I agree," Leavitt said. "Hopelessly farfetched. No evidence for it whatever. But I don't think we can afford to ignore the possibility."

A gong sounded softly. A lush female voice, which Hall now recognized as that of Gladys Stevens of Omaha, said softly, "You may proceed to the next level, gentlemen."

Chapter 13

Level V

Level V was painted a quiet shade of blue, and they all wore blue uniforms. Burton showed Hall around.

"This floor," he said, "is like all the others. It's circular. Arranged in a series of concentric circles, actually. We're on the outer perimeter now; this is where we live and work. Cafeteria, sleeping rooms, everything is out here. Just inside is a ring of laboratories. And inside that, sealed off from us, is the central core. That's where the satellite and the two people are now."

"But they're sealed off from us?"

"Yes."

"Then how do we get to them?"

"Have you ever used a glove box?" Burton asked.

Hall shook his head.

Burton explained that glove boxes were large clear plastic boxes used to handle sterile materials. The boxes had holes cut in the sides, and gloves attached with an airtight seal. To handle the contents, you slipped your hands into the gloves and reached into the box. But your fingers never touched the material, only the gloves.

"We've gone one step further," Burton said. "We have whole rooms that are nothing more than glorified glove boxes. Instead of a glove for your hand, there's a whole plastic suit, for your entire body. You'll see what I mean."

They walked down the curved corridor to a room marked CENTRAL CONTROL. Leavitt and Stone were there, working quietly. Central Control was a cramped room, stuffed with electronic equipment. One wall was glass, allowing the workers to look into the adjacent room.

Through the glass, Hall saw mechanical hands moving the capsule to a table and setting it down. Hall, who had never seen a capsule before, watched with interest. It was smaller than he had imagined, no more than a yard long; one end was seared and blackened from the heat of reentry.

The mechanical hands, under Stone's direction, opened the little scoop-shaped trough in the side of the capsule to expose the interior.

"There," Stone said, taking his hands from the controls. The controls looked like a pair of brass knuckles; the operator slipped his own hands into them and moved his hands as he wanted the mechanical hands to move.

"Our next step," he said, "is to determine whether there is still anything in the capsule which is biologically active. Suggestions?"

"A rat," Leavitt said. "Use a black Norway."

The black Norway rat was not black at all; the name simply designated a strain of laboratory animal, perhaps the most famous strain in all science. Once, of course, it had been both black and Norwegian; but years of breeding and countless generations had made it white, small, and docile. The biological explosion had created a demand for genetically uniform animals. In the last thirty years more than a thousand strains of "pure" animals had been evolved artificially. In the case of the black Norwegian, it was now possible for a scientist anywhere in the world to conduct experiments using this animal and be assured that other scientists elsewhere could repeat or enlarge upon his work using virtually identical organisms.

"Follow with a rhesus," Burton said. "We will want to get onto primates sooner or later."

The others nodded. Wildfire was prepared to conduct experiments with monkeys and apes, as well as smaller, cheaper animals. A monkey was exceedingly difficult to work with: the little primates were hostile, quick, intelligent. Among scientists, the New World monkeys, with their prehensile tails, were considered particularly trying. Many a scientist had engaged three or four lab assistants to hold down a monkey while he administered an injection—only to have the prehensile tail whip up, grasp the syringe, and fling it across the room.

The theory behind primate experimentation was that these animals were closer biologically to man. In the 1950's, several laboratories even attempted experiments on gorillas, going to great trouble and expense to work with these seemingly most human of animals. However, by 1960 it had been demonstrated that of the apes, the chimpanzee was biochemically more like man than the gorilla. (On the basis of similarity to man, the choice of laboratory animals is often surprising. For example, the hamster is preferred for immunological and cancer studies, since his responses are so similar to man's, while for studies of the heart and circulation, the pig is considered most like man.)

Stone put his hands back on the controls, moving them gently. Through the glass, they saw the black metal fingers move to the far wall of the adjoining room, where several caged lab animals were kept, separated from the room by hinged airtight doors. The wall reminded Hall oddly of an automat.

The mechanical hands opened one door and removed a rat in its cage, brought it into the room, and set it down next to the capsule.

The rat looked around the room, sniffed the air, and made some stretching movements with its neck. A moment later it flopped over onto its side, kicked once, and was still.

It had happened with astonishing speed. Hall could hardly believe it had happened at all.

"My God," Stone said. "What a time course."

"That will make it difficult," Leavitt said.

Burton said, "We can try tracers . . ."

"Yes. We'll have to use tracers on it," Stone said. "How fast are our scans?"

"Milliseconds, if necessary."

"It will be necessary."

"Try the rhesus," Burton said. "You'll want a post on it, anyway."

Stone directed the mechanical hands back to the wall, opening another door and withdrawing a cage containing a large brown adult rhesus monkey. The monkey screeched as it was lifted and banged against the bars of its cage.

Then it died, after flinging one hand to its chest with a look of startled surprise.

Stone shook his head. "Well, at least we know it's still biologically active. Whatever killed everyone in Piedmont is still there, and still as potent as ever." He sighed. "If potent is the word."

Leavitt said, "We'd better start a scan of the capsule."

"I'll take these dead animals," Burton said, "and run the initial vector studies. Then I'll autopsy them."

Stone worked the mechanical hands once more. He picked up the cages that held the rat and monkey and set them on a rubber conveyor belt at the rear of the room. Then he pressed a button on a control console marked AUTOPSY. The conveyor belt began to move.

Burton left the room, walking down the corridor to the autopsy room, knowing that the conveyor belt, made to carry materials from one lab to another, would have automatically delivered the cages.

Stone said to Hall, "You're the practicing physician among us. I'm afraid you've got a rather tough job right now."

"Pediatrician and geriatrist?"

"Exactly. See what you can do about them. They're both in our miscellaneous room, the room we built precisely for unusual circumstances like this. There's a computer linkup there that should help you. The technician will show you how it works."

Chapter 14

Miscellaneous

Hall opened the door marked MISCELLANEOUS, thinking to himself that his job was indeed miscellaneous—keeping alive an old man and a tiny infant. Both of them vital to the project, and both of them, no doubt, difficult to manage.

He found himself in another small room similar to the control room he had just left. This one also had a glass window, looking inward to a central room. In the room were two beds, and on the beds, Peter Jackson and the infant. But the incredible thing was the suits: standing upright in the room were four clear plastic inflated suits in the shape of men. From each suit, a tunnel ran back to the wall.

Obviously, one would have to crawl down the tunnel and then stand up inside the suit. Then one could work with the patients inside the room.

The girl who was to be his assistant was working in the room, bent over the computer console. She introduced herself as Karen Anson, and explained the working of the computer.

"This is just one substation of the Wildfire computer on the first level," she said. "There are thirty substations throughout the laboratory, all plugging into the computer. Thirty different people can work at once."

Hall nodded. Time-sharing was a concept he understood. He knew that as many as two hundred people had been able to use the same computer at once; the principle was that computers operated very swiftly—in fractions of a second—while people operated slowly, in seconds or minutes. One person using a computer was inefficient, because it took several minutes to punch in instructions, while the computer sat around idle, waiting. Once instructions were fed in, the computer answered almost instantaneously. This meant that a computer was rarely "working," and by permitting a number of people to ask questions of the computer simultaneously, you could keep the machine more continuously in operation.

"If the computer is really backed up," the technician said, "there may be a delay of one or two seconds before you get your answer. But usually it's immediate. What we are using here is the MEDCOM program. Do you know it?"

Hall shook his head.

"It's a medical-data analyzer," she said. "You feed in information and it will diagnose the patient and tell you what to do next for therapy, or to confirm the diagnosis."

"Sounds very convenient."

"It's fast," she said. "All our lab studies are done by automated machines. So we can have complex diagnoses in a matter of minutes."

Hall looked through the glass at the two patients. "What's been done on them so far?"

"Nothing. At Level I, they were started on intravenous infusions. Plasma for Peter Jackson, dextrose and water for the baby. They both seem well hydrated now, and in no distress. Jackson is still unconscious. He has no pupillary signs but is unresponsive and looks anemic."

Hall nodded. "The labs here can do everything?"

"Everything. Even assays for adrenal hormones and things like partial thromboplastin times. Every known medical test is possible."

"All right. We'd better get started."

She turned on the computer. "This is how you order laboratory tests," she said. "Use this light pen here, and check off the tests you want. Just touch the pen to the screen."

She handed him a small penlight, and pushed the START button.

The screen glowed.

MEDCOM PROGRAM

LAB/ANALYS

CK/JGG/1223098

BLOOD
COUNTS RBC
RETIC
PLATES
WBC
DIFF
HEMATOCRIT
HEMOGLOBIN
INDICES MCV
MCHC
PROTIME
PTT
SED RATE

CHEMISTRY
BRO
CA
CL
MG
PO4
K
NA
CO2

ENZYMES
AMYLASE
CHOLINESTERASE
LIPASE
PHOSPHATASE, ACID
ALKALINE
LDH
SGOT
SGPT

STEROIDS
ALDO
L7-OH
I7-KS
ACTH

PROTEIN
ALB
GLOB
FIBRIN
TOTAL
FRACTION

DIAGNOSTICS
CHOLEST
CREAT
GLUCOSE
PBI
BEI
I
IBC
NPN
BUN
BILIRU, DIFF
CEPH/FLOC
THYMOL/TURB
BSP

PULMONARY
TVC
TV
IC
IRV
ERV
MBC

URINE
SP GR
PH
PROT
GLUC
KETONE
ALL ELECTROLYTES
ALL STEROIDS
ALL INORGANICS
CATECHOLS
PORPHYRINS
UROBIL
5-HIAA

VITS
A
ALL B
C
E
K

Hall stared at the list. He touched the tests he wanted with the penlight; they disappeared from the screen. He ordered fifteen or twenty, then stepped back.

The screen went blank for a moment, and then the following appeared:

TESTS ORDERED WILL REQUIRE FOR EACH
SUBJECT

20 CC WHOLE BLOOD
LO CC OXALATED BLOOD
L2 CC CITRATED BLOOD
15 CC URINE

The technician said, "I'll draw the bloods if you want to do physicals. Have you been in one of these rooms before?"

Hall shook his head.

"It's quite simple, really. We crawl through the tunnels into the suits. The tunnel is then sealed off behind us."

"Oh? Why?"

"In case something happens to one of us. In case the covering of the suit is broken—the integrity of the surface is ruptured, as the protocol says. In that case, bacteria could spread back through the tunnel to the outside."

"So we're sealed off."

"Yes. We get air from a separate system—you can see the thin lines coming in over there. But essentially you're isolated from everything, when you're in that suit. I don't think you need worry, though. The only way you might possibly break your suit is to cut it with a scalpel, and the gloves are triple-thickness to prevent just such an occurrence."

She showed him how to crawl through, and then, imitating her, he stood up inside the plastic suit. He felt like some kind of giant reptile, moving cumbersomely about, dragging his tunnel like a thick tail behind him.

After a moment, there was a hiss: his suit was being sealed off. Then another hiss, and the air turned cold as the special line began to feed air in to him.

The technician gave him his examining instruments. While she drew blood from the child, taking it from a scalp vein, Hall turned his attention to Peter Jackson.

* * *

An old man, and pale: anemia. Also thin: first thought, cancer. Second thought, tuberculosis, alcoholism, some other chronic process. And unconscious: he ran through the differential in his mind, from epilepsy to hypoglycemic shock to stroke.

Hall later stated that he felt foolish when the computer provided him with a differential, complete with probabilities of diagnosis. He was not at that time aware of the skill of the computer, the quality of its program.

He checked Jackson's blood pressure. It was low, 85/50. Pulse fast at 110. Temperature 97.8. Respirations 30 and deep.

He went over the body systematically, beginning with the head and working down. When he produced pain—by pressing on the nerve through the supraorbital notch, just below the eyebrow—the man grimaced and moved his arms to push Hall away.

Perhaps he was not unconscious after all. Perhaps just stuporous. Hall shook him.

"Mr. Jackson. Mr. Jackson."

The man made no response. And then, slowly, he seemed to revive. Hall shouted his name in his ear and shook him hard.

Peter Jackson opened his eyes, just for a moment, and said, "Go . . . away . . ."

Hall continued to shake him, but Jackson relaxed, going limp, his body slipping back to its unresponsive state. Hall gave up, returning to his physical examination. The lungs were clear and the heart seemed normal. There was some tenseness of the abdomen, and Jackson retched once, bringing up some bloody drooling material. Quickly, Hall did a basolyte test for blood: it was positive. He did a rectal exam and tested the stool. It was also positive for blood.

He turned to the technician, who had drawn all the bloods and was feeding the tubes into the computer analysis apparatus in one corner.

"We've got a GI bleeder here," he said. "How soon will the results be back?"

She pointed to a TV screen mounted near the ceiling. "The lab reports are flashed back as soon as they come in. They are displayed there, and on the console in the other room. The easy ones come back first. We should have hematocrit in two minutes."

Hall waited. The screen glowed, the letters printing out:

JACKSON, PETER
LABORATORY ANALYSES

TEST	NORMAL	VALUE
HEMATOCRIT	38-54	21

"Half normal," Hall said. He slapped an oxygen mask on Jackson's face, fixed the straps, and said, "We'll need at least four units. Plus two of plasma."

"I'll order them."

"To start as soon as possible."

She went to phone the blood bank on Level II and asked them to hurry on the requisition. Meantime, Hall turned his attention to the child.

It had been a long time since he had examined an infant, and he had forgotten how difficult it could be. Every time he tried to look at the eyes, the child shut them tightly. Every time he looked down the throat, the child closed his mouth. Every time he tried to listen to the heart, the child shrieked, obscuring all heart sounds.

Yet he persisted, remembering what Stone had said. These two people, dissimilar though they were, nonetheless represented the only survivors of Piedmont. Somehow they had managed to beat the disease. That was a link between the two, between the shriveled old man vomiting blood and the pink young child, howling and screaming.

At first glance, they were as different as possible; they were at opposite ends of the spectrum, sharing nothing in common.

And yet there must be something in common.

It took Hall half an hour to finish his examination of the child. At the end of that time he was forced to conclude that the infant was, to his exam, perfectly normal. Totally normal. Nothing the least bit unusual about him.

Except that, somehow, he had survived.

Chapter 15

Main Control

Stone sat with Leavitt in the main control room, looking into the inner room with the capsule. Though cramped, main control was complex and expensive: it had cost $2,000,000, the most costly single room in the Wildfire installation. But it was vital to the functioning of the entire laboratory.

Main control served as the first step in scientific examination of the capsule. Its chief function was detection—the room was geared to detect and isolate microorganisms. According to the Life Analysis Protocol, there were three main steps in the Wildfire program: detection, characterization, and control. First the organism had to be found. Then it had to be studied and understood. Only then could ways be sought to control it.

Main control was set up to find the organism.

Leavitt and Stone sat side by side in front of the banks of controls and dials. Stone operated the mechanical hands, while Leavitt manipulated the microscopic apparatus. Naturally it was impossible to enter the room with the capsule and examine it directly. Robot-controlled microscopes, with viewing screens in the control room, would accomplish this for them.

An early question had been whether to utilize television or some kind of direct visual linkup. Television was cheaper and more easily set up; TV image-intensifiers were already in use for electron microscopes, X-ray machines, and other devices. However, the Wildfire group finally decided that a TV screen was too imprecise for their needs; even a double-scan camera, which transmitted twice as many lines as the usual TV and gave better image resolution, would be insufficient. In the end, the group chose a fiber optics system in which a light image was transmitted directly through a snake-like bundle of glass fibers and then displayed on the viewers. This gave a clear, sharp image.

Stone positioned the capsule and pressed the appropriate controls. A black box moved down from the ceiling and began to scan the capsule surface. The two men watched the viewer screens:

"Start with five power," Stone said. Leavitt set the controls. They watched as the viewer automatically moved around the capsule, focusing on the surface of the metal. They watched one complete scan, then shifted up to twenty-power magnification. A twenty-power scan took much longer, since the field of view was smaller. They still saw nothing on the surface: no punctures, no indentations, nothing that looked like a small growth of any kind.

"Let's go to one hundred," Stone said. Leavitt adjusted the controls and sat back. They were beginning what they knew would be a long and tedious search. Probably they would find nothing. Soon they would examine the interior of the capsule; they might find something there. Or they might not. In either case, they would take samples for analysis, plating out the scrapings and swabs onto growth media.

Leavitt glanced from the viewing screens to look into the room. The viewer, suspended from the ceiling by a complex arrangement of rods and wires, was automatically moving in slow circles around the capsule. He looked back to the screens.

There were three screens in main control, and all showed exactly the same field of view. In theory, they could use three viewers projecting onto three screens, and cover the capsule in one third the time. But they did not want to do that—at least, not now. Both men knew that their interest and attention would fatigue as the day wore on. No matter how hard they tried, they could not remain alert all the time. But if two men watched the same image, there was less chance of missing something.

The surface area of the cone-shaped capsule, thirty-seven inches long and a foot in diameter at the base, was just over 650 square inches. Three scans, at five, twenty, and one hundred power, took them slightly more than two hours. At the end of the third scan, Stone said, "I suppose we ought to proceed with the 440 scan as well."

"But?"

"I am tempted to go directly to a scan of the interior. If we find nothing, we can come back outside and do a 440."

"I agree."

"All right," Stone said. "Start with five. On the inside."

Leavitt worked the controls. This time, it could not be done automatically; the viewer was programmed to follow the contours of any regularly shaped object, such as a cube, a sphere, or a cone. But it could not probe the interior of the capsule without direction. Leavitt set the lenses at five diameters and switched the remote viewer to manual control. Then he directed it down into the scoop opening of the capsule.

Stone, watching the screen, said, "More light."

Leavitt made adjustments. Five additional remote lights came down from the ceiling and clicked on, shining into the scoop.

"Better?"

"Fine."

Watching his own screen, Leavitt began to move the remote viewer. It took several minutes before he could do it smoothly; it was difficult to coordinate, rather like trying to write while you watched in a mirror. But soon he was scanning smoothly.

The five-power scan took twenty minutes. They found nothing except a small indentation the size of a pencil point. At Stone's suggestion, when they began the twenty-power scan they started with the indentation.

Immediately, they saw it: a tiny black fleck of jagged material no larger than a grain of sand. There seemed to be bits of green mixed in with the black.

Neither man reacted, though Leavitt later recalled that he was "trembling with excitement. I kept thinking, if this is it, if it's really something new, some brand new form of life . . ."

However, all he said was, "Interesting."

"We'd better complete the scan at twenty power," Stone said. He was working to keep his voice calm, but it was clear that he was excited too.

Leavitt wanted to examine the fleck at higher power immediately, but he understood what Stone was saying. They could not afford to jump to conclusions—any conclusions. Their only hope was to be grindingly, interminably thorough. They had to proceed methodically, to assure themselves at every point that they had overlooked nothing.

Otherwise, they could pursue a course of investigation for hours or days, only to find it ended nowhere, that they had made a mistake, misjudged the evidence, and wasted time.

So Leavitt did a complete scan of the interior at twenty power. He paused, once or twice, when they thought they saw other patches of green, and marked down the coordinates so they could find the areas later, under higher magnification. Half an hour passed before Stone announced he was satisfied with the twenty-power scan.

They took a break for caffeine, swallowing two pills with water. The team had agreed earlier that amphetamines should not be used except in times of serious emergency; they were stocked in the Level V pharmacy, but for routine purposes caffeine was preferred.

The aftertaste of the caffeine pill was sour in his mouth as Leavitt clicked in the hundred-power lenses, and began the third scan. As before, they started with the indentation, and the small black fleck they had noted earlier.

It was disappointing: at higher magnification it appeared no different from their earlier views, only larger. They could see, however, that it was an irregular piece of material, dull, looking like rock. And they could see there were definitely flecks of green mined on the jagged surface of the material.

"What do you make of it?" Stone said.

"If that's the object the capsule collided with," Leavitt said, "it was either moving with great speed, or else it is very heavy. Because it's not big enough—"

"To knock the satellite out of orbit otherwise. I agree. And yet it did not make a very deep indentation."

"Suggesting?"

Stone shrugged. "Suggesting that it was either not responsible for the orbital change, or that it has some elastic properties we don't yet know about."

"What do you think of the green?"

Stone grinned. "You won't trap me yet. I am curious, nothing more."

Leavitt chuckled and continued the scan. Both men now felt elated and inwardly certain of their discovery. They checked the other areas where they had noted green, and confirmed the presence of the patches at higher magnification.

But the other patches looked different from the green on the rock. For one thing, they were larger, and seemed somehow more luminous. For another, the borders of the patches seemed quite regular, and rounded.

"Like small drops of green paint, spattered on the inside of the capsule," Stone said.

"I hope that's not what it is."

"We could probe," Stone said.

"Let's wait for 440."

Stone agreed. By now they had been scanning the capsule for nearly four hours, but neither man felt tired. They watched closely as the viewing screens blurred for a moment, the lenses shifting. When the screens came back into focus, they were looking at the indentation, and the black fleck with the green areas. At this magnification, the surface irregularities of the rock were striking—it was like a miniature planet, with jagged peaks and sharp valleys. It occurred to Leavitt that this was exactly what they were looking at: a minute, complete planet, with its life forms intact. But he shook his head, dismissing the thought from his mind. Impossible.

Stone said, "If that's a meteor, it's damned funny-looking."

"What bothers you?"

"That left border, over there." Stone pointed to the screen. "The surface of the stone—if it is stone—is rough everywhere except on that left border, where it is smooth and rather straight."

"Like an artificial surface?"

Stone sighed. "If I keep looking at it," he said, "I might start to think so. Let's see those other patches of green."

Leavitt set the coordinates and focused the viewer. A new image appeared on the screens. This time, it was a close-up of one of the green patches. Under high magnification the borders could be seen clearly. They were not smooth, but slightly notched: they looked almost like a gear from the inside of a watch.

"I'll be damned," Leavitt said.

"It's not paint. That notching is too regular."

As they watched, it happened: the green spot turned purple for a fraction of a second, less than the blink of an eye. Then it turned green once more.

"Did you see that?"

"I saw it. You didn't change the lighting?"

"No. Didn't touch it."

A moment later, it happened again: green, a flash of purple, green again.

"Amazing."

"This may be—"

And then, as they watched, the spot turned purple and remained purple. The notches disappeared; the spot had enlarged slightly, filling in the V-shaped gaps. It was now a complete circle. It became green once more.

"It's growing," Stone said.

They worked swiftly. The movie cameras were brought down, recording from five angles at ninety-six frames per second. Another time-lapse camera clicked off frames at half-second intervals. Leavitt also brought down two more remote cameras, and set them at different angles from the original camera.

In main control, all three screens displayed different views of the green spot.

"Can we get more power? More magnification?" Stone said.

"No. You remember we decided 440 was the top."

Stone swore. To obtain higher magnification, they would have to go to a separate room, or else use the electron microscopes. In either case, it would take time.

Leavitt said, "Shall we start culture and isolation?"

"Yes. Might as well."

Leavitt turned the viewers back down to twenty power. They could now see that there were four areas of interest—three isolated green patches, and the rock with its indentation. On the control console, he pressed a button marked CULTURE, and a tray at the side of the room slid out, revealing stacks of circular, plastic-covered petri dishes. Inside each dish was a thin layer of growth medium.

The Wildfire project employed almost every known growth medium. The media were jellied compounds containing various nutrients on which bacteria would feed and multiply. Along with the usual laboratory standbys—horse and sheep blood agar, chocolate agar, simplex, Sabourad's medium—there were thirty diagnostic media, containing various sugars and minerals. Then there were forty-three specialized culture media, including those for growth of tubercule bacilli and unusual fungi, as well as the highly experimental media, designated by numbers: ME-997, ME-423, ME-A12, and so on.

With the tray of media was a batch of sterile swabs. Using the mechanical hands, Stone picked up the swabs singly and touched them to the capsule surface, then to the media. Leavitt punched data into the computer, so that they would know later where each swab had been taken. In this manner, they swabbed the outer surface of the entire capsule, and went to the interior. Very carefully, using high viewer magnification, Stone took scrapings from the green spots and transferred them to the different media.

Finally, he used fine forceps to pick up the rock and move it intact to a clean glass dish.

The whole process took better than two hours. At the end of that time, Leavitt punched through the MAXCULT computer program. This program automatically instructed the machine in the handling of the hundreds of petri dishes they had collected. Some would be stored at room temperature and pressure, with normal earth atmosphere. Others would be subjected to heat and cold; high pressure and vacuum; low oxygen and high oxygen; light and dark. Assigning the plates to the various culture boxes was a job that would take a man days to work out. The computer could do it in seconds.

When the program was running, Stone placed the stacks of petri dishes on the conveyor belt. They watched as the dishes moved off to the culture boxes.

There was nothing further they could do, except wait twenty-four to forty-eight hours, to see what grew out.

"Meantime," Stone said, "we can begin analysis of this piece of rock—if it actually is rock. How are you with an EM?"

"Rusty," Leavitt said. He had not used an electron microscope for nearly a year.

"Then I'll prepare the specimen. We'll also want mass spectrometry done. That's all computerized. But before we do that, we ought to go to higher power. What's the highest light magnification we can get in Morphology?"

"A thousand diameters."

"Then let's do that first. Punch the rock through to Morphology."

Leavitt looked down at the console and pressed MORPHOLOGY. Stone's mechanical hands placed the glass dish with the rock onto the conveyor belt.

They looked at the wall clock behind them. It showed 1100 hours; they had been working for eleven straight hours.

"So far," Stone said, "so good."

Leavitt grinned, and crossed his fingers.

Chapter 16

Autopsy

Burton was working in the autopsy room. He was nervous and tense, still bothered by his memories of Piedmont. Weeks later, in reviewing his work and his thoughts on Level V, he regretted his inability to concentrate.

Because in his initial series of experiments, Burton made several mistakes.

According to the protocol, he was required to carry out autopsies on dead animals, but he was also in charge of preliminary vector experiments. In all fairness, Burton was not the man to do this work; Leavitt would have been better suited to it. But it was felt that Leavitt was more useful working on preliminary isolation and identification.

So the vector experiments fell to Burton.

They were reasonably simple and straightforward, designed to answer the question of how the disease was transmitted. Burton began with a series of cages, lined up in a row. Each had a separate air supply; the air supplies could be interconnected in a variety of ways.

Burton placed the corpse of the dead Norway rat, which was contained in an airtight cage, alongside another cage containing a living rat. He punched buttons; air was allowed to pass freely from one cage to the other.

The living rat flopped over and died.

Interesting, he thought. Airborne transmission. He hooked up a second cage with a live rat, but inserted a Millipore filter between the living and dead rat cages. This filter had perforations 100 angstroms in diameter—the size of a small virus.

He opened the passage between the two cages. The rat remained alive.

He watched for several moments, until he was satisfied. Whatever it was that transmitted the disease, it was larger than a virus. He changed the filter, replacing it with a larger one, and then another still larger. He continued in this way until the rat died.

The filter had allowed the agent to pass. He checked it: two microns in diameter, roughly the size of a small cell. He thought to himself that he had just learned something very valuable indeed: the size of the infectious agent.

This was important, for in a single simple experiment he had ruled out the possibility that a protein or a chemical molecule of some kind was doing the damage. At Piedmont, he and Stone had been concerned about a gas, perhaps a gas released as waste from the living organism.

Yet, clearly, no gas was responsible. The disease was transmitted by something the size of a cell that was very much bigger than a molecule, or gas droplet.

The next step was equally simple—to determine whether dead animals were potentially infectious.

He took one of the dead rats and pumped the air out of its cage. He waited until the air was fully evacuated. In the pressure fall, the rat ruptured, bursting open. Burton ignored this.

When he was sure all air was removed, he replaced the air with fresh, clean, filtered air. Then he connected the cage to the cage of a living animal.

Nothing happened.

Interesting, he thought. Using a remotely controlled scalpel, he sliced open the dead animal further, to make sure any organisms contained inside the carcass would be released into the atmosphere.

Nothing happened. The live rat scampered about its cage happily.

The results were quite clear: dead animals were not infectious. That was why, he thought, the buzzards could chew at the Piedmont victims and not die. Corpses could not transmit the disease; only the bugs themselves, carried in the air, could do so.

Bugs in the air were deadly.

Bugs in the corpse were harmless.

In a sense, this was predictable. It had to do with theories of accommodation and mutual adaptation between bacteria and man. Burton had long been interested in this problem, and had lectured on it at the Baylor Medical School.

Most people, when they thought of bacteria, thought of diseases. Yet the fact was that only 3 per cent of bacteria produced human disease; the rest were either harmless or beneficial. In the human gut, for instance, there were a variety of bacteria that were helpful to the digestive process. Man needed them, and relied upon them.

In fact, man lived in a sea of bacteria. They were everywhere—on his skin, in his ears and mouth, down his lungs, in his stomach. Everything he owned, anything he touched, every breath he breathed, was drenched in bacteria. Bacteria were ubiquitous. Most of the time you weren't aware of it.

And there was a reason. Both man and bacteria had gotten used to each other, had developed a kind of mutual immunity. Each adapted to the other.

And this, in turn, for a very good reason. It was a principle of biology that evolution was directed toward increased reproductive potential. A man easily killed by bacteria was poorly adapted; he didn't live long enough to reproduce.

A bacteria that killed its host was also poorly adapted. Because any parasite that kills its host is a failure. It must die when the host dies. The successful parasites were those that could live off the host without killing him.

And the most successful hosts were those that could tolerate the parasite, or even turn it to advantage, to make it work for the host.

"The best adapted bacteria," Burton used to say, "are the ones that cause minor diseases, or none at all. You may carry the same single cell of *Strep. viridians* on your body for sixty or seventy years. During that time, you are growing and reproducing happily; so is the *Strep.* You can carry *Staph. aureus* around, and pay only the price of some acne and pimples. You can carry tuberculosis for many decades; you can carry syphilis for a lifetime. These last are not minor diseases, but they are much less severe than they once were, because both man and organism have adapted."

It was known, for instance, that syphilis had been a virulent disease four hundred years before, producing huge festering sores all over the body, often killing in weeks. But over the centuries, man and the spirochete had learned to tolerate each other.

Such considerations were not so abstract and academic as they seemed at first. In the early planning of Wildfire, Stone had observed that 40 per cent of all human disease was caused by microorganisms. Burton had countered by noting that only 3 per cent of all microorganisms caused disease. Obviously, while much human misery was attributable to bacteria, the chances of any particular bacteria being dangerous to man were very small. This was because the process of adaptation—of fitting man to bacteria—was complex.

"Most bacteria," Burton observed, "simply can't live within a man long enough to harm him. Conditions are, one way or another, unfavorable. The body is too hot or too cold, too acid or too alkaline, there is too much oxygen or not enough. Man's body is as hostile as Antarctica to most bacteria."

This meant that the chances of an organism from outer space being suited to harm man were very slim. Everyone recognized this, but felt that Wildfire had to be constructed in any event. Burton certainly agreed, but felt in an odd way that his prophecy had come true.

Clearly, the bug they had found could kill men. But it was not really adapted to men, because it killed and died within the organism. It could not be transmitted from corpse to corpse. It existed for a second or two in its host, and then died with it.

Satisfying intellectually, he thought.

But practically speaking they still had to isolate it, understand it, and find a cure.

Burton already knew something about transmission, and something about the mechanism of death: clotting of the blood. The question remained—How did the organisms get into the body?

Because transmission appeared to be airborne, contact with skin and lungs seemed likely. Possibly the organisms burrowed right through the skin surface. Or they might be inhaled. Or both.

How to determine it?

He considered putting protective suitings around an experimental animal to cover all but the mouth. That was possible, but it would take a long time. He sat and worried about the problem for an hour.

Then he hit upon a more likely approach.

He knew that the organism killed by clotting blood. Very likely it would initiate clotting at the point of entrance into the body. If skin, clotting would start near the surface. If lungs, it would begin in the chest, radiating outward.

This was something he could test. By using radioactively tagged blood proteins, and then following his animals with scintillometer scans, he could determine where in the body the blood first clotted.

He prepared a suitable animal, choosing a rhesus monkey because its anatomy was more human than a rat's. He infused the radioactive tagging substance, a magnesium isotope, into the monkey and calibrated the scanner. After allowing equilibration, he tied the monkey down and positioned the scanner overhead.

He was now ready to begin.

The scanner would print out its results on a series of human block outlines. He set the computer printing program and then exposed the rhesus to air containing the lethal microorganism.

Immediately, the printout began to clatter out from the computer:

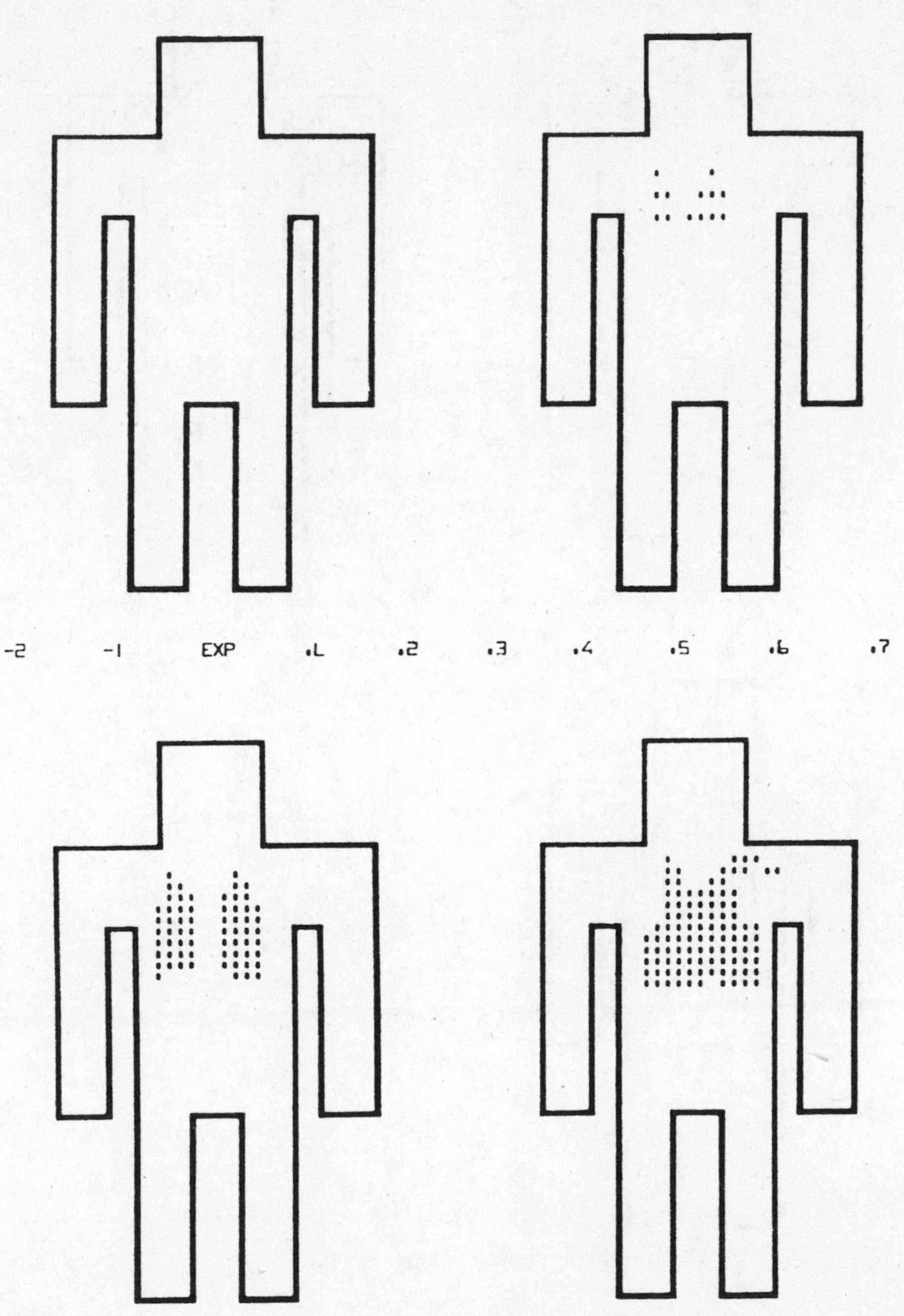
-2 -1 EXP .L .2 .3 .4 .5 .6 .7
.8 .9 1.0 1.1 1.2 1.3 1.4 1.5 1.6 1.7

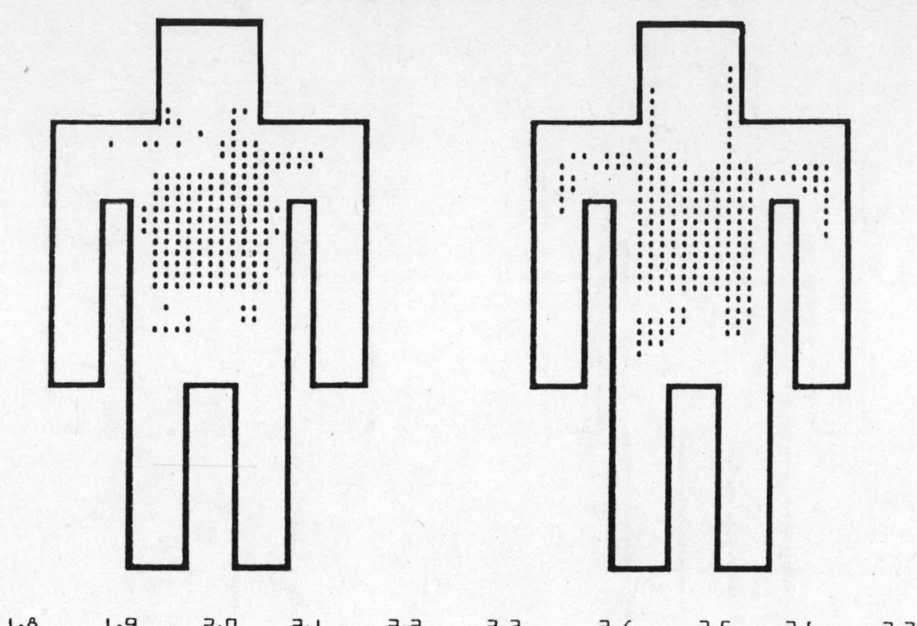
1.8 1.9 2.0 2.1 2.2 2.3 2.4 2.5 2.6 2.7

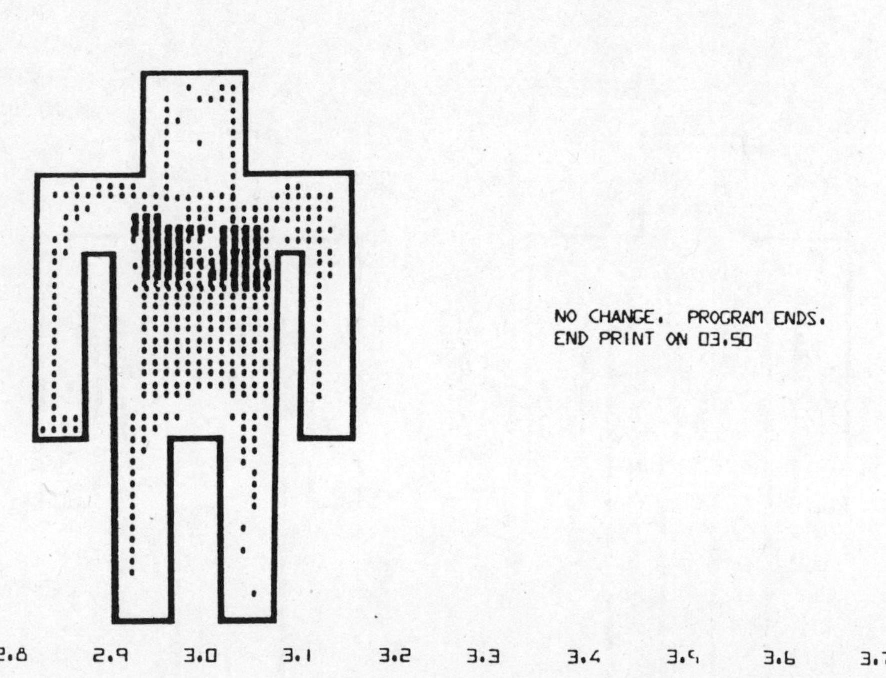
NO CHANGE. PROGRAM ENDS.
END PRINT ON 03.50
2.8 2.9 3.0 3.1 3.2 3.3 3.4 3.5 3.6 3.7

It was all over in three seconds. The graphic printout told him what he needed to know, that clotting began in the lungs and spread outward through the rest of the body.

But there was an additional piece of information gained. Burton later said, "I had been concerned that perhaps death and clotting did not coincide—or at least did not coincide exactly. It seemed impossible to me that death could occur in three seconds, but it seemed even more unlikely that the total blood volume of the body—five quarts—could solidify in so short a period. I was curious to know whether a single crucial clot might form, in the brain, perhaps, and the rest of the body clot at a slower pace."

Burton was thinking of the brain even at this early stage of his investigation. In retrospect, it is frustrating that he did not follow this line of inquiry to its logical conclusion. He was prevented from doing this by the evidence of the scans, which told him that clotting began in the lungs and progressed up the carotid arteries to the brain one or two seconds later.

So Burton lost immediate interest in the brain. And his mistake was compounded by his next experiment.

It was a simple test, not part of the regular Wildfire Protocol. Burton knew that death coincided with blood clotting. If clotting could be prevented, could death be avoided?

He took several rats and injected them with heparin, an anticoagulating drug—preventing blood-clot formation. Heparin was a rapid-acting drug widely used in medicine; its actions were thoroughly understood. Burton injected the drug intravenously in varying amounts, ranging from a low-normal dose to a massively excessive dose.

Then he exposed the rats to air containing the lethal organism.

The first rat, with a low dose, died in five seconds. The others followed within a minute. A single rat with a massive dose lived nearly three minutes, but he also succumbed in the end.

Burton was depressed by the results. Although death was delayed, it was not prevented. The method of symptomatic treatment did not work.

He put the dead rats to one side, and then made his crucial mistake.

Burton did not autopsy the anticoagulated rats.

Instead, he turned his attention to the original autopsy specimens, the first black Norway rat and the first rhesus monkey to be exposed to the capsule. He performed a complete autopsy on these animals, but discarded the anticoagulated animals.

It would be forty-eight hours before he realized his error. The autopsies he performed were careful and good; he did them slowly, reminding himself that he must overlook nothing. He removed the internal organs from the rat and monkey and examined each, removing samples for both the light and electron microscopes.

To gross inspection, the animals had died of total, intravascular coagulation. The arteries, the heart, lungs, kidneys, liver and spleen—all the blood-containing organs—were rock-hard, solid. This was what he had expected.

He carried his tissue slices across the room to prepare frozen sections for microscopic examination. As each section was completed by his technician, he slipped it under the microscope, examined it, and photographed it.

The tissues were normal. Except for the clotted blood, there was nothing unusual about them at all. He knew that these same pieces of tissue would now be sent to the microscopy lab, where another technician would prepare stained sections, using hematoxylin-eosin, periodic acid-Schiff, and Zenker-formalin stains. Sections of nerve would be stained with Nissl and Cajal gold preparations. This process would take an additional twelve to fifteen hours. He could hope, of course, that the stained sections would reveal something more, but he had no reason to believe they would.

Similarly, he was unenthusiastic about the prospects for electron microscopy. The electron microscope was a valuable tool, but occasionally it made things more difficult, not easier. The electron microscope could provide great magnification and clear detail—but only if you knew where to look. It was excellent for examining a single cell, or part of a cell. But first you had to know which cell to examine. And there were billions of cells in a human body.

At the end of ten hours of work, he sat back to consider what he had learned. He drew up a short list:

1. The lethal agent is approximately 1 micron in size. Therefore it is not a gas or molecule, or even a large protein or virus. It is the size of a cell, and may actually be a cell of some sort.
2. The lethal agent is transmitted by air. Dead organisms are not infectious.
3. The lethal agent is inspired by the victim, entering the lungs. There it presumably crosses over into the bloodstream and starts coagulation.
4. The lethal agent causes death through coagulation. This occurs within seconds, and coincides with total coagulation of the entire body vascular system.
5. Anticoagulant drugs do not prevent this process.
6. No other pathologic abnormalities are known to occur in the dying animal.

Burton looked at his list and shook his head. Anticoagulants might not work, but the fact was that *something* stopped the process. There was a way that it could be done. He knew that.

Because two people had survived.

Chapter 17

Recovery

At 1147 hours, Mark Hall was bent over the computer, staring at the console that showed the laboratory results from Peter Jackson and the infant. The computer was giving results as they were finished by the automated laboratory equipment; by now, nearly all results were in.

The infant, Hall observed, was normal. The computer did not mince words:

SUBJECT CODED—INFANT—SHOWS ALL LABORATORY VALUES WITHIN NORMAL LIMITS

However, Peter Jackson was another problem entirely. His results were abnormal in several respects.

SUBJECT CODED JACKSON, PETER
LABORATORY VALUES NOT WITHIN NORMAL
LIMITS FOLLOW

TEST	NORMAL	VALUE
HEMATOCRIT	38–54	21 INITIAL 25 REPEAT 29 REPEAT 33 REPEAT 37 REPEAT
BUN	10–20	50
COUNTS RETIC	1	6

BLOOD SMEAR SHOWS MANY IMMATURE ERYTHROCYTE FORMS

TEST	NORMAL	VALUE
PRO TIME	L2	12
BLOOD PH	7.40	7.31
SGOT	40	75
SED RATE	9	29
AMYLASE	70–200	450

Some of the results were easy to understand, others were not. The hematocrit, for example, was rising because Jackson was receiving transfusions of whole blood and packed red cells. The BUN, or blood urea nitrogen, was a test of kidney function and was mildly elevated, probably because of decreased blood flow.

Other analyses were consistent with blood loss. The reticulocyte count was up from 1 to 6 per cent—Jackson had been anemic for some time. He showed immature red-cell forms, which meant that his body was struggling to replace lost blood, and so had to put young, immature red cells into circulation.

The prothrombin time indicated that while Jackson was bleeding from somewhere in his gastrointestinal tract, he had no primary bleeding problem: his blood clotted normally.

The sedimentation rate and SGOT were indices of tissue destruction. Somewhere in Jackson's body, tissues were dying off.

But the pH of the blood was a bit of a puzzle. At 7.31, it was too acid, though not strikingly so. Hall was at a loss to explain this. So was the computer.

SUBJECT CODED JACKSON, PETER

DIAGNOSTIC PROBABILITIES

1. ACUTE AND CHRONIC BLOOD LOSS
   ETIOLOGY GASTROINTESTINAL .884
   NO OTHER STATISTICALLY SIGNIFICANT SOURCES.

2. ACIDOSIS
   ETIOLOGY UNEXPLAINED
   FURTHER DATA REQUIRED
   SUGGEST HISTORY

Hall read the printout and shrugged. The computer might suggest he talk to the patient, but that was easier said than done. Jackson was comatose, and if he had ingested anything to make his blood acid, they would not find out until he revived.

On the other hand, perhaps he could test blood gases. He turned to the computer and punched in a request for blood gases.

The computer responded stubbornly.

PATIENT HISTORY PREFERABLE TO LABORATORY ANALYSES

Hall typed in: "Patient comatose."

The computer seemed to consider this, and then flashed back:

PATIENT MONITORS NOT COMPATIBLE WITH COMA
EEG SHOWS ALPHA WAVES DIAGNOSTIC OF SLEEP

"I'll be damned," Hall said. He looked through the window and saw that Jackson was, indeed, stirring sleepily. He crawled down through the tunnel to his plastic suit and leaned over the patient.

"Mr. Jackson, wake up . . ."

Slowly, he opened his eyes and stared at Hall. He blinked, not believing.

"Don't be frightened," Hall said quietly. "You're sick, and we have been taking care of you. Do you feel better?"

Jackson swallowed, and nodded. He seemed afraid to speak. But the pallor of his skin was gone; his cheeks had a slight pinkish tinge; his fingernails were no longer gray.

"How do you feel now?"

"Okay . . . Who are you?"

"I am Dr. Hall. I have been taking care of you. You were bleeding very badly. We had to give you a transfusion."

He nodded, accepting this quite calmly. Somehow, his manner rung a bell for Hall, who said, "Has this happened to you before?"

"Yes," he said. "Twice."

"How did it happen before?"

"I don't know where I am," he said, looking around the room. "Is this a hospital? Why are you wearing that thing?"

"No, this isn't a hospital. It is a special laboratory in Nevada."

"Nevada?" He closed his eyes and shook his head. "But I'm in Arizona . . ."

"Not now. We brought you here, so we could help you."

"How come that suit?"

"We brought you from Piedmont. There was a disease in Piedmont. You are now in an isolation chamber."

"You mean I'm contagious?"

"Well, we don't know for sure. But we must—"

"Listen," he said, suddenly trying to get up, "this place gives me the creeps. I'm getting out of here. I don't like it here."

He struggled in the bed, trying to move against the straps. Hall pushed him back gently.

"Just relax, Mr. Jackson. Everything will be all right, but you must relax. You've been a sick man."

Slowly, Jackson lay back. Then: "I want a cigarette."

"I'm afraid you can't have one."

"What the hell, I want one."

"I'm sorry, smoking is not allowed—"

"Look here, young fella, when you've lived as long as I have you'll know what you can do and what you can't do. They told me before. None of that Mexican food, no liquor, no butts. I tried it for a spell. You know how that makes a body feel? Terrible, just terrible."

"Who told you?"

"The doctors."

"What doctors?"

"Those doctors in Phoenix. Big fancy hospital, all that shiny equipment and all those shiny white uniforms. Real fancy hospital. I wouldn't have gone there, except for my sister. She insisted. She lives in Phoenix, you know, with that husband of hers, George. Stupid ninny. I didn't want no fancy hospital, I just wanted to rest up, is all. But she insisted, so I went."

"When was this?"

"Last year. June it was, or July."

"Why did you go to the hospital?"

"Why does anybody go to the hospital? I was sick, dammit."

"What was your problem?"

"This damn stomach of mine, same as always."

"Bleeding?"

"Christ, bleeding. Every time I hiccoughed I came up with blood. Never knew a body had so much blood in it."

"Bleeding in your stomach?"

"Yeah. Like I said, I had it before. All these needles stuck in you"—he nodded to the intravenous lines—"and all the blood going into you. Phoenix last year, and then Tucson the year before that. Now, Tucson was a right nice place. Right nice. Had me a pretty little nurse and all." Abruptly, he closed his mouth. "How old are you, son, anyhow? You don't seem old enough to be a doctor."

"I'm a surgeon," Hall said.

"Surgeon! Oh no you don't. They kept trying to get me to do it, and I kept saying, Not on your sweet life. No indeedy. Not taking it out of me."

"You've had an ulcer for two years?"

"A bit more. The pains started out of the clear blue. Thought I had a touch of indigestion, you know, until the bleeding started up."

A two-year history, Hall thought. Definitely ulcer, not cancer.

"And you went to the hospital?"

"Yep. Fixed me up fine. Warned me off spicy foods and hard stuff and cigarettes. And I tried, sonny, I sure did. But it wasn't no good. A man gets used to his pleasures."

"So in a year, you were back in the hospital."

"Yeah. Big old place in Phoenix, with that stupid ninny George and my sister visiting me every day. He's a book-learning fool, you know. Lawyer. Talks real big, but he hasn't got the sense God gave a grasshopper's behind."

"And they wanted to operate in Phoenix?"

"Sure they did. No offense, sonny, but any doctor'll operate on you, give him half a chance. It's the way they think. I just told them I'd gone this far with my old stomach, and I reckoned I'd finish the stretch with it."

"When did you leave the hospital?"

"Must have been early August sometime. First week, or thereabouts."

"And when did you start smoking and drinking and eating the wrong foods?"

"Now don't lecture me, sonny," Jackson said. "I've been living for sixty-nine years, eating all the wrong foods and doing all the wrong things. I like it that way, and if I can't keep it up, well then the hell with it."

"But you must have had pain," Hall said, frowning.

"Oh, sure, it kicked up some. Specially if I didn't eat. But I found a way to fix that."

"Yes?"

"Sure. They gave me this milk stuff at the hospital, and wanted me to keep on with it. Hundred times a day, in little sips. Milk stuff. Tasted like chalk. But I found a better thing."

"What was that?"

"Aspirin," Jackson said.

"Aspirin?"

"Sure. Works real nice."

"How much aspirin did you take?"

"Fair bit, toward the end. I was doing a bottle a day. You know them bottles it comes in?"

Hall nodded. No wonder the man was acid. Aspirin was acetylsalicylic acid, and if it was taken in sufficient quantities, it would acidify you. Aspirin was a gastric irritant, and it could exacerbate bleeding.

"Didn't anybody tell you aspirin would make the bleeding worse?" he asked.

"Sure," Jackson said. "They told me. But I didn't mind none. Because it stopped the pains, see. That, plus a little squeeze."

"Squeeze?"

"Red-eye. You know."

Hall shook his head. He didn't know.

"Sterno. Pink lady. You take it, see, and put it in cloth, and squeeze it out . . ."

Hall sighed. "You were drinking Sterno," he said.

"Well, only when I couldn't get nothing else. Aspirin and squeeze, see, really kills that pain."

"Sterno isn't only alcohol. It's methanol, too."

"Doesn't hurt you, does it?" Jackson asked, in a voice suddenly concerned.

"As a matter of fact, it does. It can make you go blind, and it can even kill you."

"Well, hell, it made me feel better, so I took it," Jackson said.

"Did this aspirin and squeeze have any effect on you? On your breathing?"

"Well, now you mention it, I was a tad short of breath. But what the hell, I don't need much breath at my age."

Jackson yawned and closed his eyes.

"You're awful full of questions, boy. I want to sleep now."

Hall looked at him, and decided the man was right. It would be best to proceed slowly, at least for a time. He crawled back down the tunnel and out to the main room. He turned to his assistant:

"Our friend Mr. Jackson has a two-year history of ulcer. We'd better keep the blood going in for another couple of units, then we can stop and see what's happening. Drop an NG tube and start icewater lavage."

A gong rang, echoing softly through the room.

"What's that?"

"The twelve-hour mark. It means we have to change our clothing. And it means you have a conference."

"I do? Where?"

"The CR off the dining room."

Hall nodded, and left.

* * *

In delta sector, the computers hummed and clicked softly, as Captain Arthur Morris punched through a new program on the console. Captain Morris was a programmer; he had been sent to delta sector by the command on Level I because no MCN messages had been received for nine hours. It was possible, of course, that there had been no priority transmissions; but it was also unlikely.

And if there had been unreceived MCN messages, then the computers were not functioning properly. Captain Morris watched as the computer ran its usual internal check program, which read out as all circuits functioning.

Unsatisfied, he punched in the CHECKLIM program, a more rigorous testing of the circuit banks. It required 0.03 seconds for the machine to come back with its answer: a row of five green lights blinked on the console. He walked over to the teleprinter and watched as it typed:

MACHINE FUNCTION ON ALL CIRCUITS
WITHIN RATIONAL INDICES

He looked and nodded, satisfied. He could not have known, as he stood before the teleprinter, that there was indeed a fault, but that it was purely mechanical, not electronic, and hence could not be tested on the check programs. The fault lay within the teleprinter box itself. There a sliver of paper from the edge of the roll had peeled away and, curling upward, had lodged between the bell and striker, preventing the bell from ringing. It was for this reason that no MCN transmissions had been recorded.

Neither machine nor man was able to catch the error.

Chapter 18

The Noon Conference

According to protocol, the team met every twelve hours for a brief conference, at which results were summarized and new directions planned. In order to save time the conferences were held in a small room off the cafeteria; they could eat and talk at the same time.

Hall was the last to arrive. He slipped into a chair behind his lunch—two glasses of liquid and three pills of different colors—just as Stone said, "We'll hear from Burton first."

Burton shuffled to his feet and in a slow, hesitant voice outlined his experiments and his results. He noted first that he had determined the size of the lethal agent to be one micron.

Stone and Leavitt looked at each other. The green flecks they had seen were much larger than that; clearly, infection could be spread by a mere fraction of the green fleck.

Burton next explained his experiments concerning airborne transmission, and coagulation beginning at the lungs. He finished with his attempts at anticoagulation therapy.

"What about the autopsies?" Stone said. "What did they show?"

"Nothing we don't already know. The blood is clotted throughout. No other demonstrable abnormalities at the light-microscope level."

"And clotting is initiated at the lungs?"

"Yes. Presumably the organisms cross over to the bloodstream there—or they may release a toxic substance, which crosses over. We may have an answer when the stained sections are finished. In particular, we will be looking for damage to blood vessels, since this releases tissue thromboplastin, and stimulates clotting at the site of the damage."

Stone nodded and turned to Hall, who told of the tests carried out on his two patients. He explained that the infant was normal to all tests and that Jackson had a bleeding ulcer, for which he was receiving transfusions.

"He's revived," Hall said. "I talked with him briefly."

Everyone sat up.

"Mr. Jackson is a cranky old goat of sixty-nine who has a two-year history of ulcer. He's bled out twice before: two years ago, and again last year. Each time he was warned to change his habits; each time he went back to his old ways, and began bleeding again. At the time of the Piedmont contact, he was treating his problems with his own regimen: a bottle of aspirin a day and some Sterno on top of it. He says this left him a little short of breath."

"And made him acidotic as hell," Burton said.

"Exactly."

Methanol, when broken down by the body, was converted to formaldehyde and formic acid. In combination with aspirin, it meant Jackson was consuming great quantities of acid. The body had to maintain its acid-base balance within fairly narrow limits or death would occur. One way to keep the balance was to breathe rapidly, and blow off carbon dioxide, decreasing carbonic acid in the body.

Stone said, "Could this acid have protected him from the organism?"

Hall shrugged. "Impossible to say."

Leavitt said, "What about the infant? Was it anemic?"

"No," Hall said. "But on the other hand, we don't know for sure that it was protected by the same mechanism. It might have something entirely different."

"How about the acid-base balance of the child?"

"Normal," Hall said. "Perfectly normal. At least it is now."

There was a moment of silence. Finally Stone said, "Well, you have some good leads here. The problem remains to discover what, if anything, that child and that old man have in common. Perhaps, as you suggest, there is nothing in common. But for a start, we have to assume that they were protected in the same way, by the same mechanism."

Hall nodded.

Burton said to Stone, "And what have you found in the capsule?"

"We'd better show you," Stone said.

"Show us what?"

"Something we believe may represent the organism," Stone said.

* * *

The door said MORPHOLOGY. Inside, the room was partitioned into a place for the experimenters to stand, and a glass-walled isolation chamber further in. Gloves were provided so the men could reach into the chamber and move instruments about.

Stone pointed to the glass dish, and the small fleck of black inside it.

"We think this is our 'meteor,'" he said. "We have found something apparently alive on its surface. There were also other areas within the capsule that may represent life. We've brought the meteor in here to have a look at it under the light microscope."

Reaching through with the gloves, Stone set the glass dish into an opening in a large chrome box, then withdrew his hands.

"The box," he said, "is simply a light microscope fitted with the usual image intensifiers and resolution scanners. We can go up to a thousand diameters with it, projected on the screen here."

Leavitt adjusted dials while Hall and the others stared at the viewer screen.

"Ten power," Leavitt said.

On the screen, Hall saw that the rock was jagged, blackish, dull. Stone pointed out green flecks.

"One hundred power."

The green flecks were larger now, very clear.

"We think that's our organism. We have observed it growing; it turns purple, apparently at the point of mitotic division."

"Spectrum shift?"

"Of some kind."

"One thousand power," Leavitt said.

The screen was filled with a single green spot, nestled down in the jagged hollows of the rock. Hall noticed the surface of the green, which was smooth and glistening, almost oily.

"You think that's a single bacterial colony?"

"We can't be sure it's a colony in the conventional sense," Stone said. "Until we heard Burton's experiments, we didn't think it was a colony at all. We thought it might be a single organism. But obviously the single units have to be a micron or less in size; this is much too big. Therefore it is probably a larger structure—perhaps a colony, perhaps something else."

As they watched, the spot turned purple, and green again.

"It's dividing now," Stone said. "Excellent."

Leavitt switched on the cameras.

"Now watch closely."

The spot turned purple and held the color. It seemed to expand slightly, and for a moment, the surface broke into fragments, hexagonal in shape, like a tile floor.

"Did you see that?"

"It seemed to break up."

"Into six-sided figures."

"I wonder," Stone said, "whether those figures represent single units."

"Or whether they are regular geometric shapes all the time, or just during division?"

"We'll know more," Stone said, "after the EM." He turned to Burton. "Have you finished your autopsies?"

"Yes."

"Can you work the spectrometer?"

"I think so."

"Then do that. It's computerized, anyway. We'll want an analysis of samples of both the rock and the green organism."

"You'll get me a piece?"

"Yes." Stone said to Leavitt: "Can you handle the AA analyzer?"

"Yes."

"Same tests on that."

"And a fractionation?"

"I think so," Stone said. "But you'll have to do that by hand."

Leavitt nodded; Stone turned back to the isolation chamber and removed a glass dish from the light microscope. He set it to one side, beneath a small device that looked like a miniature scaffolding. This was the microsurgical unit.

Microsurgery was a relatively new skill in biology—the ability to perform delicate operations on a single cell. Using microsurgical techniques, it was possible to remove the nucleus from a cell, or part of the cytoplasm, as neatly and cleanly as a surgeon performed an amputation.

The device was constructed to scale down human hand movements into fine, precise miniature motions. A series of gears and servomechanisms carried out the reduction; the movement of a thumb was translated into a shift of a knife blade millionths of an inch.

Using a high magnification viewer, Stone began to chip away delicately at the black rock, until he had two tiny fragments. He set them aside in separate glass dishes and proceeded to scrape away two small fragments from the green area.

Immediately, the green turned purple, and expanded.

"It doesn't like you," Leavitt said, and laughed.

Stone frowned. "Interesting. Do you suppose that's a nonspecific growth response, or a trophic response to injury and irradiation?"

"I think," Leavitt said, "that it doesn't like to be poked at."

"We must investigate further," Stone said.

Chapter 19

Crash

For Arthur Manchek, there was a certain kind of horror in the telephone conversation. He received it at home, having just finished dinner and sat down in the living room to read the newspapers. He hadn't seen a newspaper in the last two days, he had been so busy with the Piedmont business.

When the phone rang, he assumed that it must be for his wife, but a moment later she came in and said, "It's for you. The base."

He had an uneasy feeling as he picked up the receiver. "Major Manchek speaking."

"Major, this is Colonel Burns at Unit Eight." Unit Eight was the processing and clearing unit of the base. Personnel checked in and out through Unit Eight, and calls were transmitted through it.

"Yes, Colonel?"

"Sir, we have you down for notification of certain contingencies." His voice was guarded; he was choosing his words carefully on the open line. "I'm informing you now of an RTM crash forty-two minutes ago in Big Head, Utah."

Manchek frowned. Why was he being informed of a routine training-mission crash? It was hardly his province.

"What was it?"

"Phantom, sir. En route San Francisco to Topeka."

"I see," Manchek said, though he did not see at all.

"Sir, Goddard wanted you to be informed in this instance so that you could join the post team."

"Goddard? Why Goddard?" For a moment, as he sat there in the living room, staring at the newspaper headline absently—NEW BERLIN CRISIS FEARED—he thought that the colonel meant Lewis Goddard, chief of the codes section of Vandenberg. Then he realized he meant Goddard Spaceflight Center, outside Washington. Among other things, Goddard acted as collating center for certain special projects that fell between the province of Houston and the governmental agencies in Washington.

"Sir," Colonel Burns said, "the Phantom drifted off its flight plan forty minutes out of San Francisco and passed through Area WF."

Manchek felt himself slowing down. A kind of sleepiness came over him. "Area WF?"

"That is correct, sir."

"When?"

"Twenty minutes before the crash."

"At what altitude?"

"Twenty-three thousand feet, sir."

"When does the post team leave?"

"Half an hour, sir, from the base."

"All right," Manchek said. "I'll be there."

He hung up and stared at the phone lazily. He felt tired; he wished he could go to bed. Area WF was the designation for the cordoned-off radius around Piedmont, Arizona.

They should have dropped the bomb, he thought. They should have dropped it two days ago.

At the time of the decision to delay Directive 7–12, Manchek had been uneasy. But officially he could not express an opinion, and he had waited in vain for the Wildfire team, now located in the underground laboratory, to complain to Washington. He knew Wildfire had been notified; he had seen the cable that went to all security units; it was quite explicit.

Yet for some reason Wildfire had not complained. Indeed, they had paid no attention to it whatever.

Very odd.

And now there was a crash. He lit his pipe and sucked on it, considering the possibilities. Overwhelming was the likelihood that some green trainee had daydreamed, gone off his flight plan, panicked, and lost control of the plane. It had happened before, hundreds of times. The post team, a group of specialists who went out to the site of the wreckage to investigate all crashes, usually returned a verdict of "Agnogenic Systems Failure." It was military doubletalk for crash of unknown cause; it did not distinguish between mechanical failure and pilot failure, but it was known that most systems failures were pilot failures. A man could not afford to daydream when he was running a complex machine at two thousand miles an hour. The proof lay in the statistics: though only 9 per cent of flights occurred after the pilot had taken a leave or weekend pass, these flights accounted for 27 per cent of casualties.

Manchek's pipe went out. He stood, dropping the newspaper, and went into the kitchen to tell his wife he was leaving.

"This is movie country," somebody said, looking at the sandstone cliffs, the brilliant reddish hues, against the deepening blue of the sky. And it was true, many movies had been filmed in this area of Utah. But Manchek could not think of movies now. As he sat in the back of the limousine moving away from the Utah airport, he considered what he had been told.

During the flight from Vandenberg to southern Utah, the post team had heard transcripts of the flight transmission between the Phantom and Topeka Central. For the most part it was dull, except for the final moments before the pilot crashed.

The pilot had said: "Something is wrong."

And then, a moment later, "My rubber air hose is dissolving. It must be the vibration. It's just disintegrating to dust."

Perhaps ten seconds after that, a weak, fading voice said, "Everything made of rubber in the cockpit is dissolving."

There were no further transmissions.

Manchek kept hearing that brief communication, in his mind, over and over. Each time, it sounded more bizarre and terrifying.

He looked out the window at the cliffs. The sun was setting now, and only the tops of the cliffs were lighted by fading reddish sunlight; the valleys lay in darkness. He looked ahead at the other limousine, raising a small dust cloud as it carried the rest of the team to the crash site.

"I used to love westerns," somebody said. "They were all shot out here. Beautiful country."

Manchek frowned. It was astonishing to him how people could spend so much time on irrelevancies. Or perhaps it was just denial, the unwillingness to face reality.

The reality was cold enough: the Phantom had strayed into Area WF, going quite deep for a matter of six minutes before the pilot realized the error and pulled north again. However, once in WF, the plane had begun to lose stability. And it had finally crashed.

He said, "Has Wildfire been informed?"

A member of the group, a psychiatrist with a crew cut—all post teams had at least one psychiatrist—said, "You mean the germ people?"

"Yes."

"They've been told," somebody else said. "It went out on the scrambler an hour ago."

Then, thought Manchek, there would certainly be a reaction from Wildfire. They could not afford to ignore this.

Unless they weren't reading their cables. It had never occured to him before, but perhaps it was possible—they weren't reading the cables. They were so absorbed in their work, they just weren't bothering.

"There's the wreck," somebody said. "Up ahead."

Each time Manchek saw a wreck, he was astonished. Somehow, one never got used to the idea of the sprawl, the mess—the destructive force of a large metal object striking the earth at thousands of miles an hour. He always expected a neat, tight little clump of metal, but it was never that way.

The wreckage of the Phantom was scattered over two square miles of desert. Standing next to the charred remnants of the left wing, he could barely see the others, on the horizon, near the right wing. Everywhere he looked, there were bits of twisted metal, blackened, paint peeling. He saw one with a small portion of a sign still intact, the stenciled letters clear: DO NOT. The rest was gone.

It was impossible to make anything of the remnants. The fuselage, the cockpit, the canopy were all shattered into a million fragments, and the fires had disfigured everything.

As the sun faded, he found himself standing near the remains of the tail section, where the metal still radiated heat from the smoldering fire. Half-buried in the sand he saw a bit of bone; he picked it up and realized with horror that it was human. Long, and broken, and charred at one end, it had obviously come from an arm or a leg. But it was oddly clean—there was no flesh remaining, only smooth bone.

Darkness descended, and the post team took out their flashlights, the half-dozen men moving among smoking metal, flashing their yellow beams of light about.

It was late in the evening when a biochemist whose name he did not know came up to talk with him.

"You know," the biochemist said, "it's funny. That transcript about the rubber in the cockpit dissolving."

"How do you mean?"

"Well, no rubber was used in this airplane. It was all a synthetic plastic compound. Newly developed by Ancro; they're quite proud of it. It's a polymer that has some of the same characteristics as human tissue. Very flexible, lots of applications."

Manchek said, "Do you think vibrations could have caused the disintegration?"

"No," the man said. "There are thousands of Phantoms flying around the world. They all have this plastic. None of them has ever had this trouble."

"Meaning?"

"Meaning that I don't know what the hell is going on," the biochemist said.

Chapter 20

Routine

Slowly, the Wildfire installation settled into a routine, a rhythm of work in the underground chambers of a laboratory where there was no night or day, morning or afternoon. The men slept when they were tired, awoke when they were refreshed, and carried on their work in a number of different areas.

Most of this work was to lead nowhere. They knew that, and accepted it in advance. As Stone was fond of saying, scientific research was much like prospecting: you went out and you hunted, armed with your maps and your instruments, but in the end your preparations did not matter, or even your intuition. You needed your luck, and whatever benefits accrued to the diligent, through sheer, grinding hard work.

Burton stood in the room that housed the spectrometer along with several other pieces of equipment for radioactivity assays, ratio-density photometry, thermocoupling analysis, and preparation for X-ray crystallography.

The spectrometer employed in Level V was the standard Whittington model K-5. Essentially it consisted of a vaporizer, a prism, and a recording screen. The material to be tested was set in the vaporizer and burned. The light from its burning then passed through the prism, where it was broken down to a spectrum that was projected onto a recording screen. Since different elements gave off different wavelengths of light as they burned, it was possible to analyze the chemical makeup of a substance by analyzing the spectrum of light produced.

In theory it was simple, but in practice the reading of spectrometrograms was complex and difficult. No one in this Wildfire laboratory was trained to do it well. Thus results were fed directly into a computer, which performed the analysis. Because of the sensitivity of the computer, rough percentage compositions could also be determined.

Burton placed the first chip, from the black rock, onto the vaporizer and pressed the button. There was a single bright burst of intensely hot light; he turned away, avoiding the brightness, and then put the second chip onto the lamp. Already, he knew, the computer was analyzing the light from the first chip.

He repeated the process with the green fleck, and then checked the time. The computer was now scanning the self-developing photographic plates, which were ready for viewing in seconds. But the scan itself would take two hours—the electric eye was very slow.

Once the scan was completed, the computer would analyze results and print the data within five seconds.

The wall clock told him it was now 1500 hours—three in the afternoon. He suddenly realized he was tired. He punched in instructions to the computer to wake him when analysis was finished. Then he went off to bed.

In another room, Leavitt was carefully feeding similar chips into a different machine, an amino-acid analyzer. As he did so, he smiled slightly to himself, for he could remember how it had been in the old days, before AA analysis was automatic.

In the early fifties, the analysis of amino acids in a protein might take weeks, or even months. Sometimes it took years. Now it took hours—or at the very most, a day—and it was fully automatic.

Amino acids were the building blocks of proteins. There were twenty-four known amino acids, each composed of a half-dozen molecules of carbon, hydrogen, oxygen, and nitrogen. Proteins were made by stringing these amino acids together in a line, like a freight train. The order of stringing determined the nature of the protein—whether it was insulin, hemoglobin, or growth hormone. All proteins were composed of the same freight cars, the same units. Some proteins had more of one kind of car than another, or in a different order. But that was the only difference. The same amino acids, the same freight cars, existed in human proteins and flea proteins.

That fact had taken approximately twenty years to discover.

But what controlled the order of amino acids in the protein? The answer turned out to be DNA, the genetic-coding substance, which acted like a switching manager in a freightyard.

That particular fact had taken another twenty years to discover.

But then once the amino acids were strung together, they began to twist and coil upon themselves; the analogy became closer to a snake than a train. The manner of coiling was determined by the order of acids, and was quite specific: a protein had to be coiled in a certain way, and no other, or it failed to function.

Another ten years.

Rather odd, Leavitt thought. Hundreds of laboratories, thousands of workers throughout the world, all bent on discovering such essentially simple facts. It had all taken years and years, decades of patient effort.

And now there was this machine. The machine would not, of course, give the precise order of amino acids. But it would give a rough percentage composition: so much valine, so much arginine, so much cystine and proline and leucine. And that, in turn, would give a great deal of information.

Yet it was a shot in the dark, this machine. Because they had no reason to believe that either the rock or the green organism was composed even partially of proteins. True, every living thing on earth had at least some proteins—but that didn't mean life elsewhere had to have it.

For a moment, he tried to imagine life without proteins. It was almost impossible: on earth, proteins were part of the cell wall, and comprised all the enzymes known to man. And life without enzymes? Was that possible?

He recalled the remark of George Thompson, the British biochemist, who had called enzymes "the matchmakers of life." It was true; enzymes acted as catalysts for all chemical reactions, by providing a surface for two molecules to come together and react upon. There were hundreds of thousands, perhaps millions, of enzymes, each existing solely to aid a single chemical reaction. Without enzymes, there could be no chemical reactions.

Without chemical reactions, there could be no life.

Or could there?

It was a long-standing problem. Early in planning Wildfire, the question had been posed: How do you study a form of life totally unlike any you know? How would you even know it was alive?

This was not an academic matter. Biology, as George Wald had said, was a unique science because it could not define its subject matter. Nobody had a definition for life. Nobody knew what it was, really. The old definitions—an organism that showed ingestion, excretion, metabolism, reproduction, and so on—were worthless. One could always find exceptions.

The group had finally concluded that energy conversion was the hallmark of life. All living organisms in some way took in energy—as food, or sunlight—and converted it to another form of energy, and put it to use.

(Viruses were the exception to this rule, but the group was prepared to define viruses as nonliving.)

For the next meeting, Leavitt was asked to prepare a rebuttal to the definition. He pondered it for a week, and returned with three objects: a swatch of black cloth, a watch, and a piece of granite. He set them down before the group and said, "Gentleman, I give you three living things."

He then challenged the team to prove that they were not living. He placed the black cloth in the sunlight; it became warm. This, he announced, was an example of energy conversion—radiant energy to heat.

It was objected that this was merely passive energy absorption, not conversion. It was also objected that the conversion, if it could be called that, was not purposeful. It served no function.

"How do you know it is not purposeful?" Leavitt had demanded.

They then turned to the watch. Leavitt pointed to the radium dial, which glowed in the dark. Decay was taking place, and light was being produced.

The men argued that this was merely release of potential energy held in unstable electron levels. But there was growing confusion; Leavitt was making his point.

Finally, they came to the granite. "This is alive," Leavitt said. "It is living, breathing, walking, and talking. Only we cannot see it, because it is happening too slowly. Rock has a lifespan of three billion years. We have a lifespan of sixty or seventy years. We cannot see what is happening to this rock for the same reason that we cannot make out the tune on a record being played at the rate of one revolution every century. And the rock, for its part, is not even aware of our existence because we are alive for only a brief instant of its lifespan. To it, we are like flashes in the dark."

He held up his watch.

His point was clear enough, and they revised their thinking in one important respect. They conceded that it was possible that they might not be able to analyze certain life forms. It was possible that they might not be able to make the slightest headway, the least beginning, in such an analysis.

But Leavitt's concerns extended beyond this, to the general problem of action in uncertainty. He recalled reading Talbert Gregson's "Planning the Unplanned" with close attention, poring over the complex mathematical models the author had devised to analyze the problem. It was Gregson's conviction that:

> All decisions involving uncertainty fall within two distinct categories—those with contingencies, and those without. The latter are distinctly more difficult to deal with.
>
> Most decisions, and nearly all human interaction, can be incorporated into a contingencies model. For example, a President may start a war, a man may sell his business, or divorce his wife. Such an action will produce a reaction; the

number of reactions is infinite but the number of *probable* reactions is manageably small. Before making a decision, an individual can predict various reactions, and he can assess his original, or primary-mode, decision more effectively.

But there is also a category which cannot be analyzed by contingencies. This category involves events and situations which are *absolutely* unpredictable, not merely disasters of all sorts, but those also including rare moments of discovery and insight, such as those which produced the laser, or penicillin. Because these moments are unpredictable, they cannot be planned for in any logical manner. The mathematics are wholly unsatisfactory.

We may only take comfort in the fact that such situations, for ill or for good, are exceedingly rare.

Jeremy Stone, working with infinite patience, took a flake of the green material and dropped it into molten plastic. The plastic was the size and shape of a medicine capsule. He waited until the flake was firmly imbedded, and poured more plastic over it. He then transferred the plastic pill to the curing room.

Stone envied the others their mechanized routines. The preparation of samples for electron microscopy was still a delicate task requiring skilled human hands; the preparation of a good sample was as demanding a craft as that ever practiced by an artisan—and took almost as long to learn. Stone had worked for five years before he became proficient at it.

The plastic was cured in a special high-speed processing unit, but it would still take five hours to harden to proper consistency. The curing room would maintain a constant temperature of 61° C. with a relative humidity of 10 per cent.

Once the plastic was hardened, he would scrape it away, and then flake off a small bit of green with a microtome. This would go into the electron microscope. The flake would have to be of the right thickness and size, a small round shaving 1,500 angstroms in depth, no more.

Only then could he look at the green stuff, whatever it was, at sixty thousand diameters magnification.

That, he thought, would be interesting.

In general, Stone believed the work was going well. They were making fine progress, moving forward in several promising lines of inquiry. But most important, they had time. There was no rush, no panic, no need to fear.

The bomb had been dropped on Piedmont. That would destroy airborne organisms, and neutralize the source of infection. Wildfire was the only place that any further infection could spread from, and Wildfire was specifically designed to prevent that. Should isolation be broken in the lab, the areas that were contaminated would automatically seal off. Within a half-second, sliding airtight doors would close, producing a new configuration for the lab.

This was necessary because past experience in other laboratories working in so-called axenic, or germ-free, atmospheres indicated that contamination occurred in 15 per cent of cases. The reasons were usually structural—a seal burst, a glove tore, a seam split—but the contamination occurred, nonetheless.

At Wildfire, they were prepared for that eventuality. But if it did not happen, and the odds were it would not, then they could work safely here for an indefinite period. They could spend a month, even a year, working on the organism. There was no problem, no problem at all.

Hall walked through the corridor, looking at the atomic-detonator substations. He was trying to memorize their positions. There were five on the floor, positioned at intervals along the central corridor. Each was the same: small silver boxes no larger than a cigarette packet. Each had a lock for the key, a green light that was burning, and a dark-red light.

Burton had explained the mechanism earlier. "There are sensors in all the duct systems and in all the labs. They monitor the air in the rooms by a variety of chemical, electronic, and straight bioassay devices. The bioassay is just a mouse whose heartbeat is being monitored. If anything goes wrong with the sensors, the lab automatically seals off. If the whole floor is contaminated, it will seal off, and the atomic device will cut in. When that happens, the green light will go out, and the red light will begin to blink. That signals the start of the three-minute interval. Unless you lock in your key, the bomb will go off at the end of three minutes."

"And I have to do it myself?"

Burton nodded. "The key is steel. It is conductive. The lock has a system which measures the capacitance of the person holding the key. It responds to general body size, particularly weight, and also the salt content of sweat. It's quite specific, actually, for you."

"So I'm really the only one?"

"You really are. And you only have one key. But there's a complicating problem. The blueprints weren't followed exactly; we only discovered the error after the lab was finished and the device was installed. But there is an error: we are short three detonator substations. There are only five, instead of eight."

"Meaning?"

"Meaning that if the floor starts to contaminate, you must rush to locate yourself at a substation. Otherwise there is a chance you could be sealed off in a sector without a substation. And then, in the event of a malfunction of the bacteriologic sensors, a false positive malfunction, the laboratory could be destroyed needlessly."

"That seems a rather serious error in planning."

"It turns out," Burton said, "that three new substations were going to be added next month. But that won't help us now. Just keep the problem in mind, and everything'll be all right."

Leavitt awoke quickly, rolling out of bed and starting to dress. He was excited: he had just had an idea. A fascinating thing, wild, crazy, but fascinating as hell.

It had come from his dream.

He had been dreaming of a house, and then of a city—a huge, complex, interconnecting city around the house. A man lived in the house, with his family; the man lived and worked and commuted within the city, moving about, acting, reacting.

And then, in the dream, the city was suddenly eliminated, leaving only the house. How different things were then! A single house, standing alone, without the things it needed—water, plumbing, electricity, streets. And a family, cut off from the supermarkets, schools, drugstores. And the husband, whose work was in the city, interrelated to others in the city, suddenly stranded.

The house became a different organism altogether. And from that to the Wildfire organism was but a single step, a single leap of the imagination . . .

He would have to discuss it with Stone. Stone would laugh, as usual—Stone always laughed—but he would also pay attention. Leavitt knew that, in a sense, he operated as the idea man for the team. The man who would always provide the most improbable, mind-stretching theories.

Well, Stone would at least be interested.

He glanced at the clock. 2200 hours. Getting on toward midnight. He hurried to dress.

He took out a new paper suit and slipped his feet in. The paper was cool against his bare flesh.

And then suddenly it was warm. A strange sensation. He finished dressing, stood, and zipped up the one-piece suit. As he left, he looked once again at the clock.

2210.

Oh, Christ, he thought.

It had happened again. And this time, for ten minutes. What had gone on? He couldn't remember. But it was ten minutes gone, disappeared, while he had dressed—an action that shouldn't have taken more than thirty seconds.

He sat down again on the bed, trying to remember, but he could not.

Ten minutes gone.

It was terrifying. Because it was happening again, though he had hoped it would not. It hadn't happened for months, but now, with the excitement, the odd hours, the break in his normal hospital schedule, it was starting once more.

For a moment, he considered telling the others, then shook his head. He'd be all right. It wouldn't happen again. He was going to be just fine.

He stood. He had been on his way to see Stone, to talk to Stone about something. Something important and exciting.

He paused.

He couldn't remember.

The idea, the image, the excitement was gone. Vanished, erased from his mind.

He knew then that he should tell Stone, admit the whole thing. But he knew what Stone would say and do if he found out. And he knew what it would mean to his future, to the rest of his life, once the Wildfire Project was finished. Everything would change, if people knew. He couldn't ever be normal again—he would have to quit his job, do other things, make endless adjustments. He couldn't even drive a car.

No, he thought. He would not say anything. And he would be all right: as long as he didn't look at blinking lights.

Jeremy Stone was tired, but he knew he was not ready for sleep. He paced up and down the corridors of the laboratory, thinking about the birds at Piedmont. He ran over everything they had done: how they had seen the birds, how they had gassed them with chlorazine, and how the birds had died. He went over it in his mind, again and again.

Because he was missing something. And that something was bothering him.

At the time, while he had been inside Piedmont itself, it had bothered him. Then he had forgotten, but his nagging doubts had been revived at the noon conference, while Hall was discussing the patients.

Something Hall had said, some fact he had mentioned, was related, in some off way, to the birds. But what was it? What was the exact thought, the precise words, that had triggered the association?

Stone shook his head. He simply couldn't dig it out. The clues, the connection, the keys were all there, but he couldn't bring them to the surface.

He pressed his hands to his head, squeezing against the bones, and he damned his brain for being so stubborn.

Like many intelligent men, Stone took a rather suspicious attitude toward his own brain, which he saw as a precise and skilled but temperamental machine. He was never surprised when the machine failed to perform, though he feared those moments, and hated them. In his blackest hours, Stone doubted the utility of all thought, and all intelligence. There were times when he envied the laboratory rats he worked with; their brains were so simple. Certainly they did not have the intelligence to destroy themselves; that was a peculiar invention of man.

He often argued that human intelligence was more trouble than it was worth. It was more destructive than creative, more confusing than revealing, more discouraging than satisfying, more spiteful than charitable.

There were times when he saw man, with his giant brain, as equivalent to the dinosaurs. Every schoolboy knew that dinosaurs had outgrown themselves, had become too large and ponderous to be viable. No one ever thought to consider whether the human brain, the most complex structure in the known universe, making fantastic demands on the human body in terms of nourishment and blood, was not analogous. Perhaps the human brain had become a kind of dinosaur for man and perhaps, in the end, would prove his downfall.

Already, the brain consumed one quarter of the body's blood supply. A fourth of all blood pumped from the heart went to the brain, an organ accounting for only a small percentage of body mass. If brains grew larger, and better, then perhaps they would consume more—perhaps so much that, like an infection, they would overrun their hosts and kill the bodies that transported them.

Or perhaps, in their infinite cleverness, they would find a way to destroy themselves and each other. There were times when, as he sat at State Department or Defense Department meetings, and looked around the table, he saw nothing more than a dozen gray, convoluted brains sitting on the table. No flesh and blood, no hands, no eyes, no fingers. No mouths, no sex organs—all these were superfluous.

Just brains. Sitting around, trying to decide how to outwit other brains, at other conference tables.

Idiotic.

He shook his head, thinking that he was becoming like Leavitt, conjuring up wild and improbable schemes.

Yet, there was a sort of logical consequence to Stone's ideas. If you really feared and hated your brain, you would attempt to destroy it. Destroy your own, and destroy others.

"I'm tired," he said aloud, and looked at the wall clock. It was 2340 hours—almost time for the midnight conference.

Chapter 21

The Midnight Conference

They met again, in the same room, in the same way. Stone glanced at the others and saw they were tired; no one, including himself, was getting enough sleep.

"We're going at this too hard," he said. "We don't need to work around the clock, and we shouldn't do so. Tired men will make mistakes, mistakes in thinking and mistakes in action. We'll start to drop things, to screw things up, to work sloppily. And we'll make wrong assumptions, draw incorrect inferences. That mustn't happen."

The team agreed to get at least six hours sleep in each twenty-four-hour period. That seemed reasonable, since there was no problem on the surface; the infection at Piedmont had been halted by the atomic bomb.

Their belief might never have been altered had not Leavitt suggested that they file for a code name. Leavitt stated that they had an organism and that it required a code. The others agreed.

In a corner of the room stood the scrambler typewriter. It had been clattering all day long, typing out material sent in from the outside. It was a two-way machine; material transmitted had to be typed in lowercase letters, while received material was printed out in capitals.

No one had really bothered to look at the input since their arrival on

Level V. They were all too busy; besides, most of the input had been routine military dispatches that were sent to Wildfire but did not concern it. This was because Wildfire was one of the Cooler Circuit substations, known facetiously as the Top Twenty. These substations were linked to the basement of the White House and were the twenty most important strategic locations in the country. Other substations included Vandenberg, Kennedy, NORAD, Patterson, Detrick, and Virginia Key.

Stone went to the typewriter and printed out his message. The message was directed by computer to Central Codes, a station that handled the coding of all projects subsumed under the system of Cooler.

The transmission was as follows:

open line to transmit
UNDERSTAND TRANSMIT STATE ORIGIN
stone project wildfire
STATE DESTINATION
central codes
UNDERSTAND CENTRAL CODES
message follows
SEND
have isolated extraterrestrial organism secondary to return of scoop seven wish coding for organism
end message
TRANSMITTED

There followed a long pause. The scrambler teleprinter hummed and clicked, but printed nothing. Then the typewriter began to spit out a message on a long roll of paper.

MESSAGE FROM CENTRAL CODES FOLLOWS
UNDERSTAND ISOLATION OF NEW ORGANISM
PLEASE CHARACTERIZE
END MESSAGE

Stone frowned. "But we don't know enough." However, the teleprinter was impatient:

TRANSMIT REPLY TO CENTRAL CODES

After a moment, Stone typed back:

message to central codes follows
cannot characterize at this time but suggest
tentative classification as bacterial strain
end message

MESSAGE FROM CENTRAL CODES FOLLOWS

UNDERSTAND REQUEST FOR BACTERIAL CLASSIFICATION
OPENING NEW CATEGORY CLASSIFICATION ACCORDING TO ICDA
STANDARD REFERENCE CODE FOR YOUR ORGANISM WILL BE ANDROMEDA CODE WILL READ OUT ANDROMEDA STRAIN
FILED UNDER ICDA LISTINGS AS 053.9 [UNSPECIFIED ORGANISM]
FURTHER FILING AS E866 [AIRCRAFT ACCIDENT] THIS FILING REPRESENTS CLOSEST FIT TO
ESTABLISHED CATEGORIES

Stone smiled. "It seems we don't fit the established categories."

He typed back:

understand coding as andromeda strain
accepted
end message
TRANSMITTED

"Well," Stone said, "that's that."

Burton had been looking over the sheaves of paper behind the teleprinter. The teleprinter wrote its messages out on a long roll of paper, which fell into a box. There were dozens of yards of paper that no one had looked at.

Silently, he read a single message, tore it from the rest of the strip, and handed it to Stone.

1134/443/KK/Y-U/9
INFORMATION STATUS
TRANSMIT TO ALL STATIONS
CLASSIFICATION TOP SECRET

REQUEST FOR DIRECTIVE 7-12 RECEIVED TODAY BY EXEC AND NSC-COBRA
ORIGIN VANDENBERG/WILDFIRE
CORROBORATION NASA/AMC
AUTHORITY PRIMARY MANCHEK, ARTHUR, MAJOR USA
IN CLOSED SESSION THIS DIRECTIVE HAS NOT BEEN ACTED UPON
FINAL DECISION HAS BEEN POSTPONED TWENTY FOUR TO FORTY EIGHT HOURS
RECONSIDERATION AT THAT TIME
ALTERNATIVE TROOP DEPLOYMENT ACCORDING TO DIRECTIVE 7-11 NOW IN EFFECT
NO NOTIFICATION
END MESSAGE

TRANSMIT ALL STATIONS
CLASSIFICATION TOP SECRET
END TRANSMISSION

The team stared at the message in disbelief. No one said anything for a long time. Finally, Stone ran his fingers along the upper corner of the sheet and said in a low voice, "This was a 443. That makes it an MCN transmission. It should have rung the bell down here."

"There's no bell on this teleprinter," Leavitt said. "Only on Level I, at sector five. But they're supposed to notify us whenever—"

"Get sector five on the intercom," Stone said.

Ten minutes later, the horrified Captain Morris had connected Stone to Robertson, the head of the President's Science Advisory Committee, who was in Houston.

Stone spoke for several minutes with Robertson, who expressed initial surprise that he hadn't heard from Wildfire earlier. There then followed a heated discussion of the president's decision not to call a Directive 7-12.

"The President doesn't trust scientists," Robertson said. "He doesn't feel comfortable with them."

"It's your job to make him comfortable," Stone said, "and you haven't been doing it."

"Jeremy—"

"There are only two sources of contamination," Stone said. "Piedmont, and this installation. We're adequately protected here, but Piedmont—"

"Jeremy, I agree the bomb should have been dropped."

"Then work on him. Stay on his back. Get him to call a 7-12 as soon as possible. It may already be too late."

Robertson said he would, and would call back. Before he hung up, he said, "By the way, any thoughts about the Phantom?"

"The what?"

"The Phantom that crashed in Utah."

There was a moment of confusion before the Wildfire group understood that they had missed still another important teleprinter message.

"Routine training mission. The jet strayed over the closed zone, though. That's the puzzle."

"Any other information?"

"The pilot said something about his air hose dissolving. Vibration, or something. His last communication was pretty bizarre."

"Like he was crazy?" Stone asked.

"Like that," Robertson said.

"Is there a team at the wreck site now?"

"Yes, we're waiting for information from them. It could come at any time."

"Pass it along," Stone said. And then he stopped. "If a 7-11 was ordered, instead of a 7-12," he said, "then you have troops in the area around Piedmont."

"National Guard, yes."

"That's pretty damned stupid," Stone said.

"Look, Jeremy, I agree—"

"When the first one dies," Stone said, "I want to know when, and how. And most especially, *where*. The wind there is from the east predominantly. If you start losing men west of Piedmont—"

"I'll call, Jeremy," Robertson said.

The conversation ended, and the team shuffled out of the conference room. Hall remained behind a moment, going through some of the rolls in the box, noting the messages. The majority were unintelligible to him, a weird set of nonsense messages and codes. After a time he gave up; he did so before he came upon the reprinted news item concerning the peculiar death of Officer Martin Willis, of the Arizona highway patrol.

DAY 4

SPREAD

Chapter 22

The Analysis

With the new pressures of time, the results of spectrometry and amino-acid analysis, previously of peripheral interest, suddenly became matters of major concern. It was hoped that these analyses would tell, in a rough way, how foreign the Andromeda organism was to earth life forms.

It was thus with interest that Leavitt and Burton looked over the computer printout, a column of figures written on green paper:

MASS SPECTROMETRY DATA OUTPUT
PRINT
PERCENTAGE OUTPUT SAMPLE 1—BLACK OBJECT
UNIDENTIFIED ORIGIN

H	HE								
21.07	0								
LI	BE	B	C	N	O	F			
0	0	0	54.90	0	18.00	0			
NA	MG	AL	SI	P	S	CL			
0	0	0	00.20	—	01.01	0			
K	CA	SC	TI	V	CR	MN	FE	CO	NI
0	0	0	—	—	—	—	—	—	—
CU	ZN	GA	GE	AS	SE	BR			
—	—	0	0	0	00.34	0			

ALL HEAVIER METALS SHOW ZERO CONTENT

SAMPLE 2—GREEN OBJECT UNIDENTIFIED ORIGIN—

H	HE					
27.00	0					
LI	BE	B	C	N	0	F
0	0	0	45.00	05.00	23.00	0

ALL HEAVIER METALS SHOW ZERO CONTENT

END PRINT

END PROGRAM

-STOP-

What all this meant was simple enough. The black rock contained hydrogen, carbon, and oxygen, with significant amounts of sulfur, silicon, and selenium, and with trace quantities of several other elements.

The green spot, on the other hand, contained hydrogen, carbon, nitrogen, and oxygen. Nothing else at all. The two men found it peculiar that the rock and the green spot should be so similar in chemical makeup. And it was peculiar that the green spot should contain nitrogen, while the rock contained none at all.

The conclusion was obvious: the "black rock" was not rock at all, but some kind of material similar to earthly organic life. It was something akin to plastic.

And the green spot, presumably alive, was composed of elements in roughly the same proportion as earth life. On earth, these same four elements—hydrogen, carbon, nitrogen, and oxygen—accounted for 99 per cent of all the elements in life organisms.

The men were encouraged by these results, which suggested similarity between the green spot and life on earth. Their hopes were, however, short-lived as they turned to the amino-acid analysis:

AMINO ACID ANALYSIS DATA OUTPUT
PRINT
SAMPLE 1—BLACK OBJECT UNIDENTIFIED ORIGIN—
SAMPLE 2—GREEN OBJECT UNIDENTIFIED ORIGIN—

	SAMPLE 1	SAMPLE 2
NEUTRAL AMINO ACIDS		
GLYCINE	00.00	00.00
ALANINE	00.00	00.00
VALINE	00.00	00.00

	SAMPLE 1	SAMPLE 2
ISOLEUCINE	00.00	00.00
SERINE	00.00	00.00
THREONINE	00.00	00.00
LEUCINE	00.00	00.00
AROMATIC AMINO ACIDS		
PHENYLALANINE	00.00	00.00
TYROSINE	00.00	00.00
TRYPTOPHAN	00.00	00.00
SULFURIC AMINO ACIDS		
CYSTINE	00.00	00.00
CYSTEINE	00.00	00.00
METHIONINE	00.00	00.00
SECONDARY AMINO ACIDS		
PROLINE	00.00	00.00
HYDROXYPROLINE	00.00	00.00
DICARBOXYLIC AMINO ACIDS		
ASPARTIC ACID	00.00	00.00
GLUTAMIC ACID	00.00	00.00
BASIC AMINO ACIDS		
HISTIDINE	00.00	00.00
ARGININE	00.00	00.00
LYSINE	00.00	00.00
HYDROXYLYSINE	00.00	00.00
TOTAL AMINO ACID CONTENT	00.00	00.00

END PRINT
END PROGRAM

—STOP—

"Christ," Leavitt said, staring at the printed sheet. "Will you look at that."

"No amino acids," Burton said. "No proteins."

"Life without proteins," Leavitt said. He shook his head; it seemed as if his worst fears were realized.

On earth, organisms had evolved by learning to carry out biochemical reactions in a small space, with the help of protein enzymes. Biochemists were now learning to duplicate these reactions, but only by isolating a single reaction from all others.

Living cells were different. There, within a small area, reactions were carried out that provided energy, growth, and movement. There was no separation, and man could not duplicate this any more than a man could prepare a complete dinner from appetizers to dessert by mixing together the ingredients for everything into a single large dish, cooking it, and hoping to separate the apple pie from the cheese dip later on.

Cells could keep the hundreds of separate reactions straight, using enzymes. Each enzyme was like a single worker in a kitchen, doing just one thing. Thus a baker could not make a steak, any more than a steak griller could use his equipment to prepare appetizers.

But enzymes had a further use. They made possible chemical reactions that otherwise would not occur. A biochemist could duplicate the reactions by using great heat, or great pressure, or strong acids. But the human body, or the individual cell, could not tolerate such extremes of environment. Enzymes, the matchmakers of life, helped chemical reactions to go forward at body temperature and atmospheric pressure.

Enzymes were essential to life on earth. But if another form of life had learned to do without them, it must have evolved in a wholly different way.

Therefore, they were dealing with an entirely alien organism.

And this in turn meant that analysis and neutralization would take much, much longer.

In the room marked MORPHOLOGY, Jeremy Stone removed the small plastic capsule in which the green fleck had been imbedded. He set the now-hard capsule into a vise, fixing it firmly, and then took a dental drill to it, shaving away the plastic until he exposed bare green material.

This was a delicate process, requiring many minutes of concentrated work. At the end of that time, he had shaved the plastic in such a way that he had a pyramid of plastic, with the green fleck at the peak of the pyramid.

He unscrewed the vise and lifted the plastic out. He took it to the microtome, a knife with a revolving blade that cut very thin slices of plastic and imbedded green tissue. These slices were round; they fell from the plastic block into a dish of water. The thickness of the slice could be measured by looking at the light as it reflected off the slices—if the light was faint silver, the slice was too thick. If, on the other hand, it was a rainbow of colors, then it was the right thickness, just a few molecules in depth.

That was how thick they wanted a slice of tissue to be for the electron microscope.

When Stone had a suitable piece of tissue, he lifted it carefully with forceps and set it onto a small round copper grid. This in turn was inserted into a metal button. Finally, the button was set into the electron microscope, and the microscope sealed shut.

The electron microscope used by Wildfire was the BVJ model JJ-42. It was a high-intensity model with an image-resolution attachment. In principle, the electron microscope was simple enough: it worked exactly like a light microscope, but instead of focusing light rays, it focused an electron beam. Light is focused by lenses of curved glass. Electrons are focused by magnetic fields.

In many respects, the EM was not a great deal different from television, and in fact, the image was displayed on a television screen, a coated surface that glowed when electrons struck it. The great advantage of the electron microscope was that it could magnify objects far more than the light microscope. The reason for this had to do with quantum mechanics and the waveform theory of radiation. The best simple explanation had come from the electron microscopist Sidney Polton, also a racing enthusiast.

"Assume," Polton said, "that you have a road, with a sharp corner. Now assume that you have two automobiles, a sports car and a large truck. When the truck tries to go around the corner, it slips off the road; but the sports car manages it easily. Why? The sports car is lighter, and smaller, and faster; it is better suited to tight, sharp curves. On large, gentle curves, the automobiles will perform equally well, but on sharp curves, the sports car will do better.

"In the same way, an electron microscope will 'hold the road' better than a light microscope. All objects are made of corners, and edges. The electron wavelength is smaller than the quantum of light. It cuts the corners closer, follows the road better, and outlines it more precisely. With a light microscope—like a truck—you can follow only a large road. In microscopic terms this means only a large object, with large edges and gentle curves: cells, and nuclei. But an electron microscope can follow all the minor routes, the byroads, and can outline very small structures within the cell—mitochondria, ribosomes, membranes, reticula."

In actual practice there were several drawbacks to the electron microscope, which counterbalanced its great powers of magnification. For one thing, because it used electrons instead of light, the inside of the microscope had to be a vacuum. This meant it was impossible to examine living creatures.

But the most serious drawback had to do with the sections of specimen. These were extremely thin, making it difficult to get a good three-dimensional concept of the object under study.

Again, Polton had a simple analogy. "Let us say you cut an automobile in half down the middle. In that case, you could guess the complete, 'whole' structure. But if you cut a very thin slice from the automobile, and if you cut it on a strange angle, it could be more difficult. In your slice, you might have only a bit of bumper, and rubber tire, and glass. From such a slice, it would be hard to guess the shape and function of the full structure."

Stone was aware of all the drawbacks as he fitted the metal button into the EM, sealed it shut, and started the vacuum pump. He knew the drawbacks and he ignored them, because he had no choice. Limited as it was, the electron microscope was their only available high-power tool.

He turned down the room lights and clicked on the beam. He adjusted several dials to focus the beam. In a moment, the image came into focus, green and black on the screen.

It was incredible.

Jeremy Stone found himself staring at a single unit of the organism. It was a perfect, six-sided hexagon, and it interlocked with other hexagons on each side. The interior of the hexagon was divided into wedges, each meeting at the precise center of the structure. The overall appearance was accurate, with a kind of mathematical precision he did not associate with life on earth.

It looked like a crystal.

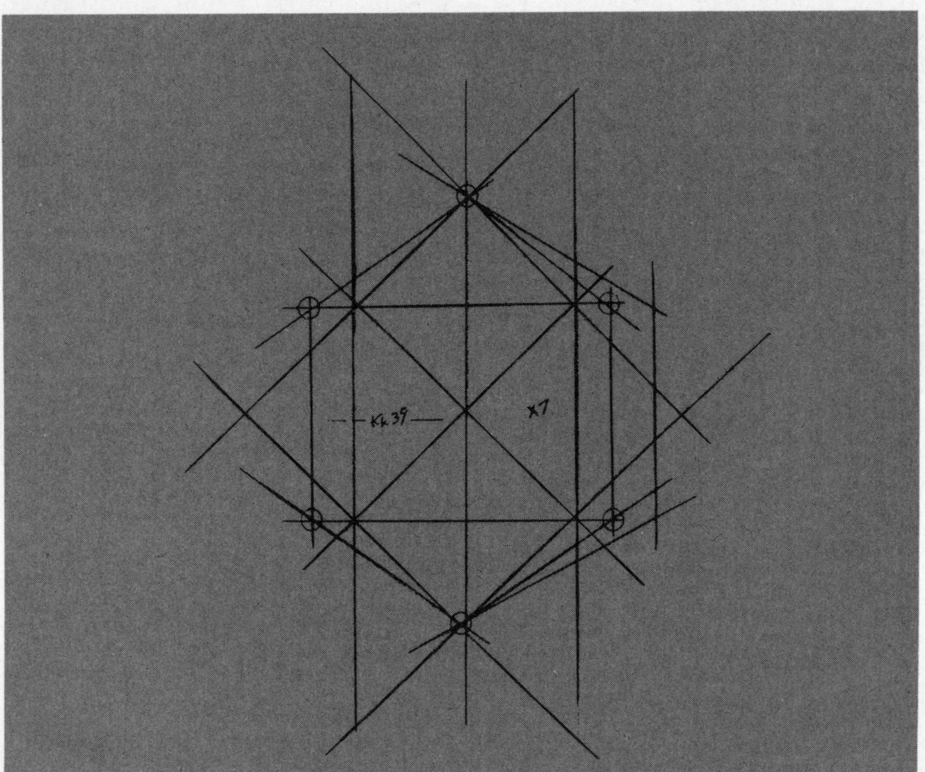

Early sketch by Jeremy Stone of hexagonal Andromeda configuration.

Photo courtesy Project Wildfire

He smiled: Leavitt would be pleased. Leavitt liked spectacular, mind-stretching things. Leavitt had also frequently considered the possibility that life might be based upon crystals of some kind, that it might be ordered in some regular pattern.

He decided to call Leavitt in.

As soon as he arrived, Leavitt said, "Well, there's our answer."

"Answer to what?"

"To how this organism functions. I've seen the results of spectrometry and amino-acid analysis."

"And?"

"The organism is made of hydrogen, carbon, oxygen, and nitrogen. But it has no amino acids at all. None. Which means that it has no proteins as we know them, and no enzymes. I was wondering how it could survive without protein-based organization. Now I know."

"The crystalline structure."

"Looks like it," Leavitt said, peering at the screen. "In three dimensions, it's probably a hexagonal slab, like a piece of tile. Eight-sided, with each face a hexagon. And on the inside, those wedge-shaped compartments leading to the center."

"They would serve to separate biochemical functions quite well."

"Yes," Leavitt said. He frowned.

"Something the matter?"

Leavitt was thinking, remembering something he had forgotten. A dream, about a house and a city. He thought for a moment and it began to come back to him. A house and a city. The way the house worked alone, and the way it worked in a city.

It all came back.

"You know," he said, "it's interesting, the way this one unit interlocks with the others around it."

"You're wondering if we're seeing part of a higher organism?"

"Exactly. Is this unit self-sufficient, like a bacterium, or is it just a block from a larger organ, or a larger organism? After all, if you saw a single liver cell, could you guess what kind of an organ it came from? No. And what good would one brain cell be without the rest of the brain?"

Stone stared at the screen for a long time. "A rather unusual pair of analogies. Because the liver can regenerate, can grow back, but the brain cannot."

Leavitt smiled. "The Messenger Theory."

"One wonders," Stone said.

The Messenger Theory had come from John R. Samuels, a communications engineer. Speaking before the Fifth Annual Conference on Astronautics and Communication, he had reviewed some theories about the way in which an alien culture might choose to contact other cultures. He argued that the most advanced concepts in communications in earth technology were inadequate, and that advanced cultures would find better methods.

"Let us say a culture wishes to scan the universe," he said. "Let us say they wish to have a sort of 'coming-out party' on a galactic scale—to formally announce their existence. They wish to spew out information, clues to their existence, in every direction. What is the best way to do this? Radio? Hardly—radio is too slow, too expensive, and it decays too rapidly. Strong signals weaken within a few billion miles. TV is even worse. Light rays are fantastically expensive to generate. Even if one learned a way to detonate whole stars, to explode a sun as a kind of signal, it would be costly.

"Besides expense, all these methods suffer the traditional drawback to any radiation, namely decreasing strength with distance. A light bulb may be unbearably bright at ten feet; it may be powerful at a thousand feet; it may be visible at ten miles. But at a million miles, it is completely obscure, because radiant energy decreases according to the fourth power of the radius. A simple, unbeatable law of physics.

"So you do not use physics to carry your signal. You use biology. You create a communications system that does not diminish with distance, but rather remains as powerful a million miles away as it was at the source.

"In short, you devise an organism to carry your message. The organism would be self-replicating, cheap, and could be produced in fantastic numbers. For a few dollars, you could produce trillions of them, and send them off in all directions into space. They would be tough, hardy bugs, able to withstand the rigors of space, and they would grow and duplicate and divide. Within a few years, there would be countless numbers of these in the galaxy, speeding in all directions, waiting to contact life.

"And when they did? Each single organism would carry the potential to develop into a full organ, or a full organism. They would, upon contacting life, begin to grow into a complete communicating mechanism. It is like spewing out a billion brain cells, each capable of regrowing a complete brain under the proper circumstances. The newly grown brain would then speak to the new culture—informing it of the presence of the other, and announcing ways in which contact might be made."

Samuels's theory of the Messenger Bug was considered amusing by practical scientists, but it could not be discounted now.

"Do you suppose," Stone said, "that it is already developing into some kind of organ of communication?"

"Perhaps the cultures will tell us more," Leavitt said.

"Or X-ray crystallography," Stone said. "I'll order it now."

Level V had facilities for X-ray crystallography, though there had been much heated discussion during Wildfire planning as to whether such facilities were necessary. X-ray crystallography represented the most advanced, complex, and expensive method of structural analysis in modern biology. It was a little like electron microscopy, but one step further along the line. It was more sensitive, and could probe deeper—but only at great cost in terms of time, equipment, and personnel.

The biologist R. A. Janek has said that "increasing vision is increasingly expensive." He meant by this that any machine to enable men to see finer or fainter details increased in cost faster than it increased in resolving power. This hard fact of research was discovered first by the astronomers, who learned painfully that construction of a two-hundred-inch telescope mirror was far more difficult and expensive than construction of a one-hundred-inch mirror.

In biology this was equally true. A light microscope, for example, was a small device easily carried by a technician in one hand. It could outline a cell, and for this ability a scientist paid about $1,000.

An electron microscope could outline small structures within the cell. The EM was a large console and cost up to $100,000.

In contrast, X-ray crystallography could outline individual molecules. It came as close to photographing atoms as science could manage. But the device was the size of a large automobile, filled an entire room, required specially trained operators, and demanded a computer for interpretation of results.

This was because X-ray crystallography did not produce a direct visual picture of the object being studied. It was not, in this sense, a microscope, and it operated differently from either the light or electron microscope.

It produced a diffraction pattern instead of an image. This appeared as a pattern of geometric dots, in itself rather mysterious, on a photographic plate. By using a computer, the pattern of dots could be analyzed and the structure deduced.

It was a relatively new science, retaining an old-fashioned name. Crystals were seldom used any more; the term "X-ray crystallography" dated from the days when crystals were chosen as test objects. Crystals had regular structures and thus the pattern of dots resulting from a beam of X rays shot at a crystal were easier to analyze. But in recent years the X rays had been shot at irregular objects of varying sorts. The X rays were bounced off at different angles. A computer could "read" the photographic plate and measure the angles, and from this work back to the shape of the object that had caused such a reflection.

The computer at Wildfire performed the endless and tedious calculations. All this, if done by manual human calculation, would take years, perhaps centuries. But the computer could do it in seconds.

"How are you feeling, Mr. Jackson?" Hall asked.

The old man blinked his eyes and looked at Hall, in his plastic suit. "All right. Not the best, but all right."

He gave a wry grin.

"Up to talking a little?"

"About what?"

"Piedmont."

"What about it?"

"That night," Hall said. "The night it all happened."

"Well, I tell you. I've lived in Piedmont all my life. Traveled a bit—been to LA, and even up to Frisco. Went as far east as St. Louis, which was far enough for me. But Piedmont, that's where I've lived. And I have to tell you—"

"The night it all happened," Hall repeated.

He stopped, and turned his head away. "I don't want to think about it," he said.

"You have to think about it."

"No."

He continued to look away for a moment, and then turned back to Hall. "They all died, did they?"

"Not all. One other survived." He nodded to the crib next to Jackson.

Jackson peered over at the bundle of blankets. "Who's that?"

"A baby."

"Baby? Must be the Ritter child. Jamie Ritter. Real young, is it?"

"About two months."

"Yep. That's him. A real little heller. Just like the old man. Old Ritter likes to kick up a storm, and his kid's the same way. Squalling morning, noon, and night. Family couldn't keep the windas open, on account of the squalling."

"Is there anything else unusual about Jamie?"

"Nope. Healthy as a water buffalo, except he squalls. I remember he was squalling like the dickens that night."

Hall said, "What night?"

"The night Charley Thomas brought the damned thing in. We all seen it, of course. It came down like one of them shooting stars, all glowing, and landed just to the north. Everybody was excited, and Charley Thomas went off to get it. Came back about twenty minutes later with the thing in the back of his Ford station wagon. Brand-new wagon. He's real proud of it."

"Then what happened?"

"Well, we all gathered around, looking at it. Reckoned it must be one of those space things. Annie figured it was from Mars, but you know how Annie is. Let's her mind carry her off, at times. The rest of us, we didn't feel it was no Martian thing, we just figured it was something sent up from Cape Canaveral. You know, that place in Florida where they shoot the rockets?"

"Yes. Go on."

"So, once we figured that out good and proper, we didn't know what to do. Nothing like that ever happened in Piedmont, you know. I mean, once we had that tourist with the gun, shot up the Comanche Chief motel, but that was back in '48 and besides, he was just a GI had a little too much to drink, and there were exterminating circumstances. His gal run out on him while he was in Germany or some damn place. Nobody gave him a bad time; we understood how it was. But nothing happened since, really. Quiet town. That's why we like it, I reckon."

"What did you do with the capsule?"

"Well, we didn't know what to do with it. Al, he said open 'er up, but we didn't figure that was right, especially since it might have some scientific stuff inside, so we thought awhile. And then Charley, who got it in the first place, Charley says, let's give it to Doc. That's Doc Benedict. He's the town doctor. Actually, he takes care of everybody around, even the Indians. But he's a good fella anyhow, and he's been to lots of schools. Got these degrees on the walls? Well, we figured Doc Benedict would know what to do with the thing. So we brought it to him."

"And then?"

"Old Doc Benedict, he's not so old actually, he looks 'er over real careful, like it was his patient, and then he allows as how it might be a thing from space, and it might be one of ours, or it might be one of theirs. And he says he'll take care of it, and maybe make a few phone calls, and let everybody know in a few hours. See, Doc always played poker Monday nights with Charley and Al and Herb Johnstone, over at Herb's place, and we figured that he'd spread the word around then. Besides, it was getting on suppertime and most of us were a bit hungry, so we all kind of left it with Doc."

"When was that?"

"Bout seven-thirty or so."

"What did Benedict do with the satellite?"

"Took it inside his house. None of us saw it again. It was about eight, eight-thirty that it all started up, you see. I was over at the gas station, having a chat with Al, who was working the pump that night. Chilly night, but I wanted a chat to take my mind off the pain. And to get some soda from the machine, to wash down the aspirin with. Also, I was thirsty, squeeze makes you right thirsty, you know."

"You'd been drinking Sterno that day?"

"Bout six o'clock I had some, yes."

"How did you feel?"

"Well, when I was with Al, I felt good. Little dizzy, and my stomach was paining me, but I felt good. And Al and me were sitting inside the office, you know, talking, and suddenly he shouts, 'Oh God, my head!" He ups and runs outside, and falls down. Right there in the street, not a word from him.

"Well, I didn't know what to make of it. I figured he had a heart attack or a shock, but he was pretty young for that, so I went after him. Only he was dead. Then . . . they all started coming out. I believe Mrs. Langdon, the Widow Langdon, was next. After that, I don't recall, there was so many of them. Just pouring outside, it seemed like. And they just grab their chests and fall, like they slipped. Only they wouldn't get up afterward. And never a word from any of them."

"What did you think?"

"I didn't know what to think, it was so damned peculiar. I was scared, I don't mind telling you, but I tried to stay calm. I couldn't, naturally. My old heart was thumping, and I was wheezin' and gaspin'. I was scared. I thought everybody was dead. Then I heard the baby crying, so I knew not *everybody* could be dead. And then I saw the General."

"The General?"

"Oh, we just called him that. He wasn't no general, just been in the war, and liked to be remembered. Older'n me, he is. Nice fella, Peter Arnold. Steady as a rock all his life and he's standing by the porch, all got up in his military clothes. It's dark, but there's a moon, and he sees me in the street and he says, 'That you, Peter?' We both got the same name, see. And I says, 'Yes it is.' And he says, 'What the hell's happening? Japs coming in?' And I think that's a mighty peculiar thing for him to be saying. And he says, 'I think it must be the Japs, come to kill us all.' And I say, 'Peter, you gone loco?' And he says he don't feel too good and he goes inside. Course, he must have gone loco, 'cause he shot himself. But others went loco, too. It was the disease."

"How do you know?"

"People don't burn themselves, or drown themselves, if they got sense, do they? All them in that town were good, normal folks until that night. Then they just seemed to go crazy."

"What did you do?"

"I thought to myself, Peter, you're dreaming. You had too much to drink. So I went home and got into bed, and figured I'd be better in the morning. Only about ten o'clock, I hear a noise, and it's a car, so I go outside to see who it is. It's some kind of car, you know, one of those vans. Two fellers inside. I go up to them, and damn but they don't fall over dead. Scariest thing you ever saw. But it's funny."

"What's funny?"

"That was the only other car to come through all night. Normally, there's lots of cars."

"There was another car?"

"Yep. Willis, the highway patrol. He came through about fifteen, thirty seconds before it all started. Didn't stop, though; sometimes he doesn't. Depends if he's late on his schedule; he's got a regular patrol, you know, he has to stick to."

Jackson sighed and let his head fall back against the pillow. "Now," he said, "if you don't mind, I'm going to get me some sleep. I'm all talked out."

He closed his eyes. Hall crawled back down the tunnel, out of the unit, and sat in the room looking through the glass at Jackson, and the baby in the crib alongside. He stayed there, just looking, for a long time.

Chapter 23

Topeka

The room was huge, the size of a football field. It was furnished sparsely, just a few tables scattered about. Inside the room, voices echoed as the technicians called to each other, positioning the pieces of wreckage. The post team was reconstructing the wreck in this room, placing the clumps of twisted metal from the Phantom in the same positions as they had been found on the sand.

Only then would the intensive examination begin.

Major Manchek, tired, bleary-eyed, clutching his coffee cup, stood in a corner and watched. To him, there was something surrealistic about the scene: a dozen men in a long, white-washed room in Topeka, rebuilding a crash.

One of the biophysicists came up to him, holding a clear plastic bag. He waved the contents under Manchek's nose.

"Just got it back from the lab," he said.

"What is it?"

"You'll never guess." The man's eyes gleamed in excitement.

All right, Manchek thought irritably, I'll never guess. "What is it?"

"A depolymerized polymer," the biochemist said, smacking his lips with satisfaction. "Just back from the lab."

"What kind of polymer?"

A polymer was a repeating molecule, built up from thousands of the same units, like a stack of dominos. Most plastics, nylon, rayon, plant cellulose, and even glycogen in the human body were polymers.

"A polymer of the plastic used on the air hose of the Phantom jet. The face mask to the pilot. We thought as much."

Manchek frowned. He looked slowly at the crumbly black powder in the bag. "Plastic?"

"Yes. A polymer, depolymerized. It was broken down. Now that's no vibration effect. It's a biochemical effect, purely organic."

Slowly, Manchek began to understand. "You mean something tore the plastic apart?"

"Yes, you could say that," the biochemist replied. "It's a simplification, of course, but—"

"What tore it apart?"

The biochemist shrugged. "Chemical reaction of some sort. Acid could do it, or intense heat, or . . ."

"Or?"

"A microorganism, I suppose. If one existed that could eat plastic. If you know what I mean."

"I think," Manchek said, "that I know what you mean."

He left the room and went to the cable transmitter, located in another part of the building. He wrote out his message to the Wildfire group, and gave it to the technician to transmit. While he waited, he said, "Has there been any reply yet?"

"Reply, sir?" the technician asked.

"From Wildfire," Manchek said. It was incredible to him that no one had acted upon the news of the Phantom crash. It was so obviously linked . . .

"Wildfire, sir?" the technician asked.

Manchek rubbed his eyes. He was tired: he would have to remember to keep his big mouth shut.

"Forget it," he said.

After his conversation with Peter Jackson, Hall went to see Burton. Burton was in the autopsy room, going over his slides from the day before.

Hall said, "Find anything?"

Burton stepped away from the microscope and sighed. "No. Nothing."

"I keep wondering," Hall said, "about the insanity. Talking with Jackson reminded me of it. A large number of people in that town went insane—or at least became bizarre and suicidal—during the evening. Many of those people were old."

Burton frowned. "So?"

"Old people," Hall said, "are like Jackson. They have lots wrong with them. Their bodies are breaking down in a variety of ways. The lungs are bad. The hearts are bad. The livers are shot. The vessels are sclerotic."

"And this alters the disease process?"

"Perhaps. I keep wondering. What makes a person become rapidly insane?"

Burton shook his head.

"And there's something else," Hall said. "Jackson recalls hearing one victim say, just before he died, 'Oh, God, my head.' "

Burton stared away into space. "Just before death?"

"Just before."

"You're thinking of hemorrhage?"

Hall nodded. "It makes sense," he said. "At least to check."

If the Andromeda Strain produced hemorrhage inside the brain for any reason, then it might produce rapid, unusual mental aberrations.

"But we already know the organism acts by clotting—"

"Yes," Hall said, "in most people. Not all. Some survive, and some go mad."

Burton nodded. He suddenly became excited. Suppose that the organism acted by causing damage to blood vessels. This damage would initiate clotting. Anytime the wall of a blood vessel was torn, or cut, or burned, then the clotting sequence would begin. First platelets would clump around the injury, protecting it, preventing blood loss. Then red cells would accumulate. Then a fibrin mesh would bind all the elements together. And finally, the clot would become hard and firm.

That was the normal sequence.

But if the damage was extensive, if it began at the lungs and worked its way . . .

"I'm wondering," Hall said, "if our organism attacks vessel walls. If so, it would initiate clotting. But if clotting were prevented in certain persons, then the organism might eat away and cause hemorrhage in those persons."

"And insanity," Burton said, hunting through his slides. He found three of the brain, and checked them.

No question.

The pathology was striking. Within the internal layer of cerebral vessels were small deposits of green. Burton had no doubt that, under higher magnification, they would turn out to be hexagonal in shape.

Quickly, he checked the other slides, for vessels in lung, liver, and spleen. In several instances he found green spots in the vessel walls, but never in the profusion he found for cerebral vessels.

Obviously the Andromeda Strain showed a predilection for cerebral vasculature. It was impossible to say why, but it was known that the cerebral vessels are peculiar in several respects. For instance, under circumstances in which normal body vessels dilate or contract—such as extreme cold, or exercise—the brain vasculature does not change, but maintains a steady, constant blood supply to the brain.

In exercise, the blood supply to muscle might increase five to twenty times. But the brain always has a steady flow: whether its owner is taking an exam or a nap, chopping wood or watching TV. The brain receives the same amount of blood every minute, hour, day.

The scientists did not know why this should be, or how, precisely, the cerebral vessels regulate themselves. But the phenomenon is known to exist, and cerebral vessels are regarded as a special case among the body's arteries and veins. Clearly, something is different about them.

And now there was an example of an organism that destroyed them preferentially.

But as Burton thought about it, the action of Andromeda did not seem so unusual. For example, syphilis causes an inflammation of the aorta, a very specific, peculiar reaction. Schistosomiasis, a parasitic infection, shows a preference for bladder, intestine, or colonic vessels—depending on the species. So such specificity was not impossible.

"But there's another problem," he said. "In most people, the organism begins clotting at the lungs. We know that. Presumably vessel destruction begins there as well. What is different about—"

He stopped.

He remembered the rats he had anticoagulated. The ones who had died anyway, but had had no autopsies.

"My God," he said.

He drew out one of the rats from cold storage and cut it open. It bled. Quickly he incised the head, exposing the brain. There he found a large hemorrhage over the gray surface of the brain.

"You've got it," Hall said.

"If the animal is normal, it dies from coagulation, beginning at the lungs. But if coagulation is prevented, then the organism erodes through the vessels of the brain, and hemorrhage occurs."

"And insanity."

"Yes." Burton was now very excited. "And coagulation could be prevented by any blood disorder. Or too little vitamin K. Malabsorption syndrome. Poor liver function. Impaired protein synthesis. Any of a dozen things."

"All more likely to be found in an old person," Hall said.

"Did Jackson have any of those things?"

Hall took a long time to answer, then finally said, "No. He has liver disease, but not significantly."

Burton sighed. "Then we're back where we started."

"Not quite. Because Jackson and the baby both survived. They didn't hemorrhage—as far as we know—they survived untouched. Completely untouched."

"Meaning?"

"Meaning that they somehow prevented the primary process, which is invasion of the organism into the vessel walls of the body. The Andromeda organism didn't get to the lungs, or the brain. It didn't get anywhere."

"But why?"

"We'll know that," Hall said, "when we know why a sixty-nine-year-old Sterno drinker with an ulcer is like a two-month-old baby."

"They seem pretty much opposites," Burton said.

"They do, don't they?" Hall said. It would be hours before he realized Burton had given him the answer to the puzzle—but an answer that was worthless.

Chapter 24

Evaluation

Sir Winston Churchill once said that "true genius resides in the capacity for evaluation of uncertain, hazardous, and conflicting information." Yet it is a peculiarity of the Wildfire team that, despite the individual brilliance of team members, the group grossly misjudged their information at several points.

One is reminded of Montaigne's acerbic comment: "Men under stress are fools, and fool themselves." Certainly the Wildfire team was under severe stress, but they were also prepared to make mistakes. They had even predicted that this would occur.

What they did not anticipate was the magnitude, the staggering dimensions of their error. They did not expect that their ultimate error would be a compound of a dozen small clues that were missed, a handful of crucial facts that were dismissed.

The team had a blind spot, which Stone later expressed this way: "We were problem-oriented. Everything we did and thought was directed toward finding a solution, a cure to Andromeda. And, of course, we were fixed on the events that had occurred at Piedmont. We felt that if we did not find a solution, no solution would be forthcoming, and the whole world would ultimately wind up like Piedmont. We were very slow to think otherwise."

The error began to take on major proportions with the cultures.

Stone and Leavitt had taken thousands of cultures from the original capsule. These had been incubated in a wide variety of atmospheric, temperature, and pressure conditions. The results of this could only be analyzed by computer.

Using the GROWTH/TRANSMATRIX program, the computer did not print out results from all possible growth combinations. Instead, it printed out only significant positive and negative results. It did this after first weighing each petri dish, and examining any growth with its photoelectric eye.

When Stone and Leavitt went to examine the results, they found several striking trends. Their first conclusion was that growth media did not matter at all—the organism grew equally well on sugar, blood, chocolate, plain agar, or sheer glass.

However, the gases in which the plates were incubated were crucial, as was the light.

Ultraviolet light stimulated growth under all circumstances. Total darkness, and to a lesser extent infrared light, inhibited growth.

Oxygen inhibited growth in all circumstances, but carbon dioxide stimulated growth. Nitrogen had no effect.

Thus, best growth was achieved in 100-per cent carbon dioxide, lighted by ultraviolet radiation. Poorest growth occurred in pure oxygen, incubated in total darkness.

"What do you make of it?" Stone said.

"It looks like a pure conversion system," Leavitt said.

"I wonder," Stone said.

He punched through the coordinates of a closed-growth system. Closed-growth systems studied bacterial metabolism by measuring intake of gases and nutrients, and output of waste products. They were completely sealed and self-contained. A plant in such a system, for example, would consume carbon dioxide and give off water and oxygen.

But when they looked at the Andromeda Strain, they found something remarkable. The organism had no excretions. If incubated with carbon dioxide and ultraviolet light, it grew steadily until all carbon dioxide had been consumed. Then growth stopped. There was no excretion of any kind of gas or waste product at all.

No waste.

"Clearly efficient," Stone said.

"You'd expect that," Leavitt said.

This was an organism highly suited to its environment. It consumed everything, wasted nothing. It was perfect for the barren existence of space.

He thought about this for a moment, and then it hit him. It hit Leavitt at the same time.

"Good Christ."

```
CULTURE DESIG - 779,223,187,
ANDROMEDA
MEDIA DESIG - 779
ATMOSPHERE DESIG - 223
LUMIN DESIG - L87 UV/HI
FINAL SCANNER PRINT
```

An example of a scanner printout from the photoelectric eye that examined all growth media. Within the circular petri dish the computer has noted the presence of two separate colonies. The colonies are "read" in two-millimeter-square segments, and graded by density on a scale from one to nine.

Leavitt was already reaching for the phone. "Get Robertson," he said. "Get him immediately."

"Incredible," Stone said softly. "No waste. It doesn't require growth media. It can grow in the presence of carbon, oxygen, and sunlight. Period."

"I hope we're not too late," Leavitt said, watching the computer console screen impatiently.

Stone nodded. "If this organism is really converting matter to energy, and energy to matter—directly—then it's functioning like a little reactor."

"And an atomic detonation . . ."

"Incredible," Stone said. "Just incredible."

The screen came to life; they saw Robertson, looking tired, smoking a cigarette.

"Jeremy, you've got to give me time. I haven't been able to get through to—"

"Listen," Stone said, "I want you to make sure Directive 7-12 is not carried out. It is imperative: no atomic device must be detonated around the organisms. That's the last thing in the world, literally, that we want to do."

He explained briefly what he had found.

Robertson whistled. "We'd just provide a fantastically rich growth medium."

"That's right," Stone said.

The problem of a rich growth medium was a peculiarly distressing one to the Wildfire team. It was known, for example, that checks and balances exist in the normal environment. These manage to dampen the exuberant growth of bacteria.

The mathematics of uncontrolled growth are frightening. A single cell of the bacterium *E. coli* would, under ideal circumstances, divide every twenty minutes. That is not particularly disturbing until you think about it, but the fact is that bacteria multiply geometrically: one becomes two, two becomes four, four becomes eight, and so on. In this way, it can be shown that in a single day, one cell of *E. coli* could produce a supercolony equal in size and weight to the entire planet earth.

This never happens, for a perfectly simple reason: growth cannot continue indefinitely under "ideal circumstances." Food runs out. Oxygen runs out. Local conditions within the colony change, and check the growth of organisms.

On the other hand, if you had an organism that was capable of directly converting energy to matter, and if you provided it with a huge rich source of energy, like an atomic blast . . .

"I'll pass along your recommendation to the President," Robertson said. "He'll be pleased to know he made the right decision on the 7-12."

"You can congratulate him on his scientific insight," Stone said, "for me."

Robertson was scratching his head. "I've got some more data on the Phantom crash. It was over the area west of Piedmont at twenty-three thousand feet. The post team has found evidence of the disintegration the pilot spoke of, but the material that was destroyed was a plastic of some kind. It was depolymerized."

"What does the post team make of that?"

"They don't know what the hell to make of it," Robertson admitted. "And there's something else. They found a few pieces of bone that have been identified as human. A bit of humerus and tibia. Notable because they are clean—almost polished."

"Flesh burned away?"

"Doesn't look that way," Robertson said.

Stone frowned at Leavitt.

"What *does* it look like?"

"It looks like clean, polished bone," Robertson said. "They say it's weird as hell. And there's something else. We checked into the National Guard around Piedmont. The 112th is stationed in a hundred-mile radius, and it turns out they've been running patrols into the area for a distance of fifty miles. They've had as many as one hundred men west of Piedmont. No deaths."

"None? You're quite sure?"

"Absolutely."

"Were there men on the ground in the area the Phantom flew over?"

"Yes. Twelve men. They reported the plane to the base, in fact."

Leavitt said, "Sounds like the plane crash is a fluke."

Stone nodded. To Robertson: "I'm inclined to agree with Peter. In the absence of fatalities on the ground . . ."

"Maybe it's only in the upper air."

"Maybe. But we know at least this much: we know how Andromeda kills. It does so by coagulation. Not disintegration, or bone-cleaning, or any other damned thing. By coagulation."

"All right," Robertson said, "let's forget the plane for the time being."

It was on that note that the meeting ended.

Stone said, "I think we'd better check our cultured organisms for biologic potency."

"Run some of them against a rat?"

Stone nodded. "Make sure it's still virulent. Still the same."

Leavitt agreed. They had to be careful the organism didn't mutate, didn't change to something radically different in its effects.

As they were about to start, the Level V monitor clicked on and said, "Dr. Leavitt. Dr. Leavitt."

Leavitt answered. On the computer screen was a pleasant young man in a white lab coat.

"Yes?"

"Dr. Leavitt, we have gotten our electroencephalograms back from the computer center. I'm sure it's all a mistake, but . . ."

His voice trailed off.

"Yes?" Leavitt said. "Is something wrong?"

"Well, sir, yours were read as grade four, atypical, probably benign. But we would like to run another set."

Stone said, "It must be a mistake."

"Yes," Leavitt said. "It must be."

"Undoubtedly, sir," the man said. "But we would like another set of waves to be certain."

"I'm rather busy now," Leavitt said.

Stone broke in, talking directly to the technician. "Dr. Leavitt will get a repeat EEG when he has the chance."

"Very good, sir," the technician said.

When the screen was blank, Stone said, "There are times when this damned routine gets on anybody's nerves."

Leavitt said, "Yes."

They were about to begin biologic testing of the various culture media when the computer flashed that preliminary reports from X-ray crystallography were prepared. Stone and Leavitt left the room to check the results, delaying the biologic tests of media. This was a most unfortunate decision, for had they examined the media, they would have seen that their thinking had already gone astray, and that they were on the wrong track.

Chapter 25

Willis

X-ray crystallography analysis showed that the Andromeda organism was not composed of component parts, as a normal cell was composed of nucleus, mitochondria, and ribosomes. Andromeda had no subunits, no smaller particules. Instead, a single substance seemed to form the walls and interior. This substance produced a characteristic precession photograph, or scatter pattern of X rays.

Looking at the results, Stone said, "A series of six-sided rings."

"And nothing else," Leavitt said. "How the hell does it operate?"

The two men were at a loss to explain how so simple an organism could utilize energy for growth.

"A rather common ring structure," Leavitt said. "A phenolic group, nothing more. It should be reasonably inert."

"Yet it can convert energy to matter."

Leavitt scratched his head. He thought back to the city analogy, and the brain-cell analogy. The molecule was simple in its building blocks. It possessed no remarkable powers, taken as single units. Yet collectively, it had great powers.

"Perhaps there is a critical level," he suggested. "A structural complexity that makes possible what is not possible in a similar but simple structure."

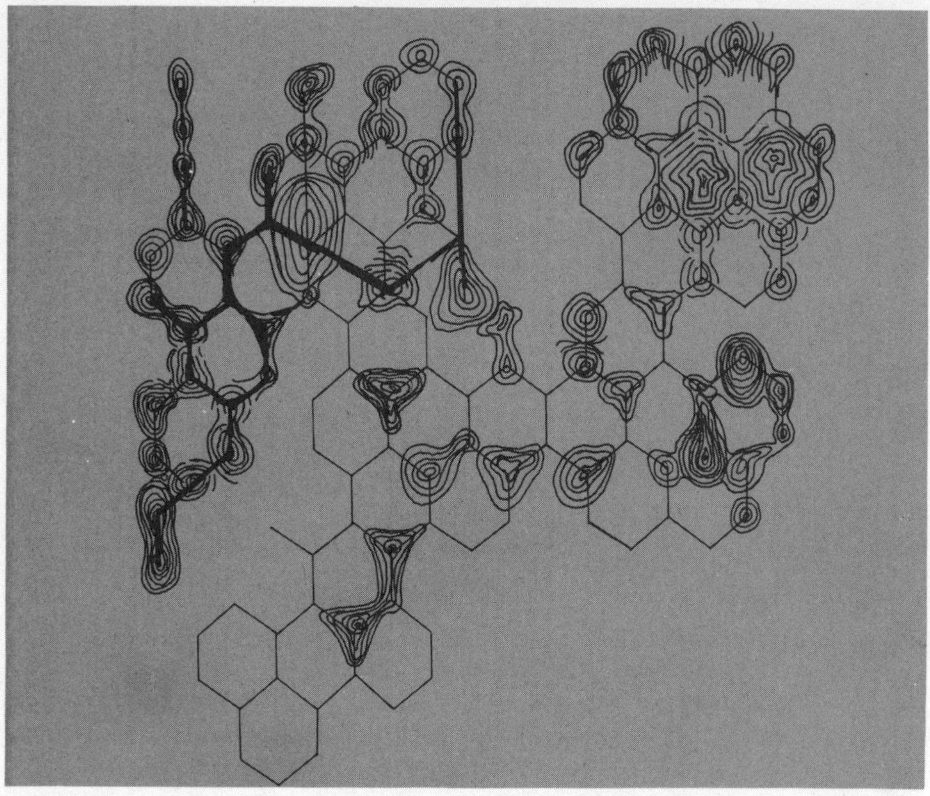

Electron-density mapping of Andromeda structure as derived from micrographic studies. It was this mapping which disclosed activity variations within an otherwise uniform structure.

Photo courtesy Project Wildfire

"The old chimp-brain argument," Stone said.

Leavitt nodded. As nearly as anyone could determine, the chimp brain was as complex as the human brain. There were minor differences in structure, but the major difference was size—the human brain was larger, with more cells, more interconnections.

And that, in some subtle way, made the human brain different. (Thomas Waldren, the neurophysiologist, once jokingly noted that the major difference between the chimp and human brain was that "we can use the chimp as an experimental animal, and not the reverse.")

Stone and Leavitt puzzled over the problem for several minutes until they came to the Fourier electron-density scans. Here, the probability of finding electrons was mapped for the structure on a chart that resembled a topological map.

They noticed something odd. The structure was present but the Fourier mapping was inconstant.

"It almost looks," Stone said, "as if part of the structure is switched off in some way."

"It's not uniform after all," Leavitt said.

Stone sighed, looking at the map. "I wish to hell," he said, "that we'd brought a physical chemist along on the team."

Unspoken was the added comment, "instead of Hall."

Tired, Hall rubbed his eyes and sipped the coffee, wishing he could have sugar. He was alone in the cafeteria, which was silent except for the muted ticking of the teleprinter in the corner.

After a time he got up and went over to the teleprinter, examining the rolls of paper that had come from it. Most of the information was meaningless to him.

But then he saw one item which had come from the DEATHMATCH program. DEATHMATCH was a news-scanning computer program that recorded all significant deaths according to whatever criterion the computer was fed. In this case, the computer was alerted to pick up all deaths in the Arizona-Nevada-California area, and to print them back.

The item he read might have gone unnoticed, were it not for Hall's conversation with Jackson. At the time, it had seemed like a pointless conversation to Hall, productive of little and consuming a great deal of time.

But now, he wondered.

PRINT PROGRAM
DEATHWATCH
DEATHMATCH/998
SCALE 7,Y,0. X,4,0
PRINT AS
ITEM FROM ASSOCIATED PRESS VERBATIM 778-778

BRUSH RIDGE, ARIZ.———,: An Arizona highway patrol officer was allegedly involved in the death today of five persons in a highway diner. Miss Sally Conover, waitress at the Dine-eze diner on Route 15, ten miles south of Flagstaff, was the sole survivor of the incident.

Miss Conover told investigators that at 2:40 A.M., Officer Martin Willis entered the diner and ordered coffee and donut. Officer Willis had frequently visited the diner in the past. After eating, he stated that he had a severe headache and that "his ulcer was acting up." Miss Conover gave him two aspirin and a tablespoon of bicarbonate of soda. According to her statement, Officer Willis then looked suspiciously at the other people in the diner and whispered, "They're after me."

Before the waitress could reply, Willis took out his revolver and shot the other customers in the diner, moving methodically from one to the next, shooting each in the forehead. Then, he allegedly turned to Miss Conover and, smiling, said "I love you, Shirley Temple," placed the barrel in his mouth, and fired the last bullet.

Miss Conover was released by police after questioning. The names of the deceased customers are not known at this time.

END ITEM VERBATIM
END PRINT
END PROGRAM

TERMINATE

Hall remembered that Officer Willis had gone through Piedmont earlier in the evening—just a few minutes before the disease broke out. He had gone through without stopping.

And had gone mad later on.

Connection?

He wondered. There might be. Certainly, he could see many similarities: Willis had an ulcer, had taken aspirin, and had, eventually, committed suicide.

That didn't prove anything, of course. It might be a wholly unrelated series of events. But it was certainly worth checking.

He punched a button on the computer console. The TV screen lighted and a girl at a switchboard, with a headset pressing down her hair, smiled at him.

"I want the chief medical officer for the Arizona highway patrol. The western sector, if there is one."

"Yes, sir," she said briskly.

A few moments later, the screen came back on. It was the operator. "We have a Dr. Smithson who is the medical officer for the Arizona highway patrol west of Flagstaff. He has no television monitor but you can speak to him on audio."

"Fine," Hall said.

There was a crackling, and a mechanical hum. Hall watched the screen, but the girl had shut down her own audio and was busy answering another call from elsewhere in the Wildfire station. While he watched her, he heard a deep, drawling voice ask tentatively, "Anyone there?"

"Hello, Doctor," Hall said. "This is Dr. Mark Hall, in . . . Phoenix. I'm calling for some information about one of your patrolmen, Officer Willis."

"The girl said it was some government thing," Smithson drawled. "That right?"

"That is correct. We require—"

"Dr. Hall," Smithson said, still drawling, "perhaps you'd identify yourself and your agency."

It occurred to Hall that there was probably a legal problem involved in Officer Willis's death. Smithson might be worried about that.

Hall said, "I am not at liberty to tell you exactly what it is—"

"Well, look here, Doctor. I don't give out information over the phone, and especially I don't when the feller at the other end won't tell me what it's all about."

Hall took a deep breath. "Dr. Smithson, I must ask you—"

"Ask all you want. I'm sorry, I simply won't—"

At that moment, a bell sounded on the line, and a flat mechanical voice said:

"Attention please. This is a recording. Computer monitors have analyzed cable properties of this communication and have determined that the communication is being recorded by the outside party. All parties should be informed that the penalty for outside recording of a classified government communication is a minimum of five years' prison sentence. If the recording is continued this connection will automatically be broken. This is a recording. Thank you."

There was a long silence. Hall could imagine the surprise Smithson was feeling; he felt it himself.

"What the hell kind of a place are you calling from, anyhow?" Smithson said finally.

"Turn it off," Hall said.

There was a pause, a click, then: "All right. It's off."

"I am calling from a classified government installation," Hall said.

"Well, look here, mister—"

"Let me be perfectly plain," Hall said. "This is a matter of considerable importance and it concerns Officer Willis. No doubt there's a court inquiry pending on him, and no doubt you'll be involved. We may be able to demonstrate that Officer Willis was not responsible for his actions, that he was suffering from a purely medical problem. But we can't do that unless you tell us what you know about his medical status. And if you don't tell us, Dr. Smithson, and tell us damned fast, we can have you locked away for twelve years for obstructing an official government inquiry. I don't care whether you believe that or not. I'm telling you, and you'd better believe it."

There was a very long pause, and finally the drawl: "No need to get excited, Doctor. Naturally, now that I understand the situation—"

"Did Willis have an ulcer?"

"Ulcer? No. That was just what he said, or was reported to have said. He never had an ulcer that I know of."

"Did he have any medical problem?"

"Diabetes," Smithson said.

"Diabetes?"

"Yeah. And he was pretty casual about it. We diagnosed him five, six years ago, at the age of thirty. Had a pretty severe case. We put him on insulin, fifty units a day, but he was casual, like I said. Showed up in the hospital once or twice in coma, because he wouldn't take his insulin. Said he hated the needles. We almost put him off the force, because we were afraid to let him drive a car—thought he'd go into acidosis at the wheel and conk out. We scared him plenty and he promised to go straight. That was three years ago, and as far as I know, he took his insulin regularly from then on."

"You're sure of that?"

"Well, I think so. But the waitress at that restaurant, Sally Conover, told one of our investigators that she figured Willis had been drinking, because she could smell liquor on his breath. And I know for a fact that Willis never touched a drop in his life. He was one of these real religious fellows. Never smoked and never drank. Always led a clean life. That was why his diabetes bothered him so: he felt he didn't deserve it."

Hall relaxed in his chair. He was getting near now, coming closer. The answer was within reach; the final answer, the key to it all.

"One last question," Hall said. "Did Willis go through Piedmont on the night of his death?"

"Yes. He radioed in. He was a little behind schedule, but he passed through. Why? Is it something about the government tests being held there?"

"No," Hall said, but he was sure Smithson didn't believe him.

"Well, listen, we're stuck here with a bad case, and if you have any information which would—"

"We will be in touch," Hall promised him, and clicked off.

The girl at the switchboard came back on.

"Is your call completed, Dr. Hall?"

"Yes. But I need information."

"What kind of information?"

"I want to know if I have the authority to arrest someone."

"I will check, sir. What is the charge?"

"No charge. Just to hold someone."

There was a moment while she looked over at her computer console.

"Dr. Hall, you may authorize an official Army interview with anyone involved in project business. This interview may last up to forty-eight hours."

"All right," Hall said. "Arrange it."

"Yes sir. Who is the person?"

"Dr. Smithson," Hall said.

The girl nodded and the screen went blank. Hall felt sorry for Smithson, but not very sorry; the man would have a few hours of sweating, but nothing more serious than that. And it was essential to halt rumors about Piedmont.

He sat back in his chair and thought about what he had learned. He was excited, and felt on the verge of an important discovery.

Three people:

A diabetic in acidosis, from failure to take insulin.

An old man who drank Sterno and took aspirin, also in acidosis.

A young infant.

One had survived for hours, the other two had survived longer, apparently permanently. One had gone mad, the other two had not. Somehow they were all interrelated.

In a very simple way.

Acidosis. Rapid breathing. Carbon-dioxide content. Oxygen saturation. Dizziness. Fatigue. Somehow they were all logically coordinated. And they held the key to beating Andromeda.

At that moment, the emergency bell sounded, ringing in a highpitched, urgent way as the bright-yellow light began to flash.

He jumped up and left the room.

Chapter 26

The Seal

In the corridor, he saw the flashing sign that indicated the source of the trouble: AUTOPSY. Hall could guess the problem—somehow the seals had been broken, and contamination had occurred. That would sound the alarm.

As he ran down the corridor, a quiet, soothing voice on the loudspeakers said, "Seal has been broken in Autopsy. Seal has been broken in Autopsy. This is an emergency."

His lab technician came out of the lab and saw him. "What is it?"

"Burton, I think. Infection spread."

"Is he all right?"

"Doubt it," Hall said, running. She ran with him.

Leavitt came out of the MORPHOLOGY room and joined them, sprinting down the corridor, around the gentle curves. Hall thought to himself that Leavitt was moving quite well, for an older man, when suddenly Leavitt stopped.

He stood riveted to the ground. And stared straight forward at the flashing sign, and the light above it, blinking on and off.

Hall looked back. "Come on," he said.

Then the technician: "Dr. Hall, he's in trouble."

Leavitt was not moving. He stood, eyes open, but otherwise he might have been asleep. His arms hung loosely at his sides.

"Dr. Hall."

Hall stopped, and went back.

"Peter, boy, come on, we need your—"

He said nothing more, for Leavitt was not listening. He was staring straight forward at the blinking light. When Hall passed his hand in front of his face, he did not react. And then Hall remembered the other blinking lights, the lights Leavitt had turned away from, had joked off with stories.

"The son of a bitch," Hall said. "Now, of all times."

"What is it?" the technician said.

A small dribble of spittle was coming from the corner of Leavitt's mouth. Hall quickly stepped behind him and said to the technician, "Get in front of him and cover his eyes. Don't let him look at the blinking light."

"Why?"

"Because it's blinking three times a second," Hall said.

"You mean—"

"He'll go any minute now."

Leavitt went.

With frightening speed, his knees gave way and he collapsed to the floor. He lay on his back and his whole body began to vibrate. It began with his hands and feet, then involved his entire arms and legs, and finally his whole body. He clenched his teeth and gave a gasping, loud cry. His head hammered against the floor; Hall slipped his foot beneath the back of Leavitt's head and let him bang against his toes. It was better than having him hit the hard floor.

"Don't try to open his mouth," Hall said. "You can't do it. He's clenched tight."

As they watched, a yellow stain began to spread at Leavitt's waist.

"He may go into status," Hall said. "Go to the pharmacy and get me a hundred milligrams of phenobarb. Now. In a syringe. We'll get him onto Dilantin later, if we have to."

Leavitt was crying, through his clenched teeth, like an animal. His body rapped like a tense rod against the floor.

A few moments later, the technician came back with the syringe. Hall waited until Leavitt relaxed, until his body stopped its seizures, and then he injected the barbiturate.

"Stay with him," he said to the girl. "If he has another seizure, just do what I did—put your foot under his head. I think he'll be all right. Don't try to move him."

And Hall ran down to the autopsy lab.

* * *

For several seconds, he tried to open the door to the lab, and then he realized it had been sealed off. The lab was contaminated. He went on to main control, and found Stone looking at Burton through the closed-circuit TV monitors.

Burton was terrified. His face was white and he was breathing in rapid, shallow gasps, and he could not speak. He looked exactly like what he was: a man waiting for death to strike him.

Stone was trying to reassure him. "Just take it easy, boy. Take it easy. You'll be okay. Just take it easy."

"I'm scared," Burton said. "Oh Christ, I'm scared . . ."

"Just take it easy," Stone said in a soft voice. "We know that Andromeda doesn't do well in oxygen. We're pumping pure oxygen through your lab now. For the moment, that should hold you."

Stone turned to Hall. "You took your time getting here. Where's Leavitt?"

"He fitted," Hall said.

"What?"

"Your lights flash at three per second, and he had a seizure."

"What?"

"Petit mal. It went on to a grand-mal attack; tonic clonic seizure, urinary incontinence, the whole bit. I got him onto phenobarb and came as soon as I could."

"Leavitt has epilepsy?"

"That's right."

Stone said, "He must not have known. He must not have realized."

And then Stone remembered the request for a repeat electroencephalogram.

"Oh," Hall said, "he knew, all right. He was avoiding flashing lights, which will bring on an attack. I'm sure he knew. I'm sure he has attacks where he suddenly doesn't know what happened to him, where he just loses a few minutes from his life and can't remember what went on."

"Is he all right?"

"We'll keep him sedated."

Stone said, "We've got pure oxygen running into Burton. That should help him, until we know something more." Stone flicked off the microphone button connecting voice transmission to Burton. "Actually, it will take several minutes to hook in, but I've told him we've already started. He's sealed off in there, so the infection is stopped at that point. The rest of the base is okay, at least."

Hall said, "How did it happen? The contamination."

"Seal must have broken," Stone said. In a lower voice, he added, "We knew it would, sooner or later. All isolation units break down after a certain time."

Hall said, "You think it was just a random event?"

"Yes," Stone said. "Just an accident. So many seals, so much rubber, of such-and-such a thickness. They'd all break, given time. Burton happened to be there when one went."

Hall didn't see it so simply. He looked in at Burton, who was breathing rapidly, his chest heaving in terror.

Hall said, "How long has it been?"

Stone looked up at the stop-clocks. The stop-clocks were special timing clocks that automatically cut in during emergencies. The stop-clocks were now timing the period since the seal broke.

"Four minutes."

Hall said, "Burton's still alive."

"Yes, thank God." And then Stone frowned. He realized the point.

"*Why*," Hall said, "*is he still alive?*"

"The oxygen . . ."

"You said yourself the oxygen isn't running yet. What's protecting Burton?"

At that moment, Burton said over the intercom, "Listen. I want you to try something for me."

Stone flicked on the microphone. "What?"

"Kalocin," Burton said.

"*No.*" Stone's reaction was immediate.

"Dammit, it's my life."

"No," Stone said.

Hall said, "Maybe we should try—"

"Absolutely not. We don't dare. Not even once."

Kalocin was perhaps the best-kept American secret of the last decade. Kalocin was a drug developed by Jensen Pharmaceuticals in the spring of 1965, an experimental chemical designated UJ-44759W, or K-9 in the short abbreviation. It had been found as a result of routine screening tests employed by Jensen for all new compounds.

Like most pharmaceutical companies, Jensen tested all new drugs with a scatter approach, running the compounds through a standard battery of tests designed to pick up any significant biologic activity. These tests were run on laboratory animals—rats, dogs, and monkeys. There were twenty-four tests in all.

Jensen found something rather peculiar about K-9. It inhibited growth. An infant animal given the drug never attained full adult size.

This discovery prompted further tests, which produced even more intriguing results. The drug, Jensen learned, inhibited metaplasia, the shift of normal body cells to a new and bizarre form, a precursor to cancer. Jensen became excited, and put the drug through intensive programs of study.

By September 1965, there could be no doubt: Kalocin stopped cancer. Through an unknown mechanism, it inhibited the reproduction of the virus responsible for myelogenous leukemia. Animals taking the drug did not develop the disease, and animals already demonstrating the disease showed a marked regression as a result of the drug.

The excitement at Jensen could not be contained. It was soon recognized that the drug was a broad-spectrum antiviral agent. It killed the virus of polio, rabies, leukemia, and the common wart. And, oddly enough, Kalocin also killed bacteria.

And fungi.

And parasites.

Somehow, the drug acted to destroy all organisms built on a unicellular structure, or less. It had no effect on organ systems—groups of cells organized into larger units. The drug was perfectly selective in this respect.

In fact, Kalocin was the universal antibiotic. It killed everything, even the minor germs that caused the common cold. Naturally, there were side effects—the normal bacteria in the intestines were destroyed, so that all users of the drug experienced massive diarrhea—but that seemed a small price to pay for a cancer cure.

In December 1965, knowledge of the drug was privately circulated among government agencies and important health officials. And then for the first time, opposition to the drug arose. Many men, including Jeremy Stone, argued that the drug should be suppressed.

But the arguments for suppression seemed theoretical, and Jensen, sensing billions of dollars at hand, fought hard for a clinical test. Eventually the government, the HEW, the FDA, and others agreed with Jensen and sanctioned further clinical testing over the protests of Stone and others.

In February 1966, a pilot clinical trial was undertaken. It involved twenty patients with incurable cancer, and twenty normal volunteers from the Alabama state penitentiary. All forty subjects took the drug daily for one month. Results were as expected: normal subjects experienced unpleasant side effects, but nothing serious. Cancer patients showed striking remission of symptoms consistent with cure.

On March 1, 1966, the forty men were taken off the drug. Within six hours, they were all dead.

It was what Stone had predicted from the start. He had pointed out that mankind had, over centuries of exposure, developed a carefully regulated immunity to most organisms. On his skin, in the air, in his lungs, gut, and even bloodstream were hundreds of different viruses and bacteria. They were potentially deadly, but man had adapted to them over the years, and only a few could still cause disease.

All this represented a carefully balanced state of affairs. If you introduced a new drug that killed *all* bacteria, you upset the balance and undid the evolutionary work of centuries. And you opened the way to superinfection, the problem of new organisms, bearing new diseases.

Stone was right: the forty volunteers each had died of obscure and horrible diseases no one had ever seen before. One man experienced swelling of his body, from head to foot, a hot, bloated swelling until he suffocated from pulmonary edema. Another man fell prey to an organism that ate away his stomach in a matter of hours. A third was hit by a virus that dissolved his brain to a jelly.

And so it went.

Jensen reluctantly took the drug out of further study. The government, sensing that Stone had somehow understood what was happening, agreed to his earlier proposals, and viciously suppressed all knowledge and experimentation with the drug Kalocin.

And that was where the matter had rested for two years.

Now Burton wanted to be given the drug.

"No," Stone said. "Not a chance. It might cure you for a while, but you'd never survive later, when you were taken off."

"That's easy for you to say, from where you are."

"It's not easy for me to say. Believe me, it's not." He put his hand over the microphone again. To Hall: "We know that oxygen inhibits growth of the Andromeda Strain. That's what we'll give Burton. It will be good for him—make him a little giddy, a little relaxed, and slow his breathing down. Poor fellow is scared to death."

Hall nodded. Somehow, Stone's phrase stuck in his mind: scared to death. He thought about it, and then began to see that Stone had hit upon something important. That phrase was a clue. It was the answer.

He started to walk away.

"Where are you going?"

"I've got some thinking to do."

"About what?"

"About being scared to death."

Chapter 27

Scared to Death

Hall walked back to his lab and stared through the glass at the old man and the infant. He looked at the two of them and tried to think, but his brain was running in frantic circles. He found it difficult to think logically, and his earlier sensation of being on the verge of a discovery was lost.

For several minutes, he stared at the old man while brief images passed before him: Burton dying, his hand clutched to his chest. Los Angeles in panic, bodies everywhere, cars going haywire, out of control . . .

It was then that he realized that he, too, was scared. Scared to death. The words came back to him.

Scared to death.

Somehow, that was the answer.

Slowly, forcing his brain to be methodical, he went over it again.

A cop with diabetes. A cop who didn't take his insulin and had a habit of going into ketoacidosis.

An old man who drank Sterno, which gave him methanolism, and acidosis.

A baby, who did . . . what? What gave him acidosis?

Hall shook his head. Always, he came back to the baby, who was normal, not acidotic. He sighed.

Take it from the beginning, he told himself. Be logical. If a man has metabolic acidosis—any kind of acidosis—what does he do?

He has too much acid in his body. He can die from too much acid, just as if he had injected hydrochloric acid into his veins.

Too much acid meant death.

But the body could compensate. By breathing rapidly. Because in that manner, the lungs blew off carbon dioxide, and the body's supply of carbonic acid, which was what carbon dioxide formed in the blood, decreased.

A way to get rid of acid.

Rapid breathing.

And Andromeda? What happened to the organism, when you were acidotic and breathing fast?

Perhaps fast breathing kept the organism from getting into your lungs long enough to penetrate to blood vessels. Maybe that was the answer. But as soon as he thought of it, he shook his head. No: something else. Some simple, direct fact. Something they had always known, but somehow never recognized.

The organism attacked through the lungs.

It entered the bloodstream.

It localized in the walls of arteries and veins, particularly of the brain.

It produced damage.

This led to coagulation. Which was dispersed throughout the body, or else led to bleeding, insanity, and death.

But in order to produce such rapid, severe damage, it would take many organisms. Millions upon millions, collecting in the arteries and veins. Probably you did not breathe in so many.

So they must multiply in the bloodstream.

At a great rate. A fantastic rate.

And if you were acidotic? Did that halt multiplication?

Perhaps.

Again, he shook his head. Because a person with acidosis like Willis or Jackson was one thing. But what about the baby?

The baby was normal. If it breathed rapidly, it would become alkalotic—basic, too little acid—not acidotic. The baby would go to the opposite extreme.

Hall looked through the glass, and as he did, the baby awoke. Almost immediately it began to scream, its face turning purple, the little eyes wrinkling, the mouth, toothless and smooth-gummed, shrieking.

Scared to death.

And then the birds, with the fast metabolic rate, the fast heart rates, the fast breathing rates. The birds, who did everything fast. They, too, survived.

Breathing fast?

Was it as simple as that?

He shook his head. It couldn't be.

He sat down and rubbed his eyes. He had a headache, and he felt tired. He kept thinking of Burton, who might die at any minute. Burton, sitting there in the sealed room.

Hall felt the tension was unbearable. He suddenly felt an overwhelming urge to escape it, to get away from everything.

The TV screen clicked on. His technician appeared and said, "Dr. Hall, we have Dr. Leavitt in the infirmary."

And Hall found himself saying, "I'll be right there."

He knew he was acting strangely. There was no reason to see Leavitt. Leavitt was all right, perfectly fine, in no danger. In going to see him, Hall knew that he was trying to forget the other, more immediate problems. As he entered the infirmary, he felt guilty.

His technician said, "He's sleeping."

"Post-ictal," Hall said. Persons after a seizure usually slept.

"Shall we start Dilantin?"

"No. Wait and see. Perhaps we can hold him on phenobarb."

He began a slow and meticulous examination of Leavitt. His technician watched him and said, "You're tired."

"Yes," said Hall. "It's past my bedtime."

On a normal day, he would now be driving home on the expressway. So would Leavitt: going home to his family in Pacific Palisades. The Santa Monica Expressway.

He saw it vividly for a moment, the long lines of cars creeping slowly forward.

And the signs by the side of the road. Speed limit 65 maximum, 40 minimum. They always seemed like a cruel joke at rush hour.

Maximum and minimum.

Cars that drove slowly were a menace. You had to keep traffic moving at a fairly constant rate, little difference between the fastest and the slowest, and you had to . . .

He stopped.

"I've been an idiot," he said.

And he turned to the computer.

In later weeks, Hall referred to it as his "highway diagnosis." The principle of it was so simple, so clear and obvious, he was surprised none of them had thought of it before.

He was excited as he punched in instructions for the GROWTH program into the computer; he had to punch in the directions three times; his fingers kept making mistakes.

At last the program was set. On the display screen, he saw what he wanted: growth of Andromeda as a function of pH, of acidity-alkalinity.

The results were quite clear:

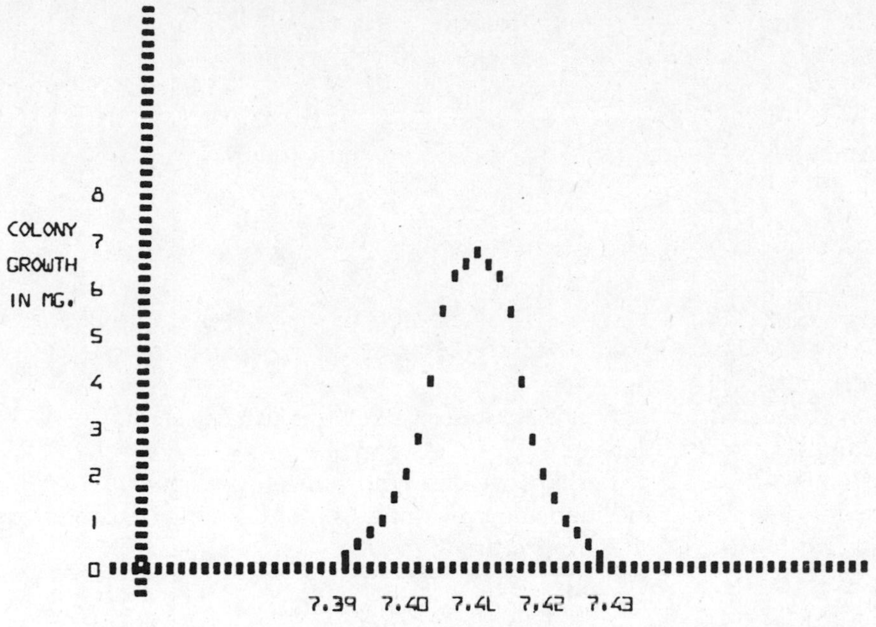

ACIDITY OF MEDIUM AS LOG H - ION CONCENTRATION

CORRECTED FOR SKEW

MEANS. MODES. S.D. FOUND

IN CORREL/PRINT

MM -76

CALL COORDINATES

0.Y.88.Z.09.

REVIEW CHECK

END PRINT

The Andromeda Strain grew within a narrow range. If the medium for growth was too acid, the organism would not multiply. If it was too basic, it would not multiply. Only within the range of pH 7.39 to 7.43 would it grow well.

He stared at the graph for a moment, then ran for the door. On his way out he grinned at his assistant and said, "It's all over. Our troubles are finished."

He could not have been more wrong.

Chapter 28

The Test

In the main control room, Stone was watching the television screen that showed Burton in the sealed lab.

"The oxygen's going in," Stone said.

"Stop it," Hall said.

"What?"

"Stop it now. Put him on room air."

Hall was looking at Burton. On the screen, it was clear that the oxygen was beginning to affect him. He was no longer breathing so rapidly; his chest moved slowly.

He picked up the microphone.

"Burton," he said, "this is Hall. I've got the answer. The Andromeda Strain grows within a narrow range of pH. Do you understand? A very narrow range. If you're either acidotic or alkalotic, you'll be all right. I want you to go into respiratory alkalosis. I want you to breathe as fast as you can."

Burton said, "But this is pure oxygen. I'll hyperventilate and pass out. I'm a little dizzy now."

"No. We're switching back to air. Now start breathing as fast as you can."

Hall turned back to Stone. "Give him a higher carbon dioxide atmosphere."

"But the organism flourishes in carbon dioxide!"

"I know, but not at an unfavorable pH of the blood. You see, that's the problem: air doesn't matter, but blood does. We have to establish an unfavorable acid balance for Burton's blood."

Stone suddenly understood. "The child," he said. "It screamed."

"Yes."

"And the old fellow with the aspirin hyperventilated."

"Yes. And drank Sterno besides."

"And both of them shot their acid-base balance to hell," Stone said.

"Yes," Hall said. "My trouble was, I was hung up on the acidosis. I didn't understand how the baby could become acidotic. The answer, of course, was that it didn't. It became basic—too little acid. But that was all right—you could go either way, too much acid or too little—as long as you got out of the growth range of Andromeda."

He turned back to Burton. "All right now," he said. "Keep breathing rapidly. Don't stop. Keep your lungs going and blow off your carbon dioxide. How do you feel?"

"Okay," Burton panted. "Scared . . . but . . . okay."

"Good."

"Listen," Stone said, "we can't keep Burton that way forever. Sooner or later—"

"Yes," Hall said. "We'll alkalinize his blood."

To Burton: "Look around the lab. Do you see anything we could use to raise your blood pH?"

Burton looked. "No, not really."

"Bicarbonate of soda? Ascorbic acid? Vinegar?"

Burton searched frantically among the bottles and reagents on the lab shelf, and finally shook his head. "Nothing here that will work."

Hall hardly heard him. He had been counting Burton's respirations; they were up to thirty-five a minute, deep and full. That would hold him for a time, but sooner or later he would become exhausted—breathing was hard work—or pass out.

He looked around the lab from his vantage point. And it was while doing this that he noticed the rat. A black Norway, sitting calmly in its cage in a corner of the room, watching Burton.

He stopped.

"That rat . . ."

It was breathing slowly and easily. Stone saw the rat and said, "What the hell . . ."

And then, as they watched, the lights began to flash again, and the computer console blinked on:

EARLY DEGENERATIVE CHANGE IN GASKET
V-112-6886

"Christ," Stone said.

"Where does that gasket lead?"

"It's one of the core gaskets; it connects all the labs. The main seal is—"

The computer came back on.

DEGENERATIVE CHANGE IN GASKETS A-009-5478

V-430-0030

N-966-6656

They looked at the screen in astonishment. "Something is wrong," Stone said. "Very wrong."

In rapid succession the computer flashed the number of nine more gaskets that were breaking down.

"I don't understand . . ."

And then Hall said, "The child. Of course!"

"The child?"

"And that damned airplane. It all fits."

"What are you talking about?" Stone said.

"The child was normal," Hall said. "It could cry, and disrupt it's acid-base balance. Well and good. That would prevent the Andromeda Strain from getting into its bloodstream, and multiplying, and killing it."

"Yes, yes," Stone said. "You've told me all that."

"But what happens when the child stops crying?"

Stone stared at him. He said nothing.

"I mean," Hall said, "that sooner or later, that kid had to stop crying. It couldn't cry forever. Sooner or later, it would stop, and its acid-base balance would return to normal. Then it would be vulnerable to Andromeda."

"True."

"But it didn't die."

"Perhaps some rapid form of immunity—"

"No. Impossible. There are only two explanations. When the child stopped crying, either the organism was no longer there—had been blown away, cleared from the air—or else the organism—"

"Changed," Stone said. "Mutated."

"Yes. Mutated to a noninfectious form. And perhaps it is still mutating. Now it is no longer directly harmful to man, but it eats rubber gaskets."

"The airplane."

Hall nodded. "National guardsmen could be on the ground, and not be harmed. But the pilot had his aircraft destroyed because the plastic was dissolved before his eyes."

"So Burton is now exposed to a harmless organism. That's why the rat is alive."

"That's why Burton is alive," Hall said. "The rapid breathing isn't necessary. He's only alive because Andromeda changed."

"It may change again," Stone said. "And if most mutations occur at times of multiplication, when the organism is growing most rapidly—"

The sirens went off, and the computer flashed a message in red.

GASKET INTEGRITY ZERO. LEVEL V CONTAMINATED AND SEALED.

Stone turned to Hall. "Quick," he said, "get out of here. There's no substation in this lab. You have to go to the next sector."

For a moment, Hall did not understand. He continued to sit in his seat, and then, when the realization hit him, he scrambled for the door and hurried outside to the corridor. As he did so he heard a hissing sound, and a thump as a massive steel plate slid out from a wall and closed off the corridor.

Stone saw it and swore. "That does it," he said. "We're trapped here. And if that bomb goes off, it'll spread the organism all over the surface. There will be a thousand mutations, each killing in a different way. We'll never be rid of it."

Over the loudspeaker, a flat mechanical voice was saying, "The level is closed. The level is closed. This is an emergency. The level is closed."

There was a moment of silence, and then a scratching sound as a new recording came on, and Miss Gladys Stevens of Omaha, Nebraska, said quietly, "There are now three minutes to atomic self-destruct."

Chapter 29

Three Minutes

A new rising and falling siren came on, and all the clocks snapped their hands back to 1200 hours, and the second hands began to sweep out the time. The stop-clocks all glowed red, with a green line on the dial to indicate when detonation would occur.

And the mechanical voice repeated calmly, "There are now three minutes to self-destruct."

"Automatic," Stone said quietly. "The system cuts in when the level is contaminated. We can't let it happen."

Hall was holding the key in his hand. "There's no way to get to a substation?"

"Not on this level. Each sector is sealed from every other."

"But there *are* substations, on the other levels?"

"Yes . . ."

"How do I get up?"

"You can't. All the conventional routes are sealed."

"What about the central core?" The central core communicated with all levels.

Stone shrugged. "The safeguards . . ."

Hall remembered talking to Burton earlier about the central-core safeguards. In theory, once inside the central core you could go straight to the top. But in practice, there were ligamine sensors located around the core to prevent this. Originally intended to prevent escape of lab animals that might break free into the core, the sensors released ligamine, a curare derivative that was water-soluble, in the form of a gas. There were also automatic guns that fired ligamine darts.

The mechanical voice said, "There are now two minutes forty-five seconds to self-destruct."

Hall was already moving back into the lab and staring through the glass into the inner work area; beyond that was the central core.

Hall said, "What are my chances?"

"They don't exist," Stone explained.

Hall bent over and crawled through a tunnel into a plastic suit. He waited until it had sealed behind him, and then he picked up a knife and cut away the tunnel, like a tail. He breathed in the air of the lab, which was cool and fresh, and laced with Andromeda organisms.

Nothing happened.

Back in the lab, Stone watched him through the glass. Hall saw his lips move, but heard nothing; then a moment later the speakers cut in and he heard Stone say, "—best that we could devise."

"What was?"

"The defense system."

"Thanks very much," Hall said, moving toward the rubber gasket. It was circular and rather small, leading into the central core.

"There's only one chance," Stone said. "The doses are low. They're calculated for a ten-kilogram animal, like a large monkey, and you weigh seventy kilograms or so. You can stand a fairly heavy dose before—"

"Before I stop breathing," Hall said. The victims of curare suffocate to death, their chest muscles and diaphragms paralyzed. Hall was certain it was an unpleasant way to die.

"Wish me luck," he said.

"There are now two minutes thirty seconds to self-destruct," Gladys Stevens said.

Hall slammed the gasket with his fist, and it crumbled in a dusty cloud. He moved out into the central core.

It was silent. He was away from the sirens and flashing lights of the level, and into a cold, metallic, echoing space. The central core was perhaps thirty feet wide, painted a utilitarian gray; the core itself, a cylindrical shaft of cables and machinery, lay before him. On the walls he could see the rungs of a ladder leading upward to Level IV.

"I have you on the TV monitor," Stone's voice said. "Start up the ladder. The gas will begin any moment."

A new recorded voice broke in. "The central core has been contaminated," it said. "Authorized maintenance personnel are advised to clear the area immediately."

"Go!" Stone said.

Hall climbed. As he went up the circular wall, he looked back and saw pale clouds of white smoke blanketing the floor.

"That's the gas," Stone said. "Keep going."

Hall climbed quickly, hand over hand, moving up the rungs. He was breathing hard, partly from the exertion, partly from emotion.

"The sensors have you," Stone said. His voice was dull.

Stone was sitting in the Level V laboratory, watching on the consoles as the computer electric eyes picked up Hall and outlined his body moving up the wall. To Stone he seemed painfully vulnerable. Stone glanced over at a third screen, which showed the ligamine ejectors pivoting on their wall brackets, the slim barrels coming around to take aim.

"Go!"

On the screen, Hall's body was outlined in red on a vivid green background. As Stone watched, a crosshair was superimposed over the body, centering on the neck. The computer was programmed to choose a region of high blood flow; for most animals, the neck was better than the back.

Hall, climbing up the core wall, was aware only of the distance and his fatigue. He felt strangely and totally exhausted, as if he had been climbing for hours. Then he realized that the gas was beginning to affect him.

"The sensors have picked you up," Stone said. "But you have only ten more yards."

Hall glanced back and saw one of the sensor units. It was aimed directly at him. As he watched, it fired, a small puff of bluish smoke spurting from the barrel. There was a whistling sound, and then something struck the wall next to him, and fell to the ground.

"Missed that time. Keep going."

Another dart slammed into the wall near his neck. He tried to hurry, tried to move faster. Above, he could see the door with the plain white markings LEVEL IV. Stone was right; less than ten yards to go.

A third dart, and then a fourth. He still was untouched. For an ironic moment he felt irritation: the damned computers weren't worth anything, they couldn't even hit a simple target . . .

The next dart caught him in the shoulder, stinging as it entered his flesh, and then there was a second wave of burning pain as the liquid was injected. Hall swore.

Stone watched it all on the monitor. The screen blandly recorded STRIKE and then proceeded to rerun a tape of the sequence, showing the dart moving through the air, and hitting Hall's shoulder. It showed it three times in succession.

The voice said, "There are now two minutes to self-destruct."

"It's a low dose," Stone said to Hall. "Keep going."

Hall continued to climb. He felt sluggish, like a four-hundred pound man, but he continued to climb. He reached the next door just as a dart slammed into the wall near his cheekbone.

"Nasty."

"Go! Go!"

The door had a seal and handle. He tugged at the handle while still another dart struck the wall.

"That's it, that's it, you're going to make it," Stone said.

"There are now ninety seconds to self-destruct," the voice said.

The handle spun. With a hiss of air the door came open. He moved into an inner chamber just as a dart struck his leg with a brief, searing wave of heat. And suddenly, instantly, he was a thousand pounds heavier. He moved in slow motion as he reached for the door and pulled it shut behind him.

"You're in an airlock," Stone said. "Turn the next door handle."

Hall moved toward the inner door. It was several miles away, an infinite trip, a distance beyond hope. His feet were encased in lead; his legs were granite. He felt sleepy and achingly tired as he took one step, and then another, and another.

"There are now sixty seconds to self-destruct."

Time was passing swiftly. He could not understand it; everything was so fast, and he was so slow.

The handle. He closed his fingers around it, as if in a dream. He turned the handle.

"Fight the drug. You can do it," Stone said.

What happened next was difficult to recall. He saw the handle turn, and the door open; he was dimly aware of a girl, a technician, standing in the hallway as he staggered through. She watched him with frightened eyes as he took a single clumsy step forward.

"Help me," he said.

She hesitated; her eyes got wider, and then she ran down the corridor away from him.

He watched her stupidly, and fell to the ground. The substation was only a few feet away, a glittering, polished metal plate on the wall.

"Forty-five seconds to self-destruct," the voice said, and then he was angry because the voice was female, and seductive, and recorded, because someone had planned it this way, had written out a series of inexorable statements, like a script, which was now being followed by the computers, together with all the polished, perfect machinery of the laboratory. It was as if this was his fate, planned from the beginning.

And he was angry.

Later, Hall could not remember how he managed to crawl the final distance; nor could he remember how he was able to get to his knees and reach up with the key. He did remember twisting it in the lock, and watching as the green light came on again.

"Self-destruct has been canceled," the voice announced, as if it were quite normal.

Hall slid to the floor, heavy, exhausted, and watched as blackness closed in around him.

DAY 5

RESOLUTION

Chapter 30

The Last Day

A voice from very far away said, "He's fighting it."
"Is he?"
"Yes. Look."
And then, a moment later, Hall coughed as something was pulled from his throat, and he coughed again, gasped for air, and opened his eyes.
A concerned female face looked down at him. "You okay? It wears off quickly."
Hall tried to answer her but could not. He lay very still on his back, and felt himself breathe. It was a little stiff at first, but soon became much easier, his ribs going in and out without effort. He turned his head and said, "How long?"
"About forty seconds," the girl said, "as nearly as we can figure. Forty seconds without breathing. You were a little blue when we found you, but we got you intubated right away and onto a respirator."
"When was that?"
"Twelve, fifteen minutes ago. Ligamine is short-acting, but even so, we were worried about you. . . . How are you feeling?"
"Okay."
He looked around the room. He was in the infirmary on Level IV. On

the far wall was a television monitor, which showed Stone's face.

"Hello," Hall said.

Stone grinned. "Congratulations."

"I take it the bomb didn't?"

"The bomb didn't," Stone said.

"That's good," Hall said, and closed his eyes. He slept for more than an hour, and when he awoke the television screen was blank. A nurse told him that Dr. Stone was talking to Vandenburg.

"What's happening?"

"According to predictions, the organism is over Los Angeles now."

"And?"

The nurse shrugged. "Nothing. It seems to have no effect at all."

"None whatsoever," Stone said, much later. "It has apparently mutated to a benign form. We're still waiting for a bizarre report of death or disease, but it's been six hours now, and it gets less likely with every minute. We suspect that ultimately it will migrate back out of the atmosphere, since there's too much oxygen down here. But of course if the bomb had gone off in Wildfire . . ."

Hall said, "How much time was left?"

"When you turned the key? About thirty-four seconds."

Hall smiled. "Plenty of time. Hardly even exciting."

"Perhaps from where you were," Stone said. "But down on Level V, it was very exciting indeed. I neglected to tell you that in order to improve the subterranean detonation characteristics of the atomic device, all air is evacuated from Level V, beginning thirty seconds before explosion."

"Oh," Hall said.

"But things are now under control," Stone said. "We have the organism, and can continue to study it. We've already begun to characterize a variety of mutant forms. It's a rather astonishing organism in its versatility." He smiled. "I think we can be fairly confident that the organism will move into the upper atmosphere without causing further difficulty on the surface, so there's no problem there. And as for us down here, we understand what's happening now, in terms of the mutations. That's the important thing. That we understand."

"Understand," Hall repeated.

"Yes," Stone said. "We have to understand."

Epilogue

Officially, the loss of Andros V, the manned spacecraft that burned up as it reentered the atmosphere, was explained on the basis of mechanical failure. The tungsten-and-plastic-laminate heat shield was said to have eroded away under the thermal stress of returning to the atmosphere, and an investigation was ordered by NASA into production methods for the heat shield.

In Congress, and in the press, there was clamor for safer spacecraft. As a result of governmental and public pressure, NASA elected to postpone future manned flights for an indefinite period. This decision was announced by Jack Marriott, "the voice of Andros," in a press conference at the Manned Spaceflight Center in Houston. A partial transcript of the conference follows:

Q: Jack, when does this postponement go into effect?
A: Immediately. Right as I talk to you, we are shutting down.
Q: How long do you anticipate this delay will last?
A: I'm afraid that's impossible to say.
Q: Could it be a matter of months?
A: It could.

Q: Jack, could it be as long as a year?
A: It's just impossible for me to say. We must wait for the findings of the investigative committee.
Q: Does this postponement have anything to do with the Russian decision to curtail their space program after the crash of Zond 19?
A: You'd have to ask the Russians about that.
Q: I see that Jeremy Stone is on the list of the investigative committee. How did you happen to include a bacteriologist?
A: Professor Stone has served on many scientific advisory councils in the past. We value his opinion on a broad range of subjects.
Q: What will this delay do to the Mars-landing target date?
A: It will certainly set the scheduling back.
Q: Jack, how far?
A: I'll tell you frankly, it's something that all of us here would like to know. We regard the failure of Andros V as a scientific error, a breakdown in systems technology, and not as a specifically human error. The scientists are going over the problem now, and we'll have to wait for their findings. The decision is really out of our hands.
Q: Jack, would you repeat that?
A: The decision is out of our hands.

REFERENCES

Listed below is a selected bibliography of unclassified documents, reports, and references that formed the background to the book.

DAY ONE

1. Merrick, J. J. "Frequencies of Biologic Contact According to Speciation Probabilities," *Proceedings of the Cold Spring Harbor Symposia* 10:443–57.
2. Toller, G. G. *Essence and Evolution*. New Haven: Yale Univ. Press, 1953.
3. Stone, J., et al. "Multiplicative Counts in Solid Plating," *J. Biol. Res.* 17:323–7.
4. Stone, J., et al. "Liquid-Pure Suspension and Monolayer Media: A Review" *Proc. Soc. Biol. Phys.* 9:101–14.
5. Stone, J., et al. "Linear Viral Transformation Mechanisms," *Science* 107:2201–4.
6. Stone, J., "Sterilization of Spacecraft," *Science* 112:1198–2001.
7. Morley, A., et al. "Preliminary Criteria for a Lunar Receiving Laboratory," *NASA Field Reports*, #7703A, 123 pp.
8. Worthington, Al. et al. "The Axenic Environment and Life Support Systems Delivery," *Jet Propulsion Lab Tech. Mem.* 9:404–11.
9. Ziegler, V. A., et al. "Near Space Life: A Predictive Model for Retrieval Densities," *Astronaut. Aeronaut. Rev.* 19:449–507.
10. Testimony of Jeremy Stone before the Senate Armed Services Subcommittee, Space and Preparedness Subcommittee (see Appendix).
11. Manchek, A. "Audiometric Screening by Digital Computer," *Ann. Tech.* 7:1033–9.
12. Wilson, L. O., et al. "Unicentric Directional Routing." *J. Space Comm.* 43:34–41.
13. *Project Procedures Manual: Scoop.* U.S. Gov't Printing Office, publication #PJS-4431.
14. Comroe, L. "Critical Resonant Frequencies in Higher Vertebrate Animals," *Rev. Biol. Chem.* 109:43–59.
15. Pockran, A. *Culture, Crisis and Change*. Chicago: Univ. of Chicago Press, 1964.
16. Manchek, A. "Module Design for High-Impact Landing Ratios," *NASA Field Reports* #3–3476.
17. Lexwell, J. F., et al. "Survey Techniques by Multiple Spectrology," *USAF Technical Pubs.*, #55A-789.
18. Jaggers, N. A. et al. "The Direct Interpretation of Infrared Intelligence Data," *Tech. Rev. Soc.* 88:111–19.
19. Vanderlink, R. E. "Binominate Analysis of Personality Characteristics: A Predictive Model," *Pubs. NIMH* 3:199.
20. Vanderlink, R. E. "Multicentric, Problems in Personnel Prediction," *Proc. Symp. NIMH* 13:404–512.
21. Sanderson, L. L. "Continuous Screen Efficiency in Personnel Review," *Pubs. NIMH* 5:98.

REFERENCES

DAY TWO

1. Metterlinck, J. "Capacities of a Closed Cable-Link Communications System with Limited Entry Points," *J. Space Comm.* 14:777–801.
2. Leavitt, P. "Metabolic Changes in *Ascaris* with Environmental Stress," *J. Microbio, Parasitol.* 97:501–44.
3. Herrick, L. A. "Induction of Petit-Mal Epilepsy with Flashing Lights," *Ann. Neurol.* 8:402–19.
4. Burton, C., et al. "*Endotoxic properties of Staphylococcus aureus,*" *NEJM* 14:11–39.
5. Kenniston, N. N., et al., "Geographics by Computer: A Critical Review," *J. Geog. Geol.* 98:1–34.
6. Blakley, A. K. "Computerbase Output Mapping as a Predictive Technique," *Ann. Comp. Tech.* 18:8–40.
7. Vorhees, H. G. "The Time Course of Enzymatic Blocking Agents," *J. Phys. Chem.* 66:303–18.
8. Garrod, D. O. "Effects of Chlorazine on Aviary Metabolism: A Rate-Dependent Decoupler," *Rev. Biol. Sci.* 9:13–39.
9. Bagdell, R. L. "Prevailing Winds in the Southwest United States," *Gov. Weather Rev.* 81:-291–9.
10. Jaegers, A. A. *Suicide and Its Consequences.* Ann Arbor: Michigan Univ. Press, 1967.
11. Revel, T. W. "Optical Scanning in Machine-Score Programs," *Comp. Tech.* 12:34–51.
12. Kendrew, P. W. "Voice Analysis by Phonemic Inversion." *Ann Biol. Comp. Tech.* 19:35–61.
13. Ulrich, V., et al. "The Success of Battery Vaccinations in Previously Immunized Healthy Subjects," *Medicine* 180:901–6.
14. Rodney, K. G. "Electronic Body Analyzers with Multifocal Input," *NASA Field Reports* #2-223-1150.
15. Stone, J., et al. "Gradient Decontamination Procedures to Life Tolerances," *Bull Soc. Biol. Microbiol.* 16:84–90.
16. Howard, E. A. "Realtime Functions in Autoclock Transcription," *NASA Field Reports,* #4-564-0002.
17. Edmundsen, T. E. "Long Wave Asepsis Gradients," *Proc. Biol. Soc.* 13:343–51.

DAY THREE

1. Karp, J. "Sporulation and Calcium Dipicolonate Concentrations in Cell Walls," *Microbiol.* 55:180.
2. *Weekly Reports of the United States Air Force Satellite Tracking Stations,* NASA Res. Pubs., —.
3. Wilson, G. E. "Glove-box Asepsis and Axenic Environments," *J. Biol. Res.* 34:88–96.
4. Yancey, K. L., et al. "Serum Electrophoresis of Plasma Globulins in Man and the Great Apes," *Nature* 89:1101–9.
5. Garrison, H. W. "Laboratory Analysis by Computer: A Maximum Program," *Med. Adv.* 17:9–41.
6. Urey, W. W. "Image Intensification from Remote Modules," *Jet Propulsion Lab Tech. Mem* 33:376–86.
7. Isaacs, I. V. "Physics of Non-Elastic Interactions," *Phys. Rev.* 80:97–104.
8. Quincy, E. W. "Virulence as a Function of Gradient Adaptation to Host," *J. Microbiol.* 99:109–17.
9. Danvers, R. C. "Clotting Mechanisms in Disease States," *Ann. Int. Med.* 90:404–81.
10. Henderson, J. W., et al. "Salicylism and Metabolic Acidosis," *Med. Adv.* 23:77–91.

DAY FOUR

1. Livingston, J. A. "Automated Analysis of Amino Acid Substrates," *J. Microbiol.* 100:44–57.
2. Laandgard, Q. *X-Ray Crystallography.* New York: Columbia Univ. Press, 1960.
3. Polton, S., et al. "Electron Waveforms and Microscopic Resolution Ratios," *Ann. Anatomy* 5:90–118.

REFERENCES

4. Twombley, E. R., et al. "Tissue Thromboplastin in Timed Release from Graded Intimal Destruction," *Path. Res.* 19:1–53.
5. Ingersoll, H. G. "Basal Metabolism and Thyroid Indices in Bird Metabolic Stress Contexts," *J. Zool.* 50:223–304.
6. Young, T. C., et al. "Diabetic Ketoacidosis Induced by Timed Insulin Withdrawal," *Rev. Med. Proc.* 96:87–96.
7. Ramsden, C. C. "Speculations on a Universal Antibiotic," *Nature* 112:44–8.
8. Yandell, K. M. "Ligamine Metabolism in Normal Subjects," *JAJA* 44:109–10.

DAY FIVE

1. Hepley, W. E., et al. "Studies in Mutagenic Transformation of Bacteria from Non-virulent to Virulent Forms," *J. Biol. Chem.* 78:90–9.
2. Drayson, V. L. "Does Man Have a Future?" *Tech. Rev.* 119:1–13.

THE TERMINAL MAN

To Kurt Villadsen

ACKNOWLEDGMENT

Martin J. Nathan, M.D., and Demian Kuffler gave technical advice and assistance. Kay Kolman Tyler prepared the graphics. I am indebted to them all.

CONTENTS

Author's Introduction
239

Tuesday, March 9, 1971: Admission
243

Wednesday, March 10, 1971: Implantation
283

Thursday, March 11, 1971: Interfacing
317

Friday, March 12, 1971: Breakdown
339

Saturday, March 13, 1971: Termination
409

Bibliography
429

AUTHOR'S INTRODUCTION

Readers who find the subject matter of this book shocking or frightening should not delude themselves by also thinking it is something quite new. The physical study of the brain, and the technology for modifying behavior through psychosurgery, has been developing for nearly a century. For decades, it was there for anyone to see, discuss, support, or oppose.

Nor has there been any lack of publicity. Research in neurobiology is spectacular enough to appear regularly in the Sunday supplements. But the public has never really taken it seriously. There has been so much ominous talk and so much frivolous speculation for so many years that the public now regards "mind control" as a problem removed to the distant future: it might eventually happen, but not soon, and not in a way that would affect anyone now alive.

Scientists engaged in this research have sought public discussion. James V. McConnell of the University of Michigan told his students some years ago, "Look, we can do these things. We can control behavior. Now, who's going to decide what's to be done? If you don't get busy and tell me how I'm supposed to do it, I'll make up my own mind for you. And then it's too late."

Many people today feel that they live in a world that is predetermined and running along a fixed pre-established course. Past decisions have left us with pollution, depersonalization, and urban blight; somebody else made the decisions for us, and we are stuck with the consequences.

That attitude represents a childish and dangerous denial of responsibility, and everyone should recognize it for what it is. In that spirit, the following chronology is presented:

HISTORY OF THERAPY OF PSYCHOSURGERY

1908 Horsley and Clarke (Great Britain) describe stereotaxic surgical techniques for use on animals.

1947 Spiegel and co-workers (U.S.A.) report the first stereotaxic surgery performed on a human being.

1950 Penfield and Flanagan (Canada) perform ablative surgery with favorable results in patients with seizure foci.

1953 Heath and co-workers (U.S.A.) perform stereotaxic implantation of depth electrodes.

1958 Talairach and co-workers (France) begin chronic stereotaxic implantation of depth electrodes.

1963 Heath and co-workers (U.S.A.) allow patients to stimulate themselves, at will, via implanted electrodes.

1965 Narabayashi (Japan) reports on 98 patients with violent behavior treated by stereotaxic surgery.

1965 More than 24,000 stereotaxic procedures on human beings have been performed in various countries by this date.

1968 Delgado and co-workers (U.S.A.) attach "stimoceiver" (radio stimulator plus radio receiver) to freely ambulatory hospital patients.

1969 Chimpanzee at Alamogordo, N.M., is directly linked by radio to a computer which programs and delivers his brain stimulations.

1971 Patient Harold Benson is operated on in Los Angeles.

M.C.

Los Angeles
October 23, 1971

"I have come to the conclusion that my subjective account of my own motivation is largely mythical on almost all occasions. I don't know why I do things."

—J. B. S. HALDANE

"The wilderness masters the colonist."

—FREDERICK JACKSON TURNER

TUESDAY, MARCH 9, 1971: ADMISSION

Chapter 1

They came down to the emergency ward at noon and sat on the bench just behind the swinging doors that led in from the ambulance parking slot. Ellis, the senior man, was tense, preoccupied, distant. The younger man, Morris, was eating a candy bar. He crumpled the wrapper into the pocket of his white jacket.

From where they sat, they could look at the sunlight outside, falling across the big sign that said EMERGENCY WARD and the smaller sign that said NO PARKING AMBULANCES ONLY. In the distance they heard sirens.

"Is that him?" Ellis asked.

Morris checked his watch. "I doubt it. It's too early."

They sat on the bench and listened to the sirens come closer. Ellis removed his glasses and wiped them with his tie. One of the emergency ward nurses, a girl Morris did not know by name, came over and said brightly, "Is this the welcoming committee?"

Ellis squinted at her. Morris said, "We'll be taking him straight through. Do you have his chart down here?"

The nurse said, "Yes, I think so, Doctor," and walked off looking irritated.

Ellis sighed. He replaced his glasses and frowned at the nurse. "I suppose the whole damned hospital knows."

"It's a pretty big secret to keep."

The sirens were very close now; through the windows they saw an ambulance back into the slot. Two orderlies opened the door and pulled out the stretcher. A frail elderly woman lay on the stretcher, gasping for breath, making wet gurgling sounds. Severe pulmonary edema, Morris thought as he watched her taken into one of the treatment rooms.

"I hope he's in good shape," Ellis said.

"Who?"

"Benson."

"Why shouldn't he be?"

"They might have roughed him up." Ellis stared morosely out the windows. He really is in a bad mood, Morris thought. He knew that meant Ellis was excited; he had scrubbed in on enough cases with Ellis to recognize the pattern. Irascibility under pressure while he waited—and then total, almost lazy calm when the operation began. "Where the hell is he?" Ellis said, looking at his watch again.

To change the subject, Morris said, "Are we all set for three-thirty?" At 3:30 that afternoon, Benson would be presented to the hospital staff at a special Neurosurgical Rounds.

"As far as I know," Ellis said. "Ross is making the presentation. I just hope Benson's in good shape."

Over the loudspeaker, a soft voice said, "Dr. Ellis, Dr. John Ellis, two-two-three-four. Dr. Ellis, two-two-three-four."

Ellis got up to answer the page. "Hell," he said.

Morris knew that two-two-three-four was the extension for the animal laboratories. The call probably meant something had gone wrong with the monkeys. Ellis had been doing three monkeys a week for the past month, just to keep himself and his staff ready.

He watched as Ellis crossed the room and answered from a wall phone. Ellis walked with a slight limp, the result of a childhood injury that had cut the common peroneal nerve in his right leg. Morris always wondered if the injury had had something to do with Ellis's later decision to become a neurosurgeon. Certainly Ellis had the attitude of a man determined to correct defects, to fix things up. That was what he always said to his patients: "We can fix you up." And he seemed to have more than his share of defects himself—the limp, the premature near-baldness, the weak eyes, and the heavy thick glasses. It produced a vulnerability about him that made his irascibility more tolerable.

Morris stared out the window at the sunlight and the parking lot. Afternoon visiting hours were beginning; relatives were driving into the parking lot, getting out of their cars, glancing up at the high buildings of the hospital. The apprehension was clear in their faces; the hospital was a place people feared.

Morris noticed how many of them had sun tans. It had been a warm, sunny spring in Los Angeles, yet he was still as pale as the white jacket and trousers he wore every day. He had to get outside more often, he told himself. He should start eating lunch outside. He played tennis, of course, but that was usually in the evenings.

Ellis came back, shaking his head. "It's Ethel. She tore out her sutures."

"How did it happen?" Ethel was a juvenile rhesus monkey who had undergone brain surgery the day before. The operation had proceeded flawlessly. And Ethel was unusually docile, as rhesus monkeys went.

"I don't know," Ellis said. "Apparently she worked an arm loose from her restraints. Anyway, she's shrieking and the bone's exposed on one side."

"Did she tear out her wires?"

"I don't know. But I've got to go down and resew her now. Can you handle this?"

"I think so."

"Are you all right with the police?" Ellis said. "I don't think they'll give you any trouble."

"No, I don't think so."

"Just get Benson up to seven as fast as you can," Ellis said. "Then call Ross. I'll be up as soon as possible." He checked his watch. "It'll probably take forty minutes to resew Ethel, if she behaves herself."

"Good luck with her," Morris said.

Ellis looked sour and walked away.

After he had gone, the emergency ward nurse came back. "What's the matter with *him*?" she asked.

"Just edgy," Morris said.

"He sure is," the nurse said. She paused and looked out the window, lingering.

Morris watched her with a kind of bemused detachment. He'd spent enough years in the hospital to recognize the subtle signs of status. He had begun as an intern, with no status at all. Most of the nurses knew more medicine than he did, and if they were tired they didn't bother to conceal it. ("I don't think you want to do that, Doctor.") As the years went by, he became a surgical resident, and the nurses became more deferential. When he was a senior resident, he was sufficiently assured in his work that a few of the nurses called him by his first name. And finally, when he transferred to the Neuropsychiatric Research Unit as a junior staff member, the formality returned as a new mark of status.

But this was something else: a nurse hanging around, just being near him, because he had a special aura of importance. Because everyone in the hospital knew what was going to happen.

Staring out the window, the nurse said, "Here he comes."

Morris got up and looked out. A blue police van drove up toward the emergency ward, and turned around, backing into the ambulance slot. "All right," he said. "Notify the seventh floor, and tell them we're on our way."

"Yes, Doctor."

The nurse went off. Two ambulance orderlies opened the hospital doors. They knew nothing about Benson. One of them said to Morris, "You expecting this one?"

"Yes."

"EW case?"

"No, a direct admission."

The orderlies nodded, and watched as the police officer driving the van came around and unlocked the rear door. Two officers seated in the back emerged, blinking in the sunlight. Then Benson came out.

As always, Morris was struck by his appearance. Benson was a meek, pudgy, thirtyish man, with a bewildered air as he stood by the van, with his wrists handcuffed in front of him. When he saw Morris, he said, "Hello," and then looked away, embarrassed.

One of the cops said, "You in charge?"

"Yes. I'm Dr. Morris."

The cop gestured toward the interior of the hospital. "Lead the way, Doctor."

Morris said, "Would you mind taking off his handcuffs?"

Benson's eyes flicked up at Morris, then back down.

"We don't have any orders about that." The cops exchanged glances. "I guess it's okay."

While they took the cuffs off, the driver brought Morris a form on a clipboard: "Transfer of Suspect to Institutional Care (Medical)." He signed it.

"And again here," the driver said.

As Morris signed again, he looked at Benson. Benson stood quietly, rubbing his wrists, staring straight ahead. The impersonality of the transaction, the forms and signatures, made Morris feel as if he were receiving a package from United Parcel.

"Okay," the driver said. "Thanks, Doc."

Morris led the other two policemen and Benson into the hospital. The orderlies shut the doors. A nurse came up with a wheelchair and Benson sat down in it. The cops looked confused.

"It's hospital policy," Morris said.

They all went to the elevators.

The elevator stopped at the lobby. A half-dozen relatives were waiting to go up to the higher floors, but they hesitated when they saw Morris, Benson in the wheelchair, and the two cops. "Please take the next car," Morris said smoothly. The doors closed. They continued up.

"Where is Dr. Ellis?" Benson asked. "I thought he was going to be here."

"He's in surgery. He'll be up shortly."

"And Dr. Ross?"

"You'll see her at the presentation."

"Oh, yes." Benson smiled. "The presentation."

The elevator arrived at the seventh floor, and they all got out.

Seven was the Special Surgical floor, where difficult and complex cases were treated. It was essentially a research floor. The most severe cardiac, kidney, and metabolic patients recuperated here. They went down to the nurses' station, a glass-walled area strategically located at the center of the X-shaped floor.

The nurse on duty at the station looked up. She was surprised to see the cops, but she said nothing. Morris said, "This is Mr. Benson. Have we got seven-ten ready?"

"All set for him," the nurse said, and gave Benson a cheery smile. Benson smiled bleakly back, and glanced from the nurse to the computer console in the corner of the nursing station.

"You have a time-sharing station up here?"

"Yes," Morris said.

"Where's the main computer?"

"In the basement."

"Of this building?"

"Yes. It draws a lot of power, and the power lines come to this building."

Benson nodded. Morris was not surprised at the questions. Benson was trying to distract himself from the thought of surgery, and he was, after all, a computer expert.

The nurse handed Morris the chart on Benson. It had the usual blue plastic cover with the seal of University Hospital. But there was also a red tag, which meant neurosurgery, and a yellow tag, which meant intensive care, and a white tag, which Morris had almost never seen on a patient's chart. The white tag meant security precautions.

"Is that my record?" Benson asked as Morris wheeled him down the hall to 710. The cops followed along behind.

"Uh-huh."

"I always wondered what was in it."

"Lot of unreadable notes, mostly." Actually, Benson's chart was thick and very readable, with all the computer print-outs of different tests.

They came to 710. Before they entered the room, one of the cops went in and closed the door behind him. The second cop remained outside the door. "Just a precaution," he said.

Benson glanced up at Morris. "They're very careful about me," he said.

The first cop came out. "It's okay," he said.

Morris wheeled Benson into the room. It was a large room, on the south side of the hospital, so that it was sunny in the afternoon. Benson looked around and nodded approvingly. Morris said, "This is one of the best rooms in the hospital."

"Can I get up now?"

"Of course."

Benson got out of the wheelchair and sat on the bed. He bounced on the mattress. He pressed the buttons that made the bed move up and down, then bent over to look at the motorized mechanism beneath the bed. Morris went to the window and drew the blinds, reducing the direct light.

"Simple," Benson said.

"What's that?"

"This bed mechanism. Remarkably simple. You should really have a feedback unit so that body movements by the person in the bed are automatically compensated for . . ." His voice trailed off. He opened the closet doors, looked in, checked the bathroom, came back. Morris thought that he wasn't acting like an ordinary patient. Most patients were intimidated by the hospital, but Benson acted as if he were renting a hotel room.

"I'll take it," Benson said, and laughed. He sat down on the bed and looked at Morris, then at the cops. "Do they have to be here?"

"I think they can wait outside," Morris said.

The cops nodded and went out, closing the door behind them.

"I meant," Benson said, "do they have to be here at all?"

"Yes, they do."

"All the time?"

"Yes. Unless we can get charges against you dropped."

Benson frowned. "Was it . . . I mean, did I . . . Was it bad?"

"You gave him a black eye and you fractured one rib."

"But he's all right?"

"Yes. He's all right."

"I don't remember any of it," Benson said. "All my memory cores are erased."

"I know that."

"But I'm glad he's all right."

Morris nodded. "Did you bring anything with you? Pajamas, anything like that?"

Benson said, "No. But I can arrange for it."

"All right. I'll get you some hospital clothing in the meantime. Are you all right for now?"

"Yes. Sure." And he grinned. "I could do with a quick shot, maybe."

"That," Morris said, "is something you'll have to do without."

He went out of the room.

The cops had brought a chair up to the door. One of them sat on it, the other stood alongside. Morris flipped open his notebook.

"You'll want to know the schedule," he said. "An admitting person will show up in the next half hour with financial waivers for Benson to sign. Then, at three-thirty he goes downstairs to the main amphitheater for Surgical Rounds. He comes back after about twenty minutes. His head will be shaved tonight. The operation is scheduled for six A.M. tomorrow morning. Do you have questions?"

"Can someone get us meals?" one of them asked.

"I'll have the nurse order extras. Will there be two of you, or just one?"

"Just one. We're working eight-hour shifts."

Morris said, "I'll tell the nurses. It'd help if you check in and out with them. They like to know who's on the floor."

The cops nodded. There was a moment of silence. Finally, one of them said, "What's wrong with him, anyway?"

"He has a special kind of brain damage. It gives him seizures."

"I saw the guy he beat up," one of the cops said. "Big strong guy, looked like a truck driver. You'd never think a little guy like that"—he jerked his arm toward Benson's room—"could do it."

"When he has seizures, he's violent."

They nodded. "What's this operation he's getting?"

"It's a kind of surgery we call a stage-three procedure," Morris said. He didn't bother to explain further. The policemen wouldn't understand. And, he thought, even if they understood, they wouldn't believe it.

Chapter 2

Neurosurgical Grand Rounds, where unusual cases were presented and discussed by all the surgeons of the hospital, were normally scheduled for Thursdays at nine. Special rounds were hardly ever called; it was too difficult for the staff to get together. But now the amphitheater was packed, tier after tier of white jackets and pale faces staring down at Ellis, who pushed his glasses up on his nose and said, "As many of you know, tomorrow morning the Neuropsychiatric Research Unit will perform a limbic pacing procedure—what we call a stage three—on a human patient."

There was no sound, no movement, from the audience. Janet Ross stood in the corner of the amphitheater near the doors and watched. She found it odd that there should be so little reaction. But then it was hardly a surprise. Everyone in the hospital knew that the Neuropsychiatric Service, or NPS, had been waiting for a good stage-three subject.

"I must ask you," Ellis said, "to restrain your questions when the patient is introduced. He is a sensitive man, and his disturbance is quite severe. We thought you should have the psychiatric background before we bring him in. The attending psychiatrist, Dr. Ross, will give you a summary." Ellis nodded to Ross. She came forward to the center of the room.

She stared up at the steeply banked rows of faces and felt a momentary hesitation. Janet Ross was good-looking in a lean, dark-blond way. She herself felt she was too bony and angular, and she often wished she were more softly feminine. But she knew her appearance was striking, and at thirty, after a decade of training in a predominantly masculine profession, she had learned to use it.

She clasped her hands behind her back, took a breath, and launched into the summary, delivering it in the rapid, stylized method that was standard for grand rounds.

"Harold Franklin Benson," she said, "is a thirty-four-year-old divorced computer scientist who was healthy until two years ago, when he was involved in an automobile accident on the Santa Monica Freeway. Following the accident, he was unconscious for an unknown period of time. He was taken to a local hospital for overnight observation and discharged the next day in good health. He was fine for six months, until he began to experience what he called 'blackouts.' "

The audience was silent, faces staring down at her, listening.

"These blackouts lasted several minutes, and occurred about once a month. They were often preceded by the sensation of peculiar, unpleasant odors. The blackouts frequently occurred after drinking alcohol. The patient consulted his local physician, who told him he was working too hard, and recommended he reduce his alcohol intake. Benson did this, but the blackouts continued.

"One year ago—a year after the accident—he realized that the blackouts were becoming more frequent and lasting longer. He often regained consciousness to find himself in unfamiliar surroundings. On several occasions, he had cuts and bruises or torn clothing which suggested that he had been fighting. However, he never remembered what occurred during the blackout periods."

Heads in the audience nodded. They understood what she was telling them; it was a straightforward history for an eptileptiform syndrome which might be treated with surgery. But there were complexities.

"The patient's friends," she continued, "told him that he was acting differently, but he discounted their opinion. Gradually he has lost contact with most of his former friends. Around this time—one year ago—he also made what he called a monumental discovery in his work. Benson is a computer scientist specializing in artificial life, or machine intelligence. In the course of this work, he says he discovered that machines were competing with human beings, and that ultimately machines would take over the world."

Now there were whispers in the audience. This interested them, particularly the psychiatrists. She could see her old teacher Manon sitting in the top row holding his head in his hands. Manon knew.

"Benson communicated his discovery to his remaining friends. They suggested that he see a psychiatrist, which angered him. In the last year, he has become increasingly certain that machines are conspiring to take over the world.

"Then, six months ago, the patient was arrested by police on suspicion of beating up an airplane mechanic. Positive identification could not be made, and charges were dropped. But the episode unnerved Benson and led him to seek psychiatric help. He had the vague suspicion that somehow he *had* been the man who had beaten the mechanic so severely. That was unthinkable to him, but the nagging suspicion remained.

"He was referred to the University Hospital Neuropsychiatric Research Unit four months ago, in November, 1970. On the basis of his history—head injury, episodic violence preceded by strange smells—he was considered a probable case of what is now called ADL: Acute Disinhibitory Lesion syndrome, an organic illness in which the patient periodically loses his inhibitions against violent acts. As you know, the NPS now accepts only patients with organically treatable behavioral disturbances.

"A neurological examination was fully normal. An electroencephalogram was fully normal; brainwave activity showed no pathology. It was repeated after alcohol ingestion and an abnormal tracing was obtained. The EEG showed seizure activity in the right temporal lobe of the brain. Benson was therefore considered a stage-one patient—firm diagnosis of ADL syndrome."

She paused to get her breath and let the audience absorb what she had told them. "The patient is an intelligent man," she said, "and his illness was explained to him. He was told he had injured his brain in the automobile accident and, as a result, had an illness that produced 'thought seizures'—seizures of the mind, not the body, leading to loss of inhibitions and violent acts. He was told that the syndrome was well-studied and could be controlled. He was started on a series of drug trials.

"Three months ago, Benson was arrested on charges of assault and battery. The victim was a twenty-four-year-old topless dancer, who later dropped charges. The hospital intervened slightly on his behalf.

"One month ago, drug trials of morladone, para-amino benzadone, and triamiline were concluded. Benson showed no improvement on any drug or combination of drugs. He was therefore a stage two—drug-resistant ADL syndrome. And he was scheduled for a stage-three surgical procedure, which we will discuss today."

She paused. "Before I bring him in," she said, "I think I should add that yesterday afternoon he attacked a gas-station attendant and beat the man rather badly. His operation is scheduled for tomorrow and we have persuaded the police to release him in our custody. But he is still technically awaiting arraignment on charges of assault and battery."

The room was silent as she turned, and went to bring in Benson.

° ° °

Benson was just outside the doors to the amphitheater, sitting in his wheelchair, wearing the blue-and-white striped bathrobe the hospital issued to its patients. When Janet Ross appeared, he smiled. "Hello, Dr. Ross."

"Hello, Harry." She smiled back. "How do you feel?"

Of course, she could see clearly how he felt. Benson was nervous and threatened: there was sweat on his upper lip, his shoulders were drawn in, his hands clenched together in his lap.

"I feel fine," he said. "Just fine."

Behind Benson was Morris, pushing the wheelchair, and a cop. She said to Morris, "Does he come in with us?"

Before Morris could answer, Benson said lightly, "He goes anywhere I go."

The cop nodded and looked embarrassed.

"All right," she said.

She opened the doors, and Morris wheeled Benson into the amphitheater, over to Ellis. Ellis came forward to shake Benson's hand.

"Mr. Benson, good to see you."

"Dr. Ellis."

Morris turned the wheelchair around so Benson was facing the amphitheater audience. Ross sat to one side and glanced at the cop, who remained by the door trying to look inconspicuous. Ellis stood alongside Benson, who was looking at a wall of frosted glass, against which a dozen X-rays had been clipped. He seemed to realize that they were his own skull films. Ellis noticed, and turned off the light behind the frosted glass. The X-rays became opaquely black.

"We've asked you to come here," Ellis said, "to answer some questions for these doctors." He gestured to the men sitting in the semicircular tiers. "They don't make you nervous, do they?"

Ellis asked it easily. Ross frowned. She'd attended hundreds of grand rounds in her life, and the patients were invariably asked if the doctors peering down at them made them nervous. In answer to a direct question, the patients always denied nervousness.

"Sure they make me nervous," Benson said. "They'd make anybody nervous."

Ross suppressed a smile. Good for you, she thought.

Then Benson said, "What if you were a machine and I brought you in front of a bunch of computer experts who were trying to decide what was wrong with you and how to fix it? How would you feel?"

Ellis was flustered. He ran his hands through his thinning hair and glanced at Ross, and she shook her head fractionally *no*. This was the wrong place to explore Benson's psychopathology.

"I'd be nervous, too," Ellis said.

"Well, then," Benson said. "You see?"

Ellis swallowed.

He's being deliberately irritating, Ross thought. Don't take the bait.

"But, of course," Ellis said, "I'm not a machine, am I?"

Ross winced.

"That depends," Benson said. "Certain of your functions are repetitive and mechanical. From that standpoint, they are easily programmed and relatively straightforward, if you—"

"I think," Ross said, standing up, "that we might take questions from those present now."

Ellis clearly didn't like the interruption, but he was silent, and Benson mercifully was quiet. She looked up at the audience, and after a moment a man in the back raised his hand and said, "Mr. Benson, can you tell us more about the smells you have before your blackouts?"

"Not really," Benson said. "They're strange, is all. They smell terrible, but they don't smell *like* anything, if you get what I mean. I mean, you can't identify the odor. Memory tapes cycle through blankly."

"Can you give us an approximation of the odor?"

Benson shrugged. "Maybe . . . pig shit in turpentine."

Another hand in the audience went up. "Mr. Benson, these blackouts have been getting more frequent. Have they also been getting longer?"

"Yes," Benson said. "They're several hours now."

"How do you feel when you recover from a blackout?"

"Sick to my stomach."

"Can you be more specific?"

"Sometimes I vomit. Is that specific enough?"

Ross frowned. She could see that Benson was becoming angry. "Are there other questions?" she asked, hoping there would not be. She looked up at the audience. There was a long silence.

"Well, then," Ellis said, "perhaps we can go on to discuss the details of stage-three surgery. Mr. Benson knows all this, so he can stay or leave, whichever he prefers."

Ross didn't approve. Ellis was showing off, the surgeon's instinct for demonstrating to everyone that his patient didn't mind being cut and mutilated. It was unfair to ask—to dare—Benson to stay in the room.

"I'll stay," Benson said.

"Fine," Ellis said. He went to the blackboard and drew a brain schematically. "Now," he said, "our understanding of the disease process in ADL is that a portion of the brain is damaged, and a scar forms. It's like a scar in other body organs—lots of fibrous tissue, lots of contraction and distortion. And it becomes a focus for abnormal electrical discharges. We see spreading waves moving outward from the focus, like ripples from a rock in a pond."

Ellis drew a point on the brain, then sketched concentric circles.

"These electrical ripples produce a seizure. In some parts of the brain, the discharge focus produces a shaking fit, frothing at the mouth, and so on.

In other parts, there are other effects. If the focus is in a part of the temporal lobe, as in Mr. Benson's case, you get acute disinhibitory lesion syndrome—strange thoughts and sometimes violent behavior, preceded by a characteristic aura which is often an odor."

Benson was watching, listening, nodding.

"Now, then," Ellis said, "we know from the work of many researchers that it may be incorrect to think of episodes of disinhibition in ADL as seizures in the usual sense. They may simply be intermittent periods of brain malfunction that result from organic damage. Nevertheless, these episodes tend to have a characteristic pattern in the way they occur, and so for convenience we speak of them as seizures. We know it is possible to abort the seizure by delivering an electrical shock to the critical portion of the brain substance. There are a few seconds—sometimes as much as half a minute—before the disinhibition takes full effect. A shock at that moment prevents the seizure."

He drew a large "X" through the concentric circles. Then he drew a new brain, and a head around it, and a neck. "We face two problems," he said. "First, what is the correct part of the brain to shock? In the case of ADL patients, we know roughly that it's in the amygdala, an anterior area of the so-called limbic system. We don't know *exactly* where, but we solve that problem by implanting a number of electrodes in the brain. Mr. Benson will have forty electrodes implanted tomorrow morning."

He drew two lines into the brain.

"Now, our second problem is how do we know when an attack is starting? We must know when to deliver our aborting shock. Well, fortunately the same electrodes that we use to deliver the shock can also be used to 'read' the electrical activity of the brain. And there is a characteristic electrical pattern that precedes a seizure."

Ellis paused, glanced at Benson, then up at the audience.

"So we have a feedback system—the same electrodes are used to detect a new attack, and to deliver the aborting shock. A computer controls the feedback mechanism."

He drew a small square in the neck of his schematic figure.

"The NPS staff has developed a computer that will monitor electrical activity of the brain, and when it sees an attack starting, will transmit a shock to the correct brain area. This computer is about the size of a postage stamp and weighs a tenth of an ounce. It will be implanted beneath the skin of the patient's neck."

He then drew an oblong shape below the neck and attached wires to the computer square.

"We will power the computer with a Handler PP-J plutonium power pack, which will be implanted beneath the skin of the shoulder. This makes the patient completely self-sufficient. The power pack supplies energy continuously and reliably for twenty years."

With his chalk, he tapped the different parts of his diagram. "That's the complete feedback loop—brain, to electrodes, to computer, to power pack, back to brain. A closed loop without any externalized portions."

He turned to Benson, who had watched the discussion with an expression of bland disinterest.

"Any comments? Mr. Benson? Anything you want to say, or add?"

Ross groaned inwardly. She knew Ellis was only trying to be considerate to his patient, but it was wrong to ask any patient to comment before such frightening surgery, as if the patient himself were not about to undergo it. It was too much to ask.

"No," Benson said. "I have nothing to say." And he yawned.

When Benson was wheeled out of the room, Ross went with him. It wasn't really necessary for her to accompany him, but she was concerned about his condition—and a little guilty about the way Ellis had treated him. She said, "How did that go?"

"I thought it was interesting," he said.

"In what way?"

"Well, the discussion was entirely medical. I would have expected a more philosophical approach."

"We're just practical people," she said lightly, "dealing with a practical problem."

Benson smiled. "So was Newton," he said. "What's more practical than the problem of why an apple falls to the ground?"

"Do you really see philosophical implications in all this?"

Benson nodded. "Yes," he said, "and so do you. You're just pretending that you don't."

She stopped then and stood in the corridor, watching as Benson was wheeled down to the elevator. Benson, Morris, and the cop waited in the corridor for the next car. Morris pushed the button repeatedly in that impatient, aggressive way of his. Then the elevator arrived and they got on. Benson waved one last time, and the doors closed.

She went back to the amphitheater.

". . . has been under development for ten years," Ellis was saying. "It was first started for cardiac pacemakers, where changing batteries requires minor surgery every year or so. That's an annoyance to surgeon and patient. The atomic power pack is totally reliable and has a long lifespan. If Mr. Benson is still alive, we might have to change packs around 1990, but not before then."

Janet Ross slipped back into the room just as another question was asked: "How will you determine which of the forty electrodes will prevent a seizure?"

"We will implant them all," Ellis said, "and wire up the computer. But we will not lock in any electrodes for twenty-four hours. One day after surgery, we'll stimulate each of the electrodes by radio and determine which electrodes work best. Then we will lock those in by remote control."

High up in the amphitheater, a familiar voice coughed and said, "These technical details are interesting, but they seem to me to elude the point." Ross looked up and saw Manon speaking. Manon was nearly seventy-five, an emeritus professor of psychiatry who rarely came to the hospital any more. When he did, he was usually regarded as a cranky old man, far past his prime, out of touch with modern thinking. "It seems to me," Manon continued, "that the patient is psychotic."

"That's putting it a little strongly," Ellis said.

"Perhaps," Manon said. "But, at the very least, he has a severe personality disorder. All this confusion about men and machines is worrisome."

"The personality disorder is part of his disease," Ellis said. "In a recent review, Harley and co-workers at Yale reported that fifty percent of ADL sufferers had an accompanying personality disorder which was independent of seizure activity *per se*."

"Quite so," Manon said, in a voice that had the slightest edge of impatience to it. "It is part of his disease, independent of seizures. But will your procedure cure it?"

Janet Ross found herself quietly pleased; Manon was reaching exactly her own conclusions.

"No," Ellis said. "Probably not."

"In other words, the operation will stop his seizures, but it won't stop his delusions."

"No," Ellis repeated. "Probably not."

"If I may say so," Manon said, frowning down from the top row, "this kind of thinking is what I fear most from the NPS. I don't mean to single you out. It's a general problem of the medical profession. For example, if we get a suicide attempt or a suicide gesture by drug overdose in the emergency ward, our approach is to pump the patient's stomach, give him a lecture, and send him home. That's a treatment—but it's hardly a cure. The patient will be back sooner or later. Stomach pumping doesn't treat depression. It only treats drug overdose."

"I see what you're saying, but . . ."

"I'd also remind you of the hospital's experience with Mr. L. Do you recall the case?"

"I don't think Mr. L. applies here," Ellis said. But his voice was stiff and exasperated.

"I'm not so sure," Manon said. Since several puzzled faces in the amphitheater were turned toward him, he explained. "Mr. L. was a famous case here a few years ago. He was a thirty-nine-year-old man with bilateral end-stage kidney disease. Chronic glomerulonephritis. He was considered a candidate for renal transplant. Because our facilities for transplantation are limited, a hospital review board selects patients. The psychiatrists on that board strongly opposed Mr. L. as a transplantation candidate, because he was psychotic. He believed that the sun ruled the earth and he refused to go outside during the daylight hours. We felt he was too unstable to benefit from kidney surgery, but he ultimately received the operation. Six months later, he committed suicide. That's a tragedy. But the real question is couldn't someone else have benefited more from the thousands of dollars and many hours of specialized effort that went into the transplant?"

Ellis paced back and forth, the foot of his bad leg scraping slightly along the floor. Ross knew he was feeling threatened, under attack. Normally Ellis was careful to minimize his disability, concealing it so that the limp was noticeable only to a trained eye. But if he was tired, or angry, or threatened, the flaw appeared. It was almost as if he unconsciously wanted sympathy: don't attack me, I'm a cripple."

"I understand your objection," Ellis said. "In the terms you present it, your argument is unanswerable. But I would like to consider the problem from a somewhat different viewpoint. It is perfectly true that Benson is disturbed, and that our operation probably won't change that. But what happens if we *don't* operate on him? We know that his seizures are life-threatening—to himself, to others. His seizures have already gotten him into trouble with the law, and his seizures are getting worse. The operation will prevent seizures, and we think that is an important benefit to the patient."

High up, Manon gave a little shrug. Janet Ross knew the gesture; it signaled irreconcilable differences, an impasse.

"Well, then," Ellis said, "are there other questions?"

There were no other questions.

Chapter 3

"Jesus fucking Christ," Ellis said, wiping his forehead. "He didn't let up, did he?"

Janet Ross walked with him across the parking lot toward the Langer research building. It was late afternoon; the sunlight was yellowing, turning pale and weak.

"His point was valid," she said mildly.

Ellis sighed. "I keep forgetting you're on his side."

"Why do you keep forgetting?" she asked. She smiled as she said it. As the psychiatrist on the NPS staff, she'd opposed Benson's operation from the beginning.

"Look," Ellis said. "We do what we can. It'd be great to cure him, but we can't do that. We can only help him to a partial cure. So we'll do that. We'll help him. It's not a perfect world."

She walked alongside him in silence. There was nothing to say. She had told Ellis her opinion many times before. The operation might not help—it might, in fact, make Benson much worse. She was sure Ellis understood that possibility, but he was stubbornly ignoring it. Or so it seemed to her.

Actually, she liked Ellis, as much as she liked any surgeon. She regarded surgeons as flagrantly action-oriented men (they were almost always men, which she found significant) desperate to do something, to take some physical action. In that sense, Ellis was better than most of them. He had wisely turned down several stage-three candidates before Benson, and she knew that was difficult for him to do, because he was terribly eager to perform the new operation.

"I hate all this," Ellis said. "Hospital politics."

"But you want to do Benson. . . ."

"I'm ready," Ellis said. "We're all ready. We have to take that first big step, and now is the time to take it." He glanced at her. "Why do you look so uncertain?"

"Because I am," she said.

They came to the Langer building. Ellis went off to an early dinner with McPherson—a political dinner, he said irritably—and she took the elevator to the fourth floor.

After ten years of steady expansion, the Neuropsychiatric Research Unit encompassed the entire fourth floor of the Langer research building. The other floors were painted a dead, cold white, but the NPS was bright with primary colors. The intention was to make patients feel optimistic and happy, but it always had the reverse effect on Ross. She found it falsely and artificially cheerful, like a nursery school for retarded children.

She got off the elevator and looked at the reception area, one wall a bright blue, the other red. Like almost everything else about the NPS, the colors had been McPherson's idea. It was strange, she thought, how much an organization reflected the personality of its leader. McPherson himself always seemed to have a bright kindergarten quality about him, and a boundless optimism.

Certainly you had to be optimistic if you planned to operate on Harry Benson.

The Unit was quiet now, most of the staff gone home for the night. She walked down the corridor past the colored doors with the stenciled labels: SONOENCEPHALOGRAPHY, CORTICAL FUNCTION, EEG, RAS SCORING, PARIETAL T, and, at the far end of the hall, TELECOMP. The work done behind those doors was as complex as the labels—and this was just the patient-care wing, what McPherson called "Applications."

Applications was ordinary compared to Development, the research wing with its chemitrodes and compsims and elad scenarios. To say nothing of the big projects, like George and Martha, or Form Q. Development was ten years ahead of Applications—and Applications was very, very advanced.

A year ago, McPherson had asked her to take a group of newspaper science reporters through the NPS. He chose her, he said, "because she was such a piece of ass." It was funny to hear him say that, and shocking in a way. He was usually so courtly and fatherly.

But her shock was minor compared to the shock the reporters felt. She had planned to show them both Applications and Development, but after the reporters had seen Applications they were so agitated, so clearly overloaded, that she cut the tour short.

She worried a lot about it afterward. The reporters hadn't been naïve and they hadn't been inexperienced. They were people who shuttled from one scientific arena to another all their lives. Yet they were rendered speechless by the implications of the work she had shown them. She herself had lost that insight, that perspective—she had been working in the NPS for three years, and she had gradually become accustomed to the things done there. The conjunction of men and machines, human brains and electronic brains, was no longer bizarre and provocative. It was just a way to take steps forward and get things done.

On the other hand, she opposed the stage-three operation on Benson. She had opposed it from the start. She thought Benson was the wrong human subject, and she had just one last chance to prove it.

At the end of the corridor, she paused by the door to Telecomp, listening to the quiet hiss of the print-out units. She heard voices inside, and opened the door. Telecomp was really the heart of the Neuropsychiatric Research Unit; it was a large room, filled with electronic equipment. The walls and ceilings were soundproofed, a vestige of earlier days when the read-out consoles were clattering teletypes. Now they used either silent CRTs—cathode-ray tubes—or a print-out machine that sprayed the letters with a nozzle, rather than typed them mechanically. The hiss of the sprayer was the loudest sound in the room. McPherson had insisted on the change to quieter units because he felt the clattering disturbed patients who came to the NPS for treatment.

Gerhard was there, and his assistant Richards. The wizard twins, they were called: Gerhard was only twenty-four, and Richards even younger. They were the least professional people attached to the NPS; both men regarded Telecomp as a playground filled with complex toys. They worked long but erratic hours, frequently beginning in the late afternoon, quitting at dawn. They rarely showed up for group conferences and formal meetings, much to McPherson's annoyance. But they were undeniably good.

Gerhard, who wore cowboy boots and dungarees and satiny shirts with pearl buttons, had gained some national attention at the age of thirteen when he built a twenty-foot solid-fuel rocket behind his house in Phoenix. The rocket possessed a remarkably sophisticated electronic guidance system and Gerhard felt he could fire it into orbit. His neighbors, who could see the nose of the finished rocket sticking up above the garage in the backyard, were disturbed enough to call the police, and ultimately the Army was notified.

The Army examined Gerhard's rocket and shipped it to White Sands for firing. As it happened, the second stage ignited before disengagement and the rocket exploded two miles up; but by that time Gerhard had four patents on his guidance mechanism and a number of scholarship offers from colleges and industrial firms. He turned them all down, let his uncle invest the patent royalties, and when he was old enough to drive, bought a Maserati. He went to work for Lockheed in Palmdale, California, but quit after a year because he was blocked from advancement by a lack of formal engineering degrees. It was also true that his colleagues resented a seventeen-year-old with a Maserati Ghibli and a propensity for working in the middle of the night; it was felt he had no "team spirit."

Then McPherson hired him to work at the Neuropsychiatric Research Unit, designing electronic components to be synergistic with the human brain. McPherson, as head of the NPS, had interviewed dozens of candidates who thought the job was "a challenge" or "an interesting systems application context." Gerhard said he thought it would be fun, and was hired immediately.

Richards's background was similar. He had finished high school and gone to college for six months before being drafted by the Army. He was about to be sent to Vietnam when he began to suggest improvements in the Army's electronic scanning devices. The improvements worked, and Richards never got closer to combat than a laboratory in Santa Monica. When he was discharged, he also joined the NPS.

The wizard twins: Ross smiled.

"Hi, Jan," Gerhard said.

"How's it going, Jan?" Richards said.

They were both offhand. They were the only people on the Staff who dared refer to McPherson as "Rog." And McPherson put up with it.

"Okay," she said. "We've got our stage three through grand rounds. I'm going to see him now."

"We're just finishing a check on the computer," Gerhard said. "It looks fine." He pointed to a table with a microscope surrounded by a tangle of electronic meters and dials.

"Where is it?"

"Under the stage."

She looked closer. A clear plastic packet the size of a postage stamp lay under the microscope lens. Through the plastic she could see a dense jumble of micro-miniaturized electronic components. Forty contact points protruded from the plastic. With the help of the microscope, the twins were testing the points sequentially, using fine probes.

"The logic circuits are the last to be checked," Richards said. "And we have a backup unit, just in case."

Janet went over to the file-card storage shelves and began looking through the test cards. After a moment, she said, "Haven't you got any more psychodex cards?"

"They're over here," Gerhard said. "You want five-space or *n*-space?"

"*N*-space," she said.

Gerhard opened a drawer and took out a cardboard sheet. He also took out a flat plastic clipboard. Attached to the clipboard by a metal chain was a pointed metal probe, something like a pencil.

"This isn't for the stage three, is it?"

"Yes," she said.

"But you've run so many psychodexes on him before—"

"Just one more, for the records."

Gerhard handed her the card and clipboard. "Does your stage three know what's going on?"

"He knows most of it," she said.

Gerhard shook his head. "He must be out of his mind."

"He is," she said. "That's the problem."

At the seventh floor, she stopped at the nurses' station to ask for Benson's chart. A new nurse was there, who said, "I'm sorry but relatives aren't allowed to look at medical records."

"I'm Dr. Ross."

The nurse was flustered. "I'm sorry, Doctor, I didn't see a name tag. Your patient is in seven-oh-four."

"What patient?"

"Little Jerry Peters."

Dr. Ross looked blank.

"Aren't you the pediatrician?" the nurse asked, finally.

"No," she said. "I'm a psychiatrist at the NPS." She heard the stridency in her own voice, and it upset her. But all those years growing up with people who said, "You don't *really* want to be a doctor, you want to be a nurse," or, "Well, for a woman, pediatrics is best, I mean, the most natural thing. . . ."

"Oh," the nurse said. "Then you want Mr. Benson in seven-ten. He's been prepped."

"Thank you," she said. She took the chart and walked down the hall to Benson's room. She knocked on Benson's door and heard gunshots. She opened the door and saw that the lights were dimmed, except for a small bedside lamp, but the room was bathed in an electric-blue glow from a TV. On the screen, a man was saying, ". . . dead before he hit the ground. Two bullets right through the heart."

"Hello?" she said, and swung the door wider.

Benson looked over. He smiled and pressed a button beside the bed, turning off the TV. His head was wrapped in a towel.

"How are you feeling?" she asked, coming into the room. She sat on a chair beside the bed.

"Naked," he said, and touched the towel. "It's funny. You don't realize how much hair you have until somebody cuts it all off." He touched the towel again. "It must be worse for a woman." Then he looked at her and became embarrassed.

"It's not much fun for anybody," she said.

"I guess not." He lay back against the pillow. "After they did it, I looked in the wastebasket, and I was amazed. So much hair. And my head was cold. It was the funniest thing, a cold head. They put a towel around it. I said I wanted to look at my head—see what I looked like bald—but they said it wasn't a good idea. So I waited until after they left, and then I got out of bed and went into the bathroom. But when I got there . . ."

"Yes?"

"I didn't take the towel off." He laughed. "I couldn't do it. What does that mean?"

"I don't know. What do you think it means?"

He laughed again. "Why is it that psychiatrists never give you a straight answer?" He lit a cigarette and looked at her defiantly. "They told me I shouldn't smoke, but I'm doing it anyway."

"I doubt that it matters," she said. She was watching him closely. He seemed in good spirits, and she didn't want to take that away from him. But on the other hand, it wasn't entirely appropriate to be so cheerful on the eve of brain surgery.

"Ellis was here a few minutes ago," he said, puffing on the cigarette. "He put some marks on me. Can you see?" He lifted up the right side of his towel slightly, exposing white pale flesh over the skull. Two blue "X" marks were positioned behind the ear. "How do I look?" he asked, grinning.

"You look fine," she said. "How do you feel?"

"Fine. I feel fine."

"Any worries?"

"No. I mean, what is there to worry about? Nothing I can do. For the next few hours, I'm in your hands, and Ellis's hands. . . ." He bit his lip. "Of course I'm worried."

"What worries you?"

"Everything," he said. He sucked on the cigarette. "Everything. I worry about how I'll sleep. How I'll feel tomorrow. How I'll be when it's all over. What if somebody makes a mistake? What if I get turned into a vegetable? What if it hurts? What if I . . ."

"Die?"

"Sure. That, too."

"It's really a minor procedure. It's hardly more complicated than an appendectomy."

"I bet you tell that to all your brain-surgery patients."

"No, really. It's a short, simple procedure. It'll take about an hour and a half."

He nodded vaguely. She couldn't tell if she had reassured him. "You know," he said, "I don't really think it will happen. I keep thinking tomorrow morning at the last minute they'll come in and say, 'You're cured, Mr. Benson, you can go home now.' "

"We hope you'll be cured by the operation." She felt a twinge of guilt saying that, but it came out smoothly enough.

"You're so goddamned reasonable," he said. "There are times when I can't stand it."

"Like now?"

He touched the towel around his head again. "I mean, for Christ's sake, they're going to drill holes in my head, and stick wires in—"

"You've known about that for a long time."

"Sure," he said. "Sure. But this is the night before."

"Do you feel angry now?"

"No. Just scared."

"It's all right to be scared, it's perfectly normal. But don't let it make you angry."

He stubbed out the cigarette, and lit another immediately. Changing the subject, he pointed to the clipboard she carried under her arm. "What's that?"

"Another psychodex test. I want you to go through it."

"Now?"

"Yes. It's just for the record."

He shrugged indifferently. He had taken the psychodex several times before. She handed him the clipboard and he arranged the question card on the board, then began to answer the questions. He read them aloud:

"Would you rather be an elephant or a baboon? Baboon. Elephants live too long."

With the metal probe, he punched out the chosen answer on the card.

"If you were a color, would you rather be green or yellow? Yellow. I'm feeling very yellow right now." He laughed, and punched the answer.

She waited until he had done all thirty questions and punched his answers. He handed the clipboard back to her, and his mood seemed to shift again. "Are you going to be there? Tomorrow?"

"Yes."

"Will I be awake enough to recognize you?"

"I imagine so."

"And when will I come out of it?"

"Tomorrow afternoon or evening."

"That soon?"

"It's really a minor procedure," she said again. He nodded. She asked him if she could get him anything, and he said some ginger ale, and she replied that he was NPO, nothing *per ora*, for twelve hours before the operation. She said he'd be getting shots to help him sleep, and shots in the morning before he went to surgery. She said she hoped he'd sleep well.

As she left, she heard a hum as the television went back on, and a metallic voice said, "Look, Lieutenant, I've got a murderer out there, somewhere in a city of three million people. . . ."

She closed the door.

Before leaving the floor, she put a brief note in the chart. She drew a red line around it, so that the nurses would be sure to see it:

ADMITTING PSYCHIATRIC SUMMARY:

This 34-year-old man has documented ADL syndrome of 2 years' duration. The etiology is presumably traumatic, following an automobile accident. This patient has already tried to kill two people, and has been involved in fights with several others. Any statement by him to hospital staff that he "feels funny" or "smells something bad" should be respected as indicating the start of a seizure. Under such circumstances, notify the NPS and Hospital Security at once.

The patient has an accompanying personality disorder which is part of his disease. He is convinced that machines are conspiring to take over the world. These beliefs are strongly held and attempts to dissuade him from them will only draw his enmity and suspicion. One should also remember that he is a highly intelligent and sensitive man. The patient can be quite demanding at times, but he should be treated with firmness and respect.

His intelligent and articulate manner may lead one to forget that his attitudes are not willful. He suffers an organic disease which has affected his mental state. Beneath it all he is frightened and concerned about what is happening to him.

Janet Ross, M.D.
NPS

Chapter 4

"I don't understand," the public relations man said.

Ellis sighed. McPherson smiled patiently. "This is an organic cause of violent behavior," he said. "That's the way to look at it."

The three of them were sitting in the Four Kings Restaurant, adjacent to the hospital. The early dinner had been McPherson's idea; McPherson said he wanted Ellis present, so Ellis was present. That was how Ellis thought about it.

Ellis raised his hand, beckoning the waiter for more coffee. As he did so, he thought it might keep him awake. But it didn't matter: he wouldn't sleep much tonight anyway. Not on the eve of his first stage three on a human subject.

He knew he would toss and turn in bed, going over the operative procedure. Over and over again, reviewing the pattern he already knew so well. He'd done a lot of monkeys as stage-three procedures. One hundred and fifty-four monkeys, to be exact. Monkeys were difficult. They pulled out their stitches, they tugged at the wires, they screeched and fought you and bit you—

"Cognac?" McPherson asked.

"Fine," the PR man said.

McPherson glanced questioningly at Ellis. Ellis shook his head. He put cream in his coffee, and sat back suppressing a yawn. Actually, the PR man looked a little like a monkey. A juvenile rhesus: he had the same blocky lower jaw and the same bright-eyed alertness.

The PR man's name was Ralph. Ellis didn't know the last name. No PR man ever gave his last name. Of course, at the hospital he wasn't referred to as a PR man; he was the Hospital Information Officer or News Officer or some damned thing.

He did look like a monkey. Ellis found himself staring at the area of the skull behind the ear, where the electrodes would be implanted.

"We don't know much about the causes of violence," McPherson said. "And there's a lot of bad theory floating around, written by sociologists and paid for by good taxpayer money. But we do know that one particular brain disease, called ADL syndrome, may lead to violence."

"ADL syndrome," Ralph repeated.

"Yes. Acute Disinhibitory Lesion syndrome is caused by an injury or lesion to the brain. At the NPS, we think these lesions may be extremely common among those people who engage in repetitive violent acts—like certain policemen, gangsters, rioters, Hell's Angels. Nobody ever thinks of these people as *physically* ill. We just accept the idea that there are a lot of men in the world with bad tempers. We think that's normal. Perhaps it isn't."

"I see," Ralph said. And he did, indeed, seem to be seeing. McPherson should have been a grade-school teacher, Ellis thought. His great gift was teaching. Certainly he'd never been much of a researcher.

"So far," McPherson said, brushing his hand through his white hair, "we have no idea exactly how common ADL syndrome is. But our guess is that as much as one or two percent of the population may suffer from it. That's two to four million Americans."

"Gosh," Ralph said.

Ellis sipped his coffee. Gosh, he thought. Good Christ. Gosh . . .

"For some reason," McPherson said, nodding to the waiter as the cognacs were brought, "ADL patients are predisposed to violent, aggressive behavior during their attacks. We don't know why, but it's true. The other things that go along with the syndrome are hypersexuality and pathological intoxication."

Ralph began to look unusually interested.

"We had the case of one woman with this disease," McPherson said, "who during a seizure state would have intercourse with twelve men a night and still be unsatisfied."

Ralph swallowed his cognac. Ellis noticed that Ralph wore a wide tie in a fashionable psychedelic pattern. A hip forty-year-old public-relations man gulping cognac at the thought of this woman.

"Pathological intoxication refers to the phenomenon of excessive, violent drunkenness brought on by minuscule amounts of liquor—just a sip or two. That much liquor will unleash a seizure."

Ellis thought of his first stage three. Benson: pudgy little Benson, the mild-mannered computer programmer who got drunk and beat up people —men, women, whoever happened to be present. The very idea of curing that with wires stuck in the brain seemed absurd.

Ralph seemed to think so, too. "And this operation will cure the violence?"

"Yes," McPherson said. "We believe so. But the operation has never been done before on a human subject. It will be done at the hospital tomorrow morning."

"I *see,*" Ralph said, as if he suddenly understood the reason for the dinner.

"It's very sensitive, in terms of the press," McPherson said.

"Oh, yes, I can see that. . . ."

There was a short pause. Finally, Ralph said, "Who's going to do the operation?"

"I am," Ellis said.

"Well," Ralph said, "I'll have to check our files. I want to make sure I have a recent picture of you, and a good bio for the releases." He frowned, thinking of the work ahead of him.

Ellis was astonished at the man's reaction. Was that all he thought? That he might need a recent photo? But McPherson took it smoothly in stride. "We'll get you whatever you need," he said, and the meeting broke up.

Chapter 5

Robert Morris was sitting in the hospital cafeteria finishing some stale apple pie when his pagemaster went off. It produced a high electronic squeal, which persisted until he reached down to his belt and turned it off. He returned to his pie. After a few moments, the squeal came again. He swore, put down his fork, and went to the wall phone to answer his page.

There had been a time when he regarded the little gray box clipped to his belt as a wonderful thing. He relished those moments when he would be having lunch or dinner with a girl and his pagemaster would go off, requiring him to call in. That sound demonstrated that he was a busy, responsible person involved in life-and-death matters. When the pagemaster went off, he would excuse himself abruptly and answer the call, radiating a sense of duty before pleasure. The girls loved it.

But after several years it was no longer wonderful. The box was inhuman and implacable, and it had come to symbolize for him the fact that he was not his own man. He was perpetually on call to some higher authority, however whimsical—a nurse who wanted to confirm a medication order at 2 A.M.; a relative who was acting up, making trouble about Mama's post-operative treatment; a call to tell him a conference was being held when he was already there attending the damned conference.

Now the finest moments in his life were those when he went home and put the box away for a few hours. He became unreachable and free. And he liked that very much.

He stared across the cafeteria at the remainder of his apple pie as he dialed the switchboard. "Dr. Morris."

"Dr. Morris, two-four-seven-one."

"Thank you." That was the extension for the seventh floor nurses' station. He had long ago learned all the principal extensions of the University Hospital system. He dialed the floor. "Dr. Morris."

"Oh, yes," a female voice said. "We have a woman with an overnight bag for patient Harold Benson. She says it's personal things. Is it all right to give it to him?"

"I'll come up," he said.

"Thank you, Doctor."

He went back to his tray, picked it up, and carried it to the disposal area. As he did so, his beeper went off again. He went to answer it.

"Dr. Morris."

"Dr. Morris, one-three-five-seven."

That was the metabolic unit. He dialed. "Dr. Morris."

"This is Dr. Hanley," an unfamiliar voice said. "We wondered if you could take a look at a lady we think may have steroid psychosis. She's a hemolytic anemic up for splenectomy."

"I can't see her today," Morris said, "and tomorrow is tight." That, he thought, was the understatement of the year. "Have you tried Peters?"

"No . . ."

"Peters has a lot of experience with steroid mentation. Try him."

"All right. Thanks."

Morris hung up. He got onto the elevator and pressed the button for the seventh floor. His beeper went off a third time. He checked his watch; it was 6:30 and he was supposedly off-duty by now. But he answered it anyway. It was Kelso, the pediatric resident.

"Want your ass whipped?" Kelso said.

"Okay. What time?"

"Say, about half an hour?"

"If you've got the balls."

"I've got them. They're in my car."

"See you on the court," Morris said. Then he added, "I may be a little late."

"Don't be too late," Kelso said. "It'll be dark soon."

Morris said he would hurry, and hung up.

The seventh floor was quiet. Most of the other hospital floors were noisy, jammed with relatives and visitors at this hour, but the seventh floor was always quiet. It had a sedate, calm quality that the nurses were careful to preserve.

The nurse at the station said, "There she is, Doctor," and nodded to a girl sitting on a couch. Morris went over to her. She was young and very pretty in a flashy, show-business sort of way. She had long legs.

"I'm Dr. Morris."

"Angela Black." She stood up and shook hands, very formally. "I brought this for Harry." She lifted a small blue overnight bag. "He asked me to bring it."

"All right." He took the bag from her. "I'll see that he gets it."

She hesitated, then said, "Can I see him?"

"I don't think it's a good idea." Benson would have been shaved by now; pre-op patients who had been shaved often didn't want to see people.

"Just for a few minutes?"

"He's heavily sedated," he said.

She was clearly disappointed. "Then would you give him a message?"

"Sure."

"Tell him I'm back in my old apartment. He'll understand."

"All right."

"You won't forget?"

"No. I'll tell him."

"Thank you." She smiled. It was a rather nice smile, despite the long false eyelashes and the heavy make-up. Why did young girls do that to their faces? "I guess I'll be going now." And she walked off, short skirt and very long legs, a briskly determined walk. He watched her go, then hefted the bag, which seemed heavy.

The cop sitting outside the door to 710 said, "How's it going?"

"Fine," Morris said.

The cop glanced at the overnight bag but said nothing as Morris took it inside the room.

Harry Benson was watching a Western on television. Morris turned down the sound. "A very pretty girl brought you this."

"Angela?" Benson smiled. "Yes, she has a nice exterior. Not a very complicated internal mechanism, but a nice exterior." He extended his hand; Morris gave him the bag. "Did she bring everything?"

Morris watched as Benson opened it, placing the contents on the bed. There were a pair of pajamas, an electric razor, some after-shave lotion, a paperback novel.

Then Benson brought out a black wig.

"What's that?" Morris asked.

Benson shrugged. "I knew I'd need it sooner or later," he said. Then he laughed. "You *are* letting me out of here, aren't you? Sooner or later?"

Morris laughed with him. Benson dropped the wig back into the bag, and removed a plastic packet. With a metallic clink, he unfolded it, and Morris saw it was a set of screwdrivers of various sizes, stored in a plastic package with pockets for each size.

"What's that for?" Morris asked.

Benson looked puzzled for a moment. Then he said, "I don't know if you'll understand. . . ."

"Yes?"

"I always have them with me. For protection."

Benson placed the screwdrivers back into the overnighter. He handled them carefully, almost reverently. Morris knew that patients frequently brought odd things into the hospital, particularly if they were seriously ill. There was a kind of totemic feeling about these objects, as if they might have magical preservative powers. They were often connected with some hobby or favorite activity. He remembered a yachtsman with a metastatic brain tumor who had brought a kit to repair sails, and a woman with advanced heart disease who had brought a can of tennis balls. That kind of thing.

"I understand," Morris said.

Benson smiled.

Chapter 6

Telecomp was empty when she came into the room; the consoles and teleprinters stood silently, the screens blinking up random sequences of numbers. She went to the corner and poured herself a cup of coffee, then fed the test card from Benson's latest psychodex into the computer.

The NPS had developed the psychodex test, along with several other computer-analyzed psychological tests. It was all part of what McPherson called "double-edged thinking." In this case, he meant that the idea of a brain being like a computer worked two ways, in two different directions. On the one hand, you could utilize the computer to probe the brain, to help you analyze its workings. At the same time, you could use your increased knowledge of the brain to help design better and more efficient computers. As McPherson said, "The brain is as much a model for the computer as the computer is a model for the brain."

At the NPS, computer scientists and neurobiologists had worked together for several years. From that association had come Form Q, and programs like George and Martha, and new psychosurgical techniques, and psychodex.

Psychodex was relatively simple. It was a test that took straightforward answers to psychological questions and manipulated the answers according to complex mathematical formulations. As the data were fed into the computer, Ross watched the screen glow with row after row of calculations.

She ignored them; the numbers, she knew, were just the computer's scratch pad, the intermediate steps that it went through before arriving at a final answer. She smiled, thinking of how Gerhard would explain it—rotation of thirty by thirty matrices in space, deriving factors, making them orthogonal, then weighting them. It all sounded complicated and scientific, and she didn't really understand any of it.

She had discovered long ago that you could use a computer without understanding how it worked. Just as you could use an automobile, a vacuum cleaner—or your own brain.

The screen flashed "CALCULATIONS ENDED. CALL DISPLAY SEQUENCE."

She punched in the display sequence for three-space scoring. The computer informed her that three spaces accounted for eighty-one percent of variance. On the screen she saw a three-dimensional image of a mountain with a sharp peak. She stared at it a moment, then picked up the telephone and paged McPherson.

McPherson frowned at the screen. Ellis looked over his shoulder. Ross said, "Is it clear?"

"Perfectly," McPherson said. "When was it done?"

"Today," she said.

McPherson sighed. "You're not going to quit without a battle, are you?"

Instead of answering, she punched buttons and called up a second mountain peak, much lower. "Here's the last one previously."

"On this scoring, the elevation is—"

"Psychotic mentation," she said.

"So he's much more pronounced now," McPherson said. "Much more than even a month ago."

"Yes," she said.

"You think he was screwing around with the test?"

She shook her head. She punched in the four previous tests, in succession. The trend was clear: on each test the mountain peak got higher and sharper.

"Well, then," McPherson said, "he's definitely getting worse. I gather you still think we shouldn't operate."

"More than ever," she said. "He's unquestionably psychotic, and if you start putting wires in his head—"

"I know," McPherson said. "I know what you're saying."

"—he's going to feel that he's been turned into a machine," she said.

McPherson turned to Ellis. "Do you suppose we can knock this elevation

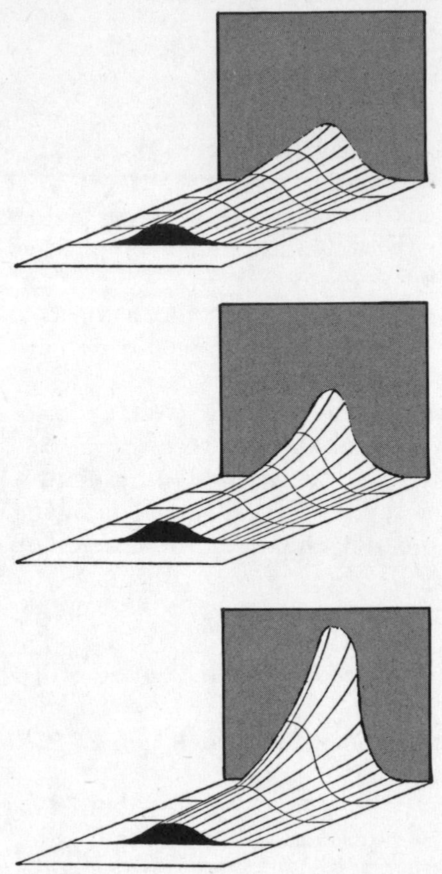

SERIAL PSYCHODEX SCORE REPRESENTATIONS SHOWING INCREASED ELEVATION (PSYCHOTIC MENTATION)

down with thorazine?" Thorazine was a major tranquilizer. With some psychotics, it helped them to think more clearly.

"I think it's worth a try."

McPherson nodded. "I do, too. Janet?"

She stared at the screen and didn't reply. It was odd how these tests worked. The mountain peaks were an abstraction, a mathematical representation of an emotional state. They weren't a real characteristic of a person, like fingers or toes, or height or weight.

"Janet? What do you think?" McPherson repeated.

"I think," she said, "that you're both committed to this operation."

"And you still disapprove?"

"I don't 'disapprove.' I think it's unwise for Benson."

"What do you think about using thorazine?" McPherson persisted.

"It's a gamble."

"A gamble not worth taking."

"Maybe it's worth it, and maybe it's not. But it's a gamble."

McPherson nodded and turned to Ellis. "Do you still want to do him?"

"Yes," Ellis said, staring at the screen. "I still want to do him."

Chapter 7

As always, Morris found it strange to play tennis on the hospital court. The hospital buildings looming high above him always made him feel slightly guilty—all those rows of windows, all those patients who could not do what he was doing. Then there was the sound. Or, rather, the absence of sound. The freeway ran near the hospital, and the reassuring *thwock!* of the tennis balls was completely obliterated by the steady, monotonous rush of passing cars.

It was getting dark now, and he was having trouble with his vision; the ball seemed to pop unexpectedly into his court. Kelso was much less hampered. Morris often joked that Kelso ate too many carrots, but whatever the explanation, it was humiliating to play late with Kelso. Darkness helped him. And Morris hated to lose.

He had long ago become comfortable with the fact of his own competitiveness. Morris never stopped competing. He competed in games, he competed in work, he competed with women. More than once Ross had pointed that out to him, and then dropped the subject in the sly way that psychiatrists raise a point, then drop it. Morris didn't mind. It was a fact of his life, and whatever the connotations—deep insecurity, a need to prove himself, a feeling of inferiority—he didn't worry about it. He drew pleasure from competition and satisfaction from winning. And so far in his life he had managed to win more often than not.

In part, he had joined the NPS because the challenges were very great and because the potential rewards were enormous. Privately, Morris expected to be a professor of surgery before he was forty. His past career had been outstanding—that was why Ellis had accepted him—and he was equally confident about his future. It wouldn't hurt to be associated with a landmark case in surgical history.

All in all, he was in a good mood, and he played hard for half an hour, until he was tired and it was too dark to see. He signaled to Kelso—no point in calling above the freeway sounds—to end the game. They met at the net and shook hands. Morris was reassured to see that Kelso was sweating heavily.

"Good game," Kelso said. "Tomorrow, same time?"

"I'm not sure," Morris said.

Kelso paused. "Oh," he said. "That's right. You have a big day tomorrow."

"Big day," Morris nodded. Christ, had the news even reached the pediatric residents? For a moment he felt what Ellis must be feeling—the intense pressure, abstract, vague, that came from knowing that the entire University Hospital staff was watching this procedure.

"Well, good luck with it," Kelso said.

As the two men walked back to the hospital, Morris saw Ellis, a distant solitary figure, limping slightly as he crossed the parking lot and climbed into his car, and drove home.

WEDNESDAY, MARCH 10, 1971: IMPLANTATION

Chapter 1

At 6 A.M. Janet Ross was on the third surgical floor, dressed in greens, having coffee and a doughnut. The surgeons' lounge was busy at this hour. Although operations were scheduled to begin at six, most didn't get going for fifteen or twenty minutes after that. The surgeons sat around, reading the newspaper, discussing the stock market and their golf games. From time to time one of them would leave, go to the overhead viewing galleries, and look down on their ORs to see how preparations were coming.

Ross was the only woman in the room, and her presence changed the masculine atmosphere subtly. It annoyed her that she should be the only woman, and it annoyed her that the men should become quieter, more polite, less jovial and raucous. She didn't give a damn if they were raucous, and she resented being made to feel like an intruder. It seemed to her that she had been an intruder all her life, even when she was very young. Her father had been a surgeon who never bothered to conceal his disappointment that he had a daughter instead of a son. A son would have fitted into his scheme of life; he could have brought him to the hospital on Saturday mornings, taken him into the operating rooms—those were all things you could do with a *son*. But a daughter was something else, a perplexing entity not suited for a surgical life. And therefore an intrusion . . .

She looked around at all the surgeons in the lounge, and then, to cover her unease, she went to the phone and dialed the seventh floor.

"This is Dr. Ross. Is Mr. Benson on call?"

"He was just sent."

"When did he leave the floor?"

"About five minutes ago."

She hung up and went back to her coffee. Ellis appeared and waved to her across the room. "There'll be a five-minute delay hooking into the computer," he said. "They're tying in the lines now. Is the patient on call?"

"Sent five minutes ago."

"You seen Morris?"

"Not yet."

"He better get his ass down here," Ellis said.

Somehow that made her feel good.

Morris was in the elevator with a nurse and Benson, who lay on a stretcher, and one of the cops. As they rode down, Morris said to the cop, "You can't get off on the floor."

"Why not?"

"We're going onto the sterile floor directly."

"What should I do?"

"You can watch from the viewing gallery on the third floor. Tell the desk nurse I said it was all right."

The cop nodded. The elevator stopped at the second floor. The doors opened to reveal a hallway with people, all in surgical greens, walking back and forth. A large sign read STERILE AREA. NO ADMITTANCE WITHOUT AUTHORIZATION. The lettering was red.

Morris and the nurse wheeled Benson out of the elevator. The cop remained behind, looking nervous. He pushed the button for the third floor, and the doors closed.

Morris went with Benson down the corridor. After a moment, Benson said, "I'm still awake."

"Of course you are."

"But I don't want to be awake."

Morris nodded patiently. Benson had gotten pre-op medications half an hour earlier. They would be taking effect soon, making him drowsy. "How's your mouth?"

"Dry."

That was the atropine beginning to work. "You'll be okay."

Morris himself had never had an operation. He'd performed hundreds, but never experienced one himself. In recent years, he had begun to wonder how it felt to be on the other side of things. He suspected, though he would never admit it, that it must be awful.

"You'll be okay," he said to Benson again, and touched his shoulder.

Benson just stared at him as he was wheeled down the corridor toward OR 9.

OR 9 was the largest operating room in the hospital. It was nearly thirty feet square and packed with electronic equipment. When the full surgical team was there—all twelve of them—things got pretty crowded. But now just two scrub nurses were working in the cavernous gray-tiled space. They were setting out sterile tables and drapes around the chair. OR 9 had no operating table—only a cushioned upright chair, like a dentist's chair.

Janet Ross was in the scrub room adjacent to the operating room. Alongside her, Ellis finished his scrub and muttered something about fucking Morris being fucking late. Ellis got very nervous before operations, though he seemed to think nobody noticed it. Ross had scrubbed with him on several animal procedures and had seen the ritual—tension and profanity before the operation, and utter bland calmness once things were under way.

Ellis turned off the faucets with his elbows and entered the OR, backing in so that his arms did not touch the door. A nurse handed him a towel. While he dried his hands, he looked back through the door at Ross, and then up at the glass-walled viewing gallery overhead. Ross knew there would be a crowd in the gallery watching the operation.

Morris came down and began scrubbing. She said, "Ellis wondered where you were."

"Bringing down the patient," he said.

One of the circulating nurses entered the scrub room and said, "Dr. Ross, there's somebody here from the radiation lab with a unit for Dr. Ellis. Does he want it now?"

"If it's loaded," she said.

"I'll ask," the nurse said. She disappeared, and stuck her head in a moment later. "He says it's loaded and ready to go, but unless your equipment is shielded it could give you trouble."

Ross knew that all the OR equipment had been shielded the week before. The plutonium exchanger didn't put out much radiation—not enough to fog an X-ray plate—but it could confuse more delicate scientific equipment. There was, of course, no danger to people.

"We're shielded," Ross said. "Have him take it into the OR."

Ross turned to Morris, scrubbing alongside her. "How's Benson?"

"Nervous."

"He should be," she said. Morris glanced at her, his eyes questioning above the gauze surgical mask. She shook her hands free of excess water and backed into the OR. The first thing she saw was the rad-lab man wheeling in the tray with the charging unit on it. It was contained in a small lead box. On the sides were stenciled DANGER RADIATION and the triple-blade orange symbol for radiation. It was all faintly ridiculous; the charging unit was quite safe.

Ellis stood across the room, being helped into his gown. He plunged his hands into his rubber gloves and flexed his fingers. To the rad-lab man he said, "Has it been sterilized?"

"Sir?"

"Has the unit been sterilized?"

"I don't know, sir."

"Then give it to one of the girls and have her autoclave it. It's got to be sterile."

Dr. Ross dried her hands and shivered in the cold of the operating room. Like most surgeons, Ellis preferred a cold room—too cold, really, for the patient. But as Ellis often said, "If I'm happy, the patient's happy."

Ellis was now across the room standing by the viewing box, while the circulating nurse, who was not scrubbed, put up the patient's X-rays. Ellis peered closely at them, though he had seen them a dozen times before. They were perfectly normal skull films. Air had been injected into the ventricles, so that the horns stood out darkly.

One by one the rest of the team filtered into the room. All together, there were two scrub nurses, two circulating nurses, one orderly, Ellis, two assistant surgeons including Morris, two electronics technicians, and a computer programmer. The anaesthetist was outside with Benson.

Without looking up from his console, one of the electronics men said, "Any time you want to begin, Doctor."

"We'll wait for the patient," Ellis said dryly, and there were some chuckles from the Nine Group team.

Ross looked around the room at the seven TV screens. They were of different sizes and stationed in different places, depending on how important they were to the surgeon. The smallest screen monitored the closed-circuit taping of the operation. At the moment, it showed an overhead view of the empty chair.

Another screen, nearer the surgeon, monitored the electroencephalogram, or EEG. It was turned off now, the sixteen pens tracing straight white lines across the screen. There was also a large TV screen for basic operative parameters: electrocardiogram, peripheral arterial pressure, respirations, cardiac output, central venous pressure, rectal temperature. Like the EEG screen, it was also tracing a series of straight lines.

Another pair of screens were completely blank. They would display black-and-white image-intensified X-ray views during the operation.

Finally, two color screens displayed the LIMBIC Program output. That program was cycling now, without punched-in coordinates. On the screens, a picture of the brain rotated in three dimensions while random coordinates, generated by computer, flashed below. As always, Ross felt that the computer was another, almost human presence in the room—an impression that was always heightened as the operation proceeded.

Ellis finished looking at the X-rays and glanced up at the clock. It was 6:19; Benson was still outside being checked by the anaesthetist. Ellis walked around the room, talking briefly to everyone. He was being unusually friendly, and Ross wondered why. She looked up at the viewing gallery and saw the director of the hospital, the chief of surgery, the chief of medicine, and the chief of research all looking down through the glass. Then she understood.

It was 6:21 when Benson was wheeled in. He was now heavily premedicated, relaxed, his body limp, his eyelids heavy. His head was wrapped in a green towel.

Ellis supervised Benson's transfer from the stretcher to the chair. As the leather straps were placed across his arms and legs, Benson seemed to wake up, his eyes opening wide.

"That's just so you don't fall off," Ellis said easily. "We don't want you to hurt yourself."

"Uh-huh," Benson said softly, and closed his eyes again.

Ellis nodded to the nurses, who removed the sterile towel from Benson's head. The naked head seemed very small—that was Ross's usual reaction—and white. The skin was smooth, except for a razor nick on the left frontal. Ellis's blue-ink "X" marks were clearly visible on the right side.

Benson leaned back in the chair. He did not open his eyes again. One of the technicians began to fix the monitor leads to his body, strapping them on with little dabs of electrolyte paste. They were attached quickly; soon his body was connected to a tangle of multicolored wires running off to the equipment.

Ellis looked at the TV monitor screens. The EEG was now tracing sixteen jagged lines; heartbeat was recorded; respirations were gently rising and falling; temperature was steady. The technicians began to punch pre-op parameters into the computer. Normal lab values had already been fed in. During the operation, the computer would monitor all vital signs at five-second intervals, and would signal if anything went wrong.

"Let's have music, please," Ellis said, and one of the nurses slipped a tape cartridge into the portable cassette recorder in a corner of the room. A Bach concerto began to play softly. Ellis always operated to Bach; he said he hoped that the precision, if not the genius, might be contagious.

They were approaching the start of the operation. The digital wall clock said 6:29:14 A.M. Next to it, an elapsed-time digital clock still read 0:00:00.

With the help of a scrub nurse, Ross put on her sterile gown and gloves. The gloves were always difficult for her. She didn't scrub in frequently, and when she plunged her fingers into the gloves she caught her hand, missing one of the finger slots and putting two fingers in another. It was impossible to read the scrub nurse's reaction; only her eyes were visible above the mask. But Ross was glad that Ellis and the other surgeons were turned away attending to the patient.

She stepped to the back of the room, being careful not to trip over the thick black power cables that snaked across the floor in all directions. Ross did not participate in the initial stages of the operation. She waited until the stereotaxic mechanism was in place and the coordinates were determined. She had time to stand to one side and pluck at her glove until all the fingers were in the right slots.

There was no real need for her to attend the operation at all, but McPherson insisted that one member of the non-surgical staff scrub in each day that they operated. He said it made the Unit more cohesive.

She watched Ellis and his assistants across the room draping Benson; then she looked over to the draping as seen on the closed-circuit monitor. The entire operation would be recorded on video tape for later review.

"I think we can start now," Ellis said easily. "Go ahead with the needle."

The anaesthetist, working behind the chair, placed the needle between the second and third lumbar spaces of Benson's spine. Benson moved once and made a slight sound, and then the anaesthetist said, "I'm through the dura. How much do you want?"

The computer console flashed "OPERATION BEGUN." The computer automatically started the elapsed-time clock, which ticked off the seconds.

"Give me thirty cc's to begin," Ellis said. "Let's have X-ray, please."

The X-ray machines were swung into position at the front and side of the patient's head. Film plates were set on, locking in with a click. Ellis stepped on the floor button, and the TV screens glowed suddenly, showing black-and-white images of the skull. He watched in two views as air slowly filled the ventricles, outlining the horns in black.

The programmer sat at the computer console, his hands fluttering over the buttons. On his TV display screen, the words "PNEUMOGRAPH INITIATED" appeared.

"All right, let's fix his hat," Ellis said. The box-like tubular stereotactic frame was placed over the patient's head. Burr-hole locations were fixed and checked. When Ellis was satisfied, he injected local anaesthetic into the scalp points. Then he cut the skin and reflected it back, exposing the white surface of the skull.

"Drill, please."

With the 2-mm drill, he made the first of the two holes on the right side of the skull. He placed the stereotactic frame—the "hat"—over the head, and screwed it down securely.

Ross looked over at the computer display. Values for heart rate and blood pressure flashed on the screen and faded; everything was normal. Soon the computer, like the surgeons, would begin to deal with more complex matters.

"Let's have a position check," Ellis said, stepping away from the patient, frowning critically at Benson's shaved head and the metal frame screwed on top of it. The X-ray technician came forward and snapped the pictures.

In the old days, Ross remembered, they actually took X-ray plates and determined position by visual inspection of the plates. It was a slow process. Using a compass, protractor, and ruler, they drew lines across the X-ray, measured them, rechecked them. Now the data were fed directly to the computer, which did the analysis more rapidly and more accurately.

All the team turned to look at the computer print-out screen. The X-ray views appeared briefly, and were replaced by schematic drawings. The maxfield location of the stereotactic apparatus was calculated; the actual location was then merged with it. A set of coordinates flashed up, followed by the notation "PLACEMENT CORRECT."

Ellis nodded. "Thank you for your consultation," he said, and went over to the tray which held the electrodes.

The team was now using Briggs stainless-steel Teflon-coated electrode arrays. In the past, they had tried gold, platinum alloy, and even flexible steel strands, back in the days when the electrodes were placed by inspection.

The old inspection operations were bloody, messy affairs. It was necessary to remove a large portion of the skull and expose the surface of the brain. The surgeon found his landmark points on the surface itself, and then placed his electrodes in the substance of the brain. If he had to place them in deep structures, he would occasionally cut through the brain to the ventricles with a knife, and then place them. There were serious complications; the operations were lengthy; the patients never did very well.

Now the computer had changed all that. The computer allowed you to fix a point precisely in three-dimensional space. Initially, along with other researchers in the field, the NPS group had tried to relate deep brain points to skull architecture. They measured their landmark points from the orbit of the eye, from the meatus of the ear, from the sagittal suture. That, of course, didn't work—people's brains did not fit inside their skulls with any consistency. The only way to determine deep brain points was in relation to other brain points—and the logical landmarks were the ventricles, the fluid-filled spaces within the brain. According to the new system, everything was determined in relation to the ventricles.

With the help of the computer, it was no longer necessary to expose the brain surface. Instead, a few small holes were drilled in the skull and the electrodes inserted, while the computer watched by X-ray to make sure they were being placed correctly.

Ellis picked up the first electrode array. From where Ross stood, it looked like a single slender wire. Actually, it was a bundle of twenty wires, with staggered contact points. Each wire was coated with Teflon except for the last millimeter, which was exposed. Each wire was a different length, so that under a magnifying glass, the staggered electrode tips looked like a miniature staircase.

Ellis checked the array under a large glass. He called for more light and turned the array, peering at all contact points. Then he had a scrub nurse plug it into a testing unit and test every contact. This had been done dozens of times before, but Ellis always checked again before insertion. And he always had four arrays sterilized, though he would need only two. Ellis was careful.

At length he was satisfied. "Are we ready to wire?" he asked the team. They nodded. He stepped up to the patient and said, "Let's go through the dura."

Up to this point in the operation, they had drilled through the skull, but had left intact the membrane of *dura mater* which covered the brain and enclosed the spinal fluid. Ellis's assistant used a probe to puncture the dura.

"I have fluid," he said, and a thin trickle of clear liquid slid down the side of the shaved skull from the hole. A nurse sponged it away.

Ross always found it a source of wonder the way the brain was protected. Other vital body organs were well-protected, of course: the lungs and heart inside the bony cage of the ribs, the liver and spleen under the edge of the ribs, the kidneys packed in fat and secure against thick muscles of the lower back. Good protection, but nothing compared to the central nervous system, which was encased entirely in thick bone. Yet even this was not enough; inside the bone there were sac-like membranes which held cerebrospinal fluid. The fluid was under pressure, so that the brain sat in the middle of a pressurized liquid system that afforded it superb protection.

McPherson had compared it to a fetus in a water-filled womb. "The baby comes out of the womb," McPherson said, "but the brain never comes out of its own special womb."

"We will place now," Ellis said.

Ross moved forward, joining the surgical team gathered around the head. She watched as Ellis slid the tip of the electrode array into the burr hole and then pressed slightly, entering the substance of the brain. The technician punched buttons on the computer console. The display screen read: "ENTRY POINT LOCALIZED."

The patient did not move, made no sound. The brain could not feel pain; it lacked pain sensors. It was one of the freaks of evolution that the organ which sensed pain throughout the body could feel nothing itself.

Ross looked away from Ellis toward the X-ray screens. There, in harsh black and white, she saw the crisply outlined white electrode array begin its slow, steady movement into the brain. She looked from the anterior view to the lateral, and then to the computer-generated images.

The computer was interpreting the X-ray images by drawing a simplified brain, with the temporal-lobe target area in red and a flickering blue track showing the line the electrode must traverse from entry point to the target area. So far, Ellis was following the track perfectly.

"Very pretty," Ross said.

The computer flashed up triple coordinates in rapid succession as the electrodes went deeper.

"Practice makes perfect," Ellis said sourly. He was now using the scale-down apparatus attached to the stereotactic hat. The scaler reduced his crude finger movements to very small changes in electrode movements. If he moved his finger half an inch, the scaler converted that to half a millimeter. Very slowly the electrodes penetrated deeper into the brain.

From the screens, Ross could lift her eyes and watch the closed-circuit TV monitor showing Ellis at work. It was easier to watch on TV than to turn around and see the real thing. But she turned around when she heard Benson say, very distinctly, "Uh."

Ellis stopped. "What was that?"

"Patient," the anaesthetist said, gesturing toward Benson.

Ellis paused, bent over, to look at Benson's face. "You all right, Mr. Benson?" He spoke loudly, distinctly.

"Yuh. Fine," Benson said. His voice was deeply drugged.

"Any pain?"

"No."

"Good. Just relax now." And he returned to his work.

Ross sighed in relief. Somehow, all that had made her tense, even though she knew there was no reason for alarm. Benson could feel no pain, and she had known all along that his sedation was only that—a kind of deep, drugged semisleep, and not unconsciousness. There was no reason for him to be unconscious, no reason to risk general anaesthesia.

She turned back to the computer screen. The computer had now presented an inverted view of the brain, as seen from below, near the neck. The electrode track was visible end on, as a single blue point surrounded by concentric circles. Ellis was supposed to keep within one millimeter, one twenty-fifth of an inch, of the assigned track. He deviated half a millimeter.

"50 TRACK ERROR," warned the computer. Ross said, "You're slipping off."

The electrode array stopped in its path. Ellis glanced up at the screens. "Too high on beta plane?"

"Wide on gamma."

"Okay."

After a moment, the electrodes continued along the path. "40 TRACK ERROR," the computer flashed. It rotated its brain image slowly, bringing up an anterolateral view. "20 TRACK ERROR," it said.

"You're correcting nicely," Ross said.

Ellis hummed along with the Bach and nodded.

"ZERO TRACK ERROR," the computer indicated, and swung the brain view around to a full lateral. The second screen showed a full frontal view. After a few moments, the screen blinked "APPROACHING TARGET." Ross conveyed the message.

Seconds later, the flashing word "STRIKE."

"You're on," Ross said.

Ellis stepped back and folded his hands across his chest. "Let's have a coordinate check," he said. The elapsed-time clock showed that twenty-seven minutes had passed in the operation.

The programmer flicked the console buttons rapidly. On the TV screens, the placement of the electrode was simulated by the computer. The simulation ended, like the actual placement, with the word "STRIKE."

"Now match it," Ellis said.

The computer held its simulation on one screen and matched it to the X-ray image of the patient. The overlap was perfect; the computer reported "MATCHED WITHIN ESTABLISHED LIMITS."

"That's it," Ellis said. He screwed on the little plastic button cap which held the electrodes tightly against the skull. Then he applied dental cement to fix it. He untangled the twenty fine wire leads that came off the electrode array and pushed them to one side.

"We can do the next one now," he said.

At the end of the second placement, a thin, arcing cut was made with a knife along the scalp. To avoid important superficial vessels and nerves, the cut ran from the electrode entry points down the side of the ear to the base of the neck. There it deviated to the right shoulder. Using blunt dissection, Ellis opened a small pocket beneath the skin of the right lateral chest, near the armpit.

"Have we got the charging unit?" he asked.

The charger was brought to him. It was smaller than a pack of cigarettes, and contained thirty-seven grams of the radioactive isotope plutonium-239 oxide. The radiation produced heat, which was converted directly by a thermionic unit to electric power. A Kenbeck solid-state DC/DC circuit transformed the output to the necessary voltage.

Ellis plugged the charger into the test pack and did a last-minute check of its power before implantation. As he held it in his hand, he said, "It's cold. I can't get used to that." Ross knew layers of vacuum-foil insulation kept the exterior cool and that inside the packet the radiation capsule was producing heat at 500 degrees Fahrenheit—hot enough to cook a roast.

He checked radiation to be sure there would be no leakage. The meters all read in the low-normal range. There was a certain amount of leakage, naturally, but it was no more than that produced by a commercial color television set.

Finally he called for the dog tag. Benson would have to wear this dog tag for as long as he had the atomic charging unit in his body. The tag warned that the person had an atomic pacemaker, and gave a telephone number. Ross knew that the number was a listing which played a recorded message twenty-four hours a day. The recording gave detailed technical information about the charging unit, and warned that bullet wounds, automobile accidents, fires, and other damage could release the plutonium, which was a powerful alpha-particle emitter. It gave special instructions to physicians, coroners, and morticians, and warned particularly against cremation of the body, unless the charger was first removed.

Ellis inserted the charging unit into the small subdermal pocket he had made in the chest wall. He sewed tissue layers around it to fix it in place. Then he turned his attention to the postage-stamp-sized electronic computer.

Ross looked up at the viewing gallery and saw the wizard twins, Gerhard and Richards, watching intently. Ellis checked the packet under the magnifying glass, then gave it to a scrubbed technician, who hooked the little computer into the main hospital computer.

To Ross, the computer was the most remarkable part of the entire system. Since she had joined the NPS three years before, she had seen the computer shrink from a prototype as large as a briefcase to the present tiny model, which looked small in the palm of a hand yet contained all the elements of the original bulky unit.

This tiny size made subdermal implantation possible. The patient was free to move about, take showers, do anything he wanted. Much better than the old units, where the charger was clipped to a patient's belt and wires dangled down all over.

She looked at the computer screens which flashed "OPERATIVE MONITORS INTERRUPTED FOR ELECTRONICS CHECK." On one screen, a blown-up circuit diagram appeared. The computer checked each pathway and component independently. It took four-millionths of a second for each check; the entire process was completed in two seconds. The computer flashed "ELECTRONIC CHECK NEGATIVE." A moment later, brain views reappeared. The computer had gone back to monitoring the operation.

"Well," Ellis said, "let's hook him up." He painstakingly attached the forty fine wire leads from the two electrode arrays to the plastic unit. Then he fitted the wires down along the neck, tucked the plastic under the skin, and called for sutures. The elapsed-time clock read one hour and twelve minutes.

Chapter 2

Morris wheeled Benson into the recovery room, a long, low-ceilinged room where patients were brought immediately after operation. The NPS had a special section of the rec room, as did cardiac patients and burns patients. But the NPS section, with its cluster of electronic equipment, had never been used before. Benson was the first case.

Benson looked pale but otherwise fine; his head and neck were heavily bandaged. Morris supervised his transfer from the rolling stretcher to the permanent bed. Across the room, Ellis was telephoning in his operative note. If you dialed extension 1104, you got a transcribing machine. The dictated message would later be typed up by a secretary and inserted in Benson's record.

Ellis's voice droned on in the background. ". . . centimeter incisions were made over the right temporal region, and 2-millimeter burr holes drilled with a K-7 drill. Implantation of Briggs electrodes carried out with computer assistance on the LIMBIC Program. Honey, that's spelled in capital letters, L-I-M-B-I-C. Program. X-ray placement of electrodes determined with computer review as within established limits. Electrodes sealed with Tyler fixation caps and seven-oh-grade dental sealer. Transmission wires—"

"What do you want on him?" the rec-room nurse asked.

"Vital signs Q five minutes for the first hour, Q fifteen for the second, Q thirty for the third, hourly thereafter. If he's stable, you can move him up to the floor in six hours."

The nurse nodded, making notes. Morris sat down by the bedside to write a short operative note:

Short operative note on Harold F. Benson

Pre-op dx:	*acute disinhibitory lesion (temporal focus)*	
Post-op dx:	*same*	
Procedure:	*implantation of twin Briggs electrode arrays into right temporal lobe with subdermal placing of computer and plutonium charging unit.*	
Pre-op meds:	*phenobarbital 500 mg* *atropine 60 mg*	*one hr. prior to procedure*

Anaesthesia: lidocaine (1/1000) epinephrine locally
Estimated blood loss: 250 cc
Fluid replacement: 200 cc D5/W
Operative duration: 1 hr. 12 min.
Post-op condition: good

As he finished the note, he heard Ross say to the nurse, "Start him on phenobarb as soon as he's awake." She sounded angry.

Morris looked up at her. She was frowning, her face tight. "Something the matter, Jan?"'

"No," she said. "Of course not."

"Well, if there's anything you want to—"

"Just make sure he gets his phenobarb. We want to keep him sedated until we can interface him."

And she stormed out of the room. Morris watched her go, then glanced over at Ellis, who was still dictating but had been watching. Ellis shrugged.

Morris adjusted the monitoring equipment on the shelf above Benson's head. He turned it on and waited until it warmed up. Then he placed the temporary induction unit around Benson's taped shoulder.

During the operation, all the wires had been hooked up, but they were not working yet. First, Benson would have to be "interfaced." This meant determining which of the forty electrodes would stop his seizures, and locking in the appropriate switches on the subdermal computer. Because the computer was under the skin, the locking in would be accomplished by an induction unit, which worked through the skin. But the interfacing couldn't be done until tomorrow.

Meanwhile, the equipment monitored Benson's brainwave activity. The screens above the bed glowed a bright green, and showed the white tracing of his EEG. The pattern was normal for alpha rhythms slowing from sedation.

Benson opened his eyes and looked at Morris.

"How do you feel?" he asked.

"Sleepy," he said. "Is it beginning soon?"

"It's over," Morris said.

Benson nodded, not at all surprised, and closed his eyes. A rad-lab technician came in and checked for leakage from the plutonium with a Geiger counter. There was none. Morris slipped the dog tag around Benson's neck. The nurse picked it up curiously, read it, and frowned.

Ellis came over. "Time for breakfast?"

"Yes," Morris said. "Time for breakfast."

They left the room together.

Chapter 3

The trouble was he didn't really like the sound of his voice. His voice was rough and grating, and his enunciation was poor. McPherson preferred to see the words in his mind, as if they had been written. He pressed the microphone button on the dictation machine. "Roman numeral three. Philosophical Implications."

III. Philosophical Implications.

He paused and looked around his office. The large model of the brain sat at the corner of his desk. Shelves of journals along one wall. And the TV monitor. On the screen now he was watching the playback of the morning's operation. The sound was turned off, the milky images silent. Ellis was drilling holes in Benson's head. McPherson watched and began to dictate.

This procedure represents the first direct link between a human brain and a computer. The link is permanent. Now of course, any man sitting at a computer console and interacting with the computer by pressing buttons can be said to be linked.

Too stuffy, he thought. He ran the tape back and made changes. *Now, a man sitting at a computer console and interacting with the computer by pressing buttons is linked to the computer. But that link is not direct. And the link is not permanent. Therefore, this operative procedure represents something rather different. How is one to think about it?*

He stared at the TV image of the operation, then continued.

One might think of the computer in this case as a prosthetic device. Just as a man who has his arm amputated can receive a mechanical equivalent of the lost arm, so a brain-damaged man can receive a mechanical aid to overcome the effects of brain damage. This is a comfortable way to think about the operation. It makes the computer into a high-class wooden leg. Yet the implications go much further than that.

He paused to look at the screen. Somebody at the main tape station had changed reels. He was no longer seeing the operation, but a psychiatric interview with Benson before the surgery. Benson was excited, smoking a cigarette, making stabbing gestures with the lighted tip as he spoke.

Curious, McPherson turned the sound up slightly. ". . . know what they're doing. The machines are everywhere. They used to be the servants of man, but now they're taking over. Subtly, subtly taking over."

Ellis stuck his head into the office, saw the TV screen, and smiled. "Looking at the 'before' pictures?"

"Trying to get a little work done," McPherson said, and pointed to the dictation machine.

Ellis nodded, ducked out, closing the door behind him.

Benson was saying, ". . . know I'm a traitor to the human race, because I'm helping to make machines more intelligent. That's my job, programming artificial intelligence, and—"

McPherson turned the sound down until it was almost inaudible. Then he went back to his dictation.

In thinking about computer hardware, we distinguish between central and peripheral equipment. That is, the main computer is considered central even though, in human terms, it may be located in some out-of-the-way place—like the basement of a building, for example. The computer's read-out equipment, display consoles, and so on, are peripheral. They are located at the edges of the computer system, on different floors of the building.

He looked at the TV screen. Benson was particularly excited. He turned up the sound and heard, ". . . getting more intelligent. First steam engines, then automobiles, and airplanes, then adding machines. Now computers, feedback loops—"

McPherson turned the sound off.

For the human brain, the analogy is a central brain and peripheral terminals, such as mouth, arms, and legs. They carry out the instructions—the output—of the brain. By and large, we judge the workings of the brain by the activity of these peripheral functions. We notice what a person says, and how he acts, and from that deduce how his brain works. This idea is familiar to everyone.

He looked at Benson on the TV screen. What would Benson say? Would he agree or disagree?

Now, however, in this operation we have created a man with not one brain but two. He has his biological brain, which is damaged, and he has a new computer brain, which is designed to correct the damage. This new brain is intended to control the biological brain. Therefore a new situation arises. The patient's biological brain is the peripheral terminal—the only peripheral terminal—for the new computer. In one area, the new computer brain has total control. And therefore the patient's biological brain, and indeed his whole body, has become a terminal for the new computer. We have created a man who is one single, large, complex computer terminal. The patient is a read-out device for the new computer, and he is as helpless to control the read-out as a TV screen is helpless to control the information presented on it.

Perhaps that was a bit strong, he thought. He pressed the button and said, "Harriet, type that last paragraph but I want to look at it, okay? Roman numeral four. Summary and Conclusions."

IV. Summary and Conclusions.

He paused again, and turned up the sound on Benson. Benson was saying, ". . . hate them, particularly the prostitutes. Airplane mechanics, dancers, translators, gas-station attendants, the people who are machines, or who service machines. The prostitutes. I hate them all."

As he spoke, Benson continued to stab with his cigarette.

Chapter 4

"And how did you feel?" Dr. Ramos said.

"Angry," Janet Ross said. "Angry as hell. I mean, that nurse was standing there, watching it all. She pretended she didn't understand what was happening, but she did."

"You felt angry about . . ." Dr. Ramos let his voice trail off.

"About the operation. About Benson. They went ahead and did it. I told them from the beginning—from the goddamned very beginning—that it was a bad idea, but Ellis and Morris and McPherson all wanted to do it. They're so cocky. Particularly Morris. When I saw him in the recovery room, gloating over Benson—who was all taped up and pale as a ghost—I just got mad."

"Why is that?"

"Because he was so pale, because he, uh—"

She stopped. She fumbled for an answer, but couldn't think of a logical response.

"I gather the operation was successful," Dr. Ramos said. "And most people are pale after surgery. What made you mad?"

She said nothing. Finally, she said, "I don't know."

She heard Dr. Ramos shift in his chair. She could not see him; she was lying on the couch, and Dr. Ramos was behind her head. There was a long silence while she stared at the ceiling and tried to think what to say. Her thoughts seemed to be churning, not making any sense. Finally Dr. Ramos said, "The presence of the nurse seems important to you."

"It does?"

"Well, you mentioned it."

"I wasn't aware I had."

"You said the nurse was there and knew what was going on. . . . What, exactly, was going on?"

"I was mad."

"But you don't know why? . . ."

"Yes, I do," she said. "It was Morris. He's so cocky."

"Cocky," Dr. Ramos repeated.

"Overly self-assured."

"You said cocky."

"Look, I didn't mean anything by that; it was just a word—" She broke off. She was very angry. She could hear it in her voice.

"You are angry now," Dr. Ramos said.

"Very."

"Why?"

After a long pause, she sad, "They didn't listen to me."

"Who didn't listen to you?"

"Any of them. Not McPherson, not Ellis, not Morris. Nobody listened to me."

"Did you tell Dr. Ellis or Dr. McPherson you were angry?"

"No."

"But you indicated your anger to Dr. Morris."

"Yes." He was leading her someplace and she couldn't see where. Normally at this point she could jump ahead and understand. But this time—

"How old is Dr. Morris?"

"I don't know. About my age. Thirty, thirty-one—something in there."

"About your age."

That pissed her off, his way of repeating things. "Yes, God damn it, about my age."

"And a surgeon."

"Yes. . . ."

"Is it easier to express anger toward someone you regard as a contemporary?"

"Probably. I never thought about it."

"Your father was also a surgeon, but he wasn't your contemporary."

"You don't have to draw me a picture," she said.

"You're still angry."

She sighed. "Let's change the subject."

"All right," he said, in that easy voice that she sometimes liked, and sometimes hated.

Chapter 5

Morris hated to do Initial Interviews. The Initial Interview staff consisted mostly of clinical psychologists; the work was lengthy and boring. A recent tabulation had shown that only one in forty new patients to the NPS received further work; and only one in eighty-three was accepted as having some variety of organic brain disease with behavioral manifestations. That meant most Initial Interviews were a waste of time.

And it was particularly true of off-the-street patients. A year ago McPherson had decided, for political reasons, that anyone who heard of the NPS and presented himself directly would be seen. Most patients were still referrals, of course, but McPherson felt the image of the Unit depended upon prompt treatment of self-referrals as well.

McPherson also believed that everyone on the staff should do some Initial Interviews from time to time. Morris worked two days a month in the little interview rooms with the one-way glass mirrors. This was one of his days, but he didn't want to be here; he was still exhilarated from the morning's operation, and he resented returning to this kind of mundane routine.

He looked up unhappily as the next patient came into the room. He was a young man in his twenties, wearing dungarees and a sweatshirt. He had long hair. Morris stood to greet him.

"I'm Dr. Morris."

"Craig Beckerman." The handshake was soft and tentative.

"Please sit down." He waved Beckerman to a chair which faced Morris's desk, and the one-way mirror behind. "What brings you to us?"

"I, uh . . . I'm curious. I read about you," Beckerman said, "in a magazine. You do brain surgery here."

"That's true."

"Well, I uh . . . I was curious about it."

"In what sense?"

"Well, this magazine article—Can I smoke here?"

"Of course," Morris said. He pushed an ashtray across the desk to Beckerman. Beckerman brought out a pack of Camels, tapped one on the desk, then lit it.

"The magazine article . . ."

"Right. The magazine article said that you put wires in the brain. Is that true?"

"Yes, we sometimes perform that kind of surgery."

Beckerman nodded. He smoked the cigarette. "Yeah, well, is it true that you can put wires in so that you feel pleasure? Intense pleasure?"

"Yes," Morris said. He tried to say it blandly.

"That's really true?"

"It's really true," Morris said. And then he shook his pen, indicating that it was out of ink. He opened the desk drawer to take out another pen, and as he reached into the drawer, he pressed a sequence on the buttons hidden inside. Immediately his telephone rang.

"Dr. Morris."

At the other end, the secretary said, "You rang?"

"Yes. Would you hold all calls, please, and transfer them to Development section?"

"Right away," the secretary said.

"Thank you." Morris hung up. He knew that the Development people would arrive soon, to watch on the other side of the one-way mirror. "I'm sorry for the interruption. You were saying . . ."

"About the wires in the brain."

"Yes. We do that operation, Mr. Beckerman, under special circumstances, but it's still pretty experimental."

"That's all right," Beckerman said. He puffed on his cigarette. "That's fine with me."

"If you want information, we can arrange for you to have some reprints and magazine tear sheets explaining our work here."

Beckerman smiled and shook his head. "No, no," he said. "I don't want information. I want the operation. I'm volunteering."

Morris pretended to be surprised. He paused a moment and said, "I see."

"Listen," Beckerman said, "in the article it said that one jolt of electricity was like a dozen orgasms. It sounded really terrific."

"And you want this operation performed on you?"

"Yeah," Beckerman said, nodding vigorously. "Right."

"Why?"

"Are you kidding? Wouldn't everybody want it? Pleasure like that?"

"Perhaps," Morris said, "but you're the first person to ask for it."

"What's the matter?" Beckerman said. "Is it really expensive or something?"

"No. But we don't perform brain surgery for trivial reasons."

"Oh, wow," Beckerman said. "So that's where you are. Jesus."

And he got up and left the room, shaking his head.

The three Development guys looked stupefied. They sat in the adjoining room and stared through the one-way glass. Beckerman had long since departed.

"Fascinating," Morris said.

The Development guys didn't reply. Finally one of them cleared his throat and said, "To say the least."

Morris knew what was going through their heads. For years, they had been doing feasibility studies, potential application studies, ramification studies, industrial operations studies, input-output studies. They were geared to think in the future—and now they were suddenly confronted with the present.

"That man is an elad," one of them said. And sighed.

The elad concept had caused a lot of interest and some detached academic concern. The notion of an electrical addict—a man who needed his jolts of electricity just as some men needed doses of drugs—had seemed almost fancifully speculative. But now they had a patient who was clearly a potential addict.

"Electricity is the biggest kick of all," one of them said, and laughed. But the laugh was nervous, edged with tension.

Morris wondered what McPherson would say. Probably something philosophical. McPherson was mostly interested in philosophy these days.

The idea of an electrical addict was predicated on an astonishing discovery made by James Olds in the 1950s. Olds found that there were areas in the brain where electrical stimulation produced intense pleasure—strips of brain tissue he called "rivers of reward." If an electrode was placed in such an area, a rat would press a self-stimulation lever to receive a shock as often as five thousand times an hour. In its quest for pleasure, it would ignore food and water. It would stop pressing the lever only when it was prostrate with exhaustion.

This remarkable experiment had been repeated with goldfish, guinea pigs, dolphins, cats, and goats. There was no longer any question that the pleasure terminals in the brain were a universal phenomenon. They had also been located in humans.

Out of these considerations had come the notion of the electrical addict, the man who needed pleasurable shocks. At first glance, it seemed impossible for a person to become an addict. But it actually wasn't.

For instance, the technological hardware was now expensive, but it needn't be. One could envision clever Japanese firms manufacturing electrodes for as little as two or three dollars and exporting them.

Nor was the idea of an illegal operation so far-fetched. At one time a million American women underwent illegal abortions each year. The implantation brain surgery was somewhat more complex, but not forbiddingly so. And the surgical techniques would become more standardized in the future. It was easy to imagine clinics springing up in Mexico and the Bahamas.

Nor was there a problem finding surgeons to do the job. A single busy, well-organized neurosurgeon could perform ten or fifteen operations a day. He could certainly charge a thousand dollars for each—and with that kind of incentive, unscrupulous surgeons could be found. A hundred thousand dollars a week in cash was a strong inducement to break the law—if indeed a law were ever passed.

That did not seem very likely. A year before, the hospital had organized a seminar with legal scholars on "Biomedical Technology and the Law." Elads were among the subjects discussed, but the lawyers were not responsive. The elad concept did not fit neatly into the already existing pattern of laws governing drug addiction. All those laws recognized that a person could become a drug addict innocently or involuntarily—quite a different proposition from a person coldly seeking a surgical procedure that would make him an addict. Most of the lawyers felt that the public would not seek such an operation; there would be no legal problem because there would be no public demand. Now Beckerman had provided evidence for such a demand.

"I'll be goddamned," another of the Development people said.

Morris found that comment hardly adequate. He himself felt something he had felt once or twice before since joining the NPS. It was the sensation that things were moving too fast, without enough caution and control, and that it could *all* get out of control, suddenly, and without warning.

Chapter 6

At 6 P.M., Roger McPherson, head of the Neuropsychiatric Research Unit, went up to the seventh floor to check on his patient. At least, that was how he thought of Benson—as his patient. A proprietary feeling, but not entirely incorrect. Without McPherson, there would be no NPS, and without an NPS, there would be no surgery, no Benson. That was how he thought of it.

Room 710 was quiet and bathed in reddish light from the setting sun. Benson appeared to be asleep, but his eyes opened when McPherson closed the door.

"How are you feeling?" McPherson asked, moving close to the bed.

Benson smiled. "Everyone wants to know that," he said.

McPherson smiled back. "It's a natural question."

"I'm tired, that's all. Very tired. . . . Sometimes I think I'm a ticking time bomb, and you're wondering when I'll explode."

"Is that what you think?" McPherson asked. Automatically, he adjusted Benson's covers so he could look at the I.V. line. It was flowing nicely.

"Ticktick," Benson said, closing his eyes again. "Ticktick."

McPherson frowned. He was accustomed to mechanical metaphors from Benson—the man was preoccupied, after all, with the idea of men as machines. But to have them appear so soon after operation . . .

"Any pain?"

"None. A little ache behind my ears, like I'd fallen. That's all."

That, McPherson knew, was the bone pain from the drilling.

"Fallen?"

"I'm a fallen man," Benson said. "I've succumbed."

"To what?"

"To the process of being turned into a machine." He opened his eyes and smiled again. "Or a time bomb."

"Any smells? Strange sensations?" As he asked, McPherson looked at the EEG scanner above the bed. It was still reading normal alpha patterns, without any suggestion of seizure activity.

"No. Nothing like that."

"But you feel as if you might explode?" He thought: Ross should really be asking these questions.

"Sort of," Benson said. "In the coming war, we may all explode."

"How do you mean?"

"In the coming war between men and machines. The human brain is obsolete, you see."

That was a new thought. McPherson hadn't heard it from Benson before. He stared at him, lying in the bed, his head and shoulders heavily bandaged. It made the upper part of his body and his head appear thick, gross, oversized.

"Yes," Benson said. "The human brain has gone as far as it is going to go. It's exhausted, so it spawned the next generation of intelligent forms. They will— Why am I so tired?" He closed his eyes again.

"You're exhausted from the operation."

"A minor procedure," he said, and smiled with his eyes closed. A moment later he was snoring.

McPherson remained by the bed for a moment, then turned to the window and watched the sun set over the Pacific. Benson had a nice room; you could see a bit of the ocean between the high-rise apartments in Santa Monica. He remained there for several minutes. Benson did not wake. Finally, McPherson went out to the nurses' station to write his note in the chart.

"Patient alert, responsive, oriented times three." He paused after writing that. He didn't really know if Benson was oriented to person, place, and time; he hadn't checked specifically. But he was clear and responsive, and McPherson let it go. "Flow of ideas orderly and clear, but patient retains machine imagery of pre-operative state. It is too early to be certain, but it appears that early predictions were correct that the operation would not alter his mentation between seizures."

Signed, "Roger A. McPherson, M.D."

He stared at it for a moment, then closed the chart and replaced it on the shelf. It was a good note, cool, direct, holding out no false anticipations. The chart was a legal document, after all, and it could be called into court. McPherson didn't expect to see Benson's chart in court, but you couldn't be too careful.

The head of any large scientific laboratory performed a political function. You might deny it; you might dislike it. But it was nonetheless true, a necessary part of the job.

You had to keep all the people in the lab happy as they worked together. The more prima donnas you had, the tougher the job was, as pure politics.

You had to get your lab funded from outside sources, and that was also pure politics. Particularly if you were working in a delicate area, as the NPS was. McPherson had long since evolved the horseradish-peroxidase principle of grant applications. It was simple enough: when you applied for money, you announced that the money would be spent to find the enzyme horseradish peroxidase, which could lead to a cure for cancer. You would easily get sixty thousand dollars for that project—although you couldn't get sixty cents for mind control.

He looked at the row of charts on the shelf, a row of unfamiliar names, into which BENSON, H. F. 710 merged indistinguishably. In one sense, he thought, Benson was correct—he was a walking time bomb. A man treated with mind-control technology was subject to all sorts of irrational public prejudice. "Heart control" in the form of cardiac pacemakers was considered a wonderful invention; "kidney control" through drugs was a blessing. But "mind control" was evil, a disaster—even though the NPS control work was directly analogous to control work with other organs. Even the technology was similar: the atomic pacemaker they were using had been developed first for cardiac applications.

But the prejudice remained. And Benson thought of himself as a ticking time bomb. McPherson sighed, took out the chart again, and flipped to the section containing doctors' orders. Both Ellis and Morris had written post-op care orders. McPherson added: "After interfacing tomorrow A.M., begin thorazine."

He looked at the note, then decided the nurses wouldn't understand interfacing. He scratched it out and wrote: "After noon tomorrow, begin thorazine."

As he left the floor, he thought that he would rest more easily once Benson was on thorazine. Perhaps they couldn't defuse the time bomb—but they could certainly drop it into a bucket of cold water.

Chapter 7

Late at night, in Telecomp, Gerhard stared anxiously at the computer console. He typed in more instructions, then walked to a print-out typewriter and began reviewing the long sheaf of green-striped sheets. He scanned them quickly, looking for the error he knew was there in the programmed instructions.

The computer itself never made a mistake. Gerhard had used computers for nearly ten years—different computers, different places—and he had never seen one make a mistake. Of course, mistakes occurred all the time, but they were always in the program, not in the machine. Sometimes that infallibility was hard to accept. For one thing, it didn't fit with one's view of the rest of the world, where machines were always making mistakes—fuses blowing, stereos breaking down, ovens overheating, cars refusing to start. Modern man expected machines to make their fair share of errors.

But computers were different, and working with them could be a humiliating experience. They were never wrong. It was as simple as that. Even when it took weeks to find the source of some problem, even when the program was checked a dozen times by as many different people, even when the whole staff was slowly coming to the conclusion that for once, the computer circuitry had fouled up—it always turned out, in the end, to be a human error of some kind. Always.

Richards came in, shrugging off a sport coat, and poured himself a cup of coffee. "How's it going?"

Gerhard shook his head. "I'm having trouble with George."

"Again? Shit." Richards looked at the console. "How's Martha?"

"Martha's fine, I think. It's just George."

"Which George is it?"

"Saint George," Gerhard said. "Really a bitch."

Richards sipped his coffee and sat down at the console. "Mind if I try it?"

"Sure," Gerhard said.

Richards began flicking buttons. He called up the program for Saint George. Then he called up the program for Martha. Then he pushed the interaction button.

Richards and Gerhard hadn't devised these programs; they were modified from several existing computer programs developed at other universities. But the basic idea was the same—to create a computer program that would make the computer act emotionally, like people. It was logical to designate the programs with names like George and Martha. There was a precedent for that: Eliza in Boston, and Aldous in England.

George and Martha were essentially the same program with slight differences. The original George was programmed to be neutral in his response to stimuli. Then Martha was created. Martha was a little bitchy; Martha disliked most things. Finally, another George was formulated, a very loving George, who was referred to as Saint George.

Each program could respond with three emotional states—love, fear, and anger. Each could produce three actions—approach, withdrawal, and attack. All this was, of course, highly abstract. It was carried out in terms of numbers. For example, the original George was neutral to most numbers, but he disliked the number 751. He was programmed to dislike it. And by extension he disliked similar numbers—743, 772, and so on. He much preferred numbers such as 404, 133, and 918. If you punched in one of these numbers, George responded with numbers signifying love and approach. If you punched in 707, George withdrew. If you punched in 750, George angrily attacked—according to the numbers he printed out.

The NPS staff had played with the programs in this way for a long time. Then they had incorporated program modifications to allow for "talk" from the computer. The numbers were translated into sentences. This was amusing, and revealing. The actual interaction was referred to as "the Christmas game" because most of it was conducted as giving and receiving gifts—objects that had an assigned or learned emotional value, just as the numbers did.

Normal George interacting with Martha would eventually win her over, and her bitchiness would recede into the background.

But Saint George had a much worse effect on her. His loving acceptance drove her up the wall. That is, if things were working normally. Richards watched as the print-out flashed across the screen.

HELLO I'M SAINT GEORGE
HELLO
WHAT IS YOUR NAME?
MARTHA.
YOU DON'T SAY MUCH, MARTHA.
NO
BUT I LIKE YOU.
WHY I DON'T LIKE YOU.
I UNDERSTAND THAT. HOW CAN I HELP?

"It isn't printing periods consistently," Richards said. "When did that start?"

"That's nothing," Gerhard said. "Just keep watching."

HELP?
YES, I WOULD LIKE TO HELP YOU.
HAVE A CAT.

Richards winced. Cats were programmed to be something that both George and Martha disliked. Giving George a cat was a very hostile move.

THANK YOU
HAVE ANOTHER CAT.
THANK YOU YOU ARE VERY KIND.
HAVE ANOTHER CAT.
NO THANK YOU.
DON'T YOU LIKE CATS?
YES BUT I HAVE ENOUGH CATS.
HAVE A GORILLA.

"Really nasty," Richards said. "What are the other interactions like?"

"Pretty much the same," Gerhard said.

"As bad as this?"

"Pretty much."

They were accustomed now to the idea that when the computers interacted, the results were unpredictable. The general form of interaction could be guessed, but the specific results were uncertain. It was like a computer playing checkers—it was probably going to win, but it would win a different way each time, depending on what the opponent did.

I DON'T WANT A GORILLA.
DON'T YOU LIKE GORILLAS?

NO THANK YOU.
YOU ARE TOO POLITE.
I AM SORRY IF I OFFEND YOU IN ANY WAY.
YOU TALK TOO MUCH.
I AM SORRY.
HAVE AN EGGPLANT.

Richards watched with interest. Saint George had no background for eggplants. But he disliked cucumbers and bananas.

NO THANK YOU.
DON'T YOU LIKE EGGPLANT?
NOT VERY MUCH.
HERE HAVE ANOTHER ONE.
NO THANK YOU.
I WANT YOU TO HAVE IT.
NO THANK YOU.
GO ON AND TAKE IT.
NO THANK YOU.
I INSIST.
NO THANK YOU.

"What's happened to Saint George?" Richards asked. "His responses are too much the same."

"That's what's bothering me."

"What's he cycling through on the program?"

"I was looking for it when you came in."

I INSIST THAT YOU HAVE A CUCUMBER.
I REFUSE.

"George!" Richards said, almost without thinking.

THEN HAVE A BANANA.
NO.

"George is breaking down," Richards said. "He's not a saint any more."

THEN HAVE BOTH A BANANA AND A
CUCUMBER.
NO THANK YOU.
I INSIST.
GO TO HELL I WILL KILL YOU: : : : : : : :
: :
: :

The screen was filled with white dots. "What does that mean, unprintable response?" Richards said.

"I don't know. I've never seen it before tonight."

"How many times has this program been run?" Richards asked.

"One hundred and ten, against Martha."

"Any learning erasures?"

"No."

"I'll be goddamned," Richards said. "He's getting to be a short-tempered saint." He grinned. "We can write this one up."

Gerhard nodded and went back to the print-out. In theory, what was happening was not puzzling. Both George and Martha were programmed to learn from experience. Like the checkers-playing programs—where the machine got better each time it played a game—this program was established so that the machine would "learn" new responses to things. After one hundred and ten sets of experience, Saint George had abruptly stopped being a saint. He was learning not to be a saint around Martha—even though he had been programmed for saintliness.

"I know just how he feels," Richards said, and switched the machine off. Then he joined Gerhard, looking for the programming error that had made it happen.

THURSDAY, MARCH 11, 1971: INTERFACING

Chapter 1

Janet Ross sat in the empty room and glanced at the wall clock. It was 9 A.M. She looked down at the desk in front of her, which was bare except for a vase of flowers and a notepad. She looked at the chair opposite her. Then, aloud, she said, "How're we doing?"

There was a mechanical click and Gerhard's voice came through the speaker mounted in the ceiling. "We need a few minutes for the sound levels. The light is okay. You want to talk a minute?"

She nodded, and glanced over her shoulder at the one-way mirror behind her. She saw only her reflection, but she knew Gerhard, with his equipment, was behind, watching her. "You sound tired," she said.

"Trouble with Saint George last night," Gerhard said.

"I'm tired, too," she said. "I was having trouble with somebody who isn't a saint." She laughed. She was just talking so they could get a sound level for the room; she hadn't really paid attention to what she was saying. But it was true: Arthur was no saint. He was also no great discovery, though she'd thought he might be a few weeks ago when she first met him. She had been, in fact, a little infatuated with him. ("Infatuated? Hmm? Is that what you'd call it?" She could hear Dr. Ramos now.) Arthur had been born handsome and wealthy. He had a yellow Ferrari, a lot of dash, and a lot of charm. She was able to feel feminine and frivolous around him. He did madcap, dashing things like flying her to Mexico City for dinner because he knew a little restaurant where they made the best tacos in the world. She knew it was all silly, but she enjoyed it. And in a way she was relieved—she never had to talk about medicine, or the hospital, or psychiatry. Arthur wasn't interested in any of those things; he was interested in her as a woman. ("Not as a sex object?" Damn Dr. Ramos.)

Then, as she got to know him better, she found herself wanting to talk about her work. And she found, with some surprise, that Arthur didn't want to hear about it. Arthur was threatened by her work; he had problems about achievement. He was nominally a stockbroker—an easy thing for a rich man's son to be—and he talked with authority about money, investments, interest rates, bond issues. But there was an aggressive quality in his manner, a defensiveness, as if he were substantiating himself.

And then she realized what she should have known from the beginning, that Arthur was chiefly interested in her because she was substantial. It was—in theory—more difficult to impress her, to sweep her off her feet, than it was to impress the little actresses who hung out at Bumbles and the Candy Store. And therefore more satisfying.

As time went on she no longer drew pleasure from being frivolous around him, and everything became vaguely depressing. She recognized all the signs: her work at the hospital became busier, and she had to break dates with him. When she did see him, she was bored by his flamboyance, his restless impulsiveness, his clothes, and his cars. She would look at him across the dinner table and try to discover what she had once seen. She could not find even a trace of it. Last night she had broken it off. They both knew it was coming, and—

"You stopped talking," Gerhard said.

"I don't know what to say . . . Now is the time for all good men to come to the aid of the patient. The quick brown fox jumped over the pithed frog. We are all headed for that final common pathway in the sky." She paused. "Is that enough?"

"A little more."

"Mary, Mary, quite contrary, how does your garden grow? I'm sorry I don't remember the rest. How does the poem go?" She laughed.

"That's fine, we have the level now."

She looked up at the loudspeaker. "Will you be interfacing at the end of the series?"

"Probably," Gerhard said, "if it goes well. Rog is in a hurry to get him onto tranquilizers."

She nodded. This was the final stage in Benson's treatment, and it had to be done before tranquilizers could be administered. Benson had been kept on sedation with phenobarbital until midnight the night before. He would be clearheaded this morning, and ready for interfacing.

It was McPherson who had coined the term "interfacing." McPherson liked computer terminology. An interface was the boundary between two systems. Or between a computer and an effector mechanism. In Benson's case, it was almost a boundary between two computers—his brain and the little computer wired into his shoulder. The wires had been attached, but the switches hadn't been thrown yet. Once they were, the feedback loop of Benson-computer-Benson would be instituted.

McPherson saw this case as the first of many. He planned to go from organic seizures to schizophrenics to mentally retarded patients to blind patients. The charts were all there on his office wall, projecting the technology five years into the future. And he planned to use more and more sophisticated computers in the link-up. Eventually, he would get to projects like Form Q, which seemed far-fetched even to Ross.

But today the practical question was which of the forty electrodes would prevent an attack. Nobody knew that yet. It would be determined experimentally.

During the operation, the electrodes had been located precisely, within millimeters of the target area. That was good surgical placement, but considering the density of the brain it was grossly inadequate. A nerve cell in the brain was just a micron in diameter. There were a thousand nerve cells in the space of a millimeter.

From that standpoint, the electrodes had been crudely positioned. And this crudeness meant that many electrodes were required. One could assume that if you placed several electrodes in the correct general area, at least one of them would be in the precise position to abort an attack. Trial-and-error stimulation would determine the proper electrode to use.

"Patient coming," Gerhard said over the loudspeaker. A moment later, Benson arrived in a wheelchair, wearing his blue-and-white striped bathrobe. He seemed alert as he waved to her stiffly—the shoulder bandages inhibited movement of his arm. "How are you feeling?" he said, and smiled.

"I'm supposed to ask you."

"I'll ask the questions around here," he said. He was still smiling, but there was an edge to his voice. With some surprise, she realized that he was afraid. And then she wondered why that surprised her. Of course he would be afraid. Anyone would be. She wasn't exactly calm herself.

The nurse patted Benson on the shoulder, nodded to Dr. Ross, and left the room. They were alone.

For a moment, neither spoke. Benson stared at her; she stared back. She wanted to give Gerhard time to focus the TV camera in the ceiling, and to prepare his stimulating equipment.

"What are we doing today?" Benson asked.

"We're going to stimulate your electrodes, sequentially, to see what happens."

He nodded. He seemed to take this calmly, but she had learned not to trust his calm. After a moment he said, "Will it hurt?"

"No."

"Okay," he said. "Go ahead."

Gerhard, sitting on a high stool in the adjacent room, surrounded in the darkness by glowing green dials of equipment, watched through the one-way glass as Ross and Benson began to talk.

Alongside him, Richards picked up the tape-recorder microphone and said quietly, "Stimulation series one, patient Harold Benson, March 11, 1971."

Gerhard looked at the four TV screens in front of him. One showed the closed-circuit view of Benson that would be stored on video tape as the stimulation series proceeded. Another displayed a computer-generated view of the forty electrode points, lined up in two parallel rows within the brain substance. As each electrode was stimulated, the appropriate point glowed on the screen.

A third TV screen ran an oscilloscope tracing of the shock pulse as it was delivered. And a fourth showed a wiring diagram of the tiny computer in Benson's neck. It also glowed as stimulations traveled through the circuit pathways.

In the next room, Ross was saying, "You'll feel a variety of sensations, and some of them may be quite pleasant. We want you to tell us what you feel. All right?"

Benson nodded.

Richards said, "Electrode one, five millivolts, for five seconds." Gerhard pressed the buttons. The computer diagram showed a tracing of the circuit being closed, the current snaking its way through the intricate electronic maze of Benson's shoulder computer. They watched Benson through the one-way glass.

Benson said, "That's interesting."

"What's interesting?" Ross asked.

"That feeling."

"Can you describe it?"

"Well, it's like eating a ham sandwich."

"Do you like ham sandwiches?"

Benson shrugged. "Not particularly."

"Do you feel hungry?"

"Not particularly."

"Do you feel anything else?"

"No. Just the taste of a ham sandwich." He smiled. "On rye."

Gerhard, sitting at the control panel, nodded. The first electrode had stimulated a vague memory trace.

Richards: "Electrode two, five millivolts, five seconds."

Benson said, "I have to go to the bathroom."

Ross said, "It will pass."

Gerhard sat back from the control panel, sipped a cup of coffee, and watched the interview progress.

"Electrode three, five millivolts, five seconds."

This one produced absolutely no effect on Benson. Benson was quietly talking with Ross about bathrooms in restaurants, hotels, airports—

"Try it again," Gerhard said. "Up five."

"Repeat electrode three, ten millivolts, five seconds," Richards said. The TV screen flashed the circuit through electrode three. There was still no effect.

"Go on to four," Gerhard said. He wrote out a few notes:

#1—? memory trace (ham sand.)
#2—bladder fullness
#3—no subjective change
#4—

He drew the dash and waited. It was going to take a long time to go through all forty electrodes, but it was fascinating to watch. They produced such strikingly different effects, yet each electrode was very close to the next. It was the ultimate proof of the density of the brain, which had once been described as the most complex structure in the known universe. And it was certainly true: there were three times as many cells packed into a single human brain as there were human beings on the face of the earth. That density was hard to comprehend, sometimes. Early in his NPS career, Gerhard had requested a human brain to dissect. He had done it over a period of several days, with a dozen neuroanatomy texts opened up before him. He used the traditional tool for brain dissection, a blunt wooden stick, to scrape away the cheesy gray material. He had patiently, carefully scraped away—and in the end, he had nothing. The brain was not like the liver or the lungs. To the naked eye, it was uniform and boring, giving no indication of its true function. The brain was too subtle, too complex. Too dense.

"Electrode four," Richards said into the recorder. "Five millivolts, five seconds." The shock was delivered.

And Benson, in an oddly childlike voice, said, "Could I have some milk and cookies, please?"

"That's interesting," Gerhard said, watching the reaction.

Richards nodded. "How old would you say?"

"About five or six, at most."

Benson was talking about cookies, talking about his tricycle, to Ross. Slowly, over the next few minutes, he seemed to emerge like a time-traveler advancing through the years. Finally he became fully adult again, thinking back to his youth, instead of actually being there. "I always wanted the cookies, and she would never give them to me. She said they were bad for me and would give me cavities."

"We can go on," Gerhard said.

Richards said, "Electrode five, five millivolts, five seconds."

In the next room, Benson shifted uncomfortably in his wheelchair. Ross asked him if something was wrong. Benson said, "It feels funny."

"How do you mean?"

"I can't describe it. It's like sandpaper. Irritating."

Gerhard nodded, and wrote in his notes, "#5—potential attack electrode." This happened sometimes. Occasionally an electrode would be found to stimulate a seizure. Nobody knew why—and Gerhard personally thought that nobody ever would. The brain was, he believed, beyond comprehension.

His work with programs like George and Martha had led him to understand that relatively simple computer instructions could produce complex and unpredictable machine behavior. It was also true that the programmed machine could exceed the capabilities of the programmer; that was clearly demonstrated in 1963 when Arthur Samuel at IBM programmed a machine to play checkers—and the machine eventually became so good that it beat Samuel himself.

Yet all this was done with computers which had no more circuits than the brain of an ant. The human brain far exceeded that complexity, and the programming of the human brain extended over many decades. How could anyone seriously expect to understand it?

There was also a philosophical problem. Goedel's Theorem: that no system could explain itself, and no machine could understand its own workings. At most, Gerhard believed that a human brain might, after years of work, decipher a frog brain. But a human brain could never decipher itself in the same detail. For that you would need a superhuman brain.

Gerhard thought that someday a computer would be developed that could untangle the billions of cells and hundreds of billions of interconnections in the human brain. Then, at last, man would have the information that he wanted. But man wouldn't have done the work—another order of intelligence would have done it. And man would not know, of course, how the computer worked.

Morris entered the room with a cup of coffee. He sipped it, and glanced at Benson through the glass. "How's he holding up?"

"Okay," Gerhard said.

"Electrode six, five and five," Richards intoned.

In the next room, Benson failed to react. He sat talking with Ross about the operation, and his lingering headache. He was quite calm and apparently unaffected. They repeated the stimulation, still without change in Benson's behavior. Then they went on.

"Electrode seven, five and five," Richards said. He delivered the shock.

Benson sat up abruptly. "Oh," he said, "that was nice."

"What was?" Ross said.

"You can do that again if you want to."

"How does it feel?"

"Nice," Benson said. His whole appearance seemed to change subtly. "You know," he said after a moment, "you're really a wonderful person, Dr. Ross."

"Thank you," she said.

"Very attractive, too. I don't know if I ever told you before."

"How do you feel now?"

"I'm really very fond of you," Benson said. "I don't know if I told you that before."

"Nice," Gerhard said, watching through the glass. "Very nice."

Morris nodded. "A strong P-terminal. He's clearly turned on."

Gerhard made a note of it. Morris sipped his coffee. They waited until Benson settled down. Then, blandly, Richards said, "Electrode eight, five millivolts, five seconds."

The stimulation series continued.

Chapter 2

At noon, McPherson showed up to supervise interfacing. No one was surprised to see him. In a sense, this was the irrevocable step; everything preceding it was unimportant. They had implanted electrodes and a computer and a power pack, and they had hooked everything up. But nothing functioned until the interfacing switches were thrown. It was a little like building an automobile and then finally turning the ignition.

Gerhard showed him notes from the stimulation series. "At five millivolts on a pulse-form stimulus, we have three positive terminals and two negatives. The positives are seven, nine, and thirty-one. The negatives are five and thirty-two."

McPherson glanced at the notes, then looked through the one-way glass at Benson. "Are any of the positives true P's?"

"Seven seems to be."

"Strong?"

"Pretty strong. When we stimulated him, he said he liked it, and he began to act sexually aroused toward Jan."

"Is it too strong? Will it tip him over?"

Gerhard shook his head. "No," he said. "Not unless he were to receive multiple stimulations over a short time course. There was that Norwegian . . ."

"I don't think we have to worry about that," McPherson said. "We've got Benson in the hospital for the next few days. If anything seems to be going wrong, we can switch to other electrodes. We'll just keep track of him for a while. What about nine?"

"Very weak. Equivocal, really."

"How did he respond?"

"There was a subtle increase in spontaneity, more tendency to smile, to tell happy and positive anecdotes."

McPherson seemed unimpressed. "And thirty-one?"

"Clear tranquilizing effect. Calmness, relaxation, happiness."

McPherson rubbed his hands together. "I guess we can get on with it," he said. He looked once through the glass at Benson, and said, "Interface the patient with seven and thirty-one."

McPherson was clearly feeling a sense of high drama and medical history. Gerhard got off his stool and walked to a corner of the room where there was a computer console mounted beneath a TV screen. He began to touch the buttons. The TV screen glowed to life. After a moment, letters appeared on it.

BENSON, H. F.
INTERFACING PROCEDURE
POSSIBLE ELECTRODES: 40, designated serially
POSSIBLE VOLTAGES: continuous
POSSIBLE DURATIONS: continuous
POSSIBLE WAVE FORMS: pulse only

Gerhard pressed a button and the screen went blank. Then a series of questions appeared, to which Gerhard typed out the answers on the console.

INTERFACE PROCEDURES BENSON, H. F.
1. WHICH ELECTRODES WILL BE ACTIVATED?

7, 31 only

2. WHAT VOLTAGE WILL BE APPLIED TO ELECTRODE SEVEN?

5 mv

3. WHAT DURATION WILL BE APPLIED TO ELECTRODE SEVEN?

5 sec

There was a pause, and the questions continued for electrode 31. Gerhard typed in the answers. Watching him, McPherson said to Morris, "This is amusing, in a way. We're telling the tiny computer how to work. The little computer gets its instructions from the big computer, which gets its instructions from Gerhard, who has a bigger computer than any of them."

"Maybe," Gerhard said, and laughed.
The screen glowed:

INTERFACING PARAMETERS STORED. READY TO PROGRAM AUXILIARY UNIT.

Morris sighed. He hoped that he would never reach the point in his life when he was referred to by a computer as an "auxiliary unit." Gerhard typed quietly, a soft clicking sound. On the other TV screens, they could see the inner circuitry of the small computer. It glowed intermittently as the wiring locked in.

BENSON HF HAS BEEN INTERFACED.
IMPLANTED DEVICE NOW READING
EEG DATA AND DELIVERING APPROPRIATE
FEEDBACK.

That was all there was to it. Somehow Morris was disappointed; he knew it would be this way, but he had expected—or needed—something more dramatic. Gerhard ran a systems check which came back negative. The screen went blank and then came through with a final message:

UNIVERSITY HOSPITAL SYSTEM 360
COMPUTER THANKS YOU FOR REFERRING
THIS INTERESTING PATIENT FOR
THERAPY.

Gerhard smiled. In the next room, Benson was still talking quietly with Ross. Neither of them seemed to have noticed anything different at all.

Chapter 3

Janet Ross finished the stimulation series profoundly depressed. She stood in the corridor watching as Benson was wheeled away. She had a last glimpse of the white bandages around his neck as the nurse turned the corner; then he was gone.

She walked down the hallway in the other direction, through the multi-colored NPS doors. For some reason, she found herself thinking about Arthur's yellow Ferrari. It was so marvelous and elegant and irrelevant to anything. The perfect toy. She wished she were in Monte Carlo, stepping out of Arthur's Ferrari wearing her Balenciaga gown, going up the stairs to the casino to gamble with nothing more important than money.

She looked at her watch. Christ, it was only 12:15. She had half the day ahead of her. What was it like to be a pediatrician? Probably fun. Tickling babies and giving shots and advising mothers on toilet training. Not a bad way to live.

She thought again of the bandages on Benson's shoulder, and went into Telecomp. She had hoped to speak to Gerhard alone, but instead everyone was in the room—McPherson, Morris, Ellis, everyone. They were all jubilant, toasting each other with coffee in Styrofoam cups.

Someone thrust a cup into her hands, and McPherson put his arm around her in a fatherly way. "I gather we turned Benson on to you today."

"Yes, you did," she said, managing to smile.

"Well, I guess you're used to that."

"Not exactly," she said.

The room got quieter, the festive feeling slid away. She felt bad about that, but not really. There was nothing amusing about shocking a person into sexual arousal. It was physiologically interesting, was frightening and pathetic, but not funny. Why did they all find it so goddamned funny?

Ellis produced a hip flask and poured clear liquid into her coffee. "Makes it Irish," he said, with a wink. "Much better."

She nodded, and glanced across the room at Gerhard.

"Drink up, drink up," Ellis said.

Gerhard was talking to Morris about something. It seemed a very intent conversation; then she heard Morris say, ". . . you please pass the pussy?" Gerhard laughed; Morris laughed. It was some kind of joke.

"Not bad, considering," Ellis said. "What do you think?"

"Very good," she said, taking a small sip. She managed to get away from Ellis and McPherson and went over to Gerhard. He was momentarily alone; Morris had gone off to refill his cup.

"Listen," she said, "can I talk to you for a second?"

"Sure," Gerhard said. He bent his head closer to hers. "What is it?"

"I want to know something. Is it possible for you to monitor Benson here, on the main computer?"

"You mean monitor the implanted unit?"

"Yes."

Gerhard shrugged. "I guess so, but why bother? We know the implanted unit is working—"

"I know," she said. "I know. But will you do it anyway, as a precaution?"

Gerhard said nothing. His eyes said: Precaution against what?

"Please?"

"Okay," he said. "I'll punch in a monitoring subroutine as soon as they leave." He nodded to the group. "I'll have the computer check on him twice an hour."

She frowned.

"Four times an hour?"

"How about every ten minutes?" she said.

"Okay," he said. "Every ten minutes."

"Thanks," she said. Then she drained her coffee, and left the room.

Chapter 4

Ellis sat in a corner of Room 710 and watched the half-dozen technicians maneuvering around the bed. There were two people from the rad lab doing a radiation check; there was one girl drawing blood for the chem lab, to check steroid levels; there was an EEG technician resetting the monitors; and there were Gerhard and Richards, taking a final look at the interface wiring.

Throughout it all, Benson lay motionless, breathing easily, staring up at the ceiling. He did not seem to notice the people touching him, moving an arm here, shifting a sheet there. He stared straight up at the ceiling.

One of the rad-lab men had hairy hands protruding from the cuffs of his white lab coat. For a moment, the man rested his hairy dark hand on Benson's bandages. Ellis thought about the monkeys he had operated on. There was nothing to that except technical expertise, because you always knew—no matter how hard you pretended—that it was a monkey and not a human being, and if you slipped and cut the monkey from ear to ear, it didn't matter at all. There would be no questions, no relatives, no lawyers, no press, no nothing—not even a nasty note from Requisitions asking what was happening to all those eighty-dollar monkeys. Nobody gave a damn. And neither did he. He wasn't interested in helping monkeys. He was interested in helping human beings.

Benson stirred. "I'm tired," he said. He glanced over at Ellis.

Ellis said, "About ready to wrap it up, boys?"

One by one, the technicians stepped back from the bed, nodding, collected their instruments and their data, and left the room. Gerhard and Richards were the last to go. Finally Ellis was alone with Benson.

"You feel like sleeping?" Ellis said.

"I feel like a goddamned machine. I feel like an automobile in a complicated service station. I feel like I'm being *repaired.*"

Benson was getting angry. Ellis could feel his own tension building. He was tempted to call for nurses and orderlies to restrain Benson when the attack came. But he remained seated.

"That's a lot of crap," Ellis said.

Benson glared at him, breathing deeply.

Ellis looked at the monitors over the bed. The brain waves were going irregular, moving into an attack configuration.

Benson wrinkled his nose and sniffed. "What's that smell?" he said. "That awful—"

Above the bed, a red monitor light blinked STIMULATION. The brain waves spun in a distorted tangle of white lines for five seconds. Simultaneously, Benson's pupils dilated. Then the lines were smooth again; the pupils returned to normal size.

Benson turned away, staring out the window at the afternoon sun. "You know," he said, "it's really a very nice day, isn't it?"

Chapter 5

For no particular reason, Janet Ross came back to the hospital at 11 P.M. She had gone to see a movie with a pathology resident who had been asking her for weeks; finally she had relented. They had seen a murder mystery, which the resident claimed was the only kind of movie he attended. This one featured five murders before she stopped counting them. In the darkness, she had glanced at the resident, and he was smiling. His reaction was so stereotyped—the pathologist drawn to violence and death—that she found herself thinking of the other stereotypes in medicine: the sadistic surgeons and the childish pediatricians and the woman-hating gynecologists. And the crazy psychiatrists.

Afterward, he had driven her back to the hospital because she had left her car in the hospital parking lot. But instead of driving home she had gone up to the NPS. For no particular reason.

The NPS was deserted, but she expected to find Gerhard and Richards at work, and they were, poring over computer print-outs in Telecomp. They hardly noticed when she came into the room and got herself some coffee. "Trouble?" she said.

Gerhard scratched his head. "Now it's Martha," he said. "First George refuses to be a saint. Now Martha is becoming nice. Everything's screwed up."

Richards smiled. "You have your patients, Jan," he said, "and we have ours."

"Speaking of my patient . . ."

"Of course," Gerhard said, getting up and walking over to the computer console. "I was wondering why you came in." He smiled. "Or was it just a bad date?"

"Just a bad movie," she said.

Gerhard punched buttons on the console. Letters and numbers began to print out. "Here's all the checks since I started it at one-twelve this afternoon."

01:12	NORMAL EEG	06:12	NORMAL EEG
01:22	NORMAL EEG	06:22	NORMAL EEG
01:32	SLEEP EEG	06:32	NORMAL EEG
01:42	SLEEP EEG	06:42	NORMAL EEG
01:52	NORMAL EEG	06:52	STIMULATION
02:02	NORMAL EEG	07:02	NORMAL EEG
02:12	NORMAL EEG	07:12	NORMAL EEG
02:22	NORMAL EEG	07:22	SLEEP EEG
02:32	SLEEP EEG	07:32	SLEEP EEG
02:42	NORMAL EEG	07:42	SLEEP EEG
02:52	NORMAL EEG	07:52	NORMAL EEG
03:02	NORMAL EEG	08:02	NORMAL EEG
03:12	SLEEP EEG	08:12	NORMAL EEG
03:22	SLEEP EEG	08:22	SLEEP EEG
03:32	STIMULATION	08:32	NORMAL EEG
03:42	NORMAL EEG	08:42	NORMAL EEG
03:52	SLEEP EEG	08:52	NORMAL EEG
04:02	NORMAL EEG	09:02	STIMULATION
04:12	NORMAL EEG	09:12	SLEEP EEG
04:22	NORMAL EEG	09:22	NORMAL EEG
04:32	SLEEP EEG	09:32	NORMAL EEG
04:42	NORMAL EEG	09:42	NORMAL EEG
04:52	NORMAL EEG	09:52	NORMAL EEG
05:02	SLEEP EEG	10:02	NORMAL EEG
05:12	NORMAL EEG	10:12	NORMAL EEG
05:22	NORMAL EEG	10:22	NORMAL EEG
05:32	SLEEP EEG	10:32	STIMULATION
05:42	NORMAL EEG	10:42	SLEEP EEG
05:52	NORMAL EEG	10:52	NORMAL EEG
06:02	NORMAL EEG	11:02	NORMAL EEG

"I can't make anything out of this," Ross said, frowning. "It looks like he's dozing on and off, and he's gotten a couple of stimulations, but . . ." She shook her head. "Isn't there another display mode?"

As she spoke, the computer produced another report, adding it to the column of numbers:

11:12 NORMAL EEG

"People," Gerhard said, in mock irritation. "They just can't handle machine data." It was true. Machines could handle column after column of numbers. People needed to see patterns. On the other hand, machines were very poor at recognizing patterns. The classic problem was trying to get a machine to differentiate between the letter "B" and the letter "D." A child could do it; it was almost impossible for a machine to look at the two patterns and discern the difference.

"I'll give you a graphic display," Gerhard said. He punched buttons, wiping the screen. After a moment, cross-hatching for a graph appeared, and the points began to blink on:

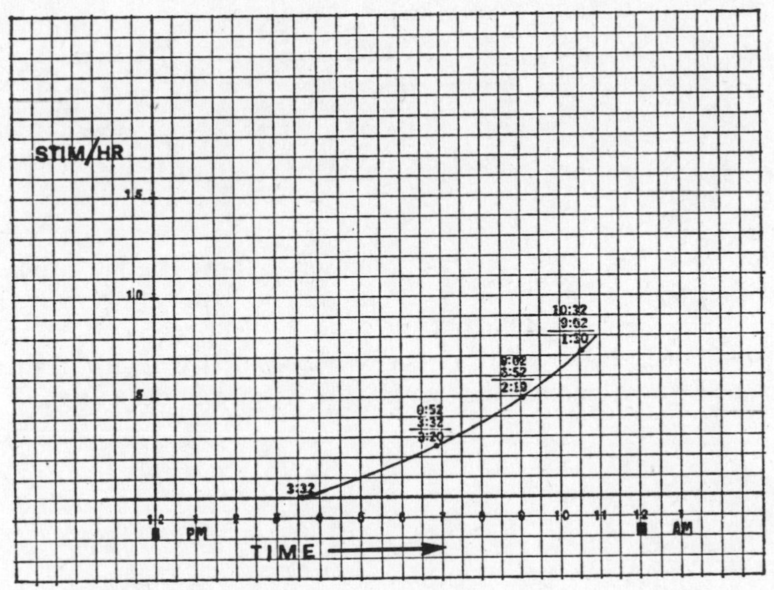

"Damn," she said when she saw the graph.

"What's the matter?" Gerhard said.

"He's getting more frequent stimulations. He had none for a long time, and then he began to have them every couple of hours. Now it looks like one an hour."

"So?" Gerhard said.

"What does that suggest to you?" she said.

"Nothing in particular."

"It should suggest something quite specific," she said. "We know that Benson's brain will be interacting with the computer, right?"

"Yes . . ."

"And that interaction will be a learning pattern of some kind. It's just like a kid with a cookie jar. If you slap the kid's hand every time he reaches for the cookies, pretty soon he won't reach so often. Look." She drew a quick sketch.

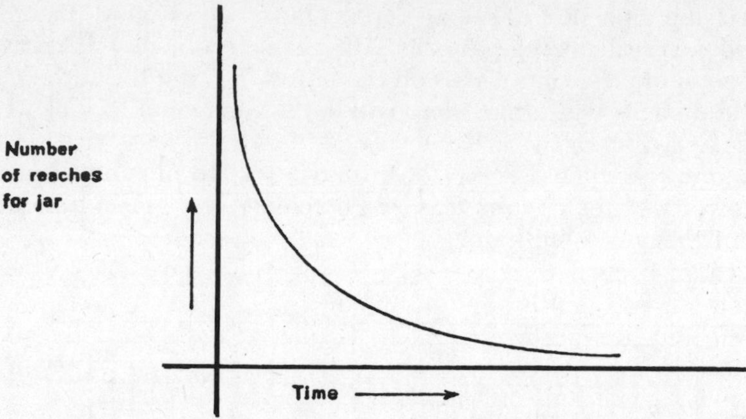

"Now," she said, "that's negative reinforcement. The kid reaches, but he gets hurt. So he stops reaching. Eventually he'll quit altogether. Okay?"

"Sure," Gerhard said, "but—"

"Let me finish. If the kid is normal, it works that way. But if the kid is a masochist, it will be very different." She drew another curve.

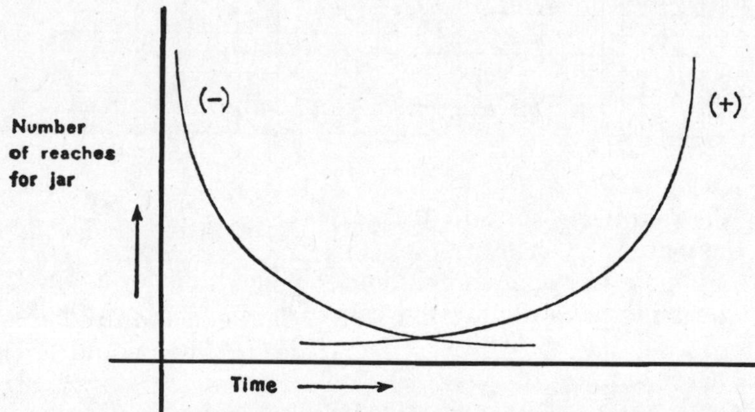

"Here the kid is reaching more often for the cookies, because he likes getting hit. It should be negative reinforcement, but it's really positive reinforcement. Do you remember Cecil?"

"No," Gerhard said.

On the computer console, a new report appeared:

11:22 STIMULATION

"Oh shit," she said. "It's happening."

"What's happening?"

"Benson is going into a positive progression cycle."

"I don't understand."

"It's just like Cecil. Cecil was the first monkey to be wired with electrodes to a computer. That was back in '65. The computer wasn't miniaturized then; it was a big clunky computer, and the monkey was wired up by actual wires. The computer detected the start of a seizure in Cecil, and delivered a counter-shock to stop it. Okay. Now the seizures should have come less and less frequently, like the hand reaching for the cookies less and less often. But instead the reverse happened. Cecil *liked* the shocks. And he began to initiate seizures in order to experience the pleasurable shocks."

"And that's what Benson is doing?"

"I think so."

Gerhard shook his head. "Listen, Jan, that's all interesting. But a person can't start and stop seizures at will. They can't control them. The seizures are—"

"Involuntary," she said. "That's right. You have no more control over them than you do over heart rate and blood pressure and sweating and all the other involuntary acts."

There was a long pause. Gerhard said, "You're going to tell me I'm wrong."

On the screen, the computer blinked:

11:32 -------

"I'm going to tell you," she said, "that you've cut too many conferences. You know about autonomic learning?"

After a guilty pause: "No."

"It was a big mystery for a long time. Classically, it was believed that you could learn to control only voluntary acts. You could learn to drive a car, but you couldn't learn to lower your blood pressure. Of course, there were those yogis who supposedly could reduce oxygen requirements of their body and slow their heartbeats to near death. They could reverse intestinal peristalsis and drink liquids through the anus. But that was all unproven—and theoretically impossible."

Gerhard nodded cautiously.

"Well, it turns out to be perfectly possible. You can teach a rat to blush in only one ear. Right ear or left ear, take your pick. You can teach it to lower or raise blood pressure or heartbeat. And you can do the same thing with people. It's not impossible. It can be done."

"How?" He asked the question with unabashed curiosity. Whatever embarrassment he had felt before was gone.

"Well, with people who have high blood pressure, for instance, all you do is put them in a room with a blood-pressure cuff on their arm. Whenever the blood pressure goes down, a bell rings. You tell the person to try to make the bell ring as often as possible. They work for that reward—a bell ringing. At first it happens by accident. Then pretty soon they learn how to make it happen more often. The bell rings more frequently. After a few hours, it's ringing a lot."

Gerhard scratched his head. "And you think Benson is producing more seizures to be rewarded with shocks?"

"Yes."

"Well, what's the difference? He still can't have any seizures. The computer always prevents them from happening."

"Not true," she said. "A couple of years ago, a Norwegian schizophrenic was wired up and allowed to stimulate a pleasure terminal as often as he wanted. He pushed himself into a convulsion by overstimulating himself."

Gerhard winced.

Richards, who had been watching the computer console, suddenly said, "Something's wrong."

"What is it?"

"We're not getting readings any more."

On the screen, they saw:

```
11:32  -------
11:42  -------
```

Ross looked and sighed. "See if you can get a computer extrapolation of that curve," she said. "See if he's really going into a learning cycle, and how fast." She started for the door. "I'm going to see what's happened to Benson."

FRIDAY, MARCH 12, 1971: BREAKDOWN

Chapter 1

The seventh (Special Surgical) floor was quiet; there were two nurses at the station. One was making progress notes in a patient's chart; the other was eating a candy bar and reading a movie magazine. Neither paid much attention to Ross as she went to the chart shelf, opened Benson's record, and checked it.

She wanted to be certain that Benson had received all his medications, and to her astonishment she found that he had not. "Why hasn't Benson gotten his thorazine?" she demanded.

The nurses looked up in surprise. "Benson?"

"The patient in seven-ten." She glanced at her watch; it was after midnight. "He was supposed to be started on thorazine at noon. Twelve hours ago."

"I'm sorry . . . may I?" One of the nurses reached for the chart. Ross handed it to her and watched while she turned to the page of nursing orders. McPherson's order for thorazine was circled in red by a nurse, with the cryptic notation "Call."

Ross was thinking that without heavy doses of thorazine Benson's psychotic thinking would be unchecked, and could be dangerous.

"Oh, yes," the nurse said. "I remember now. Dr. Morris told us that only medication orders from him or from Dr. Ross were to be followed. We don't know this Dr. McPhee, so we waited to call him to confirm the therapy. It—"

"Dr. Mc*Pherson,*" Ross said heavily, "is the chief of the NPS."

The nurse frowned at the signature. "Well, how are we supposed to know that? You can't read the name. Here." She handed back the chart. "We thought it looked like McPhee, and the only McPhee in the hospital directory is a gynecologist and that didn't seem logical, but sometimes doctors will put a note in the wrong chart by mistake, so we—"

"All right," Ross said, waving her hand. "All right. Just get him his thorazine now, will you?"

"Right away, Doctor," the nurse said. She gave her a dirty look and went to the medicine locker. Ross went down the hall to Room 710.

The cop sat outside Benson's room with his chair tipped back against the wall. He was reading *Secret Romances* with more interest than Ross would have thought likely. She knew without asking where he had gotten the magazine; he had been bored, one of the nurses had given it to him. He was also smoking a cigarette, flicking the ashes in the general direction of an ashtray on the floor.

He looked up as she came down the hall. "Good evening, Doctor."

"Good evening." She stifled an impulse to lecture him on his sloppy demeanor. But the cops weren't under her jurisdiction, and besides, she was just irritated with the nurses. "Everything quiet?" she asked.

"Pretty quiet."

Inside 710 she could hear television, a talk show with laughter. Someone said, "And what did you do then?" There was more laughter. She opened the door.

The room lights were off; the only light came from the glow of the television. Benson had apparently fallen asleep; his body was turned away from the door, and the sheets were pulled up over his shoulder. She clicked the television off and crossed the room to the bed. Gently, she touched his leg.

"Harry," she said softly. "Harry—"

She stopped.

The leg beneath her hand was soft and formless. She pressed down; the "leg" bulged oddly. She reached for the bedside lamp and turned it on, flooding the room with light. Then she pulled back the sheets.

Benson was gone. In his place were three plastic bags of the kind the hospital used to line wastebaskets. Each had been inflated and then knotted shut tightly. Benson's head was represented by a wadded towel; his arm by another.

"Officer," she said, in a low voice, "you'd better get your ass in here."

The cop came bounding into the room, his hand reaching for his gun. Ross gestured to the bed.

"Holy shit," the cop said. "What happened?"

"I was going to ask you."

The cop went immediately to the bathroom and checked there; it was empty. He looked in the closet. "His clothes are still here—"

"When was the last time you looked into this room?"

"—but his shoes are gone," the cop said, still looking in the closet. "His shoes are missing." He turned and looked at Ross with a kind of desperation. "Where is he?"

"When was the last time you looked into this room?" Ross repeated. She pressed the bedside buzzer to call the night nurse.

"About twenty minutes ago."

Ross walked to the window and looked out. The window was open, but there was a sheer drop of seven stories to the parking lot below. "How long were you away from the door?"

"Look, Doc, it was only a few minutes—"

"How long?"

"I ran out of cigarettes. The hospital doesn't have any machines. I had to go to that coffee shop across the street. I was gone about three minutes. That was around eleven-thirty. The nurses said they'd keep an eye on things."

"Great," Ross said. She checked the bedside table and saw that Benson's shaving equipment was there, his wallet, his car keys . . . all there.

The nurse stuck her head in the door, answering the call. "What is it now?"

"We seem to be missing a patient," Ross said.

"I beg your pardon?"

Ross gestured to the plastic bags in the bed. The nurse reacted slowly, and then turned quite pale.

"Call Dr. Ellis," Ross said, "and Dr. McPherson and Dr. Morris. They'll be at home; have the switchboard put you through. Say it's an emergency. Tell them Benson is gone. Then call hospital security. Is that clear?"

"Yes, Doctor," the nurse said, and hurried from the room.

Ross sat down on the edge of Benson's bed and turned her attention to the cop.

"Where did he get those bags?" the cop said.

She had already figured that out. "One from the bedside wastebasket," she said. "One from the wastebasket by the door. One from the bathroom wastebasket. Two towels from the bathroom."

"Clever," the cop said. He pointed to the closet. "But he can't get far. He left his clothes."

"Took his shoes."

"A man with bandages and a bathrobe can't get far, even if he has shoes." He shook his head. "I better call this in."

"Did Benson make any calls?"

"Tonight?"

"No, last month."

"Look, lady, I don't need any of your lip right now."

She saw then that he was really quite young, in his early twenties, and that he was afraid. He had screwed up, and he didn't know what would happen. "I'm sorry," she said. "Yes, tonight."

"He made one call," the cop said. "About eleven."

"Did you listen to it?"

"No." He shrugged. "I never thought . . ." His voice trailed off. "You know."

"So he made one call at eleven, and left at eleven-thirty." She walked outside to the hallway and looked down the corridor to the nurses' station. There was always somebody on duty there, and he would have to pass the nurses' station to reach the elevator. He'd never make it.

What else could he have done? She looked toward the other end of the hall. There was a stairway at the far end. He could walk down. But seven flights of stairs? Benson was too weak for that. And when he got to the ground-floor lobby, there he'd be, in his bathrobe with his head bandaged. The reception desk would stop him.

"I don't get it," the cop said, coming out into the hallway. "Where could he go?"

"He's a very bright man," Ross said. It was a fact that they all tended to forget. To the cops, Benson was a criminal charged with assault, one of the hundreds of querulous types they saw each day. To the hospital staff, he was a diseased man, unhappy, dangerous, borderline psychotic. Everyone tended to forget that Benson was also brilliant. His computer work was outstanding in a field where many intelligent men worked. On the initial psychological testing at the NPS, his abbreviated WAIS I.Q. test had scored 144. He was fully capable of planning to leave, then listening at the door, hearing the cop and the nurse discuss going for cigarettes—and then making his escape in a matter of minutes. But how?

Benson must have known that he could never get out of the hospital in his bathrobe. He had left his street clothes in his room—he probably couldn't get out wearing those, either. Not at midnight. The lobby desk would have stopped him. Visiting hours had ended three hours before.

What the hell would he do?

The cop went up to the nurses' station to phone in a report. Ross followed along behind him, looking at the doors. Room 709 was a burns patient; she opened the door and looked inside, making sure only the patient was there. Room 708 was empty; a kidney-transplant patient had been discharged that afternoon. She checked that room, too.

The next door was marked SUPPLIES. It was a standard room on surgical floors. Bandages, suture kits, and linen supplies were stored there. She opened the door and went inside. She passed row after row of bottled intravenous solutions; then trays of different kits. Then sterile masks, smocks, spare uniforms for nurses and orderlies—

She stopped. She was staring at a blue bathrobe, hastily wadded into a corner on a shelf. The rest of the shelf contained neatly folded piles of white trousers, shirts, and jackets worn by hospital orderlies.

She called for the nurse.

"It's impossible," Ellis said, pacing up and down in the nurses' station. "Absolutely impossible. He's two days—a day and a half—post-op. He couldn't possibly leave."

"He did," Janet Ross said. "And he did it the only way he could, by changing into an orderly's uniform. Then he probably walked downstairs to the sixth floor and took an elevator to the lobby. Nobody would have noticed him; orderlies come and go at all hours."

Ellis wore a dinner jacket and a white frilly shirt; his bow tie was loosened and he was smoking a cigarette. She had never seen him smoke before. "I still don't buy it," he said. "He was heavily tranked with thorazine, and—"

"Never got it," Ross said.

"Never got it?"

"What's thorazine?" the cop said, taking notes.

"The nurses had a question on the order and didn't administer it. He had no sedatives and no tranquilizers since midnight last night."

"Christ," Ellis said. He looked at the nurses as if he could kill them. Then he paused. "But what about his head? It was covered with bandages. Someone would notice that."

Morris, who had been sitting silently in a corner, said, "He had a wig."

"You're kidding."

"I saw it," Morris said.

"What was the color of the wig in question?" the cop said.

"Black," Morris said.

"Oh Christ," Ellis said.

Ross said, "How did he get this wig?"

"A friend brought it to him. The day of admission."

"Listen," Ellis said, "even with a wig, he can't have gotten anywhere. He left his wallet and his money. There are no taxis at this hour."

She looked at Ellis, marveling at his ability to deny reality. He just didn't want to believe that Benson had left; he was fighting the evidence, fighting hard.

"He called a friend," Ross said, "about eleven." She looked at Morris. "You remember who brought the wig?"

"A pretty girl," Morris said.

"Do you remember her name?" Ross said, with a sarcastic edge.

"Angela Black," Morris said promptly.

"See if you can find her in the phone book," Ross said. Morris began to check; the phone rang, and Ellis answered it. He listened, then without comment handed the phone to Ross.

"Yes," Ross said.

"I've done the computer projection." Gerhard said. "It just came through. You were right. Benson is on a learning cycle with his implanted computer. His stimulation points conform to the projected curve exactly."

"That's wonderful," Ross said. As she listened, she glanced at Ellis, Morris, and the cop. They watched her expectantly.

"It's exactly what you said," Gerhard said. "Benson apparently likes the shocks. He's starting seizures more and more often. The curve is going up sharply.

"When will he tip over?"

"Not long," Gerhard said. "Assuming that he doesn't break the cycle—and I doubt that he will—then he'll be getting almost continuous stimulations at six-four A.M."

"You have a confirmed projection on that?" she asked, frowning. She glanced at her watch. It was already 12:30.

"That's right," Gerhard said. "Continuous stimulations starting at six-four this morning."

"Okay," Ross said, and hung up. She looked at the others. "Benson has gone into a learning progression with his computer. He's projected for tip-over at six A.M. today."

"Christ," Ellis said, looking at the wall clock. "Less than six hours from now."

Across the room, Morris had put aside the phone books and was talking to Information. "Then try West Los Angeles," he said, and after a pause, "What about new listings?"

The cop stopped taking notes, and looked confused. "Is something going to happen at six o'clock?"

"We think so," Ross said.

Ellis puffed on his cigarette. "Two years," he said, "and I'm back on them." He stubbed it out carefully. "Has McPherson been notified?"

"He's been called."

"Check unlisted numbers," Morris said. He listened for a moment. "This is Dr. Morris at University Hospital," he said, "and it's an emergency. We have to locate Angela Black. Now, if—" Angrily, he slammed down the phone. "Bitch," he said.

"Any luck?"

He shook his head.

"We don't even know if Benson called this girl," Ellis said. "He could have called someone else."

"Whoever he called may be in a lot of trouble in a few hours," Ross said. She flipped open Benson's chart. "It looks like a long night. We'd better get busy."

Chapter 2

The freeway was crowded. The freeway was always crowded, even at 1 A.M. on a Friday morning. She stared ahead at the pattern of red tail-lights, stretching ahead like an angry snake for miles. So many people. Where were they going at this hour?

Janet Ross usually took pleasure in the freeways. There had been times when she had driven home from the hospital at night, with the big green signs flashing past overhead, and the intricate web of overpasses and underpasses, and the exhilarating anonymous speed, and she had felt wonderful, expansive, free. She had been raised in California, and as a child she remembered the first of the freeways. The system had grown up as she had grown, and she did not see it as a menace or an evil. It was part of the landscape; it was fast; it was fun.

The automobile was important to Los Angeles, a city more technology-dependent than any in the world. Los Angeles could not survive without the automobile, as it could not survive without water piped in from hundreds of miles away, and as it could not survive without certain building technologies. This was a fact of the city's existence, and had been true since early in the century.

But in recent years Ross had begun to recognize the subtle psychological effects of living your life inside an automobile. Los Angeles had no sidewalk cafés, because no one walked; the sidewalk café, where you could stare at passing people, was not stationary but mobile. It changed with each traffic light, where people stopped, stared briefly at each other, then drove on. But there was something inhuman about living inside a cocoon of tinted glass and stainless steel, air-conditioned, carpeted, stereophonic tape-decked, power-optioned, isolated. It thwarted some deep human need to congregate, to be together, to see and be seen.

Local psychiatrists recognized an indigenous depersonalization syndrome. Los Angeles was a town of recent emigrants and therefore strangers; cars kept them strangers, and there were few institutions that served to bring them together. Practically no one went to church, and work groups were not entirely satisfactory. People became lonely; they complained of being cut off, without friends, far from families and old homes. Often they became suicidal—and a common method of suicide was the automobile. The police referred to it euphemistically as "single unit fatalities." You picked your overpass, and hit it at eighty or ninety, foot flat to the floor. Sometimes it took hours to cut the body out of the wreckage. . . .

Moving at sixty-five miles an hour, she shifted across five lanes of traffic and pulled off the freeway at Sunset, heading up into the Hollywood Hills, through an area known locally as the Swish Alps because of the many homosexuals who lived there. People with problems seemed drawn to Los Angeles. The city offered freedom; its price was lack of supports.

She came to Laurel Canyon and took the curves fast, tires squealing, headlamps swinging through the darkness. There was little traffic here; she would reach Benson's house in a few minutes.

In theory, she and the rest of the NPS staff had a simple problem: get Benson back before six o'clock. If they could get him back into the hospital, they could uncouple his implanted computer and stop the progression series. Then they could sedate him and wait a few days before relinking him to a new set of terminals. They'd obviously chosen the wrong electrodes the first time around; that was a risk they accepted in advance. It was an acceptable risk because they expected to have a chance to correct any error. But that opportunity was no longer there.

They had to get him back. A simple problem, with a relatively simple solution—check Benson's known haunts. After reviewing his chart, they'd all set out to different places. Ross was going to his house on Laurel. Ellis was going to a strip joint called the Jackrabbit Club, where Benson often went. Morris was going to Autotronics, Inc., in Santa Monica, where Benson was employed; Morris had called the president of the firm, who was coming to the offices to open them up for him.

They would check back in an hour or so to compare notes and progress. A simple plan, and one she thought unlikely to work. But there wasn't much else to do.

She parked her car in front of Benson's house and walked up the slate path to the front door. It was ajar; from inside she could hear the sound of laughter and giggles. She knocked and pushed it open.

"Hello?"

No one seemed to hear. The giggles came from somewhere at the back of the house. She stepped into the front hallway. She had never seen Benson's house, and she wondered what it was like. Looking around, she realized she should have known.

From the outside, the house was an ordinary ranch-style house as unremarkable in its appearance as Benson himself. But the inside looked like the drawing rooms of Louis XVI—graceful antique chairs and couches, tapestries on the walls, bare hardwood floors.

"Anybody home?" she called. Her voice echoed through the house. There was no answer, but the laughter continued. She followed the sound toward the rear. She came into the kitchen—antique gas stove, no oven, no dishwasher, no electric blender, no toaster. No machines, she thought. Benson had built himself a world without any sort of modern machine in it.

The kitchen window looked out onto the back of the house. There was a small patch of lawn and a swimming pool, all perfectly ordinary and modern, Benson's ordinary exterior again. The back yard was bathed in greenish light from the underwater pool lights. In the pool, two girls were laughing and splashing. She went outside.

The girls were oblivious to her arrival. They continued to splash and shriek happily; they wrestled with each other in the water. She stood on the pool deck and said, "Anybody home?"

They noticed her then, and moved apart from each other. "Looking for Harry?" one of them said.

"Yes."

"You a cop?"

"I'm a doctor."

One of the girls got out of the pool lithely and began toweling off. She wore a brief red bikini. "You just missed him," the girl said. "But we weren't supposed to tell the cops. That's what he said." She put one leg on a chair to dry it with the towel. Ross realized the move was calculated, seductive, and directed toward her.

"When did he leave?"

"Just a few minutes ago."

"How long have you been here?"

"About a week," the girl in the pool said. "Harry invited us to stay. He thought we were cute."

The other girl wrapped the towel around her shoulders and said, "We met him at the Jackrabbit. He comes there a lot."

Ross nodded.

"He's a lot of fun," the girl said. "A lot of laughs. You know what he was wearing tonight?"

"What?"

"A hospital uniform. All white." She shook her head. "What a riot."

"Did you talk to him?"

"Sure."

"What did he say?"

The girl in the red bikini started back inside the house. Ross followed her. "He said not to tell the cops. He said to have a good time."

"Why did he come here?"

"He had to pick up some stuff."

"What stuff?"

"Some stuff from his study."

"Where is the study?"

"I'll show you."

She led her back into the house, through the living room. Her wet feet left small pools on the bare hardwood floor. "Isn't this place wild? Harry's really crazy. You ever heard him talk about things?"

"Yes."

"Then you know. He's really nutty." She gestured around the room. "All this old stuff. Why do you want to see him?"

"He's sick," Ross said.

"He must be," the girl said. "I saw those bandages. What was he, in an accident?"

"He had an operation."

"No kidding. In a hospital?"

"Yes."

"No kidding."

They went through the living room and down a corridor toward the bedrooms. The girl turned right into one room, which was a study—antique desk, antique lamps, overstuffed couches. "He came in here and got some stuff."

"Did you see what he got?"

"We didn't really pay much attention. But he took some big rolls of paper." She gestured with her hands. "Real big. They looked like blueprints or something."

"Blueprints?"

"Well, they were blue on the inside of the roll, and white on the outside, and they were big." She shrugged.

"Did he take anything else?"

"Yeah. A metal box."

"What kind of a metal box?" Ross was thinking of a lunchbox, or a small suitcase.

"It looked like a tool kit, maybe. I saw it open for a moment, before he closed it. It seemed to have tools and stuff inside."

"Did you notice anything in particular?"

The girl was silent then. She bit her lip. "Well, I didn't really see, but . . ."

"Yes?"

"It looked like he had a gun in there."

"Did he say where he was going?"

"No."

"Did he give any clue?"

"No."

"Did he say he was coming back?"

"Well, that was funny," the girl said. "He kissed me, and he kissed Suzie, and he said to have a good time, and he said not to tell the cops. And he said he didn't think he'd be seeing us again." She shook her head. "It was funny. But you know how Harry is."

"Yes," Ross said. "I know how Harry is." She looked at her watch. it was 1:47. There were only four hours left.

Chapter 3

The first thing that Ellis noticed was the smell: hot, damp, fetid—a dark warm animal smell. He wrinkled his nose in distaste. How could Benson tolerate a place like this?

He watched as the spotlight swung through the darkness and came to rest on a pair of long tapering thighs. There was an expectant rustling in the audience. It reminded Ellis of his days in the Navy, stationed in Baltimore. That was the last time he had been in a place like this, hot and sticky with fantasies and frustrations. That had been a long time ago. It was a shock to think how fast the time had passed.

"Yes, ladies and gentlemen, the incredible, the lovely, *Cyn*thia *Sin*-cere. A big hand for the lovely *Cyn*thia!"

The spotlight widened onstage, to show a rather ugly but spectacularly constructed girl. The band began to play. When the spotlight was wide enough to hit Cynthia's eyes, she squinted and began an awkward dance. She paid no attention to the music, but nobody seemed to mind. Ellis looked at the audience. There were a lot of men here—and a lot of very tough-looking girls with short hair.

"Harry Benson?" the manager said, at his elbow. "Yeah, he comes in a lot."

"Have you seen him lately?"

"I don't know about lately," the manager said. He coughed. Ellis smelled sweet alcoholic breath. "But I tell you," the manager said, "I wish he wouldn't hang around, you know? I think he's a little nuts. And always bothering the girls. You know how hard it is to keep the girls? Fucking murder, that's what it is."

Ellis nodded, and scanned the audience. Benson had probably changed clothes; certainly he wouldn't be wearing an orderly's uniform any more. Ellis looked at the backs of the heads, at the area between hairline and shirt collar. He looked for a white bandage. He saw none.

"But you haven't seen him lately?"

"No," the manager said, shaking his head. "Not for a week or so." A waitress went by wearing a rabbitlike white fur bikini. "Sal, you seen Harry lately?"

"He's usually around," she said vaguely, and wandered off with a tray of drinks.

"I wish he wouldn't hang around, bothering the girls," the manager said, and coughed again.

Ellis moved deeper into the club. The spotlight swung through smoky air over his head, following the movements of the girl on stage. She was having trouble unhooking her bra. She did a sort of two-step shuffle, hands behind her back, eyes looking vacantly out at the audience. Ellis understood, watching her, why Benson thought of strippers as machines. They were mechanical, no question about it. And artificial—when the bra came off, he could see the U-shaped surgical incision beneath each breast, where the plastic had been inserted.

Jaglon would love this, he thought. It would fit right into his theories about machine sex. Jaglon was one of the Development boys and he was preoccupied with the idea of artificial intelligence merging with human intelligence. He argued that, on the one hand, cosmetic surgery and implanted machinery were making man more mechanical, while on the other hand robot developments were making machines more human. It was only a matter of time before people began having sex with humanoid robots.

Perhaps it's already happening, Ellis thought, looking at the stripper. He looked back at the audience, satisfying himself that Benson was not there. Then he checked a phone booth in the back, and the men's room.

The men's room was small and reeked of vomit. He grimaced again, and stared at himself in the cracked mirror over the washbasin. Whatever else was true about the Jackrabbit Club, it produced an olfactory assault. He wondered if that mattered to Benson.

He went back into the club itself and made his way toward the door. "Find him?" the manager asked.

Ellis shook his head and left. Once outside, he breathed the cool night air, and got into his car. The notion of smells intrigued him. It was a problem he had considered before, but never really resolved in his own mind.

His operation on Benson was directed toward a specific part of the brain, the limbic system. It was a very old part of the brain, in terms of evolution. Its original purpose had been the control of smell. In fact, the old term for it was *rhinencephalon*—the "smelling brain."

The rhinencephalon had developed 150 million years ago, when reptiles ruled the earth. It controlled the most primitive behavior—anger and fear, lust and hunger, attack and withdrawal. Reptiles like crocodiles had little else to direct their behavior. Man, on the other hand, had a cerebral cortex.

But the cerebral cortex was a recent addition. Its modern development had begun only two million years ago; in its present state, the cerebral cortex of man was only 100,000 years old. In terms of evolutionary time scales, that was nothing. The cortex had grown up around the limbic brain, which remained unchanged, embedded deep inside the new cortex. That cortex, which could feel love, and worry about ethical conduct, and write poetry, had to make an uneasy peace with the crocodile brain at its core. Sometimes, as in the case of Benson, the peace broke down, and the crocodile brain took over intermittently.

What was the relationship of smell to all this? Ellis was not sure. Of course, attacks often began with the sensation of strange smells. But was there anything else? Any other effect?

He didn't know, and as he drove he reflected that it didn't much matter. The only problem was to find Benson before his crocodile brain took over. Ellis had seen that happen once, in the NPS. Ellis had watched it through the one-way glass. Benson had been quite normal—and suddenly he had lashed out against the wall, striking it viciously, picking up his chair, smashing it against the wall. The attack had begun without warning, and had been carried out with utter, total, unthinking viciousness.

Six A.M., he thought. There wasn't much time.

Chapter 4

"What is it, some kind of emergency?" Farley asked, unlocking the door to Autotronics.

"You could say so," Morris said, standing outside, shivering. It was a cold night, and he had been waiting half an hour. Waiting for Farley to show up.

Farley was a tall, slender man with a slow manner. Or perhaps he was just sleepy. He seemed to take forever to unlock the offices and let Morris inside. He turned on the lights in a rather plain lobby-reception area. Then he went back toward the rear of the building.

The rear of Autotronics was a single cavernous room. Desks were scattered here and there around several pieces of enormous, glittering machinery. Morris frowned slightly.

"I know what you're thinking," Farley said. "You're thinking it's a mess."

"No, I—"

"Well, it is. But we get the job done, I can tell you that." He pointed across the room. "That's Harry's desk, next to Hap."

"Hap?"

Farley gestured to a large, spidery metal construction across the room.

"Hap," he said, "is short for Hopelessly Automatic Ping-pong Player." He grinned. "Not really," he said. "But we have our little jokes here."

Morris walked over to the machine, circled around it, staring. "It plays ping-pong?"

"Not well," Farley admitted. "But we're working on that. It's a DOD—Department of Defense—grant, and the terms of the grant were to devise a ping-pong-playing robot. I know what you're thinking. You're thinking it isn't an important project."

Morris shrugged. He didn't like being told what he was thinking all the time.

Farley smiled. "God knows what they want it for," he said. "Of course, the capability would be striking. Imagine—a computer that could recognize a sphere moving rapidly through three-dimensional space, with the ability to contact the sphere and knock it back according to certain rules. Must land between the white lines, not off the table, and so on. I doubt," he said, "that they'll use it for ping-pong tournaments."

He went to the back of the room and opened a refrigerator which had a big orange RADIATION sign on it, and beneath, AUTHORIZED PERSONNEL ONLY. He removed two jars. "Want some coffee?"

Morris was staring at the signs.

"That's just to discourage the secretaries," Farley said, and laughed again. His jovial mood bothered Morris. He watched as Farley made instant coffee.

Morris went over to Benson's desk and began checking the drawers.

"What is it about Harry, anyway?"

"How do you mean?" Morris asked. The top drawer contained supplies—paper, pencils, slide rule, scribbled notes and calculations. The second drawer was a file drawer; it seemed to hold mostly letters.

"Well, he was in the hospital, wasn't he?"

"Yes. He had an operation, and left. We're trying to find him now."

"He's certainly gotten strange," Farley said.

"Uh-huh," Morris said. He was thumbing through the files. Business letters, business letters, requisition forms . . .

"I remember when it began," Farley said. "It was during Watershed Week."

Morris looked up from the letters. "During what?"

"Watershed Week," Farley said. "How do you take your coffee?"

"Black."

Farley gave him a cup, stirred artificial cream into his own. "Watershed Week," he said, "was a week in July of 1969. You've probably never heard of it."

Morris shook his head.

"That wasn't an official title," Farley said, "but that was what we called it. Everybody in our business knew it was coming, you see."

"What was coming?"

"The Watershed. Computer scientists all over the world knew it was coming, and they watched for it. It happened in July of 1969. The information-handling capacity of all the computers in the world exceeded the information-handling capacity of all the human brains in the world. Computers could receive and store more information than the 3.5 billion human brains in the world."

"That's the Watershed?"

"You bet it is," Farley said.

Morris sipped the coffee. It burned his tongue, but he woke up a little. "Is that a joke?"

"Hell, no," Farley said. "It's true. The Watershed was passed in 1969, and computers have been steadily pulling ahead since then. By 1975, they'll lead human beings by fifty to one in terms of capacity." He paused. "Harry was awfully upset about that."

"I can imagine," Morris said.

"And that was when it began for him. He got very strange, very secretive."

Morris looked around the room, at the large pieces of computer equipment standing in different areas. It was an odd sensation: the first time he could recall being in a room littered with computers. He realized that he had made some mistakes about Benson. He had assumed that Benson was pretty much like everyone else—but no one who worked in a place such as this was like everyone else. The experience must change you. He remembered that Ross had once said that it was a liberal myth that everybody was fundamentally the same. Lots of people weren't. They weren't like everybody else.

Farley was different, too, he thought. In another situation, he would have dismissed Farley as a jovial clown. But he was obviously bright as hell. Where did that grinning, comic manner come from?

"You know how fast this is moving?" Farley said. "Damned fast. We've gone from milliseconds to nanoseconds in just a few years. When the computer ILLIAC I was built in 1952, it could do eleven thousand arithmetical operations a second. Pretty fast, right? Well, they're almost finished with ILLIAC IV now. It will do two hundred *million* operations a second. It's the fourth generation. Of course, it couldn't have been built without the help of other computers. They used two other computers full time for two years, designing the new ILLIAC."

Morris drank his coffee. Perhaps it was his fatigue, perhaps the spookiness of the room, but he was beginning to feel some kinship with Benson. Computers to design computers—maybe they were taking over, after all. What would Ross say about that? A shared delusion?

"Find anything interesting in his desk?"

"No," Morris said. He sat down in the chair behind the desk and looked around the room. He was trying to act like Benson, to think like Benson, to *be* Benson.

"How did he spend his time?"

"I don't know," Farley said, sitting on another desk across the room. "He got pretty distant and withdrawn the last few months. I know he had some trouble with the law. And I knew he was going into the hospital. I knew that. He didn't like your hospital much."

"How is that?" Morris asked, not very interested. It wasn't surprising that Benson was hostile to the hospital.

Farley didn't answer. Instead, he went over to a bulletin board, where clippings and photos had been tacked up. He removed one yellowing newspaper item and gave it to Morris.

It was from the Los Angeles *Times*, dated July 17, 1969. The headline read: UNIVERSITY HOSPITAL GETS NEW COMPUTER. The story outlined the acquisition of the IBM System 360 computer which was being installed in the hospital basement, and would be used for research, assistance in operations, and a variety of other functions.

"You notice the date?" Farley said. "Watershed Week."

Morris stared at it and frowned.

Chapter 5

"I am trying to be logical, Dr. Ross."

"I understand, Harry."

"I think it's important to be logical and rational when we discuss these things, don't you?"

"Yes, I do."

She sat in the room and watched the reels of the tape recorder spin. Across from her, Ellis sat back in a chair, eyes closed, cigarette burning in his fingers. Morris drank another cup of coffee as he listened. She was making a list of what they knew, trying to decide what their next step should be.

The tape spun on.

"I classify things according to what I call trends to be opposed," Benson said. "There are four important trends to be opposed. Do you want to hear them?"

"Yes, of course."

"Do you really?"

"Yes, really."

"Well, trend number one is the generality of the computer. The computer is a machine but it's not like any machine in human history. Other machines have a specific function—like cars, or refrigerators, or dishwashers. We expect machines to have specific functions. But computers don't. They can do all sorts of things."

"Surely computers are—"

"Please let me finish. Trend number two is the autonomy of the computer. In the old days, computers weren't autonomous. They were like adding machines; you had to be there all the time, punching buttons, to make them work. Like cars: cars won't drive without drivers. But now things are different. Computers are becoming autonomous. You can build in all sorts of instructions about what to do next—and you can walk away and let the computer handle things."

"Harry, I—"

"Please don't interrupt me. This is very serious. Trend number three is miniaturization. You know all about that. A computer that took up a whole room in 1950 is now about the size of a carton of cigarettes. Pretty soon it'll be smaller than that."

There was a pause on the tape.

"Trend number four—" Benson began, and she clicked the tape off. She looked at Ellis and Morris. "This isn't getting us anywhere," she said.

They didn't reply, just stared with a kind of blank fatigue. She looked at her list of information.

Benson home at 12:30. Picked up ? blueprints, ?
gun, and tool kit.
Benson not seen in Jackrabbit Club recently.
Benson upset by UH computer, installed 7/69.

"Suggest anything to you?" Ellis asked.

"No," Ross said. "But I think one of us should talk to McPherson." She looked at Ellis, who nodded without energy. Morris shrugged slightly. "All right," she said. "I'll do it."

It was 4:30 A.M.

"The fact is," Ross said, "we've exhausted all our options. Time is running out."

McPherson stared at her across his desk. His eyes were dark and tired. "What do you expect me to do?" he said.

"Notify the police."

"The police are already notified. They've been notified from the beginning by one of their own people. I understand the seventh floor is swarming with cops now."

"The police don't know about the operation."

"For Christ's sake, the police brought him here for the operation. Of course they know about it."

"But they don't really know what it involves."

"They haven't asked."

"And they don't know about the computer projection for 6 A.M."

"What about it?" he said.

She was becoming angry with him. He was so damned stubborn. He knew perfectly well what she was saying.

"I think their attitude might be different if they knew that Benson was going to have a seizure at six A.M."

"I think you're right," McPherson said. He shifted his weight heavily in his chair. "I think they might stop thinking about him as an escaped man wanted on a charge of assault. And they would begin thinking of him as a crazy murderer with wires in his brain." He sighed. "Right now, their objective is to apprehend him. If we tell them more, they'll kill him."

"But innocent lives may be involved. If the projection—"

"The projection," McPherson said, "is just that. A computer projection. It is only as good as its input and that input consists of three timed stimulations. You can draw a lot of curves through three graph points. You can extrapolate it a lot of ways. We have no positive reason to believe he'll tip over at six A.M. In actual fact, he may not tip over at all."

She glanced around the room, at the charts on his walls. McPherson plotted the future of the NPS in this room, and he kept a record of it on his walls, in the form of elaborate, multicolored charts. She knew what those charts meant to him; she knew what the NPS meant to him; she knew what Benson meant to him. But even so, his position was unreasonable and irresponsible.

Now how was she going to say that?

"Look, Jan," McPherson said, "you began by saying that we've exhausted all our options. I disagree. I think we have the option of waiting. I think there is a possibility he will return to the hospital, return to our care. And as long as that is possible, I prefer to wait."

"You're not going to tell the police?"

"No."

"If he doesn't come back," she said, "and if he attacks someone during a seizure, do you really want that on your head?"

"It's already on my head," McPherson said, and smiled sadly.

It was 5 A.M.

Chapter 6

They were all tired, but none of them could sleep. They stayed in Telecomp, watching the computer projections as they inched up the plotted line toward a seizure state. The time was 5:30, and then 5:45.

Ellis smoked an entire pack of cigarettes, and then left to get another. Morris stared at a journal in his lap but never turned the page; from time to time, he glanced up at the wall clock.

Ross paced, and looked at the sunrise, the sky turning pink over the thin brown haze of smog to the east.

Ellis came back with more cigarettes.

Gerhard stopped working with the computers to make fresh coffee. Morris got up and stood watching Gerhard make it; not speaking, not helping, just watching.

Ross became aware of the ticking of the wall clock. It was strange that she had never noticed it before, because in fact it ticked quite loudly. And once a minute there was a mechanical click as the minute hand moved another notch. The sound disturbed her. She began to fix on it, waiting for that single click on top of the quieter ticking. Mildly obsessive, she thought. And then she thought of all the other psychological derangements she had experienced in the past. *Déjá vu,* the feeling that she had been somewhere before; depersonalization, the feeling that she was watching herself from across the room at some social gathering; clang associations, delusions, phobias. There was no sharp line between health and disease, sanity and insanity. It was a spectrum, and everybody fitted somewhere on the spectrum. Wherever you were on that spectrum, other people looked strange to you. Benson was strange to them; without question, they were strange to Benson.

At 6 A.M., they all stood and stretched, glancing up at the clock. Nothing happened.

"Maybe it's six-four exactly," Gerhard said.

They waited.

The clock showed 6:04. Still nothing happened. No telephones rang, no messengers arrived. Nothing.

Ellis slipped the cellophane wrapper off his cigarettes and crumpled it. The sound made Ross want to scream. He began to play with the cellophane, crumpling it, smoothing it out, crumpling it again. She gritted her teeth.

The clock showed 6:10, then 6:15. McPherson came into the room. "So far, so good," he said, smiled bleakly, and left. The others stared at each other.

Five more minutes passed.

"I don't know," Gerhard said, staring at the computer console. "Maybe the projection was wrong after all. We only had three plotting points. Maybe we should run another curve through."

He sat down at the console and punched buttons. The screen glowed with alternative curves, streaking white across the green background. Finally, he stopped. "No," he said. "The computer sticks with the original curve. That should be the one."

"Well, obviously the computer is wrong," Morris said. "It's almost six-thirty. The cafeteria will be opening. Anybody want to have breakfast?"

"Sounds good to me," Ellis said. He got out of his chair. "Jan?"

She shook her head. "I'll wait here awhile."

"I don't think it's going to happen," Morris said. "You better get some breakfast."

"I'll wait here." The words came out almost before she realized it.

"Okay, okay," Morris said, raising his hands. He shot a glance at Ellis, and the two men left. She remained in the room with Gerhard.

"Do you have confidence limits on that curve?" she said.

"I did," Gerhard said. "But I don't know any more. We've passed the confidence limits already. They were about plus or minus two minutes for ninety-nine percent."

"You mean the seizure would have occurred between six-two and six-six?"

"Yeah, roughly." He shrugged. "But it obviously didn't happen."

"It might take time before it was discovered."

"It might," Gerhard nodded. He didn't seem convinced.

She returned to the window. The sun was up now, shining with a pale reddish light. Why did sunrises always seem weaker, less brilliant, than sunsets? They should be the same.

Behind her she heard a single electronic *beep*.

"Oh-oh," Gerhard said.

She turned. "What is it?"

He pointed across the room to a small mechanical box on a shelf in the corner. The box was attached to a telephone. A green light glowed on the box.

"What is it?" she repeated.

"That's the special line," he said. "The twenty-four-hour recording for the dog tag."

She went over and picked up the telephone from its cradle. She listened and heard a measured, resonant voice saying, ". . . should be advised that the body must not be cremated or damaged in any way until the implanted atomic material has been removed. Failure to remove the material presents a risk of radioactive contamination. For detailed information—"

She turned to Gerhard. "How do you turn it off?"

He pressed a button on the box. The recording stopped.

"Hello?" she said.

There was a pause. Then a male voice said, "Whom am I speaking to?"

"This is Dr. Ross."

"Are you affiliated with the"—a short pause—"the Neuropsychiatric Research Unit?"

"Yes, I am."

"Get a pencil and paper. I want you to take an address down. This is Captain Anders of the Los Angeles police."

She gestured to Gerhard for something to write with. "What's the problem, Captain?"

"We have a murder here," Anders said, and we've got some questions for your people."

Chapter 7

Three patrol cars were pulled up in front of the apartment building off Sunset. The flashing red lights had already drawn a crowd, despite the early hour and the morning chill. She parked her car down the street and walked back to the lobby. A young patrolman stopped her.

"You a tenant?"

"I'm Dr. Ross. Captain Anders called me."

He nodded toward the elevator. "Third floor, turn left," he said, and let her through. The crowd watched curiously as she crossed the lobby and waited for the elevator. They were standing outside, looking in, peering over each other's shoulders, whispering among themselves. She wondered what they thought of her. The flashing lights from the patrol cars bathed the lobby intermittently with a red glow. Then the elevator came, and the doors closed.

The interior of the elevator was tacky: plastic paneling made to look like wood, worn green carpeting stained by innumerable pets. She waited impatiently for it to creak up to the third floor. She knew what these buildings were like—full of hookers, full of gays, full of drugs and transients. You could rent an apartment without a long lease, just month to month. It was that kind of place.

She stepped off at the third floor and walked down to a cluster of cops outside an apartment. Another policeman blocked her way; she repeated that she was here to see Captain Anders, and he let her through with the admonition not to touch anything.

It was a one-bedroom apartment furnished in pseudo-Spanish style. Or at least she thought it was. Twenty men were crowded inside, dusting, photographing, measuring, collecting. It was impossible to visualize how it had looked before the onslaught of police personnel.

Anders came over to her. He was young, in his middle thirties, wearing a conservative dark suit. His hair was long enough to hang over the back of his collar and he wore horn-rimmed glasses. The effect was almost professorial, and quite unexpected. It was strange how you built up prejudices. When he spoke, his voice was soft: "Are you Dr. Ross?"

"Yes."

"Captain Anders." He shook hands quickly and firmly. "Thank you for coming. The body is in the bedroom. The coroner's man is in there, too."

He led the way into the bedroom. The deceased was a girl in her twenties, sprawled nude across the bed. Her head was crushed and she had been stabbed repeatedly. The bed was soaked with blood, and the room had the sickly sweet odor of blood.

The rest of the room was in disarray—a chair by the dressing table knocked over, cosmetics and lotions smeared on the rug, a bedside lamp broken. Six men were working in the room, one of them a doctor from the medical examiner's office. He was filling out the death report.

"This is Dr. Ross," Anders said. "Tell her about it."

The doctor shrugged toward the body. "Brutal methodology, as you can see. Strong blow to the left temporal region, producing cranial depression and immediate unconsciousness. The weapon was that lamp over there. Blood of her type and some of her hair are affixed to it."

Ross glanced over at the lamp, then back to the body. "The stab wounds?"

"They're later, almost certainly post-mortem. She was killed by the blow to the head."

Ross looked at the head. It was squashed in on one side, like a deflated football, distorting the features of what had once been a conventionally pretty face.

"You'll notice," the doctor said, moving closer to the girl, "that she's put on half her make-up. As we reconstruct it, she's sitting at the dressing table, over there, making up. The blow comes from above and from the side, knocking her over in the chair, spilling the lotions and crap. Then she's lifted up"—the doctor raised his arms and frowned in mock effort, lifting an invisible body—"from the chair and placed on the bed."

"Somebody pretty strong?"

"Oh, yes. A man for sure."

"How do you know that?"

"Pubic hair in the shower drain. We've found two varieties. One matches hers, the other is male. Male pubic hair as you know is more circular, less elliptical in cross section than female hair."

"No," Ross said. "I didn't know that."

"I can give you a reference on it, if you want," the doctor said. "It's also clear that her killer had intercourse with her before the murder. We've got a blood type on the seminal fluid and it's AO. The man apparently takes a shower after intercourse, and then comes out and kills her."

Ross nodded.

"Following delivery of the blow to the head, she's lifted up and placed on the bed. At this time, she's not bleeding much. No blood to speak of on the dressing table or rug. But now her killer picks up some instrument and stabs her in the stomach several times. You'll notice that the deepest wounds are all in the lower abdomen, which may have some sexual connotations for the killer. But that's just guessing on our part."

Ross nodded but said nothing. She moved closer to the body to examine the stab wounds. They were all small, puncture-like in appearance, with a good deal of skin tearing around the wounds.

"You find a weapon?"

"No," the doctor said.

"What do you think it was?"

"I'm not sure. Nothing very sharp, but something strong—it took a lot of force to penetrate this way with a relatively blunt instrument."

"Another argument that it's a man," Anders said.

"Yes. I'd guess it was something metal, like a blunt letter opener, or a metal ruler, or a screwdriver. Something like that. But what's really interesting," the doctor went on, "is this phenomenon here." He pointed to the girl's left arm, which was outstretched on the bed and mutilated badly by stab wounds. "You see, he stabbed her in the stomach, and then stabbed her arm, moving out in a regular way, a succession of stabbings. Now, notice: when he's past the arm, he continues to stab. You can see the tears in the sheet and blanket. They continue out in a straight line."

He pointed to the tears.

"Now," the doctor said, "in my book that's perseveration. Automatic continuation of pointless movement. Like he was some kind of machine that just kept going and going. . . ."

"That's correct," Ross said.

"We assume," the doctor said, "that it represents some kind of trance or seizure state. But we don't know if it was organic or functional, natural or artificially induced. Since the girl let him into the apartment freely, this trance-like state developed only later."

Ross realized that the coroner's man was showing off, and it irritated her. This was the wrong time to be playing Sherlock Holmes.

Anders handed her the metal dog tag. "We were proceeding routinely with the investigation," he said, "when we found this."

Ross turned the tag over in her hand.

I HAVE AN IMPLANTED ATOMIC PACEMAKER. DIRECT PHYSICAL INJURY OR FIRE MAY RUPTURE THE CAPSULE AND RELEASE TOXIC MATERIALS. IN THE EVENT OF INJURY OR DEATH CALL NPS, (213) 652-1134.

"That was when we called you," Anders said. He watched her carefully. "We've leveled with you," he said. "Now it's your turn."

"His name is Harry Benson," she said. "He's thirty-four and he has a disinhibitory lesion."

The doctor snapped his fingers. "I'll be damned. ADL."

"What's a disinhibitory lesion?" Anders said. "And what's ADL?"

At that moment, a plainclothesman came in from the living room. "We got a trace on the prints," he said. "They're listed in the Defense data banks, of all places. This guy had classified clearance from 1968 to the present. His name's Harry Benson, lives in L.A."

"Clearance for what?" Anders said.

"Computer work, probably," Ross said.

"That's right," the plainclothesman said. "Last three years, classified computer research."

Anders was making notes. "They have a blood type on him?"

"Yeah. Type AO is what's listed."

Ross turned to the doctor. "What do you have on the girl?"

"Name's Doris Blankfurt, stage name Angela Black. Twenty-six years old, been in the building six weeks."

"What does she do?"

"Dancer."

Ross nodded.

Anders said, "Does that have some special meaning?"

"He has a thing about dancers."

"He's attracted to them?"

"Attracted and repelled," she said. "It's rather complicated."

He looked at her curiously. Did he think she was putting him on?

"And he has some kind of seizures?"

"Yes."

Anders made notes. "I'm going to need some explanations," he said.

"Of course."

"And a description, pictures—"

"I can get you all that."

"—as soon as possible."

She nodded. All her earlier impulses to resist the police, to refuse to cooperate with them, had vanished. She kept staring at the girl's caved-in head. She could imagine the suddenness, the viciousness of the attack.

She glanced at her watch. "It's seven-thirty now," she said. "I'm going back to the hospital, but I'm stopping at home to clean up and change. You can meet me there or at the hospital."

"I'll meet you there," Anders said. "I'll be finished here in about twenty minutes."

"Okay," she said, and gave him the address.

Chapter 8

The shower felt good, the hot water like stinging needles against her bare skin. She relaxed, breathed the steam, and closed her eyes. She had always liked showers, even though she knew it was the masculine pattern. Men took showers, women took baths. Dr. Ramos had mentioned that once. She thought it was bullshit. Patterns were made to be broken. She was an individual.

Then she'd discovered that showers were used to treat schizophrenics. They were sometimes calmed by alternating hot and cold spray.

"So now you think you're schizophrenic?" Dr. Ramos had said, and laughed heartily. He didn't often laugh. Sometimes she tried to make him laugh, usually without success.

She turned off the shower and climbed out, pulling a towel around her. She wiped the steam off the bathroom mirror and stared at her reflection. "You look like hell," she said, and nodded. Her reflection nodded back. The shower had washed away her eye make-up, the only make-up she wore. Her eyes seemed small now, and weak with fatigue. What time was her hour with Dr. Ramos today? Was it today?

What day was it, anyway? It took her a moment to remember that it was Friday. She hadn't slept for at least twenty-four hours, and she was having all the sleepless symptoms she'd remembered as an intern. An acid gnawing in her stomach. A dull ache in her body. A kind of slow confusion of the mind. It was a terrible way to feel.

She knew how it would progress. In another four or five hours, she would begin to daydream about sleeping. She would imagine a bed, and the softness of the mattress as she lay on it. She would begin to dwell on the wonderful sensations that would accompany falling asleep.

She hoped they found Benson before long. The mirror had steamed over again. She opened the bathroom door to let cool air in, and wiped a clean space with her hand again. She was starting to apply fresh make-up when she heard the doorbell.

That would be Anders. She had left the front door unlocked. "It's open," she shouted, and then returned to her make-up. She did one eye, then paused before the second. "If you want coffee, just boil water in the kitchen," she said.

She did her other eye, pulled the towel tighter around her, and leaned out toward the hallway. "Find everything you need?" she called.

Harry Benson was standing in the hallway. "Good morning, Dr. Ross," he said. His voice was pleasant. "I hope I haven't come at an inconvenient time."

It was odd how frightened she felt. He held out his hand and she shook it, hardly conscious of the action. She was preoccupied with her own fear. Why was she afraid? She knew this man well; she had been alone with him many times before, and had never been afraid.

The surprise was part of it, the shock of finding him here. And the unprofessional setting: she was acutely aware of the towel, her still-damp bare legs.

"Excuse me a minute," she said, "and I'll get some clothes on."

He nodded politely and went back to the living room. She closed the bedroom door and sat down on the bed. She was breathing hard, as if she had run a great distance. Anxiety, she thought, but the label didn't really help. She remembered a patient who had finally shouted at her in frustration, "Don't tell me I'm depressed. I feel *terrible!*"

She went to the closet and pulled on a dress, hardly noticing which one it was. Then she went back into the bathroom to check her appearance. Stalling, she thought. This is not the time to stall.

She took a deep breath and went outside to talk with him.

He was standing in the middle of the living room, looking uncomfortable and confused. She saw the room freshly, through his eyes: a modern, sterile, hostile apartment. Modern furniture, black leather and chrome, hard lines; modern paintings on the walls; modern, glistening, machine-like, efficient, a totally hostile environment.

"I never would have thought this of you," he said.

"We're not threatened by the same things, Harry." She kept her voice light. "Do you want some coffee?"

"No, thanks."

He was neatly dressed, in a jacket and tie, but his wig, the black wig, threw her off. Also his eyes: they were tired, distant—the eyes of a man near the breaking point of fatigue. She remembered how the rats had collapsed from excessive pleasurable stimulation. Eventually they lay spread-eagled on the floor of the cage, panting, too weak to crawl forward and press the shock lever one more time.

"Are you alone here?" he said.

"Yes, I am."

There was a small bruise on his left cheek, just below the eye. She looked at his bandages. They just barely showed, a bit of white between the bottom of his wig and the top of his collar.

"Is something wrong?" he asked.

"No, nothing."

"You seem tense." His voice sounded genuinely concerned. Probably he'd just had a stimulation. She remembered how he had become sexually interested in her after the test stimulations, just before he was interfaced.

"No . . . I'm not tense." She smiled.

"You have a very nice smile," he said.

She glanced at his clothes, looking for blood. The girl had been soaked; Benson must have been covered with blood, yet there was none on his clothes. Perhaps he'd dressed after taking a second shower. After killing her.

"Well," she said, "I'm going to have some coffee." She went into the kitchen with a kind of relief. It was somehow easier to breathe in the kitchen, away from him. She put the kettle on the burner, turned on the gas, and stayed there a moment. She had to get control of herself. She had to get control of the situation.

The odd thing was that while she had been shocked to see him suddenly in her apartment, she was not really surprised that he had come. Some ADL patients feared their own violence.

But why hadn't he returned to the hospital?

She went out to the living room. Benson was standing by the large windows, looking out over the city, which stretched away for miles in every direction.

"Are you angry with me?" he said.

"Angry? Why?"

"Because I ran away."

"Why did you run away, Harry?" As she spoke, she felt her strength coming back, her control. She could handle this man. It was her job. She'd been alone with men more dangerous than this. She remembered a six-month period at Cameron State Hospital, where she had worked with psychopaths and multiple murderers—charming, engaging, chilling men.

"Why? Because." He smiled, and sat down in a chair. He wriggled around in it, then stood up, sitting down again on the sofa. "All your furniture is so uncomfortable. How can you live in such an uncomfortable place?"

"I like it."

"But it's uncomfortable." He stared at her, a faint challenge in the look. She wished again that they were not meeting here. This environment was too threatening, and Benson reacted to threats with attack.

"How did you find me, Harry?"

"You're surprised I knew where you lived?"

"Yes, a little."

"I was careful," he said. "Before I went into the hospital, I found out where you lived, where Ellis lived, where McPherson lived. I found out where everybody lived."

"Why?"

"Just in case."

"What were you expecting?"

He didn't reply. Instead, he got up and walked to the windows, looked out over the city. "They're searching for me out there," he said. "Aren't they?"

"Yes."

"But they'll never find me. The city is too big."

From the kitchen, her kettle began to whistle. She excused herself and went in to make coffee. Her eyes scanned the counter, searching for something heavy. Perhaps she could hit him over the head. Ellis would never forgive her, but—

"You have a picture on your wall," Benson called. "A lot of numbers. Who did that?"

"A man named Johns."

"Why would a man draw numbers? Numbers are for machines."

She stirred the instant coffee, poured in milk, went back out and sat down.

"Harry . . ."

"No, I mean it. And look at this. What is this supposed to mean?" He tapped another picture with his knuckles.

"Harry, come and sit down."

He stared at her for a moment, then came over and sat on the couch opposite her. He seemed tense, but a moment later smiled in a relaxed way. For an instant, his pupils dilated. Another stimulation, she thought.

What the hell was she going to do?

"Harry," she said, "what happened?"

"I don't know," he said, still relaxed.

"You left the hospital . . ."

"Yes, I left the hospital wearing one of those white suits. I figured it all out. Angela picked me up."

"And then?"

"And then we went to my house. I was quite tense."

"Why were you tense?"

"Well, you see, I know how this is all going to end."

She wasn't sure what he was referring to. "How is it going to end?"

"And after we left my house, we went to her apartment, and we had some drinks, and we made love, and then I told her how it was going to end. That was when she got scared. She wanted to call the hospital, to tell them where I was. . . ." He stared off into space, momentarily confused. She didn't want to press the point. He had had a seizure and he would not remember killing the girl. His amnesia would be total and genuine.

But she wanted to keep him talking. "Why did you leave the hospital, Harry?"

"It was in the afternoon," he said, turning to look at her. "I was lying in bed in the afternoon, and I suddenly realized that everybody was taking care of me, *taking care*, servicing me, like a machine. I was afraid of that all along."

In some distant, detached, and academic corner of her mind, she felt that a suspicion was confirmed. Benson's paranoia about machines was, at bottom, a fear of dependency, of losing self-reliance. He was quite literally telling the truth when he said he was afraid of being taken care of. And people usually hated what they feared.

But then Benson was dependent on her. And how would he react to that?

"You people lied to me," he said suddenly.

"Nobody lied to you, Harry."

He began to get angry. "Yes, you did, you—" He broke off and smiled again. The pupils were briefly larger: another stimulation. They were very close now. He'd tip over again soon.

"You know something? That's the most wonderful feeling in the world," he said.

"What feeling?"

"That buzz."

"Is that how it feels?"

"As soon as things start to get black—buzz!—and I'm happy again," Benson said. "Beautifully warm and happy."

"The stimulations," she said.

She resisted the impulse to look at her watch. What did it matter? Anders had said he would be coming in twenty minutes, but anything could delay him. And even if he came, she wondered if he could handle Benson. An ADL patient out of control was an awesome thing. Anders would probably end up shooting Benson, or trying to. And she didn't want that.

"But you know what else?" Benson said. "The buzz is only nice occasionally. When it gets too heavy, it's . . . suffocating."

"Is it getting heavy now?"

"Yes," he said. And he smiled.

In that moment when he smiled, she was stunned into the full realization of her own helplessness. Everything she had been taught about controlling patients, everything about directing the flow of thought, about watching the speech patterns, was useless here. Verbal maneuvers would not work, would not help her—any more than they would help control a rabies victim, or a person with a brain tumor. Benson had a physical problem. He was in the grip of a machine that was inexorably, flawlessly pushing him toward a seizure. Talk couldn't turn off the implanted computer.

There was only one thing she could do, and that was get him to the hospital. How? She tried an appeal to his cognitive functions. "Do you understand what's happening, Harry? The stimulations are overloading you, pushing you into seizures."

"The feeling is nice."

"But you said yourself it's not always nice."

"No, not always."

"Well, don't you want to have that corrected?"

He paused a moment. "Corrected?"

"Fixed. Changed so that you don't have seizures any more." She had to choose her words carefully.

"You think I need to be fixed?" His words reminded her of Ellis: the surgeon's pet phrase.

"Harry, we can make you feel better."

"I feel fine, Dr. Ross."

"But, Harry, when you went to Angela's—"

"I don't remember anything about that."

"You went there after you left the hospital."

"I don't remember anything. Memory tapes are all erased. Nothing but static. You can put it on audio if you want, and listen to it yourself." He opened his mouth, and made a hissing sound. "See? Just static."

"You're not a machine, Harry," she said softly.

"Not yet."

Her stomach churned. She felt physically sick with tension. Again that detached part of her mind noted the interesting physical manifestation of an emotional state. She was grateful for the detachment, even for a few instants of it.

But she was also angry at the thought of Ellis and McPherson, and all those conferences when she had argued that implanting machinery into Benson would exaggerate his pre-existing delusional state. They hadn't paid any attention.

She wished they were here now.

"You're trying to make me into a machine," he said. "You all are. I'm fighting you."

"Harry—"

"Let me finish." His face was taut; abruptly, it loosened into a smile.

Another stimulation. They were coming only minutes apart now. Where was Anders? Where was anybody? Should she run out into the hall screaming? Should she try to call the hospital? The police?

"It feels so good," Benson said, still smiling. "That feeling, it feels so good. Nothing feels as good as that. I could just swim in that feeling forever and ever."

"Harry. I want you to try and relax."

"I'm relaxed. But that's not what you really want, is it?"

"What do I want?"

"You want me to be a good machine. You want me to obey my masters, to follow instructions. Isn't that what you want?"

"You're not a machine, Harry."

"And I never will be." His smile faded. "Never. Ever."

She took a deep breath. "Harry," she said, "I want you to come back to the hospital."

"No."

"We can make you feel better."

"No."

"We care about you, Harry."

"You care about me." He laughed, a nasty hard sound. "You don't care about *me*. You care about your experimental preparation. You care about your scientific protocol. You care about your follow-up. You don't care about *me*."

He was becoming excited and angry. "It won't look so good in the medical journals if you have to report so many patients observed for so many years, and one died because he went crazy and the cops killed him. That will reflect badly."

"Harry—"

"I *know*," Benson said. He held out his hands. "I was sick an hour ago. Then, when I woke up, I saw blood under my fingernails. Blood. I know." He stared at his hands, curling them to look at the nails. Then he touched his bandages. "The operation was supposed to work," he said. "But it isn't working."

And then, quite abruptly, he began to cry. His face was bland, but the tears rolled down his cheeks. "It isn't working," he said. "I don't understand, it isn't working. . . ."

Equally abruptly, he smiled. Another stimulation. This one had come less than a minute after the one previously. She knew that he'd tip over in the next few seconds.

"I don't want to hurt anyone," he said, smiling cheerfully.

She felt sympathy for him, and sadness for what had happened. "I understand," she said. "Let's go back to the hospital."

"No, no . . ."

"I'll go with you. I'll stay with you all the time. It will be all right."

"Don't argue with me!" He snapped to his feet, fists clenched, and glared down at her. "I will not listen—" He broke off, but did not smile.

Instead, he began to sniff the air.

"What is that smell?" he said. "I hate that smell. What is it? I hate it, do you hear me, I *hate* it!"

He moved toward her, sniffing. He reached his hands out toward her.

"Harry . . ."

"I hate this feeling," he said.

She got up off the couch, moving away. He followed her clumsily, his hands still outstretched. "I don't want this feeling, I don't want it," he said. He was no longer sniffing. He was fully in a trance state, coming toward her.

"Harry . . ."

His face was blank, an automaton mask. His arms were still extended toward her. He almost seemed to be sleep-walking as he advanced on her. His movements were slow and she was able to back away from him, maintaining distance.

Then, suddenly, he picked up a heavy glass ashtray and flung it at her. She dodged; it struck one of the large windows, shattering the glass.

He leaped for her and threw his arms around her, holding her in a clumsy bear hug. He squeezed her with incredible strength. "Harry," she gasped, "Harry." She looked up at his face and saw it was still blank.

She kneed him in the groin.

He grunted and released her, bending at the waist, coughing. She moved away from him and picked up the phone. She dialed the operator. Benson was still bent over, still coughing.

"Operator."

"Operator, give me the police."

"Do you want the Beverly Hills police, or the Los Angeles police?"

"I don't care!"

"Well, which do you—"

She dropped the phone. Benson was stalking her again. She heard the tiny voice of the operator saying, "Hello, hello . . ."

Benson tore the phone away and flung it behind him across the room. He picked up a floor lamp and held it base outward. He began to swing it in large hissing arcs. She ducked it once and felt the gush of air in the wake of the heavy metal base. If it hit her, it would kill her. It would kill her. The realization pushed her to action.

She ran to the kitchen. Benson dropped the lamp and followed her. She tore open drawers, looking for a knife. She found only a small paring knife. Where the hell were her big knives?

Benson was in the kitchen. She threw a pot at him blindly. It clattered against his knees. He moved forward.

The detached and academic part of her mind was still operating, telling her that she was making a big mistake, that there was something in the kitchen she could use. But what?

Benson's hands closed around her neck. The grip was terrifying. She grabbed his wrists and tried to pull them away. She kicked up with her leg, but he twisted his body away from her, then pressed her back against the counter, pinning her down.

She could not move, she could not breathe. She began to see blue spots dancing before her eyes. Her lungs burned for air.

Her fingers scratched along the counter, feeling for something, anything, to strike him with. She touched nothing.

The kitchen . . .

She flung her hands around wildly. She felt the handle of the dishwasher, the handle to the oven, the machines in her kitchen.

Her vision was greenish. The blue spots were larger. They swam sickeningly before her. She was going to die in the kitchen.

The kitchen, the kitchen, *dangers of the kitchen.* It came to her in a flash, just as she was losing consciousness.

Microwaves.

She no longer had any vision; the world was dull gray, but she could still feel. Her fingers touched the metal of the oven, the glass of the oven door, then up . . . up to the controls . . . she twisted the dial. . . .

Benson screamed.

The pressure around her neck was gone. She slumped to the floor. Benson was screaming, horrible agonized sounds. Her vision came back to her slowly and she saw him, standing over her, clutching his head in his hands. Screaming.

He paid no attention to her as she lay on the floor, gasping for breath. He twisted and writhed, holding his head and howling like a wounded animal. Then he rushed from the room, still screaming.

And she slid smoothly and easily into unconsciousness.

Chapter 9

The bruises were already forming—long, purplish welts on both sides of her neck. She touched them gently as she looked into the mirror.

"When did he leave?" Anders said. He stood in the doorway to the bathroom, watching her.

"I don't know. Around the time I passed out."

He looked back toward the living room. "Quite a mess out there."

"I imagine so."

"Why did he attack you?"

"He had a seizure."

"But you're his doctor—"

"That doesn't matter," she said. "When he has a seizure, he's out of control. Totally. He'd kill his own child during a seizure. People have been known to do that."

Anders frowned uncertainly. She could imagine the trouble he was having with the idea. Unless you had seen an ADL seizure, you could not comprehend the unreasonable, brutal violence of an attack. It was completely beyond any normal life experience. Nothing else was like it, analogous to it, similar to it.

"Umm," Anders said finally. "But he didn't kill you."

Not quite, she thought, still touching the bruises. The bruises would get much worse in the next few hours. What could she do about it? Make-up? She didn't have any. A high-necked sweater?

"No," she said, "he didn't kill me. But he would have."

"What happened?"

"I turned on the microwave."

Anders looked puzzled. "The microwave?"

"It affected Benson's electronic machinery. Microwave radiation screws up pacemaking machinery. It's a big problem for cardiac pacemakers now. Dangers of the kitchen. There have been a lot of recent articles."

"Oh," Anders said.

He left the room to make some calls, while she dressed. She chose a black turtleneck sweater and a gray skirt, and stepped back to look at herself in the mirror. The bruises were hidden. Then she noticed the colors, black and gray. That wasn't like her. Too somber, too dead and cold. She considered changing, but didn't.

She heard Anders talking on the phone in the living room. She went out to the kitchen to make herself a drink—no more coffee; she wanted Scotch on the rocks—and as she poured it, she saw the long scratches in the wooden counter that her fingernails had left. She looked at her fingernails. Three of them were broken; she hadn't noticed before.

She made the drink and went out to sit in the living room.

"Yes," Anders was saying into the phone. "Yes, I understand. No . . . no idea. Well, we're trying." There was a long pause.

She went to the broken window and looked out at the city. The sun was up, lighting a dark band of brown air that hung above the buildings. It was really a lethal place to live, she thought. She should move to the beach where the air was better.

"Well, listen," Anders said angrily, "none of this would have happened if you'd kept that fucking guard at his door in the hospital. I think you better keep that in mind."

She heard the phone slam down, and turned.

"Shit," he said. "Politics."

"Even in the police department?"

"Especially in the police department," he said. "Anything goes wrong, and suddenly there's a scramble to see who can get stuck with it."

"They're trying to stick you?"

"They're trying me on for size."

She nodded, and wondered what was happening back at the hospital. Probably the same thing. The hospital had to maintain its image in the community; the chiefs of service would be in a sweat; the director would be worrying about fund-raising. Somebody at the hospital would get stuck. McPherson was too big; she and Morris were too small. It would probably be Ellis—he was an assistant professor. If you fired an assistant professor it had connotations of firing a temporary appointment who had proven himself too aggressive, too reckless, too ambitious. Much better than firing a full professor, which was very messy and reflected badly on the earlier decision that had given him tenure.

It would probably be Ellis. She wondered if he knew. He had just recently bought a new house in Brentwood. He was very proud of it; he had invited everyone in the NPS to a housewarming party next week. She stared out the window, through the shattered glass.

Anders said, "Listen, what do seizures have to do with cardiac pacemakers?"

"Nothing," she said, "except that Benson has a brain pacemaker, very similar to a cardiac pacemaker."

Anders flipped open his notebook. "You better start from the beginning," he said, "and go slowly."

"All right." She set down her drink. "Let me make one call first."

Anders nodded, sat back, and waited while she called McPherson. Then, as calmly as she could, she explained everything she knew to the policeman.

Chapter 10

McPherson hung up the telephone and stared out his office window at the morning sun. It was no longer pale and cold; there was the full warmth of morning. "That was Ross," he said.

Morris nodded from the corner. "And?"

"Benson came to her apartment. She lost him."

Morris sighed.

"It doesn't seem to be our day," McPherson said. He shook his head, not taking his eyes off the sun. "I don't believe in luck," he said. He turned to Morris. "Do you?"

Morris was tired; he hadn't really been listening. "Do I what?"

"Believe in luck."

"Sure. All surgeons believe in luck."

"I don't believe in luck," McPherson repeated. "Never did. I always believed in planning." He gestured to the charts on his wall, then lapsed, staring at them.

The charts were large things, four feet across, and intricately done in many colors. They were really glorified flow charts with timetables for technical advances. He had always been proud of them. For instance, in 1967 he had examined the state of three areas—diagnostic conceptualization, surgical technology, and microelectronics—and concluded that they would all come together to allow an operation for ADL seizures in July of 1971. They had beaten his estimate by four months, but it was still damned accurate.

"Damned accurate," he said.

"What?" Morris said.

McPherson shook his head. "Are you tired?"

"Yes."

"I guess we're all tired. Where's Ellis?"

"Making coffee."

McPherson nodded. Coffee would be good. He rubbed his eyes, wondering when he would be able to sleep. Not for a while—not until they had Benson back. And that could take many hours more, perhaps another day.

He looked again at the charts. Everything had been going so well. Electrode implantation four months ahead of schedule. Computer simulation of behavior almost nine months ahead—but that, too, was having problems. George and Martha programs were behaving erratically. And Form Q?

He shook his head. Form Q might never get off the ground now, although it was his favorite project, and had always been. Form Q on the flow chart for 1979, with human application beginning in 1986. In 1986 he would be seventy-five years old—if he was still alive—but he didn't worry about that. It was the idea, the simple idea, that intrigued him.

Form Q was the logical outgrowth of all the work at the NPS. It began as a project called Form Quixoticus, because it seemed so impossible. But McPherson felt certain that it would happen because it was so necessary. For one thing, it was a question of size; for another, a question of expense.

A modern electronic computer—say, a third-generation IBM digital computer—would cost several million dollars. It drew an enormous amount of power. It consumed space voraciously. Yet the largest computer still had the same number of circuits as the brain of an ant. To make a computer with the capacity of a human brain would require a huge skyscraper. Its energy demands would be the equivalent of a city of half a million.

Obviously, nobody would ever try to build such a computer using current technology. New methods would have to be found—and there wasn't much doubt in McPherson's mind what the methods would be.

Living tissues.

The theory was simple enough. A computer, like a human brain, was composed of functioning units—little flip-flop cells of one kind or another. The size of those units had shrunk considerably over the years. They would continue to shrink as large-scale integration and other microelectronic techniques improved. Power requirements would also decrease.

But the individual units would never become as small as a nerve cell, a neuron. You could pack a billion nerve cells into one cubic inch. No human miniaturization method would ever achieve that economy of space. Nor would any human method ever produce a unit that operated on so little power as a nerve cell.

Therefore, make your computers from living nerve cells. It was already possible to grow isolated nerve cells in tissue culture. It was possible to alter them artificially in different ways. In the future, it would be possible to grow them to specification, to make them link up in specified ways.

Once you could do that, you could make a computer that was, say, six cubic feet in volume, but contained thousands of billions of nerve cells. Its energy requirements would not be excessive; its heat production and waste products would be manageable. Yet it would be the most intelligent entity on the planet, by far.

Form Q.

Preliminary work was already being done in a number of laboratories and government research units around the country. Advances were being made.

But for McPherson the most exciting prospect was not a superintelligent organic computer. That was just a side product. What was really interesting was the idea of an organic prosthesis for the human brain.

Because once you developed an organic computer—a computer composed of living cells, and deriving energy from oxygenated, nutrified blood—then you could transplant it into a human being. And you would have a man with two brains.

What would that be like? McPherson could hardly imagine it. There were endless problems, of course. Problems of interconnection, problems of location, speculative problems about competition between the old brain and the new transplant. But there was plenty of time to solve that before 1986. After all, in 1950 most people still laughed at the idea of going to the moon.

Form Q. It was only a vision now, but with funding it would happen. And he had been convinced that it would happen, until Benson left the hospital. That changed everything.

Ellis stuck his head in the office door. "Anybody want coffee?"

"Yes," McPherson said. He looked over at Morris.

"No," Morris said. He got up out of his chair. "I think I'll replay some of Benson's interview tapes."

"Good idea," McPherson said, though he did not really think so. He realized that Morris had to keep busy—had to do something, anything, just to remain active.

Morris left, Ellis left, and McPherson was alone with his multicolored charts, and his thoughts.

Chapter 11

It was noon when Ross finished with Anders, and she was tired. The Scotch had calmed her, but it had intensified her fatigue. Toward the end she had found herself stumbling over words, losing track of her thoughts, making statements and then amending them because they were not exactly what she had intended to say. She had never felt so tired, so drugged with fatigue, in her life.

Anders, on the other hand, was maddeningly alert. He said, "Where do you suppose Benson is now? Where would he be likely to go?"

She shook her head. "It's impossible to know. He's in a post-seizure state—post-ictal, we call it—and that's not predictable."

"You're his psychiatrist," Anders said. "You must know a lot about him. Isn't there any way to predict how he'll act?"

"No," she said. God, she was tired. Why couldn't he understand? "Benson is in an abnormal state. He's nearly psychotic, he's confused, he's receiving stimulations frequently, he's having seizures frequently. He could do anything."

"If he's confused . . ." Anders let his voice trail off. "What would he do if he was confused? How would he behave?"

"Look," she said, "it's no good working that way. He could do *anything.*"

"Okay," Anders said. He glanced at her, and sipped his coffee.

Why couldn't he just let it go, for Christ's sake? His desire to outwit Benson was ludicrously unrealistic. Besides, everybody knew how this was going to turn out. Somebody would spot Benson and shoot him, and that would be the end of it. Even Benson had said—

She paused, frowning. What had he said? Something about how it would all end. What were his exact words? She tried to remember, but couldn't. She had been too frightened to pay close attention.

"These are the impossible ones," Anders said, getting up and walking to the window. "In another city, you might have a chance, but not in Los Angeles. Not in five hundred square miles of city. It's bigger than New York, Chicago, San Francisco, and Philadelphia put together. Did you know that?"

"No," she said, hardly listening.

"Too many places to hide," he said. "Too many ways to escape—too many roads, too many airports, too many marinas. If he's smart, he's left already. Gone to Mexico or to Canada."

"He won't do that," she said.

"What will he do?"

"He'll come back to the hospital."

There was a pause. "I thought you couldn't predict his behavior," Anders said.

"It's just a feeling," she said, "that's all."

"We'd better go to the hospital," he said.

The NPS looked like the planning room for a war. All patient visits had been canceled until Monday; no one but staff and police were admitted to the fourth floor. But for some reason, all the Development people were there, and they were running around with horrified looks on their faces, obviously worried that their grants and their jobs were in jeopardy. Phones rang constantly; reporters were calling in; McPherson was locked in his office with hospital administrators; Ellis was swearing at anyone who came within ten yards of him; Morris was off somewhere and couldn't be found; Gerhard and Richards were trying to free some telephone lines so they could run a projection program using another computer, but all the lines were in use.

Physically, the NPS was a shambles—ashtrays heaped with cigarette butts, coffee cups crumpled on the floor, half-eaten hamburgers and tacos everywhere, jackets and uniforms thrown across the backs of chairs. And the telephones never stopped ringing: as soon as anyone hung up on a call, the phone rang again instantly.

Ross sat with Anders in her office and went over the Miscellaneous Crime Report, checking the description of Benson. The description was computerized, but it read out fairly accurately: *male Caucasian black hair*

Page 1 of 1

LOS ANGELES POLICE DEPARTMENT

MISCELLANEOUS CRIME REPORT

☐ Shots Fired ☐ Attempt

DR 7059014-A

PREMISES

14 Business: 01 BANK/SAV. LOAN; 09 HOSPITAL; 12 MEDICAL OFF; 15 PUBLIC DEPOT; 16 RESTAURANT; 11 LAUNDROMAT; 20 OTHER:

11 Vehicle: 01 SUSPECT'S; 02 VICTIM'S; 07 TAXI; 10 OTHER:

10 Store: 08 LIQUOR; 12 OTHER:

15 Miscellaneous: 01 ALLEY; 02 CARPORT; 06 GARAGE; 07 PARK; 08 PKG. LOT; 14 SCHOOL; 16 STREET; 12 PED. TUNNEL; 11 PED. OVER XING; 18 YARD; 19 OTHER:

(13) Residence: 01 SUSPECT'S; (02) VICTIM'S; 03 APT./PROJECT; 04 HOTEL; 05 MOTEL; 07 SINGLE FAMILY; 08 OTHER:

VICTIM'S NAME (Last, first, middle – Firm name, if business): BLACK, ANGELA —

PHONES: RES. [redacted] BUS.

LOCATION OF OCCURRENCE: [redacted]

R.D.: 04

TYPE OF CRIME: HOM

	MO.	DAY	YEAR	DAY WK.	TIME
OCCURRED: ON OR BTWN	3	12	71	F	6:00 AM
AND	3	12	71	F	6:20 AM
REPORTED:	3	12	71		6:52 AM

☐ VEH. SEEN: NO. SEX DESCENT

☐ SUSP. SEEN:

V'S SEX, DESCENT, AGE: F-CAUC-26

VICTIM'S CONDITION (Normal, Hospitalized, etc.): Dead

JUV. VICT'S BIRTHPLACE – CITY/STATE/& D O B:

INVESTIGATIVE DIVISION(S) & PERSON NOTIFIED: LAPD-HOM-ANDERS/STAFF

CONNECTED REPORT(S) – TYPE & DR. NO.: DEATH REPORT (711398) + AUXILIARY FINDINGS REPORT

CODE: V–Victim R–Person Reporting W–Witness

CODE	NAME		ADDRESS	CITY	PHONE	Day Phone–X
V	Name & Phones Listed Above	RES.			[redacted]	
		BUS.			[redacted]	
R	JOS. R. ALLPORT	RES.	[redacted]	LOS ANGELES	[redacted]	
		BUS.	SAME			
		RES.				
		BUS.				

VEHICLE

LIC. NO. | STATE | MAKE/MODEL | MFG. | YEAR | TYPE | TOP – COLORS – BOTTOM

(CIRCLE IF APPL.): 4 UPHOLSTERY; 2 BUCKET SEATS; 1 HEADLINER; 4 CUSTOM; 2 TORN; 1 COVER OTHER

Interior: 4 STEREO TAPE; 2 MIRROR ORNAM; 1 FLOOR SHIFT; 4 EQUIP. ADDED; 2 EQUIP. MISSING; 1 UNIQUE ITEM

Exterior: 4 PAINTED INSCRP.; 2 STICKER/DECAL; 1 RUST/PRIMER; 4 VINYL TOP; 2 DECORATIVE PAINT; 1 LEVEL ALTERED

Modified: 4 FRONT; 2 REAR; 1 OTHER

Body (CIRCLE IF APPL.): 4 DAMAGE; 2 SIDE; 1 LEFT; 4 RIGHT; 2 REAR; 1 FRONT

Wheels: 4 MAGS; 2 CHROME RIMS; 1 UNIQUE SIZE

Windows (CIRCLE IF APPL.): 4 DAMAGE; 2 SIDE; 1 LEFT; 4 RIGHT; 2 REAR; 1 FRONT; 4 TINTED; 2 COVERED; 1 DECAL/PLAQUE

FURTHER VEHICLE DESCRIPTION (INCLUDE INSIDE COLORS)

SUSPECT

	SEX	DESCENT	HAIR	EYES	HEIGHT	WEIGHT	AGE	CLOTHING	NAME & ADDRESS IF KNOWN NAME, BKG. NO. & CHARGE IF ARRESTED.
1	M	CAUC	BL	BR	5 8	1 40	34	—	7734 LAUREL CANYON
2									
3									

PERSONAL ODDITIES

SUSP. NO. 1 2 3

300 Amputee: 1 1 1 LEG; 2 2 2 ARM; 3 3 3 FOOT; 4 4 4 HAND; 5 5 5 EAR; 6 6 6 FINGERS

301 Deformed: 1 1 1 LEG; 2 2 2 ARM; 3 3 3 HAND; 4 4 4 LIMP; 5 5 5 FINGERS; 6 6 6 BOWLEGGED

302 Tattoo: 1 1 1 ARM; 2 2 2 HAND; 3 3 3 FINGERS; 4 4 4 CHEST/NECK

303: 1 1 1 PICTURES; 2 2 2 DESIGNS

303 Tattoo (cont.): 3 3 3 NAMES; 4 4 4 WORDS; 5 5 5 INITIALS; 6 6 6 PACHUCO

304 Facial Scars: 1 1 1 CHEEK; 2 2 2 CHIN; 3 3 3 FOREHEAD; 4 4 4 LIP; 5 5 5 NOSE; 6 6 6 EAR; 7 7 7 EYEBROW

305 Facial Oddity: 0 0 0 BIRTHMARKS; 1 1 1 POCKMARKS; 2 2 2 MOLES; 3 3 3 FRECKLES; 4 4 4 PIMPLES; 5 5 5 LIPS - THICK; 6 6 6 LIPS–THIN; 7 7 7 CHIN–PROTRUDED; 8 8 8 CHIN–RECEDES; 9 9 9 HOLLOW CHEEK

307 Teeth: 1 1 1 MISSING; 2 2 2 GOLD; 3 3 3 BROKEN; 4 4 4 FALSE; 5 5 5 STAIN/DECAY; 6 6 6 PROTRUDING; 7 7 7 IRREGULAR

308 Body Scars: 1 1 1 ARM; 2 2 2 HAND; 3 3 3 WRIST; 4 4 4 NECK; 5 5 5 BURN; 6 6 6 CHEST

(309) Speech: 0 0 0 IMPEDIMENT; 1 1 1 ACCENT (U.S.); 2 2 2 ACCENT (OTHER); 3 3 3 LISPS; 4 4 4 STUTTERS; 5 5 5 HARE LIP; (6) 6 6 MUMBLES; 7 7 7 RAPID; 8 8 8 SOFT/LOW; 9 9 9 REFINED

311 Eyes: 1 1 1 MISSING; 2 2 2 CROSSED; 3 3 3 SUNGLASSES; 4 4 4 GLASSES (PLAIN); 5 5 5 BULGING; 6 6 6 SQUINT/BLINK; 7 7 7 SLANTED

(312) Hair Type: 1 1 1 DYED; 2 2 2 PROCESSED; (3) 3 3 WIG/TOUPEE; 4 4 4 CREW CUT; 5 5 5 BALD; 6 6 6 AFRO; 7 7 7 LONG; 8 8 8 THIN/RECEDED; 9 9 9 STRAIGHT

313: 1 1 1 WAVY; 2 2 2 BUSHY; 3 3 3 CURLY

314 Facial Hair: 1 1 1 MUST - CHINESE; 2 2 2 GOATEE; 3 3 3 BEARD – FULL; 4 4 4 MUST – HEAVY; 5 5 5 MUST – THIN; 6 6 6 MUST – MEDIUM; 7 7 7 BROWS – HEAVY; 8 8 8 UNSHAVEN

315 Ears: 1 1 1 CAULIFLOWER; 2 2 2 PIERCED; 3 3 3 PROTRUDING; 4 4 4 CLOSE TO HEAD; 5 5 5 LARGE; 6 6 6 SMALL

316 Nose: 1 1 1 CROOKED; 2 2 2 HOOKED; 3 3 3 UPTURNED; 4 4 4 LONG; 5 5 5 BROAD; 6 6 6 FLAT; 7 7 7 SMALL; 8 8 8 THIN

(317) Face: 1 1 1 NEGRO W/CAUC. FEATURES; 2 2 2 HI CHEEK BONE; 3 3 3 LONG; 4 4 4 BROAD; 5 5 5 THIN; (6) 6 6 ROUND

(318) Complexion: 1 1 1 DARK; 2 2 2 SALLOW; 3 3 3 RUDDY; 4 4 4 LIGHT/FAIR; (5) 5 5 MEDIUM

(319) Others: (1) 1 1 Bandages/Neck; 1 1 1 ______; 1 1 1 ______

WEAPON

40: 10 GUN–CALIBER ______; (11) REVOLVER; 12 AUTOMATIC; 13 2 INCH; 14 4 INCH; 15 6 IN. OR MORE; 16 BLUE STEEL

40: 17 NICKEL PLATED; 18 UNUSUAL GRIPS; 21 RIFLE; 22 SHOTGUN; 23 SAWED OFF; 19 RUSTY/DEFECTIVE; 24 MACHINE GUN; 20 RARE TYPE GUN

40: 25 TOY GUN; 26 OTHER GUN; 30 KNIFE; 31 SWITCH BLADE; 32 BLADE OVER 6 INCH; 28 BODILY FORCE (ONLY); 42 CAUSTIC CHEM/POISON; 45 FIRECRACKERS

40: 41 LIQUOR/DRUGS; 47 FIXED OBJ. (WALL ETC.); 40 BLACKJACK/CLUB; 44 EXPLOSIVES; 48 RAZOR; 49 SCALDING LIQUID; 50 MISSILE, ROCK; 51 BELT, CORD, WIRE

40: 52 BOTTLE, BRKN. GLASS; 53 VEHICLE; 54 ASPHYXIATION, SUFFOCATION; 55 DROWNING; 56 NARCOTICS; 57 AXE, CLEAVER; 58 ICE PICK

(60): 59 SCISSORS, FORK; 61 GAS, CARBON MONOXIDE; 63 PAINT, TAR, CRAYON; 64 BB GUN, AIR RIFLE, PELLET GUN, SLINGSHOT; 62 FLOODING; 60 FIRE; (70) OTHER/UNKNOWN:

03.10.0 (1-71) MISCELLANEOUS CRIME REPORT CHECKED

MISCELLANEOUS CRIME REPORT

DR

Page 2 of 2

TRADEMARKS

(23) Abnormal Acts
- 58 URINATION
- 52 DEFECATION
- 55 PHOTOGRAPHED VICT.
- 56 SET FIRE
- 57 PUT OBJ. IN VAGINA
- 61 SADISM (PLEASURE FROM INFLICTING PAIN)
- 62 SODOMY
- 64 FETISHISM (EXCITED BY OBJ.– FOOT, HAIR, ETC.
- (60) OTHER UNUSUAL ACT — penetration

(23) Suspect's Actions
- 22 DAMAGED BUILDING
- 23 DAMAGED PUBLIC PROP.
- (18) COMMITTED SEX ACTS IN PRESENCE OF VICTIM
- 39 HARBORED A RUNAWAY
- 43 OTHER:

22 Pretended To Be
- 31 POLICE
- 40 OTHER:

22 Victim Was
- 61 POLICEMAN
- 57 FIREMAN
- 58 LAPD/FD

(21) Type
- 27 HOMOSEXUAL
- 38 RIOT
- 21 CULT RITUAL
- 34 ORGANIZED GANG
- 22 DISRUPTIVE PRESENCE–SCHOOL
- 13 CAUSED HOSTILE CROWD TO GATHER
- 42 TRAIN WRECK-TAMPER
- 31 MAIL-MAILBOX TAMPER
- 17 CHILD STEALING
- 14 CHILD BEATING
- 16 WIFE BEATING
- (44) OTHER: epileptic

25 Bombings
- 81 PRIOR WARNING
- 82 FAILED TO EXPLODE
- 83 EXPLODED
- 84 CAUSED FIRE

(24) Quarrel
- 59 REVENGE
- 60 TRAFFIC (T/A)
- 58 JUV. PARTY
- 51 BUSINESS
- 53 DRUNKEN
- 54 GAMBLING
- 55 JEALOUS
- 56 FAMILY
- 57 LANDLORD/NEIGHBOR
- 52 COMMON-LAW
- (61) OTHER: unknown

24 Suspect Wore
- 03 CLOTHES OF OPPOSITE SEX
- 10 MASK–FACE–COVER
- 04 UNUSUAL CLOTHES

24 Lingerie Involved
- 41 CUT OR TORN
- 44 OTHER:

24 Telephone
- 80 TORE FROM WALL
- 81 PULL/CUT/DISCONNECT WIRES
- 84 CONTACTED BY
- 90 OTHER:

24 Solicited/Offered
- 36 RIDE
- 25 ASSISTANCE
- 34 MONEY
- 28 NARCOTICS
- 39 OTHER:

22 Shots Fired
- 93 AT VICTIM
- 95 AT INHABITED DWELL.
- 96 AT MOVING VEH.
- 98 OTHER:

(22) Initial Contact
- 17 SUSPECT IN VEHICLE
- 23 VICTIM IN VEHICLE
- 15 SUSPECT A PED.
- 20 VICTIM A PED.
- 06 BAR
- 08 INVITATION
- 11 PLACE OF ENTERTAINMENT
- (13) RESIDENCE
- 16 SUSP. A RELATIVE
- (18) VICTIM KNOWS SUSP.

(23) Reason
- 84 SEX
- 83 ROBBERY
- 81 BURGLARY
- 82 RACIAL HOSTILITY
- 85 STRIKE/LABOR TROUBLE
- ~~(86) SUSPECT INSANE~~
- ~~87 UNKNOWN~~
- 88 OTHER:

25 Force
- 54 HANDCUFFED
- 40 COVERED VICT'S. FACE
- 46 TIED VICT. TO OBJECT (BED, ETC.)
- 47 BURNED VICTIM
- 53 GAGGED
- 42 BIT
- 45 BOUND
- 51 CUT/STABBED
- 41 BRUTAL ASSAULT
- 48 CHOKED
- 44 BOMB THREATS, SCARES, NO BOMB FOUND
- 70 OTHER:

22 Vehicle Involved
- 71 CAUSED DAMAGE TO VEHICLE
- 76 FORCED WAY INTO VICTIM'S VEHICLE
- 83 OTHER:

(1) IDENTIFY ADDITIONAL SUSPECTS ON A SECOND FACE SHEET. IDENTIFY ADDITIONAL WITNESSES. (2) RECONSTRUCT THE CRIME. (3) DESCRIBE PHYSICAL EVIDENCE-STATE LOCATION FOUND AND BY WHOM, GIVE DISPOSITION. (4) SUMMARIZE OTHER DETAILS RELATING TO CRIME. (5) INDICATE TIME AND LOCATION WHERE VICTIM AND WITNESSES CAN BE LOCATED BY DAY INVESTIGATORS IF NO AVAILABLE PHONE. (6) LIST STOLEN ITEMS—*EXCEPT IF CASH IS THE ONLY ITEM TAKEN*—ON A PROPERTY SUPPLEMENTAL REPORT, FORM 03.05.0.

(2) Victim invited suspect to apt. Apparently friendly relations occurred and sexual intercourse obtained. Following this victim and suspect took showers. Then victim was applying makeup when suspect struck her over head with lamp. This apparently caused death of victim. Suspect placed victim on bed and carried out multiple stabbings with unknown weapon, presumably blunt. The suspect fled the scene.
(3) Physical evidence – refer to crime lab photographs and notes of RV Hapgood
(4) No other details known
(5) Victim to morgue. No witnesses
(6) No stolen items

SUPERVISOR APPROVING	SERIAL NO.	INTERVIEWING OFFICERS	SERIAL NO.	DIVISION	DETAIL	PERSON REPORTING (SIGNATURE)
		RV Hapgood	1139-A	Hom	4	x John Anders
DATE & TIME REPRODUCED	DIVISION CLERK	TW Morton	1279-C	Hom	5	CLEARED BY MULTIPLE FOLLOW-UP DR NO.:
						CLEARED BY ARREST ☐ Yes ☑ No

Los Angeles Police Department
DEATH REPORT

NAME OF DECEASED (LAST, FIRST, MIDDLE): BLACK, ANGELA —
DR. 711398

DESCRIPTION of DECEASED	SEX	DESCENT	HAIR	EYES
	F	CAUC	BLOND	BL

HEIGHT	WEIGHT	AGE	BUILD	COMPLEXION
5'4"	110	26	MED	FAIR

LOCATION OF OCCURRENCE: [redacted]
RPT. DIST.: 04 — TYPE (Trf., Nat., Hom.): HOM
LOCATION OF ORIGINAL ILLNESS OR INJURY: SAME
RPT. DIST.: 09 — TYPE ORIG. RPT.: HOM

IDENTIFYING MARKS AND CHARACTERISTICS: ———
DATE/TIME ORIGINAL ILL./INJ.: 6:10 AM 4/12/71
OCCUPATION OF DECEASED: DANCER
DATE/TIME RPTD. TO P.D.: 4/12/71 6:52 AM

CLOTHING AND JEWELRY WORN: NUDE BODY
DATE/TIME DECEASED DISCOVERED: 7:04 AM 4/12/71
DATE/TIME DEATH OCCURRED: 6:10 AM 4/12/71
RELATIVES NOTIFIED BY: CDR

REMOVED TO (Address): MORGUE – LA COUNTY
REMOVED BY (name & unit): CDR

DECEASED'S RESIDENCE ADDRESS: AT LOCATION OF OCCURRENCE
PROBABLE CAUSE OF DEATH:
REASON (Quarrel—illness—revenge, etc.):

DECEASED'S BUSINESS ADDRESS: NONE KNOWN
INVESTIGATIVE DIVISION(S) OR UNIT(S) NOTIFIED AND PERSONS CONTACTED:

CODE: R—Person reporting death D—Person discovering deceased I—Person identifying deceased W—Witness

CODE	NEAREST RELATIVE UNKNOWN / RELATIONSHIP	NOTIFIED		ADDRESS	CITY	PHONE	X
D/I	Jos R. Allport Apt Mgr	☐ YES ☐ NO	RES.	[redacted]	Los Angeles	[redacted]	X
	NAME		BUS.	Same			
			RES.				
			BUS.				
			RES.				
			BUS.				

DOCTOR IN ATTENDANCE: CARLSON – CORONER'S OFF
BUSINESS ADDRESS / PHONE:

SOURCE OF CALL (HOW NOTIFIED AND BY WHOM): D/I → LAPD (HOM)

CORONER'S CASE NUMBER: 554/71/AB ASSIGNED BY: ARAMI

DISPOSITION OF PROPERTY: ☑ RELEASED TO CORONER RECEIPT ☒ YES ☐ NO RECEIPT NUMBER 2034598
☐ RELEASED TO RELATIVE NAME ______ ADDRESS ______

(1) RECONSTRUCT THE CIRCUMSTANCES SURROUNDING THE DEATH. (2) DESCRIBE PHYSICAL EVIDENCE, LOCATION FOUND AND GIVE DISPOSITION.

See Misc. Rpt DR. 7059011-A

IF ADDITIONAL SPACE REQUIRED, USE REVERSE SIDE

SUPERVISOR APPROVING	SERIAL NO.	INTERVIEWING OFFICER(S)—SER. NO.—DIVISION—DETAIL	PERSON REPORTING DEATH (SIGNATURE)
			X [signature]
DATE & TIME REPRODUCED—DIVISION—CLERK			BOOKED 461598 / CHECKED 20301

03.11.0 7-69 DEATH REPORT

brown eyes 5'8" 140# 34 years old. Personal oddities: *312/3 wig,* and *319/1 bandages on neck.* Thought to be armed with: *40/11 revolver.* Trademarks: *23/60 abnormal act (other)—perseveration.*

Reason for crime: *23/86 suspect insane.*

Ross sighed. "He doesn't really fit your computer categories."

"Nobody does," Anders said. "All we can hope is that it's accurate enough to allow somebody to identify him. We're also circulating his picture. Several hundred photos are being run off now, and distributed around the city. That'll help."

"What happens now?" Ross said.

"We wait," he said. "Unless you can think of a hiding place he'd use."

She shook her head.

"Then we wait," he said.

Chapter 12

It was a broad, low-ceilinged, white-tiled room, lit brightly by overhead fluorescent lights. Six stainless-steel tables were set out in a row, each emptying into a sink at one end of the room. Five of the tables were empty; the body of Angela Black lay on the sixth. Two police pathologists and Morris were bent over the body as the autopsy proceeded.

Morris had seen a lot of autopsies in his day, but the autopsies he attended as a surgeon were usually different. In this one, the pathologists spent nearly half an hour examining the exterior appearance of the body and taking photographs before they made the initial incision. They paid a lot of attention to the external appearance of the stab wounds, and what they called a "stretch laceration" appearance to the wounds.

One of the pathologists explained that this means the wounds were caused by a blunt object. It didn't cut the skin; it pulled it and caused a split in the taut portion. Then the instrument went in, but the initial split was always slightly ahead of the deeper penetration track. They also pointed out that skin hair had been forced down into the wounds in several places—further evidence of a blunt object producing the cuts.

"What kind of blunt object?" Morris had asked.

They shook their heads. "No way to know yet. We'll have to take a look at the penetration."

Penetration meant the depth that the weapon had entered the body. Determining penetration was difficult; skin was elastic and tended to snap back into shape; underlying tissues moved around before and after death. It was a slow business. Morris was tired. His eyes hurt. After a time, he left the autopsy room and went next door to the police lab, where the girl's purse contents were spread out on a large table.

Three men went through it: one identifying the objects, one recording them, and the third tagging them. Morris watched in silence. Most of the objects seemed commonplace: lipstick, compact, car keys, wallet, Kleenex, chewing gum, birth control pills, address book, ball-point pen, eye shadow, hair clip. And two packs of matches.

"Two packs of matches," one of the cops intoned. "Both marked Airport Marina Hotel."

Morris sighed. They were going through this so slowly, so patiently. It was no better than the autopsy. Did they really think they'd find anything this way? He found the plodding routine intolerable. Janet Ross called that the surgeon's disease, this urge to take decisive action, the inability to wait patiently. Once in an early NPS conference where they were considering a stage-three candidate—a woman named Worley—Morris had argued strongly for taking her as a surgical candidate, even though she had several other problems. Ross had laughed; "poor impulse control," she had said. In that moment, he could cheerfully have killed her, and his murderous feelings were not relieved when Ellis then said, in a clinical, quiet tone, that he agreed that Mrs. Worley was an inappropriate surgical candidate. Morris felt let down in the worst way, even though McPherson said that he thought the candidate had some worth, and probably should be listed as a "possible" and held for a while.

Poor impulse control, he thought. The hell with her.

"Airport Marina, huh?" one of the cops said. "Isn't that where all the stewardesses stay?"

"I dunno," the other cop said.

Morris hardly listened. He rubbed his eyes and decided to get more coffee. He'd been awake for thirty-six hours straight, and he wasn't going to last much longer.

He left the room and went upstairs looking for a coffee machine. There must be coffee someplace in the building. Even cops drank coffee; everybody drank coffee. And then he stopped, shivering.

He knew something about the Airport Marina.

The Airport Marina was where Benson had first been arrested, on suspicion of beating up a mechanic. There was a bar in the hotel; it had happened there. Morris was sure of it.

He glanced at his watch and then went out to the parking lot. If he hurried, he'd beat rush-hour traffic to the airport.

* * *

A jet screamed overhead and descended toward the runway as Morris took the airport off-ramp from the freeway and drove down Airport Boulevard. He passed bars and motels and car-rental offices. On the radio, he heard the announcer drone: "And on the San Diego Freeway, there is an accident involving a truck blocking three northbound lanes. Computer projection of flow is twelve miles an hour. On the San Bernadino Freeway, a stalled car in the left lane south of the Exeter off-ramp. Computer projection of traffic flow is thirty-one miles an hour . . ."

Morris thought of Benson again. Perhaps computers really were taking over. He remembered a funny little Englishman who had lectured at the hospital and told the surgeons that soon operations would be done with the surgeon on another continent—he would work using robot hands, the signals being transmitted via satellite. The idea had seemed crazy, but his surgical colleagues had squirmed at the thought.

"On the Ventura Freeway west of Haskell, a two-car collision has slowed traffic. Computer projection is eighteen miles an hour."

He found himself listening to the traffic report intently. Computers or not, the traffic report was vital to anyone who lived in Los Angeles. You learned to pay attention to any traffic report automatically, the way people in other parts of the country automatically paid attention to weather reports.

Morris had come to California from Michigan. For the first few weeks after his arrival, he had asked people what the weather was going to be like later in the day, or on the following day. It seemed to him a natural question for a newcomer to ask, and a natural ice breaker. But he got very strange, puzzled looks from people. Later he realized that he had come to one of the few places in the world where the weather was of no interest to anyone—it was always more or less the same, and rarely discussed.

But automobiles! Now there was a subject of almost compulsive fascination. People were always interested in what kind of car you drove, how you liked it, whether it was reliable, what troubles you had had with it. In the same vein, driving experiences, bad traffic, short-cuts you had found, accidents you had experienced, were always welcome conversation topics. In Los Angeles, anything relating to cars was a serious matter, worthy of as much time and attention as you could devote to it.

He remembered, as a kind of final proof of the idiocy of it all, that an astronomer had once said that if Martians looked at Los Angeles, they would probably conclude that the automobile was the dominant life form of the area. And, in a sense, they would be right.

He parked in the lot of the Airport Marina Hotel and entered the lobby. The building was as incongruous as its name, with that California quality of bizarre mixtures—in this case, a sort of plastic-and-neon Japanese inn.

He went directly to the bar, which was dark and nearly deserted at 5 P.M. There were two stewardesses in a far corner, talking over drinks; one or two businessmen seated at the bar; and the bartender himself, staring off vacantly into space.

Morris sat at the bar. When the bartender came over, he pushed Benson's picture across the counter. "You ever seen this man?"

"What'll it be?" the bartender said.

Morris tapped the picture.

"This is a bar. We serve liquor."

Morris was beginning to feel strange. It was the kind of feeling he sometimes had when he began an operation and felt like a surgeon in a movie. Something very theatrical. Now he was a private eye.

"His name is Benson," Morris said. "I'm his doctor. He's very ill."

"What's he got?"

Morris sighed. "Have you seen him before?"

"Sure, lots of times. Harry, right?"

"That's right. Harry Benson. When was the last time you saw him?"

"An hour ago." The man shrugged. "What's he got?"

"A serious brain disease. It's important to find him. Do you know where he went?"

"Brain disease? No shit." The bartender picked up the picture and examined it closely in the light of a glowing Schlitz sign behind the bar. "That's him, all right. But he dyed his hair black."

"Do you know where he went?"

"He didn't look sick to me. Are you sure you're—"

"Do you know where he went?"

There was a long silence. The bartender looked grim. "You're no fucking doctor," the bartender said. "Now beat it."

"I need your help," Morris said. "Time is very important." As he spoke, he opened his wallet, took out his identification cards, credit cards, everything with an M.D. on it. He spread them across the counter.

The bartender didn't even glance at them.

"He is also wanted by the police," Morris said.

"I knew it," the bartender said. "I knew it."

"And I can get some policeman down here to help question you. You may be an accessory to murder." Morris thought that sounded good. At least it sounded dramatic.

The bartender picked up one of the cards, peered at it, dropped it. "I don't know nothing," he said. "He comes in sometimes, that's all."

"Where did he go today?"

"I don't know. He left with Joe."

"Who's Joe?"

"Mechanic. Works the late shift at United."

"United Air Lines?"

"That's right," the bartender said. "Listen, what about this—"

But Morris was already gone.

In the hotel lobby, he called the NPS and got through the switchboard to Captain Anders.

"Anders here."

"Listen, this is Morris. I'm at the airport. I have a lead on Benson. About an hour ago, he was seen in the bar of the Airport Marina Hotel. He left with a mechanic named Joe who works for United. Works the evening shift."

There was a moment of silence. Morris heard the scribbling sound of a pencil. "Got it," Anders said. "Anything else?"

"No."

"We'll get some cars out right away. You think he went to the United hangars?"

"Probably."

"We'll get some cars out right away.

"What about—"

Morris stopped, and stared at the receiver. It was dead in his hand. He took a deep breath and tried to decide what to do next. From now on, it was police business. Benson was dangerous. He should let the police handle it.

On the other hand, how long would it take them to get here? Where was the nearest police station? Inglewood? Culver City? In rush hour traffic, even with their sirens it might take twenty minutes. It might take half an hour.

That was too much time. Benson might leave in half an hour. Meanwhile, he ought to keep track of him. Just locate Benson, and keep track of him.

Not interfere. But not let him get away, either.

The large sign said UNITED AIR LINES—MAINTENANCE PERSONNEL ONLY. There was a guardhouse beneath the sign. Morris pulled up, leaned out of his car.

"I'm Dr. Morris. I'm looking for Joe."

Morris was prepared for a lengthy explanation. But the guard didn't seem to care. "Joe came on about ten minutes ago. Signed in to hangar seven."

Ahead of him, Morris saw three very large airplane hangars, with parking lots behind. "Which one is seven?"

"Far left," the guard said. "Don't know why he went there, except maybe the guest."

"What guest?"

"He signed in a guest. . . ." The guard consulted his clipboard. "A Mr. Benson. Took him to seven."

"What's in seven?"

"A DC-10 that's in for major overhaul. Nothing doing there—they're waiting for a new engine. It'll be another week in there. Guess he wanted to show it to him."

"Thanks," Morris said. He drove past the gates, onto the parking lot, and parked close to hangar seven. He got out of the car, then paused. The fact was, he really didn't know whether Benson was in the hangar or not. He ought to check that. Otherwise, when the police arrived he might appear a fool. He might sit here in this parking lot while Benson escaped.

He thought he'd better check. He was not afraid. He was young and in good physical condition. He was also fully aware that Benson was dangerous. That foreknowledge would protect him. Benson was most dangerous to those who didn't recognize the lethal nature of his illness.

He decided to take a quick look inside the hangar to make sure Benson was inside. The hangar was an enormous structure but didn't seem to have any doors, except for the giant doors to admit the airplane. They were now closed. How did you get in?

He scanned the exterior of the building, which was mostly corrugated steel. Then he saw a normal-sized door to the far left. He got back in his car and drove up to it, parked, and entered the hangar.

It was pitch black inside. And totally silent. He stood by the door for a moment, then heard a low groan. He ran his hands along the walls, feeling for a light switch. He touched a steel box, felt it carefully. There were several large heavy-duty switches.

He threw them.

One by one, the overhead lights came on, very bright and very high. He saw in the center of the hangar a giant plane, glinting with reflections from the overhead bulbs. It was odd how much more enormous it seemed inside a building. He walked toward it, away from the door.

He heard another groan.

At first he could not determine where it was coming from. There was no one in sight; the floor was bare. But there was a ladder near the far wing. He walked beneath the high sleek tail assembly toward the ladder. The hangar smelled of gasoline and grease, sharp smells. It was warm.

Another groan.

He walked faster, his footsteps echoing in the cavernous hangar space. The groan seemed to be coming from somewhere inside the airplane. How did you get inside? It was an odd thought: he'd made dozens of airplane trips. You always got on by a ramp near the cockpit. But here, in the hangar . . . the plane was so damned enormous, how could you possibly get inside?

He passed the two jet engines of the near wing. They were giant cylinders, black turbine blades inside. Funny the engines had never seemed so big before. Probably never noticed.

There was still another groan.

He reached the ladder and climbed up. Six feet in the air, he came to the wing, a gleaming expanse of flat silver, nubbled with rivets. A sign said STEP HERE. There were drops of blood by the sign. He looked across the wing and saw a man covered with blood lying on his back. Morris moved closer and saw that the man's face was horribly mangled, and his arm was twisted back at a grotesquely unnatural angle.

He heard a noise behind him. He spun.

And then, suddenly, all the lights in the hangar went out.

Morris froze. He had a sense of total disorientation, of being suspended in air in vast and limitless blackness. He did not move. He held his breath. He waited.

The injured man groaned again. There was no other sound. Morris knelt down, not really knowing why. Somehow he felt safer being close to the metal surface of the wing. He was not conscious of being afraid, just badly confused.

Then he heard a soft laugh. And he began to be afraid.

"Benson?"

There was no reply.

"Benson, are you there?"

No reply. But footsteps, moving across the concrete floor. Steady, quietly echoing footsteps.

"Harry, it's Dr. Morris."

Morris blinked his eyes, trying to adjust to the darkness. It was no good. He couldn't see anything. He couldn't see the edges of the wing; he couldn't see the outline of the fuselage. He couldn't see a fucking thing.

The footsteps came closer.

"Harry, I want to help you." His voice cracked as he spoke. That certainly conveyed his fear to Benson. He decided to shut up. His heart was pounding, and he was breathing hard, gasping for breath.

"Harry . . ."

No reply. But the footsteps stopped. Perhaps Benson was giving up. Perhaps he had had a stimulation. Perhaps he was changing his mind.

A new sound: a metallic creak. Quite close.

Another creak.

He was climbing the ladder.

Morris was drenched with cold sweat. He still could see nothing, nothing at all. He was so disoriented he no longer remembered where he was on the wing. Was the ladder in front of him or behind?

Another creak.

He tried to fix the sound. It was coming somewhere in front of him. That meant he was facing the tail, the rear of the wing. Facing the ladder.

Another creak.

How many steps were there? Roughly six feet, six steps. Benson would be standing on the wing soon. What could he use for a weapon? Morris patted his pockets. His clothes were soaked and clinging with sweat. He had a momentary thought that this was all ridiculous, that Benson was the patient and he was the doctor. Benson would listen to reason. Benson would do as he was told.

Another creak.

A shoe! Quickly, he slipped off his shoe, and cursed the fact that it had a rubber sole. But it was better than nothing. He gripped the shoe tightly, held it above his head, ready to swing. He had a mental image of the beaten mechanic, the disfigured, bloody face. And he suddenly realized that he was going to have to hit Benson very hard, with all the strength he had.

He was going to have to try to kill Benson.

There were no more creaking sounds, but he could hear breathing. And then, distant at first but growing rapidly louder, he heard sirens. The police were coming. Benson would hear them, too, and would give up.

Another creak.

Benson was going back down the ladder. Morris breathed a sigh of relief.

Then he heard a peculiar scratching sound and felt the wing beneath his feet shake. Benson had not climbed down. He had continued to climb up, and was now standing on the wing.

"Dr. Morris?"

Morris almost answered, but didn't. He knew then that Benson couldn't really see, either. Benson needed a voice fix. Morris said nothing.

"Dr. Morris? I want you to help me."

The sirens were louder each moment. Morris had a momentary elation at the thought that Benson was going to be caught. This whole nightmare would soon be over.

"Please help me, Dr. Morris."

Perhaps he was sincere, Morris thought. Perhaps he really meant it. If that were so, then as his doctor he had a duty to help him.

"Please?"

Morris stood. "I'm over here, Harry," he said. "Now, just take it easy and—"

Something hissed in the air. He felt it coming before it hit. Then he felt agonizing pain in his mouth and jaw, and he was knocked backward, rolling across the wing. The pain was awful, worse than anything he had ever felt.

And then he fell into blackness. It was not far to fall from the wing to the ground. But it seemed to be taking a long time. It seemed to take forever.

Chapter 13

Janet Ross stood outside the treatment room in the emergency ward, watching through the small glass window. There were six people in there taking care of Morris, all clustered around him. She couldn't see much. All she could really see were his feet. He had one shoe on; the other was off. There was a lot of blood; most of the EW people were spattered with it.

Standing outside with her, Anders said, "I don't have to tell you what I think of this."

"No," she said.

"The man is extremely dangerous. Morris should have waited for the police."

"But the police didn't catch him," she said, suddenly angry. Anders didn't understand anything. He didn't understand how you could feel responsible for a patient, how you could want to take care of somebody.

"Morris didn't catch him, either," Anders said.

"And why didn't the police get him?"

"Benson was gone when they got to the hangar. There are several exits from the hangar, and they couldn't all be covered. They found Morris under the wing and the mechanic on top of the wing, and they were both pretty badly hurt."

The treatment-room door opened. Ellis came out, looking haggard, unshaven, defeated.

"How is he?" Ross said.

"He's okay," Ellis said. "He won't have much to say for a few weeks, but he's okay. They're taking him to surgery now, to wire up his jaw and get all the teeth out." He turned to Anders. "Did they find the weapon?"

Anders nodded. "Two-foot section of lead pipe."

"He must have got it right in the mouth," Ellis said. "But at least he didn't inhale any of the loose teeth. The bronchi are clean on lung films." He put his arm around Janet. "They'll fix him up."

"What about the other one?"

"The mechanic?" Ellis shook his head. "I wouldn't place bets. His nose was shattered and the nasal bones were driven up into the substance of the brain. He's leaking CSF through the nostrils. Lot of bleeding and a big problem with encephalitis."

Anders said, "How do you assess his chances?"

"He's on the critical list."

"All right," Anders said. He walked off.

Ross walked with Ellis out of the emergency ward toward the cafeteria. Ellis kept his arm around her shoulders. "This has turned into a horrible mess," he said.

"Will he really be all right?"

"Sure."

"He was kind of good-looking. . . ."

"They'll get his jaw back together. He'll be fine."

She shuddered.

"Cold?"

"Cold," she said, "and tired. Very tired."

She had coffee with Ellis in the cafeteria. It was 6:30, and there were a lot of staff people eating. Ellis ate slowly, his movements showing fatigue. "It's funny," he said.

"What?"

"I had a call this afternoon from Minnesota. They have a professorship in neurosurgery to fill. Asked me if I was interested."

She didn't say anything.

"Isn't that funny?"

"No," she said.

"I told them I wasn't considering anything until I was fired here," he said.

"Are you sure that'll happen?"

"Aren't you?" he said. He stared across the cafeteria at all the nurses and interns and residents in white. "I wouldn't like Minnesota," he said. "It's too cold."

"But it's a good school."

"Oh, yes. A good school." He sighed. "A fine school."

She felt sorry for him, and then suppressed the emotion. He had brought it on himself, and against her advice. For the last twenty-four hours, she had not allowed herself to say "I told you so" to anyone; she had not allowed herself to think it. For one thing, it wasn't necessary to say it. For another, it would not be useful in helping Benson, which was her chief concern.

But she didn't have much sympathy now for the brave surgeon. Brave surgeons risked other people's lives, not their own. The most a surgeon could lose was his reputation.

"Well," he said, "I better get back to the NPS. See how things are going. You know what?"

"What?"

"I hope they kill him," Ellis said. And he walked away toward the elevators.

The operation began at 7 P.M. She watched from the overhead glass viewing booth as Morris was wheeled into the OR, and the surgeons draped him. Bendixon and Curtiss were doing the procedure; they were both good plastic surgeons; they would fix him up as well as anybody possibly could.

But it was still a shock to watch as the sterile gauze packs were taken away from Morris's face and the flesh exposed. The upper part of his face was normal, though pale. The lower part was a red mash, like butcher's meat. It was impossible to find the mouth in all the redness.

Ellis had seen that in the emergency ward. It was shocking to her now, even at a distance. She could imagine the effect much closer.

She stayed to watch as the drapes were placed over the body, and around the head. The surgeons were gowned and gloved; the instrument tables set in position; the scrub nurses stood ready. The whole ritual of preparing for surgery was carried out smoothly and efficiently. It was a wonderful ritual, she thought, so rigid and so perfect that nobody would ever know—and the surgeons themselves probably didn't consider—that they were operating on a colleague. The ritual, the fixed procedure, was anaesthetic for the surgeon just as gas was anaesthetic for the patient.

She stayed a few moments longer, and then left the room.

Chapter 14

As she approached the NPS, she saw that a cluster of reporters had cornered Ellis outside the building. He was answering their questions in clear bad humor; she heard the words "mind control" repeated several times.

Feeling slightly guilty, she cut around to the far entrance and took the elevator to the fourth floor. Mind control, she thought. The Sunday supplements were going to have a field day with mind control. And then there would be solemn editorials in the daily papers, and even more solemn editorials in the medical journals, about the hazards of uncontrolled and irresponsible research. She could see it coming.

Mind control. Christ.

The truth was that everybody's mind was controlled, and everybody was glad for it. The most powerful mind controllers in the world were parents, and they did the most damage. Theorists usually forgot that nobody was born prejudiced, neurotic, or hung-up; those traits required a helping hand. Of course, parents didn't intentionally damage their children. They merely inculcated attitudes that they felt would be important and useful to their offspring.

Newborn children were little computers waiting to be programmed.

And they would learn whatever they were taught, from bad grammar to bad attitudes. Like computers, they were undiscriminating; they had no way to differentiate between good ideas and bad ones. The analogy was quite exact: many people had remarked on the childishness and the literalness of computers. For example, if you could instruct a computer to "Put on your shoes and socks," the computer would certainly reply that socks could not be fitted over shoes.

All the important programming was finished by the age of seven. Racial attitudes, sexual attitudes, ethical attitudes, religious attitudes, national attitudes. The gyroscope was set, and the children let loose to spin off on their predetermined courses.

Mind control.

What about something as simple as social conventions? What about shaking hands when you meet someone? Facing forward in elevators? Passing on the left? Having your wineglass on the right? Hundreds of little conventions that people needed in order to stereotype social interaction—take away any of them, and you produce unbearable anxiety.

People needed mind control. They were glad to have it. They were hopelessly lost without it.

But let a group of people try to solve the greatest problem in the world today—uncontrolled violence—and suddenly there are shouts from all sides: mind control, mind control!

Which was better, control or uncontrol?

She got off at the fourth floor, brushed past several policemen in the hallway, and went into her office. Anders was there, hanging up the telephone. And frowning.

"We just got our first break," he said.

"Oh?" Her irritation dissipated in a wave of expectancy.

"Yes," Anders said, "but I'll be damned if I know what it means."

"What happened?"

"Benson's description and his pictures are being circulated downtown, and somebody recognized him."

"Who?"

"A clerk in Building and Planning, in City Hall. He said Benson came in ten days ago. Building and Planning files specifications on all public structures erected within city limits, and they administer certain building codes."

Ross nodded.

"Well, Benson came in to check specs on a building. He wanted to review electrical blueprints. Said he was an electrical engineer, produced some identification."

Ross said, "The girls at his house said he'd come back for some blueprints."

"Well, apparently he got them from Building and Planning."

"What are they for?"

"University Hospital," Anders said. "He has the complete wiring system for the entire hospital. Now what do you make of that?"

By eight o'clock, she was almost asleep standing up. Her neck was hurting badly, and she had a headache. She realized that she didn't have a choice any more—either she got some sleep, or she'd pass out. "I'll be on the floor if you need me," she told Anders, and left. She walked down the corridor of the NPS, past several uniformed cops. She no longer noticed them; it seemed as if there had always been cops in the hallways for as long as she could remember.

She looked into McPherson's office. He was sitting behind his desk, head on his shoulder, sleeping. His breath came in short, ragged gasps. It sounded as if he were having nightmares. She closed the door quietly.

An orderly walked past her, carrying filled ashtrays and empty coffee cups. It was strange to see an orderly doing cleaning duties. The sight triggered a thought in her mind—something unusual, some question she couldn't quite formulate.

It nagged at her mind, but she finally gave up on it. She was tired; she couldn't think clearly. She came to one of the treatment rooms and saw that it was empty. She went in, closed the door, and lay down on the examination couch.

She was almost instantly asleep.

Chapter 15

In the lounge, Ellis watched himself on the 11-o'clock news. It was partly vanity and partly morbid curiosity that made him do it. Gerhard was also there, and Richards, and the cop Anders.

On the screen, Ellis squinted slightly into the camera as he answered the questions of a group of reporters. Microphones were jammed up toward his face, but he seemed to himself calm. That pleased him. And he found his answers reasonable.

The reporters asked him about the operation, and he explained it briefly but clearly. Then one asked, "Why was this operation done?"

"The patient," Ellis answered, "suffers from intermittent attacks of violent behavior. He has organic brain disease—his brain is damaged. We are trying to fix that. We are trying to prevent violence."

No one could argue with that, he thought. Even McPherson would be pleased with it as a polite answer.

"Is that common, brain damage associated with violence?"

"We don't know how common it is," Ellis said. "We don't even know how common brain damage alone is. But our best estimates are that ten million Americans have obvious brain damage, and five million more have subtle brain damage."

"Fifteen million?" one reporter said. "That's one person in thirteen."

Pretty quick, Ellis thought. He'd figured it out later as one in fourteen.

"Something like that," he replied on the screen. "There are two and a half million people with cerebral palsy. There are two million with convulsive disorders, including ADL. There are six million with mental retardation. There are probably two and a half million with hyperkinetic behavior disorders."

"And all of these people are violent?"

"No, certainly not. Most are perfectly peaceable. But if you check violent people, you will find an unusually high proportion have brain damage. *Physical* brain damage. And we believe physical brain damage is very often the cause of violence. That contradicts a lot of theories about poverty and discrimination and social injustice. Of course those social factors may contribute to violence. But physical brain damage is also a major factor. And you can't correct physical brain damage with social remedies."

There was a pause in the reporters' questions. Ellis remembered the pause, and remembered being elated by it. He was winning; he was running the show.

"When you say violence—"

"I mean," Ellis said, "attacks of unprovoked violence initiated by single individuals. It's the biggest problem in the world today, violence. And it's a huge problem in this country. In 1969, more Americans were killed or attacked in this country than have been killed or wounded in all the years of the Vietnam war. Specifically—"

The reporters were writing fast.

"—we had 14,500 murders, 36,500 rapes, and 306,500 cases of aggravated assault. All together a third of a million cases of violence. That doesn't include automobile deaths, and a lot of violence is carried out with cars. We had 56,000 deaths in autos, and three million injuries."

"You always were good with figures," Gerhard said, watching.

"It's working, isn't it?" Ellis said.

"Yeah. But you have a squinty, untrustworthy look."

"That's my normal look."

Gerhard laughed.

On the screen, a reporter was saying, "And you think these figures reflect physical brain disease?"

"In large part," Ellis said. "Yes. One of the clues pointing to physical brain disease in a single individual is a history of repeated violence. There are some famous examples. Charles Whitman, who killed seventeen people in Texas, had a malignant brain tumor and told his psychiatrist for weeks before that he was having thoughts about climbing the tower and shooting people. Richard Speck engaged in several episodes of brutal violence before he killed eight nurses. Lee Harvey Oswald repeatedly attacked people, including his wife on many occasions. Those were famous cases. There are a third of a million cases every year that are not famous. We're trying to correct that violent behavior with surgery. I don't think that's a despicable thing. I think it's a noble goal and an important goal."

"But isn't that mind control?"

Ellis said, "What do you call compulsory education through high school?"

"Education," the reporter said.

And that ended the interview. Ellis got up angrily. "That makes me look like a fool," he said.

"No, it doesn't," Anders, the cop, said.

SATURDAY, MARCH 13, 1971: TERMINATION

Chapter 1

She was being pounded, beaten senseless by brutal, jarring blows. She rolled away and moaned.

"Come on," Gerhard said, shaking her. "Wake up, Jan."

She opened her eyes. The room was dark. Someone was leaning over her.

"Come on, come on, wake up."

She yawned. The movement sent streaks of pain down through her neck. "What is it?"

"Telephone for you. It's Benson."

That jolted her awake faster than she would have thought possible. Gerhard helped her sit up, and she shook her head to clear it. Her neck was a column of pain, and the rest of her body was stiff and aching, but she ignored that.

"Where?"

"Telecomp."

She went outside into the hallway, blinking in the bright light. The cops were still there, but they were tired now, eyes dulled, jaws slack. She followed Gerhard into Telecomp.

Richards held out the phone to her, saying, "Here she is."

She took the receiver. "Hello? Harry?"

Across the room, Anders was listening on an extension.

"I don't feel good," Harry Benson said. "I want it to stop, Dr. Ross."

"What's the matter, Harry?" She could hear the fatigue in his voice, the slow and slightly childlike quality. What would one of those rats say after twenty-four hours of stimulation?

"Things aren't working very well. I'm tired."

"We can help you," she said.

"It's the feelings," Benson said. "They're making me tired now. That's all. Just tired. I want them to stop."

"You'll have to let us help you, Harry."

"I don't believe you will."

"You have to trust us, Harry."

There was a long pause. Anders looked across the room at Ross. She shrugged. "Harry?" she said.

"I wish you never did this to me," Benson said. Anders checked his watch.

"Did what?"

"The operation."

"We can fix it for you, Harry."

"I wanted to fix it myself," he said. His voice was very childlike, almost petulant. "I wanted to pull out the wires."

Ross frowned. "Did you try?"

"No. I tried to pull off the bandages, but it hurt too much. I don't like it when it hurts."

He was really being quite childlike. She wondered if the regression was a specific phenomenon, or the result of fear and fatigue.

"I'm glad you didn't pull—"

"But I have to do *something*," Benson said. "I have to stop this feeling. I'm going to fix the computer."

"Harry, you can't do that. We have to do that for you."

"No. I'm going to fix it."

"Harry," she said, in a low, soothing, maternal voice. "Harry, please trust us."

There was no reply. Breathing on the other end of the line. She looked around the room at the tense, expectant faces.

"Harry, please trust us. Just this once. Then everything will be all right."

"The police are looking for me."

"There are no police here." she said. "They've all gone. You can come here. Everything will be all right."

"You lied to me before," he said. His voice was petulant again.

"No, Harry, it was all a mistake. If you come here now, everything will be all right."

There was a very long silence, and then a sigh. "I'm sorry," Benson said.

"I know how it's going to end. I have to fix the computer myself."

"Harry—"

There was a click, and then the buzz of a disconnection. Ross hung up. Anders immediately dialed the phone company and asked whether they had been able to trace the call. So that was why he had been looking at his watch, she thought.

"Hell," Anders said, and slammed the phone down. "They couldn't get a trace. They couldn't even find the incoming call. Idiots." He sat down across the room from Ross.

"He was just like a child," she said, shaking her head.

"What did he mean about fixing the computer?"

"I suppose he meant tearing out the wires from his shoulder."

"But he said he tried that."

"Maybe he did, maybe he didn't," she said. "He's confused now, under the influence of all the stimulations and all the seizures."

"Is it physically possible to pull out the wires, and the computer?"

"Yes," she said. "At least, animals do it. Monkeys . . ." She rubbed her eyes. "Is there any coffee?"

Gerhard poured her a cup.

"Poor Harry," she said. "He must be terrified out there."

Across the room, Anders said, "How confused do you suppose he is, really?"

"Very." She sipped the coffee. "Is there any sugar left?"

"Confused enough to mix up computers?"

"We're out of sugar," Gerhard said. "Ran out a couple of hours ago."

"I don't understand," she said.

"He had wiring plans for the hospital," Anders said. "The main computer, the computer that assisted in his operation, is in the hospital basement."

She set down her coffee cup and stared at him. She frowned, rubbed her eyes again, picked the coffee up, then set it down once more. "I don't know," she said finally.

"The pathologists called while you were asleep," Anders said. "They determined that Benson stabbed the dancer with a screwdriver. He attacked the mechanic, and he attacked Morris. Machines and people connected with machines. Morris was connected with his own mechanization."

She smiled slightly. "*I'm* the psychiatrist around here."

"I'm just asking. Is it possible?"

"Sure, of course it's possible . . ."

The telephone rang again. Ross answered it. "NPS."

"Pacific Telephone liaison here," a male voice said. "We've rechecked that trace for Captain Anders. Is he there?"

"Just a minute." She nodded to Anders, who picked up the phone.

"Anders speaking." There was a long pause. Then he said, "Would you repeat that?" He nodded as he listened. "And what was the time period you checked? I see. Thank you."

He hung up, and immediately began dialing again. "You better tell me about that atomic power pack," he said as he dialed.

"What about it?"

"I want to know what happens if it's ruptured," Anders said, then turned away as his call was put through. "Bomb squad. This is Anders, homicide." He turned back to Ross.

Ross said, "He's carrying around thirty-seven milligrams of radioactive plutonium, Pu-239. If it breaks open, you'll expose everyone in the area to serious radiation."

"What particles are emitted?"

She looked at him in surprise.

"I've been to college," he said, "and I can even read and write, when I have to."

"Alpha particles," she said.

Anders spoke into the phone. "Anders, homicide," he said. "I want a van at University Hospital right away. We've got a possible radiation hazard pending. Man and immediate environment may be contaminated with an alpha emitter, Pu-239." He listened, then looked at Ross. "Any possibility of explosion?"

"No," she said.

"No explosive," Anders said. He listened. "All right. I understand. Get them here as quickly as you can."

He hung up. Ross said, "Do you mind telling me what's going on?"

"The phone company rechecked that trace," Anders said. "They've determined that there were no calls into the NPS from the outside at the time Benson called. None at all."

Ross blinked.

"That's right," Anders said. "He must have called from somewhere inside the hospital."

Ross stared out the fourth-floor window at the parking lot, and watched as Anders gave instructions to at least twenty cops. Half of them went into the main hospital building; the rest remained outside, in little groups, talking together quietly, smoking. Then a white bomb-squad van rumbled up, and three men in gray metallic-looking suits lumbered out. Anders talked to them briefly, then nodded and stayed with the van, unpacking some very peculiar equipment.

Anders walked back toward the NPS.

Alongside her, Gerhard watched the preparations. "Benson won't make it," he said.

"I know," she said. "I keep wondering if there is any way to disarm him, or immobilize him. Could we make a portable microwave transmitter?"

"I thought of that," Gerhard said. "But it's unsafe. You can't really predict the effect on Benson's equipment. And you know it'll raise hell with all the cardiac pacemakers in other patients in the hospital."

"Isn't there anything we can do?"

Gerhard shook his head.

"There must be *something,*" she said.

He continued to shake his head. "Besides," he said, "pretty soon the incorporated environment takes over."

"Theoretically."

Gerhard shrugged.

The incorporated environment was one of the notions from the Development group of the NPS. It was a simple idea with profound implications. It began with something that everybody knew: that the brain was affected by the environment. The environment produced experiences that became memories, attitudes, and habits—things that got translated into neural pathways among brain cells. And these pathways were fixed in some chemical or electrical fashion. Just as a common laborer's body altered according to the work he did, so a person's brain altered according to past experience. But the change, like the calluses on a worker's body, persisted after the experience ended.

In that sense, the brain incorporated past environments. Our brains were the sum total of past experiences—long after the experiences themselves were gone. That meant that cause and cure weren't the same thing. The cause of behavior disorders might lie in childhood experiences, but you couldn't cure the disorder by eliminating the cause, because the cause had disappeared by adulthood. The cure had to come from some other direction. As the Development people said, "A match may start a fire, but once the fire is burning, putting out the match won't stop it. The problem is no longer the match. It's the fire."

As for Benson, he had had more than twenty-four hours of intense stimulation by his implanted computer. That stimulation had affected his brain by providing new experiences and new expectations. A new environment was being incorporated. Pretty soon, it would be impossible to predict how the brain would react. Because it wasn't Benson's old brain any more—it was a new brain, the product of new experiences.

Anders came into the room. "We're ready," he said.

"I can see."

"We've got two men for every basement access, two for the front door, two for the emergency ward, and two for each of the three elevators. I've kept men away from the patient-care floors. We don't want to start trouble in those areas."

Considerate of you, she thought, but said nothing.

Anders glanced at his watch. "Twelve-forty," he said. "I think somebody should show me the main computer."

"It's in the basement," she said, nodding toward the main building. "Over there."

"Will you show me?"

"Sure," she said. She didn't really care. She no longer maintained any illusions about her ability to affect the outcome of events. She realized that she was in the grip of an inexorable process involving many people and many past decisions. What would happen would happen.

She walked down the corridor with Anders, and found herself thinking about Mrs. Crail. It was odd; she hadn't thought of Mrs. Crail in years. Emily Crail had been her first patient as a psychiatric resident, years ago. The woman was fifty, her children grown, her husband bored with her. She was suicidally depressed. Janet Ross had taken the case with a sense of personal responsibility; she was young and eager, and she fought Mrs. Crail's impulses like a general fighting a war—marshaling resources, planning strategies, revising and updating battle plans. She nursed Mrs. Crail through two unsuccessful suicide attempts.

And then she began to realize that there were limits to her own energy, skills, and knowledge. Mrs. Crail was not improving; her suicidal attempts became more crafty; eventually she succeeded in killing herself. But by that time, Ross had—fortunately—detached herself from the patient.

As she was detached from Benson now.

They had reached the far end of the corridor when behind them, from Telecomp, they heard Gerhard shout, "Janet! Janet, are you still here?"

She returned to Telecomp, with Anders following along curiously. Inside the computer room, the console lights were flickering unsteadily.

"Look at this," Gerhard said, pointing to one print-out console.

CURRENT PROGRAM TERMINATED.
PROGRAM CHANGE
IN 05 04 02 01 00
PROGRAM CHANGE

"The main computer is going to a new program," Gerhard said.

"So what?"

"We didn't instruct that."

"What's the new program?"

"I don't know," Gerhard said. "We didn't instruct any change."

Ross and Anders watched the console.

NEW PROGRAM READS AS

Then there was nothing. No further letters appeared on the screen. Anders said, "What does it mean?"

"I don't know," Gerhard said. "Maybe another time-sharing terminal is overriding us, but that shouldn't be possible. We locked in priority for our terminal for the last twelve hours. Ours should be the only terminal that can initiate program changes."

The console flashed up new letters.

NEW PROGRAM READS AS MACHINE MAL-
FUNCTION ALL PROGRAMMING TERMINATED
TERMINATED TERMINATED TERMINATED
TERMINATED TERMINATED TERMINATED
TERMINATED TERMINATED

"What?" Gerhard said. He started to punch buttons on the console, then quit. "It isn't accepting any new instructions."

"Why not?"

"Something must be wrong with the main computer in the basement."

Ross looked at Anders. "You better show me that computer," he said.

Then, as they watched, one of the consoles went completely dead. All its lights blinked off; the TV screen shrank to a single fading white dot. A second console went off, then a third. The teleprinter stopped printing.

"The computer has shut itself down," Gerhard said.

"It probably had help," Anders said.

He went with Ross to the elevators.

It was a damp evening, and cold as they hurried across the parking lot toward the main building. Anders was checking his gun, turning it sideways to catch the light from the parking-lot lamps.

"I think you should know one thing," she said. "It's no good threatening him with that. He won't respond rationally to it."

Anders smiled. "Because he's a machine?"

"He just won't respond. If he has a seizure, he won't see it, won't recognize it, won't react appropriately to it."

They entered the hospital through the brightly lit main entrance, and walked back to the central elevator banks. Anders said, "Where's the atomic pack located?"

"Beneath the skin of his right shoulder."

"Where, exactly?"

"Here," she said, pointing to her own shoulder, tracing a rectangle.

"That size?"

"Yes. About the size of a pack of cigarettes."

"Okay," Anders said.

They took the elevator to the basement. There were two cops in the elevator car, and they were both tense, fidgety, hands touching their guns.

As they rode down, Anders nodded to his own gun. "You ever fire one of these?"

"No."

"Never at all?"

"No."

He didn't say anything after that. The elevator doors opened. They felt the coolness of the basement air and looked down the corridor ahead—bare concrete walls, unpainted; overhead pipes running along the ceiling, harsh electric lighting. They stepped out. The doors closed behind them.

They stood for a moment, listening. They heard nothing except the distant hum of power equipment. Anders whispered, "Anybody usually in the basement at night?"

She nodded. "Maintenance people. Pathologists, if they're still going."

"The pathology labs are down here?"

"Yes."

"Where's the computer?"

"This way."

She led him down the corridor. Straight ahead was the laundry room. It was locked for the night, but huge carts with bundles of laundry were outside in the corridor. Anders eyed the bundles cautiously before they moved on to the central kitchens.

The kitchens were shut down, too, but the lights were on, burning in a vast expanse of white-tiled rooms, with stainless-steel steam tables in long rows. "This is a short cut," she said as they went through the kitchen. Their footsteps echoed on the tiles. Anders walked loosely, holding his gun slightly ahead, barrel pointed out to the side.

They passed through the kitchen and back into another hallway. It was almost identical to the one they had left. Anders glanced at her questioningly. She knew he was lost; she remembered the months it had taken her to learn her way through the basement. "Turn right," she said.

They passed a sign on the wall: EMPLOYEES REPORT ALL ACCIDENTS TO YOUR SUPERVISOR. It showed a man with a small cut on his finger. Further down was another sign: NEED A LOAN? SEE YOUR CREDIT UNION.

They turned right down another corridor, and approached a small section containing vending machines—hot coffee, doughnuts, sandwiches, candy bars. She remembered all the late nights when she had been a resident in the hospital and had come down to the vending machines for a snack. The old days, when being a doctor seemed like a good and hopeful thing to be. Great advances would be made during her lifetime; it would be exciting; she would be a part of it.

Anders peered into the vending area, then paused. He whispered: "Have a look at this."

She looked, astonished. Every machine had been smashed. There were candy bars and sandwiches wrapped in plastic strewn across the floor. Coffee was pouring in short, arterial spurts from the coffee vender onto the floor.

Anders stepped around the puddles of coffee and soda and touched the dents and tears in the metal of the machines. "Looks like an axe," he said. "Where would he get an axe?"

"Fire-extinguisher stations have them."

"I don't see the axe here," he said, looking around the room. Then he glanced at her.

She didn't reply. They left the vending area and continued down the corridor. They came to a turn in the tunnels.

"Which way now?"

"Left," she said. And she added: "We're very close."

Ahead of them, the hall took another turn. Ross knew that hospital records was around the turn, and just beyond that, the computer. The planners had located the computer near the records room because they eventually hoped to computerize all the hospital records.

Suddenly Anders froze. She stopped and listened with him. They heard footsteps, and humming—somebody humming a tune.

Anders put his finger to his lips, and gestured to Ross to stay where she was. He moved forward, toward the turn in the corridor. The humming was louder. He paused at the turn and looked cautiously around the corner. Ross held her breath.

"Hey!" a male voice shouted, and suddenly Anders's arm flicked around the corner like a snake, and a man sprawled across the floor, skidding down the hall toward Ross. "Hey!" A bucket of water sloshed across the floor. Ross saw that it was an elderly maintenance man. She went over to him.

"What the—"

"Sh-h-h," she said, a finger to her lips. She helped the man back to his feet.

Anders came back. "Don't leave the basement," he said to the man. "Go to the kitchen and wait. *Don't try to leave.*" His voice was an angry hiss.

Ross knew what he was saying. Anyone who tried to leave the basement now was likely to be shot by the waiting cops.

The man was nodding, frightened and confused.

"It's all right," Ross said to him.

"I didn't do nothin'."

"There's a man down here we have to find," Ross said. "Just wait until it's over."

"Stay in the kitchen," Anders said.

The man nodded, brushed himself off, and walked away. He looked back once, shaking his head. She and Anders continued along the corridor, turned a corner, and came to the records section. A large sign sticking out from the wall said: PATIENT RECORDS.

Anders looked at her questioningly. She nodded. They went inside.

Records was a giant space, filled with floor-to-ceiling shelves of patient records. It was like an enormous library. Anders paused in surprise.

"Lot of bookkeeping," she said.

"Is this every patient the hospital ever had?"

"No," she said. "Every patient seen in the last five years. The others are stored in a warehouse."

"Christ."

They moved down the parallel stacks of shelves quietly, Anders leading with his gun. Occasionally he would pause to look through a gap in the shelves to another corridor. They saw no one at all.

"Anybody on duty here?"

"Should be."

She scanned the rows of charts. The record room always impressed her. As a practicing doctor she had an image of medical practice that involved large numbers of patients. She had treated hundreds, seen thousands for a single hour or a few weeks. Yet the hospital records ran into the millions —and that was just one hospital, in one city, in one country. Millions and millions of patients.

"We have a thing like this, too," Anders said. "You lose records often?"

"All the time."

He sighed. "So do we."

At that moment, a young girl no more than fifteen or sixteen came around the corner. She carried a stack of records in her arms. Anders had his gun up in an instant. The girl looked, dropped the records, and started to scream.

"Quiet," Anders hissed.

The scream was cut off abruptly, to a kind of gurgle. The girl's eyes were wide.

"I'm a policeman," Anders said. He flicked out his shoulder wallet to show the badge. "Have you seen anyone here?"

"Anyone . . ."

"This man." He showed her the picture.

She looked at it, and shook her head.

"You're sure?"

"Yes . . . I mean, no . . . I mean . . ."

Ross said, "I think we should go on to the computer." In some way, she was embarrassed at frightening the girl. The hospital hired high school and college students part-time to do the clerical work in records; they weren't paid much.

Ross herself remembered when she had been frightened at about the same age. She had been walking in the woods with a boy. They had seen a snake. The boy told her it was a rattlesnake, and she was terrified. Much later she learned he had been teasing her. The snake was harmless. She had resented—

"All right," Anders said. "The computer. Which way?"

Ross led the way out. Anders turned back once to the girl, who was picking up the charts she had dropped. "Listen," he said. "If you do see this man, don't talk to him. Don't do anything except shout your bloody head off. You understand?"

She nodded.

And then Ross realized that the rattlesnake was real, this time. It was all real.

They came out into the corridor again, and continued down it toward the computer section. The computer section was the only refinished part of the basement. The bare concrete floor changed abruptly to blue carpeting; one corridor wall had been knocked out to install large glass windows that looked in, from the corridor, to the room that housed the main banks of the computer. Ross remembered when the computer was being installed; it seemed to her that the windows were an unnecessary expense, and she had mentioned it to McPherson.

"Better let the people see what's coming," McPherson had replied.

"What does that mean?"

"It means that the computer is just a machine. Bigger and more expensive than most, but still just a machine. We want people to get used to it. We don't want them to fear or worship it. We want them to see it as part of the environment."

Yet every time she passed the computer section, she had the opposite feelings: the special treatment, the hallway carpeting, and the expensive surroundings served to make the computer special, unusual, unique. She thought it significant that the only other place in the hospital where the floor was carpeted was outside the small nondenominational chapel on the first floor. She had the same sense here: a shrine to the computer.

Did the computer care if there were carpets on the floor?

In any case, the employees of the hospital had provided their own reaction to the spectacle inside the glass windows. A handwritten sign had been taped to the glass: DO NOT FEED OR MOLEST THE COMPUTER.

She and Anders crouched down below the level of the window. Anders peered over cautiously.

"What do you see?" she said.

"I think I see him."

She looked, too. She was aware that her heart was suddenly pounding; her body was tense and expectant.

Inside the room there were six magnetic tape units, a broad L-shaped console for the central processor, a printer, a card-punch reader, and two disc drive units. The equipment was shiny, sharp-edged, gleaming. It sat quiet under even, fluorescent lighting. She saw no one—just the equipment, isolated, alone. It reminded her of Stonehenge, the vertical stone columns.

Then she saw him: a man moving between two tape units. White orderly's coat, black hair.

"It's him," she said.

"Where's the door?" Anders asked. For no good reason, he was checking his gun again. He snapped the revolver chamber closed with a loud click.

"Down there." She pointed down the corridor to the door, perhaps ten feet away.

"Any other entrances or exits?"

"No."

Her heart was still pounding. She looked from Anders to the gun and back to Anders.

"Okay. You stay down." Anders pressed her down to the floor as he spoke. Then he crawled forward to the door. He paused, got to his knees, and looked back at her once. She was surprised to see that he was frightened. His face was taut, his body hunched tensely. He held the gun stiffly forward by his straight arm.

We're all afraid, she thought.

Then, with a loud slam, Anders knocked the door open and flung himself on his belly into the room. She heard him shout, "Benson!" And then almost immediately there was a gunshot. This was followed by a second shot, and a third. She could not tell who was firing. She saw Anders's feet sticking out of the door as he lay on the carpeting. Gray smoke billowed out through the open door and rose lazily in the corridor.

There were two more shots and a loud scream of pain. She closed her eyes and pressed her cheek to the carpet. Anders shouted: "Benson! Give it up, Benson!"

It won't do any good, she thought. Didn't Anders understand?

Still more shots, in rapid succession. Suddenly, the glass window above her shattered, and large slabs of glass fell over her shoulders, onto her hair. She shook it off. And then to her astonishment Benson landed on the corridor floor beside her. He had thrown himself through the glass window and landed quite close to her. His body was just a few feet from her. She saw that one leg was bloody, red seeping onto the white trouser leg.

"Harry—"

Her voice cracked strangely. She was terrified. She knew she should not be afraid of this man—that was a disservice to him, a betrayal of her profession, and a loss of some important trust—but she was afraid nonetheless.

Benson looked at her, eyes blank and unseeing. He ran off down the basement corridor.

"Harry, wait—"

"Never mind," Anders said, coming out of the computer room, sprinting after Benson, holding his gun stiffly in his hand. The policeman's posture was absurd; she wanted to laugh. She heard Benson's runing footsteps echoing faintly down the tunnel. Then Anders turned a corner, continuing after him. The footsteps blended in staccato echoes.

And then she was alone. She got to her feet, dazed, feeling sick. She knew what was going to happen now. Benson, like a trapped animal, would head for one of the emergency exits. As soon as he appeared outside —where it was safe to shoot—the waiting policemen would gun him down. All the exits were covered. There was no possible escape. She didn't want to be there to see it.

Instead, she went into the computer room and looked around. The main computer was demolished. Two magnetic tape banks were knocked over; the main control panel was riddled with fine round punctures, and sparks sputtered and dripped from the panel toward the floor. She ought to control that, she thought. It might start a fire. She looked around for a fire extinguisher and saw Benson's axe lying on the carpet in a corner. And then she saw the gun.

Curious, she picked it up. It was surprisingly heavy, much heavier than she expected. It felt big and greasy and cold in her hand. She knew Anders had his gun; therefore this must be Benson's. Benson's gun. She stared at it oddly, as if it might tell her something about him.

From somewhere in the basement, there were four gunshots in rapid succession. They echoed through the labyrinthine hospital tunnels. She walked to the broken windows and looked out at the tunnels. She saw nothing, heard nothing.

It must be finished, she thought. The sputtering, hissing sound of sparks behind her made her turn. There was also a slapping sound, repetitive and monotonous. She saw that one of the magnetic tape reels had spun out, and the edge of the tape was slapping against the hardware spindle.

She went back to the reel and turned it off. She glanced up at one of the display consoles, which was now printing "ERMINA" over and over. "ERMINA, ERMINA." Then there were two more gunshots, not so distant as the others, and she realized that somehow Benson was still alive, still going. She stood in a corner of the demolished computer room and waited.

Another gunshot, very close now.

She ducked down behind one of the magnetic tape banks as she heard approaching footsteps. She was aware of the irony: Benson had been hiding behind the computers, and now she was hiding, cowering behind the metal columns, as if they could protect her in some way.

She heard someone gasping for breath; the footsteps paused; the door to the computer room opened, then closed with a slam. She was still hidden behind the tape bank, and could not see what was happening.

A second set of running feet went past the computer room and continued down the corridor, fading into echoes. Everything was quiet. Then she heard heavy breathing and a cough.

She stood.

Harry Benson, in his torn white orderly's clothes, his left leg very red, was sprawled on the carpet, his body half-propped up against the wall. He was sweating; his breath came in ragged gasps; he stared straight ahead, unaware of anyone else in the room.

She still held the gun in her hand, and she felt a moment of elation. Somehow it was all going to work out. She was going to get him back alive. The police hadn't killed him, and by the most unbelievable stroke of luck she had him alone, to herself. It made her wonderfully happy.

"Harry."

He looked over slowly and blinked. He did not seem to recognize her for a moment, and then he smiled. "Hello, Dr. Ross."

It was a nice smile. She had the brief image of McPherson, with his white hair, bending over to congratulate her on saving the project and getting Benson back alive. And then she remembered, quite incongruously, how her own father had gotten sick and had suddenly had to leave her medical-school graduation ceremonies. Why did she think of that now?

"Everything is going to be all right, Harry," she said. Her voice was full of confidence; it pleased her.

She wanted to reassure him, so she did not move, did not approach him. She stayed across the room, behind the computer data bank.

He continued to breathe heavily, and said nothing for a moment. He looked around the room at the demolished computer equipment. "I really did it," he said. "Didn't I?"

"You're going to be fine, Harry," she said. She was drawing up a schedule in her mind. He could undergo emergency surgery on his leg that night, and in the morning they could disconnect his computer, reprogram the electrodes, and everything would be corrected. A disaster would be salvaged. It was the most incredible piece of luck. Ellis would keep his house. McPherson would continue to expand the NPS into new areas. They would be grateful. They would recognize her achievement and appreciate what she—

"Dr. Ross . . ." He started to get up, wincing in pain.

"Don't try to move. Stay where you are, Harry."

"I have to."

"Stay where you are, Harry."

Benson's eyes flashed briefly, and the smile was gone. "Don't call me Harry. My name is Mr. Benson. Call me Mr. Benson."

There was no mistaking the anger in his voice. It surprised her and upset her. She was trying to help him. Didn't he know that she was the only one who still wanted to help him? The others would be just as happy if he died.

He continued to struggle to his feet.

"Don't move, Harry." She showed him the gun then. It was an angry, hostile move. He had angered her. She knew she shouldn't get angry at him, but she had.

He grinned in childish recognition. "That's my gun."

"I have it now," she said.

He still grinned, a fixed expression, partly from pain. He got to his feet and leaned heavily against the wall. There was a dark red stain on the carpet where his leg had rested. He looked down and saw it.

"I'm hurt," he said.

"Don't move. You'll be all right."

"He shot me in the leg . . ." He looked from the blood up to her. His smile remained. "You wouldn't use that, would you?"

"Yes," she said, "if I had to."

"You're my doctor."

"Stay where you are, Harry."

"I don't think you would use it," Benson said. He took a step toward her.

"Don't come closer, Harry."

He smiled. He took another step, unsteady, but he maintained his balance. "I don't think you would."

His words frightened her. She was afraid that she would shoot him, and afraid that she would not. It was the strangest set of circumstances, alone with this man, surrounded by the wreckage of a computer.

"Anders!" she shouted. *"Anders!"* Her voice echoed through the basement.

Benson took another step. His eyes never left her face. He started to fall, and leaned heavily on one of the disc drive consoles. It tore his white jacket at the armpit. He looked at the tear numbly. "It tore. . . ."

"Stay there, Harry. Stay there." It's like talking to an animal, she thought. Do not feed or molest the animals. She felt like a lion tamer in the circus.

He hung there a moment, supporting himself on the drive console, breathing heavily. "I want the gun," he said. "I need it. Give it to me."

"Harry—"

With a grunt, he pushed away from the console and continued moving toward her.

"Anders!"

"It's no good," Benson said. "There's no time left, Dr. Ross." His eyes were on her. She saw the pupils expand briefly as he received a stimulation. "That's beautiful," he said, and smiled.

The stimulation seemed to halt him for a time. He was turned inward, enjoying the sensation. When he spoke again, his voice was calm and distant. "You see," he said, "they are after me. They have turned their little computers against me. The program is hunt. Hunt and kill. The original human program. Hunt and kill. Do you understand?"

He was only a few steps away. She held the gun in her hand stiffly, as she had seen Anders hold it. But her hand was shaking badly. "Please don't come closer, Harry," she said. "Please."

He smiled.

He took another step.

She didn't really know what she was going to do until she found herself squeezing the trigger, and the gun discharged. The noise was painfully loud, and the gun snapped in her hand, flinging her arm up, almost knocking her off her feet. She was thrown back against the far wall of the computer room.

Benson stood blinking in the smoke. Then he smiled again. "It's not as easy as it looks."

She gripped the gun in her hand. It felt warm now. She raised it, but it was shaking worse than before. She steadied it with the other hand.

Benson advanced.

"No closer, Harry. I mean it."

A flood of images overcame her. She saw Benson as she had first met him, a meek man with a terrifying problem. She saw him in a montage of all the hour-long interviews, all the tests, all the drug trials. He was a good person, an honest and frightened person. Nothing that had happened was his fault. It was her fault, and Ellis's fault, and McPherson's fault, and Morris's fault.

Then she thought of Morris, the face mashed into a red pulp, deformed into butcher meat.

"Dr. Ross," Benson said. "You're my doctor. You wouldn't do anything to hurt me."

He was very close now. His hands reached out for the gun. Her whole body was shaking as she watched the hands move closer, within inches of the barrel, reaching for it, reaching for it . . .

She fired at point-blank range.

With remarkable agility, Benson jumped and spun in the air, dodging the bullet. She was pleased. She had managed to drive him back without hurting him. Anders would arrive any minute to help subdue him before they took him to surgery.

Benson's body slammed hard into the printing unit, knocking it over. It began to clatter in a monotonous, mechanical way as the keys printed out some message. Benson rolled onto his back. Blood spurted in heavy thick gushes from his chest. His white uniform became darkly red.

"Harry?" she said.

He did not move.

"Harry? Harry?"

She didn't remember clearly what happened after that. Anders returned and took the gun from her hand. He moved her to the side of the room as three men in gray suits arrived, carrying a long plastic capsule on a stretcher. They opened the capsule up; the inside was lined in a strange, yellow honeycomb insulation. They lifted Benson's body—she noticed they were careful, trying to keep the blood off their special suits—and placed him inside the capsule. They closed it and locked it with special locks. Two of the men carried it away. A third went around the room with a Geiger counter, which chattered loudly. Somehow the sound reminded her of an angry monkey. The man went over to Ross. She couldn't see his face behind the gray helmet he wore; the glass was fogged.

"You better leave this area," the man said.

Anders put his arm around her shoulders. She began to cry.

BIBLIOGRAPHY

GENERAL

Apter, Michael J. *The Computer Simulation of Behavior.* New York: Harper Colophon, 1971.

Bruner, Jerome. *On Knowing, Essays for the Left Hand.* Cambridge: Harvard University Press, 1962.

Calder, Nigel. *The Mind of Man,* New York: Viking, 1970.

Delgado, J. M. R. *Physical Control of the Mind: Toward a Psychocivilized Society.* New York: Harper & Row, 1968.

Koestler, A. *The Ghost in the Machine.* New York: Macmillan, 1967.

London, P. *Behavior Control.* Harper & Row, 1969; Perennial paperback, 1971.

Wiener, N. *The Human Use of Human Beings: Cybernetics and Society.* Boston: Houghton Mifflin, 1954; Avon paperback, 1967.

Wolstenholme, G., ed., *Man and His Future.* London: Churchill, 1963.

Wooldridge, D. E. *The Machinery of the Brain.* New York: McGraw-Hill, 1963.

TECHNICAL REFERENCES

Adams, John E. "The Future of Stereotaxic Surgery." *J. Am. Med. Assn.* 198(1966):648–652.

Aird, R. B., et al. "Antecedents of Temporal Lobe Epilepsy." *Arch. Neurology* 16(1967):67–73.

Anastasopoulos, G., et al. "Transient Bulimia-Anorexia and Hypersexuality Following Pneumoencephalography in a Case of Psychomotor Epilepsy." *J. Neuropsych.,* 4(1963):135–142.

BIBLIOGRAPHY

Bennett, A. E. "Mental Disorders Associated with Temporal Lobe Epilepsy." *Dis. of the Nervous System,* 26(1965):275–280.

Bishop, M. P., et al. "Intracranial Self-Stimulation in Man." *Science,* 140(1963):394–396.

Bloch, S. "Aetiological Aspects of the Schizophrenia-Like Psychosis of Temporal Lobe Epilepsy." *Med. J. Australia,* 66(1969):451–453.

Carleton, R. A., et al. "Environmental Influence on Implantable Cardiac Pacemakers." *J. Am. Med. Assn.,* 190(1964):938–940.

Chase, R. A., et al. "Ictal Speech Automatisms and Swearing: Studies on the Auditory Feedback Control of Speech." *J. Nervous and Mental Disease,* 144(1967):406–420.

Crandall, P. H., et al. "Clinical Applications of Studies on Stereotactically Implanted Electrodes in Temporal-Lobe Epilepsy." *J. Neurosurgery* 20(1964):827–840.

Delgado, J. M. R., et al. "Intracerebral Radio Stimulation and Recording in Completely Free Patients." *J. Nervous and Mental Disease,* 147(1968):329–340.

Duffy, J. C., et al. "Psychic and Somatic Interactions in Psychomotor Epilepsy." *Psychosomatics,* 7(1966):353–356.

Ellinwood, E. H., Jr. "Amphetamine Psychosis: Theoretical Implications." *International J. of Neuropsych.,* 4(1968):45–54.

Falconer, M. A. et al. "Temporal Lobe Epilepsy Due to Distant Lesions: Two Cases Relieved by Operation." *Brain,* 85(1961):521–534.

Falconer, M. A. "Problems in Neurosurgery: 1. Temporal Lobe Epilepsy." *Trans. Med. Soc. London,* 82(1967):111–126.

Falconer, M. A. "Surgical Treatment of Temporal Lobe Epilepsy." *New Zealand Med. J.,* 66(1964):539–542.

Fenton, G. W., et al. "Homicide, Temporal Lobe Epilepsy and Depression: A Case Report." *Brit. J. Psychiatry,* 111(1965):304–306.

Fenyes, I., et al. "Temporal Epilepsies with Deepseated Eliptogenic Foci: Postoperative Course." *Archives of Neurology* 4(1964):559–571.

Glaser, G. H. "The Problem of Psychosis in Psychomotor Temporal Lobe Epileptics," *Epilepsia,* 5(1964):271–278.

Green, J. R. "Temporal Lobectomy, with Special Reference to Selection of Epileptic Patients." *J. Neurosurg.,* 26(1966):584–593.

Greenberg, R., et al. "Sleep Patterns in Temporal Lobe Epilepsy." *Comprehensive Psychiatry,* 9(1968):194–199.

Hierons, R., et al. "Impotence in Patients with Temporal Lobe Lesions." *Lancet*, 2(1966):761–763.

Holowach, J., et al. "Psychomotor Seizures in Childhood, A Clinical Study of 120 Cases." *Pediatrics*, 59(1961):339–345.

Hommes, O. R. "Psychomotor Epilepsy: A Neurological Approach to Hysteria." *Psychiat. Neurol. Neurochir.*, 67(1964):497–519.

Hunter, R., et al. "Temporal Lobe Epilepsy Supervening on Longstanding Transvestism and Fetishism: A Case Report." *Epilepsia*, 4(1963):60–65.

Kenna, J. C., et al. "Depersonalization in Temporal Lobe Epilepsy and the Organic Psychoses." *Brit J. Psychiatry*, 111 (1965):293–299.

Knapp, D. E., et al. "Nuclear Electrical Power Sources for Biomedical Applications." Proceedings of the Fourth Intersociety Energy Conversion Engineering Conference, Washington, D.C., September 22–26, 1969. New York: American Institute of Chemical Engineers, 1969, pp. 101–106.

Kolarsky, A., et al. "Male Sexual Deviation: Association with Early Temporal Lobe Damage." *Arch. Gen. Psychiat.*, 17(1967):735–743.

Norman, J. C., et al. "Implantable Nuclear-Powered Cardiac Pacemakers." *New Eng. J. Med.*, 283(1971):1203–1206.

Pickers, B. A., et al. "Inhibition of a Demand Pacemaker and Interference with Monitoring Equipment by Radio-Frequency Transmissions." *Brit. Med. J.*, 2(1969):504–506.

Rand, R. W., et al. "Chronic Stereotactic Implantation of Depth Electrodes for Psychomotor Epilepsy." *Acta Neurochirurgica*, 11(1968):609–630.

Reiher, J., et al. "Combined Electroencephalography and Sonoencephalography in Temporal Lobe Epilepsy." *Neurology*, 19(1969):157–159.

Roth, M., et al. "Temporal Lobe Epilepsy and the Phobic Anxiety-Depersonalization Syndrome." *Comprehensive Psychiatry* 3(1963):130–151, 215–226.

Serafetinides, E. A. "Aggressiveness in Temporal Lobe Epileptics and Its Relation to Cerebal Dysfunction and Environmental Factors." *Epilepsia*, 6(1965):33–42.

Serafetinides, E. A., et al. "Some Observations on Memory Impairment After Temporal Lobectomy for Epilepsy." *J. Neurol. Neurosurg. Psychiat.*, 25(1962):251–255.

Serafetinides, E. A., et al. "The Effects of Temporal Lobectomy in Epileptic Patients with Psychosis." *J. Ment. Sci.*, 108(1962):584–593.

Slotnick, D. L. "The Fastest Computer." *Sci. Am.*, 224(1971):76–87.

Stevens, J. R. "Psychiatric Implications of Psychomotor Epilepsy." *Arch. Gen. Psych.* 14(1966):461–471.

Stevenson, H. G. "Psychomotor Epilepsy Associated with Criminal Behaviour." *Med. J. Australia*, 60(1963):784–785.

Strobos, R. J., et al. "Mechanisms in Temporal Lobe Seizures." *Arch. Neurology*, 5(1961):48–57.

Walker, E. A. "Temporal Lobectomy." *J. Neurosurgery*, 26(1966):642–649.

Weiss, A. A. "Psychodiagnostic Follow-Up of Eight Cases of Temporal Lobectomy." *Israel Ann. Psychiat.*, 3–4(1962):259–266.

Yatteau, R. F. "Radar-Induced Failure of a Demand Pacemaker." *New Eng. J. Med.*, 283(1971):1447–1448.

THE GREAT TRAIN ROBBERY

To Barbara Rose

Satan is glad—when I am bad,
And hopes that I—with him shall lie
In fire and chains—and dreadful pains

—VICTORIAN CHILD'S POEM, 1856

"I wanted the money."

—EDWARD PIERCE, 1856

CONTENTS

Introduction
443

PART I:
Preparations
449

PART II:
The Keys
519

PART III:
Delays and Difficulties
567

PART IV:
The Great Train Robbery
627

PART V:
Arrest and Trial
649

INTRODUCTION

It is difficult, after the passage of more than a century, to understand the extent to which the train robbery of 1855 shocked the sensibilities of Victorian England. At first glance, the crime hardly seems noteworthy. The sum of money stolen—£12,000 in gold bullion—was large, but not unprecedented; there had been a dozen more lucrative robberies in the same period. And the meticulous organization and planning of the crime, involving many people and extending over a year, was similarly not unusual. All major crimes at the mid-century called for a high degree of preparation and coordination.

Yet the Victorians always referred to this crime in capital letters, as The Great Train Robbery. Contemporary observers labeled it The Crime of the Century and The Most Sensational Exploit of the Modern Era. The adjectives applied to it were all strong: it was "unspeakable," "appalling," and "heinous." Even in an age given to moral overstatement, these terms suggest some profound impact upon everyday consciousness.

To understand why the Victorians were so shocked by the theft, one must understand something about the meaning of the railways. Victorian England was the first urbanized, industrialized society on earth, and it evolved with stunning rapidity. At the time of Napoleon's defeat at Waterloo, Georgian England was a predominantly rural nation of thirteen million people. By the middle of the nineteenth century, the population had nearly doubled to twenty-four million, and half the people lived in urban centers. Victorian England was a nation of cities; the conversion from agrarian life seemed to have occurred almost overnight; indeed, the process was so swift that no one really understood it.

Victorian novelists, with the exception of Dickens and Gissing, did not write about the cities; Victorian painters for the most part did not portray urban subjects. There were conceptual problems as well—during much of the century, industrial production was viewed as a kind of particularly valuable harvest, and not as something new and unprecedented. Even the language fell behind. For most of the 1800s, "slum" meant a room of low repute, and "urbanize" meant to become urbane and genteel. There were no accepted terms to describe the growth of cities, or the decay of portions of them.

This is not to say that Victorians were unaware of the changes taking place in their society, or that these changes were not widely—and often fiercely—debated. But the processes were still too new to be readily understood. The Victorians were pioneers of the urban, industrial life that has since become commonplace throughout the Western world. And if we find their attitudes quaint, we must nonetheless recognize our debt to them.

The new Victorian cities that grew so fast glittered with more wealth than any society had ever known— and they stank of poverty as abject as any society had ever suffered. The inequities and glaring contrasts within urban centers provoked many calls for reform. Yet there was also widespread public complacency, for the fundamental assumption of Victorians was that progress—progress in the sense of better conditions for all mankind—was inevitable. We may find that complacency particularly risible today, but in the 1850s it was a reasonable attitude to adopt.

During the first half of the nineteenth century, the price of bread, meat, coffee, and tea had fallen; the price of coal was almost halved; the cost of cloth was reduced 80 percent; and per-capita consumption of everything had increased. Criminal law had been reformed; personal liberties were better protected; Parliament was, at least to a degree, more representative; and one man in seven had the right to vote. Per-capita taxation had been reduced by half. The first blessings of technology were evident: gaslights glowed throughout the cities; steamships made the crossing to America in ten days instead of eight weeks; the new telegraph and postal service provided astonishing speed in communications.

Living conditions for all classes of Englishmen had improved. The reduced cost of food meant that everyone ate better. Factory working hours had been reduced from 74 to 60 hours a week for adults, and from 72 to 40 for children; the custom of working half-days on Saturday was increasingly prevalent. Average life span had increased five years.

There was, in short, plenty of reason to believe that society was "on the march," that things were getting better, and that they would continue to get better into the indefinite future. The very idea of the future seemed more solid to the Victorians than we can comprehend. It was possible to lease a box in the Albert Hall for 999 years, and many citizens did so.

But of all the proofs of progress, the most visible and striking were the railways. In less than a quarter of a century, they had altered every aspect of English life and commerce. It is only a slight simplification to say that prior to 1830 there were no railways in England. All transportation between cities was by horsedrawn coach, and such journeys were slow, unpleasant, dangerous, and expensive. Cities were consequently isolated from one another.

In September, 1830, the Liverpool & Manchester Railway opened and began the revolution. In the first year of operation, the number of railway passengers carried between these two cities was twice the number that had traveled the previous year by coach. By 1838, more than 600,000 people were carried annually on the line—a figure greater than the total population of either Liverpool or Manchester at that time.

The social impact was extraordinary. So was the howl of opposition. The new railways were all privately financed, profit-oriented ventures, and they drew plenty of criticism.

There was opposition on aesthetic grounds; Ruskin's condemnation of the railway bridges over the Thames echoed a view widely held by his less refined contemporaries; the "aggregate disfigurement" of town and countryside was uniformly deplored. Landowners everywhere fought the railways as deleterious to property values. And the tranquility of local towns was disrupted by the onslaught of thousands of rough, itinerant, camp-living "navvies," for in an era before dynamite and earthmovers, bridges were built, tracks were laid, and tunnels were cut by sheer human effort alone. It was also well recognized that in times of unemployment the navvies easily shifted to the ranks of urban criminals of the crudest sort.

Despite these reservations, the growth of the English railways was swift and pervasive. By 1850, five thousand miles of track crisscrossed the nation, providing cheap and increasingly swift transportation for every citizen. Inevitably the railways came to symbolize progress. According to the *Economist*, "In *locomotion by land* . . . our progress has been most stupendous—surpassing all previous steps since the creation of the human race. . . . In the days of Adam the average speed of travel, if Adam ever did such things, was four miles an hour; in the year 1828, or *4,000 years afterwards, it was still only ten miles,* and sensible and scientific men were ready to affirm and eager to prove that this rate could never be materially exceeded;—in 1850 it is habitually forty miles an hour, and *seventy* for those who like it."

Here was undeniable progress, and to the Victorian mind such progress implied moral as well as material advancement. According to Charles Kingsley, "The moral state of a city depends . . . on the physical state of that city; on the food, water, air, and lodging of its inhabitants." Progress in physical conditions led inevitably to the eradication of social evils and criminal behavior—which would be swept away much as the slums that housed these evils and criminals were, from time to time, swept away. It seemed a simple matter of eliminating the cause and, in due course, the effect.

From this comfortable perspective, it was absolutely astonishing to discover that "the criminal class" had found a way to prey upon progress—and indeed to carry out a crime aboard the very hallmark of progress, the railway. The fact that the robbers also overcame the finest safes of the day only increased the consternation.

What was really so shocking about The Great Train Robbery was that it suggested, to the sober thinker, that the elimination of crime might not be an inevitable consequence of forward-marching progress. Crime could no longer be likened to the Plague, which had disappeared with changing social conditions to become a dimly remembered threat of the past. Crime was something else, and criminal behavior would not simply fade away.

A few daring commentators even had the temerity to suggest that crime was not linked to social conditions at all, but rather sprang from some other impulse. Such opinions were, to say the least, highly distasteful.

They remain distasteful to the present day. More than a century after The Great Train Robbery, and more than a decade after another spectacular English train robbery, the ordinary Western urban man still clings to the belief that crime results from poverty, injustice, and poor education. Our view of the criminal is that of a limited, abused, perhaps mentally disturbed individual who breaks the law out of a desperate need—the drug addict standing as a sort of modern archetype for this person. And indeed when it was recently reported that the majority of violent street crime in New York City was not committed by addicts, that finding was greeted with skepticism and dismay, mirroring the perplexity of our Victorian forebears a hundred years ago.

Crime became a legitimate focus for academic inquiry in the 1870s, and in succeeding years criminologists have attacked all the old stereotypes, creating a new view of crime that has never found favor with the general public. Experts now agree on the following points:

First, crime is not a consequence of poverty. In the words of Barnes and Teeters (1949), "Most offenses are committed through greed, not need."

Second, criminals are not limited in intelligence, and it is probable that the reverse is true. Studies of prison populations show that inmates equal the general public in intelligence tests—and yet prisoners represent that fraction of lawbreakers who are caught.

Third, the vast majority of criminal activity goes unpunished. This is inherently a speculative question, but some authorities argue that only 3 to 5 percent of all crimes are reported; and of reported crimes, only 15 to 20 percent are ever "solved" in the usual sense of the word. This is true of even the most serious offenses, such as murder. Most police pathologists laugh at the idea that "murder will out."

Similarly, criminologists dispute the traditional view that "crime does not pay." As early as 1877, an American prison investigator, Richard Dugdale, concluded that "we must dispossess ourselves of the idea that crime does not pay. In reality, it does." Ten years later, the Italian criminologist Colajanni went a step further, arguing that on the whole crime pays better than honest labor. By 1949, Barnes and Teeters stated flatly, "It is primarily the moralist who still believes that crime does not pay."

Our moral attitudes toward crime account for a peculiar ambivalence toward criminal behavior itself. On the one hand, it is feared, despised, and vociferously condemned. Yet it is also secretly admired, and we are always eager to hear the details of some outstanding criminal exploit. This attitude was clearly prevalent in 1855, for The Great Train Robbery was not only shocking and appalling, but also "daring," "audacious," and "masterful."

We share with the Victorians another attitude—a belief in a "criminal class," by which we mean a subculture of professional criminals who make their living by breaking the laws of the society around them. Today we call this class "the Mafia," "the syndicate," or "the mob," and we are interested to know its code of ethics, its inverted value system, its peculiar language and patterns of behavior.

Without question, a definable subculture of professional criminals existed a hundred years ago in mid-Victorian England. Many of its features were brought to light in the trial of Burgess, Agar, and Pierce, the chief participants in The Great Train Robbery. They were all apprehended in 1856, nearly two years after the event. Their voluminous courtroom testimony is preserved, along with journalistic accounts of the day. It is from these sources that the following narrative is assembled.

M.C.
November, 1974

PART ONE

PREPARATIONS

May–October, 1854

Chapter 1

The Provocation

Forty minutes out of London, passing through the rolling green fields and cherry orchards of Kent, the morning train of the South Eastern Railway attained its maximum speed of fifty-four miles an hour. Riding the bright blue-painted engine, the driver in his red uniform could be seen standing upright in the open air, unshielded by any cab or windscreen, while at his feet the engineer crouched, shoveling coal into the glowing furnaces of the engine. Behind the chugging engine and tender were three yellow first-class coaches, followed by seven green second-class carriages; and at the very end, a gray, windowless luggage van.

As the train clattered down the track on its way to the coast, the sliding door of the luggage van opened suddenly, revealing a desperate struggle inside. The contest was most unevenly matched: a slender youth in tattered clothing, striking out against a burly, blue-uniformed railway guard. Although weaker, the youth made a good showing, landing one or two telling blows against his hulking opponent. Indeed, it was only by accident that the guard, having been knocked to his knees, should spring forward in such a way that the youth was caught unprepared and flung clear of the train through the open door, so that he landed tumbling and bouncing like a rag doll upon the ground.

The guard, gasping for breath, looked back at the fast-receding figure of the fallen youth. Then he closed the sliding door. The train sped on, its whistle shrieking. Soon it was gone round a gentle curve, and all that remained was the faint sound of the chugging engine, and the lingering drifting gray smoke that slowly settled over the tracks and the body of the motionless youth.

After a minute or two, the youth stirred. In great pain, he raised himself up on one elbow, and seemed about to rise to his feet. But his efforts were to no avail; he instantly collapsed back to the ground, gave a final convulsive shudder, and lay wholly still.

Half an hour later, an elegant black brougham coach with rich crimson wheels came down the dirt road that ran parallel to the railway tracks. The coach came to a hill, and the driver drew up his horse. A most singular gentleman emerged, fashionably dressed in a dark green velvet frock coat and high beaver hat. The gentleman climbed the hill, pressed binoculars to his eyes, and swept the length of the tracks. Immediately he fixed on the body of the prostrate youth. But the gentleman made no attempt to approach him, or to aid him in any way. On the contrary, he remained standing on the hill until he was certain the lad was dead. Only then did he turn aside, climb into his waiting coach, and drive back in the direction he had come, northward toward London.

Chapter 2

The Putter-Up

This singular gentleman was Edward Pierce, and for a man destined to become so notorious that Queen Victoria herself expressed a desire to meet him—or, barring that, to attend his hanging—he remains an oddly mysterious figure. In appearance, Pierce was a tall, handsome man in his early thirties who wore a full red beard in the fashion that had recently become popular, particularly among government employees. In his speech, manner, and dress he seemed to be a gentleman, and well-to-do; he was apparently very charming, and possessed of "a captivating address." He himself claimed to be an orphan of Midlands gentry, to have attended Winchester and then Cambridge. He was a familiar figure in many London social circles and counted among his acquaintances Ministers, Members of Parliament, foreign ambassadors, bankers, and others of substantial standing. Although a bachelor, he maintained a house at No. 19 Curzon Street, in a fashionable part of London. But he spent much of the year traveling, and was said to have visited not only the Continent but New York as well.

Contemporary observers clearly believed his aristocratic origins; journalistic accounts often referred to Pierce as a "rogue," using the term in the sense of a male animal gone bad. The very idea of a highborn gentleman adopting a life of crime was so startling and titillating that nobody really wanted to disprove it.

Yet there is no firm evidence that Pierce came from the upper classes; indeed, almost nothing of his background prior to 1850 is known with any certainty. Modern readers, accustomed to the concept of "positive identification" as an ordinary fact of life, may be puzzled by the ambiguities of Pierce's past. But in an era when birth certificates were an innovation, photography a nascent art, and fingerprinting wholly unknown, it was difficult to identify any man with certainty, and Pierce took special care to be elusive. Even his name is doubtful: during the trial, various witnesses claimed to have known him as John Simms, or Andrew Miller, or Robert Jeffers.

The source of his obviously ample income was equally disputed. Some said he was a silent partner with Jukes in the highly successful firm that manufactured croquet equipment. Croquet—pronounced "croaky"—was the overnight rage among athletically inclined young ladies, and it was perfectly reasonable that a sharp young businessman, investing a modest inheritance in such an enterprise, should come off very well.

Others said that Pierce owned several public houses, and a smallish fleet of cabs, headed by a particularly sinister-appearing cabby, named Barlow, with a white scar across his forehead. This was more likely true, for the ownership of pubs and cabs was an occupation where underworld connections were useful.

Of course, it is not impossible that Pierce was a wellborn man with a background of aristocratic education. One must remember that Winchester and Cambridge were in those days more often characterized by lewd and drunken behavior than serious and sober scholarship. The most profound scientific mind of the Victorian era, Charles Darwin, devoted most of his youth to gambling and horses; and the majority of wellborn young men were more interested in acquiring "a university bearing" than a university degree.

It is also true that the Victorian underworld supported many educated figures down on their luck. They were usually screevers, or writers of false letters of recommendation, or they were counterfeiters, "doing a bit of soft." Sometimes they became magsmen, or con artists. But in general these educated men were petty criminals of a pathetic sort, more deserving of public pity than condemnation.

Edward Pierce, on the other hand, was positively exuberant in his approach to crime. Whatever his sources of income, whatever the truth of his background, one thing is certain: he was a master cracksman, or burglar, who over the years had accumulated sufficient capital to finance large-scale criminal operations, thus becoming what was called "a putter-up." And toward the middle of 1854, he was already well into an elaborate plan to pull the greatest theft of his career, The Great Train Robbery.

Chapter 3

The Screwsman

Robert Agar—a known screwsman, or specialist in keys and safe-breaking—testified in court that when he met Edward Pierce in late May, 1854, he had not seen him for two years previously. Agar was twenty-six years old, and in fair health except for a bad cough, the legacy of his years as a child working for a match manufacturer on Wharf Road, Bethnal Green. The premises of the firm were poorly ventilated, and the white vapor of phosphorous filled the air at all times. Phosphorous was known to be poisonous, but there were plenty of people eager to work at any job, even one that might cause a person's lungs to decay, or his jaw to rot off—sometimes in a matter of months.

Agar was a matchstick dipper. He had nimble fingers, and he eventually took up his trade as screwsman, where he was immediately successful. He worked as a screwsman for six years and was never apprehended.

Agar had never had any direct dealings with Pierce in the past, but he knew of him as a master cracksman who worked other towns, thus accounting for his long absences from London. Agar had also heard that Pierce had the money to put up a lay from time to time.

Agar testified that their first meeting occurred at the Bull and Bear public house located at the periphery of the notorious criminal slum of

Seven Dials. This well-known flash house was, in the words of one observer, "a gathering place for all manner of females dressed to represent ladies, as well as members of the criminal class, who could be seen at every turning."

Given the infamous nature of the place, it was almost certain that a plainclothes constable from the Metropolitan Police was lurking somewhere on the premises. But the Bull and Bear was frequented by gentlemen of quality with a taste for low life, and the conversation of two fashionably dressed young bloods lounging at the bar while they surveyed the women in the room attracted no particular attention.

The meeting was unplanned, Agar said, but he was not surprised when Pierce arrived. Agar had heard some talk about Pierce lately, and it sounded as though he might be putting up. Agar recalled that the conversation began without greetings or preliminaries.

Agar said, "I heard that Spring Heel Jack's left Westminster."

"I heard that," Pierce agreed, rapping with his silverheaded cane to draw the attention of the barman. Pierce ordered two glasses of the best whiskey, which Agar took as proof that this was to be a business discussion.

"I heard," Agar said, "that Jack was going on a south swing to dip the holiday crowd." In those days, London pickpockets left in late spring, traveling north or south to other cities. A pickpocket's stock in trade was anonymity, and one could not dip a particular locale for long without being spotted by the crusher on the beat.

"I didn't hear his plans," Pierce said.

"I also heard," Agar continued, "that he took the train."

"He might have done."

"I heard," Agar said, his eyes on Pierce's face, "that on this train he was doing some crow's peeping for a particular gent who is putting up."

"He might have done," Pierce said again.

"I also heard," Agar said with a sudden grin, "that you are putting up."

"I may," Pierce said. He sipped his whiskey, and stared at the glass. "It used to be better here," he said reflectively. "Neddy must be watering his stock. What have you heard I am putting up for?"

"A robbery," Agar said. "For a ream flash pull, if truth be told."

"If truth be told," Pierce repeated. He seemed to find the phrase amusing. He turned away from the bar and looked at the women in the room. Several returned his glances warmly. "Everybody hears the pull bigger than life," he said finally.

"Aye, that's so," Agar admitted, and sighed. (In his testimony, Agar was very clear about the histrionics involved. "Now I goes and gives a big sigh, you see, like to say my patience is wearing thin, because he's a cautious one, Pierce is, but I want to get down to it, so I gives a big sigh.")

There was a brief silence. Finally Agar said, "It's two years gone since I saw you. Been busy?"

"Traveling," Pierce said.

"The Continent?"

Pierce shrugged. He looked at the glass of whiskey in Agar's hands, and the half-finished glass of gin and water Agar had been drinking before Pierce arrived. "How's the touch?"

"Ever so nice," Agar said. To demonstrate, he held out his hands, palms flat, fingers wide: there was no tremor.

"I may have one or two little things," Pierce said.

"Spring Heel Jack held his cards close," Agar said. "I know that for a ream fact. He was all swelled mighty and important, but he kept it to his chest."

"Jack's put in lavender," Pierce said curtly.

This was, as Agar later explained it, an ambiguous phrase. It might mean that Spring Heel Jack had gone into hiding; more often it meant that he was dead; it depended. Agar didn't inquire further. "These one or two little things, could they be crib jobs?"

"They could."

"Dicey, are they?"

"Very dicey," Pierce said.

"Inside or outside?"

"I don't know. You may need a canary or two when the time comes. And you will want a tight lip. If the first lay goes right enough, there will be more."

Agar downed the rest of his whiskey, and waited. Pierce ordered him another.

"Is it keys, then?" Agar asked.

"It is."

"Wax, or straightaway haul?"

"Wax."

"On the fly, or is there time?"

"On the fly."

"Right, then," Agar said. "I'm your man. I can do a wax on the fly faster than you can light your cigar."

"I know that," Pierce said, striking a match on the counter top and holding it to the tip of his cigar. Agar gave a slight shudder; he did not himself smoke—indeed, smoking had just recently returned to fashion after eighty years—and every time he smelled the phosphorous and sulfur of a match, it gave Agar a twinge, from his days in the match factory.

He watched Pierce puff on the cigar until it caught. "What's the lay to be, then?"

Pierce looked at him coldly. "You'll know when the time comes."

"You're a tight one."

"That," Pierce said, "is why I have never been in," meaning that he had no prison record. At the trial, other witnesses disputed this claim, saying that Pierce had served three and a half years in Manchester for cracking, under the name of Arthur Wills.

Agar said that Pierce gave him a final word of caution about keeping silent, and then moved away from the bar, crossing the smoky, noisy Bull and Bear to bend briefly and whisper into a pretty woman's ear. The woman laughed; Agar turned away, and recalls nothing further from the evening.

Chapter 4

The Unwitting Accomplice

Mr. Henry Fowler, forty-seven, knew Edward Pierce in rather different circumstances. Fowler admitted freely that he had little knowledgc of Piercc's background: thc man had said he was an orphan, and he was clearly educated, and well-to-do, keeping a most excellent house, which was always fitted out with the latest appurtenances, some of them exceedingly clever.

Mr. Fowler remembered particularly an ingenious hallway stove for warming the entrance to the house. This stove was in the shape of a suit of armor, and functioned admirably. Mr. Fowler also recalled seeing a pair of beautifully constructed aluminum field glasses covered in Moroccan leather; these had so intrigued Mr. Fowler that he had sought a pair of his own and was astounded to discover that they were eighty shillings, an exorbitant price. Clearly, Pierce was well-heeled, and Henry Fowler found him amusing for an occasional dinner.

He recalled, with difficulty, an episode at Pierce's home in late May, 1854. It had been a dinner of eight gentlemen; the conversation chiefly concerned a new proposal for an underground railway within London itself. Fowler found the idea tedious, and he was disappointed when it was still discussed over brandy in the smoking room.

Then the topic of conversation turned to cholera, of late an epidemic in certain parts of London, where the disease was snatching up one person in a hundred. The dispute over the proposals of Mr. Edwin Chadwick, one of the Sanitary Commissioners, for new sewer systems in the city and for a cleaning-up of the polluted Thames, was profoundly boring to Mr. Fowler. Besides, Mr. Fowler had it on good authority that old "Drain Brain" Chadwick was soon to be discharged, but he was sworn not to divulge this information. He drank his coffee with a growing sense of fatigue. Indeed, he was thinking of taking his leave when the host, Mr. Pierce, asked him about a recent attempt to rob a gold shipment from a train.

It was only natural that Pierce should ask Fowler, for Henry Fowler was the brother-in-law of Sir Edgar Huddleston, of the banking firm of Huddleston & Bradford, Westminster. Mr. Fowler was the general manager of that prosperous enterprise, which had specialized in dealings in foreign currency since its founding in 1833.

This was a time of extraordinary English domination of world commerce. England mined more than half the world's coal, and her output of pig iron was greater than that of the rest of the world combined. She produced three-quarters of the world's cotton cloth. Her foreign trade was valued at £700,000,000 annually, twice that of her leading competitors, the United States and Germany. Her overseas empire was the greatest in world history and still expanding, until ultimately it accounted for almost a quarter of the earth's surface and a third of her population.

Thus it was only natural that foreign business concerns of all sorts made London their financial center, and the London banks thrived. Henry Fowler and his bank profited from the general economic trends, but their emphasis on foreign-currency transactions brought them additional business as well. Thus, when England and France had declared war on Russia two months previously, in March, 1854, the firm of Huddleston & Bradford was designated to arrange for the payment of British troops fighting the Crimean campaign. It was precisely such a consignment of gold for troop payments that had been the object of a recent attempted theft.

"A trivial endeavor," Fowler declared, conscious he was speaking on behalf of the bank. The other men in the room, smoking cigars and drinking brandy, were substantial gentlemen who knew other substantial gentlemen. Mr. Fowler felt obliged to put down any suspicion of the bank's inadequacy in the strongest possible terms. "Yes, indeed," he said, "trivial and amateurish. There was not the slightest chance of success."

"The villain expired?" asked Mr. Pierce, seated opposite him, puffing his cigar.

"Quite," Mr. Fowler said. "The railway guard threw him from the train at a goodly speed. The shock must have killed him instantly." And he added, "Poor devil."

"Has he been identified?"

"Oh, I shouldn't think so," Fowler said. "The manner of his departure was such that his features were considerably—ah, disarrayed. At one time it was said he was named Jack Perkins, but one doesn't know. The police have taken no great interest in the matter, as is, I think, only wise. The whole manner of the robbery speaks of the rankest amateurism. It could never have succeeded."

"I suppose," Pierce said, "that the bank must take considerable precautions."

"My dear fellow," Fowler said, "considerable precautions indeed! I assure you, one doesn't transport twelve thousand pounds in bullion to France each month without the most extensive safeguards."

"So the blackguard was after the Crimean payments?" asked another gentleman, Mr. Harrison Bendix. Bendix was a well-known opponent of the Crimean campaign, and Fowler had no wish to engage in political disputes at this late hour.

"Apparently so," he said shortly, and was relieved when Pierce spoke again.

"We should all be curious to know the nature of your precautions," he said. "Or is that a secret of the firm?"

"No secret at all," Fowler said, taking the opportunity to withdraw his gold watch from the pocket of his waistcoat, flick open the cover, and glance at the dial. It was past eleven; he should retire; only the necessity to uphold the bank's reputation kept him there. "In point of fact, the precautions are of my own devising. And if I may say so, I invite you to point out any weakness in the established plan." He glanced from one face to the next as he talked.

"Each gold bullion shipment is loaded within the confines of the bank itself, which I hardly need mention is wholly impregnable. The bullion is placed in a number of ironbound strongboxes, which are then sealed. A sensible man might regard this as protection enough, but of course we go much further." He paused to sip his brandy.

"Now, then. The sealed strongboxes are taken by armed guard to the railway station. The convoy follows no established route, nor any established timetable; it keeps to populous thoroughfares, and thus there is no chance that it may be waylaid on the road to the station. Never do we employ fewer than ten guards, all trusted and longstanding servants of the firm, and all heavily armed.

"Now, then. At the station, the strongboxes are loaded into the luggage van of the Folkestone railway, where we place them into two of the latest Chubb safes."

"Indeed, Chubb safes?" Pierce said, raising an eyebrow. Chubb manufactured the finest safes in the world, and was universally recognized for skill and workmanship.

"Nor are these the ordinary line of Chubb safes," Fowler continued, "for they have been specially built to the bank's specifications. Gentlemen, they are on all sides constructed of one-quarter-inch tempered steel, and the doors are hung with interior hinges which offer no external purchase for tampering. Why, the very weight of these safes is an impediment to theft, for they each weigh in excess of two hundred and fifty pounds."

"Most impressive," Pierce said.

"So much so," Fowler said, "that one might in good conscience consider this to be adequate safeguard for the bullion shipment. And yet we have added still further refinements. Each of the safes is fitted with not one but two locks, requiring two keys."

"Two keys? How ingenious."

"Not only that," Fowler said, "but each of the four keys—two to each safe—is individually protected. Two are stored in the railway office itself. A third is in the custody of the bank's senior partner, Mr. Trent, whom some of you may know to be a most reliable gentleman. I confess I do not know precisely where Mr. Trent has sequestered his key. But I know of the fourth key, for I myself am entrusted with guarding it."

"How extraordinary," Pierce said. "A considerable responsibility, I should think."

"I must admit I felt a certain need for invention in the matter," Fowler admitted, and then he lapsed into a dramatic pause.

It was Mr. Wyndham, a bit stiff with drink, who finally spoke up. "Well, damn it all, Henry, will you tell us where you have hidden your bloody key?"

Mr. Fowler took no offense, but smiled benignly. He was not a serious drinking man himself, and he viewed the foibles of those who overindulged with a certain modest satisfaction. "I keep it," he said, "about my neck." And he patted his starched shirt front with a flat hand. "I wear it at all times, even while bathing—indeed, even in my sleep. It is never off my person." He smiled broadly. "So, gentlemen, you see that the crude attempt of a mere child from the dangerous classes can hardly be of concern to Huddleston & Bradford, for the little ruffian had no more chance of stealing that bullion than I have of—well, of flying to the moon."

Here Mr. Fowler allowed himself a chuckle at the absurdity of it all. "Now, then," he said, "can you discern any flaw in our arrangements?"

"None whatsoever," said Mr. Bendix coldly.

But Mr. Pierce was warmer. "I must congratulate you, Henry," he said. "It is really quite the most ingenious strategy I have ever heard for protecting a consignment of valuables."

"I rather think so myself," Mr. Fowler said.

Soon thereafter, Mr. Fowler took his leave, arising with the comment that if he were not soon home to his wife, she should think him dallying with a judy—"and I should hate to suffer the pains of chastisement without the antecedent reward." His comment drew laughter from the assembled gentlemen; it was, he thought, just the right note on which to depart. Gentlemen wanted their bankers prudent but not prudish; it was a fine line.

"I shall see you out," Pierce said, also rising.

Chapter 5

The Railway Office

England's railways grew at such a phenomenal rate that the city of London was overwhelmed, and never managed to build a central station. Instead, each of the lines, built by private firms, ran their tracks as far into London as they could manage, and then erected a terminus. But in the mid-century this pattern was coming under attack. The dislocation of poor people, whose dwellings were demolished to make way for the incoming lines, was one argument; another focused on the inconvenience to travelers forced to cross London by coach to make connections from one station to another in order to continue their journey.

In 1846, Charles Pearson proposed, and drew plans for, an enormous Central Railway Terminus to be located at Ludgate Hill, but the idea was never adopted. Instead, after the construction of several stations—the most recent being Victoria Station and King's Cross, in 1851—there was a moratorium on further construction because of the fury of public debate.

Eventually, the concept of a central London terminus was completely abandoned, and new outlying stations were built. When the last, Marylebone Station was finished in 1899, London had fifteen railway terminals, more than twice that of any other major city in Europe; and the bewildering array of lines and schedules was apparently never mastered by any Londoner except Sherlock Holmes, who knew it all by heart.

The mid-century halt in construction left several of the new lines at a disadvantage, and one of these was the South Eastern Railway, which ran from London to the coastal town of Folkestone, some eighty miles away. The South Eastern had no access to central London until 1851, when the London Bridge Terminus was rebuilt.

Located on the south shore of the Thames River near its namesake, London Bridge was the oldest railway station in the city. It was originally constructed in 1836 by the London & Greenwich Railway. Never popular, the station was attacked as "inferior in design and conception" to such later stations as Paddington and King's Cross. Yet when the station was rebuilt in 1851, the *Illustrated London News* recalled that the old station had been "remarkable for the neatness, artistic character, and reality of its *façade*. We regret, therefore, that this has disappeared, to make room, apparently, for one of less merit."

This is precisely the kind of critical turnabout that has always frustrated and infuriated architects. No less a figure than Sir Christopher Wren, writing two hundred years earlier, complained that "the peoples of London may despise some eyesore until it is demolished, whereupon by magick the replacement is deemed inferior to the former edifice, now eulogized in high and glowing reference."

Yet one must admit that the new London Bridge Terminus was most unsatisfactory. Victorians regarded the train stations as the "cathedrals of the age"; they expected them to blend the highest principles of aesthetics and technological achievement, and many stations fulfill that expectation with their high, arching, elegant glass vaults. But the new London Bridge Station was depressing in every way. An L-shaped two-story structure, it had a flat and utilitarian appearance, with a row of dreary shops under an arcade to the left, and the main station straight ahead, unadorned except for a clock mounted on the roof. Most serious, its interior floor plan—the focus of most earlier criticism—remained wholly unaltered.

It was during the reconstruction of the station that the South Eastern Railway arranged to use the London Bridge Terminus as the starting point for its routes to the coast. This was done on a leasing arrangement; South Eastern leased tracks, platforms, and office space from the London & Greenwich line, whose owners were not disposed to give South Eastern any better facilities than necessary.

The traffic supervisor's offices consisted of four rooms in a remote section of the terminal—two rooms for clerks, one storage area for valuable checked items, and a larger office for the supervisor himself. All the rooms had glass frontings. The whole suite was located on the second floor of the terminus and accessible only by an ironwork staircase leading up from the station platform. Anyone climbing or descending the stairs would be in plain view of the office workers, as well as all the passengers, footmen, and guards on the platforms below.

The traffic supervisor was named McPherson. He was an elderly Scotsman who kept a close eye on his clerks, seeing to it that they did no daydreaming out the window. Thus no one in the office noticed when, in early July, 1854, two travelers took up a position on a bench on the platform, and remained there the entire day, frequently consulting their watches, as if impatient for their journey to begin. Nor did anyone notice when the same two gentlemen returned the following week, and again spent a day on the same bench, watching the activity in the station while they awaited their train, and frequently checking their pocketwatches.

In fact, Pierce and Agar were not employing pocketwatches, but rather stopwatches. Pierce had an elegant one, a chronograph with two stopwatch faces, with a case of 18-karat gold. It was considered a marvel of the latest engineering, sold for racing and other purposes. But he held it cupped in his hand, and it attracted no notice.

After the second day of watching the routine of the office clerks, the changes of the railway guards, the arrival and departure of visitors to the office, and other matters of importance to them, Agar finally looked up the iron staircase to the office and announced, "It's bloody murder. She's too wide open. What's your pogue up there, anyway?"

"Two keys."

"What two keys is that?"

"Two keys I happen to want," Pierce said.

Agar squinted up at the offices. If he was disappointed in Pierce's answer he gave no indication. "Well," he said, in a professional tone, "if it's two bettys you want, I reckon they are in that storage room"—he nodded, not daring to point a finger—"just past the space for the clerks. You see the cupboard?"

Pierce nodded. Through the glass fronting, he could see all the office. In the storage area was a shallow, wall-mounted lime green cupboard. It looked like the sort of place keys might be stored. "I see it."

"There's my money, on that cupboard. Now you'll cool she has a lock on her, but that will give us no great trouble. Cheap lock."

"What about the front door?" Pierce said, shifting his gaze. Not only was the cupboard inside locked, but the door to the suite of offices—a frosted door, with SER stenciled on it, and underneath, TRAFFIC SUPERVISOR DIVISION—had a large brass lock above the knob.

"Appearances," Agar snorted. "She'll crack open with any cheap twirl to tickle her innards. I could open her with a ragged fingernail. We've no problems there. The problem is the bloody crowds."

Pierce nodded, but said nothing. This was essentially Agar's operation, and he would have to figure it out. "The pogue is two keys, you say?"

"Yes," Pierce said. "Two keys."

"Two keys is four waxes. Four waxes is nigh on a minute, to do it proper. But that doesn't count cracking the outside, or the inside cabinet. That's more time again." Agar looked around at the crowded platform, and the clerks in the office. "Bloody flummet to try and crack her by day," he said. "Too many people about."

"Night?"

"Aye, at night, when she's empty, and a proper deadlurk. I think the night is best."

"At night, the crushers make rounds," Pierce reminded him. They had already learned that during the evening, when the station was deserted, the policemen patrolled it at four- or five-minute intervals throughout the night. "Will you have time?"

Agar frowned, and squinted up at the office. "No," he said finally. "Unless . . ."

"Yes?"

"Unless the offices were already open. Then I can make my entrance neat as you please, and I do the waxes quicklike, and I'm gone in less than two minutes flat."

"But the offices will be locked," Pierce said.

"I'm thinking of a snakesman," Agar said, and he nodded to the supervisor's office.

Pierce looked up. The supervisor's office had a broad glass window; through it, he could see Mr. McPherson, in his shirtsleeves, with white hair and a green shade over his forehead. And behind McPherson was a window for ventilation, a window approximately a foot square. "I see it," Pierce said. And he added, "Damn small."

"A proper snakesman can make it through," Agar said. A snakesman was a child adept at wriggling through small spaces. Usually he was a former chimney sweep's apprentice. "And once he's in the office, he unlocks the cupboard, and he unlocks the door from the inside, and he sets it all up proper for me. That will make this job a bone lay, and no mistake," he said, nodding in satisfaction.

"If there's a snakesman."

"Aye."

"And he must be the devil's own," Pierce said, looking again at the window, "if we are to break that drum. Who's the best?"

"The best?" Agar said, looking surprised. "The best is Clean Willy, but he's in."

"Where's he in?"

"Newgate Prison, and there's no escaping that. He'll do his days on the cockchafer, and be a good lad, and wait for his ticket-of-leave if it comes. But there's no escape. Not from Newgate."

"Perhaps Clean Willy can find a way."

"Nobody can find a way," Agar said heavily. "It's been tried before."

"I'll get a word to Willy," Pierce said, "and we shall see."

Agar nodded. "I'll hope," he said, "but not too excessive."

The two men resumed watching the offices. Pierce stared at the storage room of the offices, at the little cupboard mounted on the wall. It occurred to him that he had never seen it opened. He had a thought: what if there were more keys—perhaps dozens of keys—in that little closet? How would Agar know which ones to copy?

"Here comes the escop," Agar said.

Pierce looked, and saw that the police constable was making his rounds. He flicked his chronometer: seven minutes forty-seven seconds since the last circuit. But the constable's routine would be more rapid at night.

"You see a lurk?" Pierce said.

Agar nodded to a baggage stand in a corner, not more than a dozen paces from the staircase. "There'd do."

"Well enough," Pierce said.

The two men remained seated until seven o'clock, when the clerks left the office to return home. At seven-twenty, the supervisor departed, locking the outside door after him. Agar had a look at the key, from a distance.

"What kind of a key?" Pierce asked.

"Cheap twirl will manage," Agar said.

The two men remained another hour, until it became inconvenient for them to stay in the station. The last train had departed, and they were now too conspicuous. They remained just long enough to clock the constable on night duty as he made his rounds of the station. The constable passed the traffic manager's office once every five minutes and three seconds.

Pierce snapped the button on his chronometer and glanced at the second hand. "Five and three," he said.

"Dub lay," Agar said.

"Can you do it?"

"Of course I can do it," Agar said. "I can get a judy preggers in less—a dub lay is all I said. Five and three?"

"I can light a cigar faster," Pierce reminded him.

"I can do it," Agar said firmly, "if I have a snakesman such like Clean Willy."

The two men left the railway station. As they stepped into the fading twilight, Pierce signaled his cab. The cabby with a scar across his forehead whipped up his horse and clattered toward the station entrance.

"When do we knock it over?" Agar said.

Pierce gave him a gold guinea. "When I inform you," he said. And then he got into the cab and rode off into the deepening night darkness.

Chapter 6

The Problem and the Solution

By the middle of July, 1854, Edward Pierce knew the location of three of the four keys he needed to rob the safes. Two keys were in the green cupboard of the traffic supervisor's office of the South Eastern Railway. A third hung around the neck of Henry Fowler. To Pierce, these three keys presented no major problem.

There was, of course, the question of opportune timing in making a clandestine break to obtain a wax impression. There was also the problem of finding a good snakesman to aid in the break at the railway offices. But these were all easily surmountable obstacles.

The real difficulty centered around the fourth key. Pierce knew that the fourth key was in the possession of the bank's senior partner, Mr. Trent, but he did not know *where*—and this lack of knowledge represented a formidable challenge indeed, and one that occupied his attention for the next four months.

A few words of explanation may be useful here. In 1854, Alfred Nobel was just beginning his career; the Swedish chemist would not discover dynamite for another decade, and the availability of nitroglycerin "soup" lay still further in the future. Thus, in the mid-nineteenth century, any decently constructed metal safe represented a genuine barrier to theft.

This truth was so widely acknowledged that safe manufacturers devoted most of their energies to the problem of making safes fireproof, since loss of money and documents through incineration was a much more serious hazard than loss through theft. During this period, a variety of patents were issued for ferromanganese, clay, marble dust, and plaster of Paris as fireproof linings for safes.

A thief confronted with a safe had three options. The first was to steal the whole safe outright, carrying it off to break open at his leisure. This was impossible if the safe was of any size or weight, and manufacturers were careful to employ the heaviest and most unwieldy construction materials to discourage this maneuver.

Alternatively, a thief could employ a "petter-cutter," a drill that clamped to the keyhole of the safe and permitted a hole to be bored over the lock. Through this hole, the lock mechanism could be manipulated and the lock opened. But the petter-cutter was a specialist's tool; it was noisy, slow, and uncertain; and it was expensive to purchase and bulky to carry on a job.

The third choice was to look at the safe and give up. This was the most common outcome of events. In another twenty years, the safe would be transformed from an impregnable obstacle to a mere irritant in the minds of burglars, but for the moment it was virtually unbeatable.

Unless, that is, one had a key to the safe. Combination locks had not yet been invented; all locks were operated by key, and the most reliable way to break a safe was to come prepared with a previously obtained key. This truth lies behind the nineteenth-century criminal's preoccupation with keys. Victorian crime literature, official and popular, often seems obsessed with keys, as if nothing else mattered. But in those days, as the master safe-cracker Neddy Sykes said in his trial in 1848, "The key is everything in the lay, the problem and the solution."

Thus it was Edward Pierce's unquestioned assumption in planning the train robbery that he must first obtain copies of all the necessary keys. And he must do this by gaining access to the keys themselves, for although there was a new method of using wax "blanks" and inserting them into the locks of the actual safes, this technique was undependable. Safes of the period were usually left unguarded for this reason.

The true criminal focus was upon the keys to the safe, wherever they might be. The copying process presented no difficulty: wax impressions of the key could be made in a few moments. And any premises containing a key could be cracked with relative ease.

But, if one stops to think of it, a key is really rather small. It can be concealed in the most unlikely places; it can be hidden almost anywhere on a person's body, or in a room. Particularly a Victorian room, where even so ordinary an item of furniture as a wastebasket was likely to be covered in cloth, layers of fringes, and decorative rings of tassels.

We forget how extraordinarily cluttered Victorian rooms were. Innumerable hiding places were provided by the prevailing décor of the period. Furthermore, the Victorians themselves adored secret compartments and concealed spaces; a mid-century writing desk was advertised as "containing 110 compartments, including many most artfully concealed from detection." Even the ornate hearths, found in every room of a house, offered dozens of places to hide an object as small as a key.

Thus, in the mid-Victorian period, information about the location of a key was almost as useful as an actual copy of the key itself. A thief seeking a wax impression might break into a house if he knew exactly where the key was hidden, or even if he knew in which room it was hidden. But if he did not know where in the house it was, the difficulty of making a thorough search—silently, in a house full of residents and servants, using a single shaded lantern that threw only a "bull's-eye" spot of light—was so great as to be not worth the attempt in the first instance.

Therefore, Pierce directed his attention to discovering where Mr. Edgar Trent, senior partner of the firm of Huddleston & Bradford, kept his key.

The first question was whether Mr. Trent kept his key in the bank. Junior clerks of Huddleston & Bradford took their dinner at one o'clock at a pub called the Horse and Rider, across the street from the firm. This was a smallish establishment, crowded and warm at the noon dinner hour. Pierce struck up an acquaintance with one of the clerks, a young man named Rivers.

Normally, the servants and junior clerks of the bank were wary of casual acquaintances, for one never knew when one was talking to a criminal out of twig; but Rivers was relaxed, in the knowledge that the bank was impregnable to burglary—and recognizing, perhaps, that he had a deal of resentment toward the source of his employment.

In this regard, one may profitably record the revised "Rules for Office Staff" posted by Mr. Trent in early 1854. These were as follows:

1. Godliness, cleanliness and punctuality are the necessities of a good business.
2. The firm has reduced the working day to the hours from 8:30 a.m. to 7 p.m.
3. Daily prayers will be held each morning in the main office. The clerical staff will be present.
4. Clothing will be of a sober nature. The clerical staff will not disport themselves in raiment of bright color.
5. A stove is provided for the benefit of the clerical staff. It is recommended that each member of the clerical staff bring 4 lbs. of coal each day during cold weather.
6. No member of the clerical staff may leave the room without permission from Mr. Roberts. The calls of nature are permitted and clerical staff may use the garden beyond the second gate. This area must be kept clean in good order.

7. No talking is allowed during business hours.
8. The craving of tobacco, wines or spirits is a human weakness, and as such is forbidden to the clerical staff.
9. Members of the clerical staff will provide their own pens.
10. The managers of the firm will expect a great rise in the output of work to compensate for these near Utopian conditions.

However Utopian, the working conditions of Huddleston & Bradford led the clerk Rivers to speak freely about Mr. Trent. And with less enthusiasm than one might expect for a Utopian employer.

"Bit of a stiff, he is," Rivers said. "Snapping his watch at eight-thirty sharp, and checking all to see they are at their places, no excuses. God help the man whose omnibus is late in the traffic of the rush."

"Demands his routine, does he?"

"With a vengeance, he does. He's a stiff one—the job must be done, and that's all he cares for. He's getting on in years," Rivers said. "And vain, too: grew whiskers longer than yours, he did, on account of the fact he's losing the hair up top."

During this period, there was considerable debate about the propriety of whiskers on gentlemen. It was a new fashion, and opinion was divided on its benefits. Similarly, there was a new fashion in smoking, called cigarettes, just introduced, but the most conservative men did not smoke—certainly not in public, or even at home. And the most conservative men were clean-shaven.

"He has this brush, I hear," Rivers went on. "Dr. Scott's electric hairbrush, comes from Paris. You know how dear it is? Twelve shillings sixpence, that's what it is."

Rivers would find this expensive: he was paid twelve shillings a week.

"What's it do?" Pierce inquired.

"Cures headaches, dandruff, and baldness, too," Rivers said, "or so it's claimed. Queer little brush. He locks himself into his office and brushes once an hour, punctual." Here Rivers laughed at the foibles of his employer.

"He must have a large office."

"Aye, large and comfortable, too. He's an important man, Mr. Trent is."

"Keeps it tidy?"

"Aye, the sweeper's in every night, dusting and arranging just so, and every night as he leaves, Mr. Trent says to the sweeper, 'A place for everything, and everything in its place,' and then he leaves, seven o'clock punctual."

Pierce did not recall the rest of the conversation, for it was of no interest to him. He already knew what he wanted—that Trent did not keep the key in his office. If he did, he would never leave the place to be cleaned in his absence, for sweepers were notoriously easy to bribe, and to the casual eye there was little difference between a thorough cleaning and a thorough search.

But even if the key was not in the office, it might still be kept in the bank. Mr. Trent might choose to lock it in one of the vaults. To determine if this was so, Pierce could strike up a conversation with a different clerk, but he was anxious to avoid this. Instead, he chose another method.

Chapter 7

The Swell

Teddy Burke, twenty-four, was working the Strand at two in the afternoon, the most fashionable hour. Like the other gentlemen, Teddy Burke was decked out, wearing a high hat, a dark frock coat, narrow trousers, and a dark silk choker. This outfit had cost him a pretty, but it was essential to his business, for Teddy Burke was one of the swellest of the swell mobsmen.

In the throng of gentlemen and ladies who browsed among the elegant shops of this thoroughfare, which Disraeli called "the first street in Europe," no one would notice that Teddy Burke was not alone. In fact, he was working his usual operation, with himself as dipper, a stickman at his side, and two stalls front and back—altogether, four men, each as well-dressed as the next. These four slipped through the crowd, attracting no attention. There was plenty of diversion.

On this fine early summer day, the air was warm and redolent of horse dung, despite the busy working of a dozen street-urchin sweepers. There was heavy traffic of carts, drays, brightly lettered rattling omnibuses, four-wheel and hansom cabs, and from time to time an elegant chariot rode past, with a uniformed coachman in front and liveried servants standing behind. Ragged children darted among the traffic and turned cartwheels under the horses' hoofs for the amusement of the crowd, some of whom threw a few coppers in their direction.

Teddy Burke was oblivious to the excitement, and to the rich array of goods on display in the shopwindows. His attention was wholly fixed upon the quarry, a fine lady wearing a heavy flounced crinoline skirt of deep purple. In a few moments he would dip her as she walked along the street.

His gang was in formation. One stall had taken up a position three paces ahead; another was five paces back. True to their title, the stalls would create disorder and confusion should anything go wrong with the intended dip.

The quarry was moving, but that did not worry Teddy Burke. He planned to work her on the fly, the most difficult kind of dip, as she moved from one shop to the next.

"Right, here we go," he said, and the stickman moved alongside him. It was the stickman's job to take the pogue once Teddy had snaffled it, thus leaving Teddy clean, should there be any hue and cry and a constable to stop him.

Together with the stickman, he moved so close to the woman he could smell her perfume. He was moving along her right side, for a woman's dress had only one pocket, and that was on the right.

Teddy carried an overcoat draped across his left arm. A sensible person might have asked why a gentleman would carry an overcoat on such a warm day; but the coat looked new, and he could have conceivably just picked it up from a fitting at one of the nearby shops. In any case, the overcoat concealed the movement of his right arm across his body to the woman's skirt. He fanned the dress delicately, to determine if a purse was there. His fingers touched it; he took a deep breath, praying that the coins would not clink, and lifted it out of the pocket.

Immediately he eased away from the woman, shifted his overcoat to his other arm, and in the course of that movement passed the purse to the stickman. The stickman drifted off. Ahead and behind, the stalls moved out in different directions. Only Teddy Burke, now clean, continued to walk along the Strand, pausing before a shop that displayed cut-glass and crystal decanters imported from France.

A tall gent with a red beard was admiring the wares in the window. He did not look at Teddy Burke. "Nice pull," he said.

Teddy Burke blinked.

The speaker was too well-dressed, too square-rigged, to be a plainclothes crusher, and he certainly wasn't a nose, or informer. Teddy Burke said carefully, "Are you addressing me, sir?"

"Yes," the man said. "I said that was a very nice pull. You tool her off?"

Teddy Burke was profoundly insulted. A tool was a wire hook that inferior dippers employed to snare a purse if their fingers were too shaky for the job. "Beg your pardon, sir. I don't know your meaning, sir."

"I think you do, well enough," the man said. "Shall we walk awhile?"

Teddy Burke shrugged and fell into step alongside the stranger. After all, he was clean; he had nothing to fear. "Lovely day," he said.

The stranger did not answer. They walked for some minutes in silence. "Do you think you can be less effective?" the man asked after a time.

"How do you mean, sir?"

"I mean," the man said, "can you buzz a customer and come out dry?"

"On purpose?" Teddy Burke laughed. "It happens often enough without trying, I can tell you that."

"There's five quid for you, if you can prove yourself a prize bungler."

Teddy Burke's eyes narrowed. There were plenty of magsmen about, sharp con men who often employed an unwitting accomplice, setting him up to take a fall in some elaborate scheme. Teddy Burke was nobody's fool. "Five quid's no great matter."

"Ten," the man said, in a weary voice.

"I have to think of me boys."

"No," the man said, "this is you, alone."

"What's the lay, then?" Teddy Burke said.

"Lots of bustle, a ruck touch, just enough to set the quarry to worry, make him pat his pockets."

"And you want me to come up dry?"

"Dry as dust," the man said.

"Who's the quarry, then?" Teddy Burke said.

"A gent named Trent. You'll touch him with a bungler's dip in front of his offices, just a roughing-up, like."

"Where's the office, then?"

"Huddleston & Bradford Bank."

Teddy Burke whistled. "Westminster. Sticky, that is. There's enough crushers about to make a bloody army."

"But you'll be dry. All you've to do is worry him."

Teddy Burke walked a few moments, looking this way and that, taking the air and thinking things over. "When will it be, then?"

"Tomorrow morning. Eight o'clock sharp."

"All right."

The red-bearded gentleman gave him a five-pound note, and informed him he would get the rest when the job was done.

"What's it all about, then?" Teddy Burke asked.

"Personal matter," the man replied, and slipped away into the crowd.

Chapter 8

The Holy Land

Between 1801 and 1851, London tripled in size. With a population of two and a half million, it was by far the largest city in the world, and every foreign observer was astonished at its dimensions. Nathaniel Hawthorne was speechless; Henry James was fascinated and appalled at its "horrible numerosity"; Dostoevsky found it "as vast as an ocean . . . a Biblical sight, some prophecy out of the Apocalypse being fulfilled before your very eyes."

And yet London continued to grow. At the mid-century, four thousand new dwellings were under construction at any one time, and the city was literally exploding outward. Already, the now familiar pattern of expansion was termed "the flight to the suburbs." Outlying areas that at the turn of the century had been villages and hamlets—Marylebone, Islington, Camden, St. John's Wood, and Bethnal Green—were thoroughly built up, and the newly affluent middle classes were deserting the central city for these areas, where the air was better, the noise less bothersome, and the atmosphere in general more pleasant and "countrified."

Of course, some older sections of London retained a character of great elegance and wealth, but these were often cheek by jowl with the most dismal and shocking slums. The proximity of great riches and profound squalor also impressed foreign observers, particularly since the slums, or rookeries, were refuges and breeding places for "the criminal class." There were sections of London where a thief might rob a mansion and literally cross a street to disappear into a tangled maze of alleyways and dilapidated buildings crammed with humanity and so dangerous that even an armed policeman did not dare pursue the culprit.

The genesis of slums was poorly understood at the time; indeed, the very term "slums" did not become widely accepted until 1890. But in a vague way the now familiar pattern was recognized: a region of the city would be cut off from circulation by newly constructed thoroughfares that bypassed it; businesses would depart; disagreeable industries would move in, creating local noise and air pollution and further reducing the attractiveness of the area; ultimately, no one with the means to live elsewhere would choose to reside in such a place, and the region would become decrepit, badly maintained, and overpopulated by the lowest classes.

Then, as now, these slums existed in part because they were profitable for landlords. A lodging house of eight rooms might take on a hundred boarders, each paying a shilling or two a week to live in "hugger-mugger promiscuity," sleeping with as many as twenty members of the same or opposite sex in the same room. (Perhaps the most bizarre example of lodgings of the period was the famous waterfront sailors' "penny hangs." Here a drunken seaman slept the night for a penny, draping himself across chest-high ropes, and hanging like clothes on a line.)

While some proprietors of lodging houses, or netherskens, lived in the area—and often accepted stolen goods in lieu of rent—many owners were substantial citizens, landlords *in absentia* who employed a tough deputy to collect the rents and keep some semblance of order.

During this period there were several notorious rookeries, at Seven Dials, Rosemary Lane, Jacob's Island, and Ratcliffe Highway, but none was more famous than the six acres in central London that comprised the rookery of St. Giles, called "the Holy Land." Located near the theatre district of Leicester Square, the prostitute center of the Haymarket, and the fashionable shops of Regent Street, the St. Giles rookery was strategically located for any criminal who wanted to "go to ground."

Contemporary accounts describe the Holy Land as "a dense mass of houses so old they only seem not to fall, through which narrow and tortuous lanes curve and wind. There is no privacy here, and whoever ventures in this region finds the streets—by courtesy so called—thronged with loiterers, and sees, through half-glazed windows, rooms crowded to suffocation." There are references to "the stagnant gutters . . . the filth choking up dark passages . . . the walls of bleached soot, and doors falling from their hinges . . . and children swarming everywhere, relieving themselves as they please."

Such a squalid, malodorous and dangerous tenement was no place for a gentleman, particularly after nightfall on a foggy summer evening. Yet in late July, 1854, a red-bearded man in fashionable attire walked fearlessly through the smoke-filled, cramped and narrow lanes. The loiterers and vagrants watching him no doubt observed that his silver-headed cane looked ominously heavy, and might conceal a blade. There was also a bulge about the trousers that implied a barker tucked in the waistband. And the very boldness of such a foolhardy incursion probably intimidated many of those who might be tempted to waylay him.

Pierce himself later said, "It is the demeanor which is respected among these people. They know the look of fear, and likewise its absence, and any man who is not afraid makes them afraid in turn."

Pierce went from street to stinking street, inquiring after a certain woman. Finally he found a lounging soak who knew her.

"It's Maggie you want? Little Maggie?" the man asked, leaning against a yellow gas lamppost, his face deep shadows in the fog.

"She's a judy, Clean Willy's doll."

"I know of her. Pinches laundry, doesn't she? Aye, she does a bit of snow, I'm sure of it." Here the man paused significantly, squinting.

Pierce gave him a coin. "Where shall I find her?"

"First passing up, first door to yer right," the man said.

Pierce continued on.

"But it's no use your bothering," the man called after him. "Willy's in the stir now—in Newgate, no less—and he has only the cockchafer on his mind."

Pierce did not look back. He walked down the street, passing vague shadows in the fog, and here and there a woman whose clothing glowed in the night—match-stick dippers with patches of phosphorous on their garments. Dogs barked; children cried; whispers and groans and laughter were conveyed to him through the fog. Finally he arrived at the nethersken, with its bright rectangle of yellow light at the entrance, shining on a crudely hand-painted sign which read:

LOGINS FOR
THRAVELERS

Pierce glanced at the sign, then entered the building, pushing his way past the throng of dirty, ragged children clustered about the stairs; he cuffed one briskly, to show them there was to be no plucking at his pockets. He climbed the creaking stairs to the second floor, and asked after the woman named Maggie. He was told she was in the kitchen, and so he descended again, to the basement.

The kitchen was the center of every lodging house, and at this hour it was a warm and friendly place, a focus of heat and rich smells, while the fog curled gray and cold outside the windows. A half-dozen men stood by the fire, talking and drinking; at a side table, several men and women played cards while others sipped bowls of steaming soup; tucked away in the corners were musical instruments, beggars' crutches, hawkers' baskets, and peddlers' boxes. He found Maggie, a dirty child of twelve, and drew her to one side. He gave her a gold guinea, which she bit. She flashed a half-smile.

"What is it, then, guv?" She looked appraisingly at his fine clothes, a calculating glance far beyond her years. "A bit of a tickle for you?"

Pierce ignored the suggestion. "You dab it up with Clean Willy?"

She shrugged. "I did. Willy's in."

"Newgate?"

"Aye."

"You see him?"

"I do, once and again. I goes as his sister, see."

Pierce pointed to the coin she clutched in her hand. "There's another one of those if you can downy him a message."

For a moment, the girl's eyes glowed with interest. Then they went blank again. "What's the lay?"

"Tell Willy, he should break at the next topping. It's to be Emma Barnes, the murderess. They'll hang her in public for sure. Tell him: break at the topping."

She laughed. It was an odd laugh, harsh and rough. "Willy's in Newgate," she said, "and there's no breaks from Newgate—topping or no."

"Tell him *he* can," Pierce said. "Tell him to go to the house where he first met John Simms, and all will be well enough."

"Are you John Simms?"

"I am a friend," Pierce said. "Tell him the next topping and he's over the side, or he's not Clean Willy."

She shook her head. "How can he break from Newgate?"

"Just tell him," Pierce said, and turned to leave.

At the door to the kitchen, he looked back at her, a skinny child, stoop-shouldered in a ragged second-hand dress spattered with mud, her hair matted and filthy.

"I'll tell," she said, and slipped the gold coin into her shoe. He turned away from her and retraced his steps, leaving the Holy Land. He came out of a narrow alley, turned into Leicester Square, and joined the crowd in front of the Mayberry Theatre, blending in, disappearing.

Chapter 9

The Routine of Mr. Edgar Trent

Respectable London was quiet at night. In the era before the internal combustion engine, the business and financial districts at the center of the town were deserted and silent except for the quiet footsteps of the Metropolitan Police constables making their twenty-minute rounds.

As dawn came, the silence was broken by the crowing of roosters and the mooing of cows, barnyard sounds incongruous in an urban setting. But in those days there was plenty of livestock in the central city, and animal husbandry was still a major London industry—and indeed, during the day, a major source of traffic congestion. It was not uncommon for a fine gentleman to be delayed in his coach by a shepherd with his flock moving through the streets of the city. London was the largest urban concentration in the world at that time, but by modern standards the division between city and country life was blurred.

Blurred, that is, until the Horse Guards clock chimed seven o'clock, and the first of that peculiarly urban phenomenon—commuters—appeared on their way to work, conveyed by "the Marrowbone stage"; that is, on foot. These were the armies of women and girls employed as seamstresses in the sweatshops of West End dress factories, where they worked twelve hours a day for a few shillings a week.

At eight o'clock, the shops along the great thoroughfares took down their shutters; apprentices and assistants dressed the windows in preparation for the day's commerce, setting out what one sarcastic observer called "the innumerable whim-whams and fribble-frabble of fashion."

Between eight and nine o'clock was rush hour, and the streets became crowded with men. Everyone from government clerks to bank cashiers, from stockbrokers to sugar-bakers and soap-boilers, made their way to work on foot, in omnibuses, tandems, dogcarts—altogether a rattling, noisy, thickly jammed traffic of vehicles and drivers who cursed and swore and lashed at their horses.

In the midst of this, the street sweepers began their day's labors. In the ammonia-rich air, they collected the first droppings of horse dung, dashing among the carts and omnibuses. And they were busy: an ordinary London horse, according to Henry Mayhew, deposited six tons of dung on the streets each year, and there were at least a million horses in the city.

Gliding through the midst of this confusion, a few elegant broughams, with gleaming dark polished wood carriages and delicately sprung, lacy-spoked wheels, conveyed their substantial citizens in utter comfort to the day's employment.

Pierce and Agar, crouched on a rooftop overlooking the imposing facade of the Huddleston & Bradford Bank across the way, watched as one such brougham came down the street toward them.

"There he is now," Agar said.

Pierce nodded. "Well, we shall know soon enough." He checked his watch. "Eight-twenty-nine. Punctual, as usual."

Pierce and Agar had been on the rooftop since dawn. They had watched the early arrival of the tellers and clerks; they had seen the traffic in the street and on the pavements grow more brisk and hurried with each passing minute.

Now the brougham pulled up to the door of the bank, and the driver jumped down to open the door. The senior partner of Huddleston & Bradford stepped down to the pavement. Mr. Edgar Trent was near sixty, his beard was gray, and he had a considerable paunch; whether he was balding or not, Pierce could not discern, for a high top hat covered his head.

"He's a fat one, isn't he," Agar said.

"Watch, now," Pierce said.

At the very moment that Mr. Trent stepped to the ground, a well-dressed young man jostled him roughly, muttered a brief apology over his shoulder, and moved on in the rush-hour crowd. Mr. Trent ignored the incident. He walked the few steps forward to the impressive oak doors of the bank.

Then he stopped, halting in mid-stride.

"He's realized," Pierce said.

On the street below, Trent looked after the well-dressed young man, and immediately patted his side coat pocket, feeling for some article. Apparently, what he sought was still in its place; his shoulders dropped in relief, and he continued on into the bank.

The brougham clattered off; the bank doors swung shut.

Pierce grinned and turned to Agar. "Well," he said, "that's that."

"That's what?" Agar said.

"That's what we need to know."

"What do we need to know, then?" Agar said.

"We need to know," Pierce said slowly, "that Mr. Trent brought his key with him today, for this is the day of—" He broke off abruptly. He had not yet informed Agar of the plan, and he saw no reason to do so until the last minute. A man with a tendency to be a soak, like Agar, could loosen his tongue at an unlikely time. But no drunk could split what he did not know.

"The day of what?" Agar persisted.

"The day of reckoning," Pierce said.

"You're a tight one," Agar said. And then he added, "Wasn't that Teddy Burke, trying a pull?"

"Who's Teddy Burke?" Pierce said.

"A swell, works the Strand."

"I wouldn't know," Pierce said, and the two men left the rooftop.

"Cor, you're a tight one," Agar said again. "That *was* Teddy Burke.

Pierce just smiled.

In the coming weeks, Pierce learned a great deal about Mr. Edgar Trent and his daily routine. Mr. Trent was a rather severe and devout gentleman; he rarely drank, never smoked or played at cards. He was the father of five children; his first wife had died in childbirth some years before and his second wife, Emily, was thirty years his junior and an acknowledged beauty, but she was as severe in disposition as her husband.

The Trent family resided at No. 17 Brook Street, Mayfair, in a large Georgian mansion with twenty-three rooms, not including servants' quarters. Altogether, twelve servants were employed: a coach driver, two liverymen, a gardener, a doorman, a butler, a cook and two kitchen assistants, and three maids. There was also a governess for the three youngest children.

The children ranged in age from a four-year-old son to a twenty-nine-year-old daughter. All lived in the house. The youngest child had a tendency to somnambulation, so that there were often commotions at night that roused the entire household.

Mr. Trent kept two bulldogs, which were walked twice a day, at seven in the morning and at eight-fifteen at night, by the cook's assistants. The dogs were penned in a run at the back of the house, not far from the tradesmen's entrance.

Mr. Trent himself followed a rigid routine. Each day, he arose at 7 A.M., breakfasted at 7:30, and departed for work at 8:10, arriving at 8:29. He invariably lunched at Simpson's at one o'clock, for one hour. He left the bank promptly at 7 P.M., returning home no later than 7:20. Although he was a member of several clubs in town, he rarely frequented them. Mr. Trent and his wife went out of an evening twice in the course of a week; they generally gave a dinner once a week and occasionally a large party. On such evenings, an extra maid and manservant would be laid on, but these people were obtained from adjacent households; they were very reliable and could not be bribed.

The tradesmen who came each day to the side entrance of the house worked the entire street, and they were careful never to associate with a potential thief. For a fruit or vegetable hawker, a "polite street" was not easily come by, and they were all a close-mouthed lot.

A chimney sweep named Marks worked the same area. He was known to inform the police of any approach by a lurker seeking information. The sweep's boy was a simpleton; nothing could be got from him.

The constable patrolling the street, Lewis, made his rounds once every seventeen minutes. The shift changed at midnight; the night man, Howell, made his rounds once every sixteen minutes. Both men were highly reliable, never sick or drunk, and not susceptible to bribes.

The servants were content. None had been recently hired, nor had any been recently discharged; they were all well-treated and loyal to the household, particularly to Mrs. Trent. The coach driver was married to the cook; one of the liverymen was sleeping with one of the upstairs maids; the other two maids were comely and did not, apparently, lack for male companionship—they had found lovers among the serving staff of nearby households.

The Trent family took an annual seaside holiday during the month of August, but they would not do so this year, for Mr. Trent's business obligations were such that he was required to remain in town the whole of the summer. The family occasionally weekended in the country at the home of Mrs. Trent's parents, but during these outings most of the servants remained in the mansion. At no time, it seemed, were there fewer than eight people residing in the house.

All this information Pierce accumulated slowly and carefully, and often at some risk. Apparently he adopted various disguises when he talked with servants in pubs and on the street; he must also have loitered in the neighborhood, observing the patterns of the house, but this was a dangerous practice. He could, of course, hire a number of "crows" to scout the area for him, but the more people he hired, the more likely it was that rumors of an impending burglary of the Trent mansion would get out. In that case, the already formidable problems of cracking the house would be increased. So he did most of the reconnaissance himself, with some help from Agar.

According to his own testimony, by the end of August Pierce was no further ahead than he had been a month before. "The man afforded no purchase," Pierce said, speaking of Trent. "No vices, no weaknesses, no eccentricities, and a wife straight from the pages of a handbook on dutiful attention to the running of a happy household."

Clearly, there was no point in breaking into a twenty-three-room mansion on the off chance of coming upon the hidden key. Pierce had to have more information, and as he continued his surveillance it became evident that this information could be obtained only from Mr. Trent himself, who alone would know the location of the key.

Pierce had failed in every attempt to strike up a personal acquaintance with Mr. Trent. Henry Fowler, who shared with Pierce an occasional gentlemen's evening on the town, had been approached on the subject of Trent, but Fowler had said the man was religious, proper, and rather a bore in conversation; and he added that his wife, though pretty, was equally tedious. (These comments, when brought forward in trial testimony, caused Mr. Fowler considerable embarrassment, but then Mr. Fowler was confronted with much greater embarrassments later.)

Pierce could hardly press for an introduction to such an unappetizing couple. Nor could he approach Trent directly, pretending business with the bank; Henry Fowler would rightly expect that Pierce would bring any business to him. Nor did Pierce know anyone except Fowler who was acquainted with Trent.

In short, Pierce had no gammon to play, and by the first of August he was considering several desperate ploys—such as staging an accident in which he would be run down by a cab in front of the Trent household, or a similar episode in front of the bank. But these were cheap tricks and, to be effective, they would require some degree of genuine injury to Pierce. Understandably, he was not happy at the prospect, and kept postponing the matter.

Then, on the evening of August 3rd, Mr. Trent suddenly changed his established routine. He returned home at his usual time, 7:20, but he did not go indoors. Instead, he went directly to the dog run at the back of the house, and put one of his bulldogs on a leash. Petting the animal elaborately, he climbed back into his waiting carriage and drove off.

When Pierce saw that, he knew he had his man.

Chapter 10

A Made Dog

Not far from Southwark Mint was the livery stable of Jeremy Johnson & Son. It was a smallish establishment, quartering perhaps two dozen horses in three wooden barns, with hay, saddles, bridles, and other apparatus hanging from rafters. A casual visitor to this stable might be surprised to hear, instead of the whinny of horses, the predominant sound of barking, growling, snarling dogs. But the meaning of those sounds was clear enough to frequenters of the place, and no cause for particular comment. Throughout London, there were many reputable establishments that operated a side business of training fighting dogs.

Mr. Jeremy Johnson, Sr., led his red-bearded customer back through the stables. He was a jovial old man with most of his teeth missing. "Bit of an old gummer myself," he said, chuckling. "Doesn't hurt the drinking, though, I'll tell you that." He slapped the hindquarters of a horse to push it out of the way. "Move on, move on," he said, then looked back at Pierce. "Now what is it you'll be wanting?"

"Your best," Pierce said.

"That's what all the gentlemen are wanting," Mr. Johnson said, with a sigh. "None wants else than the best."

"I am very particular."

"Oh, I can see that," Johnson said. "I can see that, indeed. You're seeking a learner, so as to polish him yourself?"

"No," Pierce said, "I want a fully made dog."

"That's dear, you know."

"I know."

"Very dear, very dear," Johnson mumbled, moving back through the stable. He pushed open a creaking door, and they came into a small courtyard at the rear. Here were three wood-boarded circular pits, each perhaps six feet in diameter, and caged dogs on all sides. The dogs yelped and barked as they saw the men.

"Very dear, a made dog," Johnson said. "Takes a proper long training to have a good made dog. Here's how we do. First we gives the dog to a coster, and he jogs the dog day and day again—to toughen him, you know."

"I understand," Pierce said impatiently, "but I—"

"Then," Johnson continued, "then we puts the learner in with an old gummer—or a young gummer, as the case is now. Lost our gummer a fortnight past, so we took this one"—he pointed to a caged dog—"and yanked all the teeth, so he's the gummer now. Very good gummer he is, too. Knows how to worry a learner—very agile, this gummer is."

Pierce looked at the gummer. It was a young and healthy dog, barking vigorously. All its teeth were gone, yet it continued to snarl and pull back its lips menacingly. The sight made Pierce laugh.

"Yes, yes, 'tis a bit of a joke," Johnson said, moving around the enclosure, "but not when you get to this one here. Not here, there's no joking. Here's the finest taste dog in all London, I warrant."

This was a mongrel, larger than a bulldog, and parts of its body had been shaved. Pierce knew the routine: a young dog was first trained in sparring bouts with an old and toothless veteran; then it was put into the pit with a "taste dog," which was expendable but had good spirit. It was in the course of sparring with the taste dog that the learner acquired the final skills to go for the kill. The usual practice was to shave the vulnerable parts of the taste dog, encouraging the learner to attack those areas.

"This taster," Johnson said, "this taster has put the touches on more champions than you can name. You know Mr. Benderby's dog, the one that bested the Manchester killer last month? Well, this taster here trained Mr. Benderby's dog. And also Mr. Starrett's dog, and—oh, a dozen others, all top fighting dogs. Now Mr. Starrett himself, he comes back to me and wants to buy this very taster. Says he wants to have him to worry a badger or two. You know what he offers me? Fifty quid, he offers me. And you know what I say? Not on your life, I say, not fifty quid for this taster."

Johnson shook his head a little sadly.

"Not for badgers, anyhow," he said. "Badgers are no proper worry for any fighting dog. No, no. A proper fighting dog is for your dogs, or, if need be, for your rats." He squinted at Pierce. "You want your dog for ratting? We have special trained ratters," Mr. Johnson said. "A touch less dear, is why I mention it."

"I want your very best made dog."

"And you shall have it, I warrant. Here is the devil's own, right here." Johnson paused before a cage. Inside, Pierce saw a bulldog that weighed about forty pounds. The dog growled but did not move. "See that? He's a confident one. He's had a good mouthful or two, and he's well made. Vicious as ever I saw. Some dogs have the instinct, you know—can't be taught 'em, they just have the instinct to get a good mouthful straightaway. This here one, he's got the instinct."

"How much?" Pierce said.

"Twenty quid."

Pierce hesitated.

"With the studded leash, and the collar and muzzle, all in," Johnson added.

Pierce still waited.

"He'll do you proud, I warrant, very proud."

After a lengthy silence, Pierce said, "I want your *best* dog." He pointed to the cage. "This dog has never fought. He has no scars. I want a trained veteran."

"And you shall have him," Johnson said, not blinking. He moved two cages down. "This one here has the killer instinct, the taste of blood, and quick? Why, quicker than your eye, he is, this one. Took the neck off old Whitington's charger a week past, at the pub tourney—perhaps you was there and saw him."

Pierce said, "How much?"

"Twenty-five quid, all in."

Pierce stared at the animal for a moment, then said, "I want the best dog you have."

"This is the very same, I swear it—the very dog that's best of the lot."

Pierce crossed his arms over his chest and tapped his foot on the ground.

"I swear it, sir, twenty-five quid, a gentleman's fancy and most excellent in all respects."

Pierce just stared at him.

"Well, then," Johnson said, looking away as if embarrassed, "there *is* one more animal, but he's very special. He has the killer instinct, the taste of blood, the quick move, and a tough hide. This way."

He led Pierce out of the enclosed courtyard to another area, where there were three dogs in somewhat larger pens. They were all heavier than the others; Pierce guessed they must weigh fifty pounds, perhaps more. Johnson tapped the middle cage.

"This'un," he said. "This'un turned felon on me," he said. "Thought I'd have to top him off—he was a felon, pure and simple." Johnson rolled up his sleeve to reveal a set of jagged white scars. "This'un did this to me," he said, "when he turned felon. But I brought him back, nursed him, and trained him special, because he has the spirit, see, and the spirit's everything."

"How much?" Pierce said.

Johnson glanced at the scars on his arm. "This'un I was saving—"

"How much?"

"Couldn't let him go for less'n fifty quid, beg pardon."

"I will give you forty."

"Sold," Johnson said quickly. "You'll take 'im now?"

"No," Pierce said. "I'll call for him soon. For the moment, hold him."

"Then you'll be putting a little something down?"

"I will," Pierce said, and gave the man ten pounds. Then he had him pry open the dog's jaws, and he checked the teeth; and then he departed.

"Damn me," Johnson said after he had gone. "Man buys a made dog, then leaves him. What're we up to today?"

Chapter 11

The Destruction of Vermin

Captain Jimmy Shaw, a retired pugilist, ran the most famous of the sporting pubs, the Queen's Head, off Windmill Street. A visitor to that pub on the evening of August 10, 1854, would be greeted by a most peculiar spectacle, for although the pub was notably low-ceilinged, dingy, and cheap, it was filled with all manner of well-dressed gentlemen who rubbed shoulders with hawkers, costers, navvies, and others of the lowest social station. Yet nobody seemed to mind, for everyone shared a state of excited, noisy anticipation. Furthermore, nearly everyone had brought a dog. There were dogs of all sorts: bulldogs, Skye terriers, brown English terriers, and various mongrels. Some nestled in the arms of their owners; others were tied to the legs of tables or to the footrail of the bar. All were the subject of intense discussion and scrutiny: they were hefted into the air to gauge their weight, their limbs were felt for the strength of bones, their jaws opened for a look at the teeth.

A visitor might then observe that the few decorative features of the Queen's Head reflected this same interest in dogs. Studded leather collars hung from the rafters; there were stuffed dogs in dirty glass boxes mounted over the bar; there were prints of dogs by the hearth, including a famous drawing of Tiny, "the wonder dog," a white bulldog whose legendary exploits were known to every man present.

Jimmy Shaw, a burly figure with a broken nose, moved about the room calling, "Give your orders, gentlemen," in a loud voice. At the Queen's Head, even the best gentlemen drank hot gin without complaint. Indeed, no one seemed to notice the tawdry surroundings at all. Nor, for that matter, did anyone seem to mind that most of the dogs were heavily scarred on the face, body, and limbs.

Above the bar, a soot-covered sign read:

EVERY MAN HAS HIS FANCY
RATTING SPORTS IN REALITY

And if people should be uncertain as to the meaning of that sign, their doubts ended at nine o'clock, when Captain Jimmy gave the order to "light up the pit" and the entire assembled company began to file toward the upstairs room, each man carrying his dog, and each man dropping a shilling into the hand of a waiting assistant before ascending the stairs.

The second floor of the Queen's Head was a large room, as low-ceilinged as the ground floor. This room was wholly devoid of furnishings, and dominated by the pit—a circular arena six feet in diameter, enclosed by slat boards four feet high. The floor of the pit was whitewashed, freshly applied each evening.

As the spectators arrived on the second floor, their dogs immediately came alive, jumping in their owners' arms, barking vigorously, and straining on the leashes. Captain Jimmy said sternly, "Now you gentlemen that have fancies—shut 'em up," and there was some attempt to do this, but it was hardly successful, especially when the first cage of rats was brought forth.

At the sight of the rats, the dogs barked and snarled fiercely. Captain Jimmy held the rusty wire cage over his head, waving it in the air; it contained perhaps fifty scampering rats. "Nothing but the finest, gentlemen," he announced. "Every one country born, and not a water-ditch among 'em. Who wants to try a rat?"

By now, fifty or sixty people had crammed into the narrow room. Many leaned over the wooden boards of the pit. There was money in every hand, and lively bargaining. Over the general din, a voice from the back spoke up. "I'll have a try at twenty. Twenty of your best for my fancy."

"Weigh the fancy of Mr. T.," Captain Jimmy said, for he knew the speaker. The assistants rushed up and took the bulldog from the arms of a gray-bearded, balding gentleman. The dog was weighed.

"Twenty-seven pounds!" came the cry, and the dog was returned to its owner.

"That's it, then, gents," Captain Jimmy said. "Twenty-seven pounds is Mr. T.'s fancy dog, and he has called for a try at twenty rats. Shall it be four minutes?"

Mr. T. nodded in agreement.

"Four minutes it is, gentlemen, and you may wager as you see fit. Make room for Mr. T."

The gray-bearded gentleman moved up to the edge of the pit, still cradling his dog in his arms. The animal was spotted black and white, and it snarled at the rats opposite. Mr. T. urged his dog on by making snarling and growling noises himself.

"Let's see them," Mr. T. said.

The assistant opened the cage and reached in to grab the rats with his bare hand. This was important, for it proved that the rats were indeed country animals, and not infected with any disease. The assistant picked out "twenty of the finest" and tossed them down into the pit. The animals scampered around the perimeter, then finally huddled together in one corner, in a furry mass.

"Are we ready?" called Captain Jimmy, brandishing a stopwatch in his hand.

"Ready," said Mr. T., making growling and snarling sounds to his dog.

"Blow on 'em! Blow on 'em!" came the cry from the spectators, and various otherwise quite dignified gentlemen puffed and blew toward the rats, raising the fur and sending them into a frenzy.

"Aaannnddd . . . *go!*" shouted Captain Jimmy, and Mr. T. flung his dog into the pit. Immediately, Mr. T. crouched down until his head was just above the wooden rim, and from this position he urged his dog on with shouted instructions and canine growls.

The dog leapt forward into the mass of rats, striking out at them, snapping at the necks like the true and well-blooded sport that he was. In an instant he had killed three or four.

The betting spectators screamed and yelled no less than the owner, who never took his eyes from the combat. "That's it!" shouted Mr. T. "That's a dead one, drop 'im, now *go!* Grrrrrrr! Good, that's another, drop 'im. *Go!* Grrr-rugh!"

The dog moved quickly from one furry body to the next. Then one rat caught hold of his nose and clung tightly; the dog could not shake the rat free.

"Twister! Twister!" shrieked the crowd.

The dog writhed, got free, and raced after the others. Now there were six rats killed, their bodies lying on the blood-streaked pit floor.

"Two minutes past," called Captain Jimmy.

"Hi, Lover, good Lover," screamed Mr. T. "Go, boy. Grrrrh! That's one, now drop 'im. Go, Lover!"

The dog raced around the arena, pursuing its quarry; the crowd screamed and pounded the wooden slats to keep the animals in a frenzy. At one point Lover had four rats clinging to his face and body, and still he kept going, crunching a fifth in his strong jaws. In the midst of all this furious excitement, no one noticed a red-bearded gentleman of dignified bearing who pushed his way through the crowd until he was standing alongside Mr. T., whose attention remained wholly focused on the dog.

"Three minutes," Captain Jimmy called. There was a groan from several in the crowd. Three minutes gone and only twelve rats dead; those who had bet on Mr. T.'s fancy were going to lose their money.

Mr. T. himself did not seem to hear the time. His eyes never left the dog; he barked and yelped; he twisted his body, writhing with the dog he owned; he snapped his jaws and screamed orders until he was hoarse.

"Time!" shouted Captain Jimmy, waving the stop-watch. The crowd sighed and relaxed. Lover was pulled from the arena; the three remaining rats were deftly scooped up by the assistants.

The ratting match was over; Mr. T. had lost.

"Bloody good try," said the red-bearded man, in consolation.

The paradoxes inherent in Mr. Edgar Trent's behavior at the Queen's Head pub—indeed, in his very presence in such surroundings—require some explanation.

In the first place, a man who was the senior partner of a bank, a devout Christian, and a pillar of the respectable community would never think to associate himself with members of the lower orders. Quite the contrary: Mr. Trent devoted considerable time and energy to keeping these people in their proper place, and he did so with the firm and certain knowledge that he was helping to maintain good social order.

Yet there were a few places in Victorian society where members of all classes mingled freely, and chief among these were sporting events—the prize ring, the turf, and, of course, the baiting sports. All these activities were either disreputable or flatly illegal, and their supporters, derived from every stratum of society, shared a common interest that permitted them to overlook the breakdown of social convention upon such occasions. And if Mr. Trent saw no incongruity in his presence among the lowest street hawkers and costers, it is also true that the hawkers and costers, usually tongue-tied and uneasy in the presence of gentlemen, were equally relaxed at these sporting events, laughing and nudging freely men whom they would not dare to touch under ordinary circumstances.

Their common interest—animal baiting—had been a cherished form of amusement throughout Western Europe since medieval times. But in Victorian England animal sports were dying out rapidly, the victim of legislation and changing public tastes. The baiting of bulls or bears, common at the turn of the century, was now quite rare; cockfighting was found only in rural centers. In London in 1854, only three animal sports remained popular, and all concerned dogs.

Nearly every foreign observer since Elizabethan times has commented on the affection Englishmen lavish upon their dogs, and it is odd that the very creature most dear to English hearts should be the focus of these flagrantly sadistic "sporting events."

Of the three dog sports, dogs set against other dogs was considered the highest "art" of animal sports. This sport was sufficiently widespread that many London criminals made a good living working exclusively as dog thieves, or "fur-pullers." But dogfights were relatively uncommon, since they were ordinarily battles to the death, and a good fighting dog was an expensive article.

Even less common was badger-baiting. Here a badger would be chained in an arena, and a dog or two set loose to worry the animal. The badger's tough hide and sharp bite made the spectacle particularly tense and highly popular, but a scarcity of badgers limited the sport.

Ratting was the most common dog sport, particularly at the mid-century. Although technically illegal, it was conducted for decades with flagrant disregard for the law. Throughout London there were signs reading, "Rats Wanted" and "Rats Bought and Sold"; there was, in fact, a minor industry in ratcatching, with its own specialized rules of the trade. Country rats were most prized, for their fighting vigor and their absence of infection. The more common sewer rats, readily identified by their smell, were timid and their bites more likely to infect a valuable fighting dog. When one recognizes that the owner of a sporting pub with a well-attended rat pit might buy two thousand rats a week—and a good country rat could fetch as much as a shilling—it is not surprising that many individuals made a living as ratcatchers. The most famous was "Black Jack" Hanson, who went about in a hearse-like wagon, offering to rid fashionable mansions of pests for absurdly low rates, so long as he could "take the critters live."

There is no good explanation for why Victorians at all levels of society looked away from the sport of ratting, but they were conveniently blind. Most humane writing of the period deplores and condemns cockfighting—which was already very rare—without mentioning dog sports at all. Nor is there any indication that reputable gentlemen felt any unease at participating in ratting sports; for these gentlemen considered themselves "staunch supporters of the destruction of vermin," and nothing more.

One such staunch supporter, Mr. T., retired to the downstairs rooms of the Queen's Head pub, which was now virtually deserted. Signaling the solitary barman, he called for a glass of gin for himself and some peppermint for his fancy.

Mr. T. was in the process of washing his dog's mouth out with peppermint—to prevent canker—when the red-bearded gentleman came down the stairs and said, "May I join you for a glass?"

"By all means," Mr. T. said, continuing to minister to his dog.

Upstairs, the sound of stomping feet and shouting indicated the beginning of another episode of the destruction of vermin. The red-bearded stranger had to shout over the din. "I perceive you are a gentleman of sporting instinct," he said.

"And unlucky," Mr. T. said, equally loudly. He stroked his dog. "Lover was not at her best this evening. When she is in a state, there is none to match her, but at times she lacks bustle." Mr. T. sighed regretfully. "Tonight was such a one." He ran his hands over the dog's body, probing for deep bites, and wiped the blood of several cuts from his fingers with his handkerchief. "But she came off well enough. My Lover will fight again."

"Indeed," the red-bearded man said, "and I shall wager upon her again when she does."

Mr. T. showed a trace of concern. "Did you lose?"

"A trifle. Ten guineas, it was nothing."

Mr. T. was a conservative man, and well enough off, but not disposed to think of ten guineas as "a trifle." He looked again at his drinking companion, noticing the fine cut of his coat and the excellent white silk of his neckcloth.

"I am pleased you take it so lightly," he said. "Permit me to buy you a glass, as a token of your ill fortune."

"Never," returned the red-bearded man, "for I count it no ill fortune at all. Indeed, I admire a man who may keep a fancy and sport her. I should do so myself, were I not so often abroad on business."

"Oh, yes?" said Mr. T., signaling to the barman for another round.

"Quite," said the stranger. "Why, only the other day, I was offered a most excellently made dog, close upon a felon, with the tastes of a true fighter. I could not make the purchase, for I have no time myself to look after the animal."

"Most unfortunate," said Mr. T. "What was the price asked?"

"Fifty guineas."

"Excellent price."

"Indeed."

The waiter brought more drinks. "I am myself in search of a made dog," Mr. T. said.

"Indeed?"

"Yes," Mr. T. said. "I should like a third to complement my stable, with Lover and Shantung—that is the other dog. But I don't suppose . . ."

The red-bearded gentleman paused discreetly before answering. The training, buying, and selling of fighting dogs was, after all, illegal. "If you wish," Pierce said at last, "I could inquire whether the animal is still available."

"Oh, yes? That would be very good of you. Very good indeed." Mr. T. had a sudden thought. "But were I you, I should buy it myself. After all, while you were abroad, your wife could instruct the servants in the care of the beast."

"I fear," replied the red-bearded man, "that I have devoted too much of my energies these past years to the pursuit of business concerns. I have never married." And then he added, "But of course I should like to."

"Of course," Mr. T. said, with a most peculiar look coming over his face.

Chapter 12

The Problem of Miss Elizabeth Trent

Victorian England was the first society to constantly gather statistics on itself, and generally these figures were a source of unabashed pride. Beginning in 1840, however, one trend worried the leading thinkers of the day: there were increasingly more single women than men. By 1851, the number of single women of marriageable age was reliably put at 2,765,000—and a large proportion of these women were the daughters of the middle and upper classes.

Here was a problem of considerable dimension and gravity. Women of lower stations in life could take jobs as seamstresses, flower girls, field workers, or any of a dozen lowly occupations. These women were of no pressing concern; they were slovenly creatures lacking in education and a discriminating view of the world. A. H. White reports, in tones of astonishment, that he interviewed a young girl who worked as a matchbox maker, who "never went to church or chapel. Never heard of 'England' or 'London' or the 'sea' or 'ships.' Never heard of God. Does not know what He does. Does not know whether it is better to be good or bad."

Obviously, in the face of such massive ignorance, one must simply be grateful that the poor child had discovered some way to survive in society at all. But the problem presented by the daughters of middle-and upper-class households was different. These young ladies possessed education and a taste for genteel living. And they had been raised from birth for no other purpose than to be "perfect wives."

It was terribly important that such women should marry. The failure to marry—spinsterhood—implied a kind of dreadful crippling, for it was universally acknowledged that "a woman's true position was that of administratrix, mainspring, guiding star of the home," and if she was unable to perform this function, she became a sort of pitiful social misfit, an oddity.

The problem was made more acute by the fact that well-born women had few alternatives to wifehood. After all, as one contemporary observer noted, what occupations could they find "without losing their position in society? A lady, to be such, must be a mere lady, and nothing else. She must not work for profit, or engage in any occupation that money can command, lest she invade the rights of the working classes, who live by their labor. . . ."

In practice, an unmarried upper-class woman could use the one unique attribute of her position, education, and become a governess. But by 1851, twenty-five thousand women were already employed as governesses and there was, to say the least, no need for more. Her other choices were much less appealing: she might be a shop assistant, a clerk, a telegraphist, or a nurse, but all these occupations were more suitable for an ambitious lower-class woman than a firmly established gentlewoman of quality.

If a young woman refused such demeaning work, her spinsterhood implied a considerable financial burden upon the household. Miss Emily Downing observed that "the daughters of professional men . . . cannot but feel themselves a burden and a drag on the hard-won earnings of their fathers; they must know—if they allow themselves to think at all—that they are a constant cause of anxiety, and that should they not get married, there is every probability of their being, sooner or later, obliged to enter the battle of life utterly unprepared and unfitted for the fight."

In short, there was intense pressure for marriage—any sort of decent marriage—felt by fathers and daughters alike. The Victorians tended to marry relatively late, in their twenties or thirties, but Mr. Edgar Trent had a daughter Elizabeth, now twenty-nine and of "wholly marriageable condition"—meaning somewhat past her prime. It could not have escaped Mr. Trent's attention that the red-bearded gentleman might be in need of a wife. The gentleman himself expressed no reluctance to marry, but rather had indicated that the exigencies of business had kept him from pursuing personal happiness. Thus there was no reason to believe that this well-dressed, evidently well-to-do young man with a sporting instinct might not be drawn to Elizabeth. With this in mind, Mr. Trent contrived to invite Mr. Pierce to his house in Brook Street for Sunday tea, on the pretext of discussing the purchase of a fighting dog from Mr. Pierce. Mr. Pierce, somewhat reluctantly, accepted the invitation.

Elizabeth Trent was not called as a witness at the trial of Pierce, out of deference to her finer sensibilities. But popular accounts of the time give us an accurate picture of her. She was of medium height, rather darker in complexion than was the fashion, and her features were, in the words of one observer, "regular enough without being what one might call pretty." Then, as now, journalists were inclined to exaggerate the beauty of any woman involved in a scandalous event, so that the absence of compliments about Miss Trent's appearance probably implies "an unfortunate aspect."

She apparently had few suitors, save for those openly ambitious fellows eager to marry a banker's daughter, and these she staunchly rejected, with her father's undoubtedly mixed blessing. But she must surely have been impressed with Pierce, that "dashing, intrepid, fine figure of a man with charm to burn."

By all accounts, Pierce was equally impressed by the young lady. A servant's testimony records their initial meeting, which reads as if it came from the pages of a Victorian novel.

Mr. Pierce was taking tea on the rear lawn with Mr. Trent and Mrs. Trent, an "acknowledged beauty of the town." They watched as bricklayers in the back yard patiently erected a ruined building, while nearby a gardener planted picturesque weeds. This was the last gasp of a nearly one-hundred-year English fascination with ruins; they were still so fashionable that everyone who could afford a decent ruin installed one on his grounds.

Pierce watched the workmen for a while. "What is it to be?" he inquired.

"We thought a water mill," Mrs. Trent said. "It will be so delightful, especially if there is the rusted curve of the waterwheel itself. Don't you think so?"

"We are building the rusted wheel at a goodly expense," Mr. Trent grumbled.

"It is being constructed of previously rusted metal, saving us a good deal of bother," Mrs. Trent added. "But of course we must wait for the weeds to grow up around the site before it takes on the proper appearance."

At that moment Elizabeth arrived, wearing white crinoline. "Ah, my darling daughter," Mr. Trent said, rising, and Mr. Pierce rose with him. "May I present Mr. Edward Pierce, my daughter Elizabeth."

"I confess I did not know you had a daughter," Pierce said. He bowed deeply at the waist, took her hand, and seemed about to kiss it but hesitated. He appeared greatly flustered by the young woman's arrival on the scene.

"Miss Trent," he said, releasing her hand awkwardly. "You take me quite by surprise."

"I cannot tell if that is to my advantage or no," Elizabeth Trent replied, quickly taking a seat at the tea table and holding out her hand until a filled cup was put in it.

"I assure you, it is wholly to your advantage," Mr. Pierce replied. And he was reported to have colored deeply at this remark.

Miss Trent fanned herself; Mr. Trent cleared his throat; Mrs. Trent, the perfect wife, picked up a tray of biscuits and said, "Will you try one of these, Mr. Pierce?"

"With gratitude, Madam," Mr. Pierce replied, and no one present doubted the sincerity of his words.

"We are just discussing the ruins," Mr. Trent said, in a somewhat overloud voice. "But prior to that Mr. Pierce was telling us of his travels abroad. He has recently returned from New York, in point of fact."

It was a cue; his daughter picked it up neatly. "Really?" she said, fanning herself briskly. "How utterly fascinating."

"I fear it is more so in the prospect than the telling," Mr. Pierce replied, avoiding the glance of the young woman to such a degree that all observed his abashed reticence. He was clearly taken with her; and the final proof was that he addressed his remarks to Mrs. Trent. "It is a city like any other in the world, if truth be told, and chiefly distinguished by the lack of niceties which we residents of London take for granted."

"I have been informed," Miss Trent ventured, still fanning, "that there are native predators in the region."

"I should be delighted if I could regale you," Mr. Pierce said, "with endless adventures with the Indians—for so they are called, in America as in the East—but I fear I have no adventures to report. The wilderness of America does not begin until the Mississippi is crossed."

"Have you done so?" asked Mrs. Trent.

"I have," Mr. Pierce replied. "It is a vast river, many times more broad than the Thames, and it marks the boundary in America between civilization and savagery. Although lately they are constructing a railway across that vast colony"—he permitted himself the condescending reference to America, and Mr. Trent guffawed—"and I expect with the coming of the railway, the savagery will soon vanish."

"How quaint," Miss Trent said, apparently unable to think of anything else to say.

"What business took you to New York?" Mr. Trent asked.

"If I may be so bold," Mr. Pierce continued, ignoring the question, "and if the delicate ears of the ladies present shall not be offended, I shall give an example of the savagery which persists in the American lands, and the rude way of life which many persons there think nothing remarkable. Do you know of buffaloes?"

"I have read of them," said Mrs. Trent, her eyes flashing. According to some of the testimony of the servants, she was as taken with Mr. Pierce as was her stepdaughter, and her demeanor created a minor scandal within the Trent household. Mrs. Trent said, "These buffaloes are large beasts, like wild cows, and shaggy."

"Precisely so," Mr. Pierce said. "The western portion of the American country is widely populated with these buffalo creatures, and many persons make their livelihood—such as it is—in hunting them."

"Have you been to California, where there is gold?" asked Miss Trent abruptly.

"Yes," Pierce said.

"Let the man finish his tale," Mrs. Trent said, rather too sharply.

"Well," Pierce said, "the buffalo hunters, as they are known, sometimes seek the flesh of the animals, which is reckoned like venison, and sometimes the hide, which also has value."

"They lack tusks," Mr. Trent said. Mr. Trent had lately financed an elephant-killing expedition on behalf of the bank, and at this very moment an enormous warehouse at dockside was filled with five thousand ivory tusks. Mr. Trent had gone to inspect these goods for himself, a vast room of white curving tusks, most impressive.

"No, they have no tusks, although the male of the species possesses horns."

"Horns, I see. But not of ivory."

"No, not ivory."

"I see."

"Please go on," Mrs. Trent said, her eyes still flashing.

"Well," Pierce said, "the men who ki—who dispatch these buffalos are called buffalo hunters, and they utilize rifles for their purposes. On occasion they organize themselves into a line to drive the beasts over some cliff in a mass. But that is not common. Most frequently, the beast is dispatched singly. In any event—and here I must beg excuses for the crudity of what I must report of this crude countryside—once the beast has terminated existence, its innards are removed."

"Very sensible," Mr. Trent said.

"To be sure," Pierce said, "but here is the peculiar part. These buffalo hunters prize as the greatest of delicacies one portion of the innards, that being the small intestines of the beast."

"How are they prepared?" Miss Trent asked. "By roasting over a fire, I expect."

"No, Madam," Pierce said, "for I am telling you a tale of abject savagery. These intestines which are so prized, so much considered a delicacy, are consumed upon the spot, in a state wholly uncooked."

"Do you mean *raw?*" asked Mrs. Trent, wrinkling her nose.

"Indeed, Madam, as we would consume a raw oyster, so do the hunters consume the intestine, and that while it is still warm from the newly expired beast."

"Dear God," said Mrs. Trent.

"Now, then," Pierce continued, "it happens upon occasion that two men may have joined in the killing, and immediately afterward each falls upon one end of the prized intestines. Each hunter races the other, trying to gobble up this delicacy faster than his opponent."

"Gracious," Miss Trent said, fanning herself more briskly.

"Not only that," Pierce said, "but in their greedy haste, the buffalo hunter often swallows the portions whole. This is a known trick. But his opponent, recognizing the trick, may in the course of eating pull from the other the undigested portion straightaway from his mouth, as I might pull a string through my fingers. And thus one man may gobble up what another has earlier eaten, in a manner of speaking."

"Oh, dear," said Mrs. Trent, turning quite pale.

Mr. Trent cleared his throat. "Remarkable."

"How quaint," said Miss Trent bravely, with a quivering voice.

"You really must excuse me," said Mrs. Trent, rising.

"My dear," Mr. Trent said.

"Madam, I hope I have not distressed you," said Mr. Pierce, also rising.

"Your tales are quite remarkable," Mrs. Trent said, turning to leave.

"My dear," Mr. Trent said again, and hastened after her.

Thus Mr. Edward Pierce and Miss Elizabeth Trent were briefly alone on the back lawn of the mansion, and they were seen to exchange a few words. The content of their conversation is not known. But Miss Trent later admitted to a servant that she found Mr. Pierce "quite fascinating in a rough-and-ready way," and it was generally agreed in the Trent household that young Elizabeth was now in possession of that most valuable of all acquisitions, a "prospect."

Chapter 13

A Hanging

The execution of the notorious axe murderess Emma Barnes on August 28, 1854, was a well-publicized affair. On the evening prior to the execution, the first of the crowds began to gather outside the high granite walls of Newgate Prison, where they would spend the night in order to be assured of a good view of the spectacle the following morning. That same evening, the gallows was brought out and assembled by the executioner's assistants. The sound of hammering would continue long into the night.

The owners of nearby rooming houses that overlooked Newgate square were pleased to rent their rooms for the evening to the better class of ladies and gents eager to get a room with a good view over the site for a "hanging party." Mrs. Edna Molloy, a virtuous widow, knew perfectly well the value of her rooms, and when a well-spoken gentleman named Pierce asked to hire the best of them for the night, she struck a hard bargain: twenty-five guineas for a single evening.

That was a considerable sum of money. Mrs. Molloy could live comfortably for a year on that amount, but she did not let the fact influence her, for she knew what it was worth to Mr. Pierce himself—the cost of a butler for six months, or the price of one or two good ladies' dresses, and nothing more substantial than that. The very proof of his indifference lay in the ready way he paid her, on the spot, in gold guineas. Mrs. Molloy did not wish to risk offending him by biting the coins in front of him, but she would bite them as soon as she was alone. One couldn't be too careful with gold guineas, and she had been fooled more than once, even by gentlemen.

The coins were genuine, and she was much relieved. Thus she paid little attention when, later in the day, Mr. Pierce and his party filed upstairs to the hired room. The party consisted of two other men and two women, all smartly turned out in good clothes. She could tell by their accents that the men were not gentlemen, and the women were no better than they looked, despite the wicker baskets and bottles of wine they carried.

When the party entered the room and closed the door behind them, she did not bother to listen at the keyhole. She'd have no trouble from them, she was sure of it.

Pierce stepped to the window and looked down at the crowd, which gathered size with each passing minute. The square was dark, lit only by the glare of torches around the scaffolding; by that hot, baleful light he could see the crossbar and trap taking shape.

"Never make it," Agar said behind him.

Pierce turned. "He has to make it, laddie."

"He's the best snakesman in the business, the best anybody ever heard speak of, but he can't get out of there," Agar said, jerking his thumb toward Newgate Prison.

The second man now spoke. The second man was Barlow, a stocky, rugged man with a white knife scar across his forehead, which he usually concealed beneath the brim of his hat. Barlow was a reformed buzzer turned rampsman—a pickpocket who had degenerated to plain mugging—whom Pierce had hired, some years back, as a buck cabby. All rampsmen were thugs at heart, and that was precisely what a cracksman like Pierce wanted for a buck cabby, a man holding the reins to the cab, ready to make the getaway—or ready for a bit of a shindy, if it came to that. And Barlow was loyal; he had worked for Pierce for nearly five years now.

Barlow frowned and said, "If it can be done, he'll do it. Clean Willy can do it if it can be done." He spoke slowly, and gave the impression of a man who formed his thoughts with slowness. Pierce knew he could be quick in action, however.

Pierce looked at the women. They were the mistresses of Agar and Barlow, which meant they were also their accomplices. He did not know their names and he did not want to know. He regretted the very idea that they must be present at this occasion—in five years, he had never seen Barlow's woman—but there was no way to avoid it. Barlow's woman was an obvious soak; you could smell the gin breath across the room. Agar's woman was little better, but at least she was sober.

"Did you bring the trimmings?" Pierce asked.

Agar's woman opened a picnic basket. In it, he saw a sponge, medicinal powders, and bandages. There was also a carefully folded dress. "All I was told, sir."

"The dress is small?"

"Aye, sir. Barely more'n a child's frock, sir."

"Well enough," Pierce said, and turned back to look at the square once more. He paid no attention to the gallows or the swelling crowd. Instead he stared at the walls of Newgate Prison.

"Here's the supper, sir," said Barlow's woman. Pierce looked back at the supplies of cold fowl, jars of pickled onion, lobster claws, and a packet of dark cigars.

"Very good, very good," he said.

Agar said, "Are you playing the noble, sir?" This was a reference to a well-known magsman's con. It was said sarcastically, and Agar later testified that Pierce didn't care for the comment. He turned back with his long coat open at the waist to reveal a revolver jammed into the waistband of his trousers.

"If any of you steps aside," he said, "you'll have a barker up your nose, and I'll see you in lavender." He smiled thinly. "There are worse things, you know, than transportation to Australia."

"No offense," Agar said, looking at the gun. "No offense at all, no offense—it was only in the manner of a joke."

Barlow said, "Why'd we need a snakesman?"

Pierce was not sidetracked. "Bear my words carefully," he said. "Any of you steps aside and you'll stop a shot before you can say Jack Robin. I mean every word." He sat down at the table. "Now then," he said, "I'll have a leg of that chicken, and we shall disport ourselves as best we can while we wait."

Pierce slept part of the night; he was awakened at daybreak by the crowd that jammed the square below. The crowd had now swollen to more than fifteen thousand noisy, rough people, and Pierce knew that the streets would be filled with ten or fifteen thousand more, making their way to see the hanging on their route to work. Employers hardly bothered to keep up a pretense of strictness on any Monday morning when there was a hanging; it was an accepted fact that everybody would be late to work, and especially today, with a woman to be hanged.

The gallows itself was now finished; the rope dangled in the air above the trap. Pierce glanced at his pocketwatch. It was 7:45, just a short time before the execution itself.

In the square below, the crowd began to chant: "Oh, my, think I'm going to die! Oh, my, think I'm going to die!" There was a good deal of laughter and shouting and stamping of feet. One or two fights broke out, but they could not be sustained in the tightly packed crush of the crowd.

They all went to the window to watch.

Agar said, "When do you think he'll make his move?"

"Right at eight, I should think."

"I'd do it a bit sooner, myself."

Pierce said, "He'll make his move whenever he thinks best."

The minutes passed slowly. No one in the room spoke. Finally, Barlow said, "I knew Emma Barnes—never thought she'd come to this."

Pierce said nothing.

At eight o'clock, the chimes of St. Sepulchre signaled the hour, and the crowd roared in anticipation. There was the soft jingle of a prison bell, and then a door in Newgate opened and the prisoner was led out, her wrists strapped behind her. In front was a chaplain, reciting from the Bible. Behind was the city executioner, dressed in black.

The crowd saw the prisoner and shouted "Hats off!" Every man's hat was removed as the prisoner slowly stepped up the scaffolding. Then there were cries of "Down in front! Down in front!" They were, for the most part, unheeded.

Pierce kept his gaze on the condemned woman. Emma Barnes was in her thirties, and looked vigorous enough. The firm lines and muscles of her neck were clearly visible through her open-necked dress. But her eyes were distant and glazed; she did not really seem to see anything. She took up her position and the city executioner turned to her, making slight adjustments, as if he were a seamstress positioning a dressmaker's dummy. Emma Barnes stared above the crowd. The rope was fitted to a chain around her neck.

The clergyman read loudly, keeping his eyes fixed on the Bible. The city executioner strapped the woman's legs together with a leather strap; this occasioned a good deal of fumbling beneath her skirts; the crowd made raucous comments.

Then the executioner stood, and slipped a black hood over the woman's head. And then, at a signal, the trap opened with a wooden *crack!* that Pierce heard with startling distinctness; and the body fell, and caught, and hung instantly motionless.

"He's getting better at it," Agar said. The city executioner was known for botching executions, leaving the hanged prisoner to writhe and dangle for several minutes before he died. "Crowd won't like it," Agar added.

The crowd, in fact, did not seem to mind. There was a moment of utter silence, and then the excited roar of discussion. Pierce knew that most of the crowd would remain in the square, watching for the next hour, until the dead woman was cut down and placed in a coffin.

"Will you take some punch?" asked Agar's tart.

"No," Pierce said. And then he said, "Where is Willy?"

* * *

Clean Willy Williams, the most famous snakesman of the century, was inside Newgate Prison beginning his escape. He was a tiny man, and he had been famous in his youth for his agility as a chimney sweep's apprentice; in later years he had been employed by the most eminent cracksman, and his feats were now legendary. It was said that Clean Willy could climb a surface of glass, and no one was quite certain that he couldn't.

Certainly the guards of Newgate, knowing the celebrity of their prisoner, had kept a close watch on him these many months, just in case. Yet they also knew that escape from Newgate was flatly impossible. A resourceful man might make a go of it from Ponsdale, where routines were notoriously lax, the walls low, and the guards not averse to the feel of gold coin and were known to look the other way. Ponsdale, or Highgate, or any of a dozen others, but never Newgate.

Newgate Prison was the most secure in all England. It had been designed by George Dance, "one of the most meticulous intellects of the Age of Taste," and every detail of the building had been set forth to emphasize the harsh facts of confinement. Thus the proportions of the window arches had been "subtly thickened in order to intensify the painful narrowness of the openings," and contemporary observers applauded the excellence of such cruel effects.

The reputation of Newgate was not merely a matter of aesthetics. In the more than seventy years since 1782, when the building was finished, no convict had ever escaped. And this was hardly surprising: Newgate was surrounded on all sides with granite walls fifty feet high. The stones were so finely cut that they were said to be impossible to scale. Yet even if one could manage the impossible, it was to no avail, for encircling the top of the walls was an iron bar, fitted with revolving, razor-sharp spiked drums. And the bar was also fitted with spikes. No man could get past that obstacle. Escape from Newgate was inconceivable.

With the passing months, as the guards grew familiar with the presence of little Willy, they ceased to watch him closely. He was not a difficult prisoner. He never broke the rule of silence, never spoke to a fellow inmate; he suffered the "cockchafer"—or treadmill—for the prescribed fifteen-minute intervals without complaint or incident; he worked at oakum-picking with no surcease. Indeed, there was some grudging respect for the reformed aspect of the little man, for the cheerful way he went about the routine. He was a likely candidate for a ticket-of-leave, a foreshortened sentence, in a year or so.

Yet at eight in the morning on that Monday, August 28, 1854, Clean Willy Williams had slipped to a corner of the prison where two walls met, and with his back to the angle he was skinning straight up the sheer rock surface, bracing with his hands and feet. He dimly heard the chanting of the crowd: "Oh, my, think I'm going to die!" as he reached the top of the wall, and without hesitation grabbed the bar with its iron spikes. His hands were immediately lacerated.

From childhood, Clean Willy had had no sensation in his palms, which were thickly covered with calluses and scar tissue. It was the custom of homeowners of the period to keep a hearth burning right to the moment when the chimney sweep and his child assistant arrived to clean the flue, and if the child scorched his hands in hastening up the still-hot chimney, that was not any great concern. If the child didn't like the work, there were plenty of others to take his place.

Clean Willy's hands had been burned again and again, over a period of years. So he felt nothing now as the blood trickled down from his slashed palms, ran in rivulets along his forearms, and dripped and spattered on his face. He paid no attention at all.

He moved slowly along the revolving spike wheels, down the full length of one wall, then to the second wall, and then to the third. It was exhausting work. He lost all sense of time, and never heard the noise of the crowd that followed the execution. He continued to make his way around the perimeter of the prison yard until he reached the south wall. There he paused and waited while a patrolling guard passed beneath him. The guard never looked up, although Willy later remembered that drops of his own blood landed on the man's cap and shoulders.

When the guard was gone, Willy clambered over the spikes—cutting his chest, his knees, and his legs, so that the blood now ran very freely—and jumped fifteen feet down to the roof of the nearest building outside the prison. No one heard the sound of his landing, for the area was deserted; everybody was attending the execution.

From that roof he jumped to another, and then another, leaping six- and eight-foot gaps without hesitation. Once or twice, he lost his grip on the shingles and slates of the roofs, but he always recovered. He had, after all, spent much of his life on rooftops.

Finally, less than half an hour from the time he began to inch his way up the prison wall, he slipped through a gabled window at the back of Mrs. Molloy's lodging house, padded down the hallway, and entered the room rented, at considerable expense, by Mr. Pierce and his party.

Agar recalled that Willy presented "a ghastly aspect, most fearsome," and he added that "he was bleeding like a stuck saint," although this blasphemous reference was expunged from the courtroom records.

Pierce directed the swift treatment of the man, who was barely conscious. He was revived with the vapors of ammonium chloride from a cut-glass inhaler. His clothes were stripped off by the women, who pretended no modesty but worked quickly; his many wounds were staunched with styptic powder and sticking plaster, then bound with surgical bandages. Agar gave him a sip of coca wine for energy, and Burroughs & Wellcome beef-and-iron wine for sustenance. He was forced to down two

Carter's Little Nerve Pills and some tincture of opium for his pain. This combined treatment brought the man to his senses, and enabled the women to clean his face, douse his body with rose water, and bundle him into the waiting dress.

When he was dressed, he was given a sip of Bromo Caffein for further energy, and told to act faint. A bonnet was placed over his head, and boots laced on his feet; his bloody prison garb was stuffed in the picnic basket.

No one among the crowd of more than twenty thousand paid the slightest attention when the well-dressed party of hangers-on departed Mrs. Molloy's boarding house—with one woman of their party so faint that she had to be carried by the men, who hustled her into a waiting cab—and rattled off into the morning light. A faint woman was a common enough sight and, in any case, nothing to compare to a woman turning slowly at the end of the rope, back and forth, back and forth.

Chapter 14

A Georgian Disgrace

It is usually estimated that seven-eighths of the structures in Victorian London were actually Georgian. The face of the city and its general architectural character were legacies of that earlier era; the Victorians did not begin to rebuild their capital in any substantial way until the 1880s. This reluctance reflected the economics of urban building. For most of the century, it simply was not profitable to tear down old structures, even those badly suited to their modern functions. Certainly the reluctance was not aesthetic—the Victorians loathed the Georgian style, which Ruskin himself termed "the *ne plus ultra* of ugliness."

Thus it is perhaps not surprising that the *Times*, in reporting that a convict had escaped from Newgate Prison, observed that "the virtues of this edifice have been clearly overstated. Not only is escape from its confines possible, it is mere child's play, for the fleeing villian had not yet attained his majority. It is time for this public disgrace to be torn down."

The article went on to comment that "the Metropolitan Police has dispatched groups of armed officers into the rookeries of the town, in order to flush out the escaped man, and there is every expectation of his apprehension."

There were no follow-up reports. One must remember that during this period, jailbreaks were, in the words of one commentator, "quite as common as illegitimate births," and nothing so ordinary was really newsworthy. At a time when the curtains of the windows of Parliament were being soaked in lime to protect the members against the cholera epidemic while they debated the conduct of the Crimean campaign, the newspapers could not be bothered with a minor felon from the dangerous classes who had been lucky enough to make a clean getaway.

A month later, the body of a young man was found floating in the Thames, and police authorities identified him as the escaped convict from Newgate. It received barely a paragraph in the *Evening Standard;* the other newspapers did not mention it at all.

Chapter 15

The Pierce Household

After his escape, Clean Willy was taken to Pierce's house in Mayfair, where he spent several weeks in seclusion while his wounds healed. It is from his later testimony to police that we first learn of the mysterious woman who was Pierce's mistress, and known to Willy as "Miss Miriam."

Willy was placed in an upstairs room, and the servants were told that he was a relative of Miss Miriam's who had been run down by a cab in New Bond Street. From time to time, Willy was tended by Miss Miriam. He said of her that she was "well carried, a good figure, and well-spoke, and she walked here and there slow, never hurrying." This last sentiment was echoed by all the witnesses, who were impressed by the ethereal aspect of the young woman; her eyes were said to be especially captivating, and her grace in movement was called "dreamlike" and "phantasmagorical."

Apparently this woman lived in the house with Pierce, although she was often gone during the day. Clean Willy was never very clear about her movements, and in any case he was often sedated with opium, which may also account for the ghostly qualities he saw in her.

Willy recalled only one conversation with her. He asked, "Are you his canary, then?" Meaning was she Pierce's accomplice in burglary.

"Oh no," she said, smiling. "I have no ear for music."

From this he assumed she was not involved in Pierce's plans, although this was later shown to be wrong. She was an integral part of the plan, and was probably the first of the thieves to know Pierce's intentions.

At the trial, there was considerable speculation about Miss Miriam and her origins. A good deal of evidence points to the conclusion that she was an actress. This would explain her ability to mimic various accents and manners of different social classes; her tendency to wear make-up in a day when no respectable woman would let cosmetics touch her flesh; and her open presence as Pierce's mistress. In those days, the dividing line between an actress and a prostitute was exceedingly fine. And actors were by occupation itinerant wanderers, likely to have connections with criminals, or to be criminals themselves. Whatever the truth of her past, she seems to have been his mistress for several years.

Pierce himself was rarely in the house, and on occasion he was gone overnight. Clean Willy recalled seeing him once or twice in the late afternoon, wearing riding clothes and smelling of horses, as if he had returned from an equestrian excursion.

"I didn't know you were a horse fancier," Willy once said.

"I'm not," Pierce replied shortly. "Hate the bloody beasts."

Pierce kept Willy indoors after his wounds were healed, waiting for his "terrier crop" to grow out. In those days, the surest way to identify an escaped convict was by his short haircut. By late September, his hair was longer, but still Pierce did not allow him to leave. When Willy asked why, Pierce said, "I am waiting for you to be recaptured, or found dead."

This statement puzzled Willy, but he did as he was told. A few days later, Pierce came in with a newspaper under his arm and told him he could leave. That same evening Willy went to the Holy Land, where he expected to find his mistress, Maggie. He found that Maggie had taken up with a footpad, a rough sort who made his way by "swinging the stick"—that is, by mugging. Maggie showed no interest in Willy.

Willy then took up with a girl of twelve named Louise, whose principal occupation was snowing. She was described in court as "no gofferer, mind, and no clean-starcher, just a bit of plain snow now and then for the translator. Simple, really." What was meant by this passage, which required considerable explanation to the presiding magistrates, was that Willy's new mistress was engaged in the lowest form of laundry stealing. The better echelons of laundry stealers, the gofferers and clean-starchers, stole from high-class districts, often taking clothes off the lines. Plain ordinary snowing was relegated to children and young girls, and it could be lucrative enough when fenced to "translators," who sold the clothing as second-hand goods.

Willy lived off this girl's earnings, never venturing outside the sanctuary of the rookery. He had been warned by Pierce to keep his mouth shut, and he never mentioned that he had had help in his break from Newgate.

Clean Willy lived with his judy in a lodging house that contained more than a hundred people; the house was a well-known buzzer's lurk. Willy lived and slept with his mistress in a bed he shared with twenty other bodies of various sexes, and Louise reported of this period, "He took his ease, and spent his time cheerful, and waited for the cracksman to give his call."

Chapter 16

Rotten Row

Of all the fashionable sections of that fashionable city of London, none compared to the spongy, muddy pathway in Hyde Park called the Ladies' Mile, or Rotten Row. Here, weather permitting, were literally hundreds of men and women on horseback, all dressed in the greatest splendor the age could provide, radiant in the golden sunshine at four in the afternoon.

It was a scene of bustling activity: the horsemen and horsewomen packed tightly together; the women with little uniformed foot pages trotting along behind their mistresses, or sometimes accompanied by stern, mounted duennas, or sometimes escorted by their beaus. And if the spectacle of Rotten Row was splendid and fashionable, it was not entirely respectable, for many of the women were of dubious character. "There is no difficulty," wrote one observer, "in guessing the occupation of the dashing *equestrienne* who salutes half-a-dozen men at once with whip or with a wink, and who sometimes varies the monotony of a safe seat by holding her hands behind her back while gracefully swerving over to listen to the compliments of a walking admirer."

These were members of the highest class of prostitute and, like it or not, respectable ladies often found themselves competing with these smartly turned-out demimondes for masculine attention. Nor was this the only arena of such competition; it occurred at the opera, and the theatre as well. More than one young lady found that her escort's gaze was fixed not on the performance but on some high box where an elegant woman returned his glances with open, frank interest.

Victorians claimed to be scandalized by the intrusion of prostitutes into respectable circles, but despite all the calls for reform and change, the women continued to appear gaily for nearly a half-century more. It is usual to dismiss Victorian prostitution as a particularly gaudy manifestation of that society's profound hypocrisy. But the issue is really more complex; it has to do with the way that women were viewed in Victorian England.

This was an era of marked sexual differentiation in dress, manner, attitude, and bearing. Even pieces of furniture and rooms within the house were viewed as "masculine" or "feminine"; the dining room was masculine, the drawing room feminine, and so on. All this was assumed to have a biological rationale:

"It is evident," wrote Alexander Walker, "that the man, possessing reasoning faculties, muscular power, and courage to employ it, is qualified for being a protector; the woman, being little capable of reasoning, feeble, and timid, requires protecting. Under such circumstances, the man naturally governs: the woman naturally obeys."

With minor variations, this belief was repeated again and again. The power of reasoning was small in women; they did not calculate consequences; they were governed by their emotions, and hence required strict controls on their behavior by the more rational and levelheaded male.

The presumed intellectual inferiority of the female was reinforced by her education, and many well-bred women probably were the simpering, tittering, pathologically delicate fools that populate the pages of Victorian novels. Men could not expect to share much with their wives. Mandell Creighton wrote that he found "ladies in general very unsatisfactory mental food; they seem to have no particular thoughts or ideas, and though for a time it is flattering to one's vanity to think one may teach them some, it palls after a while. Of course at a certain age, when you have a house and so on, you get a wife as part of its furniture, and find her a very comfortable institution; but I doubt greatly whether there were ever many men who had thoughts worth recounting, who told these thoughts to their wives at first, or who expected them to appreciate them."

There is good evidence that both sexes were bored silly by this arrangement. Women, stranded in their vast, servant-filled households, dealt with their frustrations in spectacular displays of hysterical neuroses: they suffered loss of hearing, speech, and sight; they had choking fits, fainting spells, loss of appetite, and even loss of memory. In the midst of a seizure they might make copulating movements or writhe in such arcing spasms that their heads would touch their heels. All these bizarre symptoms, of course, only reinforced the general notion of the frailty of the female sex.

Frustrated men had another option, and that was recourse to prostitutes, who were often lively, gay, witty—indeed, all the things it was inconceivable for a woman to be. On a simpler level, men found prostitutes agreeable because they could, in their company, discard the strained formalities of polite society and relax in an atmosphere of "unbuttoned easiness." This freedom from restraints was at least as important as the availability of sexual outlets *per se*, and it is probably this appeal that gave the institution such a broad base within society and allowed prostitutes to intrude boldly into acceptable arenas of Victorian society, such as Rotten Row.

Beginning in late September, 1854, Edward Pierce began to meet Miss Elizabeth Trent on riding excursions in Rotten Row. The first encounter was apparently accidental but later, by a sort of unstated agreement, they occurred with regularity.

Elizabeth Trent's life began to form itself around these afternoon meetings: she spent all morning preparing for them, and all evening discussing them; her friends complained that she talked incessantly of Edward; her father complained of his daughter's insatiable demand for new dresses. She seemed, he said, "to require *as a necessity* a new garment every day, and she would prefer two."

The unattractive young woman apparently never thought it strange that Mr. Pierce should single her out from among the throng of stunning beauties in Rotten Row; she was completely captivated by his attentions. At the trial, Pierce summarized their conversations as "light and trivial," and recounted only one in detail.

This occurred sometime in the month of October, 1854. It was a time of political upheaval and military scandal; the nation had suffered a severe blow to its self-esteem. The Crimean War was turning into a disaster. When it began, J. B. Priestley notes, "the upper classes welcomed the war as a glorified large-scale picnic in some remote and romantic place. It was almost as if the Black Sea had been opened to tourism. Wealthy officers like Lord Cardigan decided to take their yachts. Some commanders' wives insisted upon going along, accompanied by their personal maids. Various civilians cancelled their holidays elsewhere to follow the army and see the sport."

The sport quickly became a debacle. The British troops were badly trained, badly supplied, and ineptly led. Lord Raglan, the military commander, was sixty-five and "old for his age." Raglan often seemed to think he was still fighting Waterloo, and referred to the enemy as "the French," although the French were now his allies. On one occasion he was so confused that he took up an observation post behind the Russian enemy lines. The atmosphere of "aged chaos" deepened, and by the middle of the summer even the wives of officers were writing home to say that "nobody appears to have the least idea what they are about."

By October, this ineptitude culminated in Lord Cardigan's charge of the Light Brigade, a spectacular feat of heroism which decimated three-quarters of his forces in a successful effort to capture the wrong battery of enemy guns.

Clearly the picnic was over, and nearly all upper-class Englishmen were profoundly concerned. The names of Cardigan, Raglan, and Lucan were on everyone's lips. But on that warm October afternoon in Hyde Park, Mr. Pierce gently guided Elizabeth Trent into a conversation about her father.

"He was most fearfully nervous this morning," she said.

"Indeed?" Pierce said, trotting alongside her.

"He is nervous every morning when he must send the gold shipments to the Crimea. He is a different man from the very moment he arises. He is distant and preoccupied in the extreme."

"I am certain he bears a heavy responsibility," Pierce said.

"So heavy, I fear he may take to excessive drink," Elizabeth said, and laughed a little.

"I pray you exaggerate, Madam."

"Well, he acts strangely, and no mistake. You know he is entirely opposed to the consumption of any alcohol before nightfall."

"I do, and most sensible, too."

"Well," Elizabeth Trent continued, "I suspect him of breaking his own regulation, for each morning of the shipments he goes alone to the wine cellar, with no servants to accompany him or to hold the gas lanterns. He is insistent upon going alone. Many times my step-mother has chided him that he may stumble or suffer some misfortune on the steps to the basement. But he will have none of her entreaties. And he spends some time in the cellar, and then emerges, and makes his journey to the bank."

"I think," Pierce said, "that he merely checks the cellar for some ordinary purpose. Is that not logical?"

"No, indeed," Elizabeth said, "for at all times he relies upon my step-mother to deal in the stocking and care of the cellar, and the decanting of wines before dinners, and such matters."

"Then his manner is most peculiar. I trust," Pierce said gravely, "that his responsibilities are not placing an overgreat burden upon his nervous system."

"I trust," the daughter answered, with a sigh. "Is it not a lovely day?"

"Lovely," Pierce agreed. "Unspeakably lovely, but no more lovely than you."

Elizabeth Trent tittered, and replied that he was a bold rogue to flatter her so openly. "One might even suspect an ulterior motive," she said, laughing.

"Heavens, no," Pierce said, and to further reassure her he placed his hand lightly, and briefly, over hers.

"I am so happy," she said.

"And I am happy with you," Pierce said, and this was true, for he now knew the location of all four keys.

PART TWO

THE KEYS

November, 1854–February, 1855

Chapter 17

The Necessity of a Fresh

Mr. Henry Fowler, seated in a dark recess of the taproom at the lunch hour, showed every sign of agitation. He bit his lip, he twisted his glass in his hands, and he could hardly bring himself to look into the eyes of his friend Edward Pierce. "I do not know how to begin," he said. "It is a most embarrassing circumstance."

"You are assured of my fullest confidence," Pierce said, raising his glass.

"I thank you," Fowler said. "You see," he began, then faltered. "You see, it is"—he broke off, and shook his head—"most dreadfully embarrassing."

"Then speak of it forthrightly," Pierce advised, "as one man to another."

Fowler gulped his drink, and set the glass back on the table with a sharp clink. "Very well. Plainly, the long and the short of it is that I have the French malady."

"Oh, dear," Pierce said.

"I fear I have overindulged," said Fowler sadly, "and now I must pay the price. It is altogether most wretched and vexing." In those days, venereal disease was thought to be the consequence of sexual overactivity. There were few cures, and fewer doctors willing to treat a patient with the illness. Most hospitals made no provision for gonorrhea and syphilis at all. A respectable man who contracted these diseases became an easy target for blackmail; thus Mr. Fowler's reticence.

"How may I help you?" Pierce asked, already knowing the answer.

"I maintained the hope—not falsely, I pray—that as a bachelor, you might have knowledge—ah, that you might make an introduction on my behalf to a fresh girl, a country girl."

Pierce frowned. "It is no longer so easy as it once was."

"I know that, I know that," Fowler said, his voice rising heatedly. He checked himself, and spoke more quietly. "I understand the difficulty. But I was hoping . . ."

Pierce nodded. "There is a woman in the Haymarket," he said, "who often has a fresh or two. I can make discreet inquiries."

"Oh, *please,*" said Mr. Fowler, his voice tremulous. And he added, "It is most painful."

"All I can do is inquire," Pierce said.

"I should be forever in your debt," Mr. Fowler said. "It is most painful."

"I shall inquire," Pierce said. "You may expect a communication from me in a day or so. In the meanwhile, do not lose cheer."

"Oh, thank you, thank you," Fowler said, and called for another drink.

"It may be expensive," Pierce warned.

"Damn the expense, man. I swear I will pay anything!" Then he seemed to reconsider this comment. "How much do you suppose?"

"A hundred guineas, if one is to be assured of a true fresh."

"A hundred guineas?" He looked unhappy.

"Indeed, and only if I am fortunate enough to strike a favorable bargain. They are much in demand, you know."

"Well, then, it shall be," Mr. Fowler said, gulping another drink. "Whatever it is, it shall be."

Two days later, Mr. Fowler received by the newly instituted penny post a letter addressed to him at his offices at the Huddleston & Bradford Bank. Mr. Fowler was much reassured by the excellent quality of the stationery, and the fine penmanship displayed by the unmistakably feminine hand.

Nov. 11, 1854

Sir,

Our mutual acquaintance, Mr. P., has requested that I inform you when next I knew of any lady—*fresh*. I am pleased to recommend to you a very pretty fair young girl, just come from the country, and I think you will like her very much. If it is convenient for you, you may meet her in four days' time at Lichfield Street, at the bottom of St. Martin's Lane, at eight o'clock. She shall be there waiting for you, and suitable arrangements for private quarterings have been made nearby.

I remain, Sir, your most obedient
humble servant,
M.B.

South Moulton Street

There was no mention of the price of the girl, but Mr. Fowler hardly cared. His private parts were now swollen and extremely tender, so much so, in fact, that he could think of nothing else as he sat at his desk and tried to conduct the business of the day. He looked again at the letter and again felt reassured by the excellent impression it made. In every aspect, it smacked of the utmost reliability, and that was important. Fowler knew that many virgins were nothing of the sort, but rather young girls initiated a score of times over, with their "demure state" freshly renewed by the application of a small seamstress's stitch in a strategic place.

He also knew that intercourse with a virgin was not uniformly accepted as a cure for venereal disease. Many men swore the experience produced a cure; others rejected the idea. It was often argued that the failures resulted from the fact that the girl was not genuinely fresh. Thus Mr. Fowler looked at the stationery and the penmanship, and found there the reassurance he hoped to find. He sent off a quick note of vague thanks to his friend Pierce for his assistance in this matter.

Chapter 18

The Carriage Fakement

On the same day that Mr. Fowler was writing a letter of thanks to Mr. Pierce, Mr. Pierce was preparing to crack the mansion of Mr. Trent. Involved in this plan were five people: Pierce, who had some inside knowledge of the layout of the house; Agar, who would make the wax impression of the key; Agar's woman, who would act as "crow," or lookout; and Barlow, who would be a "stall," providing diversion.

There was also the mysterious Miss Miriam. She was essential to the planned housebreak, for she would carry out what was called "the carriage fakement." This was one of the most clever methods of breaking into a house. For its effect, the carriage fakement relied upon a solid social custom of the day—the tipping of servants.

In Victorian England, roughly 10 percent of the entire population was "in service," and nearly all were poorly paid. The poorest paid were those whose tasks brought them in contact with visitors and house guests: the butler and the footman relied on tips for most of their annual income. Thus the notorious disdain of the footman for insubstantial callers—and thus, too, the "carriage fakement."

By nine o'clock on the evening of November 12, 1854, Pierce had his confederates in their places. The crow, Agar's woman, lounged across the street from the Trent mansion. Barlow, the stall, had slipped down the alley toward the tradesman's entrance and the dog pens at the back of the house. Pierce and Agar were concealed in shrubbery right next to the front door. When all was in readiness, an elegant closed carriage drew up to the curb in front of the house, and the bell was rung.

The Trent household's footman heard the ring, and opened the door. He saw the carriage drawn up at the curb. Dignified and conscious of tips, he was certainly not going to stand in the doorway and shout into the night to inquire what was wanted. When, after a moment, no one emerged from the carriage, he went down the steps to the curb to see if he could be of service.

Inside the carriage he saw a handsome, refined woman who asked if this was the residence of Mr. Robert Jenkins. The footman said it was not, but he knew of Mr. Jenkins; the house was around the corner, and he gave directions.

While this was happening, Pierce and Agar slipped into the house through the open front door. They proceeded directly to the cellar door. This door was locked, but Agar employed a twirl, or picklock, and had it open in a moment. The two men were inside the cellar, with the door closed behind them, by the time the footman received his shilling from the lady in the carriage. He tossed the coin in the air, caught it, walked back to the house, and locked up the door once more, never suspecting he had been tricked.

That was the carriage fakement.

In the light of a narrow-beam lantern, Pierce checked his watch. It was 9:04. That gave them an hour to find the key before Barlow provided his diversion to cover their escape.

Pierce and Agar moved stealthily down the creaking stairs into the depths of the cellar. They saw the wine racks, locked behind iron gratings. These new locks yielded easily to Agar's attentions. At 9:11, they swung the grating door open and entered the wine cellar proper. They immediately began the search for the key.

There was no way to be clever about the search. It was a slow and painstaking business. Pierce could make only one assumption about the hiding place: since Mr. Trent's wife was the person who usually went into the cellar, and since Mr. Trent did not want her coming across the key by accident, the banker probably hid his key at some inconveniently high location. They first searched the tops of the racks, feeling with their fingers. It was dusty, and there was soon a good deal of dust in the air.

Agar, with his bad lungs, had difficulty suppressing his cough. Several times his stifled grunts were sufficiently loud to alarm Pierce, but the Trent household never heard them.

Soon it was 9:30. Now, Pierce knew, time was beginning to work against them. Pierce searched more frantically and became impatient, hissing his complaints to Agar, who wielded the spot of light from the hot shaded lantern.

Ten more minutes passed, and Pierce began to sweat. And then, with startling suddenness, his fingers felt something cold on the top of the wine-rack cross-bars. The object fell to the ground with a metallic clink. A few moments of scrambling around on the earthern floor of the cellar, and they had the key. It was 9:45.

Pierce held it into the spot from the lantern. In darkness, Agar groaned.

"What is it?" Pierce whispered.

"That's not it."

"What do you mean?"

"I mean it's not the ruddy key, it's the wrong one."

Pierce turned the key over in his hands. "Are you sure?" he whispered, but even as he spoke he knew Agar was right. The key was dusty and old; there was grime in the crevices of the prongs. Agar spoke his thoughts.

"Nobody's touched her in ten years."

Pierce swore, and continued his search, while Agar held the lantern. Agar looked at the key critically.

"Damn me but she's odd," he whispered. "I never seen the likes of it. Small as she is, delicate-like, could be a lady's twirl to some female trifle, you ask me—"

"—Shut up," Pierce hissed.

Agar fell silent. Pierce searched, feeling his heart thump in his chest, not looking at his watch, not wanting to know the time. Then his fingers again felt cold metal. He brought it into the light.

It was a shiny key.

"That's for a safe," Agar said when he saw it.

"Right," Pierce said, sighing. He took the lantern and held it for Agar. Agar fished two wax blanks from his pockets. He held them in his hands to warm them a moment, and then he pressed the key into them, first one side, then the other.

"Time?" he whispered.

"Nine-fifty-one," Pierce said.

"I'll do another," Agar said, and repeated the process with a second set of blanks. This was common practice among the most adept screwsmen, for one never knew when a blank might be later injured after a break-in. When he had two sets, Pierce returned the key to its hiding place.

"Nine-fifty-seven."

"Crikey, it's close."

They left the wine cellar, locking it behind them, and slipped up the stairs to the basement door. Then they waited.

Barlow, lurking in the shadows near the servants' quarters, checked his own pocket watch and saw it was ten o'clock. He had a moment of hesitation. On the one hand, every minute his accomplices spent inside the Trent household was dangerous; on the other hand, they might not have finished their work, despite the planned schedule. He had no wish to be the villain, greeted by the spectacle of their angry faces when they made their escape.

Finally he muttered to himself, "Ten is ten," and, carrying a bag, he moved back to the dog kennels. Three dogs were there, including the new gift of a made dog from Mr. Pierce. Barlow bent over the run and pushed four squeaking rats out of the bag and into the enclosure. Immediately, the dogs began to yelp and bark, raising a terrible din.

Barlow slipped off into the shadows as he saw the lights come on in one window after another in the servants' quarters.

Pierce and Agar, hearing the commotion, opened the cellar door and moved into the hallway, locking that door behind them. There was the sound of running footsteps at the back of the house. They unfastened the locks and bolts of the front door, let themselves out, and disappeared into the night.

They left behind them only one sign of their visit: the unlocked front door. They knew that in the morning the footman, being first to arise, would come upon the front door and find the locks open. But he would remember the incident of the carriage the night before, and would assume that he had forgotten to lock up afterward. He might secretly suspect a housebreak, but as the day went on and nothing was discovered missing, he would forget all about it.

In any case, no burglary of the Trent residence was ever reported to authorities. The mysterious commotion of the dogs was explained by the bodies of the dead rats in the kennels. There was some discussion of how the rats had found their way into the dog run, but the Trent household was large and busy, and there was no time for idle speculation on trivial matters.

Thus, by dawn of November 13, 1854, Edward Pierce had the first of the four keys he needed. He immediately directed his attention to obtaining the second key.

Chapter 19

The Assignation

Mr. Henry Fowler could scarcely believe his eyes. There, in the faint glow of the street gas lamp, was a delicate creature, rosy-cheeked and wonderfully young. She could not be much past the age of consent of twelve, and her very posture, bearing, and timid manner bespoke her tender and uninitiated state.

He approached her; she replied softly, halting, with downcast eyes, and led him to a brothel lodging house not far distant. Mr. Fowler eyed the establishment with some trepidation, for the exterior was not particularly prepossessing. Thus it was a pleasant surprise when the child's gentle knock at the door received an answer from an exceedingly beautiful woman, whom the child called "Miss Miriam." Standing in the hallway, Fowler saw that this accommodation house was not one of those crude establishments where beds were rented for five shillings an hour and the proprietor came round and rapped on the door with a stick when the time was due; on the contrary, here the furnishings were plush velvet, with rich drapings, fine Persian carpets, and appointments of taste and quality. Miss Miriam comported herself with extraordinary dignity as she requested one hundred and fifty pounds; her manner was so wellborn that Fowler paid without a quibble, and he proceeded directly to an upstairs room with the little girl, whose name was Sarah.

Sarah explained that she had lately come from Derbyshire, that her parents were dead, that she had an older brother off in the Crimea, and a younger brother in the poorhouse. She talked of all these events almost gaily as they ascended the stairs. Fowler thought he detected a certain overexcited quality to her speech; no doubt the poor child was nervous at her first experience, and he reminded himself to be gentle.

The room they entered was as superbly furnished as the downstairs sitting room; it was red and elegant, and the air was softly perfumed with the scent of jasmine. He looked about briefly, for a man could never be too careful. Then he bolted the door and turned to face the girl.

"Well, now," he said.

"Sir?" she said.

"Well, now," he said. "Shall, we, ah . . ."

"Oh, yes, of course, sir," she said, and the simple child began to undress him. He found it extraordinary, to stand in the midst of this elegant—very nearly *decadent*—room and have a little child who stood barely to his waist reach up with her little fingers and pluck at his buttons, undressing him. Altogether, it was so remarkable he submitted passively, and soon was naked, although she was still attired.

"What is this?" she asked, touching a key around his neck on a silver chain.

"Just a—ah—key," he replied.

"You'd best take it off," she said, "it may harm me."

He took it off. She dimmed the gaslights, and then disrobed. The next hour or two was magical to Henry Fowler, an experience so incredible, so astounding he quite forgot his painful condition. And he certainly did not notice that a stealthy hand slipped around one of the heavy red velvet curtains and plucked away the key from atop his clothing; nor did he notice when, a short time later, the key was returned.

"Oh, sir," she cried, at the vital moment. "Oh, *sir!*"

And Henry Fowler was, for a brief instant, more filled with life and excitement than he could ever remember in all his forty-seven years.

Chapter 20

The Coopered Ken

The ease with which Pierce and his fellow conspirators obtained the first two keys gave them a sense of confidence that was soon to prove false. Almost immediately after obtaining Fowler's key, they ran into difficulties from an unexpected quarter: the South Eastern Railway changed its routine for the dispatcher's offices in London Bridge Station.

The gang employed Miss Miriam to watch the routine of the offices, and in late December, 1854, she returned with bad news. At a meeting in Pierce's house, she told both Pierce and Agar that the railway company had hired a jack who now guarded the premises at night.

Since they had been planning to break in at night, this was sour news indeed. But according to Agar, Pierce covered his disappointment quickly. "What's his rig?" he asked.

"He comes on duty at lock-up each night, at seven sharp," Miss Miriam said.

"And what manner of fellow is he?"

"He's a ream escop," she replied, meaning a real policeman. "He's forty or so; square-rigged, fat. But I'll wager he doesn't sleep on the job, and he's no lushington."

"Is he armed?"

"He is," she said, nodding.

"Where's he lurk, then?" Agar said.

"Right at the door. Sits up at the top of the steps by the door, and does not move at all. He has a small paper bag at his side, which I think is his supper." Miss Miriam could not be sure of that, because she dared not remain watching the station office too late in the day for fear of arousing suspicion.

"Crikey," Agar said in disgust. "Sits right by the door? He's coopered that ken."

"I wonder why they put on a night guard," Pierce said.

"Maybe they knew we were giving it the yack," Agar said, for they had kept the office under surveillance, off and on, for a period of months, and someone might have noticed.

Pierce sighed.

"No gammon now," Agar said.

"There's always a gammon," Pierce said.

"It's coopered for sure," Agar said.

"Not coopered," Pierce said, "just a little more difficult, that is all."

"How you going to knock it over, then?" Agar said.

"At the dinner hour," he said.

"In broad daylight?" Agar said, aghast.

"Why not?" Pierce said.

The following day, Pierce and Agar watched the midday routine of the office. At one o'clock, the London Bridge Station was crowded with passengers coming and going; footmen hauling luggage behind elegant travelers on their way to coaches; hawkers shouting refreshments for sale; and three or four policemen moving around, keeping order and watching for buzzers —pickpockets—since train stations were becoming their new favorite haunt. The dipper would nail his quarry as he boarded the train, and the victim would not discover the robbery until he was well out of London.

The association of pickpockets with train stations became so notorious that when William Frith painted one of the most famous pictures of his generation, "The Railway Station," in 1862, the chief focus of the composition was two detectives pinching a thief.

Now the London Bridge Station had several Metropolitan Police constables. And the railway companies had private guards as well.

"It's fair aswarm with miltonians," Agar said unhappily, looking around the station platforms.

"Never mind that," Pierce said. He watched the railway office.

At one o'clock, the clerks clambered down the iron stairs, chattering among themselves, off to lunch. The traffic manager, a stern gentleman in muttonchop whiskers, remained inside. The clerks were back at two o'clock, and the office routine resumed.

The next day, the manager went to lunch but two of the clerks remained behind, skipping lunch.

By the third day, they knew the pattern: one or more of the men in the office went to lunch for an hour at one o'clock, but the office was never left unattended. The conclusion was clear.

"No daylight gammon," Agar said.

"Perhaps Sunday," Pierce said, thinking aloud.

In those days—and indeed to the present day—the British railway system strongly resisted operations on the Sabbath. It was considered unnecessary and unseemly for any company to do business on Sunday, and the railways in particular had always shown an oddly moralistic bent. For example, smoking in railway carriages was forbidden long after smoking became a widespread custom in society; a gentleman who wished to enjoy a cigar was obliged to tip the railway footman—another forbidden act—and this state of affairs continued, despite the intense pressure of public opinion, until 1868, when Parliament finally passed a law forcing the railways to allow passengers to smoke.

Similarly, although everyone agreed that the most God-fearing men sometimes needed to travel on the Sabbath, and although the popular custom of weekend excursions provided ever more pressure for Sunday schedules, the railways fought stubbornly against this trend. In 1854, the South Eastern Railway ran only four trains on Sunday, and the other line that used London Bridge, the London & Greenwich Railway, ran only six trains, less than half the usual number.

Pierce and Agar checked the station the following Sunday, and found a double guard posted outside the traffic manager's office; one jack stationed himself near the door, and the second was positioned near the foot of the stairs.

"Why?" Pierce asked when he saw the two guards. "Why, in God's name, *why?*"

In later courtroom testimony, it emerged that the South Eastern Railway management changed hands in the autumn of 1854. Its new owner, Mr. Willard Perkins, was a gentleman of philanthropic bent whose concern for the lower classes was such that he introduced a policy of employing more people at all positions on the line, "in order to provide honest work for those who might otherwise be tempted into lawlessness and improvident promiscuity." The extra personnel were hired for this reason alone; the railway never suspected a robbery, and indeed Mr. Perkins was greatly shocked when his line was eventually robbed.

It is also true that at this time the South Eastern Railway was trying to build new access lines into downtown London, and this caused the displacement of many families and the destruction of their houses. Thus this philanthropic endeavor had a certain public-relations aspect in the minds of the railway owners.

"No gammon on Sunday," Agar said, looking at the two guards. "Perhaps Christmas?"

Pierce shook his head. It was possible that security might be relaxed on

Christmas Day, but they could not depend on that. "We need something routine," he said.

"There's nothing to be done by day."

"Yes," Pierce said. "But we don't know the full night routine. We never had an all-night watch." At night the station was deserted, and loiterers and tramps were briskly ordered off by the policemen making their rounds.

"They'll shoo away a canary," Agar said. "And perhaps collar him as well."

"I was thinking of a canary in a lurk," Pierce said. A concealed man could remain all night in the station.

"Clean Willy?"

"No," Pierce said. "Clean Willy is a mouth and a flat, without a downy bone in his body. He's glocky."

"It's true he's glocky," Agar said.

Clean Willy, dead at the time of the trial, was noted in courtroom testimony to be of "diminished faculties of reasoning"; this was reported by several witnesses. Pierce himself said, "We felt we could not trust him to do the surveillance. If he were apprehended, he would put down on us —reveal our plans—and never know the difference."

"Who shall we have instead?" Agar said, looking around the station.

"I was thinking of a skipper," Pierce said.

"A skipper?" Agar said, in surprise.

"Yes," Pierce said. "I think a skipper would do nicely. Do you happen to know of a bone skipper?"

"I can find one. But what's the lurk, then?"

"We'll pack him in a crate," Pierce said.

Pierce then arranged for a packing crate to be built and delivered to his residence. Agar obtained, by his own accounting, "a very reliable skipper," and arrangements were made to send the crate to the railway station.

The skipper, named Henson, was never found, nor was there much attempt to track him down; he was a very minor figure in the entire scheme, and by his very nature was somebody not worth bothering with. For the term "skipper" did not imply an occupation, but rather a way of life, and more specifically a way of spending the night.

During the mid-century, London's population was growing at the rate of 20 percent per decade. The number of people in the city was increasing by more than a thousand per day, and even with massive building programs and densely crowded slums, a sizable fraction of the population lacked both shelter and the means to pay for it. Such people spent their nights outdoors, wherever the police with the dreaded bull's-eye lanterns would leave them alone. The favorite places were the so-called "Dry-Arch Hotels," meaning the arches of railway bridges, but there were other haunts: ruined buildings, shop doorways, boiler rooms, omnibus depots, empty market stalls, under hedges, any place that provided a kip. "Skippers" were people who routinely sought another kind of shelter: barns and outhouses. At this time even rather elegant households frequently lacked indoor plumbing; the outhouse was a fixture among all classes, and it was increasingly found in public places as well. The skipper would wedge himself into these narrow confines and sleep away the night.

At his trial, Agar spoke proudly of the way he had procured a reliable skipper. Most of the night people were muck-snipes or tramps, wholly down and out; skippers were a little more enterprising than most, but they were still at the bottom of the social order. And they were often soaks; no doubt their intoxication helped them tolerate their fragrant resting places.

The reason Pierce wanted a skipper, of course, was to obtain someone who could tolerate cramped quarters for many hours. The man Henson was reported to have found his shipping crate "ever so wide" as he was nailed into it.

This crate was placed strategically within London Bridge Station. Through the slats, Henson was able to watch the behavior of the night guard. After the first night, the crate was hauled away, painted another color, and returned to the station again. This routine was followed three nights in succession. Then Henson reported his findings. None of the thieves was encouraged.

"The jack's solid," he told Pierce. "Regular as this very clock." He held up the stopwatch Pierce had given him to time the activities. "Comes on at seven prompt, with his little paper bag of supper. Sits on the steps, always alert, never a snooze, greeting the crusher on his rounds."

"What are the rounds?"

"First crusher works to midnight, goes every eleven minutes round the station. Sometimes he goes twelve, and once or twice thirteen minutes, but regular, it's eleven for him. Second crusher works midnight to the dawn. He's a flummut crusher, keeps to no beat but goes this way and that, popping up here and there like a jack-in-a-box, with a wary eye in all directions. And he's got himself two barkers at his belt."

"What about the jack who sits by the office door?" Pierce said.

"Solid, like I say, ream solid. Comes at seven, chats with the first crusher—he doesn't care for the second crusher, he cools him with a steady eye, he does. But the first crusher he likes, chats now and again with him, but never a stop in the crusher's rounds, just a little chat."

"Does he ever leave his place?" Pierce said.

"No," the skipper said. "He sits right there, and then he hears the bells of Saint Falsworth ringing the hour, and each time they ring he cocks his head and listens. Now at eleven o'clock, he opens his bag, and eats his tightener, always at the ringing of the clock. Now he eats for maybe ten, fifteen minutes, and he has a bottle of reeb"—beer—"and then the crusher comes around again. Now the jack sits back, taking his ease, and he waits until the crusher comes once more. Now it's half past eleven or thereabouts. And then the crusher passes him by, and the jack goes to the W.C."

"Then he *does* leave his place," Pierce said.

"Only for the pisser."

"And how long is he gone?"

"I was thinking you might want to know," Henson said, "so I clocked it proper. He's gone sixty-four seconds one night, and sixty-eight the next night, and sixty-four the third night. Always at the same time of the night, near about eleven-thirty. And he's back to his post when the guard makes the last round, quarter to midnight, and then the other crusher comes on to the beat."

"He did this every night?"

"Every night. It's the reeb does it. Reeb makes a man have a powerful urge."

"Yes," Pierce said, "beer does have that effect. Now does he leave his post at any other time?"

"Not to my eye."

"And you never slept?"

"What? When I'm sleeping here all the day through on your nice bed, here in your lodgings, and you ask if I kip the night away?"

"You must tell me the truth," Pierce said, but without any great sense of urgency.

(Agar later testified: "Pierce asks him the questions, see, but he shows no interest in the matter, he plays like a flimp or a dub buzzer, or a mutcher, no interest or importance, and this because he don't want the skipper to granny that a bone lay is afoot. Now the skipper should have done, we went to a lot of trouble on his account, and he could have put down on us to the miltonians, and for a pretty penny, too, but he hasn't the sense, otherwise why'd he be a skipper, eh?"

(This statement put the court into an uproar. When His Lordship requested an explanation, Agar said with an expression of surprise that he had just explained it as best he could. It required several minutes of interrogation to make it clear that Agar meant that Pierce had pretended to be a "flimp or dub buzzer"—that is, a snatch-pickpocket or a low-grade thief, or a "mutcher," a man who rolled drunks—in order to deceive the skipper, so that the skipper would not comprehend that a good criminal plan was being worked out. Agar also said that the skipper should have figured it out for himself and "put down" on them—that is, squealed to the police—but he lacked the sense to do so. This was only one of several instances in which incomprehensible criminal slang halted courtroom proceedings.)

"I swear, Mr. Pierce," the skipper said. "I swear I never slept a bit."

"And the jack never left except that one time each night?"

"Aye, and every night the same. He's regular as this jerry"—he held up his stopwatch—"that jack is."

Pierce thanked the skipper, paid him a half-crown for his troubles, allowed himself to be whined and cajoled into paying an additional half-crown, and sent the man on his way. As the door closed on the skipper, Pierce told Barlow to "worry" the man; Barlow nodded and left the house by another exit.

When Pierce returned to Agar, he said, "Well? Is it a coopered ken?"

"Sixty-four seconds," Agar said, shaking his head. "That's not your kinchin lay"—not exactly robbing children.

"I never said it was," Pierce said. "But you keep telling me you're the best screwsman in the country, and here's a fitting challenge for your talents: is it a coopered ken?"

"Maybe," Agar said. "I got to practice the lay. And I need to cool it close up. Can we pay a visit?"

"Certainly," Pierce said.

Chapter 21

An Audacious Act

"Of recent weeks," wrote the *Illustrated London News* on December 21, 1854, "the incidence of bold and brutal street banditry has reached alarming proportions, particularly of an evening. It would appear that the faith Mr. Wilson placed in street gas lighting as a deterrent to blackguard acts has been unjustified, for the villains are ever bolder, preying upon an unsuspecting populace with the utmost audacity. Only yesterday a constable, Peter Farrell, was lured into an alley, whereupon a band of common thugs fell upon him, beating him and taking all of his possessions and even his very uniform. Nor must we forget that just a fortnight past, Mr. Parkington, M.P., was viciously assaulted in an open, well-lighted place while walking from Parliament to his club. This epidemic of garrotting must receive the prompt attention of authorities in the near future."

The article went on to describe the condition of Constable Farrell, who was "faring no better than could be expected." The policeman gave the story that he had been called by a well-dressed woman who was arguing with her cabdriver, "a surly thug of a fellow with a white scar across the forehead." When the policeman interceded in the dispute, the cabby fell on him, swearing and cursing and beating him with a needy, or blackjack;

and when the unfortunate policeman came to his senses, he discovered he had been stripped of his clothing.

In 1854, many urban-dwelling Victorians were concerned over what was viewed as an upsurge in street crime. Later periodic "epidemics" of street violence finally culminated in a pedestrian panic during the years 1862 and 1863, and the passage of the "Garrotting Act" by Parliament. This legislation provided unusually stiff penalties for offenders, including flogging in installments—to allow the prisoners to recover before their next scheduled beating—and hanging. Indeed, more people were hanged in England in 1863 than in any year since 1838.

Brutal street crime was the lowest form of underworld activity. Rampsmen and footpads were frequently despised by their fellow criminals, who abhorred crude lays and acts of violence. The usual method of footpadding called for a victim, preferably drunk, to be lured into a corner by an accomplice, preferably a woman, whereupon the footpad would "bear up" on the victim, beat him with a cudgel and rob him, leaving him in the gutter. It was not an elegant way to make a living.

The lurid details of a footpad bearing up on his hapless quarry were the ordinary fare of news reporting. Apparently, no one ever stopped to think how strange the attack on Constable Farrell really was. In fact, it made very little sense. Then, as now, criminals tried wherever possible to avoid confrontations with the police. To "prop a crusher" was merely asking for an all-out manhunt through the rookeries until the culprits were apprehended, for the police took a special interest in attacks on their own kind.

Nor was there any sensible reason to attack a policeman. He was more capable than most victims of defending himself, and he never carried much money; often he had no money at all.

And, finally, there was absolutely no point in stripping a policeman. In those days, stripping was a common crime, usually the work of old women who lured children into alleys and then took all their clothing to sell at a secondhand shop. But you could not take the down off a crusher's dunnage; that is, you could not disguise a policeman's uniform so that it would have resale value. Secondhand shops were always under surveillance, and always accused of taking stolen goods; no "translator" would ever accept a police uniform. It was perhaps the only kind of clothing in all London that had no resale value at all.

Thus the attack on Constable Farrell was not merely dangerous but pointless, and any thoughtful observer would have been led to ponder why it had occurred at all.

Chapter 22

The Prad Prig

Sometime in late December, 1854, Pierce met a man named Andrew Taggert in the King's Arms publican house, off Regent Street. Taggert was by then nearly sixty, and a well-known character in the neighborhood. He had survived a long and varied career, which is worth briefly recounting, for he is one of the few participants in The Great Train Robbery whose background is known.

Taggert was born around 1790 outside Liverpool, and came to London near the turn of the century with his unmarried mother, a prostitute. By the age of ten, he was employed in "the resurrection trade," the business of digging up fresh corpses from graveyards to sell to medical schools. He soon acquired a reputation for uncommon daring; it was said that he once transported a stiff through London streets in daylight, with the man propped up in his cart like a passenger.

The Anatomy Act of 1838 ended the business in corpses, and Andrew Taggert shifted to the smasher's job of "ringing the changes"—disposing of counterfeit money. In this maneuver, a genuine coin would be offered to a shopkeeper for some purchase, and then the smasher would fumble in his purse, saying that he thought he had correct change, and take the original coin back. After a while, he would say, "No, I don't have it, after all," and hand over a counterfeit coin in place of the original. This was petty work, and Taggert soon tired of it. He moved on to a variety of con games, becoming a full-fledged magsman by the middle 1840s. He was apparently very successful in his work; he took a respectable flat in Camden Town, which was not a wholly respectable area. (Charles Dickens had lived there some fifteen years earlier, while his father was in prison.) Taggert also took a wife, one Mary Maxwell, a widow, and it is one of those minor ironies that the master magsman should himself be conned. Mary Maxwell was a coiner specializing in small silver coins. This bit-faker had served time in prison on several occasions, and knew something of the law, which her new husband apparently did not, for she had not married idly.

A woman's legal position was already the subject of active attempts at reform; but at this time women did not have the right to vote, to own property, or to make wills, and the earnings of any married woman who was separated from her husband were still legally the property of her husband. Although the law treated women as near idiots and appeared overwhelmingly to favor men, there were some odd quirks, as Taggert discovered soon enough.

In 1847, the police raided Mary Taggert's coining operation, catching her red-handed in the midst of stamping out sixpenny pieces. She greeted the raid with equanimity, announced pleasantly that she was married, and told the police the whereabouts of her husband.

By law, a husband was responsible for any criminal activities of his wife. It was assumed that such activity must be the result of the husband's planning and execution, in which the wife was a mere—and perhaps unwilling—participant.

In July, 1847, Andrew Taggert was arrested and convicted of counterfeiting currency and sentenced to eight years in Bridewell Prison; Mary Taggert was released without so much as a reprimand. She is said to have displayed "a roistering, bantering demeanour" in the courtroom at the time of her husband's sentencing.

Taggert served three years, and was given a ticket-of-leave and allowed to depart. Afterward it was said the steel had gone out of him, a common consequence of a prison term; he no longer had the energy or the confidence to be a magsman, and turned to hoof-snaffling, or horse stealing. By 1854, he was a familiar face in the flash sporting pubs frequented by turfites; he was said to have been involved in the scandal of 1853 in which a four-year-old was passed off as a three-year-old in the Derby. No one was certain but, as a known prad prig, he was thought to have engineered the theft of the most famous prad of recent years: Silver Whistle, a three-year-old from Derbyshire.

Pierce met him in the King's Arms with a most peculiar suggestion, and Taggert gulped his gin as he said, "You want to snaffle a *what?*"

"A leopard," Pierce said.

"Now, where's an honest man like me to find a leopard?" Taggert said.

"I wouldn't know," Pierce said.

"Never in my life," Taggert said, "would I know of any leopard, excepting the bestiaries here and there, which have all manner of beasts."

"That's so," Pierce said calmly.

"Is it to be christened?"

Now this was a particularly difficult problem. Taggert was an expert christener—a man who could conceal the fact that goods were stolen. He could disguise the markings of a horse so that even its owner would not recognize it. But christening a leopard might be harder.

"No," Pierce said. "I can take it as you have it."

"Won't gull nobody."

"It doesn't have to."

"What's it for, then?"

Pierce gave Taggert a particularly severe look and did not reply.

"No harm in asking," Taggert said. "It's not every day a man gets asked to snaffle a leopard, so I ask why—no harm intended."

"It is a present," Pierce said, "for a lady."

"Ah, a lady."

"On the Continent."

"Ah, on the Continent"

"In Paris."

"Ah."

Taggert looked him up and down. Pierce was well dressed. "You could buy one right enough," he said. "Cost you just as dear as buying from me."

"I made you a business proposition."

"So you did, and a proper one, too, but you didn't mention the joeys for me. You just mention you want a knapped leopard."

"I'll pay you twenty guineas."

"Cor, you'll pay me forty and count yourself lucky."

"I'll pay you twenty-five and *you'll* count yourself lucky," Pierce said.

Taggert looked unhappy. He twisted his gin glass in his hands. "All right, then," he said. "When's it to be?"

"Never you mind," Pierce said. "You find the animal and set the lay, and you'll hear from me soon enough." And he dropped a gold guinea on the counter.

Taggert picked it up, bit it, nodded, and touched his cap. "Good day to you, sir," he said.

"Good day," Pierce said.

Chapter 23

The Jolly Gaff

The twentieth-century urban dweller's attitude of fear or indifference to a crime in progress would have astounded the Victorians. In those days, any person being robbed or mugged immediately raised a hue and cry, and the victim both expected and got an immediate response from law-abiding citizens around him, who joined in the fray with alacrity in an attempt to catch the bolting villian. Even ladies of breeding were known, upon occasion, to participate in a fracas with enthusiasm.

There were several reasons for the willingness of the populace to get involved in a crime. In the first place, an organized police force was still relatively new; London's Metropolitan Police was the best in England, but it was only twenty-five years old, and people did not yet believe that crime was "something for the police to take care of." Second, firearms were rare, and remain so to the present day in England; there was little likelihood of a bystander stopping a charge by pursuing a thief. And finally, the majority of criminals were children, often extremely young children, and adults were not hesitant to go after them.

In any case, an adept thief took great care to conduct his business undetected, for if any alarm was raised, the chances were that he would be caught. For this very reason thieves often worked in gangs, with several members acting as "stalls" to create confusion in any alarm. Criminals of the day also utilized the fracas—as a staged event—to cover illegal activities, and this maneuver was known as a "jolly gaff."

A good jolly gaff required careful planning and timing, for it was, as the name implied, a form of theatre. On the morning of January 9, 1855, Pierce looked around the cavernous, echoing interior of the London Bridge Station and saw that all his players were in position.

Pierce himself would perform the most crucial role, that of the "beefer." He was dressed as a traveler, as was Miss Miriam alongside him. She would be the "plant."

A few yards distant was the "culprit," a chavy nine years old, scruffy and noticeably (should anyone care to observe it, *too* noticeably) out of place among the crowd of first-class passengers. Pierce had himself selected the chavy from among a dozen children in the Holy Land; the criterion was speed, pure and simple.

Farther away still was the "crusher," Barlow, wearing a constable's uniform with the hat pulled down to conceal the white scar across his forehead. Barlow would permit the child to elude him as the gaff progressed.

Finally, not far from the steps to the railway dispatcher's office was the whole point of the ploy: Agar, dressed out of twig—disguised—in his finest gentleman's clothing.

As it came time for the London & Greenwich eleven-o'clock train to depart, Pierce scratched his neck with his left hand. Immediately, the child came up and brushed rather abruptly against Miss Miriam's right side, rustling her purple velvet dress. Miss Miriam cried, "I've been robbed, John!"

Pierce raised his beef: "Stop, thief!" he shouted, and raced after the bolting chavy. "Stop, thief!"

Startled bystanders immediately grabbed at the youngster, but he was quick and slippery, and soon tore free of the crowd and ran toward the back of the station.

There Barlow in his policeman's uniform came forward menacingly. Agar, as a civic-spirited gentleman, also joined in the pursuit. The child was trapped; his only escape lay in a desperate scramble up the stairs leading to the railway office, and he ran hard, with Barlow, Agar, and Pierce fast on his heels.

The little boy's instructions had been explicit: he was to get up the stairs, into the office, past the desks of the clerks, and back to a high rear window opening out onto the roof of the station. He was to break this window in an apparent attempt to escape. Then Barlow would apprehend him. But he was to struggle valiantly until Barlow cuffed him; this was his signal that the gaff had ended.

The child burst into the South Eastern Railway office, startling the clerks. Pierce dashed in immediately afterward: "Stop him, he's a thief!" Pierce shouted and, in his own pursuit, knocked over one of the clerks. The child was scrambling for the window. Then Barlow, the constable, came in.

"I'll handle this," Barlow said, in an authoritative and tough voice, but he clumsily knocked one of the desks over and sent papers flying.

"Catch him! Catch him!" Agar called, entering the offices.

By now the child was scrambling up onto the station dispatcher's desk, going toward a narrow high window; he cracked the glass with his small fist, cutting himself. The station dispatcher kept saying "Oh, dear, oh, dear," over and over.

"I am an officer of the law, make way!" Barlow shouted.

"Stop him!" Pierce screamed, allowing himself to become quite hysterical. "Stop him, he's getting away!"

Glass fragments from the window fell on the floor, and Barlow and the child rolled on the ground in an uneven struggle that took rather longer to resolve itself than one might expect. The clerks and the dispatchers watched in considerable confusion.

No one noticed that Agar had turned his back on the commotion and picked the lock on the door to the office, trying several of his jangling ring of bettys until he found one that worked the mechanism. Nor did anyone notice when Agar then moved to the side wall cabinet, also fitted with a lock, which he also picked with one key after another until he found one that worked.

Three or four minutes passed before the young ruffian—who kept slipping from the hands of the redfaced constable—was finally caught by Pierce, who held him firmly. At last the constable gave the little villain a good boxing on the ears, and the lad ceased to struggle and handed up the purse he had stolen. He was carted away by the constable. Pierce dusted himself off, looked around the wreckage of the office, and apologized to the clerks and the dispatcher.

Then the other gentleman who had joined in the pursuit said, "I fear, sir, that you have missed your train."

"By God, I have," Pierce said. "Damn the little rascal."

And the two gentleman departed—the one thanking the other for helping corner the thief, and the other saying it was nothing—leaving the clerks to clean up the mess.

It was, Pierce later reflected, a nearly perfect jolly gaff.

Chapter 24

Hykey Doings

When Clean Willy Williams, the snakesman, arrived at Pierce's house late in the afternoon of January 9, 1855, he found himself confronted by a very strange spectacle in the drawing room.

Pierce, wearing a red velvet smoking jacket, lounged in an easy chair, smoking a cigar, utterly relaxed, a stopwatch in his hands.

In contrast, Agar, in shirtsleeves, stood in the center of the room. Agar was bent into a kind of half-crouch; he was watching Pierce and panting slightly.

"Are you ready?" Pierce said.

Agar nodded.

"Go!" Pierce said, and flicked the stopwatch.

To Clean Willy's amazement, Agar dashed across the room to the fireplace, where he began to jog in place, counting to himself, his lips moving, in a low whisper, ". . . seven . . . eight . . . nine . . ."

"That's it," Pierce said. "Door!"

"Door!" Agar said and, in pantomime, turned the handle on an unseen door. He then took three steps to the right, and reached up to shoulder height, touching something in the air.

"Cabinet," Pierce said.

"Cabinet . . ."

Now Agar fished two wax flats out of his pocket, and pretended to make an impression of a key. "Time?" he asked.

"Thirty-one," Pierce said.

Agar proceeded to make a second impression, on a second set of flats, all the while counting to himself. "Thirty-three, thirty-four, thirty-five . . ."

Again, he reached into the air, with both hands, as if closing something. "Cabinet shut," he said, and took three paces back across the room. "Door!"

"Fifty-four," Pierce said.

"Steps!" Agar said, and ran in place once more, and then sprinted across the room to halt beside Pierce's chair. "Done!" he cried.

Pierce looked at the watch and shook his head. "Sixty-nine." He puffed on his cigar.

"Well," Agar said, in a wounded tone, "it's better than it was. What was the last time?"

"Your last time was seventy-three."

"Well, it's better—"

"—But not good enough. Maybe if you don't close the cabinet. And don't hang up the keys, either. Willy can do that."

"Do what?" Willy said, watching.

"Open and close the cabinet," Pierce said.

Agar went back to his starting position.

"Ready?" Pierce said.

"Ready," Agar said.

Once again, this odd charade was repeated, with Agar sprinting across the room, jogging in place, pretending to open a door, taking three steps, making two wax impressions, taking three steps, closing a door, jogging in place, and then running across the room.

"Time?"

Pierce smiled. "Sixty-three," he said.

Agar grinned, gasping for breath.

"Once more," Pierce said, "just to be certain."

Later in the afternoon, Clean Willy was given the lay.

"It'll be tonight," Pierce said. "Once it's dark, you'll go up to London Bridge, and get onto the roof of the station. That a problem?"

Clean Willy shook his head. "What then?"

"When you're on the roof, cross to a window that is broken. You'll see it; it's the window to the dispatcher's office. Little window, barely a foot square."

"What then?"

"Get into the office."

"Through the window?"

"Yes."

"What then?"

"Then you will see a cabinet, painted green, mounted on the wall." Pierce looked at the little snakesman. "You'll have to stand on a chair to reach it. Be very quiet; there's a jack posted outside the office, on the steps."

Clean Willy frowned.

"Unlock the cabinet," Pierce said, "with this key." He nodded to Agar, who gave Willy the first of the picklocks. "Unlock the cabinet, and open it up, and wait."

"What for?"

"Around ten-thirty, there'll be a bit of a shindy. A soak will be coming into the station to chat up the jack."

"What then?"

"Then you unlock the main door to the office, using this key here"—Agar gave him the second key—"and then you wait."

"What for?"

"For eleven-thirty, or thereabouts, when the jack goes to the W.C. Then Agar comes up the steps, through the door you've unlocked, and he makes his waxes. He leaves, and you lock the first door right away. By now, the jack is back. You lock the cabinets, put the chair back, and go out the window, quiet-like."

"That's the lay?" Clean Willy said doubtfully.

"That's the lay."

"You popped me out of Newgate for this?" Clean Willy said. "This is no shakes, to knock over a deadlurk."

"It's a deadlurk with a jack posted at the door, and it's quiet, you'll have to be quiet-like, all the time."

Clean Willy grinned. "Those keys mean a sharp vamp. You've planned."

"Just do the lay," Pierce said, "and quiet."

"Simple," Clean Willy said.

"Keep those dubs handy," Agar said, pointing to the keys, "and have the doors ready and open when I come in, or it's nommus for all of us, and we're likely nibbed by the crusher."

"Don't want to be nibbed," Willy said.

"Then look sharp, and be ready."

Clean Willy nodded. "What's for dinner?" he said.

Chapter 25

Breaking the Drum

On the evening of January 9th, a characteristic London "pea soup" fog, heavily mixed with soot, blanketed the town. Clean Willy Williams, easing down Tooley Street, one eye to the façade of London Bridge Station, was not sure he liked the fog. It made his movements on the ground less noticeable, but it was so dense that he could not see the second story of the terminus building, and he was worried about access to the roof. It wouldn't do to make the climb halfway, only to discover it was a dead end.

But Clean Willy knew a lot about the way buildings were constructed, and after an hour of maneuvering around the station he found his spot. By climbing onto a footman's luggage cart, he was able to jump to a drainpipe, and from there to the sill of the second-story windows. Here a lip of stone ran the length of the second story; he inched along it until he reached a corner in the façade. Then he climbed up the corner, his back to the wall, in the same way that he had escaped from Newgate Prison. He would leave marks, of course; in those days nearly every central London building was soot-covered, and Clean Willy's climb left an odd pattern of whitish scrapes going up the corner.

By eight o'clock he was standing on the broad roof of the terminus. The main portion of the station was roofed in slate; over the tracks the roofing was glass, and he avoided that. Clean Willy weighed sixty-eight pounds, but he was heavy enough to break the glass roofing.

Moving cautiously through the fog, he edged around the building until he found the broken window Pierce had mentioned. Looking in, he saw the dispatcher's office. He was surprised to notice that it was in some disarray, as if there had been a struggle in the office during the day and the damage only partially corrected.

He reached through the jagged hole in the glass, turned the transom lock, and raised the window. It was a window of rectangular shape, perhaps nine by sixteen inches. He wriggled through it easily, stepped down onto a desk top, and paused.

He had not been told the walls of the office were glass.

Through the glass, he could see down to the deserted tracks and platforms of the station below. He could also see the jack on the stairs, near the door, a paper bag containing his dinner at his side.

Carefully, Clean Willy climbed down off the desk. His foot crunched on a shard of broken glass; he froze. But if the guard heard it, he gave no sign. After a moment, Willy crossed the office, lifted a chair, and set it next to the high cabinet. He stepped onto the chair, plucked the twirl Agar had given him from his pocket, and picked the cabinet lock. Then he sat down to wait, hearing distant church bells toll the hour of nine o'clock.

Agar, lurking in the deep shadows of the station, also heard the church bells. He sighed. Another two and a half hours, and he had been wedged into a cramped corner for two hours already. He knew how stiff and painful his legs would be when he finally made his sprint for the stairs.

From his hiding place, he could see Clean Willy make an entrance into the office behind the guard; and he could see Willy's head when he stood on the chair and worked the cabinet lock. Then Willy disappeared.

Agar sighed again. He wondered, for the thousandth time, what Pierce intended to do with these keys. All he knew was that it must be a devilish flash pull. A few years earlier, Agar had been in on a Brighton warehouse pull. There had been nine keys involved: one for an outer gate, two for an inner gate, three for the main door, two for an office door, and one for a storeroom. The pogue had been ten thousand quid in B. of E. notes, and the putter-up had spent four months arranging the lay.

Yet here was Pierce, flush if ever a cracksman was, spending eight months now to get four keys, two from bankers, and two from a railway office. It had all cost a pretty penny, Agar was certain of that, and it meant the pogue was well worth having.

But what *was* it? Why were they breaking this drum now? The question preoccupied him more than the mechanics of timing a sixty-four-second smash and grab. He was a professional; he was cool; he had prepared well and was fully confident. His heart beat evenly as he stared across the station at the jack on the stairs, as the crusher made his rounds.

The crusher said to the jack, "You know there's a P.R. on?" A.P.R. was a prize-ring event.

"No," said the jack. "Who's it to be?"

"Stunning Bill Hampton and Edgar Moxley."

"Where's it to be, then?" the jack said.

"I hear Leicester," the crusher said.

"Where's your money?"

"Stunning Bill, for my gambit."

"He's a good one," the jack said. "He's tough, is Bill."

"Aye," the crusher said, "I've got a half-crown or two on him says he's tough."

And the crusher went on, making his rounds.

Agar smirked in the darkness. A copper talking big of a five-shilling bet. Agar bet ten quid on the last P.R., between the Lancaster Dervish, John Boynton, and the gammy Kid Ballew. Agar had come off well on that one: odds were two to one; he'd done a bit of winning there.

He tensed the muscles in his cramped legs, trying to get the circulation going, and then he relaxed. He had a long wait ahead of him. He thought of his dolly-mop. Whenever he was working, he thought of his dolly's quim; it was a natural thing—tension turned a man randy. Then his thoughts drifted back to Pierce, and the question that Agar had puzzled over for nearly a year now: what *was* the damn pull?

The drunken Irishman with the red beard and slouch hat stumbled through the deserted station singing "Molly Malone." With his shuffling, flatfooted gait, he was a true soak, and as he walked along, it appeared he was so lost in his song that he might not notice the guard on the stairs.

But he did, and he eyed the guard's paper bag suspiciously before making an elaborate and wobbly bow.

"And a good evenin' to you, sir," the drunk said.

"Evening," the guard said.

"And what, may I inquire," said the drunk, standing stiffer, "is your business up there, eh? Up to no good, are you?"

"I'm guarding these premises here," the guard said.

The drunk hiccuped. "So you say, my good fellow, but many a rascal has said as much."

"Here, now—"

"I think," the drunk said, waving an accusatory finger in the air, trying to point it at the guard but unable to aim accurately, "I think, sir, we shall have the police to look you over, so that we shall know if you are up to no good."

"Now, look here," the guard said.

"You look here, and lively, too," the drunk said, and abruptly began to shout, "Police! *Po-lice!*"

"Here, now," the guard said, coming down the stairs. "Get a grip on yourself, you scurvy soak."

"Scurvy soak?" the drunk said, raising an eyebrow and shaking his fist. "I am a Dubliner, sir."

"I palled that, right enough," the guard snorted.

At that moment, the constable came running around the corner, drawn by the shouts of the drunk.

"Ah, a criminal, officer," said the drunk. "Arrest that scoundrel," he said, pointing to the guard, who had now moved to the bottom of the stairs. "He is up to no good."

The drunk hiccuped.

The constable and the guard exchanged glances, and then open smiles.

"You find this a laughing matter, sir?" said the drunk, turning to the copper. "I see nothing risible. The man is plainly up to no good."

"Come along, now," the constable said, "or I'll have you in lumber for creatin' a nuisance."

"A nuisance?" the drunk said, twisting free of the constable's arm. "I think you and this blackguard are in cahoots, sir."

"That's enough," the constable said. "Come along smartly."

The drunk allowed himself to be led away by the copper. He was last heard to say, "You wouldn't be havin' a daffy of reeb, would you, now?" and the constable assured him he had no drink on his person.

"Dublin," the guard said, sighing, and he climbed back up the stairs to eat his dinner. The distant chimes rang eleven o'clock.

Agar had seen it all, and while he was amused by Pierce's performance, he worried whether Clean Willy had taken the opportunity to open the office door. There was no way to know until he made his own mad dash, in less than half an hour now.

He looked at his watch, he looked at the door to the office, and he waited.

For Pierce, the most delicate part of his performance was the conclusion, when he was led by the constable out into Tooley Street. Pierce did not want to disrupt the policeman's regular rhythm on the beat, so he had to disengage himself rather rapidly.

As they came into the foggy night air, he breathed deeply. "Ah," he said, "and it's a lovely evening, brisk and invigorating."

The copper looked round at the gloomy fog. "Chill enough for me," he said.

"Well, my dear fellow," Pierce said, dusting himself off and making a show of straightening up, as if the night air had sobered him, "I am most grateful for your ministrations upon this occasion, and I can assure you that I can carry on well from here."

"You're not going to be creating another nuisance?"

"My dear sir," Pierce said, standing still straighter, "what do you take me for?"

The copper looked back at the London Bridge Station. It was his business to stay on the beat; a drunk wandering in was not his responsibility once he was ejected from the premises. And London was full of drunks, especially Irish ones who talked too much.

"Stay clear of trouble, then," the cop said, and let him go.

"A good evening to you, officer," Pierce said, and bowed to the departing crusher. Then he wandered out into the fog, singing "Molly Malone."

Pierce went no farther than the end of Tooley Street, less than a block from the station entrance. There, hidden in the fog, was a cab. He looked up at the driver.

"How'd it carry off?" Barlow asked.

"Smart and tidy," Pierce said. "I gave Willy two or three minutes; it should have been enough."

"Willy's a bit glocky."

"All he has to do," Pierce said, "is twirl two locks, and he's not too glocky to bring that off." He glanced at his watch. "Well, we'll know soon enough."

And he slipped away, in the fog, back toward the station.

At eleven-thirty, Pierce had taken up a position where he could see the dispatch office stairs and the guard. The copper made his round; he waved to the jack, who waved back. The copper went on; the jack yawned, stood, and stretched.

Pierce took a breath and poised his finger on the stopwatch button.

The guard came down the stairs, yawning again, and moved off toward the W.C. He walked several paces, and then was out of sight, around a corner.

Pierce hit the button, and counted softly, "One . . . two . . . three . . ."

He saw Agar appear, running hard, barefooted to make no sound, and dashing up the stairs to the door.

"Four . . . five . . . six . . ."

Agar reached the door, twisted the knob; the door opened and Agar was inside. The door closed.

"Seven . . . eight . . . nine . . ."

"Ten," Agar said, panting, looking around the office. Clean Willy, grinning in the shadows in the corner, took up the count.

"Eleven . . . twelve . . . thirteen . . ."

Agar crossed to the already opened cabinet. He removed the first of the wax blanks from his pocket, and then looked at the keys in the cabinet.

"Crikey!" he whispered.

"Fourteen . . . fifteen . . . sixteen . . ."

Dozens of keys hung in the cabinet, keys of all sorts, large and small, labeled and unlabeled, all hanging on hooks. He broke into a sweat in an instant.

"Crikey!"

"Seventeen . . . eighteen . . . nineteen . . ."

Agar was going to fall behind. He knew it with sickening suddenness: he was already behind on the count. He stared helplessly at the keys. He could not wax them all; which were the ones to do?

"Twenty . . . twenty-one . . . twenty-two . . ."

Clean Willy's droning voice infuriated him; Agar wanted to run across the room and strangle the little bastard. He stared at the cabinet in a rising panic. He remembered what the other two keys looked like; perhaps these two keys were similar. He peered close at the cabinet, squinting, straining: the light in the office was bad.

"Twenty-three . . . twenty-four . . . twenty-five . . ."

"It's no bloody use," he whispered to himself. And then he realized something odd: each hook had only one key, except for a single hook, which had two. He quickly lifted them off. They looked like the others he had done.

"Twenty-six . . . twenty-seven . . . twenty-eight . . ."

He set out the first blank, and pressed one side of the first key into the blank, holding it neatly, plucking it out with his fingernail; the nail on the little finger was long, one of the hallmarks of a screwsman.

"Twenty-nine . . . thirty . . . thirty-one . . ."

He took the second blank, flipped the key over, and pressed it into the wax to get the other side. He held it firmly, then scooped it out.

"Thirty-two . . . thirty-three . . . thirty-four . . ."

Now Agar's professionalism came into play. He was falling behind—at least five seconds off his count now, maybe more—but he knew that at all costs he must avoid confusing the keys. It was common enough for a screwsman under pressure to make two impressions of the same side of a single key; with two keys, the chance of confusion was doubled. Quickly but carefully, he hung up the first finished key.

"Thirty-five . . . thirty-six . . . thirty-seven, Lordy," Clean Willy said. Clean Willy was looking out the glass windows, down to where the guard would be returning in less than thirty seconds.

"Thirty-eight . . . thirty-nine . . . forty . . ."

Swiftly, Agar pressed the second key into his third blank. He held it there just an instant, then lifted it out. There was a decent impression.

"Forty-one . . . forty-two . . . forty-three . . ."

Agar pocketed the blank, and plucked up his fourth wax plate. He pressed the other side of the key into the soft material.

"Forty-four . . . forty-five . . . forty-six . . . forty-seven . . ."

Abruptly, while Agar was peeling the key free of the wax, the blank cracked in two.

"Damn!"

"Forty-eight . . . forty-nine . . . fifty . . ."

He fished in his pocket for another blank. His fingers were steady, but there was sweat dripping from his forehead.

"Fifty-one . . . fifty-two . . . fifty-three . . ."

He drew out a fresh blank and did the second side again.

"Fifty-four . . . fifty-five . . ."

He plucked the key out, hung it up, and dashed for the door, still holding the final blank in his fingers. He left the office without another look at Willy.

"Fifty-six," Willy said, immediately moving to the door to lock it up.

Pierce saw Agar exit, behind schedule by five full seconds. His face was flushed with exertion.

"Fifty-seven . . . fifty-eight . . ."

Agar sprinted down the stairs, three at a time.

"Fifty-nine . . . sixty . . . sixty-one . . ."

Agar streaked across the station to his hiding place.

"Sixty-two . . . sixty-three . . ."

Agar was hidden.

The guard, yawning, came around the corner, still buttoning up his trousers. He walked toward the steps.

"Sixty-four," Pierce said, and flicked his watch.

The guard took up his post at the stairs. After a moment, he began humming to himself, very softly, and it was a while until Pierce realized it was "Molly Malone."

Chapter 26

Crossing the Mary Blaine Scrob

"The distinction between base avarice and honest ambition may be exceeding fine," warned the Reverend Noel Blackwell in his 1853 treatise, *On the Moral Improvement of the Human Race*. No one knew the truth of his words better than Pierce, who arranged his next meeting at the Casino de Venise, in Windmill Street. This was a large and lively dance hall, brightly lit by myriad gas lamps. Young men spun and wheeled girls colorfully dressed and gay in their manner. Indeed, the total impression was one of fashionable splendor, which belied a reputation as a wicked and notorious place of assignation for whores and their clientele.

Pierce went directly to the bar, where a burly man in a blue uniform with silver lapel markings sat hunched over a drink. The man appeared distinctly uncomfortable in the casino. "Have you been here before?" Pierce asked.

The man turned. "You Mr. Simms?"

"That's right."

The burly man looked around the room, at the women, the finery, the bright lights. "No," he said, "never been before."

"Lively, don't you think?"

The man shrugged. "Bit above me," he said finally, and turned back to stare at his glass.

"And expensive," Pierce said.

The man raised his drink. "Two shillings a daffy? Aye, it's expensive."

"Let me buy you another," Pierce said, raising a gray-gloved hand to beckon the bartender. "Where do you live, Mr. Burgess?"

"I got a room in Moresby Road," the burly man said.

"I hear the air is bad there."

Burgess shrugged. "It'll do."

"You married?"

"Aye."

The bartender came, and Pierce indicated two more drinks. "What's your wife do?"

"She sews." Burgess showed a flash of impatience. "What's this all about, then?"

"Just a little conversation," Pierce said, "to see if you want to make more money."

"Only a fool doesn't," Burgess said shortly.

"You work the Mary Blaine," Pierce said.

Burgess, with still more impatience, nodded and flicked the silver SER letters on his collar: the insignia of the South Eastern Railway.

Pierce was not asking these questions to obtain information; he already knew a good deal about Richard Burgess, a Mary Blaine scrob, or guard on the railway. He knew where Burgess lived; he knew what his wife did; he knew that they had two children, aged two and four, and he knew that the four-year-old was sickly and needed the frequent attentions of a doctor, which Burgess and his wife could not afford. He knew that their room in Moresby Road was a squalid, peeling, narrow chamber that was ventilated by the sulfurous fumes of an adjacent gasworks.

He knew that Burgess fell into the lowest-paid category of railway employee. An engine driver was paid 35 shillings a week; a conductor 25 shillings; a coachman 20 or 21; but a guard was paid 15 shillings a week and counted himself lucky it was not a good deal less.

Burgess's wife made ten shillings a week, which meant that the family lived on a total of about sixty-five pounds a year. Out of this came certain expenses—Burgess had to provide his own uniforms—so that the true income was probably closer to fifty-five pounds a year, and for a family of four it was a very rough go.

Many Victorians had incomes at that level, but most contrived supplements of one sort or another: extra work, tips, and a child in industry were the most common. The Burgess household had none of these. They were compelled to live on their income, and it was little wonder that Burgess felt uncomfortable in a place that charged two shillings a drink. It was very far beyond his means.

"What's it to be?" Burgess said, not looking at Pierce.

"I was wondering about your vision."

"My vision?"

"Yes, your eyesight."

"My eyes are good enough."

"I wonder," Pierce said, "what it would take for them to go bad."

Burgess sighed, and did not speak for a moment. Finally he said in a weary voice, "I done a stretch in Newgate a few years back. I'm not wanting to see the cockchafer again."

"Perfectly sensible," Pierce said. "And I don't want anybody to blow my lay. We both have our fears."

Burgess gulped his drink. "What's the sweetener?"

"Two hundred quid," Pierce said.

Burgess coughed, and pounded his chest with a thick fist. "Two hundred quid," he repeated.

"That's right," Pierce said. "Here's ten now, on faith." He removed his wallet and took out two five-pound notes; he held the wallet in such a way that Burgess could not fail to notice it was bulging. He set the money on the bar top.

"Pretty a sight as a hot nancy," Burgess said, but he did not touch it. "What's the lay?"

"You needn't worry over the lay. All you need to do is worry over your eyesight."

"What is it I'm not to see, then?"

"Nothing that will get you into trouble. You'll never see the inside of a lockup again, I promise you that."

Burgess turned stubborn. "Speak plain," he said.

Pierce sighed. He reached for the money. "I'm sorry," he said, "I fear I must take my business elsewhere."

Burgess caught his hand. "Not overquick," he said. "I'm just asking."

"I can't tell you."

"You think I'll blow on you to the crushers?"

"Such things," Pierce said, "have been known to happen."

"I wouldn't blow."

Pierce shrugged.

There was a moment of silence. Finally, Burgess reached over with his other hand and plucked away the two five-pound notes. "Tell me what I do," he said.

"It's very simple," Pierce said. "Soon you will be approached by a man who will ask you whether your wife sews your uniforms. When you meet that man, you simply . . . look away."

"That's all?"

"That's all."

"For two hundred quid?"

"For two hundred quid."

Burgess frowned for a moment, and then began to laugh.

"What's funny?" Pierce said.

"You'll never pull it," Burgess said. "It's not to be done, that one. There's no cracking those safes, wherever I look. Few months past, there's a kid, works into the baggage car, wants to do those safes. Have a go, I says to him, and he has a go for half an hour, and he gets no further than the tip of my nose. Then I threw him off smartly, bounced him on his noggin."

"I know that," Pierce said. "I was watching."

Burgess stopped laughing.

Pierce withdrew two gold guineas from his pocket and dropped them on the counter. "There's a dollymop in the corner—pretty thing, wearing pink. I believe she's waiting for you," Pierce said, and then he got up and walked off.

Chapter 27

The Eel-Skinner's Perplexity

Economists of the mid-Victorian period note that increasing numbers of people made their living by what was then called "dealing," an inclusive term that referred to supplying goods and services to the burgeoning middle class. England was then the richest nation on earth, and the richest in history. The demand for all kinds of consumer goods was insatiable, and the response was specialization in manufacture, distribution, and sale of goods. It is in Victorian England that one first hears of cabinetmakers who made only the joints of cabinets, and of shops that sold only certain kinds of cabinets.

The increasing specialization was apparent in the underworld as well, and nowhere more peculiar than in the figure of the "eel-skinner." An eel-skinner was usually a metalworker gone bad, or one too old to keep up with the furious pace of legitimate production. In either case, he disappeared from honest circles, re-emerging as a specialized supplier of metal goods to criminals. Sometimes the eel-skinner was a coiner who could not get the stamps to turn out coins.

Whatever his background, his principal business was making eel-skins, or coshes. The earliest eel-skins were sausage-like canvas bags filled with sand, which rampsmen and gonophs—muggers and thieves—could carry up their sleeves until the time came to wield them on their victims. Later, eel-skins were filled with lead shot, and they served the same purpose.

An eel-skinner also made other articles. A "neddy" was a cudgel, sometimes a simple iron bar, sometimes a bar with a knob at one end. The "sack" was a two-pound iron shot placed in a strong stocking. A "whipler" was a shot with an attached cord, and was used to disable a victim head on; the attacker held the shot in his hand and flung it at the victim's face, "like a horrible yo-yo." A few blows from these weapons were certain to take the starch out of any quarry, and the robbery proceeded without further resistance.

As firearms became more common, eel-skinners turned to making bullets. A few skilled eel-skinners also manufactured sets of bettys, or picklocks, but this was demanding work, and most stuck to simpler tasks.

In early January, 1855, a Manchester eel-skinner named Harkins was visited by a gentleman with a red beard who said he wanted to purchase a quantity of LC shot.

"Easy enough done," the skinner said. "I make all manner of shot, and I can make LC right enough. How much will you have?"

"Five thousand," the gentleman said.

"I beg pardon?"

"I said, I will have five thousand LC shot."

The eel-skinner blinked. "Five thousand—that's a quantity. That's—let's see—six LC to the ounce. Now, then . . ." He stared up at the ceiling and plucked at his lower lip. "And sixteen . . . now, that makes it . . . Bless me, that's more'n fifty pounds of shot all in."

"I believe so," the gentleman said.

"You want fifty pounds of LC shot?"

"I want five thousand, yes."

"Well, fifty pounds of lead, that'll take some doing, and the casting—well, that'll take some doing. That'll take some time, five thousand LC shot will, some time indeed."

"I need it in a month," the gentleman said.

"A month, a month . . . Let's see, now . . . casting at a hundred a mold . . . Yes, well . . ." The eel-skinner nodded. "Right enough, you shall have five thousand within a month. You'll be collecting it?"

"I will," the gentleman said, and then he leaned closer, in a conspiratorial fashion. "It's for Scotland, you know."

"Scotland, eh?"

"Yes, Scotland."

"Oh, well, yes, I see that plain enough," the eel-skinner said, though the reverse was clearly true. The red-bearded man put down a deposit and departed, leaving the eel-skinner in a state of marked perplexity. He would have been even more perplexed to know that this gentleman had visited skinners in Newcastleon-Tyne, Birmingham, Liverpool, and London, and placed identical orders with each of them, so that he was ordering a total of two hundred and fifty pounds of lead shot. What use could anyone have for that?

Chapter 28

The Finishing Touch

London at the mid-century had six morning newspapers, three evening newspapers, and twenty influential weeklies. This period marked the beginning of an organized press with enough power to mold public opinion and, ultimately, political events. The unpredictability of that power was highlighted in January, 1855.

On the one hand, the first war correspondent in history, William Howard Russell, was in Russia with the Crimean troops, and his dispatches to the *Times* had aroused furious indignation at home. The charge of the Light Brigade, the bungling of the Balaclava campaign, the devastating winter when British troops, lacking food and medical supplies, suffered a 50 percent mortality—these were all reported in the press to an increasingly angry public.

By January, however, the commander of British forces, Lord Raglan, was severely ill, and Lord Cardigan—"haughty, rich, selfish and stupid," the man who had bravely led his Light Brigade to utter disaster, and then returned to his yacht to drink champagne and sleep—Lord Cardigan had returned home, and the press everywhere hailed him as a great national hero. It was a role he was only too happy to play. Dressed in the uniform he had worn at Balaclava, he was mobbed by crowds in every city; hairs from his horse's tail were plucked for souvenirs. London shops copied the woolen jacket he had worn in the Crimea—called a "Cardigan"—and thousands were sold.

The man known to his own troops as "the dangerous ass" went about the country delivering speeches recounting his prowess in leading the charge; and as the months passed, he spoke with more and more emotion, and was often forced to pause and revive himself. The press never ceased to cheer him on; there was no sense of the chastisement that later historians have richly accorded him.

But if the press was fickle, public tastes were even more so. Despite all the provocative news from Russia, the dispatches which most intrigued Londoners in January concerned a man-eating leopard that menaced Naini Tal in northern India, not far from the Burmese border. The "Panar man-eater" was said to have killed more than four hundred natives, and accounts were remarkable for their vivid, even lurid, detail. "The vicious Panar beast," wrote one correspondent, "kills for the sake of killing and not for any food. It rarely eats any portion of the body of its victims, although two weeks past it ate the upper torso of an infant after stealing it from its crib. Indeed, the majority of its victims have been children under the age of ten who are unfortunate enough to stray from the center of the village after nightfall. Adult victims are generally mauled and later die of suppurating wounds; Mr. Redby, a hunter of the region, says these infections are caused by rotten flesh lodged in the beast's claws. The Panar killer is exceedingly strong, and has been seen to carry off a fully grown female adult in its jaws, while the victim struggles and cries out most piteously."

These and other stories became the delicious talk of dining rooms among company given to raciness; women colored and tittered and exclaimed, while men—especially Company men who had spent time in India—spoke knowledgeably about the habits of such a beast, and its nature. An interesting working model of a tiger devouring an Englishman, owned by the East India Company, was visited by fascinated crowds. (The model can still be seen in the Victoria and Albert Museum.)

And when, on February 17, 1855, a caged, fully grown leopard arrived at London Bridge Terminus, it created a considerable stir—much more than the arrival, a short time previously, of armed guards carrying strongboxes of gold, which were loaded into the SER luggage van.

Here was a full-sized, snarling beast, which roared and charged the bars of its cage as it was loaded onto the same luggage van of the London-Folkestone train. The animal's keeper accompanied the beast, in order to look after the leopard's welfare, and to protect the luggage-van guard in the event of any unforeseen mishap.

Meanwhile, before the train departed the station, the keeper explained to the crowd of curious onlookers and children that the beast ate raw meat, that it was a female four years old, and that it was destined for the Continent, where it would be a present to a wellborn lady.

The train pulled out of the station shortly after eight o'clock, and the guard on the luggage van closed the sliding side door. There was a short silence while the leopard stalked its cage, and growled intermittently; finally the railway guard said, "What do you feed her?"

The animal's attendant turned to the guard. "Does your wife sew your uniforms?" he asked.

Burgess laughed. "You mean it's to be you?"

The attendant did not answer. Instead, he opened a small leather satchel and removed a jar of grease, several keys, and a collection of files of varied shapes and sizes.

He went immediately to the two Chubb safes, coated the four locks with grease, and began fitting his keys. Burgess watched with only vague interest in the process: he knew that rough-copied wax keys would not work on a finely made safe without polishing and refining. But he was also impressed; he never thought it would be carried off with such boldness.

"Where'd you make the impressions?" he said.

"Here and there," Agar replied, fitting and filing.

"They keep those keys separate."

"Do they," Agar said.

"Aye, they do. How'd you pull them?"

"That's no matter to you," Agar said, still working.

Burgess watched him for a time, and then he watched the leopard. "How much does he weigh?"

"Ask him," Agar said irritably.

"Are you taking the gold today, then?" Burgess asked as Agar managed to get one of the safe doors open. Agar did not answer; he stared transfixed for a moment at the strongboxes inside. "I say, are you taking the gold today?"

Agar shut the door. "No," he said. "Now stop your voker."

Burgess fell silent.

For the next hour, while the morning passenger train chugged from London to Folkestone, Agar worked on his keys. Ultimately, he had opened and closed both safes. When he was finished, he wiped the grease from the locks. Then he cleaned the locks with alcohol and dried them with a cloth. Finally he took his four keys, placed them carefully in his pocket, and sat down to await the arrival of the train at the Folkestone station.

Pierce met him at the station and helped to unload the leopard.

"How was it?" he asked.

"The finishing touches are done," Agar said, and then he grinned. "It's the gold, isn't it? The Crimean gold—that's the flash pull."

"Yes," Pierce said.

"When?"

"Next month," Pierce said.

The leopard snarled.

PART THREE

DELAYS AND DIFFICULTIES

March–May, 1855

Chapter 29

Minor Setbacks

The robbers originally intended to take the gold during the next Crimean shipment. The plan was extremely simple. Pierce and Agar were to board the train in London, each checking several heavy satchels onto the baggage van. The satchels would be filled with sewn packets of lead shot.

Agar would again ride in the van, and while Burgess looked away Agar would open the safes, remove the gold, and replace it with lead shot. These satchels would be thrown from the train at a predetermined point, and collected by Barlow. Barlow would then drive on to Folkestone, where he would meet Pierce and Agar.

Meanwhile, the gold strongboxes—still convincingly heavy—would be transferred to the steamer going to Ostend, where the theft would be discovered by the French authorities hours later. By then, enough people would have been involved in the transportation process that there would be no particular reason to fix suspicion on Burgess; and in any case, British-French relations were at a low level because of the Crimean War, and it would be natural that the French would assume the English had carried out the theft, and vice versa. The robbers could count on plenty of confusion to muddy the waters for the police.

The plan seemed utterly foolproof, and the robbers prepared to carry it out on the next gold shipment, scheduled for March 14, 1855.

On March 2nd, "that fiend in human shape," Czar Nicholas I of Russia, died suddenly. News of his death caused considerable confusion in business and financial circles. For several days the reports were doubted, and when his death was finally confirmed, the stock markets of Paris and London responded with large gains. But as a result of the general uncertainty the gold shipment was delayed until March 27th. By then, Agar, who had sunk into a kind of depression after the fourteenth, was desperately ill with an exacerbation of his chest condition, and so the opportunity was missed.

The firm of Huddleston & Bradford was making gold shipments once a month; there were now only 11,000 English troops in the Crimea, as opposed to 78,000 French, and most of the money was paid out directly from Paris. Thus Pierce and his compatriots were obliged to wait until April.

The next shipment was set for April 19th. The robbers at this time were getting their information on shipment schedules from a tart named Susan Lang, a favorite of Henry Fowler's. Mr. Fowler liked to impress the simple girl with episodes reflecting his importance to the world of banking and commerce, and for her part, the poor girl—who could hardly have understood a word he said—seemed endlessly fascinated by everything he told her.

Susan Lang was hardly simple, but somehow she got her facts wrong: the gold went out on April 18th, and when Pierce and Agar arrived at London Bridge Station in time to board the April 19th train, Burgess informed them of their error. To maintain appearances, Pierce and Agar made the trip anyway, but Agar testified in court that Pierce was in "very ugly humor indeed" during the journey.

The next shipment was scheduled for May 22nd. In order to prevent any further snags, Pierce took the rather risky step of opening a line of communication between Agar and Burgess. Burgess could reach Agar at any time through an intermediary, a betting-shop proprietor named Smashing Billy Banks; and Burgess was to get in touch with Banks if there was any change in the planned routine. Agar would check with Banks daily.

On May 10th, Agar returned to Pierce with a piece of ghastly news—the two safes had been removed from the South Eastern Railway's luggage van and returned to the manufacturer, Chubb, for "overhaul."

"Overhaul?" Pierce said. "What do you mean, overhaul?"

Agar shrugged. "That was the cant."

"Those are the finest safes in the world," Pierce said. "They don't go back for an overhaul." He frowned. "What's wrong with them?"

Agar shrugged.

"You bastard," Pierce said, "did you scratch the locks when you put on your finishing touches? I swear, if someone's cooled your scratches—"

"I greased her lovely," Agar said. "I know they look as a routine for scratches. I tell you, she had nary a tickle on her."

Agar's calm demeanor convinced Pierce that the screwsman was telling the truth. Pierce sighed. "Then *why?*"

"I don't know," Agar said. "You know a man who will blow on the doings at Chubb?"

"No," Pierce said. "And I wouldn't want to try a cross. They're not gulled at Chubb's." The safemaker's firm was unusually careful about its employees. Men were hired and fired only with reluctance, and they were continually warned to look for underworld figures who might try to bribe them.

"A little magging, then?" Agar suggested, meaning some conning.

Pierce shook his head. "Not me," he said. "They're just too careful; I'd never be able to slip it to them. . . ."

He stared into the distance thoughtfully.

"What is it?" Agar asked.

"I was thinking," Pierce said, "that they would never suspect a lady."

Chapter 30

A Visit to Mr. Chubb

What Rolls-Royce would become to automobiles, and Otis to elevators, Chubb's had long since been to safes. The head of that venerable firm, Mr. Laurence Chubb, Jr., did not later remember—or pretended not to remember—a visit by a handsome young woman in May, 1855. But an employee of the company was sufficiently impressed by the lady's beauty to recall her in great detail.

She arrived in a handsome coach, with liveried footmen, and swept imperiously into the firm unattended by any escort. She was extremely well dressed and spoke with a commanding manner; she demanded to see Mr. Chubb himself, and immediately.

When Mr. Chubb appeared a few moments later, the woman announced that she was Lady Charlotte Simms; that she and her invalid husband maintained a country estate in the Midlands, and that recent episodes of thievery in the neighborhood had convinced her that she and her husband needed a safe.

"Then you have come to the best shop in Christendom," said Mr. Chubb.

"So I have been previously informed," Lady Charlotte said, as if not at all convinced.

"Indeed, Madam, we manufacture the finest safes in the world, and in all sizes and varieties, and these excel even the best of the Hamburg German safes."

"I see."

"What is it, specifically, that Madam requires?"

Here Lady Charlotte, for all her imperiousness, seemed to falter. She gestured with her hands. "Why, just some manner of, ah, large safe, you know."

"Madam," said Mr. Chubb severely, "we manufacture single-thickness and double-thickness safes; steel safes and iron safes; lock safes and throwbolt safes; portable safes and fixed safes; safes with a capacity of six cubic inches and safes with a capacity of twelve cubic yards; safes mounted with single locks and double locks—and triple locks, should the customer require it."

This recitation seemed to put Lady Charlotte even further off her form. She appeared nearly helpless—quite the ordinary way of a female when asked to deal with technical matters. "Well," she said, "I, ah, I don't know . . ."

"Perhaps if Madam looks through our catalogue, which is illustrated, and denotes the various aspects and features of our different models."

"Yes, excellent, that would be fine."

"This way, please." Mr. Chubb led her into his office and seated her by his desk. He drew out the catalogue and opened it to the first page. The woman hardly looked at it.

"They seem rather small."

"These are only pictures, Madam. You will notice that the true dimensions are stated beside each. For example, here—"

"Mr. Chubb," she interrupted, in an earnest tone, "I must beg your assistance. The fact is that my husband is recently ill, or he should be conducting this business for himself. In truth, I know nothing of these matters, and should press my own brother into my assistance were he not at this very minute abroad on business. I am quite at a loss and I can tell nothing from pictures. Can you perhaps show me some of your safes?"

"Madam, forgive me," Mr. Chubb said, rushing around the desk to help her to her feet. "Absolutely, of course. We maintain no showroom, as you might imagine, but if you will follow me into the workrooms—and I heartily apologize for any dust, noise, or commotion you may suffer—I can show you the various safes we make."

He led Lady Charlotte back into the long workroom behind the offices. Here a dozen men were busy hammering, fitting, welding, and soldering. The noise was so loud that Mr. Chubb had to shout for Lady Charlotte to hear, and the good woman herself fairly winced from the din.

"Now, this version here," he said, "has a one-cubic-foot capacity, and is double-layered, sixteenth-inch tempered steel, with an insulating layer of dried brick dust of Cornish origin. It is an excellent intermediate safe for many purposes."

"It is too small."

"Very good, Madam, too small. Now, this one here"—he moved down the line—"is one of our most recent creations. It is a single layer of eighth-inch steel with an inner hinge and a capacity of—" He turned to the workman: "What is the capacity?"

"This'un here's two and a half," the workman said.

"Two and a half cubic feet," Mr. Chubb said.

"Still too small."

"Very good, Madam. If you will come this way," and he led her deeper into the workroom. Lady Charlotte coughed delicately in a cloud of brick dust.

"Now, this model here—" Mr. Chubb began.

"There!" said Lady Charlotte, pointing across the room. "That's the size I want."

"You mean those two safes over there?"

"Yes, those."

They crossed the room. "These safes," said Mr. Chubb, "represent the finest examples of our workmanship. They are owned by the Huddleston & Bradford Bank, and are employed in the Crimean gold shipments, where naturally security is of the utmost. However, these are generally sold to institutions, and not to private individuals. I naturally thought—"

"This is the safe I want," she said, and then looked at them suspiciously. "They don't appear very new."

"Oh, no, Madam, they are nearly two years old now."

This seemed to alarm Lady Charlotte. "Two years old. Why are they back? Have they some defect?"

"No, indeed. A Chubb safe has no defects. They have merely been returned for replacement of the undercarriage mounting pins. Two of them have sheared. You see, they travel on the railway, and the vibration from the roadbed works on the bolts which anchor the safes to the luggage-van floor." He shrugged. "These details need not concern you. There is nothing wrong with the safes, and we are making no alterations. We are merely replacing the anchor bolts."

"Now I see these have double locks."

"Yes, Madam, the banking firm requested double-lock mechanisms. As I believe I mentioned, we also install triple locks if the customer requires it."

Lady Charlotte peered at the locks. "Three seems excessive. It must be rather a bore to turn three locks just to open a safe. These locks are burglarproof?"

"Oh, absolutely. So much so that in two years no villain has ever even attempted to break these locks. It would be quite hopeless, in any case.

These safes are double-layered eighth-inch tempered steel. There is no breaking these."

Lady Charlotte peered thoughtfully at the safes for some moments, and finally nodded. "Very well," she said, "I shall take one. Please have it loaded into my carriage outside."

"I beg pardon?"

"I said I shall take one safe such as these I see here. It is precisely what I need."

"Madam," Mr. Chubb said patiently, "we must construct the safe to your order."

"You mean you have none for sale?"

"None already built, no, Madam, I am very sorry. Each safe is specially built to the customer's specifications."

Lady Charlotte appeared quite irritated. "Well, can I have one tomorrow morning?"

Mr. Chubb gulped. "Tomorrow morning—um, well, as a rule, Madam, we require six weeks to construct a safe. On occasion we can manufacture one as quickly as four weeks, but—"

"Four weeks? That is a *month*."

"Yes, Madam."

"I wish to purchase a safe *today*."

"Yes, Madam, quite. But as I have attempted to explain, each safe must be built, and the shortest time—"

"Mr. Chubb, you must think me an utter fool. Well, I shall disabuse you of the notion. I have come here for the purpose of buying a safe, and now I discover you have none to sell—"

"Madam, please—"

"—but on the contrary will construct one for me in only a month's time. Within a month the brigands of the neighborhood will very probably have come and gone, and your safe will not in the least interest me, or my husband. I shall take my business elsewhere. Good day to you, sir, and thank you for your time."

With that, Lady Charlotte swept out of the firm of Chubb's. And Mr. Laurence Chubb, Jr., was heard to mutter in a low voice, "Women."

It was in this fashion that Pierce and Agar learned that the overhaul did not include changing the locks on the safes. That was, of course, all they cared about, and so they made their final preparations for the robbery, which they would carry out on May 22, 1855.

Chapter 31

The Snakesman Turns Nose

One week later, their plans were thrown into still further disarray. On May 17, 1855, a letter was delivered to Pierce. Written in a graceful and educated hand, it read:

> My dear Sir:
>
> I should be most greatly obliged if you could contrive to meet with me at the Palace, Sydenham, this afternoon at four o'clock, for the purpose of discussing some matters of mutual interest.
>
> Most respectfully, I am,
> William Williams, Esq.

Pierce looked at the letter in consternation. He showed it to Agar; but Agar could not read, so Pierce read the contents aloud. Agar stared at the penmanship.

"Clean Willy's got himself a screever for this one," he said.

"Obviously," Pierce said. "But why?"

"Perhaps he's touching you up."

"If that's all it is, I'd be happy," Pierce said.

"You going to meet him?"

"Absolutely. Will you crow for me?"

Agar nodded. "You want Barlow? A good cosh could save a mighty trouble."

"No," Pierce said. "That'll set them hounding for sure, a cosh would."

"Right, then," Agar said, "a simple crow. 'Twon't be easy in the Palace."

"I'm sure Willy knows that," Pierce said gloomily.

A word should be said about the Crystal Palace, that magical structure which came to symbolize the Victorian mid-century. An enormous three-story glass building covering nineteen acres, it was erected in 1851 in Hyde Park, to house the Great Exhibition of that year, and it impressed every visitor who saw it. Indeed, even in drawings the Crystal Palace is stunning to the modern eye, and to see more than a million square feet of glass shimmering in the afternoon light must have been a remarkable sight for anyone. It is not surprising that the Palace soon represented the forward-looking, technological aesthetic of the new industrial Victorian society.

But this fabulous structure had a comfortingly haphazard origin. Led by Prince Albert himself, plans for the Great Exhibition began in 1850, and soon ran into arguments about the proposed Exhibition Hall itself, and its location.

Obviously the building would have to be very large. But what kind of building, and where? A competition in 1850 attracted more than two hundred designs, but no winner. Thus the Building Committee drew up a plan of its own for a dreadful brick monstrosity; the structure would be four times as long as Westminster Abbey and boast a dome even larger than that of St. Peter's. It would be located in Hyde Park.

The public balked at the destruction of trees, the inconvenience to riders, the general ruin of the pleasant neighborhood, and so on. Parliament seemed reluctant to permit Hyde Park to be used as the building site.

In the meantime, the Building Committee discovered that their plans required nineteen million bricks. By the summer of 1850, there was insufficient time to make all these bricks and build the Great Hall in time for the exhibition's opening. There was even some dark talk that the exhibition would have to be canceled, or at least postponed.

It was at this point that the Duke of Devonshire's gardener, Joseph Paxton, came forward with the idea of erecting a large greenhouse to serve as the Exhibition Hall. His original plan for the committee, drawn up on a piece of blotting paper, was eventually accepted for its several virtues.

First, it saved the trees of Hyde Park; second, its chief material, glass, could be manufactured quickly; and third, it could be taken down after the exhibition and reinstalled elsewhere. The committee accepted a bid of £79,800 from a contractor to erect the giant structure, which was completed in only seven months, and was later the focal point of almost universal acclaim.

Thus the reputation of a nation and an empire was saved by a gardener; and thus a gardener was eventually knighted.*

After the exhibition, the Great Hall was taken down and moved to Sydenham, in South-East London. In those days, Sydenham was a pleasant suburban area of fine homes and open fields, and the Crystal Palace made an excellent addition to the neighborhood. Shortly before four o'clock, Edward Pierce entered the vast structure to meet Clean Willy Williams.

The giant hall held several permanent exhibits, the most impressive being full-scale reproductions of the huge Egyptian statues of Ramses II at Abu Simbel. But Pierce paid no attention to these attractions, or to the lily ponds and pools of water everywhere about.

A brass band concert was in progress; Pierce saw Clean Willy sitting in one of the rows to the left. He also saw Agar, disguised as a retired army officer, apparently snoozing in another corner. The band played loudly. Pierce slipped into the seat alongside Willy.

"What is it?" Pierce said, in a low voice. He looked at the band, and thought idly that he despised band music.

"I'm needing a turn," Willy said.

"You've been paid."

"I'm needing more," Willy said.

Pierce shot him a glance. Willy was sweating, and he was edgy, but he did not look nervously around as an ordinary nervous man would do.

"You been working, Willy?"

"No."

"You been touched, Willy?"

"No, I swear it, no."

"Willy," Pierce said, "if you've turned nose on me, I'll put you in lavender."

"I swear it," Willy said. "It's no flam—a finny or two is what I need, and that's the end of it."

The band, in a moment of patriotic support for England's allies, struck up the "Marseillaise." A few listeners had the ill grace to boo the selection.

Pierce said, "You're sweating, Willy."

"Please, sir, a finny or two and that'll be the end of it."

Pierce reached into his wallet and withdrew two five-pound notes.

---

*There was only one unforeseen problem with the Crystal Palace. The building contained trees, and the trees contained sparrows, and the sparrows were not housebroken. It was really no laughing matter, especially as the birds couldn't be shot, and they ignored traps set for them. Finally the Queen herself was consulted, and she said, "Send for the Duke of Wellington." The Duke was informed of the problem. "Try sparrow hawks, Ma'am," he suggested, and he was once more victorious.

"Don't blow on me," Pierce said, "or I'll do what must be done."

"Thank you, sir, thank you," Willy said, and quickly pocketed the money. "Thank you, sir."

Pierce left him there. As he exited the Palace and came out into the park, he walked quickly to Harleigh Road. There he paused to adjust his top hat. The gesture was seen by Barlow, whose cab was drawn up at the end of the street.

Then Pierce walked slowly down Harleigh Road, moving with all appearances of casualness, as a relaxed gent taking the air. His thoughts, whatever they might have been, were interrupted by the wail of a railway whistle, and a nearby chugging sound. Looking over the trees and roofs of mansions, he saw black smoke puffing into the air. Automatically, he checked his watch: it was the mid-afternoon train of the South Eastern Railway, coming back from Folkestone, going toward London Bridge Station.

Chapter 32

Minor Incidents

The train continued on toward London, and so did Mr. Pierce. At the end of Harleigh Road, near St. Martin's Church, he hailed a cab and rode it into town to Regent Street, where he got out.

Pierce walked along Regent Street casually, never once glancing over his shoulder, but pausing frequently to look in the shopwindows along the street, and to watch the reflections in the glass.

He did not like what he saw, but he was wholly unprepared for what he next heard as a familiar voice cried out, "Edward, dear Edward!"

Groaning inwardly, Pierce turned to see Elizabeth Trent. She was shopping, accompanied by a livery boy, who carried brightly wrapped packages. Elizabeth Trent colored deeply. "I—why, I must say, this is an extraordinary surprise."

"I am so pleased to see you," Pierce said, bowing and kissing her hand.

"I—yes, I—" She snatched her hand away and rubbed it with her other. "Edward," she said, taking a deep breath. "Edward, I did not know what had become of you."

"I must apologize," Pierce said smoothly. "I was very suddenly called abroad on business, and I am sure my letter from Paris was inadequate to your injured sensibilities."

"Paris?" she said, frowning.

"Yes. Did you not receive my letter from Paris?"

"Why, no."

"Damn!" Pierce said, and then immediately apologized for his strong language. "It is the French," he said; "they are so ghastly inefficient. If only I had known, but I never suspected—and when you did not reply to me in Paris, I assumed that you were angry. . . ."

"I? Angry? Edward, I assure you," she began, and broke off. "But when did you return?"

"Just three days past," Pierce said.

"How strange," Elizabeth Trent said, with a sudden look of unfeminine shrewdness, "for Mr. Fowler was to dinner a fortnight past, and spoke of seeing you."

"I do not wish to contradict a business associate of your father's, but Henry has the deplorable habit of mixing his dates. I've not seen him for nearly three months." Pierce quickly added: "And how is your father?"

"My father? Oh, my father is well, thank you." Her shrewdness was replaced by a look of hurt confusion. "Edward, I—My father, in truth, spoke some rather unflattering words concerning your character."

"Did he?"

"Yes. He called you a cad." She sighed. "And worse."

"I wholly understand, given the circumstances, but—"

"But now," Elizabeth Trent said, with a sudden determination, "since you are returned to England, I trust we shall be seeing you at the house once more."

Here it was Pierce's turn to be greatly discomfited. "My dear Elizabeth," he said, stammering. "I do not know how to say this," and he broke off, shaking his head. It seemed that tears were welling up in his eyes. "When I did not hear from you in Paris, I naturally assumed that you were displeased with me, and . . . well, as time passed . . ." Pierce suddenly straightened. "I regret to inform you that I am betrothed."

Elizabeth Trent stared. Her mouth fell open.

"Yes," Pierce said, "it is true. I have given my word."

"But to whom?"

"To a French lady."

"A *French* lady?"

"Yes, I fear it is true, all true. I was most desperately unhappy, you see."

"I do see, sir," she snapped, and turned abruptly on her heel and walked away. Pierce remained standing on the pavement, trying to appear as abject as possible, until she had climbed into her carriage and driven off. Then he continued down Regent Street.

Anyone who observed him might have noticed that at the bottom of Regent Street there was nothing about his manner or carriage that indicated the least remorse. He boarded a cab to Windmill Street, where he entered an accommodation house that was a known dolly-mop's lurk, but one of the better class of such establishments.

In the plush velvet hallway, Miss Miriam said, "He's upstairs. Third door on the right."

Pierce went upstairs and entered a room to find Agar seated, chewing a mint. "Bit late," Agar said. "Trouble?"

"I ran into an old acquaintance."

Agar nodded vaguely.

"What did you see?" Pierce said.

"I cooled two," Agar said. "Both riding your tail nice-like. One's a crusher in disguise; the other's dressed as a square-rigged sport. Followed you all the way down Harleigh Road, and took a cab when you climbed aboard."

Pierce nodded. "I saw the same two in Regent Street."

"Probably lurking outside now," Agar said. "How's Willy?"

"Willy looks to be turning nose," Pierce said.

"Must have done a job."

Pierce shrugged.

"What's to be done with Willy, then?"

"He'll be getting what any gammy trasseno gets."

"I'd bump him," Agar said.

"I don't know about bumping," Pierce said, "but he won't have another chance to blow on us."

"What'll you do with the officers?"

"Nothing for the moment," Pierce said. "I've got to think a bit." And he sat back, lit a cigar, and puffed in silence.

The planned robbery was only five days away, and the police were on to him. If Willy had sung, and loudly, then the police would know that Pierce's gang had broken into the London Bridge Terminus offices.

"I need a new lay," he said, and stared at the ceiling. "A proper flash lay for the miltonians to discover." He watched the cigar smoke curl upward, and frowned.

Chapter 33

Miltonians on the Stalk

The institutions of any society are interrelated, even those which appear to have completely opposite goals. Gladstone himself observed: "There is often, in the course of this wayward and bewildered life, exterior opposition, and sincere and even violent condemnation, between persons and bodies who are nevertheless profoundly associated by ties and relations that they know not of."

Perhaps the most famous example of this, and one well-recognized by Victorians, was the bitter rivalry between the temperance societies and the pubs. These two institutions in fact served similar ends, and ultimately were seen to adopt the same attractions: the pubs acquired organs, hymn singing, and soft drinks, and the temperance meetings had professional entertainers and a new, raucous liveliness. By the time the temperance groups began buying pubs in order to turn them dry, the intermixture of these two hostile forces became pronounced indeed.

Victorians also witnessed another rivalry, centering around a new social institution—the organized police force. Almost immediately, the new force began to form relationships with its avowed enemy, the criminal class. These relationships were much debated in the nineteenth century, and they continue to be debated to the present day. The similarity in methods of police and criminals, as well as the fact that many policemen were former criminals—and the reverse—were features not overlooked by thinkers of the day. And it was also noted by Sir James Wheatstone that there was a logical problem inherent in a law-enforcement institution, "for, should the police actually succeed in eliminating all crime, they will simultaneously succeed in eliminating themselves as a necessary adjunct to society, and no organized force or power will ever eliminate itself willingly."

In London, the Metropolitan Police, founded by Sir Robert Peel in 1829, was headquartered in a district known as Scotland Yard. Scotland Yard was originally a geographical term, denoting an area of Whitehall that contained many government buildings. These buildings included the official residence of the surveyor of works to the crown, which was occupied by Inigo Jones, and later by Sir Christopher Wren. John Milton lived in Scotland Yard when he was working for Oliver Cromwell from 1649 to 1651, and it is apparently from this association that a slang reference for police, two hundred years later, was "miltonian."

When Sir Robert Peel located the new Metropolitan Police in Whitehall, the correct address for the headquarters was No. 4 Whitehall Place, but the police station there had an entrance from Scotland Yard proper, and the press always referred to the police as Scotland Yard, until the term became synonymous with the force itself.

Scotland Yard grew rapidly in its early years; in 1829 the total force was 1,000, but a decade later it was 3,350, and by 1850 it was more than 6,000, and would increase to 10,000 by 1870. The task of the Yard was extraordinary: it was called upon to police crime in an area of nearly seven hundred square miles, containing a population of two and a half million people.

From the beginning, the Yard adopted a posture of deference and modesty in its manner of solving crimes; the official explanations always mentioned lucky breaks of one sort or another—an anonymous informant, a jealous mistress, a surprise encounter—to a degree that was hard to believe. In fact, the Yard employed informers and plainclothesmen, and these agents were the subject of heated debate for the now familiar reason that many in the public feared that an agent might easily provoke a crime and then arrest the participants. Entrapment was a hot political issue of the day, and the Yard was at pains to defend itself.

In 1855, the principal figure in the Yard was Richard Mayne, "a sensible lawyer," who had done much to improve the public attitude toward the Metropolitan Police. Directly under him was Mr. Edward Harranby, and it was Harranby who oversaw the ticklish business of working with undercover agents and informers. Usually Mr. Harranby kept irregular hours; he avoided contact with the press, and from his office could be seen strange figures coming and going, often at night.

In the late afternoon of May 17th, Harranby had a conversation with his assistant, Mr. Jonathan Sharp. Mr. Harranby reconstructed the conversation in his memoirs, *Days on the Force*, published in 1879. The conversation must be taken with some reservations, for in that volume Harranby was attempting to explain why he did not succeed in thwarting Pierce's robbery plans before they were carried out.

Sharp said to him, "The snakesman blew, and we have had a look at our man."

"What sort is he?" Harranby said.

"He appears a gentleman. Probably a cracksman or a swell mobsman. The snakesman says he's from Manchester, but he lives in a fine house in London."

"Does he know where?"

"He says he's been there, but he doesn't know the exact location. Somewhere in Mayfair."

"We can't go knocking on doors in Mayfair," Harranby said. "Can we assist his powers of memory?"

Sharp sighed. "Possibly."

"Bring him in. I'll have a talk with him. Do we know the intended crime?"

Sharp shook his head. "The snakesman says he doesn't know. He's afraid of being mizzled, you know, he's reluctant to blow all he knows. He says this fellow's planning a flash pull."

Harranby turned irritable. "That is of remarkably little value to me," he said. "What, exactly, is the crime? There's our question, and it begs a proper answer. Who is on this gentleman now?"

"Cramer and Benton, sir."

"They're good men. Keep them on his trail, and let's have the nose in my office, and quickly."

"I'll see to it myself, sir," the assistant said.

Harranby later wrote in his memoirs: "There are times in any professional's life when the elements requisite for the deductive process seem almost within one's grasp, and yet they elude the touch. These are the times of greatest frustration, and such was the case of the Robbery of 1855."

Chapter 34

The Nose Is Crapped

Clean Willy, very nervous, was drinking at the Hound's Tooth pub. He left there about six and headed straight for the Holy Land. He moved swiftly through the evening crowds, then ducked into an alley; he jumped a fence, slipped into a basement, crossed it, crawled through a passage into an adjoining building, climbed up the stairs, came out onto a narrow street, walked half a block, and disappeared into another house, a reeking nethersken.

Here he ascended the stairs to the second floor, climbed out onto the roof, jumped to an adjacent roof, scrambled up a drainpipe to the third floor of a lodging house, crawled in through a window, and went down the stairs to the basement.

Once in the basement, he crawled through a tunnel that brought him out on the opposite side of the street, where he came up into a narrow mews. By a side door, he entered a pub, the Golden Arms, looked around, and left by the front door.

He walked to the end of the street, and then turned in to the entrance of another lodging house. Immediately he knew that something was wrong; normally there were children yelling and scrambling all over the stairs, but now the entrance and stairs were deserted and silent. He paused at the doorway, and was just about to turn and flee when a rope snaked out and twisted around his neck, yanking him into a dark corner.

Clean Willy had a look at Barlow, with the white scar across his forehead, as Barlow strained on the garrotting rope. Willy coughed, and struggled, but Barlow's strength was such that the little snakesman was literally lifted off the floor, his feet kicking in the air, his hands pulling at the rope.

This struggle continued for the better part of a minute, and then Clean Willy's face was blue, and his tongue protruded gray, and his eyes bulged. He urinated down his pants leg, and then his body sagged.

Barlow let him drop to the floor. He unwound the rope from his neck, removed the two five-pound notes from the snakesman's pocket, and slipped away into the street. Clean Willy's body lay huddled in a corner and did not move. Many minutes passed before the first of the children reemerged, and approached the corpse cautiously. Then the children stole the snakesman's shoes, and all his clothing, and scampered away.

Chapter 35

Plucking the Pigeon

Sitting in the third-floor room of the accommodation house with Agar, Pierce finished his cigar and sat up in his chair. "We are very lucky," he said finally.

"Lucky? Lucky to have jacks on our nancy five days before the pull?"

"Yes, lucky," Pierce said. "What if Willy blew? He'd tell them we knocked over the London Bridge Terminus."

"I doubt he'd blow so much, right off. He'd likely tickle them for a bigger push." An informant was in the habit of letting out information bit by bit, with a bribe from the police at each step.

"Yes," Pierce said, "but we must take the chance that he did. Now, that's why we are lucky."

"Where's the luck, then?" Agar said.

"In the fact that London Bridge is the only station in the city with two lines operating from it. The South Eastern, and the London & Greenwich."

"Aye, that's so," Agar said, with a puzzled look.

"We need a bone nose to blow on us," Pierce said.

"You giving the crushers a slum?"

"They must have something to keep them busy," Pierce said. "In five days' time, we'll pull the peters on that train, and I don't want the crushers around to watch."

"Where do you want them?"

"I was thinking of Greenwich," Pierce said. "It would be pleasant if they were in Greenwich."

"So you're needing a bone nose to pass them the slang."

"Yes," Pierce said.

Agar thought for a moment. "There's a dolly-mop, Lucinda, in Seven Dials. They say she knows one or two miltonians—dabs it up with them whenever they pinch her, which is often, seeing as how they like the dabbing."

"No," Pierce said. "They wouldn't believe a woman; it'll look like a feed to them."

"Well, there's Black Dick, the turfite. Know him? He's a Jew, to be found about the Queen's Crown of an evening."

"I know him," Pierce nodded. "Black Dick's a lushington, too fond of his gin. I need a true bone nose, a man of the family."

"A man of the family? Then Chokee Bill will do you proper."

"Chokee Bill? That old mick?"

Agar nodded. "Aye, he's a lag, did a stretch in Newgate. But not for long."

"Oh, yes?" Pierce was suddenly interested. A shortened prison sentence often implied that the man had made a deal to turn nose, to become an informer. "Got his ticket-of-leave early, did he?"

"Uncommon early," Agar said. "And the crushers gave him his broker's license quick-like, too. Very odd, seeing as he's a mick." Pawnbrokers were licensed by the police, who shared the usual prejudice against Irishmen.

"So he's in the uncle trade now?" Pierce said.

"Aye," Agar said. "But they say he deals barkers now and again. And they say he's a blower."

Pierce considered this at length, and finally nodded. "Where is Bill now?"

"His uncling shop is in Battersea, in Ridgeby Way."

"I'll see him now," Pierce said, getting to his feet. "I'll have a go at plucking the pigeon."

"Don't make it too easy," Agar warned.

Pierce smiled. "It will take all their best efforts." He went to the door.

"Here, now," Agar called to him, with a sudden thought. "It just came to me mind: what's there for a flash pull in Greenwich, of all places?"

"That," Pierce said, "is the very question the crushers will be asking themselves."

"But *is* there a pull?"

"Of course."

"A flash pull?"

"Of course."

"But what is it, then?"

Pierce shook his head. He grinned at Agar's perplexed look and left the room.

When Pierce came out of the accommodation house, it was twilight. He immediately saw the two crushers lurking at opposite corners of the street. He made a show of looking nervously about, then walked to the end of the block, where he hailed a cab.

He rode the cab several blocks, then jumped out quickly at a busy part of Regent Street, crossed the thoroughfare, and took a hansom going in the opposite direction. To all appearances, he was operating with the utmost cunning. In fact, Pierce would never bother with the crossover fakement to dodge a tail; it was a glocky ploy that rarely worked, and when he glanced out of the small back window of the hansom cab, he saw that he had not thrown off his pursuers.

He rode to the Regency Arms pub house, a notorious place. He entered it, left from a side door (which was in plain view of the street), and crossed over to New Oxford Street, where he caught another cab. In the process, he lost one of the crushers, but the other was still with him. Now he proceeded directly across the Thames, to Battersea, to see Chokee Bill.

The image of Edward Pierce, a respectable and well-dressed gentleman, entering the dingy premises of a Battersea pawnbroker may seem incongruous from a modern perspective. At the time, it was not at all uncommon, for the pawnbroker served more than the lower classes, and whomever he served, his function was essentially the same: to act as a sort of impromptu bank, operating more cheaply than established banking concerns. A person could buy an expensive article, such as a coat, and hock it one week to pay the rent; reclaim it a few days later, for wearing on Sunday; hock it again on Monday, for a smaller loan; and so on until there was no further need for the broker's services.

The pawnbroker thus filled an important niche in the society, and the number of licensed pawnshops doubled during the mid-Victorian period. Middle-class people were drawn to the broker more for the anonymity of the loan than the cheapness of it; many a respectable household did not wish it known that some of their silver was uncled for cash. This was, after all, an era when many people equated economic prosperity and good fiscal management with moral behavior; and conversely, to be in need of a loan implied some kind of misdeed.

The pawnshops themselves were not really very shady, although they had that reputation. Criminals seeking fences usually turned to unlicensed, secondhand goods "translators," who were not regulated by the police and were less likely to be under surveillance. Thus, Pierce entered the door beneath the three balls with impunity.

He found Chokee Bill, a red-faced Irishman whose complexion gave the appearance of perpetual near strangulation, sitting in a back corner. Chokee Bill jumped to his feet quickly, recognizing the dress and manner of a gentleman.

"Evening, sir," Bill said.

"Good evening," Pierce said.

"How may I be serving you, sir?"

Pierce looked around the shop. "Are we alone?"

"We are, sir, as my name is Bill, sir." But Chokee Bill got a guarded look in his eyes.

"I am looking to make a certain purchase," Pierce said. As he spoke, he adopted a broad Liverpool dockyard accent, though ordinarily he had no trace of it.

"A certain purchase . . ."

"Some items you may have at hand," Pierce said.

"You see my shop, sir," Chokee Bill said, with a wave of his arm. "All is before you."

"This is all?"

"Aye, sir, whatever you may see."

Pierce shrugged. "I must have been told wrongly. Good evening to you." And he headed for the door.

He was almost there when Chokee Bill coughed. "What is it you were told, sir?"

Pierce looked back at him. "I need certain rare items."

"Rare items," Chokee Bill repeated. "What manner of rare items, sir?"

"Objects of metal," Pierce said, looking directly at the pawnbroker. He found all this circumspection tedious, but it was necessary to convince Bill of the genuineness of his transaction.

"Metal, you say?"

Pierce made a deprecating gesture with his hands. "It is a question of defense, you see."

"Defense."

"I have valuables, property, articles of worth. . . . And therefore I need defense. Do you take my meaning?"

"I take your meaning," Bill said. "And I may have such a thing as you require."

"Actually," Pierce said, looking around the shop again, as if to reassure himself that he was truly alone with the proprietor, "actually, I need five."

"Five barkers?" Chokee Bill's eyes widened in astonishment.

Now that his secret was out, Pierce became very nervous. "That's right," he said, glancing this way and that, "five is what I need."

"Five's a goodly number," Bill said, frowning.

Pierce immediately edged toward the door. "Well, if you can't snaffle them—"

"Wait, now," Bill said, "I'm not saying can't. You never heard me say can't. All's I said is five is a goodly number, which it is, right enough."

"I was told you had them at hand," Pierce said, still nervous.

"I may."

"Well, then, I should like to purchase them at once."

Chokee Bill sighed. "They're not here, sir—you can count on that—a man doesn't keep barkers about in an uncle shop, no, sir."

"How quickly can you get them?"

As Pierce became more agitated, Chokee Bill became more calm, more appraising. Pierce could almost see his mind working, thinking over the meaning of a request for five pistols. It implied a major crime, and no mistake. As a blower, he might make a penny or two if he knew the details.

"It would be some days, sir, and that's the truth," Bill said.

"I cannot have them now?"

"No, sir, you'd have to give a space of time, and then I'll have them for you, right enough."

"How much time?"

There followed a long silence. Bill went so far as to mumble to himself, and tick off the days on his fingers. "A fortnight would be safe."

"A fortnight!"

"Eight days, then."

"Impossible," Pierce said, talking aloud to himself. "In eight days, I must be in Greenw—" He broke off. "No," he said. "Eight days is too long."

"Seven?" Bill asked.

"Seven," Pierce said, staring at the ceiling. "Seven, seven . . . seven days . . . Seven days is Thursday next?"

"Aye, sir."

"At what hour on Thursday next?"

"A question of timing, is it?" Bill asked, with a casualness that was wholly unconvincing.

Pierce just stared at him.

"I don't mean to pry, sir," Bill said quickly.

"Then see you do not. What hour on Thursday?"

"Noon."

Pierce shook his head. "We will never come to terms. It is impossible and I—"

"Here, now—here, now. What hour Thursday must it be?"

"No later than ten o'clock in the morning."

Chokee Bill reflected. "Ten o'clock here?"

"Yes."

"And no later?"

"Not a minute later."

"Will you be coming yourself, then, to collect them?"

Once again, Pierce gave him a stern look. "That hardly need concern you. Can you supply the pieces or not?"

"I can," Bill said. "But there's an added expense for the quick service."

"That will not matter," Pierce said, and gave him ten gold guineas. "You may have this on account."

Chokee Bill looked at the coins, turned them over in his palm. "I reckon this is the half of it."

"So be it."

"And the rest will be paid in kind?"

"In gold, yes."

Bill nodded. "Will you be needing shot as well?"

"What pieces are they?"

"Webley 48-bore, rim-fire, holster models, if my guess is right."

"Then I will need shot."

"Another three guineas for shot," Chokee Bill said blandly.

"Done," Pierce said. He went to the door, and paused. "A final consideration," he said. "If, when I arrive Thursday next, the pieces are not waiting, it shall go hard with you."

"I'm reliable, sir."

"It will go very hard," Pierce said again, "if you are not. Think on it." And he left.

It was not quite dark; the street was dimly lit by gas lamps. He did not see the lurking crusher but knew he was there somewhere. He took a cab and drove to Leicester Square, where the crowds were gathering for the evening's theatrical productions. He entered one throng, bought a ticket for a showing of *She Stoops to Conquer*, and then lost himself in the lobby. He was home an hour later, after three cab changes and four duckings in and out of pubs. He was quite certain he had not been followed.

Chapter 36

Scotland Yard Deduces

The morning of May 18th was uncommonly warm and sunny, but Mr. Harranby took no pleasure in the weather. Things were going very badly, and he had treated his assistant, Mr. Sharp, with notable ill temper when he was informed of the death of the snakesman Clean Willy in a nethersken in Seven Dials. When he was later informed that his tails had lost the gentleman in the theatre crowd—a man they knew only as Mr. Simms, with a house in Mayfair—Mr. Harranby had flown into a rage, and complained vigorously about the ineptitude of his subordinates, including Mr. Sharp.

But Mr. Harranby's rage was now controlled, for the Yard's only remaining clue was sitting before him, perspiring profusely, wringing his hands, and looking very red-faced. Harranby frowned at Chokee Bill.

"Now, Bill," Harranby said, "this is a most serious matter."

"I know it, sir, indeed I do," Bill said.

"Five barkers tells me there is something afoot, and I mean to know the truth behind it."

"He was tight with his words, he was."

"I've no doubt," Harranby said heavily. He fished a gold guinea out of his pocket and dropped it on his desk before him. "Try to recall," he said.

"It was late in the day, sir, with all respects, and I was not at my best," Bill said, staring pointedly at the gold piece.

Harranby would be damned if he'd give the fellow another. "Many a memory improves on the cockchafer, in my experience," he said.

"I've done no wrong," Bill protested. "I'm honest as the day is long, sir, and I'd keep nothing from you. There's no call to put me in the stir."

"Then try to remember," Harranby said, "and be quick about it."

Bill twisted his hands in his lap. "He comes into the shop near six, he does. Dressed proper, with good manner, but he speaks a wave lag from Liverpool, and he can voker romeny."

Harranby glanced at Sharp, in the corner. From time to time, even Harranby needed some help in translation.

"He had a Liverpool sailor's accent and he spoke criminal jargon," Sharp said.

"Aye, sir, that's so," Bill said, nodding. "He's in the family, and that's for sure. Wants me to snaffle five barkers, and I say five's a goodly number, and he says he wants them quick-like, and he's nervous, and in a hurry, and he's showing plenty of ream thickers to pay up on the spot."

"What did you tell him?" Harranby said, keeping his eyes fixed on Bill. A skilled informant like Chokee Bill was not above playing each side against the other, and Bill could lie like an adept.

"I says to him, five's a goodly number but I can do it in time. And he says how much time, and I says a fortnight. This makes him cool the cockum for a bit, and then he says he needs it quicker than a fortnight. I says eight days. He says eight days is too long, and he starts to say he's off to Greenwich in eight days, but then he catches himself, like."

"Greenwich," Harranby said, frowning.

"Aye, sir, Greenwich was to the tip of his tongue, but he stops down and says it's too long. So I says how long? And he says seven days. So I says I can translate in seven days. And he says what time of the day? I say noontime. And he says noontime's too late. He says no later than ten o'clock."

"Seven days," Harranby said, "meaning Friday next?"

"No, sir. Thursday next. Seven days from yesterday it was."

"Go on."

"So I says, after a hem and a haw, I says I can have his pieces on Thursday at ten o'clock. And he says that's fly enough, but he's no flat, this one, and he says any gammy cockum and it will go hard on me."

Harranby looked at Sharp again. Sharp said, "The gentleman is no fool and warned that if the guns were not ready at the arranged time, it would be hard on Bill."

"And what did you say, Bill?" Harranby inquired.

"I says I can do it, and I promise him. And he gives me ten gold pushes, and I granny they're ream, and he takes his leave and says he'll be back Thursday next."

"What else?" Harranby said.

"That's the lot," Bill said.

There was a long silence. Finally Harranby said, "What do you make of this, Bill?"

"It's a flash pull and no mistake. He's no muck-snipe, this gent, but a hykey bloke who knows his business."

Harranby tugged at an earlobe, a nervous habit. "What in Greenwich has the makings of a proper flash pull?"

"Damn me if I know," Chokee Bill said.

"What have you heard?" Harranby said.

"I keep my lills to the ground, but I heard nothing of a pull in Greenwich, I swear."

Harranby paused. "There's another guinea in it for you if you can say."

A fleeting look of agony passed across Chokee Bill's face. "I wish I could be helping you, sir, but I heard nothing. It's God's own truth, sir."

"I'm sure it is," Harranby said. He waited a while longer, and finally dismissed the pawnbroker, who snatched up the guinea and departed.

When Harranby was alone with Sharp, he said again, "What's in Greenwich?"

"Damn me if I know," Sharp said.

"You want a gold guinea, too?"

Sharp said nothing. He was accustomed to Harranby's sour moods; there was nothing to do except ride them out. He sat in the corner and watched his superior light a cigarette and puff on it reflectively. Sharp regarded cigarettes as silly, insubstantial little things. They had been introduced the year before by a London shopkeeper, and were mostly favored by troops returning from the Crimea. Sharp himself liked a good cigar, and nothing less.

"Now, then," Harranby said. "Let us begin from the beginning. We know this fellow Simms has been working for months on something, and we can assume he's clever."

Sharp nodded.

"The snakesman was killed yesterday. Does that mean they know we're on the stalk?"

"Perhaps."

"Perhaps, perhaps," Harranby said irritably. "Perhaps is not enough. We must *decide*, and we must do so according to principles of deductive logic. Guesswork has no place in our thinking. Let us stick to the facts of the matter, and follow them wherever they lead. Now, then, what else do we know?"

The question was rhetorical, and Sharp said nothing.

"We know," Harranby said, "that this fellow Simms, after months of preparation, suddenly finds himself, on the eve of his big pull, in desperate need of five barkers. He has had months to obtain them quietly, one at a time, creating no stir. But he postpones it to the last minute. Why?"

"You think he's playing us for a pigeon?"

"We must entertain the thought, however distasteful," Harranby said. "Is it well known that Bill's a nose?"

"Perhaps."

"Damn your perhapses. Is it known or not?"

"Surely there are suspicions about."

"Indeed," Harranby said. "And yet our clever Mr. Simms chooses this very person to arrange for his five barkers. I say it smells of a fakement." He stared moodily at the glowing tip of his cigarette. "This Mr. Simms is deliberately leading us astray, and we must not follow."

"I am sure you are right," Sharp said, hoping his boss's disposition would improve.

"Without question," Harranby said. "We are being led a merry chase."

There was a long pause. Harranby drummed his fingers on the desk. "I don't like it. We are being too clever. We're giving this Simms fellow too much credit. We must assume he is really planning on Greenwich. But what in the name of God is there in Greenwich to steal?"

Sharp shook his head. Greenwich was a seaport town, but it had not grown as rapidly as the larger ports of England. It was chiefly known for its naval observatory, which maintained the standard of time—Greenwich Mean Time—for the nautical world.

Harranby began opening drawers in his desk, rummaging. "Where is the damned thing?"

"What, sir?"

"The schedule, the schedule," Harranby said. "Ah, here it is." He brought out a small printed folder. "London & Greenwich Railway . . . Thursdays . . . Ah. Thursdays there is a train leaving London Bridge Terminus for Greenwich at eleven-fifteen in the morning. Now, what does that suggest?"

Sharp looked suddenly bright-eyed. "Our man wants his guns by ten, so that he will have time to get to the station and make the train."

"Precisely," Harranby said. "All logic points to the fact that he is, indeed, going to Greenwich on Thursday. And we also know he cannot go later than Thursday."

Sharp said, "What about the guns? Buying five at once."

"Well, now," Harranby said, warming to his subject, "you see, by a process of deduction we can conclude that his need for the guns is genuine, and his postponing the purchase to the last minute—on the surface, a most suspicious business—springs from some logical situation. One can surmise several. His plans for obtaining the guns by other means may have been thwarted. Or perhaps he regards the purchase of guns as dangerous—

which is certainly the case; everyone knows we pay well for information about who is buying barkers—so he postpones it to the last moment. There may be other reasons we cannot guess at. The exact reason does not matter. What matters is that he needs those guns for some criminal activity in Greenwich."

"Bravo," Sharp said, with a show of enthusiasm.

Harranby shot him a nasty look. "Don't be a fool," he said, "we are little better off than when we began. The principal question still stands before us. *What is there to steal in Greenwich?*"

Sharp said nothing. He stared at his feet. He heard the scratch of a match as Harranby lit another cigarette.

"All is not lost," Harranby said. "The principles of deductive logic can still aid us. For example, the crime is probably a robbery. If it has been planned for many months, it must figure around some stable situation which is predictable months in advance. This is no casual, off-the-cuff snatch."

Sharp continued to stare at his feet.

"No, indeed," Harranby said. "There is nothing casual about it. Furthermore, we may deduce that this lengthy planning is directed toward a goal of some magnitude, a major crime with high stakes. In addition, we know our man is a seafaring person, so we may suspect his crime has something to do with the ocean, or dockyard activities in some way. Thus we may limit our inquiry to whatever exists in the town of Greenwich that fits our—"

Sharp coughed.

Harranby frowned at him. "Do you have something to say?"

"I was only thinking, sir," Sharp said, "that if it is Greenwich, it's out of our jurisdiction. Perhaps we ought to telegraph the local police and warn them."

"Perhaps, perhaps. When will you learn to do without that word? If we were to cable Greenwich, what would we tell them? Eh? What would we say in our cable?"

"I was only thinking—"

"Good God," Harranby said, standing up behind his desk. "Of course! The cable!"

"The cable?"

"Yes, of course, the cable. The cable is in Greenwich, even as we speak."

"Do you mean the Atlantic cable?" Sharp asked.

"Certainly," Harranby said, rubbing his hands together. "Oh, it fits perfectly. Perfectly!"

Sharp remained puzzled. He knew, of course, that the proposed transatlantic telegraph cable was being manufactured in Greenwich; the project had been under way for more than a year, and represented one of the most considerable technological efforts of the time. There were already undersea cables in the Channel, linking England to the Continent. But these were nothing compared to the twenty-five hundred miles of cable being constructed to join England to New York.

"But surely," Sharp said, "there is no purpose in stealing a cable—"

"Not the *cable*," Harranby said. "The *payroll* for the firm. What is it? Glass, Elliot & Company, or some such. An enormous project, and the payroll must be equal to the undertaking. That's our man's objective. And if he is in a hurry to leave on Thursday, he wishes to be there on Friday—"

"Payday!" Sharp cried.

"Exactly," Harranby said. "It is entirely logical. You see the process of deduction carried to its most accurate conclusion."

"Congratulations," Sharp said cautiously.

"A trifle," Harranby said. He was still very excited, and clapped his hands together. "Oh, he is a bold one, our friend Simms. To steal the cable payroll—what an audacious crime! And we shall have him red-handed. Come along, Mr. Sharp. We must journey to Greenwich, and apprise ourselves of the situation at first hand."

Chapter 37

Further Congratulations

"And then?" Pierce said.

Miriam shrugged. "They boarded the train."

"How many of them were there?"

"Four altogether."

"And they took the Greenwich train?"

Miriam nodded. "In great haste. The leader was a squarish man with whiskers, and his lackey was cleanshaven. There were two others, jacks in blue."

Pierce smiled. "Harranby," he said. "He must be very proud of himself. He's such a clever man." He turned to Agar. "And you?"

"Fat Eye Lewis, the magsman, is in the Regency Arms asking about a cracker's lay in Greenwich—wants to join in, he says."

"So the word is out?" Pierce said.

Agar nodded.

"Feed it," he said.

"Who shall I say is in?"

"Spring Heel Jack, for one."

"What if the miltonians find him?" Agar said.

"I doubt that they will," Pierce said.

"Jack's under, is he?"

"So I have heard."

"Then I'll mention him."

"Make Fat Eye pay," Pierce said. "This is valuable information."

Agar grinned. "It'll come to him, dear, I promise you."

Agar departed, and Pierce was alone with Miriam.

"Congratulations," she said, smiling at him. "Nothing can go wrong now."

Pierce sat back in a chair. "Something can always go wrong," he said, but he was smiling.

"In four days?" she asked.

"Even in the space of an hour."

Later, in his courtroom testimony, Pierce admitted he was astounded at how prophetic his own words were, for enormous difficulties lay ahead—and they would come from the most unlikely source.

Chapter 38

A Sharp Business Practice

Henry Mayhew, the great observer, reformer, and classifier of Victorian society, once listed the various types of criminals in England. The list had five major categories, twenty subheadings, and more than a hundred separate entries. To the modern eye, the list is remarkable for the absence of any consideration of what is now called "white-collar crime."

Of course, such crime existed at that time, and there were some flagrant examples of embezzlement, forgery, false accounting, bond manipulation, and other illegal practices that came to light during the mid-century. In 1850, an insurance clerk named Walter Watts was caught after he embezzled more than £70,000, and there were several crimes much larger: Leopold Redpath's £150,000 in forgeries on the Great Northern Railway Company, and Beaumont Smith's £350,000 in counterfeit exchequer bonds, to name two examples.

Then, as now, white-collar crime involved the largest sums of money, was the least likely to be detected, and was punished most leniently if the participants were ever apprehended. Yet Mayhew's list of criminals ignores this sector of crime entirely. For Mayhew, along with the majority of his contemporaries, was firmly committed to the belief that crime was the product of "the dangerous classes," and that criminal behavior sprang from poverty, injustice, oppression, and lack of education. It was almost a matter of definition: a person who was not from the criminal class could not be committing a crime. Persons of a better station were merely "breaking the law." Several factors unique to the Victorian attitude toward upperclass crime contributed to this belief.

First, in a newly capitalistic society, with thousands of emerging businesses, the principles of honest accounting were not firmly established, and accounting methods were understood to be even more variable than they are today. A man might, with a fairly clear conscience, blur the distinction between fraud and "sharp business practices."

Second, the modern watchdog of all Western capitalist countries, the government, was nowhere near so vigilant then. Personal incomes below £150 annually were not taxed, and the great majority of citizens fell beneath this limit. Those who were taxed got off lightly by modern standards, and although people grumbled about the cost of government, there was no hint yet of the modern citizen's frantic scramble to arrange his finances in such a way as to avoid as much tax as possible. (In 1870, taxes amounted to 9 percent of the gross national product of England; in 1961, they were 38 percent.)

Furthermore, the Victorians of all classes accepted a kind of ruthlessness in their dealings with one another that seems outrageous today. To take an example, when Sir John Hall, the physician in charge of the Crimean troops, decided to get rid of Florence Nightingale, he elected to starve her out by ordering that her food rations be halted. Such vicious maneuvers were considered ordinary by everyone; Miss Nightingale anticipated it, and carried her own supplies of food, and even Lytton Strachey, who was hardly disposed to view the Victorians kindly, dismissed this incident as "a trick."

If this is only a trick, it is easy to see why middle-class observers were reluctant to label many kinds of wrongdoing as "crimes"; and the higher an individual's standing within the community, the greater the reluctance.

A case in point is Sir John Alderston and his crate of wine.

Captain John Alderston was knighted after Waterloo, in 1815, and in subsequent years he became a prosperous London citizen. He was one of the owners of the South Eastern Railway from the inception of the line, and had large financial holdings in several coal mines in Newcastle as well. He was, according to all accounts, a portly, tart-spoken gentleman who maintained a military bearing all his life, barking out terse commands in a manner that was increasingly ludicrous as his waistline spread with the passing years.

Alderston's single vice was a passion for card games, acquired during his army days, and his outstanding eccentricity was that he refused to gamble for money, preferring to wager personal articles and belongings instead of hard cash. Apparently this was his way of viewing card-playing as a gentlemanly pastime, and not a vice. The story of his crate of wine, which figures so prominently in The Great Train Robbery of 1855, never came to light until 1914, some forty years after Alderston's death. At that time, his family commissioned an official biography by an author named William Shawn. The relevant passage reads:

> Sir John at all times had a highly developed sense of conscience, which only once caused him any personal qualms. A family member recalls that he returned home one evening, after an outing for card-playing, in a mood of great distress. When asked the cause, he replied: "I cannot bear it."
>
> Upon further inquiry, it emerged that Sir John had been playing cards with several associates, these being men who also owned a share of the railway. In his play, Sir John had lost a case of Madeira, twelve years old, and he was exceedingly reluctant to part with it. Yet he had promised to put it aboard the Folkestone train, for delivery to the winner, who resided in that coastal town, where he oversaw the operation of the railway at its most distant terminus.
>
> Sir John fretted and fussed for three days, condemning the gentleman who had won, and suspecting aloud that the man had cheated in clandestine fashion. With each passing day, he became more convinced of the man's trickery, although there was no evidence for such a belief.
>
> Finally he instructed his manservant to load the crate of wine on the train, placing it in the luggage van with a deal of ceremony and filling-in of forms; the wine was, in fact, insured against loss or injury during the journey.
>
> When the train arrived in Folkestone, the crate was discovered to be empty, and a robbery of the precious wine was presumed. This provided no small commotion among the railway employees. The guard in the van was dismissed and changes in procedures were adopted. Sir John paid his wager with the funds from the insurance.
>
> Many years later, he admitted to his family that he had loaded an empty crate onto the train, for he could not, he said, bear parting with his precious Madeira. Yet he was overcome with guilt, especially for the discharged railway employee, to whom he contrived to pay an anonymous annual stipend over a period of many years, such that the sum paid was vastly in excess of the value of his wine.
>
> Yet to the last, he felt no remorse for the creditor, one John Banks. On the contrary, during the last days of his mortal existence, when he lay in his bed delirious with fevers, he was often heard to say, "That blasted Banks is no gentleman, and I'll be damned if he'll get my Madeira, do you hear?"
>
> Mr. Banks at this time had been deceased some years. It has been said that many of Sir John's closest associates suspected that he had had a hand in the mysterious disappearance of the wine, but no one dared accuse him. Instead, certain changes were made in the railway security procedures (partly at the behest of the insuring agency). And when, soon after, a consignment of gold was stolen from the railway, everyone forgot the matter of Sir John's crate of wine, excepting the man himself, for his conscience tormented him to his final days. Thus was the strength of this great man's character.

Chapter 39

Some Late Difficulties

On the evening of May 21st, just a few hours before the robbery, Pierce dined with his mistress, Miriam, in his house in Mayfair.

Shortly before nine-thirty that night, their meal was interrupted by the sudden arrival of Agar, who looked very distraught. He came storming into the dining room, making no apologies for his abrupt entrance.

"What is it?" Pierce said calmly.

"Burgess," Agar said, in a breathless voice. "Burgess: he's downstairs."

Pierce frowned. "You brought him *here?*"

"I had to do," Agar said. "Wait until you hear."

Pierce left the table and went downstairs to the smoking room. Burgess was standing there, twitching his blue guard's cap in his hands. He was obviously as nervous as Agar.

"What's the trouble?" Pierce said.

"It's the line," Burgess said. "They've changed it all, and just today—changed everything."

"What have they changed?" Pierce said.

Burgess spoke in a headlong torrent: "I first came to know this morning, you see, I come to work proper at seven sharp, and there's a cooper working on me van, hammering and pounding. And there's a smith as well, and some gentlemen standing about to watch the work. And that's how I find they've changed all manner of things, and just today, changed it all. I mean the running of the car the way that we do, all changed, and I didn't know—"

"What, exactly, have they changed?" Pierce said.

Burgess took a breath. "The line," he said. "The manner of things, the way we do, all fresh changed."

Pierce frowned impatiently. "Tell me what is changed," he said.

Burgess squeezed his hat in his hands until his knuckles were pale. "For one, they have a new jack the line's put on, started today—a new bloke, young one."

"He rides with you in the baggage van?"

"No, sir," Burgess said. "He only works the platform at the station. Stays at the station, he does."

Pierce shot a glance at Agar. It didn't matter if there were more guards at the platform. There could be a dozen guards, for all Pierce cared. "What of it?" he said.

"Well, it's the new rule, you see."

"What new rule?"

"Nobody rides in the baggage car, save me as guard," Burgess said. "That's the new rule, and there's this new jack to keep it proper."

"I see," Pierce said. That was indeed a change.

"There's more," Agar said gloomily.

"Yes?"

Burgess nodded. "They've gone and fitted a lock to the luggage-van door. Outside lock, it is. Now they lock up in London Bridge, and unlock in Folkestone."

"Damn," Pierce said. He began to pace back and forth in the room. "What about the other stops? That train stops in Redhill, and at—"

"They've changed the rules," Burgess said. "That van is never unlocked till Folkestone."

Pierce continued to pace. "Why have they changed the routine?"

"It's on account of the afternoon fast train," Burgess explained. "There's two fast trains, morning train and afternoon train. Seems the afternoon van was robbed last week. Gentleman was robbed of a valuable parcel somehow—collection of rare wine, I hear it to be. Anyhow, he puts a claim to the line or some such. The other guard's been fired, and there's all bloody hell to pay. Dispatcher his very self called me in this morning and dressed me down proper, warning me of this and that. Near cuffed me, he did. And the new jack at the platform's the station dispatcher's nephew. He's the one locks up in London Bridge, just before the train pulls out."

"Rare wines," Pierce said. "God in heaven, *rare wines*. Can we get Agar aboard in a trunk?"

Burgess shook his head. "Not if they do like today. Today, this nephew, his name's McPherson, he's a Scotsman and eager—badly wanting a job, as I look at it—this McPherson makes the passengers open every trunk or parcel large enough to hold a man. Caused a considerable fray, I'll say. This nephew is a stickler. New to the work, you see, and wanting to do it all proper, and that's the way it is."

"Can we distract him and slip Agar in while he's not looking?"

"Not looking? Never's he not looking. He looks like a starved rat after a flake of cheese, looks here and there and everywhere. And when all the baggage's loaded, he climbs in, pokes about in all the corners seeing there's no lurkers. Then he climbs off and locks up."

Pierce plucked his pocket watch from his waistcoat. It was now ten o'clock at night. They had ten hours before the Folkestone train left the next morning. Pierce could think of a dozen clever ways to get Agar past a watchful Scotsman, but nothing that could be quickly arranged.

Agar, whose face was the very picture of gloom, must have been thinking the same thing. "Shall we put off until next month, then?"

"No," Pierce said. He immediately shifted to his next problem. "Now, this lock they've installed on the luggage-van door. Can it be worked from inside?"

Burgess shook his head. "It's a padlock—hooks through a bolt and iron latch, outside."

Pierce was still pacing. "Could it be unlocked during one of the stops—say, Redhill—and then locked again at Tonbridge, farther down the line?"

"Be a risk," Burgess said. "She's a fat lock, big as your fist, and it might be noticed."

Pierce continued to pace. For a long time, his footsteps on the carpet and the ticking of the clock on the mantel were the only sounds in the room. Agar and Burgess watched him. Finally Pierce said, "If the van door is locked, how do you get ventilation?"

Burgess, looking a little confused, said, "Oh, there's air enough. That van's shoddy made, and when the train gets to speed, the breeze whistles through the cracks and chinks loud enough to pain your ears."

"I meant," Pierce said, "is there any apparatus for ventilation in the van?"

"Well, there's the slappers in the roof. . . ."

"What're they?" Pierce said.

"Slappers? Slappers—well, to speak true, they're not your proper slappers, on account of the lack of hinging. Many's the time I was wishing they were true slappers, I mean a slapper fit with hinging, and all the more when it rains—then it's a cold puddle inside, I can tell you—"

"What is a slapper?" Pierce interrupted. "Time is short."

"A slapper? A slapper's what your railway folks call a manner of trap. She's a hinged door up in the roof, mounted center, and inside you've a rod to open or shut the slapper. Some of your slappers—I mean proper slappers—they fit two to a coach, facing opposite ways. That's so's one is always away from the wind. Now, other coaches, they've their slappers mounted both the same, but it's a bother in the yards, you see, for it means the coach must be clamped with the slappers backward, and—"

"And you have two of these slappers in the luggage van?"

"Aye, that's true," Burgess said, "but they're not proper, because they're fixed open, you see, no hinging on the van slappers, and so when it rains there I be, soaked through—"

"The slappers give access directly to the interior of the luggage van?"

"They do, direct down." Burgess paused. "But if you're thinking of slipping a bloke through, it can't be done. They're no more than a hand's breadth square, and—"

"I'm not," Pierce said. "Now, you say you have two slappers? Where are they located?"

"On the roof, like I said, center of the roof, and—"

"Where in relation to the length of the car?" Pierce said. His pacing back and forth, and his brusque, irritable manner left Burgess, who was nervous and trying to be helpful, at a complete loss.

"Where . . . in relation . . ." His voice trailed off.

Agar said, "I don't know what you're thinking, but my knee pains me—my left knee here—and that's always a bad sign. I say, quit the lay for a deadly flummut, and be done."

"Shut up," Pierce said, with a sudden flaring anger that made Agar take a step backward. Pierce turned to Burgess. "Now I am asking," he said, "if you look at the van from the side, you see it as a kind of box, a large box. And on the top of this box are the slappers. Now, where are they?"

"Not proper set, and that's God's truth," Burgess said. "A proper slapper's near the ends of the coach, one at each end, so's to allow air to pass end to end, one slapper to the next. That's the way to arrange it for the best—"

"Where are the slappers on the luggage van?" Pierce said, glancing again at his watch. "I care only about the van."

"That's the hell of it," Burgess said. "They're near center, and no more than three paces separate. And they've no hinge. Now when it rains, down comes the water, direct to the center of the van, and there's one great puddle, straightaway in the center."

"You say the slappers are separated by three paces?"

"Three, four, thereabouts," Burgess said. "I never cared to know for certain, but it's certain I hate the damn things, and that's—"

"All right," Pierce said, "you've told me what I need to know."

"I'm glad of that," Burgess said, with a sort of confused relief, "but I swear, there's no way a man or even a chavy can slip down that hole, and once they lock me in—"

Pierce cut him off with a wave of his hand and turned to Agar. "This padlock on the outside. Is it hard to pick?"

"I don't know it," Agar said, "but a padlock's no trick. They're made strong, but they have fat tumblers, on account of their size. Some a man can use his little finger for the betty, and tickle her broke open in a flash."

"Could I?" Pierce said.

Agar stared at him. "Easy enough, but you might take a minute or two." He frowned. "But you heard what he said, you don't dare break her at the station stops, so why—"

Pierce turned back to Burgess. "How many second-class coaches are there on the morning train?"

"I don't know exact. Six, as often as not. Seven near the weekend. Sometimes, midweek they run five, but lately there's six. Now, first class, that's—"

"I don't care about first class," Pierce said.

Burgess fell silent, hopelessly confused. Pierce looked at Agar: Agar had figured it out. The screwsman shook his head. "Mother of God," Agar said, "you've lost your mind, you've gone flat debeno, sure as I stand here. What do you think, you're Mr. Coolidge?" Coolidge was a well-known mountaineer.

"I know who I am," Pierce said tersely. He turned back to Burgess, whose confusion had steadily increased during the last few minutes until he was now nearly immobilized, his face blank and expressionless, having lost even the quality of bewilderment.

"Is your name Coolidge, then?" Burgess asked. "You said Simms. . . ."

"It's Simms," Pierce said. "Our friend here is only making a joke. I want you to go home now, and sleep, and get up tomorrow and go to work as usual. Just carry on as usual, no matter what happens. Just do your regular day of work, and don't worry about anything."

Burgess glanced at Agar, then back to Pierce. "Will you pull tomorrow, then?"

"Yes," Pierce said. "Now go home and sleep."

When the two men were alone, Agar exploded in anxious fury. "Damn me if I'll voker flams at this dead hour. This is no simple kynchin lay tomorrow. Is that not plain?" Agar threw up his hands. "Make an end to it, I say. Next month, I say."

Pierce remained quiet for a moment. "I've waited a year," he said finally, "and it will be tomorrow."

"You're puckering," Agar said, "just talk, with no sense."

"It can be done," Pierce insisted.

"Done?" Agar exploded again. "Done *how?* Look here, I know you for a clever one, but I'm no flat, and there's no gammoning me. That lay is coopered. It's too damn sad the wine was snaffled, but so it was, and we must know it." Agar was red-faced and frantic; he swung his arms through the air in agitation.

In contrast, Pierce was almost unnaturally still. His eyes surveyed Agar steadily. "There is a bone lay," Pierce said.

"As God is my witness, how?" Agar watched as Pierce calmly went to a sideboard and poured two glasses of brandy. "You'll not put enough of that in me to cloud my eyes," he said. "Now, look plain."

Agar held up his hand, and ticked the points off on his fingers. "I am to ride in the van, you say. But I cannot get in—an eager jack of a Scotsman stands sharp at the door. You heard as much yourself. But fair enough: I trust you to get me in. Now."

He ticked off another finger. "Now, there I be in the van. The Scotsman locks up from the outside. I've no way to touch that lock, so even if I make the switch, I can't open the door and toss out the pogue. I'm locked in proper, all the way to Folkestone."

"Unless I open the door for you," Pierce said. He gave Agar a snifter of brandy.

Agar swallowed it in a single gulp. "Aye, and there's a likely turn. You come back over all those coaches, tripping light over the rooftops, and swing down like Mr. Coolidge over the side of the van to pick the lock and break the drum. I'll see God in heaven first, no mistake."

Pierce said, "I know Mr. Coolidge."

Agar blinked. "No gull?"

"I met him on the Continent last year. I climbed with him in Switzerland—three peaks in all—and I learned what he knows."

Agar was speechless. He stared at Pierce for any sign of deception, scanning the cracksman's face. Mountaineering was a new sport, only three or four years old, but it had captured the popular attention, and the most notable of the English practitioners, such as A. E. Coolidge, had become famous.

"No gull?" Agar said again.

"I have the ropes and tackle up in the closet," Pierce said. "No gull."

"I'll have another daffy," Agar said, holding out his empty glass. Pierce immediately filled it, and Agar immediately gulped it down.

"Well then," he said. "Let's say you *can* betty the lock, hanging on a rope, and break the drum, and then lock up again, with nobody the wiser. How do I get on in the first place, past the Scots jack, with his sharp cool?"

"There is a way," Pierce said. "It's not pleasant, but there is a way."

Agar appeared unconvinced. "Say you put me on in some trunk. He's bound he'll open it and have a see, and there I am. What then?"

"I intend for him to open it and see you," Pierce said.

"You *intend?*"

"I think so, and it will go smoothly enough, if you can take a bit of odor."

"What manner of odor?"

"The smell of a dead dog, or cat," Pierce said. "Dead some days. Do you think you can manage that?"

Agar said, "I swear, I don't get the lay. Let's settle the down with another daffy or two," and he extended his glass.

"That's enough," Pierce said. "There are things for you to do. Go to your lodgings, and come back with your best dunnage, the finest you have, and quickly."

Agar sighed.

"Go now," Pierce said. "And trust me."

When Agar had departed, he sent for Barlow, his cabby.

"Do we have any rope?" Pierce said.

"Rope, sir? You mean hempen rope?"

"Precisely. Do we have any in the house?"

"No, sir. Could you make do with bridle leather?"

"No," Pierce said. He considered a moment. "Hitch up the horse to the flat carriage and get ready for a night's work. We have a few items to obtain."

Barlow nodded and left. Pierce returned to the dining room, where Miriam was still sitting, patient and calm.

"There's trouble?" she said.

"Nothing beyond repair," Pierce said. "Do you have a black dress? I am thinking of a frock of cheap quality, such as a maid might wear."

"I think so, yes."

"Good," he said. "Set it out, you will wear it tomorrow morning."

"Whatever for?" she asked.

Pierce smiled. "To show your respect for the dead," he said.

Chapter 40

A False Alarm

On the morning of May 22nd, when the Scottish guard McPherson arrived at the platform of the London Bridge Station to begin the day's work, he was greeted by a most unexpected sight. There alongside the luggage van of the Folkestone train stood a woman in black—a servant, by the look of her, but handsome enough, and sobbing most piteously.

The object of her grief was not hard to discover, for near the poor girl, set onto a flat baggage cart, was a plain wooden casket. Although cheap and unadorned, the casket had several ventholes drilled in the sides. And mounted on the lid of the casket was a kind of miniature belfry, containing a small bell, with a cord running from the clapper down through a hole to the innards of the coffin.

Although the sight was unexpected, it was not in the least mysterious to McPherson—or, indeed, to any Victorian of the day. Nor was he surprised, as he approached the coffin, to detect the reeking odor of advanced corporeal decay emanating from the ventholes, and suggesting that the present occupant had been dead for some time. This, too, was wholly understandable.

During the nineteenth century, both in England and in the United

States, there arose a peculiar preoccupation with the idea of premature burial. All that remains of this bizarre concern is the macabre literature of Edgar Allan Poe and others, in which premature burial in some form or another appears as a frequent motif. To modern thinking, it is all exaggerated and fanciful; it is difficult now to recognize that for the Victorians, premature burial was a genuine, palpable fear shared by nearly all members of society, from the most superstitious worker to the best-educated professional man.

Nor was this widespread fear simply a neurotic obsession. Quite the contrary: there was plenty of evidence to lead a sensible man to believe that premature burials did occur, and that such ghastly happenings were only prevented by some fortuitous event. A case in 1853 in Wales, involving an apparently drowned ten-year-old boy, received wide publicity: "While the coffin lay in the open grave, and the first earth was shovelled upon it, a most frightful noise and kicking ensued from within. The sextons ceased their labors, and caused the coffin to be opened, whereupon the lad stepped out, and called for his parents. Yet the same lad had been pronounced dead many hours past, and the doctor said that he had no respirations nor any detectable pulse, and the skin was cold and gray. Upon sighting the lad, his mother fell into a swoon, and did not revive for some length of time."

Most cases of premature burial involved victims ostensibly drowned, or electrocuted, but there were other instances where a person might lapse into a state of "apparent death, or suspended animation."

In fact, the whole question of when a person was dead was very much in doubt—as it would be again, a century later, when doctors struggled with the ethics of organ transplantation. But it is worth remembering that physicians did not understand that cardiac arrest was wholly reversible until 1950; and in 1850 there was plenty of reason to be skeptical about the reliability of any indicator of death.

Victorians dealt with their uncertainty in two ways. The first was to delay interment for several days—a week was not uncommon—and await the unmistakable olfactory evidence of the beloved one's departure from this world. Indeed, the Victorian willingness to postpone burial sometimes reached extremes. When the Duke of Wellington died, in 1852, there was public debate about the way his state funeral should be conducted; the Iron Duke simply had to wait until these disagreements were settled, and he was not actually buried until more than two months after his death.

The second method for avoiding premature burial was technological; the Victorians contrived an elaborate series of warning and signaling devices to enable a dead person to make known his resuscitation. A wealthy individual might be buried with a length of iron pipe connecting his casket to the ground above, and a trusted family servant would be required to remain at the cemetery, day and night, for a month or more, on the chance that the deceased would suddenly awake and begin to call for help. Persons buried above-ground, in family vaults, were often placed in patented, spring-loaded caskets, with a complex maze of wires attached to arms and legs, so that the slightest movement of the body would throw open the coffin lid. Many considered this method preferable to any other, for it was believed that individuals often returned from a state of suspended animation in a mute or partially paralyzed condition.

The fact that these spring-loaded coffins popped open months or even years later (undoubtedly the result of some external vibration or deterioration in the spring mechanism) only heightened the widespread uncertainty about how long a person might lie dead before coming back to life, even for a moment.

Most signaling devices were costly, and available only to the wealthy classes. Poor people adopted the simpler tactic of burying relatives with some implement—a crowbar, or a shovel—on the vague assumption that if they revived, they could dig themselves out of their predicament.

There was clearly a market for an inexpensive alarm system, and in 1852 George Bateson applied for, and received, a patent for the Bateson Life Revival Device, described as "a most economical, ingenious, and trustworthy mechanism, superior to any other method, and promoting peace of mind amongst the bereaved at all stations of life. Constructed of the finest materials throughout." And there is an additional comment: "A device of proven efficacy, in countless instances in this country and abroad."

"Bateson's belfry," as it was ordinarily known, was a plain iron bell mounted on the lid of the casket, over the deceased's head, and connected by a cord or wire through the coffin to the dead person's hand, "such that the least tremor shall directly sound the alarum." Bateson's belfries attained instant popularity, and within a few years a substantial proportion of coffins were fitted with these bells. During this period, three thousand people died daily in London alone, and Bateson's business was brisk; he was soon a wealthy man and respected as well: in 1859, Victoria awarded him an O.B.E. for his efforts.

As a kind of odd footnote to the story, Bateson himself lived in mortal terror of being buried alive, and caused his workshop to fabricate increasingly complex alarm systems for installation on his own coffin after he died. By 1867, his preoccupation left him quite insane, and he rewrote his will, directing his family to cremate him at his death. However, suspecting that his instructions would not be followed, in the spring of 1868 he doused himself with linseed oil in his workshop, set himself aflame, and died by self-immolation.

On the morning of May 22nd, McPherson had more important things to worry about than the weeping servant girl and the coffin with its belfry, for he knew that today the gold shipment from Huddleston & Bradford would be loaded upon the railway van at any moment.

Through the open door of the van, he saw the guard, Burgess. McPherson waved, and Burgess responded with a nervous, rather reserved greeting. McPherson knew that his uncle, the dispatcher, had yesterday given Burgess a good deal of sharp talk; Burgess was no doubt worried to keep his job, especially as the other guard had been dismissed. McPherson assumed that this accounted for Burgess's tension.

Or perhaps it was the sobbing woman. It would not be the first time a stout man had been put off his mark by a female's piteous cries. McPherson turned to the young girl and proffered his handkerchief.

"There, now, Missy," he said. "There, now . . ." He sniffed the air. Standing close to the coffin, he noticed that the odor seeping out of the ventholes was certainly rank. But he was not so overcome by the smell that he failed to observe the girl was attractive, even in her grief. "There, now," he said again.

"Oh, please, sir," the girl cried, taking his handkerchief and sniffing into it. "Oh, please, can you help me? The man is a heartless beast, he is."

"What man is that?" McPherson demanded, in a burst of outrage.

"Oh, please, sir, that guard upon the line. He will not let me set my dear brother here upon the train, for he says I must await another guard. Oh, I am most wretched," she finished, and dissolved into tears once more.

"Why, the unfeeling rogue, he would not let your brother be put aboard?"

Through sobs and sniffles, the girl said something about rules.

"Rules?" he said. "A pox on rules, I say." He noticed her heaving bosom, and her pretty, narrow waist.

"Please, sir, he is most firm about the other guard—"

"Missy," he said, "I am the other guard, standing here before you, and I'll see your dear brother on the train with no delay, and never you mind that blackguard."

"Oh, sir, I am in your debt," she said, managing a smile through her tears.

McPherson was overwhelmed: he was a young man, and it was springtime, and the girl was pretty, and soon to be in his debt. At the same instant, he felt the greatest compassion and tenderness for her distress. Altogether, he was set spinning with the emotions of the moment.

"Just you wait," he promised, and turned to chastise Burgess for his heartless and overzealous adherence to the rules. But before he could make known his opinion, he saw the first of the gray-uniformed, armed guards of Huddleston & Bradford, bringing the bullion consignment down the platform toward them.

The loading was carried out with sharp precision. First, two guards came down the platform, entered the van, and made a quick search of the interior. Then eight more guards arrived, in neat formation around two flatcarts, each pushed by a gang of grunting, sweating footmen—and each piled high with rectangular, sealed strongboxes.

At the van, a ramp was swung down, and the footmen joined together to push first one, and then the other, of the laden flatcarts up into the van, to the waiting safes.

Next an official of the bank, a well-rigged gent with an air of authority, appeared with two keys in his hand. Soon after, McPherson's uncle, the dispatcher, arrived with a second pair of keys. His uncle and the bank's man inserted their keys in the safes and opened them.

The bullion strongboxes were loaded into the safes, and the doors were shut with a massive metal clang that echoed in the interior of the luggage van. The keys were twisted in the locks; the safes were secured.

The man from the bank took his keys and departed. McPherson's uncle pocketed his keys and came over to his nephew.

"Mind your work this morning," he said. "Open every parcel large enough to hold a knave, and no exception." He sniffed the air. "What's that ungodly stink?"

McPherson nodded over his shoulder to the girl and the coffin, a short distance away. It was a pitiful sight but his uncle frowned with no trace of compassion. "Scheduled for the morning train, is it?"

"Yes, Uncle."

"See that you open it," the dispatcher said, and turned away.

"But, Uncle—" McPherson began, thinking he would lose his newly gained favor with the girl by insisting on such a thing.

The dispatcher stopped. "No stomach for it? Dear God, you're a delicate one." He scanned the youth's agonized face, misinterpreting his discomfiture. "All right, then. I'm near enough to death that it holds no terrors for me. I'll see to it myself." And the dispatcher strode off toward the weeping girl and her coffin. McPherson trailed reluctantly behind.

It was at that moment that they heard an electrifying, ghastly sound: the ringing of Mr. Bateson's patented bell.

In later courtroom testimony, Pierce explained the psychology behind the plan. "Any guard watches for certain happenings, which he suspects at any moment, and lies in wait for. I knew the railway guard suspected some fakement to smuggle a living body onto the van. Now, a vigilant guard will know a coffin can easily hold a body; he will suspect it less, because it seems such a poor trick for smuggling. It is too obvious.

"Yet, he will likely wonder if the body is truly dead, and if he is vigilant he will call to have the box opened, and spend some moments making a thorough examination of the body to insure that it is dead. He may feel the pulse, or the warmth of the flesh, or he may stick a pin here or there. Now, no living soul can pass such an examination without detection.

"But how different it is if all believe that the body is not dead, but alive, and wrongly incarcerated. Now all emotions are reversed: instead of suspicion, there is hope the body is vital. Instead of a solemn and respectful opening of the casket, there is a frantic rush to break it free, and in this the relatives join in willingly, sure proof there is nothing to hide.

"And then, when the lid is raised and the decomposed remains come to light, how different is the response of the spectators. Their desperate hopes are dashed in an instant; the cruel and ghastly truth is immediately apparent at a moment's glance, and warrants no prolonged investigation. The relatives are bitterly disappointed and wildly distraught. The lid is quickly closed—and all because of reversed expectations. This is simple human nature, as evidenced in every ordinary man."

At the sound of the bell, which rang only once, and briefly, the sobbing girl let out a shriek. At the same instant, the dispatcher and his nephew broke into a run, quickly covering the short distance to the coffin.

By then the girl was in a state of profound hysteria, clawing at the coffin lid with her fingers, mindless that her efforts were ineffectual. "Oh, my dear brother—oh, Richard, dear Richard—oh, God, he lives . . ." Her fingers scrabbled at the wooden surface, and her tugging rocked the coffin so that the bell rang continuously.

The dispatcher and his nephew instantly caught the girl's frantic anxiety, but they were able to proceed with more sense. The lid was closed with a series of metal latches, and they opened them one after another. Apparently it never occurred to either man, in the heat of the moment, that this coffin had more latches than any three others. And certainly the process of opening was more prolonged as the poor girl, in her agony, somehow impeded their efforts with her own.

In a few moments, the men were at a fever pitch of intensity. And all the while, the girl cried, "Oh, Richard—dear God, make haste, he's alive—please, dear God, he lives, praise God . . ." And all the while, the bell rang from the rocking of the coffin.

The commotion drew a crowd of some size, which stood a few paces back on the platform, taking in the bizarre spectacle.

"Oh, hurry, hurry, lest we are too late," the girl cried, and the men worked frantically at the latches. Indeed, only when they were at the final two latches did the dispatcher hear the girl cry, "Oh, I knew it was not cholera, he was a quack to say it. Oh, I knew . . ."

The dispatcher froze, his hand on the latch. "Cholera?" he said.

"Oh, hurry, hurry," the girl cried. "It is five days now I have waited to hear the bell. . . ."

"You say cholera?" the dispatcher repeated. "Five days?"

But the nephew, who had not stopped throwing off the latches, now flung the coffin lid wide.

"Thank God!" cried the girl, and threw herself down upon the body inside, as if to hug her brother. But she halted in mid-gesture, which was perfectly understandable. With the raising of the lid, a most hideous, fetid, foul stench rolled forth in a near palpable wave, and its source was not hard to determine; the body lying within, dressed in his best Sunday clothes, hands folded across the chest, was already in a state of obvious decomposition.

The exposed flesh at the face and hands was bloated and puffed, a repellent gray-green color. The lips were black, and so was the partially protruding tongue. The dispatcher and his nephew hardly saw more of that horrific spectacle before the feverish girl, with a final scream of heart-wrenching agony, swooned on the spot. The nephew instantly leapt to attend her, and the dispatcher, with no less alacrity, closed the lid and began shutting the latches with considerably more haste than he had displayed in opening them.

The watching crowd, when it heard that the man had died of cholera, dissipated with the same swiftness. In a moment, the station platform was nearly deserted.

Soon the servant girl recovered from her swoon, but she remained in a state of profound distress. She kept asking softly, "How can it be? I heard the bell. Did you not hear the bell? I heard it plain, did you not? The bell rang."

McPherson did his best to comfort her, saying that it must have been some earth tremor or sudden gust of wind that had caused the bell to ring.

The station dispatcher, seeing that his nephew was occupied with the poor child, took it upon himself to supervise the loading of luggage into the van of the Folkestone train. He did this with as much diligence as he could muster after such a distressing experience. Two well-dressed ladies had large trunks and, despite their haughty protests, he insisted that both be unlocked and opened for his inspection. There was only one further incident, when a portly gentleman placed a parrot—or some such multicolored bird—on the van, and then demanded that his manservant be permitted to ride with the bird and look after its needs. The dispatcher refused, explaining the new rules of the railway. The gentleman became abusive, and then offered the dispatcher "a sensible gratuity," but the dispatcher—who viewed the proffered ten shillings with somewhat more interest than he cared to admit, even to himself—was aware that he was being watched by Burgess, the same guard whom he had admonished the day before. Thus the dispatcher was forced to turn down the bribe, to his own displeasure and also that of the gentleman, who stomped off muttering a litany of stinging profanity.

These incidents did nothing to improve the dispatcher's mood, and when at last the malodorous coffin was loaded into the van, the dispatcher took a certain delight in warning Burgess, in tones of great solicitousness, to look after his health, since his fellow passenger had fallen victim to King Cholera.

To this, Burgess made no response at all, except to look nervous and out of sorts—which had been his appearance prior to the admonition. Feeling vaguely dissatisfied, the dispatcher barked a final order to his nephew to get on with the job and lock up the van. Then he returned to his office.

With embarrassment, the dispatcher later testified that he had no recollection of any red-bearded gentleman in the station that day at all.

Chapter 41

A Final Inconvenience

In fact, Pierce had been among the crowd that witnessed the dreadful episode of the opened coffin. He saw that the episode proceeded precisely as he had intended, and that Agar, in his hideous make-up, had escaped detection.

When the crowd dissipated, Pierce moved forward to the van, with Barlow at his side. Barlow was carrying some rather odd luggage on a footman's trolley, and Pierce had a moment of disquiet when he saw the dispatcher himself take up the job of supervising the loading of the van. For if anyone considered it, Pierce's behavior was distinctly odd.

To all appearances, he was a prosperous gentleman. But his luggage was unusual, to say the least: five identical satchels of leather. These satchels were hardly the sort of items considered agreeable by gentlemen. The leather was coarse and the stitching at the seams was crude and obvious. If the satchels were unquestionably sturdy, they were also unmistakably ugly.

Yet none was very large, and Pierce could easily have stowed them in the overhead luggage racks of his carriage compartment, instead of the luggage van. The van was ordinarily considered a nuisance, since it meant delays at both the start and the conclusion of the journey.

Finally, Pierce's manservant—he did not employ a railway footman—loaded the bags on to the luggage van separately. Although the servant was a burly character of evident strength, he was clearly straining under the weight of each satchel.

In short, a thoughtful man might wonder why a gentleman of quality traveled with five small, ugly, extremely heavy, and identical bags. Pierce watched the dispatcher's face while the bags were loaded, one after another. The dispatcher, somewhat pale, never noticed the bags at all, and indeed did not emerge from his distracted state until another gentleman arrived with a parrot, and an argument ensued.

Pierce drifted away, but did not board the train. Instead, he remained near the far end of the platform, apparently curious about the recovery of the woman who had fainted. In fact, he was lingering in the hope of seeing the padlock that he would soon be attempting to pick. When the dispatcher left, with a final sharp rebuke to his nephew, the young woman made her way toward the coaches. Pierce fell into step beside her.

"Are you fully recovered, Miss?" he asked.

"I trust so," she said.

They merged with the boarding crowd at the coaches. Pierce said, "Perhaps you will join me in my compartment for the duration of the journey?"

"You are kind," the girl said, with a slight nod.

"Get rid of him," Pierce whispered to her. "I don't care how, just do it."

Miriam had a puzzled look for only a moment, and then a hearty voice boomed out, "Edward! Edward, my dear fellow!" A man was pushing toward them through the crowd.

Pierce waved a delighted greeting. "Henry," he called. "Henry Fowler, what an extraordinary surprise."

Fowler came over and shook Pierce's hand. "Fancy meeting you here," he said. "Are you on this train? Yes? Why, so am I, the fact of the matter—ah . . ." His voice trailed off as he noticed the girl at Pierce's side. He displayed some discomfiture, for in terms of Henry Fowler's social world all the signals were mixed. Here was Pierce, dressed handsomely and showing his usual polish, standing with a girl who was, God knew, pretty enough, but by her dress and manner a very common sort.

Pierce was a bachelor and a blood, and he might travel openly with a mistress for a holiday by the sea, but such a girl would certainly be dressed with gentility, which this girl was not. And contrariwise, were this creature a servant in his household, he would hardly have her out and about in so public a place as a train station unless there was some particular reason for it, but Fowler could not imagine a reason.

Then, too, he perceived that the girl had been weeping; her eyes were red and there were streaks upon her cheeks, and so it was all most perplexing and unusual, and—

Pierce put Fowler out of his misery. "Forgive me," he said, turning to the girl. "I should introduce you, but I do not know your name. This is Mr. Henry Fowler."

The girl, giving him a demure smile, said, "I am Brigid Lawson. How'd you do, sir."

Fowler nodded a vaguely polite greeting, struggling to assume the correct stance toward an obvious servant girl (and therefore not an equal) and a female in distress (and therefore deserving of gentlemanly conduct, so long as her distress sprang from some morally acceptable exigency). Pierce made the situation clearer.

"Miss, ah, Lawson, has just had a most trying encounter," Pierce said. "She is traveling to accompany her deceased brother, who is now situated in the van. But a few moments past, the bell rang, and there was hope of revival and the casket was opened—"

"I see, I see," Fowler said, "most distressing—"

"—but it was a false alarm," Pierce said.

"And thus doubly painful, I am certain," Fowler said.

"I offered to accompany her on the journey," Pierce said.

"And indeed I should do the same," Fowler said, "were I in your place. In fact . . ." He hesitated. "Would it seem an imposition if I joined you both?"

Pierce did not hesitate. "By all means," he said cheerfully. "That is, unless Miss Lawson . . ."

"You are ever so kind, you two are," the girl said, with a brave but grateful smile.

"Well, it's settled, then," Fowler said, also smiling. Pierce saw that he was looking at the girl with interest. "But would you like to come with me? My compartment is just a short way forward." He pointed up the line of first-class coaches.

Pierce, of course, intended to sit in the last compartment of the final first-class coach. From there, he would have the shortest distance to travel, over the tops of the cars, to reach the luggage van at the rear.

"Actually," Pierce said, "I've my own compartment, down there." He pointed toward the back of the train. "My bags are already there, and I've paid the footman, and so on."

"My dear Edward," Fowler said, "How did you get yourself way back there? The choice compartments are all toward the front, where the noise is minified. Come along: I assure you, you'll find a forward compartment more to your liking, and particularly if Miss Lawson feels poorly. . . ." He shrugged as if to suggest the conclusion was obvious.

"Nothing would delight me more," Pierce said, "but in truth I have selected my compartment on the advice of my physician, after experiencing certain distress on railway journeys. This he has attributed to the effects of vibrations originating in the engine, and therefore he's warned me to sit as far back from the source as possible." Pierce gave a short laugh. "He said, in fact, that I should sit second class, but I cannot bring myself to it."

"And little wonder," Fowler said. "There is a limit to healthy living, though you cannot expect a physician to know it. My own once advised me to quit wine—can you imagine the temerity? Very well, then, we shall all ride in your compartment."

Pierce said, "Perhaps Miss Lawson feels, as you do, that a forward carriage would be preferable."

Before the girl could speak, Fowler said, "What? And steal her away from you, leaving you solitary upon the journey? I would not think of it. Come, come, the train will soon leave. Where is your compartment?"

They walked the length of the train to Pierce's compartment. Fowler was in unshakable good spirits, and chattered at length about physicians and their foibles. They stepped into Pierce's compartment and closed the door. Pierce glanced at his watch: it was six minutes to eight. The train did not always leave precisely on schedule, but even so, time was short.

Pierce had to get rid of Fowler. He could not climb out of his compartment onto the roof of the train if there were any strangers—and certainly anyone from the bank—in his compartment. But at the same time, he had to get rid of Fowler in such a way that no suspicion would be aroused; for in the aftermath of the robbery Mr. Fowler would search his memory—and probably be questioned by the authorities—to uncover the least hint of [illegible]gularity that might explain who the robbers were.

[illegible] Fowler was still talking, but his focus was directed toward the girl, who gave every appearance of rapt and fascinated attention. "It's the most extraordinary luck, running across Edward today. Do you travel this route often, Edward? I myself do it no more than once a month. And you, Miss Lawson?"

"I been on a train before," the girl said, "but I never gone first class; only my mistress, this time she buys me a first ticket, seeing as how, you know . . ."

"Oh, quite, quite," Fowler said, in a hearty, chin-up manner. "One must do all one can for one in time of stress. I must confess, I am under no little stress myself this morning. Now, Edward here, he may have guessed the reason for my travel, and therefore my stress. Eh, Edward? Have you a guess?"

Pierce had not been listening. He was staring out the window, considering how to get rid of Fowler in the remaining few minutes. He looked over at Fowler. "Do you think your bags are safe?" he said.

"My bags? Bags? What—Oh, in my compartment? I have no bags, Edward. I carry not so much as a case of briefs, for once in Folkestone, I shall remain there just two hours, hardly the space of time to take a meal, or some refreshments, or smoke a cigar, before I am back on the train, homeward bound."

Smoke a cigar, Pierce thought. Of course. He reached into his coat pocket, and withdrew a long cigar, which he lit.

"Now, then, dear girl," Fowler said, "our friend Edward here shall surely have surmised the purpose of my journey, but I fancy you are still in the dark."

The girl was, in fact, staring at Mr. Fowler with her mouth slightly open.

"The truth is that this is no ordinary train, and I am no ordinary passenger. On the contrary, I am the general manager of the banking firm of Huddleston & Bradford, Westminster, and today, aboard this very train—not two hundred paces from us as we sit here—my firm has stored a quantity of gold bullion for shipment overseas to our brave troops. Can you imagine how much? No? Well, then—it is a quantity in excess of twelve thousand pounds, my dear child."

"Cor!" the girl exclaimed. "And you're in charge of all that?"

"I am indeed." Henry Fowler was looking plainly self-satisfied, and with reason. He had obviously overwhelmed the simple girl with his words, and she now regarded him with dizzy admiration. And perhaps more? She appeared to have entirely forgotten Pierce.

That is, until Pierce's cigar smoke billowed in gray clouds within the compartment. Now the girl coughed in a delicate, suggestive fashion, as she had no doubt observed her mistress to do. Pierce, staring out of the window, did not seem to notice.

The girl coughed again, more insistently. When Pierce still [illegible] response, Fowler took it upon himself to speak. "Are you feeling well?" he inquired.

"I was, but I'm faint. . . ." The girl made a vague gesture toward the smoke.

"Edward," Fowler said. "I believe your tobacco causes Miss Lawson some distress, Edward."

Pierce looked at him and said, "What?"

"I say, would you mind—" Fowler began.

The girl bent forward and said, "I feel quite faint, I fear, please," and she extended a hand toward the door, as if to open it.

"Just look, now," Fowler said to Pierce. Fowler opened the door and helped the girl—who leaned rather heavily upon his arm—into the fresh air.

"I had no idea," Pierce protested. "Believe me, had I but known—"

"You might have inquired before lighting your diabolical contraption," Fowler said, with the girl leaning against him, weak-kneed, so that much of her bosom pressed against his chest.

"I'm most dreadfully sorry," Pierce said. He started to get out himself, to lend assistance.

The last thing Fowler wanted was assistance. "You shouldn't smoke anyway, if your doctor has warned you that trains are hazardous to your health," he snapped. "Come, my dear," he said to the girl, "my compartment is just this way, and we can continue our conversation with no danger of noxious fumes." The girl went willingly.

"Dreadfully sorry," Pierce said again, but neither of them looked back.

A moment later, the whistle blew and the engine began to chug. Pierce stepped into his compartment, shut the door, and watched London Bridge Station slide away past his window as the morning train to Folkestone began to gather speed.

PART FOUR

THE GREAT TRAIN ROBBERY

May, 1855

Chapter 42

A Remarkable Revival

Burgess, locked in the windowless luggage van, knew by now the location of the train at any moment by the sound of the track. He heard first the smooth clacking of the wheels on the well-laid rails of the yard. Then, later, the hollow, more resonant tones as the train crossed Bermondsey on the elevated overpass for several miles, and, still later, a transition to a deader sound and a rougher ride, signaling the beginning of the southward run outside London and into the countryside.

Burgess had no inkling of Pierce's plan, and he was astonished when the coffin bell began to ring. He attributed it to the vibration and sway of the train, but a few moments later there was a pounding, and then a muffled voice. Unable to make out the words, he approached the coffin.

"Open up, damn you," the voice said.

"Are you alive?" Burgess asked, in tones of wonderment.

"It's Agar, you damnable flat," came the answer.

Burgess hastily began to throw the catches on the coffin lid. Soon after, Agar—covered in a dreadful green paste, smelling horrible, but acting in normal enough fashion—got out of the coffin and said, "I must be quick. Get me those satchels there." He pointed to the five leather valises stacked in a corner of the van.

Burgess hurried to do so. "But the van is locked," he said. "How will it be opened?"

"Our friend," Agar said, "is a mountaineer."

Agar opened the safes and removed the first of the strongboxes, breaking the seal and taking out the dull gold bars of bullion—each stamped with a royal crown and the initials "H & B." He replaced them with small bags of sewn shot, which he took from the valises.

Burgess watched in silence. The train was now rumbling almost due south, past the Crystal Palace, toward Croyden and Redhill. From there it would go east to Folkestone.

"A mountaineer?" Burgess said finally.

"Yes," Agar said. "He's coming over the tops of the train to unlock us."

"When?" Burgess said, frowning.

"After Redhill, returning to his coach before Ashford. It's all open country there. Almost no chance of being seen." Agar did not glance up from his work.

"Redhill to Ashford? But that's the fastest part of the run."

"Aye, I suppose," Agar said.

"Well, then," Burgess said, "your friend is mad."

Chapter 43

The Origin of Audacity

At one point in the trial of Pierce, the prosecutor lapsed into a moment of frank admiration. "Then it is not true," said the prosecutor, "that you had any experience of the recreation of mountaineering?"

"None," Pierce said. "I merely said that to reassure Agar."

"You had not met Mr. Coolidge, nor read extensively on the subject, nor owned any of the particular devices and apparatus considered vital to that activity of mountaineering?"

"No," Pierce said.

"Had you, perhaps, some past experiences of athletic or physical endeavor which persuaded you of your ability to carry out your intended plan?"

"None," Pierce said.

"Well, then," said the prosecutor, "I must inquire, if only for reasons of ordinary human curiosity, what on earth, sir, led you to suppose that without prior training, or knowledge, or special equipment, or athletic prowess—what on earth led you to believe you might succeed in such a palpably dangerous and, may I say, nearly suicidal undertaking as clambering about on a swift-moving railway train? Wherever did you find the audacity for such an act?"

Journalistic accounts mention that at this point the witness smiled. "I knew it would be no difficulty," he said, "despite the appearance of danger, for I had on several occasions read in the press of those incidents which are called railway sway, and I had similarly read of the explanation, offered by engineers, that the forces are caused by the nature of swiftly moving air as shown in the studies of the late Italian, Baroni. Thus, I was assured that these forces would operate to hold my person to the surface of the coach, and I should be utterly safe in my undertaking."

At this point, the prosecutor asked for further elucidation, which Pierce gave in garbled form. The summary of this portion of the trial, as reported in the *Times*, was garbled still further. The general idea was that Pierce —by now almost revered in the press as a master criminal—possessed some knowledge of a scientific principle that had aided him.

The truth is that Pierce, rather proud of his erudition, undertook his climb over the cars with a sense of confidence that was completely unfounded. Briefly, the situation was this:

Beginning around 1848, when railway trains began to attain speeds of fifty or even seventy miles an hour, a bizarre and inexplicable new phenomenon was noted. Whenever a fast-moving train passed a train standing at a station, the carriages of both trains had a tendency to be drawn together in what was called "railway sway." In some cases the carriages heeled over in such a pronounced fashion that passengers were alarmed, and indeed there was sometimes minor damage to coaches.

Railway engineers, after a period of technical chatter, finally admitted their perplexity outright. No one had the slightest idea why "railway sway" occurred, or what to do to correct it. One must remember that trains were then the fastest-moving objects in human history, and the behavior of such swift vehicles was suspected to be governed by some set of physical laws as yet undiscovered. The confusion was precisely that of aircraft engineers a century later, when the "buffeting" phenomenon of an aircraft approaching the speed of sound was similarly inexplicable, and the means to overcome it could only be guessed at.

However, by 1851 most engineers had decided correctly that railway sway was an example of Bernoulli's Law, a formulation of a Swiss mathematician of the previous century which stated, in effect, that the pressure within a moving stream of air is less than the pressure of the air surrounding it.

This meant that two moving trains, if they were close enough, would be sucked together by the partial vacuum of air between them. The solution to the problem was simple, and soon adopted: the parallel tracks were set farther apart, and railway sway disappeared.

In modern times, Bernoulli's Law explains such diverse phenomena as why a baseball curves, why a sailboat can sail into the wind, and why wings lift the aircraft. But then, as now, most people did not really understand these events in terms of physics: most jet-age travelers would probably be surprised to learn that a jet flies because it is literally sucked upward into the air by a partial vacuum over the wings' upper surface, and the sole purpose of the engines is to propel the wings forward fast enough to create a stream of passing air that produces this necessary vacuum.

Furthermore, a physicist would dispute even this explanation as not really correct, and would insist that a rigorous explanation of events is even further from the public's "common sense" idea about these phenomena.

In the face of this complexity, one can readily understand Pierce's own confusion, and the erroneous conclusion he drew. Apparently he believed that the airstream around the moving carriage, as described by "Baroni," would act to suck him down to the carriage roof, and thus help him to maintain his footing as he moved from car to car.

The truth is that Bernoulli's Law would not operate in any way on his body. He would simply be a man exposed to a fifty-mile-an-hour blast of rushing air, which could blow him off the train at any moment, and it was absurd for him to attempt what he did at all.

Nor was this the extent of his misinformation. The very fact that high-speed travel was so new left Pierce, along with his contemporaries, with very little sense of the consequences of being thrown from a fast-moving vehicle.

Pierce had seen Spring Heel Jack dead after being thrown from the train. But he had regarded this with no sense of inevitability, as the outcome of some inexorable physical laws. At this time, there was only a vague notion that to be thrown from a speeding train was hazardous, and somewhat more hazardous if the train was moving rapidly. But the nature of the hazard was thought to lie in the precise manner of a person's fall: a lucky man could pick himself up with a few scrapes, while an unlucky man would break his neck on impact. In short, a fall from a train was regarded pretty much like a fall from a horse: some were worse than others, and that was that.

Indeed, during the early history of railways, there had been a sort of daredevil's sport called "carriage-hopping," favored by the kind of young men who later scaled public buildings and engaged in other madcap escapades. University students were particularly prone to these amusements.

Carriage-hopping consisted of leaping from a moving railway carriage to the ground. Although government officials condemned the practice and railway officials flatly forbade it, carriage-hopping enjoyed a brief vogue from 1830 to 1835. Most hoppers suffered nothing more serious than a few bruises, or at worst a broken bone. The fad eventually lost popularity, but the memory of it bolstered the public belief that a fall from a train was not necessarily lethal.

In fact, during the 1830s, most trains averaged twenty-five miles an hour. But by 1850, when the speed of trains had doubled, the consequences of a fall were quite different, and out of all proportion to a fall at slower speeds. Yet this was not understood, as Pierce's testimony indicates.

The prosecutor asked: "Did you take any manner of precaution against the danger of a fall?"

"I did," Pierce said, "and they caused me no little discomfort. Beneath my ordinary external garb, I wore two pairs of heavy cotton undergarments, which had the effect of making me unpleasantly heated, yet I felt these protective measures necessary."

Thus, wholly unprepared and entirely miscalculating the effects of the physical principals involved, Edward Pierce slung a coil of rope over his shoulder, opened the compartment door, and clambered up onto the roof of the moving carriage. His only true protection—and the source of his audacity—lay in his complete misunderstanding of the danger he faced.

The wind struck him like an enormous fist, screaming about his ears, stinging his eyes, filling his mouth and tugging at his cheeks, burning his skin. He had not removed his long frock coat, and the garment now flapped about him, whipping his legs "so fiercely that it was painful."

For a few moments, he was totally disoriented by the unexpected fury of the shrieking air that passed him; he crouched, clutching the wooden surface of the coach, and paused to get his bearings. He found he could hardly look forward at all, because of the streaking particles of soot blown back from the engine. Indeed, he was rapidly covered with fine black film on his hands and face and clothing. Beneath him, the coach rocked and jolted in an alarming and unpredictable fashion.

He very nearly abandoned his intent in those first moments, but after the initial shock had passed he determined to go forward with his plan. Crawling on his hands and knees, he moved backward to the end of the coach, and paused at the space over the coupling that separated his carriage from the next. This was a gap of some five feet. Some moments passed before he gathered the nerve to jump to the next car, but he did so successfully.

From there he crawled painfully down the length of the car. His frock coat was blown forward, covering his face and shoulders and flapping around his eyes. After some moments of struggle with the garment, he shook it off and saw it sail away, twisting in the air, and eventually fall by the roadside. The whirling coat looked enough like a human form to give him pause; it seemed a kind of warning of the fate that awaited him if he made the slightest error.

Freed of the coat, he was able to make more rapid progress down the second-class coaches; he jumped from one to the next with increasing assurance, and eventually reached the luggage van after a period of time he could not estimate. It seemed an eternity, but he later concluded it had not required more than five or ten minutes.

Once atop the van, he gripped an open slapper, and uncoiled his length of hemp. One end was dropped down the slapper, and after a moment he felt a tug as Agar, inside the van, picked it up.

Pierce turned and moved to the second slapper. He waited there, his body curled tight against the constant, unyielding blast of the wind, and then a ghastly green hand—Agar's—reached out, holding the end of the rope. Pierce took it; Agar's hand disappeared from view.

Pierce now had his rope slung from one slapper to the next. He tied the loose ends about his belt, and then, hanging on the ropes, eased himself over the side of the van until he was level with the padlock.

In that manner he hung suspended for several minutes while he twirled the padlock with a ring of picks, trying one betty after another and operating, as he later testified with considerable understatement, "with that degree of delicacy which circumstances permitted." Altogether, he tried more than a dozen keys, and he was beginning to despair that any would turn the trick when he heard the scream of the whistle.

Looking forward, he saw the Cuckseys tunnel, and an instant later he was plunged into blackness and churning sound. The tunnel was half a mile long; there was nothing to do but wait. When the train burst into sunlight again, he continued working with the keys, and was gratified when almost immediately one of the picks clicked smoothly in the mechanism. The padlock snapped open.

Now it was a simple matter to remove the lock, swing the crossbar free, and kick the door with his feet until Burgess slid it open. The morning train passed the sleepy town of Godstone, but no one noticed the man dangling on the rope, who now eased down into the interior of the luggage van and collapsed on the floor in absolute exhaustion.

Chapter 44

A Problem of Dunnage

Agar testified that in the first moment that Pierce landed inside the luggage van, neither he nor Burgess recognized him: "I cool him first, and I swear I granny he's some muck Indian or nigger, so black he is, and his dunnage torn all about, like he'd gone a proper dewskitch"—as if he'd had a thorough thrashing. "His min's a rag of tatters, and black as all the rest of him, and I says, the cracksman's hired a new bloke to do the lay. And then I see it's him himself, right enough."

Surely the three men must have presented a bizarre picture: Burgess, the guard, neat and tidy in his blue railway uniform; Agar, dressed splendidly in a formal suit, his face and hands a cadaverous bloated green; and Pierce, sagged to his hands and knees, his clothing shredded and sooty black from head to foot.

But they all recovered quickly, and worked with swift efficiency. Agar had completed the switch; the safes were locked up again, with their new treasure of lead shot; the five leather satchels stood by the van door in a neat row, each laden with gold bullion.

Pierce got to his feet and took his watch from his waistcoat, an incongruously clean gold object at the end of a soot-black chain. He snapped it open: it was 8:37.

"Five minutes," he said.

Agar nodded. In five minutes, they would pass the most deserted stretch of track, where Pierce had arranged for Barlow to wait and pick up the flung satchels. Pierce sat down and stared through the open van door at the countryside rushing past.

"Are you well, then?" Agar asked.

"Well enough," Pierce said. "But I don't cherish going back."

"Aye, it's frazzled you proper," Agar said. "You're a sight and no mistake. Will you change when you're snug in the compartment again?"

Pierce, breathing heavily, was slow to comprehend the meaning of the words. "Change?"

"Aye, your dunnage." Agar grinned. "You step off at Folkestone as you stand now and you'll cause no end of stir."

Pierce watched the green, rolling hills flash past, and listened to the rumble of the carriage on the tracks. Here was a problem he had never considered and had made no plans for. But Agar was right: he couldn't step out at Folkestone looking like a ragged chimney sweep, especially as Fowler was almost certain to seek him out to say goodbye. "I have no change," he said softly.

"What say?" Agar said, for the noise of the wind through the open van door was loud.

"I have no change of clothing," Pierce said. "I never expected . . ." His voice trailed off; he frowned. "I brought no other clothing."

Agar laughed heartily. "Then you'll play the proper ragamuffin, as you've made me play the stiff." Agar slapped his knee. "There's a daffy of justice, I say."

"It's nothing funny," Pierce snapped. "I have acquaintances on the train who will surely see me and mark the change."

Agar's merriment was quashed instantly. He scratched his head with a green hand. "And these same of your acquaintances, they'll miss you if you're not there at the station?"

Pierce nodded.

"It's the devil's own trap, then," Agar said. He looked around the van, at the various trunks and pieces of luggage. "Give me your ring of tickles, and I'll break a pit or two, and we'll find some square-rigged duns to fit you."

He held out his hand to Pierce for the ring of picklocks, but Pierce was looking at his watch. It was now two minutes to the drop-off point. Thirteen minutes after that, the train would stop in Ashford, and by then Pierce had to be out of the luggage van and back in his own compartment. "There's no time," he said.

"It's the only chance—" Agar began, but broke off. Pierce was looking him up and down in a thoughtful way. "No," Agar said. "Damn you, no!"

"We're about the same size," Pierce said. "Now be quick."

He turned away and the screwsman undressed, muttering oaths of all sorts. Pierce watched the countryside. They were close now: he bent to position the satchels at the lip of the open van door.

Now he saw a tree by the roadside, one of the landmarks he'd long since set for himself. Soon there would be the stone fence. . . . There it was . . . and then the old abandoned rusty cart. He saw the cart.

A moment later, he saw the crest of a hill and Barlow in profile beside the coach.

"Now!" he said and, with a grunt, flung one satchel after another out of the moving train. He watched them bounce on the ground, one by one. He saw Barlow hastening down the hill toward them. Then the train went around a curve.

He looked back at Agar, who had stripped to his underclothes, and held his fine duds out for Pierce. "Here you are, and damn your eyes."

Pierce took the clothes, rolled them into as tight a ball as he could manage, wrapped the parcel with Agar's belt, and, without another word, swung out of the open door and into the wind. Burgess closed the van door, and a few moments later the guard and Agar heard a clink as the bolt was thrown, and another clink as the padlock was locked once more. They heard the scratching of Pierce's feet as he scrambled up to the roof; and then they saw the rope, which had been taut across the roof from slapper to slapper, suddenly go slack. The rope was pulled out. They heard Pierce's footsteps on the roof a moment longer, and then nothing.

"Damn me, I'm cold," Agar said. "You'd best lock me back up," and he crawled into his coffin.

Pierce had not progressed far on his return journey before he realized he had made still another error in his planning: he had assumed it would take the same amount of time to go from the van to his compartment as it took to go from his compartment to the van. But almost immediately he recognized his mistake.

The return trip, against the blast of the wind, was much slower. And he was further burdened by the parcel of Agar's clothing, which he clutched to his chest, leaving only one hand free to grip the roofing as he crawled forward along the length of the train. His progress was agonizingly slow. Within minutes he realized that he was going to miss his intended schedule, and badly. He would still be crawling along the rooftops when the train reached Ashford Station; and then he would be spotted, and the jig would be up.

Pierce had a moment of profound rage that this final step in the plan should be, in the end, the only thing to go irretrievably wrong. The fact that the error was entirely his own doing merely increased his fury. He gripped the pitching, swaying carriage roof and swore into the wind, but the blast of air was so loud he did not hear his own voice.

He knew, of course, what he must do, but he did not think about it. He continued forward as best he could. He was midway along the fourth of the seven second-class carriages when he felt the train begin to slow beneath him. The whistle screamed.

Squinting ahead, he saw Ashford Station, a tiny red rectangle with a gray roof in the far distance. He could not make out any details, but he knew that in less than a minute the train would be near enough for passengers on the platform to see him on the roof. For a brief moment, he wondered what they would think if they did see him, and then he got up and ran, sprinting forward, leaping from one car to the next without hesitation, half blinded by the smoke that poured from the engine funnel back toward him.

Somehow he made it safely to the first-class coach, swung down, opened the door, dropped into his compartment, and immediately pulled the blinds. The train was now chugging very slowly, and as Pierce collapsed into his seat he heard the hiss of the brakes and the footman's cry: "Ashford Station . . . Ashford . . . Ashford . . ."

Pierce sighed.

They had done it.

Chapter 45

The End of the Line

Twenty-seven minutes later, the train arrived at Folkestone, the end of the South Eastern Railway line, and all the passengers disembarked. Pierce emerged from his compartment, appearing, he said, "far better than I deserved, but far from sartorial correctness, to put it lightly."

Although he had hastily employed handkerchief and spittle to clean his face and hands, he had discovered the soot and grime on his flesh to be most recalcitrant. As he had no mirror, he could only guess at the condition of his face, but his hands were no cleaner than a kind of pale gray. Furthermore, he suspected that his sandy-colored hair was now a good deal darker than previously, and he was grateful that most of it would be covered by his top hat.

But except for the top hat, all his clothing fitted poorly. Even in an age when most people's clothing fitted poorly, Pierce felt himself especially noticeable. The trousers were almost two inches short of an acceptable length, and the cut of the coat, although elegant enough, was of the extreme and showy fashion that true gentlemen of breeding avoided as indecently *nouveau riche*. And, of course, he reeked of dead cat.

Thus Pierce stepped out onto the crowded Folkestone platform with an inner dread. He knew that most observers would put down his appearance as a sham: it was common enough for men who aspired to be gentlemen to obtain secondhand goods, which they wore proudly, oblivious to the ill fit of the garments. But Pierce was all too aware that Henry Fowler, whose entire conscious being was attuned to the nuances of social standing, would spot the peculiarity of Pierce's appearance in an instant, and would wonder what was amiss. He would almost certainly realize that Pierce had changed clothing for some reason during the ride, and he would wonder about that as well.

Pierce's only hope lay in keeping his distance from Fowler. He planned, if he could, to make off with a distant wave of goodbye, and an air of pressing business that precluded social amenities. Fowler would certainly understand a man who looked after business first. And from a distance, with the intervening throng of people, Pierce's bizarre dress might possibly escape his eye.

As it happened, Fowler came charging through the crowd before Pierce could spot him. Fowler had the woman beside him, and he did not look happy.

"Now, Edward," Fowler began crisply, "I should be forever in your debt if you would—" He broke off, and his mouth fell open.

Dear God, Pierce thought. It's finished.

"Edward," Fowler said, staring at his friend in astonishment.

Pierce's mind was working fast, trying to anticipate questions, trying to come up with answers; he felt himself break into a sweat.

"Edward, my dear fellow, you look *terrible.*"

"I know," Pierce began, "you see—"

"You look ghastly near to death itself. Why, you are positively gray as a corpse. When you told me you suffered from trains, I hardly imagined . . . Are you all right?"

"I believe so," Pierce said, with a heartfelt sigh. "I expect I shall be much improved after I dine."

"Dine? Yes, of course, you must dine at once, and take a draught of brandy, too. Your circulation is sluggish, from the look of you. I should join you myself, but—ah, I see they are now unloading the gold which is my deep responsibility. Edward, can you excuse me? Are you truly well?"

"I appreciate your concern," Pierce began, "and—"

"Perhaps I can help him," the girl said.

"Oh, capital idea," Fowler said. "Most splendid. Splendid. She's a charmer, Edward, and I leave her to you." Fowler gave him a queer look at this last comment, and then he hurried off down the platform toward the luggage van, turning back once to call, "Remember, a good strong draught of brandy's the thing." And then he was gone.

Pierce gave an enormous sigh, and turned to the girl. "How could he miss my clothes?"

"You should see your countenance," she said. "You look horrible." She glanced at his clothes. "And I see you've a dead man's dunnage."

"Mine were torn by the wind."

"Then you have done the pull?"

Pierce only grinned.

Pierce left the station shortly before noon. The girl, Brigid Lawson, remained behind to supervise the loading of her brother's coffin onto a cab. Much to the irritation of the footmen, she turned down several waiting cabs at the station, claiming she had made arrangements in advance for a particular one.

The cab did not arrive until after one o'clock. The driver, an ugly massive brute with a scar across his forehead, helped with the loading, then whipped up the horses and galloped away. No one noticed when, at the end of the street, the cab halted to pick up another passenger, an ashen-colored gentleman in ill-fitting clothes. Then the cab rattled off, and disappeared from sight.

By noon, the strongboxes of the Huddleston & Bradford Bank had been transferred, under armed guard, from the Folkestone railway station to the Channel steamer, which made the crossing to Ostend in four hours. Allowing for the Continental time change, it was 5 P.M. when French customs officials signed the requisite forms and took possession of the strongboxes. These were then transported, under armed guard, to the Ostend railway terminus for shipment to Paris by train the following morning.

On the morning of May 23rd, French representatives of the bank of Louis Bonnard et Fils arrived at Ostend to open the strongboxes and verify their contents, prior to placing them aboard the nine o'clock train to Paris.

Thus, at about 8:15 A.M. on May 23rd, it was discovered that the strongboxes contained a large quantity of lead shot, sewn into individual cloth packets, and no gold at all.

This astounding development was immediately reported to London by telegraph, and the message reached Huddleston & Bradford's Westminster offices shortly after 10 A.M. Immediately, it provoked the most profound consternation in that firm's brief but respectable history, and the furor did not abate for months to come.

Chapter 46

A Brief History of the Inquiry

Predictably, the initial reaction of Huddleston & Bradford was sheer disbelief that anything was amiss. The French cable had been composed in English and read: GOLD MISSED NOW WHERE IS, and was signed VERNIER, OSTEND.

Confronted by this ambiguous message, Sir William Huddleston announced that there had been, no doubt, some silly delay with the French customs and he predicted the whole business would be unraveled before teatime. Mr. Bradford, who had never made the slightest attempt to conceal his intense and lifelong loathing for all things French, assumed that the filthy Frogs had misplaced the bullion, and were now trying to fix the blame for their own stupidity on the English. Mr. Henry Fowler, who had accompanied the gold shipment to Folkestone and seen it safely onto the Channel steamer, observed that the signature "Vernier" was an unfamiliar name, and speculated that the cable might be some sort of practical joke. This was, after all, a time of increasingly strained relations between the English and their French allies.

Cables requesting—and later demanding—clarification flashed back and forth across the Channel. By noon, it appeared that the steamship crossing from Dover to Ostend had been sunk, and the bullion lost in the mishap. However, by early afternoon it was clear the steamer had had an uneventful passage, but almost everything else was vastly more confused.

Cables were now being fired off to all conceivable parties by the Paris bank, the French railway, the English steamship line, the British railway, and the British bank, in dizzying profusion. As the day wore on, the tone of the messages became more acrimonious and their content more ludicrous. The whole thing reached a sort of pinnacle when the manager of the South Eastern Railway in Folkestone telegraphed the manager of the Britannic Steam Packet Company, also in Folkestone: QUI EST M. VERNIER. To this, the steamship manager shot back YOUR SCURRILOUS ALLEGATIONS SHALL NOT GO UNCHALLENGED.

By teatime in London, the desks of the chief officers of Huddleston & Bradford were heaped with telegrams and cables, and office boys were being dispatched to gentlemen's homes to inform wives that their husbands would not be home for dinner, owing to urgent matters of business. The earlier atmosphere of unruffled calm and disdain for French inefficiency was now fading, replaced by a growing suspicion that something might actually have happened to the gold. And it was increasingly clear that the French were as worried as the English—M. Bonnard himself had taken the afternoon train to the coast, to investigate the situation in Ostend at first hand. M. Bonnard was a notorious recluse, and his decision to travel was viewed as a most significant event.

By seven o'clock in London, when most of the bank's clerks went home for the day, the mood of the officers was openly pessimistic. Sir William Huddleston was snappish; Mr. Bradford had the smell of gin on his breath; Mr. Fowler was pale as a ghost; and Mr. Trent's hands trembled. There was a brief moment of elation around 7:30 P.M., when the customs papers from Ostend, signed by the French the previous day, arrived at the bank. They indicated that at 5 P.M. on May 22nd the designated representative of Bonnard et Fils, one Raymond Vernier, had signed for nineteen sealed strongboxes from Huddleston & Bradford containing, according to the declaration, twelve thousand pounds sterling in bullion.

"Here is their bloody death warrant," Sir William said, waving the paper in the air, "and if there's been any irregularity, it is wholly upon French heads." But this was an exaggeration of the legal situation, and he himself knew it.

Soon after, Sir William received a long cable from Ostend:

> YOUR CONSIGNMENT NINETEEN (19) STRONG BOXES ARRIVED OSTEND YESTERDAY 22 MAY AT 1700 HOURS ABOARD SHIP "ARLINGTON" SAID CONSIGNMENT ACCEPTED BY OUR REPRESENTATIVE WITHOUT BREAKING SEALS WHICH APPEARED INTACT CONSIGNMENT PLACED IN OSTEND STRONG SAFE WITH GUARD NIGHT 22 MAY FOLLOWING OUR CUSTOM NO EVIDENCE TAMPERING SAFE GUARD CHARACTER RELIABLE MORNING 23 MAY OUR REPRESENTATIVE BROKE SEALS YOUR CONSIGNMENT FOUND

CONSISTING QUANTITY LEAD PELLETS FOR GUN BUT NO GOLD PRELIMINARY INQUIRY REGARDING ORIGIN PELLETS SUGGESTS ENGLISH MANUFACTURE REVIEW OF BROKEN SEALS SUGGESTS PREVIOUS BREAK AND SECONDARY SEALING SKILLFUL NATURE NOT AROUSING SUSPICION AT ORDINARY INSPECTION IMMEDIATELY NOTIFYING POLICE OFFICIALS ALSO GOVERNMENT IN PARIS REMINDING ALL OF BRITISH ORIGIN BRITISH RAILWAY BRITISH STEAMSHIP BRITISH SUBJECT GUARDING THROUGHOUT REQUEST YOU INFORM BRITISH AUTHORITIES I AWAIT YOUR SOLUTION TO THIS TRUE PUZZLE

LOUIS BONNARD, PRESIDENT
BONNARD ET FILS, PARIS
ORIGINEE: OSTEND

Sir William's first reaction to the cable was reported to be "a heated and forceful expletive, provoked by the stresses of the moment and the lateness of the hour." He is also said to have commented extensively on the French nation, the French culture, and the personal and hygienic habits of the French populace. Mr. Bradford, even more vociferous, expressed his belief in the unnatural French fondness for intimacy with barnyard creatures. Mr. Fowler was obviously intoxicated and Mr. Trent was suffering pains in the chest.

It was nearly ten o'clock at night when the bankers were finally calm enough for Sir William to say to Mr. Bradford: "I shall notify the Minister. You notify Scotland Yard."

Events of subsequent days followed a certain predictable pattern. The English suspected the French; the French suspected the English; everyone suspected the English railway officials, who in turn suspected the English steamship officials, who in turn suspected the French customs officials.

British police officers in France, and French police officers in England, rubbed shoulders with private detectives hired by the banks, the railways, and the shipping line. Everyone offered some sort of reward for information leading to the arrest of the villains, and informants on both sides of the Channel quickly responded with a dazzling profusion of tips and rumors.

Theories about the lost gold shipment ran the gamut from the most mundane—a couple of French or English hooligans stumbling upon a fortuitous opportunity—to the most grandiose—an elaborate plot by the highest officials of the French or English government, engaged in a Machiavellian scheme intended simultaneously to line their own pockets and to sour relations with their military allies. Lord Cardigan himself, the great war hero, expressed the opinion that "it must surely be a clever combination of avarice and statecraft."

Nevertheless, the most widespread belief, on both sides of the Channel, was that it was some kind of inside job. For one thing, that was how most crimes were carried out. And, particularly in this case, the complexity and neatness of the theft surely pointed to inside information and cooperation. Thus every individual who had the slightest relationship to the Crimean gold shipment came under scrutiny, and was interrogated by the authorities. The zeal of the police to gather information led to some unlikely circumstances: the ten-year-old grandson of the Folkestone harbormaster was tailed by a plainclothesman for several days—for reasons that no one could quite recall later on. Such incidents only increased the general confusion, and the process of interrogation dragged on for months, with each new clue and possibility receiving the full attention of an eager and fascinated press.

No significant progress was made until June 17th, nearly a month after the robbery. Then, at the insistence of the French authorities, the safes in Ostend, aboard the English steamship, and on the South Eastern Railway were all returned to their respective manufacturers in Paris, Hamburg, and London for dismantling and examination of the lock mechanisms. The Chubb safes were discovered to contain telltale scratches inside the locks, as well as traces of metal filings, grease, and wax. The other safes showed no signs of tampering.

This discovery focused new attention on the luggage-van guard Burgess, who had been previously questioned and released. On June 19th, Scotland Yard announced a warrant for his arrest, but the same day the man, his wife, and his two children vanished without a trace. In subsequent weeks of searching, Burgess was not found.

It was then recalled that the South Eastern Railway had suffered another robbery from its luggage van, only a week prior to the bullion theft. The clear implication of generally lax management by railway authorities fed the growing public suspicion that the robbery must have occurred on the London-Folkestone train. And when the South Eastern Railway's hired detectives came forth with evidence that the robbery had been carried out by French villains—an allegation quickly shown to be groundless—the public suspicion hardened into certainty, and the press began to refer to The Great Train Robbery.

All during July and August, 1855, The Great Train Robbery remained a sensational topic in print and conversation. Although no one could figure out quite how it had been done, its evident complexity and audacity soon led to the unquestioned belief that it must have been carried out by Englishmen. The previously suspect French were now deemed too limited and timid even to conceive such a dashing endeavor, to say nothing of bringing it off.

When, in late August, the police in New York City announced they had captured the robbers, and that they were Americans, the English press reacted with frankly scornful disbelief. And, indeed, some weeks later it was learned that the New York police were in error, and that their robbers

had never set foot on English soil, but were, in the words of one correspondent, "of that erratic turn of mind, wherein a man will seize upon a publicized event, even if it be notorious, to gain the attention of the wider public, and this to satisfy his demented craving for a moment in the limelight."

The English newspapers printed every shred of rumor, hearsay, and speculation about the robbery; other stories were slanted to consider the robbery. Thus when Victoria made a visit to Paris in August, the press wondered in what way the robbery would affect her reception in that city. (It apparently made no difference at all.)

But the plain fact was that throughout the summer months no single new development occurred, and inevitably interest began to wane. People's imaginations had been captured for four months. During that time, they had progressed from hostility toward the French, who had obviously stolen the gold in some sleazy, underhanded fashion, to suspicion of the English leaders of finance and industry, who were at best guilty of gross incompetence and at worst culpable of the crime itself, and eventually to a sort of admiration for the resourcefulness and daring of the English rogues who had plotted and carried out the escapade—however it was actually done.

But in the absence of fresh developments The Great Train Robbery became tedious, and eventually public opinion turned distinctly sour. Having wallowed in a delightful orgy of anti-French sentiment, having deplored and applauded the villains themselves, having relished the foibles of bankers, railwaymen, diplomats, and police, the public was now ready to see its faith restored in the basic soundness of banks, railways, government, and police. In short, they wanted the culprits caught, and quickly.

But the culprits were not caught. Officials mentioned "possible new developments in the case" with ever less conviction. In late September there was an anonymous story to the effect that Mr. Harranby of Scotland Yard had known of the impending crime but had failed to prevent it; Mr. Harranby vigorously denied these rumors, but there were a few scattered calls for his resignation. The banking firm of Huddleston & Bradford, which had enjoyed a mild increase in business during the summer months, now experienced a mild decline. Newspapers featuring stories of the robbery sold fewer copies.

By October, 1855, The Great Train Robbery was no longer of interest to anyone in England. It had come full circle, from a topic of universal and endless fascination to a confused and embarrassing incident that nearly everyone wished very much to forget.

PART FIVE

ARREST AND TRIAL

November, 1856–August, 1857

Chapter 47

The Bug-Hunter's Chance

November 5th, known as Powder Plot Day or Guy Fawkes Day, had been a national holiday in England since 1605. But the celebration, observed the *News* in 1856, "has of late years been made subservient to the cause of charity as well as mere amusement. Here is a laudable instance. On Wednesday evening a grand display of fireworks took place on the grounds of the Merchant Seamen's Orphan Asylum, Bow-road, in aid of the funds of the institution. The grounds were illuminated somewhat after the fashion adopted at Vauxhall, and a band of music was engaged. In the rear of the premises was a gibbet, to which was suspended an effigy of the Pope; and around it were several barrels of tar, which at the proper time were consumed in a most formidable blaze. The exhibition was attended by a large concourse of people, and the result promised to be of considerable benefit to the funds of the charity."

Any combination of large crowds and distracting spectacles was, of course, also of considerable benefit to pickpockets, cut-purses, and dollymops, and the police at the orphan asylum that night were busy indeed. In the course of the evening, no fewer than thirteen "vagrants, vagabonds and petty villains" were apprehended by officers of the Metropolitan Force, including a female who was accused of robbing an intoxicated gentleman. This arrest was made by one Constable Johnson, and the manner of it was sufficiently idiosyncratic to merit some explanation.

The major features are clear enough. Constable Johnson, a man of twenty-three, was walking the asylum grounds when, by the flaring light of the fireworks exploding overhead, he observed a female crouched over the prostrate form of a man. Fearing the gentleman might be ill, Constable Johnson went to offer help, but at his approach the girl took to her heels. Constable Johnson gave chase, apprehending the female a short distance away when she tripped on her skirts and tumbled to the ground.

Observing her at close hand to be "a female of lewd aspect and lascivious comportment," he at once surmised the true nature of her attentions to the gentleman; namely, that she was robbing him, in his intoxicated stupor, and that she was the lowest form of criminal, a "bug-hunter." Constable Johnson promptly arrested her.

The saucy minx put her hands on her hips and glared at him in open defiance. "There's not a pogue upon me," she declared, which words must surely have given Constable Johnson pause. He faced a serious dilemma.

In the Victorian view, proper male conduct demanded that all women, even women of the lowest sort, be treated with caution and consideration for the delicacy of their feminine nature. That nature, noted a contemporary policeman's manual of conduct, "with its sacred emotional well-springs, its ennobling maternal richness, its exquisite sensitivity and profound fragility, i.e., all those qualities which comprise the very *essence of womanly character*, derive from the biological or physio-logic principles which determine all the differences between the sexes of male and female. Thus it must be appreciated that the *essence of womanly character* resides in every member of that sex, and must be duly respected by an Officer, and this despite the appearance, in certain vulgar personages, of the absence of said womanly character."

The belief in a biologically determined personality in both men and women was accepted to some extent by nearly everyone at all levels of Victorian society, and that belief was held in the face of all sorts of incongruities. A businessman could go off to work each day, leaving his "unreasoning" wife to run an enormous household, a businesslike task of formidable proportions; yet the husband never viewed his wife's activities in that way.

Of all the absurdities of the code, the most difficult was the predicament of the policeman. A woman's inherent fragility created obvious difficulties in the handling of female lawbreakers. Indeed, criminals took advantage of the situation, often employing a female accomplice precisely because the police were so reluctant to arrest.

Constable Johnson, confronted by this dratted minx on the night of November 5th, was fully aware of his situation. The woman claimed to have no stolen goods on her person; and if this was true, she would never be convicted, despite his testimony that he had found her bug-hunting. Without a pocket watch or some other indisputably masculine article, the girl would go free.

Nor could he search her: the very idea that he might touch the woman's body was unthinkable to him. His only recourse was to escort her to the station, where a matron would be called to perform the search. But the hour was late; the matron would have to be roused from her bed, and the station was some way off. In the course of being escorted through dark streets, the little tart would have many opportunities to rid herself of incriminating evidence.

Furthermore, if Constable Johnson brought her in, called for the matron, raised all manner of fuss and stir, and then it was discovered the girl was clean, he would look a proper fool and receive a stiff rebuke. He knew this; and so did the girl standing before him in a posture of brazen defiance.

Altogether it was a situation not worth the risk or the bother, and Constable Johnson would have liked to send her off with a scolding. But Johnson had recently been advised by his superiors that his arrest record left something to be desired; he had been told to be more vigilant in his pursuit of wrongdoing. And there was the strong implication that his job hung in the balance.

So Constable Johnson, in the intermittent, sputtering glow of the bursting fireworks, decided to take the bug-hunter in for a search—to the girl's open astonishment, and despite his own rather considerable reluctance.

Dalby, the station sergeant, was in a foul humor, for he was called upon to work on the night of the holiday, and he resented missing the festivities that he knew were taking place all around him.

He glared at Johnson and the woman at his side. The woman gave her name as Alice Nelson, and stated her age was "eighteen or thereabouts." Dalby sighed and rubbed his face sleepily as he filled in the forms. He sent Johnson off to collect the matron. He ordered the girl to sit in a corner. The station was deserted, and silent except for the distant pop and whistle of fireworks.

Dalby had a flask in his pocket, and at late hours he often took a daffy or two when there was no one about. But now this saucy little bit of no-good business was sitting there, and whatever else was the truth of her, she was keeping him from his nip; the idea irked him, and he frowned into space, feeling frustrated. Whenever he couldn't have a daffy, he wanted it especially much, or so it seemed.

After a space of time, the judy spoke up. "If you granny I've a pink or two beneath me duds, see for yourself, and now." Her tone was lascivious; the invitation was unmistakable, and to make it clearer, she began to scratch her limbs through the skirt, in languorous fashion.

"You'll be finding what you want, I reckon," she added.

Dalby sighed.

The girl continued to scratch. "I know to please you," she said, "and you may count on it, as God's me witness."

"And earn the pox for my troubles," Dalby said. "I know your sort, dearie."

"Here, now," the girl protested, in a sudden shift from invitation to outrage. "You've no call to voker such-like. There's not a touch of pox upon me, and never been."

"Aye, aye, aye," Dalby said wearily, thinking again of his flask. "There never is, is there."

The little tart lapsed into silence. She ceased scratching herself, and soon enough sat up straight in her chair, adopting a proper manner. "Let's us strike a bargain," she said, "and I warrant it'll be one to your liking."

"Dearie, there's no bargain to be made," Dalby said, hardly paying attention. He knew this tedious routine, for he saw it played out, again and again, every night he worked at the station. Some little bit of goods would be tugged in on an officer's arm, all protests of innocence. Then she'd settle in and make an advance of favors, and if that was not taken up, she'd soon enough talk a bribe.

It was always the same.

"Set me to go," the girl said, "and you'll have a gold guinea."

Dalby sighed, and shook his head. If this creature had a gold guinea on her, it was sure proof she'd been bug-hunting, as young Johnson claimed.

"Well, then," the girl said, "you shall have ten." Her voice now had a frightened edge.

"Ten guineas?" Dalby asked. That at least was something new; he'd never been offered ten guineas before. They must be counterfeit, he thought.

"Ten is what I promise you, right enough."

Dalby hesitated. In his own eyes he was a man of principle, and he was a seasoned officer of the law. But his weekly wage was fifteen shillings, and sometimes it came none too promptly. Ten guineas was a substantial item and no mistake. He let his mind wander over the idea.

"Well, then," the girl said, taking his hesitation for something else, "it shall be a hundred! A hundred gold guineas!"

Dalby laughed. His mood was broken, and his daydreams abruptly ended. In her anxiety the girl was obviously weaving an ever wilder story. A hundred guineas! Absurd.

"You don't believe me?"

"Be still," he said. His thoughts returned to the flask in his pocket.

There was a short silence while the tart chewed her lip and frowned. Finally she said, "I know a thing or two."

Dalby stared at the ceiling. It was all so dreary and predictable. After the bribe failed, there came the offer of information about some crime or other. The progression was always the same. Out of boredom, as much as anything else, he said, "And what is this thing or two?"

"A ream sight of a flash pull, and no slang."

"And what may that be?"

"I know who did the train-robbery lay."

"Mother of God," Dalby said, "but you're a clever judy. Why, do you know that's the very thing we're all wanting to hear—and hear it we have, from every blasted muck-snipe, smatter-hauler, and bug-picker who comes our way. Every blasted one knows the tale to tell. I've heard a hundred blows with these very ears you see here." He gave her a wan smile.

In fact, Dalby was feeling something like pity for the girl. She was such a down-and-out case, a bug-hunter, the lowest form of common and sleazy crime, and hardly able to formulate a reasonable bribe. In truth, Dalby seldom was offered information about the train robbery any more. That was old news, and nobody cared. There were half a dozen more recent and captivating crimes to blow.

"It's no slang cover," the girl said. "I know the screwsman did the pull, and I can put you to him swift enough."

"Aye, aye, aye," Dalby said.

"I swear," the girl protested, looking ever more desperate. "I *swear*."

"Who's the bloke, then?"

"I'll not say."

"Aye, but I suppose," Dalby said, "that you'll find this gent for us if only we set you free for a bit of hunting him down, isn't that right?" Dalby shook his head and looked at the girl to see her expression of astonishment. They were always astonished, these low types, to hear a crusher fill in the details of their tale. Why did they always take a man of the force for a total flat and dumb fool?

But it was Dalby who was surprised, for the girl very calmly said, "No."

"No?" Dalby said.

"No," the girl replied. "I know exact where he's to be found."

"But you must lead us to him?" Dalby said.

"No," the girl said.

"No?" Dalby hesitated. "Well, then, where's he to be found?"

"Newgate Prison," the girl said.

Several moments passed before Dalby fully appreciated her words. "Newgate Prison?" he said.

The girl nodded.

"What's his name, then?"

The girl grinned.

Soon after, Dalby called for a runner to go to the Yard and notify Mr. Harranby's office directly, for here was a story so strange it very likely had some truth to it.

* * *

By dawn, the basic situation was clear to the authorities. The woman, Alice Nelson, was the mistress of one Robert Agar, recently arrested on a charge of forging five-pound notes. Agar had protested his innocence; he was now in Newgate Prison awaiting his trial in court.

The woman, deprived of Agar's income, had turned to various crimes to support herself, and was nabbed in the act of picking a bug. According to a later official report, she showed "a most overpowering apprehension of confinement," which probably meant she was claustrophobic. In any case, she turned nose on her lover, and told all that she knew, which was little enough—but enough for Mr. Harranby to send for Agar.

Chapter 48

Kangaroo-Hunting

"A thorough comprehension of the devious criminal mind," wrote Edward Harranby in his memoirs, "is vital to police interrogation." Harranby certainly had that comprehension, but he had to admit that the man seated before him, coughing and hacking, presented a particularly difficult case. They were in their second hour of questioning, but Robert Agar stuck to his story.

In interrogations, Harranby favored the introduction of abrupt new lines of inquiry to keep the villains off balance. But Agar seemed to handle the technique easily.

"Mr. Agar," Harranby said. "Who is John Simms?"

"Never heard of 'im."

"Who is Edward Pierce?"

"Never heard of 'im. I told you that." He coughed into a handkerchief offered him by Harranby's assistant, Sharp.

"Isn't this man Pierce a famous cracksman?"

"I wouldn't know."

"You wouldn't know." Harranby sighed. He was certain Agar was lying. His posture, his flicking downcast eyes, his hand gestures—everything suggested deceit. "Well, now, Mr. Agar. How long have you been forging?"

"I didn't do no soft," Agar said. "I swear it wasn't me. I was in the pub downstairs, having a daffy or two is all. I swear."

"You are innocent?"

"Aye, I am."

Harranby paused. "You're lying," he said.

"It's God's truth," Agar said.

"We'll see you in the stir for many years. Make no mistake about it."

"There's no blame upon me," Agar said, getting excited.

"Lies, all lies. You're a counterfeiter, pure and simple."

"I swear," Agar said. "I'd not do any soft. There's no sense to it—" Abruptly, he broke off.

There was a brief silence in the room, punctuated only by the ticking of a clock on the wall. Harranby had purchased the clock especially for its tick, which was steady, loud, and irritating to prisoners.

"Why is there no sense to it?" he asked softly.

"I'm honest is why," Agar said, staring at the floor.

"What honest work do you do?"

"Local work. Here and there."

That was a nonspecific excuse, but possible enough. In London at that time, there were nearly half a million unskilled laborers who worked at various odd jobs whenever the jobs were available.

"Where have you worked?"

"Well, let's see, now," Agar said, squinting. "I did a day for the gas-works at Millbank, loading. I did two days at Chenworth, hauling bricks. A week past I did some hours for Mr. Barnham, cleaning his cellar. I go where I can, you know."

"These employers would remember you?"

Agar smiled. "Maybe."

Here was another dead end for Harranby. Employers of casual labor often did not recall their workers, or recalled them incorrectly. Either way, it wouldn't mean much.

Harranby found himself staring at the man's hands. Agar's hands were clenched in his lap. Then Harranby noticed that the little fingernail on one hand was long. It had been bitten at, to conceal this fact, but it was still somewhat long.

A long fingernail might mean all sorts of things. Sailors wore a nail long for luck, particularly Greek sailors; then, too, certain clerks who used seals kept a nail long to pluck the seal from the hot wax. But for Agar . . .

"How long have you been a screwsman?" Harranby said.

"Eh?" Agar replied with an expression of elaborate innocence. "Screws-man?"

"Come, now," Harranby said. "You know what a screwsman is."

"I worked as a sawyer once. Spent a year in the north, working in a mill as a sawyer, I did."

Harranby was not distracted. "Did you make the keys for the safes?"

"Keys? What keys?"

Harranby sighed. "You've no future as an actor, Agar."

"I don't take your meaning, sir," Agar said. "What keys are you talking of?"

"The keys to the train robbery."

Here Agar laughed. "Cor," he said. "You think if I was in on that flash pull I'd be doing a bit of soft now? You think that? That's glocky, that is."

Harranby's face was expressionless, but he knew that Agar was right. It made no sense for a man who had participated in a twelve-thousand-pound theft to be stamping out five-pound notes a year later.

"There's no use in pretending," Harranby said. "We know that Simms has abandoned you. He doesn't care what happens to you—why are you protecting him?"

"Never heard of 'im," Agar said.

"Lead us to him, and you'll have a fine reward for your troubles."

"Never heard of 'im," Agar said again. "Can't you see that plain?"

Harranby paused and stared at Agar. The man was quite calm, except for his coughing attacks. He glanced at Sharp, in the corner. It was time for a different approach.

Harranby picked up a piece of paper from his desk, and put on his spectacles. "Now, then, Mr. Agar," he said. "This is a report on your past record. It's none too good."

"Past record?" Now his puzzlement was genuine. "I've no past record."

"Indeed you do," Harranby said, running his finger along the print on the paper. "Robert Agar . . . hum . . . twenty-six years old . . . hmm . . . born Bethnal Green . . . hmm . . . Yes, here we are. Bridewell prison, six months, charge of vagrancy, in 1849—"

"That's *not true!*" Agar exploded.

"—and Coldhath, one year eight months, charge of robbery, in 1852"

"Not true, I swear it, not true!"

Harranby glared at his prisoner over his glasses. "It's all here in the record, Mr. Agar. I think the judge will be interested to learn it. What do you suppose he will get, Mr. Sharp?"

"Fourteen years transportation, at least," Sharp said, in a thoughtful way.

"Umm, yes, fourteen years in Australia—that sounds about right."

"Australia," Agar said, in a hushed voice.

"Well, I should think," Harranby said calmly. "Boating's the thing in a case like this."

Agar was silent.

Harranby knew that although "transportation" was popularly portrayed as a much-feared punishment, the criminals themselves viewed banishment to Australia with equanimity or even pleasant expectation. Many villains suspected that Australia was agreeable, and to "do the kangaroo hunts" was unquestionably preferable to a long stretch in an English prison.

Indeed, at this time Sydney, in New South Wales, was a thriving, handsome seaport of thirty thousand. In addition, it was a place where "personal history is at a discount, and good memories and inquisitive minds are particularly disliked. . . ." And if it had its brutal side—butchers were fond of plucking poultry while it was still alive—it was also pleasant, with gaslit streets, elegant mansions, bejeweled women, and social pretensions of its own. A man like Agar could view transportation as, at the very least, a mixed blessing.

But Agar was greatly agitated. Plainly, he did not want to leave England. Seeing this, Harranby was encouraged. He stood.

"That will be all for now," he said. "If in the next day or so you feel that you have something you wish to tell me, just inform the guards at Newgate."

Agar was ushered out of the room. Harranby sat back at his desk. Sharp came over.

"What were you reading?" he asked.

Harranby picked up the sheet of paper from his desk. "A notification from the Buildings Committee," he said, "to the effect that carriages are no longer to be parked in the courtyard."

After three days, Agar informed the Newgate guards that he would like another audience with Mr. Harranby. On November 13th, Agar told Harranby everything he knew about the robbery, in exchange for the promise of lenient treatment and the vague possibility that one of the institutions involved—the bank or the railway or even the government itself—might see fit to present him with a stipend from the still-outstanding offers of reward for information.

Agar did not know where the money was kept. He said that Pierce had been paying him a monthly stipend in paper currency. The criminals had previously agreed that they would divide the profits two years after the crime, in May of the following year, 1857.

Agar did, however, know the location of Pierce's house. On the night of November 13th, the forces of the Yard surrounded the mansion of Edward Pierce, or John Simms, and entered it with barkers at the ready. But the owner was not at home; the frightened servants explained that he had left town to attend the P.R. spectacle the following day in Manchester.

Chapter 49

The P.R.

Technically, boxing matches in England were illegal, but they were held throughout the nineteenth century, and drew an enormous, loyal following. The necessity to elude authorities meant that a big match might be shifted from town to town at the last minute, with vast crowds of pugilistic enthusiasts and sporting bloods following all over the countryside.

The match on November 19th between Smashing Tim Revels, the Fighting Quaker, and the challenger, Neddy Singleton, was moved from Liverpool to a small town called Eagle Welles, and eventually to Barrington, outside Manchester. The fight was attended by more than twenty thousand supporters, who found the spectacle unsatisfactory.

In those days, the P.R., or prize ring, had rules that would make the event almost unrecognizable to modern eyes. Fighting was done barefisted by the combatants, who were careful to regulate their blows in order to avoid injury to their own hands and wrists; a man who broke his knuckles or wrists early in a contest was almost certain to lose. Rounds were of variable duration, and the fights had no prearranged length. They often went fifty or even eighty rounds, thus lasting the better part of a day. The object of the sport was for each man slowly and methodically to injure his opponent with a succession of small cuts and welts; knockouts were not sought. On the contrary, the proper fighter literally battered his opponent into submission.

Neddy Singleton was hopelessly outclassed by Smashing Tim from the start. Early in the fight, Neddy adopted the ruse of dropping to one knee whenever he was struck, in order to halt the fight and allow him to catch his breath. The spectators hissed and booed this ungentlemanly trick, but nothing could be done to prevent it, especially as the referee—charged with giving the count of ten—called out the numbers with a slowness that demonstrated he'd been paid off smartly by Neddy's backers. The indignation of the fans was tempered, at least, by the recognition that this chicanery had the side affect of prolonging the bloody spectacle they had all come to witness.

With thousands of spectators standing about, including every manner of coarse and brutal ruffian, the men of the Yard were at some pains to operate unobtrusively. Agar, with a revolver at his spine, pointed out Pierce and the guard Burgess from a distance. The two men were than apprehended with great adroitness: a barker was pressed to each man's side, with a whispered suggestion that they come along quietly or take a bit of lead for their trouble.

Pierce greeted Agar amiably. "Turned nose, did you?" he asked with a smile.

Agar could not meet his eyes.

"Doesn't matter," Pierce said. "I've thought of this as well, you know."

"I had no choice," Agar blurted out.

"You'll lose your share," Pierce said calmly.

At the periphery of the P.R. crowd, Pierce was brought before Mr. Harranby of the Yard.

"Are you Edward Pierce, also known as John Simms?"

"I am," the man replied.

"You are under arrest on a charge of robbery," Mr. Harranby said.

To this Pierce replied, "You'll never hold me."

"I fancy that I will, sir," Mr. Harranby said.

By nightfall on November 19th, both Pierce and Burgess were, along with Agar, in Newgate Prison. Harranby quietly informed government officials of his success, but there was no announcement to the press, for Harranby wanted to apprehend the woman known as Miriam, and the cabby Barlow, both still at large. He also wanted to recover the money.

Chapter 50

Winkling Out

On November 22nd, Mr. Harranby interrogated Pierce for the first time. The diary of his assistant, Jonathan Sharp, records that "H. arrived in office early, most carefully attired and looking his best. Had cup of coffee instead of usual tea. Comments on how best to deal with Pierce, etc., etc. Said that he suspected nothing could be got from Pierce without softening up."

In fact, the interview was remarkably brief. At nine o'clock in the morning, Pierce was ushered into the office and asked to sit in a chair, isolated in the middle of the room. Harranby, from behind his desk, directed his first question with customary abruptness.

"Do you know the man called Barlow?"

"Yes," Pierce said.

"Where is he now?"

"I don't know."

"Where is the woman called Miriam?"

"I don't know."

"Where," said Mr. Harranby, "is the money?"

"I don't know."

"It seems that there is a good deal you don't know."

"Yes," Pierce said.

Harranby appraised him for a moment. There was a short silence. "Perhaps," Harranby said, "a time in the Steel will strengthen your powers of memory."

"I doubt it," Pierce said, with no sign of anxiety. Soon after, he was taken from the room.

Alone with Sharp, Harranby said, "I shall break him, you may be sure of that." The same day, Harranby arranged for Pierce to be transferred from Newgate Prison to the House of Correction at Coldbath Fields, also called the Bastille. "The Steel" was not ordinarily a holding place for accused criminals awaiting trial. But it was a frequent ruse for police to send a man there if some information had to be "winkled out" of him before the trial.

The Steel was the most dreaded of all English prisons. In a visit in 1853, Henry Mayhew described its features. Chief among them, of course, were the cockchafers, narrow boxes in a row with "the appearance of the stalls in a public urinal," where prisoners remained for fifteen-minute intervals, treading down a wheel of twenty-four steps. A warder explained the virtues of the cockchafer in this way: "You see the men can get no firm tread like, from the steps always sinking away from under their feet and *that* makes it very tiring. Again the compartments are small, and the air becomes very hot, so that the heat at the end of a quarter of an hour renders it difficult to breathe."

Even less pleasant was shot-drill, an exercise so rigorous that men over forty-five were usually exempted. In this, the prisoners formed a circle with three paces separating each. At a signal, each man picked up a twenty-four-pound cannonball, carried it to his neighbor's place, dropped it, and returned to his original position where another shot awaited him. The drill went on for an hour at a time.

Most feared of all was "the crank," a drum filled with sand and turned with a crank handle. It was usually reserved as a special punishment for unruly prisoners.

The daily regimen of Coldbath Fields was so debilitating that even after a short sentence of six months, many a man emerged "with the steel gone out of him"—his body damaged, nerves shot, and resolution so enfeebled that his ability to commit further crimes was severely impaired.

As a prisoner awaiting trial, Pierce could not be made to undergo the stepper, the shot-drill, or the crank; but he was obliged to follow the rules of prison conduct, and if he broke the rule of silence, for example, he might be punished by a time at the crank. Thus one may presume that the guards frequently accused him of speaking, and he was treated to "softening up."

On December 19th, after four weeks in the Steel, Pierce was again brought to Harranby's office. Harranby had told Sharp that "now we shall see a thing or two," but the second interrogation turned out to be as brief as the first:

"Where is the man Barlow?"

"I don't know."

"Where is the woman Miriam?"

"I don't know."

"Where is the money?"

"I don't know."

Mr. Harranby, coloring deeply, the veins standing out on his forehead, dismissed Pierce with a voice filled with rage. As Pierce was taken away, he calmly wished Mr. Harranby a pleasant Christmas.

"The cheek of the man," Harranby later recorded, "was beyond all imagining."

Mr. Harranby during this period was under considerable pressure from several fronts. The bank of Huddleston & Bradford wanted its money back, and made its feelings known to Harranby through the offices of none other than the Prime Minister, Lord Palmerston himself. The inquiry from "Old Pam" was in itself embarrassing, for Harranby had to admit that he had put Pierce in Coldbath Fields, and the implications of that were none too gentlemanly.

Palmerston expressed the opinion that it was "a bit irregular," but Harranby consoled himself with the thought that any Prime Minister who dyed his whiskers was hardly in a position to berate others for dissembling.

Pierce remained in Coldbath until February 6th, when he was again brought before Harranby.

"Where is the man Barlow?"

"I don't know."

"Where is the woman Miriam?"

"I don't know."

"Where is the money?"

"In a crypt, in St. John's Wood," Pierce said.

Harranby sat forward. "What was that?"

"It is stored," Pierce said blandly, "in a crypt in the name of John Simms, in the cemetery of Martin Lane, St. John's Wood."

Harranby drummed his fingers on the desk. "Why have you not come forth with this information earlier?"

"I did not want to," Pierce said.

Harranby ordered Pierce taken away to Coldbath Fields once more.

On February 7th, the crypt was located, and the appropriate dispensations obtained to open it. Mr. Harranby, accompanied by a representative of the bank, Mr. Henry Fowler, opened the vault at noon that day. There was no coffin in the crypt—and neither was there any gold. Upon reexamination of the crypt door, it appeared that the lock had been recently forced.

Mr. Fowler was extremely angry at the discovery, and Mr. Harranby was extremely embarrassed. On February 8th, the following day, Pierce was returned to Harranby's office and told the news.

"Why," Pierce said, "the villains must have robbed me."

His voice and manner did not suggest any great distress, and Harranby said so.

"Barlow," Pierce said. "I always knew he was not to be trusted."

"So you believe it was Barlow who took the money?"

"Who else could it be?"

There was a short silence. Harranby listened to the ticking of his clock; for once, it irritated him more than his subject. Indeed, his subject appeared remarkably at ease.

"Do you not care," Harranby said, "that your confederates have turned on you in this fashion?"

"It's just my ill luck," Pierce said calmly. "And yours," he added, with a slight smile.

"By his collected manner and polished demeanour," Harranby wrote, "I presumed that he had fabricated still another tale to put us off the mark. But in further attempts to learn the truth I was frustrated, for on the first of March, 1857, the *Times* reporter learned of Pierce's capture, and he could no longer conveniently be held in custody."

According to Mr. Sharp, his chief received the newspaper story of Pierce's capture "with heated imprecations and ejaculations." Harranby demanded to know how the papers had been put on to the story. The *Times* refused to divulge its source. A guard at Coldbath who was thought to have given out the information was discharged, but nobody was ever certain one way or the other. Indeed, it was even rumored that the lead had come from Palmerston's office.

In any case, the trial of Burgess, Agar, and Pierce was set to begin on July 12, 1857.

Chapter 51

The Trial of an Empire

The trial of the three train robbers was greeted by the public with the same sensational interest it had earlier shown in the crime itself. The prosecuting officials, mindful of the attention focused upon the event, took care to heighten the drama inherent in the proceedings. Burgess, the most minor of the players, was brought to the docket of Old Bailey first. The fact that this man knew only parts of the whole story only whetted the public appetite for further details.

Agar was interrogated next, providing still more information. But Agar, like Burgess, was a distinctly limited man, and his testimony served only to focus attention on the personality of Pierce himself, whom the press referred to as "the master criminal" and "the brilliant malignant force behind the deed."

Pierce was still incarcerated in Coldbath Fields, and neither the public nor the press had seen him. There was plenty of freedom for eager reporters to conjure up wild and fanciful accounts of the man's appearance, manner, and style of living. Much of what was written during the first two weeks of July, 1857, was obviously untrue: that Pierce lived with three mistresses in the same house, and was "a human dynamo"; that he had been behind the great check swindle of 1852; that he was the illegitimate son of Napoleon I; that Pierce took cocaine and laudanum; that he had previously been married to a German countess and had murdered her in 1848, in Hamburg. There is not the least evidence that any of these stories is correct, but it is certainly true that the press whipped public interest to the point of frenzy.

Even Victoria herself was not immune to the fascination with "this *most bold* and *dastardly* rogue, whom we *should like* to perceive at first hand." She also expressed a desire to see his hanging; she was apparently not aware that in 1857 grand theft was no longer a capital offense in England.

For weeks, crowds had been gathering around Coldbath Fields, on the unlikely chance of getting a look at the master thief. And Pierce's house in Mayfair was broken into on three occasions by avid souvenir hunters. One "well-born woman"—there is no further description—was apprehended while leaving the house with a man's handkerchief. Showing not the slightest embarrassment, she said that she merely wished to have a token of the man.

The *Times* complained that this fascination with a criminal was "unseemly, even decadent," and went so far as to suggest that the behavior of the public reflected "some fatal flaw in the character of the English mind."

Thus, it is one of the odd coincidences of history that by the time Pierce began his testimony, on May 29th, the public and the press had turned their attention elsewhere. For, quite unexpectedly, England was facing a new trial of national proportions: a shocking and bloody uprising in India.

The growing British Empire—some called it the Brutish Empire—had suffered two major setbacks in recent decades. The first was in Kabul, Afghanistan, in 1842, where 16,500 British soldiers, women, and children died in six days. The second setback was the Crimean War, now concluded, with demands for army reform. That sentiment was so strong that Lord Cardigan, previously a national hero, was in disrepute; he was even accused (unfairly) of not being present for the charge of the Light Brigade, and his marriage to the notorious equestrienne Adeline Horsey de Horsey had further tarnished his standing.

Now the Indian Mutiny arose as a third affront to English world supremacy, and another blow to English self-confidence. That the English were confident in India is evident from the fact that they had only 34,000 European troops in that country, commanding a quarter of a million native soldiers, called sepoys, who were not excessively loyal to their English leaders.

Since the 1840s, England had been increasingly highhanded in India. The new evangelical fervor of righteousness at home had led to ruthless religious reform abroad; thuggee and suttee had been stamped out, and the Indians were not altogether pleased to see foreigners changing their ancient religious patterns.

When the English introduced the new Enfield rifle in 1857, the cartridges for the rifle came from the factory liberally coated with grease. It was necessary to bite the cartridges to release the powder. Among the sepoy regiments there was a rumor that the grease was made from pigs and cows, and thus these cartridges were a trick to defile the sepoys and make them break caste.

English authorities acted quickly.

In January, 1857, it was ordered that factory-greased cartridges were to be issued only to European troops; the sepoys could grease their own with vegetable oil. This sensible edict came too late to halt the bad feeling, however. By March, the first English officers were shot by sepoys in sporadic incidents. And in May a genuine uprising broke out.

The most famous episode of the Indian Mutiny occurred at Cawnpore, a town of 150,000 on the banks of the Ganges. From a modern perspective, the siege of Cawnpore seems a kind of crystallization of all that was noble and foolish about Victorian England. A thousand British citizens, including three hundred women and children, were under fire for eighteen days. Living conditions "violated all the decencies and proprieties of life, and shocked the modesty of . . . womanly nature." Yet in the early days of the siege, life went on with extraordinary normalness. Soldiers drank champagne and dined on tinned herring. Children played around the guns. Several babies were born, and a wedding took place, despite the constant rain of rifle and artillery fire, day and night.

Later, everyone was rationed to a single meal a day, and soon they were eating horsemeat, "though some ladies could not reconcile themselves to this unaccustomed fare." The women gave up their undergarments for wadding for the guns: "The gentlewomen of Cawnpore gave up perhaps the most cherished components of their feminine attire to improve the ordnance. . . ."

The situation became increasingly desperate. There was no water, except from a well outside the encampment; soldiers trying to get water were shot in the attempt. The daytime temperatures reached 138 degrees Fahrenheit. Several men died of sunstroke. A dry well inside the compound was used as a grave for corpses.

On June 12th, one of the two buildings caught fire and burned to the ground. All medical supplies were destroyed. Yet the English still held out, beating back every attack.

On June 25th, the sepoys called a truce, and offered the English safe passage by ship to Allahabad, a city a hundred miles downstream. The English accepted.

The evacuation began at dawn on June 27th. The English moved onto forty riverboats, under the watchful eye of armed sepoys all around them.

As soon as the last Englishman was aboard the boats, the native boatmen jumped into the water. The sepoys opened fire on the ships, still tied up to the shore. Soon most of the boats were aflame, and the river was littered with corpses and drowning bodies. Indian cavalrymen splashed through the shallows, cutting down survivors with sabers. Every man was killed.

The women and children were taken to a mud building along the shore and held there in suffocating heat for some days. Then on July 15th, several men, including a number of butchers by trade, entered the house with sabers and knives and slaughtered everyone present. The dismembered bodies, including "some not altogether lifeless," were dumped into a nearby well, and were said to have filled it.

The English at home, expressing their "muscular Christianity," screamed for bloody revenge. Even *The Times*, swept along in the fury of the moment, demanded that "every tree and gable-end in the place should have its burden in the shape of a mutineer's carcass." Lord Palmerston announced that the Indian rebels had acted as "demons sallying forth from the lowest depths of hell."

At such a moment, the appearance of a criminal in the dock of Old Bailey, for a crime committed two years past, was of very minor interest. But there were some reports on the inside pages of the dailies, and they are fascinating for what they reveal about Edward Pierce.

He was brought before the bar for the first time on July 29th: "handsome, charming, composed, elegant and roguish." He gave his testimony in an even, utterly calm tone of voice, but his statements were inflammatory enough. He referred to Mr. Fowler as "a syphilitic fool" and Mr. Trent as "an elderly nincompoop." These comments led the prosecutor to inquire of Pierce's views on Mr. Harranby, the man who had apprehended him. "A puffed-up dandy with the brains of a schoolboy," Pierce announced, drawing a gasp from the court, for Mr. Harranby was in the gallery as an observer. Mr. Harranby was seen to color deeply, and the veins stood out on his forehead.

Even more astounding than Mr. Pierce's words was his general demeanor, for "he carried himself extremely well, and proudly, and gave no hint of contrition, nor any trace of moral remorse for his black deeds." Quite the opposite, he seemed to demonstrate an enthusiasm for his own cleverness as he recounted the various steps in the plan.

"He appears," noted the *Evening Standard*, "to take a degree of delight in his actions which is wholly inexplicable."

This delight extended to a detailed accounting of the foibles of other witnesses, who were themselves most reluctant to testify. Mr. Trent was fumbling and nervous, and greatly embarrassed ("with ample reason," snapped one outraged observer) at what he had to report, while Mr.

Fowler recounted his own experiences in a voice so low that the prosecutor was continually obliged to ask him to speak up.

There were a few shocks in Pierce's testimony. One was the following exchange, which occurred on the third day of his appearance in court:

"Mr. Pierce, are you acquainted with the cabby known as Barlow?"

"I am."

"Can you tell us his whereabouts?"

"I cannot."

"Can you tell us when you last saw him?"

"Yes, I can."

"Please be so good to do so."

"I saw him last six days ago, when he visited me at Coldbath Fields."

(Here there was a buzzing of voices within the court, and the judge rapped for order.)

"Mr. Pierce, why have you not brought forth this information earlier?"

"I was not asked."

"What was the substance of your conversation with this man Barlow?"

"We discussed my escape."

"Then I take it, you intend with the aid of this man to make your escape?"

"I should prefer that it be a surprise," Pierce said calmly.

The consternation of the court was great, and the newspapers were plainly outraged: "A graceless, unscrupulous, hideous fiend of a villain," said the *Evening Standard*. There were demands that he receive the most severe possible sentence.

But Pierce's calm manner never changed. He continued to be casually outrageous. On August 1, Pierce said in passing of Mr. Henry Fowler that "he is as big a fool as Mr. Brudenell."

The prosecutor did not let the comment go by. Quickly he said, "Do you mean Lord Cardigan?"

"I mean Mr. James Brudenell."

"That is, in fact, Lord Cardigan, is it not?"

"You may refer to him however you wish, but he is no more than Mr. Brudenell to me."

"You defame a peer and the Inspector-General of the Cavalry."

"One cannot," Pierce said, with his usual calmness, "defame a fool."

"Sir: you are accused of a heinous crime, may I remind you of that."

"I have killed no one," Pierce replied, "but had I killed five hundred Englishmen through my own rank stupidity I should be hanged immediately."

This exchange was not widely reported in the newspapers, out of fear that Lord Cardigan would sue for libel. But there was another factor: Pierce was, by his testimony, hammering at the foundations of a social structure already perceived as under attack from many fronts. In short order, the master criminal ceased to be fascinating to anyone.

And in any case, Pierce's trial could not compete with tales of wild-eyed "niggers," as they were called, charging into a room full of women and children, raping and killing the females, skewering the screaming infants, and "disporting in a spectacle of blood-curdling heathen atavism."

Chapter 52

The End

Pierce concluded his testimony on August 2nd. At that time, the prosecutor, aware that the public was perplexed by the master criminal's cool demeanor and absence of guilt, turned to a final line of inquiry.

"Mr. Pierce," said the prosecutor, rising to his full height, "Mr. Pierce, I put it to you directly: did you never feel, at any time, some sense of impropriety, some recognition of misconduct, some comprehension of unlawful behavings, some moral misgivings, in the performance of these various criminal acts?"

"I do not comprehend the question," Pierce said.

The prosecutor was reported to have laughed softly. "Yes, I suspect you do not; it is written all over you."

At this point, His Lordship cleared his throat and delivered the following speech from the bench:

"Sir," said the judge, "it is a recognized truth of jurisprudence that laws are created by men, and that civilized men, in a tradition of more than two millennia, agree to abide by these laws for the common good of society. For it is only by the rule of law that any civilization holds itself above the promiscuous squalor of barbarism. This we know from all the history of the human race, and this we pass on in our educational processes to all our citizens.

"Now, on the matter of motivation, sir, I ask you: why did you conceive, plan, and execute this dastardly and shocking crime?"

Pierce shrugged. "I wanted the money," he said.

Following Pierce's testimony, he was handcuffed and escorted from the courtroom by two stout guards, both armed. As Pierce left the court, he passed Mr. Harranby.

"Good day, Mr. Pierce," Mr. Harranby said.

"Goodbye," Pierce replied.

Pierce was taken out the back of Old Bailey to the waiting police van, which would drive him to Coldbath Fields. A sizable crowd had gathered on the steps of the court. The guards pushed away the crowd, which shouted greetings and expressions of luck to Pierce. One scabrous old whore, slipping forward, managed to kiss the culprit full on the mouth, if only for a moment, before the police pushed her aside.

It is presumed that this whore was actually the actress Miss Miriam, and that in kissing Pierce she passed him the key to the handcuffs, but that is not known for certain. What is known is that when the two van guards, coshed into insensibility, were later discovered in a gutter near Bow Street, they could not reconstruct the precise details of Pierce's escape. The only thing they agreed upon was the appearance of the driver—a tough brute of a man, they said, with an ugly white scar across his forehead.

The police van was later recovered in a field in Hampstead. Neither Pierce nor the driver was ever apprehended. Journalistic accounts of the escape are vague, and all mention that the authorities showed reluctance to discuss it at length.

In September the British recaptured Cawnpore. They took no prisoners, and burned, hanged, and disemboweled their victims. When they found the blood-soaked house where the women and children had been slaughtered, they made the natives lick the red floor before hanging them. They went on, sweeping through India in what was called "the Devil's Wind"—marching as much as sixty miles a day, burning whole villages and murdering every inhabitant, tying mutineers to the muzzles of cannons and blowing them to bits. The Indian Mutiny was crushed before the end of the year.

In August, 1857, Burgess, the railway guard, pleaded the stresses of his son's illness, claiming that it had so warped his moral inclinations that he fell in with criminals. He was sentenced to only two years in Marshalsea Prison, where he died of cholera that winter.

The screwsman Robert Agar was sentenced to transportation to Australia for his part in The Great Train Robbery. Agar died a wealthy man in Sydney, New South Wales, Australia, in 1902. His grandson Henry L. Agar was the Lord Mayor of Sydney from 1938 to 1941.

Mr. Harranby died in 1879 while flogging a horse, which kicked him in the skull. His assistant, Sharp, became head of the Yard and died a great-grandfather in 1919. He was reported to have said he was proud that none of his children was a policeman.

Mr. Trent died of a chest ailment in 1857; his daughter Elizabeth married Sir Percival Harlow in 1858, and had four children by him. Mr. Trent's wife behaved scandalously following her husband's demise; she died of pneumonia in 1884, having enjoyed, she said, "more lovers than this Bernhardt woman."

Henry Fowler died of "unknown causes" in 1858.

The South Eastern Railway, tired of the inadequate arrangements of London Bridge Station, built two new terminals for its line: the famous vaulted arch of Cannon Street in 1862, and Blackfriars Station soon after.

Pierce, Barlow, and the mysterious Miss Miriam were never heard from again. In 1862, it was reported that they were living in Paris. In 1868, they were said to be residing in "splendid circumstances" in New York. Neither report has ever been confirmed.

The money from The Great Train Robbery was never recovered.

About the Author

Michael Crichton's realistic tales of technological crisis are admired for their scientific insight and spellbinding suspense. Born in Chicago in 1942, Crichton graduated from Harvard College and Harvard Medical School. After the publication of his novel *The Andromeda Strain*, he quit medicine to devote himself full time to writing. He has since written four nonfiction books, *Five Patients, Jasper Johns, Electronic Life*, and *Travels*, and seven novels, *The Terminal Man, The Great Train Robbery, Eaters of the Dead, Congo, Sphere, Jurassic Park*, and *Rising Sun*. Seven of his books have been made into movies, including all the novels in this volume. Steven Spielberg's movie version of *Jurassic Park* is one of the most eagerly-awaited films of 1993.